The King, The Wyvern, and I
by Amy Seeling

Copyright © 2025 by Amy Seeling

Second Edition, 2025

ISBN (Paperback): 979-8-9995431-0-3
ISBN (eBook): 979-8-9995431-1-0

For information, contact:

Inner Light Warrior
www.amyseeling.com

THE KING, THE WYVERN, AND I

Amy Seeling

Acknowledgments and Dedication

I want to thank my beautiful sister-in-law Lorri and my brother David for helping me with this endeavor. Lorri is the most brilliant and patient woman I have ever met; she is a catalyst that makes every human interaction better and stronger. I look up to my sister as an editor, a scientist, and a beloved friend.

I want to thank my equally brilliant brother David, the author of *The Kingsblood Chronicles* and scientist in his own right who gifted me with a love of fantasy. Your advice throughout writing this book was priceless and much appreciated! Thank you to two amazing people brought together on this earth, I always think of you two with love, sitting on a hilltop overlooking your castle.

Thank you to my sister-in-law Michelle Noland Houpt, ranch woman extraordinaire who I modeled Phoenix the horse and Isladora's great love of everything equine after and my brother Jeff who takes care of us all. Thank you to my daughters-in-law Miranda and Mezianna who helped me greatly in my writing, artwork, and inspiration for the characters Kaigen and Mezzi.

I would also like to thank my best friend Lisa for our discussions on religion. Your faith has inspired me from the moment I met you. Thank you to my husband Mel and the saviors of my life, my sons, Troy and Aaron who are always lifting me up with their strength and in turn making me a strong woman.

Thank you to my martial arts community, North Texas Karate Academy, you keep me on my toes, young in heart and strong in mind and body.

Mostly, I would like to thank God for making my life purposeful and showered in so many blessings. I dedicate this book to my most precious blessings, my grandchildren Seth, Jeremiah and Joshua David and to my parents, Dave and Ann.

Contents

Part I—The King

Chapter 1: Thrace Dies

In the waning summer's light, the wounded warrior lay on his back, trying to draw a breath of air through a tube hastily inserted into his trachea. To the onlookers, it seemed too peaceful an evening for such a tragedy, their king with mortal wounds, the sun setting, summer scents lazily floating in the air as a rainstorm gathered. King Thrace's war horse, still frothy and winded from being run hard, pawed at the ground, nickering, outside. No one knew the full story of what had happened to the king yet, the details were still hazy like the late summer sun.

King Thrace's daughter Isladora watched from the sidelines, the rivulets of blood flowing on the stone floor too much for her. She looked out the window at the agitated horse pacing and restless, his beautiful chestnut coat flecked with sweat. The horse knew what had happened; if only she could speak to him. All they knew right now was that King Thrace had been suddenly attacked by the very men he and his warriors pursued.

Isladora sat quietly listening to the servants as they whispered about what might have befallen the great warrior, her father, her king. As she leaned closer to catch the faint words, she overheard that Thrace had endangered himself riding recklessly, as he did, always wanting to be at the front line of the action.

As it became increasingly apparent that the King would not rise again, Isladora, who hardly spoke in a crowd but was near bursting with emotion softly protested, "He was never reckless; this you know. He was a warrior." She didn't care if anyone heard her or not, but she knew very well that every move Thrace made was calculated and careful. He used to threaten to tear her to pieces for stepping too far to the right when his voice, rough and fierce, said left, or for not responding quickly enough to his command. Isladora knew he wouldn't really tear her to pieces and that it was for her own good, but truth be told she was not a very quick child. She was quiet and sensitive, afraid of her own shadow, regardless of Thrace's efforts.

The Regis King couldn't utter a word now; he could hardly draw a breath. The forest scents, dampened by a quick rain, filtered into the room but gave no peace to the fallen warrior. As he lay with his chest crushed and his right leg bent at an odd angle, his first wife, the Queen Mother, shook her head. She knew that from this he would not recover. The Queen Mother's physician with all his healing knowledge was helpless to assist. Death's approach already clouded the eyes of the dying king.

This would be the second tragedy the Juna royal line had suffered. The Juna stronghold had been founded by three brothers, Elijashen the eldest, then Thrace, and the youngest, Tonsaku. It was a great mystery to the Juna what had happened to King Elijashen. He had been a king of legends, smart and understanding, willing and able; he had brought great prosperity to the Juna tribe. He had founded their stronghold and under him, the nomadic tribe became a prospering community. Thrace had been called the Regis King because King Elijashen disappeared, his body never found, and it could not be proven that he was truly deceased.

Since the disappearance of King Elijashen, the Juna had known great sorrow. They had been attacked repeatedly by the neighboring tribe, a band of barbarians led by a man who called himself Emperor Zhu. The bloodshed went on and on, and during the last battle, Zhu had poisoned their wells and attacked with poisoned darts and arrows to slay a majority of the Juna men. The Juna had no recourse but to surrender. In the aftermath, Zhu joined his daughter, the cunning and shrewd woman who the Juna called the Queen Mother, to the Regis King Thrace in marriage. As queen, she ruled the domain with a calculating fist. And now Thrace had been killed.

Isladora's mother, Aceptye, the second wife of Thrace, was still young and strong. She whispered the blessing of the Heron in Thrace's ears, her tears bathing his cheek, it was the blessing of the peaceful way she followed and had implanted in her young daughter's heart. Aceptye and Isladora were isolated from the battles here in the stronghold, and although they had imagined that men could be as bent and broken as their Regis King, they had never witnessed it happening to someone they loved.

Isladora saw the Queen Mother shake her head in defeat. Disturbed, Isladora ran outside and gazed toward the mountains, wishing she could slip away through the forest with its glistening trunks and scramble through the birch trees, losing herself in the forest sounds.

The forest was her secret place where she could contemplate. Isladora never liked being in the middle of things. The middle of the room meant the middle of unwanted attention. She loved the edges and the way time felt different there. She loved the murmur of voices as her subconscious kept track of what was happening so her conscious self could think and examine. No one fit in this space between real and imagined as well as she did. She stayed outside, gazing at the mountains, listening faintly to the trauma inside, noting the newly washed clay and vivid peaks until the moon began to rise and the bell began to toll. And so he had died. Frightened, she went back inside.

"*Isladora*, there you are, now listen!" her mother emphatically whispered her birth name. "Regis King Thrace has left us." Her mother's face was wet with tears. "The Queen Mother's men are whispering suicide, and if those charges are brought against the royal family, we will have even more trouble on our hands."

Isladora hid her own trembling hands in her robe. "King Thrace would never commit suicide," Isladora forcefully whispered. She had never called him father, really, and she regretted that their relationship had not been close. Her breathing turned heavy. "He was the bravest of men, a hero to the tribe," her soft voice was laden with grief, her auburn hair falling across her features.

Her mother's sable eyes revealed her strain and her fear. She choked back a sob, "The Intermediaries are power-hungry and bristling with menace. They are saying his ride to the battle front was a suicidal move." She let out a soft moan. "They are declaring that his actions demonstrate the mental instability of our line, our people, Isladora." Lines furrowed her mother's brow as a tear traveled down her cheek. "No Juna will be safe until a new crown prince takes his place," she said as she gazed at Tonsaku, the youngest brother, lost in his own grief. Aceptye's look was one of pure fear, knowing that as second wife she and Isladora would certainly be cast out by the Queen Mother and that Tonsaku was now their only hope. "We are not safe. I must talk to Tonsaku. I want you to go straight to your rooms and stay there until the interment tomorrow."

"Yes mother," Isladora turned to leave.

The next day was upon them quickly and when the sun began to rise and light the way, driving out the shadows and bringing life to the dark earth cliffs, the Juna walked in a long procession through the forest and up into the hills. The royal family came first, the Queen Mother, Prince Tonsaku, Aceptye and Isladora, and then the priests, followed by Thrace's top fighting men.

The morning air was chill, and Isladora could feel the roots and the rocks beneath her leather sandals. When the wind blew under her thin robe, she shivered. Up ahead she could see the Regis King's body, carefully washed and prepared for interment, covered in a thin gauze and borne by the Commander's steed. Phoenix's haunches were set tight and hardened not because of the strain—he was a powerful animal, sixteen hands high, his shoulders twice as wide as his master—he labored to not unload his precious cargo on this last trip together.

Isladora, who was often closer to animals than humans, knew that the horse was grieving, and she thought that she might comfort him when they got home, if he would let her near.

The funeral procession was long. Isladora felt as if she had stepped across into another world, a world parallel yet like her own. Her ankles and legs strained as they climbed, not accustomed to the physical exertion. Her head was numb, and her eyes swollen from crying. In truth, she was frightened of this place with its eerie cliffs and the strange carvings that decorated the entrance to the Juna's most sacred burial tombs. The air here seemed charged with energy, causing the hair on her arms to tingle.

As the men unhooked the harness and carefully unloaded the burden from Phoenix, he lowered his noble head to nuzzle his master one last time. His neck quivered as he was commanded to stand steady. When the men carried the King's body into the tomb entrance, Phoenix snorted and pawed the ground, then broke and ran recklessly further up the mountain trail and out of sight, his hooves kicking up clods of earth in his haste and grief. He would have to come to terms with this death in his own equine way.

Inside the tomb of kings, a narrow staircase led down into the earth. Isladora gripped her mother's hand and fought to quell her fear as they began the descent into a place so dark that the torches could not light it completely. Her mother said quietly, "Be glad you cannot smell little one, for this tomb has a terrible odor that living human beings should not witness; it makes me fearful inside." Isladora was already fearful, so she was doubly thankful she could not smell such horrors; Isladora could not remember ever being able to smell.

Inside the burial chamber, paintings on the walls showed warriors in fighting poses, dancers, noblemen hunting, royal servants providing moist fruits and wine, and already added, beautiful and fierce images of King Thrace. Each image was marked with royal symbols Isladora could not yet read, but she had seen some of them before in her uncle's library.

As they gathered in the center of the chamber, one image drew her eyes again and again. It was a man she had never seen before, yet she felt she knew him. The picture disturbed her in a way that she struggled to understand. A line through the middle of his face divided the left side, where his eye was closed as if he were sleeping, from the right, where he was awake, shouting and painted for war. His features were fierce, even in rest. Isladora saw her mother's head bent towards the dark earth as she offered silent prayers for the dearly departed. Shamed, Isladora began to do the same.

The head priest began to read the last rites and passages for the dead King. "Do you accept and acknowledge King Thrace's death?"

The solemn group answered, "We do." Isladora looked at the priest's weathered face; it showed no emotion at all.

As the priest spoke on, her eyes sought out King Thrace's younger brother Tonsaku. The burden of leadership would pass to him, and it was Tonsaku who would make the final statement of the burial rites.

Tonsaku was one summer shy of passing into manhood. He was becoming a brave warrior, known more for his strategy and skill than his brute strength. He read incessantly, to Isladora's benefit, as he turned a blind eye when she borrowed his books. In this way she felt closer to Tonsaku than most people. She could tell he was nervous and suffering profound grief, the emotions forming a swirling void he tried hard to control. Isladora focused her gaze upon him and willed strength into him. He looked at her for a long moment, as if he had come to a hard decision, and then he calmed, settled, and spoke. "We are here to lie to rest a valiant man. A man who was called to the tremendous task of uniting our kingdom; he was not afraid of this task. He had courage through peace, through wartime, and through famine, courage that endured to his untimely end."

The head priest was tapping his cane on the floor, his habit when he was nervous. Or impatient.

"We cannot leave the throne empty until I turn of age next summer, so I will marry Aceptye, my brother's second wife, and take the throne on the next full moon, which will occur nine days hence."

Those in the chamber gasped as one and looked to the Queen Mother to see her reaction. Outnumbered by the Juna, she remained silent, her jade eyes calculating. The tapping became louder and more distracting until it drew Tonsaku's attention.

With a heavy heart and no sign of the affront Isladora felt toward the head priest, Tonsaku said, "Silence." The tapping ceased. "We cannot resolve that it shall be a happy marriage," he paused, "but we can and will resolve that it shall be a noble bond formed from our mutual love for my brother and the homeland he fought and died for."

Tonsaku sighed deeply and held out his hand, extending his fingertips towards my mother. "Aceptye, please come and stand by my side."

Aceptye looked confused, her eyes brimming with tears, her heart torn by the death of the man she honored above all others. Isladora knew that her mother's unfailing sense of service and duty would stay any refusal that was forming in her mind. She would commit to this new life.

Now Tonsaku, who was only five years older than Isladora, would be her stepfather instead of her uncle. Her mother's hand left hers to hang, cold and alone, as she crossed the room to stand by Tonsaku.

Isladora knew not how Aceptye stood so proudly, so bravely, with her heart breaking in two. The man she knew intimately was dead, never to return. Isladora wasn't close to him like a daughter should be, yet he had been a part of her life for as long as she could remember. Isladora thought that he must have loved her mother deeply to care for them so.

Isladora began to cry then, deep sobs wracking her body, as she tried hard not to make a scene and instead to be the daughter he should have had. She slowly raised her head and rolled her shoulders back, steeling her heart and her mind. Aceptye was watching her daughter closely, and as their eyes met, Aceptye gave a slight nod, telling Isladora to be strong. Isladora's face said, *I will be strong; I will be anything you ask me to be.*

The silent, somber group began to file from the chamber. Isladora looked back and watched her mother's fingertips graze lightly over the divided-face image of the disturbing man. Her fingers moved slowly, lovingly, from temple to jawline, her thumb pausing to run along the lower lip. Isladora was both entranced by her mother's reaction and insanely jealous.

Her stomach growled, and her mind immediately focused on the honeyed date cake and thickly buttered bread her nursemaid had given her for breakfast. Food always gave Isladora solace, and needing it now, she would find her nursemaid and her comfort there.

Chapter 2: Isladora Must Flee

Several long days passed in mourning, but the days were not unlike any other to Isladora, who rarely joined in anything public. Still, the stronghold had been strangely quiet, and she used this time to research the Juna symbols that she could remember from the cave, getting lost in her literary world.

That night, Isladora had strange dreams of the painting in the royal tomb, and she awoke in the morning with her heart racing, her mind consumed by the disturbing man's image. She wondered who he was and especially what he meant to her mother. She decided to ask Aceptye but not until after she ate the breakfast that Lepola provided for her, walnut- and raisin-filled pancakes and thick syrup made from the trees on their mountain. Her mouth watered.

"Ah my pet, you are awake!" her nursemaid Lepola said as she rolled over and stretched. Lepola was opening the curtains to allow the daylight into the room. "Today we need to make sure you have a nice gown to wear to your mother's wedding to Prince Tonsaku. Something somber but not too drab," her voice took on a reflective tone. "I think the pale lavender Porta Fina gown will do nicely." The styles from the coastal town were constructed of silk with twisted bodices that looked like drapery to Isladora.

Isladora's face turned stony as she climbed out of bed; she did not like to dress up. With an impish smile she said, "I will agree only after my requested breakfast, my dear Lepola," as she saw to her delight that the breakfast Lepola brought her included maple sausage.

Isladora finished her breakfast quickly, knowing that Lepola was waiting for her to try on the dress. As Lepola's strong arms drew the dress around her figure, it was quite apparent that Isladora's thickened waist and arms would not fit. "I don't feel any bigger," Isladora complained.

"Well, you may not feel any bigger but yet you are," Lepola sighed. She fought a little longer with the material before saying, "Let's go with the lawn green dress with wider stays."

As Isladora dressed herself in the tunic and tights that Lepola selected for her to wear that day, she felt depressed about her increasing weight. Seeing her downturned face, Lepola told her, "All children go through growth spurts. Soon you will shoot up in height and it will all even out."

"I guess so, Lepola." Setting her depressed feelings aside, she remembered she had a mystery to solve, and with that thought she left her rooms to find her mother. She walked down the breezy hallways, enjoying the architectural design, then under the beautiful arch that began Aceptye's first chamber, but it was empty. Confused, she had expected to find her mother's ladies there sewing and chatting in preparation, with only a few more days until her wedding.

The hushed darkness of the room invaded her senses as she suffered the unwelcome sensation of an outsider unable to influence events. *Where could my mother be?* she wondered as she knocked on her mother's private door. She gasped when she heard the Queen Mother's sultry voice say, "She is gone."

Isladora's hand flew to her chest, as her heart threatened to leap from it. The Queen Mother had always frightened her with her exotic beauty and her evil nature; Isladora's sugary breakfast turned in her stomach. "G...gone where? What do you mean? I don't understand."

The Queen Mother sighed at Isladora's ignorance but decided to lie to her anyway, "Aceptye is gone, preparing for her wedding." She looked down, examining her lacquered nails, finally pasting a beatific smile on her face, "She has sequestered herself in prayer and cannot be interrupted by anyone."

Isladora's hurt quickly deepened. The loss of her father, her mother's strange actions in touching the images in the burial chamber, and now she had left without telling her?

"Go back to your chamber, child, and eat some more sweets." With a long finger she pointed to the door.

Isladora was crushed. The Queen Mother had never spoken like that to her before; her mother would have set her straight immediately. Isladora did what any normal youngling would do; she ran away crying.

She always felt that her presence was unwanted and immaterial, small talk and friendship were difficult for her, and her social efforts were always two steps behind and would catch up much later when she was alone. Then she would think, *I should have said this, I should have done that.* There was no one to cry to and even if she didn't prefer being alone, she did not know how to break free from it.

Another two days went by, which Isladora spent eating and reading, her two favorite ways to repel depressing thoughts. She began with a browse through *Theory and Practice of Great Integrity*; it was one of the most widely translated books in history. It was very old, written many years ago. She loved its passages, which described pathways to a more harmonious life.

The copy Isladora was reading had the same symbology she had seen in the burial chamber, personal writings in the margins, and page markers that someone had once made. She often studied these scratchings as much as the text, wishing she knew who the author was.

> *The wise teach without telling.*

> *I tried this with Alejandro today. He never responds to my words anyway. I used gestures and extended thoughts to show him how to pull back the longbow, how to breathe out, steady the heart, and shoot to kill. To my surprise, he hit his mark!*

Isladora then turned to the last pages of *Strategies and Battles* and immersed herself in the Battle of the Juna, where the indigenous people of this area were defeated with poisons and treachery, and all were slaughtered.

> *The Juna front line infantry were small and wiry, they could twist and move in ways that were unexpected in a fight. We lost many men as they thrust and hacked, only to find that the Juna warriors had slipped underneath and severed their windpipe with a single upward thrust of a pointed knife.*

Isladora pictured herself ducking under the Queen Mother's arm, twisting and coming up for the kill. She exclaimed, "Oh wouldn't our lives be so much easier!" She put the book down and stood, trying out the movement. As she ducked and twisted, she fell into a graceless heap, bumping her chin on the table on the way down. Wrong steps, she berated herself, rubbing her chin. She stood up and realized that she was soft, spoiled, and hefty. Thinking that her mother should be back by now, she left the room, needing to talk to her about her plight.

Entering her mother's chambers, she saw they remained empty—no fire burning in her fireplace, no servants, all was dark and silent. Her heart pounded hard in her chest; this was not right, and she grew afraid for her mother. Isladora crossed to her mother's bed, a large canopied thing, and sat down on the side her mother usually slept on. The ring Aceptye always wore sat in a dish on her bedside table. She never went anywhere without it. Isladora began to worry that she wasn't sequestered in prayer but instead was in trouble. She picked up the ring and slid it on her third finger, where it hung loosely. She examined the strange metal, which glinted from bronze to silver to gold as it moved in the light. It was a wide ring; it ran almost halfway to her middle knuckle, and the metal strands were intricately woven. It had three small stones in the center, two green and one red.

"*What a scared little bird*," the old spirit in the ring thought to itself. "*I am too precious a gift for such a frightened, timid thing.*" The ring intended to reject her, but something fit, something that must be explored, that must be examined at length. Isladora felt like Aceptye to the spirit in the ring but somehow younger and more pliable. "*Laugh or die little bird, I will make you stronger,*" it thought.

As Isladora thought about tying it around her neck for safekeeping, the ring seemed to come alive, changing. It shimmered and vibrated, some dark and private language drew warmth from her human blood through the finger that it encircled. Isladora panicked, and then felt a calming in her mind beyond her control as the ring settled into the perfect size and slightly thicker width on her third finger.

"What are you doing here?"

Isladora jumped upon hearing Malagard's voice, although she was glad it wasn't the Queen Mother. Malagard was the Queen Mother's advisor, a dark humorless man who had grown greedy and corrupt. He had a long beakish nose and yellow-stained teeth that he tried to hide under an overgrown mustache and beard. His strange eyes often seemed cloudy, uneven, and full of malcontent.

"I'm looking for my mother, Princess Aceptye, soon to be wife of Tonsaku, our Prince Regis," Isladora told him, as she stood to her full height of five feet, six inches. She was a definite inch or two taller than he, which he hated, and she wanted to remind him of his place.

"That whore your mother will never be allowed to marry Tonsaku!" he spat at her. "The Queen Mother was King Thrace's first wife. The honor belongs to her and will go to her."

Isladora gasped in disbelief that he would utter such words! "My mother is a perfect Lady!"

Her mind was already formulating an escape from this horrible mess. She quickly calculated five steps to the door for him and seven for her. "What have you done with my mother?" She cried out as she circled around to a better position, now four steps for her, five for him. His beady eyes matched her pace as they preyed upon her.

"Your mother will never touch the soil of this kingdom again, and neither will you!" Quick as a weasel, he reached out and grabbed a handful of her hair. Isladora fell, screaming at the pain as he tore her hair from her scalp. She scrambled to her knees, looking back in terror. Seeing his legs, she kicked out as brutally as she could, aiming for his knee and remembering the words from the book *Indirect Strategies*:

*To stop an attacker, take away his mode of transport. The knee is
extremely vulnerable to straight-on strikes. Strike hard and repetitive-
ly until the attacker is disabled.*

The impact of her kneeling back-kick threw her forward, but it worked,
and Malagard screeched in pain. She scrambled to her feet and stumbled
out the door. She had to find someplace safe to hide, somewhere she could
think things through until she could find her mother. Fortunately, living on
the edges meant that she had plenty of inconspicuous places to choose
from. The first place they would look for her was her rooms, so she ran
towards the safest place she knew, Tonsaku's library. She ran through the
door, not knowing if Malagard had followed, to the very back bookshelf.
Isladora knew that the bottom shelf was empty, and she crammed herself
into the too-small space. It was dusty, but well hidden.

She stayed there until late afternoon, listening to the scuffle of boots
outside the door. Her heart pounded every time they sounded near, but no
one entered the room. Eventually her bladder forced her to brave leaving
the shelf to look for a chamber pot. She couldn't find one, but she did find
a nice urn and hoped Tonsaku would forgive her for using it thusly. On the
table were some apples and a banana. Starved, she ate the banana, adding
the peel to the urn, and then stuffed the apples into her pocket. She
grabbed the nearest book and went back to her hiding place on the shelf.

"No, I don't know where Isladora is. Am I her keeper?" Tonsaku's
voice jolted her awake.

"My liege, she has been missing since yesterday, we are so worried!" It
was her nurse, Lepola.

Tonsaku sighed, "It is no longer safe here; you must leave and go back
to your tribe Juha Lepola."

Isladora's mind was whirling, wondering why he called her Juha, a title
given to the elder women of the Juna tribe. The Juna tribe had been conquered and massacred; no one had survived. The history books said so.

"I will never leave her; she cannot survive without me!" Lepola cried.
Isladora was about to show herself when she heard Malagard and the
Queen Mother's henchmen in the hall.

"Ah, there you are, Prince Tonsaku," Malagard said in his reedy voice.
"It seems mother and child have fled the palace rather than be married to
you."

"What do you mean mother and child?" Tonsaku asked calmly.

Malagard sneered, "Princess Aceptye has pledged herself to Emperor
Zhu as a peace offering to our neighboring country. Her marriage to you

cannot become a reality; the Queen Mother has that right as the first wife."

"Get out Malagard, before I throw you out!" Isladora heard metal ring as Tonsaku unsheathed his sword.

As the Queen Mother's guard stepped forward to protect him, Malagard replied, "There is nothing you can do. Aceptye has left, and the Queen Mother will be your rightful bride, as is meant to be."

Isladora almost screamed from her hidden shelf—her mother given to Emperor Zhu? Horrendous acts of sin were performed in that country. Zhu was widely known for his fascination with cruelty and his dark barbarian ways. They were a crude and nomadic race, and they took what they wanted. Tears streamed down her face and she bit her arm to keep from crying out. Malagard and his men finally left the room and Isladora was wild with grief.

"Come out now, Isladora." Isladora gasped as she heard Tonsaku's voice. "I know you're hiding in here, and you are safe for now." He paused, "Next time, don't eat all the fruit and I might not notice."

Isladora crawled from her hiding space, tears and dust streaking her face. Lepola rushed across the room and hugged her to her bosom. "Oh, you're safe little dove, I was so frightened!"

"Listen to me, Lepola." Tonsaku's face was more serious than Isladora had ever seen it. "You must take Isladora and flee the stronghold."

"But my mother!" Isladora cried.

"Yes, I know Isladora. If indeed she has been given to Zhu, I will get her back somehow," Tonsaku rubbed his face, breathing deeply.

"No, no, it is too dangerous and you are too important!" Lepola would have none of it.

"There is no one else, Lepola. If I do not go, she will be lost. And if I do not marry her, our kingdom will be lost." Tonsaku looked at Aceptye's daughter for a long time. "Isladora is the last remaining seed of the One True King that my brother, God rest his soul, was sworn to protect, as must I. Protecting him means protecting his wife and child with my life until his return. You go and gather the Juna warriors who live in the mountains and the forest, and I will go retrieve Aceptye with the few loyal men we have left." Tonsaku's face took on a determined look, his eyebrows knitting together as he commanded, "Isladora will be safe with your people Lepola. You must do this."

A single tear trickled down Lepola's face, then she straightened and quietly said, "Your will be done, your majesty." Tonsaku had not yet been coroneted, but that mattered little to the nursemaid.

Chapter 3: Escape

Lepola turned Isladora toward the door and gave her a push. When she didn't respond, her nursemaid grabbed her wrist and pulled her from the room. Isladora gasped at the strength of Lepola's grip on her arm, firmly anchored where Isladora's hand widened just above the wrist, as she staggered along behind her. She had no choice but to follow as they ran cautiously back toward Isladora's rooms.

Isladora had so many questions, "What did Tonsaku mean I was the last remaining seed of the One True King?" she huffed as she was pulled through the corridors. Lepola shushed her and she asked again in a quieter tone, "My mother was the wife of Thrace. What did he mean protect us until the King's return? Our King is dead!" She let out a hysterical moan. Lepola jerked her arm and hushed her again as they approached her room.

Two guards stood outside the door, their backs turned away, talking. Lepola quickly stopped and pulled Isladora out of their line of sight. Isladora whispered, "They're waiting for us!"

"We have no time, so listen and do not speak!" Lepola whispered. "We must not let them capture us! Hide here behind this curtain." Lepola pulled the heavy curtain away from the wall. "I will try to get our things and come back for you as quick as I can." When Isladora looked at her bewildered, not understanding what things she was referring to, she said, "I have provisions that I have kept ready for us in an emergency such as this. We will need them if we are to survive!"

Isladora was so scared, she grabbed her pained stomach, hurting from the stress, and her head throbbed where Malagard had ripped her hair out. She simply could not process a thought logical enough to speak. When Lepola shook her, she nodded and moved silently behind the heavy curtain. Her shoes but nothing else stuck out. Isladora thought about how she once saw a mouse sneak into the kitchen with no one wiser but her. *Slow, listening, silent. Running close to the baseboards.* She slowly turned her feet so they would run along the baseboards and blend in with the wall. Her pained stomach clenched in agony. The curtains were unwashed and dusty and made her nose itch, so she clamped down on her nose.

Lepola slowed her rush and tried to walk past the guards as if nothing were amiss. "I am here to retrieve the laundry, has something happened?"

she affected a look of motherly concern and directed her inquiry to the guard most familiar to her.

The guard frowned; his orders were to bring Isladora to the Queen Mother immediately. He shifted his hand to the sword at his side and questioned, "You're Isladora's nursemaid. Why is she not with you?"

Lepola looked nonplussed as she smiled at him, "Today is laundry day, a task which Isladora abhors. She usually escapes to the rookery to avoid such drudgery."

With a quick look to the other guard and an order to remain there, he hastened off in the direction of the rookery. Lepola entered the room and grabbed her pack, placing it at the bottom of her basket, and piled dirty clothing on top.

Lepola returned to Isladora, pulling her from the curtains, and began to strap the pack to her torso. It was as long as Isladora's torso, flat, and made of leather. "This fits front or back," she explained. "You pull these straps tight, like this, and when you want to release it, squeeze these other straps together and pull." And with a deft pull, the pack held snug to her body.

"Aren't you coming with me?" Isladora squeaked, trembling at the thought of being alone.

"Yes, of course I am, but if we get separated at least you will have the pack; it is you they are looking for, not me," she explained wisely. "Someone is coming, quickly now, hide!" The guard was already returning from the rookery. Lepola could have kicked herself; she should have sent him somewhere farther away.

Lepola quickly picked up the basket and Isladora settled back behind the curtain and, in a moment that Isladora would not forget for a long time, she sneezed explosively! She was immediately found, grabbed, and held in the brutish arms of the guard. He began to drag her towards the other guard, his hand bruising her upper arm.

Lepola reacted immediately and without reservation, tossing the laundry to the side as her lithe body arced, her head falling towards the floor and her foot connecting under the guard's jaw. He staggered back with the surprise blow, teeth cracking.

"Run, Isladora!" she yelled as she attacked again, striking his windpipe with the inside of her forearm as his head weaved back up. Isladora was spellbound. Her nurse, whose hands were as gentle as a warm breeze, who brushed her hair and fed her sweets, was fighting a full-grown armed man! She turned and kicked his heel out from under his large body and he fell. "For God's sake Isladora, go!"

The second guard ran towards them, drawing his sword. That broke her spell, and Isladora took off at a run. He raised his sword as he charged, bellowing at Lepola and swinging down to take her head off! Isladora ran as fast as she could down the hall towards the back of the keep and out the door. She tore past the stables, scaring the small goats and chickens, and then ran through the gate and into the forest. When she was well into the trees, she paused for breath, her chest heaving, tears she didn't remember crying rolling down her face. She looked back but saw no sign of Lepola. She could hear men shouting and gathering in the keep.

Isladora knew that she had to keep going, so she ran the path that she knew so well, deeper and deeper into the forest that edged the mountains. Unfortunately, everyone knew of her love for the forest, so the guards had little trouble following. Realizing her stupid mistake, she hid behind some brush as the guards drew closer, and then as they passed by, she ran as quickly as she could in the other direction. She climbed and climbed, dodging fallen tree limbs and rocks. Her chest heaved and her legs burned; she wasn't fast, and her hefty size wore her down quickly with each step.

As she stopped to rest against a tree with her heart pounding in her ears, she heard them coming back. Tamping down her nausea, she took off again, this time towards the cliffs and praying for a hiding place. The path was gone now, leaving only undergrowth that tore at her arms and made them bleed. She twisted her ankles and jarred her knees on the rocky footing. She could hear the guards crashing behind her. When she dared to look back, she realized that she had made another mistake. She could go no further. She stood at the edge of a cliff, a long way down with nothing but a rock-filled river and death below.

The guards halted and waited for some time, saying nothing. Isladora got the impression that they hadn't wanted to chase her through the woods. Finally, the Queen Mother rode up on her horse, riding right to her and not caring if the horse twisted its foreleg on the rocks. Isladora felt unnaturally calm as she faced her.

"There you are, filth!" the Queen Mother exclaimed. "Witness the end of the line of Elijashen!" Her terribly beautiful eyes turned a cloudy grey as her lips pursed. Isladora's chest compressed and she felt the air leave her lungs, as if it was sucked from her. Isladora's body twisted, stumbling on the rocks as her footing shifted precariously, and then she fell to the ground. She couldn't do anything but writhe, rolling back and forth, the pain was so intense, nor could she draw a breath. Feeling her world about to darken, Isladora panicked and thrashed sideways, then she was suddenly airborne as the rocks gave way and she fell to the next cliff shelf. Upon impact, she had never felt so much pain in her life. Her momentum and churning body rolled off that shelf, scraping the wall as she fell to the bottom of the cliff, and finally into the rapids of the river. Then everything went dark.

*****

Isladora opened her eyes, her lips curving upwards in a gentle smile, as she had never seen a more welcome or beautiful sight than his muscled limbs. She knew not how she ended up face down in mud mixed with blood, hers or someone else's, but she knew she could happily die watching those rippling muscles. She coughed weakly and water sputtered from her mouth. At that moment, she knew she was in love. She rolled slowly and painfully to her side so she could fully gaze at him.

Her legs were in the river and the pain was pure agony. Then darkness again as she blacked out. Time passed. When she woke again, she tried to move, but the pain in her head and neck was so severe that she lay breathless, trying not to move as waves of nausea swept over her.

She lay there a long time, remembering how she got to this place, the cliff, the river, and her dream about her true love come to save her. She almost cried. thinking that she would die here and that wretched witch, the Queen Mother, would take her mother's place. She pushed her cheek further into the mud, wishing she would suffocate and it would be over.

Alas, Isladora found she was not to die this day. She woke again and laid with her eyes open until visions of her mother helped her brave sitting up. She winced and slowly pushed herself to a seated position; she was very nauseous. Dozens of cuts and abrasions and bruises covered her legs. She thought of Lepola, so brave, and she began to cry; her nursemaid was most likely dead. Her mother taken, her father dead. She was utterly alone with no one to help heal her broken heart and body.

Then she saw him again, her dream approaching her, his deep muscular chest, his proud manner, how the air seemed to clear and expand around him to make room for his beauty. Isladora was not alone. Gladdened, she said, "You could save me if I could just stand up."

She spoke to him softly, the practiced words she always said to him. "A sundry of times I have thought how I am in love with you." He gazed at her knowingly with his beautiful brown eyes, his neck arching. He loved her praise. "My heart knew yours at the dawning of time. I need your help my love, I need your strong back."

His gentle wicker was his reply. He moved to her, his hooves carefully choosing their place in the mud. He bent his glorious head close to Isladora, allowing her to grasp his head and mane as he pulled her up. She stood slowly, leaning heavily on his neck. Phoenix, the great warhorse of kings, allowed her to lean on his chest. He was warm and smelled so good. Isladora stood that way for a long time, longer than she needed to, and let his strength flow into her. He didn't mind that she took so much; he was grieving, too.

Phoenix eventually took a step back and nudged her towards a rock tall enough to climb on his back. "Okay, my friend, I will try." Isladora slowly climbed the rock, nausea making her weak in the knees, and slid onto his strong back. She had to lean down and hold his neck; she could not sit up straight.

Phoenix began to walk slowly, keeping his head and neck as still as he could, and Isladora held on, focusing all her remaining strength on not falling off. She drifted in and out of awareness, once throwing up over his shoulder. He simply stopped, waited patiently for her to finish, then began walking again. Isladora was ashamed that she had soiled his beautiful coat, but she was helpless to do anything about it.

Isladora did not remember how long they rode, nor was she strong enough worry that he would take her back to the only home they both knew. She knew it became night, and in her pain and grief she did not care where they were going. Her world now was Phoenix.

Chapter 4: Malagard and the Queen Mother's Plot

"Ah, you are deadly and beautiful, my Queen," Malagard murmured, appreciatively viewing the expanse of leg exposed by the Queen Mother's exquisite gown. "I like a ruler who knows what she wants; I find myself quite happy in your service."

The Queen Mother's eyes razed over him in unceasing scrutiny; in her imagination she cleaved his head from his body with her sword. He was a turncoat to the Juna, beneficial to her but untrustworthy. When he no longer proved useful, she would rid herself of him. She ignored his depraved stare and the way he licked his lips. Malagard shifted uncomfortably under her gaze, pasting a more subservient look onto his visage, eyes downcast. She sighed, for now she still had need of him, no matter how disgusting he was. He was also disgustingly loyal to her and that counted for something.

She looked in the mirror. Her long black hair was piled high upon her head and artfully arranged with a red lotus blossom and five sharp hair pieces standing up on the top. Each hair ornament was dipped in poison, effective weapons for short-distance throwing and piercing.

The Queen Mother was immune to large doses of this poison through skin contact. Her father had slowly exposed her to it for years. If it pierced her skin directly into her blood stream, she would probably die, but touching it didn't faze her. Anyone else would fall ill, vomiting and disoriented upon contact; it was a lethal poison. The Queen Mother had lost many a chamber maid to the toxin as they dressed her hair. Until she got smarter and found a chamber maid that could withstand contact with the poison, her pathetic little Phoebe. Quiet as a mouse and as brown as one. "You are dismissed Phoebe, well done as always, my dear."

The maid bowed and avoided looking at Malagard. Since the Queen Mother seemed to be in an agreeable mood, Phoebe thought about telling her how badly Malagard had been treating her but, too intimidated by him, she only muttered, "Yes milady," and left the room.

Having been trained since childhood in the deadly art of warfare at the cruel hands of her father, the Queen Mother had grown to become a weapon to be used at his will. She was part assassin, part courtier, master of poisons, and trained for deception. Oddly, the latter part of her life had been the better part; her younger years, not so much. Not having her own mother around, she had demanded to be called the Queen Mother here at the Juna stronghold, her latest conquest. She laughed to herself—it wasn't the Juna who were strong any longer.

"Your people will love you," Malagard told her. "You are the image of royalty."

Again, she didn't bother to respond, remembering how totally she had learned when she was young, that love was nothing but a cruel mirage. Evening meals had been the worst, when Zhu and his men drank, and what few fatherly filters he had were completely erased.

When she was ten years old, a dog birthed a litter of puppies in the room outside the eating hall. She fell in love with them and spent hours hiding in the corner playing with her new friends, the only friends she had ever really known.

"Where is that worthless she-child of mine?" Emperor Zhu queried one day, noticing that she was absent once more from the evening meal.

"She's playing with the pups, your highness," Ascendi, his first warrior replied.

Emperor Zhu's eyebrows merged into a frown. "What pups?"

Ascendi knew that look, but he had learned long ago not to try to protect Emperor Zhu's daughter from her parental tormenter. "A stray dog had a litter your highness, and the little one is playing with them in the yard room."

Zhu grunted, nonplussed. "Bring them here, all of them."

The pups and Zhu's daughter were brought into the room, the pups whining pathetically at being taken from their mother.

"So, young whelp, you like puppies, do you?" Zhu asked his daughter.

She didn't even look up at him, "Yes sir, oh they are grand!" she exclaimed, smiling at the pups, her eyes full of love. Zhu was disgusted with the glee on her face. He knew that all weakness came through love. He would expunge it immediately. When he didn't answer, his daughter looked up and her face fell as she saw his look of disgust. Oh, how she knew that look well. Her smile became a visage of fearful anxiety, but surely his cruelty wouldn't extend to young pups, she thought.

"See that pot over there?" Zhu pointed towards a heavy soup cauldron. It weighed half as much as she did, and it was hot and brimming full of soup.

"I'm very hungry today. Bring the soup to me. Now don't spill a drop! For each drop you spill, a puppy will die."

The details of that evening were a source of anguish and dark power for the Queen Mother. She learned the lesson well; it marked the last time she allowed herself to love anything. Yet, examining her perfect face, she knew that lesson was part of what made her the powerful woman she was today.

Seizing power over this stronghold in the High Country had taken patience and ruthless scheming. But she had done it, and finally her father would reward her with his devotion. She had rid the kingdom of Thrace, and before him one of the greatest warriors of all time, Elijashen. Thrace was dead and Elijashen trapped forever in the most complicated enchantment she had ever devised.

A string of glittering diamonds hung from the red lotus blossom in her hair, a king's ransom in jewels. Her jade-colored satin gown was embroidered with golden cherry blossoms and had a high neck and fitted cups for her breasts, leaving little to the imagination. Her sleeves were long and wide to conceal her hands and intentions. Her eyelids were colored with glittering jade pastels, and black kohl lined the lids. Her lips were the most delicious color of red cherries. She gave herself a slight teasing smile. The Queen Mother was well aware of her prowess and beauty; she didn't need Malagard to describe them to her.

Tonight she would rid her inner court of anyone she could not control. They would all kneel and swear fealty to her or die like helpless puppies. She knew that some would have to be killed, some would not roll over to serve her like Malagard did.

"My Queen, we have not found Princess Isladora's body," Malagard reported.

"Don't worry that you can't find the brat." The Queen Mother gave Malagard a sharp look. "A soft, fat little thing like her will not survive long; she fell off a cliff with no air in her lungs." She affixed her eyes back on her image in the mirror.

Malagard considered this. "Also, Tonsaku has escaped with a group of his warriors." Malagard grew nervous waiting for her answer, hoping she would not kill the messenger.

"Tonsaku is a brash young man gone on a fool's quest to save his brother's love, Aceptye," the Queen Mother said. "He will never survive my father." Thinking of her father, Zhu, the Queen Mother fingered the poisoned darts; Malagard's eyes followed every move of her hand. While she may be immune to the poison's effects, he knew he was not.

"And if Tonsaku survives and returns, we will kill him." She turned to Malagard with her icy cold stare. "And if by some act of God, Isladora survived her fall, we will kill her too." Her beautiful eyes turned thoughtful. "The kingdom is ours and we shall celebrate."

The Queen Mother thought back to the days when Elijashen ruled the High Country with his beautiful wife Anyumay. She had never met Anyumay, but she knew the queen had successfully practiced the healing arts and was therefore, in her eyes, pathetic. Elijashen had been hard to re-move; her attempts at assassination outside of the stronghold had all been fruitless. Some kind of magic surrounded and protected him, but she had finally found a way. She had ingeniously trapped Elijashen in a spell that kept his body frozen in time and his consciousness ensnared in a small sphere that she hid in a mountain cave some miles away. She had interred his body in the one place that no one would look, his own sarcophagus. As long as she lived, maintained the spell, and kept his body and prescience separated, he would remain spellbound in oblivion.

The Queen Mother recalled her cunning. Her father Zhu had not yet taken over the stronghold, and she had been sent as an assassin to kill Eli-jashen. She monitored his coming and going until one day she was lucky enough to catch him alone as he rode out. She pretended to be a farm girl, wild with agony, fearing for the life of her only child. She convinced Eli-jashen that her child had fallen into a hole exploring a cave in the mountain. She tearfully begged for his help, pulling on her hair and touching her head to his foot, begging him to help. "Please, please sirrah, I beg of you, she is scared and I could hear her cries for help, we must hurry!" She cried, "Please, follow me, there is no time!" It was a time of peace and Elijashen had no reason to be alarmed. It was simple trickery leading him into the cave, which she had already prepared for her magic. So simple. The end of a great and powerful King.

Shortly after, her father Zhu attacked the stronghold with treachery and poisons until the Juna were at their breaking point, lost without King Eli-jashen. It was then simple enough with her beauty and charm to show up as an Emissary from Emperor Zhu and marry the brother Thrace to keep the peace. That Thrace already had a wife, Aceptye, was no matter to her as long as Aceptye was second wife. Now Thrace had been killed and Zhu would make sure Aceptye was out of the Queen Mother's way. He was on his way to capture her even now.

No one, not even Malagard, knew what had happened to Elijashen, on-ly that he had one day disappeared from existence. The foolish people still waited for his return. The Queen Mother did not know what became of Anyumay, and she didn't care. The Queen Mother married Thrace, Elijash-en's heir, to become Queen of the High Country. As Zhu's daughter she was very marriageable indeed, a way to unite Zhu's kingdom with the warriors of the High Country.

"Send a message to my father," she told Malagard. "Tell him that all is well, that we are firmly in control here, and to prepare our men to clean house if the officers won't bow down."

"Yes, my Queen," Malagard replied with a snide smile. He did enjoy ordering the men around, knowing their fear of Zhu and his mephitic daughter kept them in line.

Chapter 5: Ariah Meets Keit

Ariah didn't harbor foolish notions about her job. She had been picked up by a group of nomadic traders in circumstances that she could not recall at a very young age. She had been with this group for seventeen years, her job to clean and cook. They were all the family she had, but she wasn't close to any of them. While she received no payment for her services, she had food to eat and shelter to sleep under. A fair trade given who and what she was. Ariah was very different from these people and she had never seen another of her kind. She was a freak and the traders avoided her for the most part. But all that, her very existence, changed because of what she saw today.

They had skin like hers. *Skin. Like hers.*

Her band of traveling merchants had stopped to set up camp near a large military village, hoping to make profitable trades and obtain infor-mation. The encampment was a base where men trained strange flying beasts. The beasts seemed like dragons, only smaller, yet still larger than any man. They had vast wings and long tails they could whip around dangerous-ly. The beasts were kept in heavy chains and inside large metal cages backed up to a cliff wall. The men referred to them as wyverns. Ariah tasted the wyrd on her lips, her long tongue snaking out to wet her lips. "Wyvern," she said, "wyverrnnn." A strange wyrd, a somehow familiar wyrd.

Ariah was an auditory being, her extended ears were long and pointed on the ends. She could raise them up to listen or keep them relaxed against her head. She turned her head slightly to one side when listening, so many people thought that she lost attention when they spoke to her. She would often turn her ear toward the speaker and defocus her eyes to concentrate on the sound of what they were saying. Her ears were sensitive, and she was repelled by loud unpleasant sounds, noises, and voices. Yet when she heard the wyvern shriek in anger for the first time today, she had been exhilarated by the noise. Her ears had perked up to full extension. The soft leathery scales of her skin along her arms had grown hard in response to their shrieks. She had felt war-like and powerful.

"Hey Ariah, quit dreaming and come clean this up!" A serving woman shouted at her, pointing to the pots and pans. Ariah scrambled to obey, she was good at pots and pans, there were many of them and it would give her ample time to think. It was the vision of those beasts she wanted to cherish, privately without intrusion.

As she scrubbed, she considered these new beasts. Most of the wyverns were dark, rich colors; some were green and some were red or yellow. Their skin looked like soft leather and they had scales running up the neck and onto their stout foreheads. They hated their captivity and thrashed their heads from side to side in anger, pulling at their chains. Black spikes grew from their heads and tails, and their necks glistened dark and foreboding in the sunlight.

After Ariah finished her chores she went to look at them again. She considered the dark green one, he was in the last cage furthest from the camp, and she saw that her scaly skin was indeed similar to his, except where the wyvern's skin was green to black, hers was red to violet. As she ran her fingers along her arm, she noted that the wyvern's scales covered their entire body. Ariah's scales began at her toes and ended at her knees in front and ran up to her buttocks in the back. They began again at her navel and covered her torso, neck, and arms.

The wyverns had no hair. Ariah's eyelashes and hair were extraordinarily long and ranged from purple to mostly red. It fell in glistening strands down to her waist. She had learned to wear clothing to cover much of her body, and she kept her long hair braided and tucked in her shirt to avoid unwanted stares.

Ariah watched the wyverns and the men throughout the day while she helped set up camp and began preparations for the evening meal. The men were trying to gentle the wyverns and harness them for flight. They used a variety of techniques from whips to tiring them by fighting them against each other for fresh meat.

The sight of the wyverns fighting and their cries of indignity, fury, and pain drew Ariah like a moth to flame. She loved the feeling of her scales tightening in response to their maddened cries. Small moaning noises escaped from her throat, noises she could not control and had never made before. As the days progressed, she crept closer and closer to the fence to watch and to learn. She taxed her brain trying to understand this connection she felt with these creatures. She needed to touch them and see if their skin felt as beautiful as it looked.

"What are you doing here? It's not safe this close to the fence." A man's voice startled Ariah from her reverie.

She jumped and hissed. Ariah was mortified, she had never hissed before in her life! The man was handsome to boot, and here she was hissing like a rabid snake. Ariah covered her mouth with her hand, lest some other humiliating noise escape.

"I'm sorry I startled you." The man smiled. Ariah studied his face. His skin was tan from hours in the sun, and he had small laugh lines around his eyes and mouth. His hair was dark brown and his eyes brown as well.

"My name is Keit. I'm Captain of the guard here. And you are?"

Ariah barely trusted her voice, and she was relieved when she answered, "Ariah," without any moaning or hissing. What the hell was wrong with her?!

Keit laughed again. "I heard there was a Sybaris with your camp, but they didn't say you were stunning." Keit's hands itched to touch her scales and see if they were soft like leather and warm in the sun like those of the wyverns. Her hair and ears were tucked into a cap, but some of the hair had escaped and what he could see was gorgeous. The strands near her cap were red, much like human redheads, running to deep purple ends that reminded him of the eggplant his grandmother grew at home in her garden.

Ariah decided to trust her voice once more. "You heard about me?" She looked directly into his eyes then quickly to the side, her gaze drawn back to the wyverns. Keit was mesmerized with the graceful way she moved her head. When he didn't answer right away, Ariah added, "I am nothing."

Nothing? Keit thought. *What would lead such a beautiful creature to think she was nothing?* Her sad gaze told him the state of her life, but her proud shoulders thrown back testified that she was not yet beaten.

Quietly, because Ariah could not control the hissing on some words, she said, "What isss a Sssybarrrisss?"

Keit replied, "A draconian woman, part woman, part dragon. They are fierce warriors, really." Keit joked, "I may be in mortal danger just talking to you."

Ariah looked to the side as he spoke, concentrating on recovering the sound 'draconian' from her mental files.

"Come on now, I was just joking about the mortal danger." Keit was worried he had offended her.

When she still didn't respond, Keit ordered, "Well go on now, away from the fences."

Ariah gave him a puzzled look, still thinking about what she just learned about herself. Her hand reached up to touch the end of her long ear and she turned to leave.

Keit could not just let her go, what if he never saw her again? "Hey!" he called, and Ariah turned at the sound. "Would you like to have dinner?" Keit smiled his most charming smile, the one that won him all the girl's hearts he wanted. "Please?"

Ariah touched her mouth, her hand running along her jaw to her ears. "No, I am ssssorry, I cannot have dinner with you." And just like that she turned away once more.

Dinner? She thought, she could not eat with anyone! She was mortified just thinking about Keit seeing her long, forked tongue. Never. She could *never* have dinner with him. Yet he held the secrets to what she was, secrets she had waited her whole life to know.

Ariah turned back to him and said, "I cannot have dinner with you, but I would love to talk with you again Keit. I will come here again tomorrow, to ssssee you." And then she purred, a mewing, gurgling sound in her throat. Hoping he didn't hear these new strange noises, Ariah retreated.

Keit watched her hips sway, completely mesmerized until she was out of sight. What a gorgeous creature she was, he thought. He would definitely see her tomorrow.

Chapter 6: Taken by Zhu

Aceptye did not know these guards, but she did know they were loyal only to the Queen Mother. Any attempt to speak to, bribe, or reason with the three men thus far had met with failure. The Queen Mother had ordered them to take Aceptye south. South to where, she did not know. She thought about trying to escape but knew they could easily catch her with their finer mounts. Aceptye was sure that she was given the small furry nag she rode on purpose. She had to get back to Isladora and get her daughter to safety. At least she knew what direction home was.

They had been on the road a day and a half and were traveling through an area forested by birch trees. As they traveled, the slight rain they had been experiencing for hours began to ease into a light mist. It left the forest eerily hazy with golden light, and the birch trees with their paper-thin bark looked like beautiful dried bones with their white bark and black veins. Aceptye shivered and grabbed a handful of her horse's mane just to feel a connection to something real. At the contact, her horse's ears perked forward. Perhaps the nag was smarter than she thought. Aceptye had never traveled this direction before. It was not considered a safe area, being too close to the barbarian kingdoms.

A few birds called from the trees. Aceptye pushed her hood back, trying to hear them better. She didn't recognize their call. "Godforsaken land," she thought aloud.

Suddenly the birds flushed through the trees, taking flight as one and startling Aceptye. Her horse stayed calm and turned to face the danger. Ahead in the clearing a horse screamed and others whinnied. The man guarding her came closer. "Quickly, lady, dismount and hide behind that tree!" He was not about to lose the gold he was promised by the Queen Mother for delivering her to Emperor Zhu. He had to deliver her alive.

Aceptye's heart was pounding like a drum as she scrambled down from her horse. "What is happening?" She peered into the clearing, trying to discern what the trouble was as arrows hissed through the air. An arrow chunked into her guard's shield and another hissed by his head, barely missing Aceptye's as well. They had come to save her! The guard brushed the arrow from his shield with his sword, spinning the broken arrow. As it landed on the ground, another arrow pierced his skull, and he fell.

His cohort grabbed her arm. "Run, these barbarians will eat you where you stand!" Aceptye's mind finally grasped that these were not Prince Tonsaku's men come to save her. Realization dawned and as her mind commanded her body to flee, the barbarians came running and leaping over the fallen trees with vicious glee. The two remaining guards threw their weapons down, raising their hands in defeat. They were grossly outnumbered. With no place to run, they were trapped, and if they tried to fight they would die. Aceptye's mount moved to stand, ears back and head lower to the ground, between her and the barbarians.

The barbarians halted some yards away. In the silence Aceptye could hear her heart pounding. She could smell their unwashed stench. Their hair and beards were unkempt, wild with all manner of tangled hell. Their eyes were hard and merciless. They were tall and muscular with thick black tattoos all over their upper torso. Many of them had leather tied around their arms in various ways.

Aceptye was too frightened to speak and stood next to the dead guard, gaping, and trembling. She placed her hands on her horse's neck to steady herself. She heard horses approaching and as they grew closer, the barbarians moved aside to create a passage.

The first horse was a giant black steed that halted upon command but pawed the ground with fierce intensity. On his back was the most fearsome and darkly handsome man Aceptye had ever laid eyes upon. The horse itself was probably worth a king's ransom. His coat was glossy and black; he was obviously well cared for, although the scars on his hide from spurs showed the cruelty of his rider.

The man was large and bare-chested, muscular and golden brown from the sun. Every part of his torso was chiseled and lean. A leather strap ran across his chest and held chain mail that covered his left arm and shoulder. His hair was long and fell wildly about his face, grey near his temples, betraying his age. He had a strong jaw and forehead, and his face was clean shaven. His eyebrows slanted down into a scowl that covered a predator's eyes. The permanent sneer on his face completely ruined any handsomeness he had.

The guards breathed a sigh of relief, realizing it was Emperor Zhu. "Your Highness!" They fell to one knee. "We are so thankful it is you!" The guard babbled on, his thankfulness and relief making the words tumble from his mouth. "We have the Princess Aceptye for you. Your daughter the Queen Mother said you would pay us in gold for her safe delivery."

"My daughter," Zhu remarked with boredom, "should be more aware of the value of gold these days." Zhu adjusted the reins carefully and methodically. "Ascendi, kill the Queen's dogs."

Before Aceptye could move, two of the archers let arrows fly, killing the guards where they stood. Her heart beat so arduously it ached. She wanted to scream but was too frightened. She could not take her eyes from the dead men. She could not look up. She was going to die. Zhu watched her with predatory stillness.

As the blood flowed from their wounds and spiraled its way back to the earth, Aceptye, head still bent towards the bloody ground, silently prayed, *"I am Elijashen's true wife, Anyumay. I am alive and he lives on through Isladora. I will survive this, I must. I will not be intimated by my enemy's appearance. This blood pouring into Mother Earth is my strength. I will be cunning and escape these barbarians. I will be crazy and wily as a fox. Fighting me will not be worth it."*

Aceptye finished her prayer and reached down and to touch the blood of the fallen guard. She wiped his blood across her breast and slowly looked up into the eyes of Zhu. She pressed her shoulders back and lifted her chin even higher, her inner strength showing like a beacon.

Impressed with the princess's bravery, Zhu gave an internal satisfied grunt. She would be interesting, and fun to break. The blood rushed through his veins in anticipation as he thought about it. She seemed to be a tough one, and he did enjoy those. They lasted longer.

"Get her on her horse," Zhu exclaimed. "We will ride hard and be home by dark."

Aceptye did not want those men touching her. She gathered her horse's reins and pulled herself into the saddle. Zhu grunted again and turned his mount, his guard gesturing for her to follow. Pressing her heels into the sides of her horse, Aceptye stepped into line and headed towards the most feared kingdom outside of the High Country, the home of Emperor Zhu. She threaded her fingers through her horse's thick mane and squeezed them tight, as if to hold on to her sanity.

Chapter 7: In the Mountain

Isladora awoke from her semi-conscious state to the realization that Phoenix had stopped moving. She slowly sat up as the horse stomped his foot, pawing the ground, impatient for her to dismount. She looked around and saw that they were at the entrance to a cave on the side of the mountain. She eased herself from his muscular back and slumped onto the ground, her numb legs betraying her. Her body was battered, and she held onto her stomach as waves of nausea caused by the lump on the back of her head permeated her being.

"Thank you, Phoenix," she murmured. He lowered his head and she gently touched his velvet muzzle. "So powerful, so gentle, my beloved friend," she bent forward and gently kissed the soft part of his nose, a few inches above his nostril. He raised his head, turned, and walked away. He looked back once and nickered at her, and then he was gone. *So beautiful,* she thought.

Isladora looked around and saw she was alone, and a torrent of feelings threatened to overwhelm her. She couldn't think of a time when she had needed her mother so badly. She couldn't remember a time when she had been truly alone. She bent her head to her knees and cried, deep sobs coming from her body as she grieved for all that had happened. Her family attacked and laid to waste by the Queen Mother, her nurse Lepola probably dead. She rolled to her side, content to die as she fell into unconsciousness at the mouth of the cave.

She woke up to a squeezing, burning sensation on her finger. It was dark outside and colder. She let out an exclamation as she looked at her hand and saw that the ring she had taken from her mother's room before she fled was glowing! It was radiant, and it was hot and tightening around her finger. She panicked and tried to remove it, but it stuck tight. She scrambled unsteadily to her feet and tried again, now in a full-blown panic. *"Run!"* She heard inside her head. *"Run into the cave, NOW, stupid girl!"*

Her head spun with dizziness until her mind became alert to a new problem—she heard a menacing growl. An old mangy wolf stared at her from less than five feet away. He hunched down, preparing to attack and gauging the distance. When he saw her look at him, he lunged, forcing her to dive into the cave. She fell to the ground and kicked out at him but he bit, clamping onto her leg. She tried to scramble further into the cave, but he held on, pulling her leg, the crushing pain making her scream. Most of his teeth were around her boot, but the nerve receptors in her calf raged as the immense pressure from his powerful jaws did not lessen. She flailed wildly in the dirt, looking for a rock. Her hand finally found purchase on a metal rod embedded in the cave wall. The rod was stuck in the rock. She pulled herself forward using it, screaming in terror, and then it suddenly broke free. She lost her purchase and was pulled back by the wolf. In her panic she swung the rod at his head, smashing it against his skull. The wolf yelped and released her leg. She scrambled further inside as the rocks shifted and began to fall, and something large and heavy slammed into the floor close by. Dust billowed all around her, creating an effective barrier between them. As a good-sized rock fell on her she curled into a ball and covered her head the best she could.

She coughed, getting a blast of gritty dust in her face. Some of the rocks had tumbled on top of her. They weren't big enough to crush her bones, but they still hurt and left scrapes on her arms and back. She crawled away from them. At least the wolf couldn't get to her now, she thought. The rocks shifted again. The ones above the cave must have loosened and were now falling. She moved further back and the cave-in sealed her in.

As the dust and noise settled, she tried to calm her racing heart. She looked down at the metal rod in her hand; it must have been some sort of brace, keeping the rocks in place, a safety mechanism.

The spirit in the ring was interested as her mind raced back to Grosberg's paper on Mechanical Advantage:

> *A lever is a beam connected to ground by a hinge, or pivot, called a fulcrum. The power into the lever equals the power out, and the ratio of output to input force is given by the ratio of the distances from the fulcrum to the points of application of these forces. This is known as the law of the lever.*

She was clever, but now she was stuck in this mountain cave. She coughed hard, her lungs full of dust, and remembering the ring, she looked at it again. It still glowed but did not tighten. It emanated some welcome light into the dark and dusty cave. She tried once more but still could not remove it. "What was that voice in my head telling me to run?" She coughed again thinking she must be losing her mind.

"You are not," she heard in her mind. She gasped. She was not alone. The implication set in—she was not alone!

"Who are you?" she whispered.

"You are such a weak little fool," she heard in the dark, in her mind, not through her ears. *"Nothing like your mother, nothing at all."*

"My mother! What do you know about my mother?" Isladora exclaimed loudly.

"See how stupid you are, yelling into the night where any creature can hear you and eat the head off your body!" The spirit in the ring was exasperated. *"I should have let that wolf eat you; he had been watching you sleep for quite some time."*

Isladora was so confused. "But…"

"Silence!" it said. She closed her mouth. *"You can talk to me through your mind, you need not speak. As long as you wear the ring we are connected."*

Isladora let out a combative snarl, "But I don't want to be connected and I do not want to wear this ring!" Again, she pulled on it.

"Take me off if you can, little idiot." The spirit chuckled and the ring stopped glowing, making the already dark cave black as pitch, leaving Isladora breathless.

Tears welled in her eyes. With anger she yanked at the ring over and over until her finger grew sore and she had to stop. It wasn't budging. Yet truth be told, she was glad to not be alone in this cavern, even though when it spoke it wasn't very nice to her.

Her mother always wore this ring, and again Isladora grieved because obviously she really didn't know her, she didn't know much about anything in her mother's life. How could she not know that this ring glowed and talked? Isladora spent her time reading and eating; her mother spent her time apart from her. Isladora suddenly realized how distant they had grown over the years. The ring listened to her mind as she questioned why her mother had allowed that distance, she was but a child. Her mother's only child. Isladora grew sullen and felt neglected. To make matters worse, her stomach growled.

Without the ring's light, Isladora could do little but wait until dawn and hope that she there would be enough light to see. She unstrapped the pack from her body and dug around in it until she found some food. It was a strange dried meat, nut, and berry mixture, and she ate it with relish. The pack contained a water skin but no water. She would have to find water soon.

Her leg ached where the wolf had bitten her. She took off her boot to examine what she could in the dark and rubbed her leg for some time. Isladora felt a puncture wound where one of its teeth had entered her skin; she thought how she would need to clean it in the morning. With what, she did not know. Hopefully the pack contained medicine.

Isladora put her boot back on and laid down using the pack as a pillow. She cried out when the back of her head touched the pack and then turned her head to the side to avoid the painful lump in her skull. Her head ached terribly and her body felt like absolute hell. She curled into the fetal position and tried not to cry, but tears ran anyway. She thought about how much their lives had changed since Thrace died.

"Ring," Isladora thought. *"Please talk to me."* She could not stop the silent tears from falling. She was scared, she hurt everywhere, she was thirsty and still hungry. Her leg was on fire.

"I must get back to my mother, Aceptye." Disciplining her thoughts with stern precision, Isladora wondered how she could make this thing understand. She would appeal to its needs, find out what it wanted. *"The Queen Mother is going to have her killed, I just know it,"* Isladora reasoned. *"You were friends with my mother, weren't you? She wore you all the time."* She needed its light if she was going to make it out of this dark place. *"That means you are honor-bound to help her, which means you must get back to her, and I am the one who will carry you. If I die here, without me to carry you, you are lost in this cave."* Her mind worked out the answers as she thought, *"If I am dead, you will be attached to bones in a place no one will ever find you."*

To his bafflement and delight in being challenged, the spirit in the ring knew that Isladora spoke the truth, that he would be left in this cavern where no one would find him. His current existence was bad enough; without any human interaction it would be unbearable. He had once spent several hundred years in that kind of isolation. Never again.

Isladora thought that maybe it in fact could not hear her thoughts. She began again, this time aloud, "Ring, are you there?"

The ring glowed softly. *"I am honor-bound to no one, but I will help."* It went dark again. *"Go to sleep, fat little Isladora,"* it whispered in her mind.

Isladora cheered inside. So it could hear her thoughts! Ignoring the ring's snide comments, she felt a tad more optimistic than before. As the room fell dark, Isladora experienced warmth like a blanket had been laid over her and she closed her eyes and fell into exhausted sleep.

Chapter 8: Learning to Survive

When morning came, Isladora awoke to dusty light filtering in through the rock-filled entrance and from the ceiling above. She was so relieved to be able to see that she forgot to be afraid and she laid still, finding comfort in the sunlight. As she looked around, she saw that the cave was not really a cave but more like a thin ravine where the mountain was enclosed at some points and made a ceiling and at some points she could see through to the sky, a blessed blue wonder. The walls were high and smooth, too smooth to climb. Isladora knew that the smoothness meant that water had flowed through here at some time, probably creating the cavern. The ravine went a long way, as far as she could see. Realizing she would have to walk, it was time to examine her wounds.

A search through the pack retrieved a small medical kit with bandages, healing salve, a sewing kit, and various herb packets labeled in a language she did not know. She quickly donned the single pair of pants, ridding herself of her torn and dirty skirt.

A fresh wave of grief hit her as she thought of Lepola and how she had fought as fiercely as any man. Isladora wondered how Lepola had known to keep a pack like this ready, while she had been oblivious to any danger in her home at all. Isladora snorted, oh, she knew she didn't like the Queen Mother and she even knew that she was dangerous; but she just didn't think that they could all be affected by her. Isladora thought about how wrong she had been. She thought about how Lepola had fought, weaponless, against armed men; her whole body was a weapon even! Isladora did not know so many things, and she grew ashamed at how spoiled and unaware she had lived her days. How could she have not known that her gentle nursemaid was a warrior? How did she not know that the Queen Mother could and would kill for the throne?

At least there was a difference in being spoiled and being ignorant. Isladora had a choice now. The veil had been lifted from her eyes. She could make a choice to learn about the world and the people in it. Isladora knew she was incredibly book smart and that would have to make up for the lack of human guidance from her parents and her nursemaid.

Isladora thought that she would not be angry with them, raising her to be inexperienced in the ways of war and men, for allowing her to be overweight and physically weak. They had their reasons, and she would ask them someday. Isladora decided she would put her keen mind and body to work to get back to the family that she dearly loved. She knelt and prayed that Lepola had not been killed, that her mother was okay, that Tonsaku had put the Queen Mother in her place.

The ring was both right and wrong, Isladora thought; she was heavy but she wasn't stupid. She set about cleaning the wolf's puncture wound and the scrapes that were all over her body the best she could. She really needed water to get the wound clean and she needed water to drink. She put a bandage over the puncture wound and put the medicine back in her pack. Her stomach grumbled and she felt horribly hungry. She ate more of the meat mixture, noting that three more packages remained. What she really wanted was a blueberry pastry and sausage. The lean meat did not taste very good now that she wasn't utterly starving like before, and she still felt hunger pains as her stomach craved the sugar and yeast from her regular poor diet. Isladora stood up and her head pounded but she was no longer nauseous.

She recalled thoughts from something she had read; water was her next crisis:

> The human body is more than 60 percent water. Blood is 92 percent water, the brain and muscles are 75 percent water, and bones are about 22 percent water. A human can survive for a month or more without eating food, but only a week or so without drinking water, and less in strenuous circumstances.

Isladora huffed, she thought *she* certainly couldn't survive a month without eating food! She felt like she was going to perish now.

Isladora stored her things in the pack and attached it securely to her body, taking the time to do it as Lepola had shown her. She picked up the metal stick she had hit the wolf with; it was cold in her hand, making her shiver, but she was glad to have a weapon of sorts. She took a few practice swings with it, attacking from all the major compass points like she had seen her father's soldiers do in sword practice. She had watched them so many times, it was easy to imagine the commands. Get a firm grip on the stick. Keep the non-active hand out of the way and be prepared to use it to brace or block. Keep your balance, feet as wide as your shoulders and staggered. Do not over-swing, leaving your side unguarded.

Isladora practiced swinging both one-handed and two-handed until her mind grew calm and her arms ached. She was ready to go. With a flourish twirl of the stick, she set off, following the cavern the only direction it allowed her to go.

As she walked, her thoughts drifted. She floated between the past and the present, thinking she had been as ignorant of the world as a newborn colt. She told herself, *"I will survive. I will learn to fight... I will avenge my family."*

"Hmmmm," thought the ring. *"Maybe this soft, fat thing has some backbone after all."* It did not have a choice of bearer in any event.

Isladora had no idea what direction she was headed. She made the decision to be more like flotsam than jetsam, one deliberate, the other in distress, both overboard, no compass, no bearing.

She had been asleep when Phoenix dumped her at the foot of the cave and had been in a delirium from hitting her head. She could only hope that it was the right direction to go home and that she would be able to find an exit. The path was clear of debris, some rocks and limbs here and there, but no other footprints or signs of life. Most times the cavern stayed lit with sunshine coming from gaps in the top; she only had to move in semi-darkness for a short while.

She traveled for what must have been a few hours before she had to sit down to rest. It was quiet and lonely; she thought about thinking to the ring, but her feelings were still hurt from its insults over her pudgy body and so she stayed silent. She was trying to be brave but was really frightened and fighting thirst and hunger. She settled down in a patch of sunlight and tried to calm herself. She thought about the last dinner she had with her mother. Aceptye always ate sparingly but Isladora had gorged on pheasant and dumplings. Isladora thought about her mother's beautiful face and her warm smile as she fell asleep.

When she woke up some time later, it was no longer light outside and the cave was dark. With no way to see, she closed her eyes and tried to fall back asleep. She had lain there for several minutes when she heard sounds that seemed like people talking. The sounds came and went, but they did sound like people. She gingerly rose to her feet, picking up her stick and checking that the pack was secure. She could make out shadows and shapes in the moonlit cavern, and she moved slowly forward for several minutes. She grew excited, thinking that if there were people in the cavern that maybe they could help her find the way out.

She traveled along, picking her way carefully, when finally she could see some light up ahead. The way the light flickered, she thought it must be coming from a fire, and a fire meant people and food! Her stomach growled in anticipation.

She edged closer to the voices, keeping her back close to the wall. As she neared, she peeked around the edge of the wall and saw three naked women. Or at least she thought they were women, but they were small, probably only two or three feet tall at most. One was bathing in a large pool lit from within with an eerie green glow; she was breathtakingly beautiful with long golden hair and firm pert breasts peeking up out of the water. The second one was just as beautiful, although her hair was red and her back was hunched over and lumpy. She was sitting on the side of the pool, her legs and feet dangling in the water. She had flowers tucked behind her ear. The third woman had long dark hair and was lying on the side of the pool sprinkling petals in the water and into the hair of the blonde one.

"I want a garland too, not just petals thrown in my hair," the one in the pool complained. The woman with the dark hair had a garland of flowers around her head and Isladora observed that the flowers came from some vines that grew down the wall.

"You don't need a garland, we all know whose hair is the most beautiful," declared the brown-haired one as she grabbed a strand of blonde hair and yanked.

Isladora watched them argue, frolic, and bathe until they were finished. She was too frightened to come out of hiding. The water ran down one wall into their pool and formed a darker river that flowed down the cavern. Her tongue felt dry and swollen; she wanted a drink of that water so badly. She thought she would drink her fill and then fill the waterskin from her pack. While adjusting the pack, her stick accidentally hit the wall and the women froze, listening. Then like fish they disappeared under the water and were gone.

Isladora sat down waited about half an hour, and when they didn't return, she rose and inched towards the pool, mesmerized by its eerie green glow. She touched the water and it was cool and inviting, and it smelled clean and fresh. Isladora marveled at the *smell* of the fresh water. Being able to smell was new to her, it was as if a new world had opened. She wondered where the fish-women had gone; perhaps an underground tunnel led out.

She gulped several handfuls of water. It felt strange as it hit her empty stomach. She washed her face and took a smaller drink and then a bigger one. She filled the waterskin and drank from it some more. She stuck her head down into the water to rub off some of the dirt and mud encrusted in her hair, being careful around the lump. Finally, she took off her pack and her boot and washed the puncture wound from the wolf and the scrapes on her leg. She reapplied some of the ointment to her wounds and re-bandaged the puncture wound and then refilled the waterskin, placing it back in her pack. Isladora started to lace her boot back up when she saw fish darting about the pool. Her stomach grumbled.

She looked through the pack for fishing line but found only a thin rope. She tried to catch a fish with her bare hands, but it went too deep. She thought how badly she needed those fish! Who knew when she would find a source of food, and she only had two packs of the meat mixture left. If only she had a net. She didn't know how to make a net with the rope, but she did know how to make lace. She would tie the same knots, just bigger, but not so big the fish could swim through. She thought it could definitely work.

She worked, tying the thin rope into her lace version of a net. When she ran out of rope, her net was only about two feet by three feet, but it would have to serve. She ate some of the meat mixture and then rubbed pieces of it into the rope to entice the fish. Since it was so small, she would have to lean down into the water and hold it ready to close when a fish swam near.

She lay on her belly and leaned down into the pool, arms holding the net ready, and waited. It didn't take long for the hungry fish to approach the net. Several were in her reach, so she closed it fast and caught a good sized one that looked like a trout. She set the fish on the ground a few feet away and got back down to catch another.

Isladora held still and let the water settle and caught two more. The fish weren't coming back as fast as they did before so she waited, and as she did her mind wandered. Suddenly, she felt a sharp bite on her forearm.

"Ouch!" Isladora yelled, pulling her arms and the net from the water. Blood was running down her arm, and the blond woman had a firm grip on the net and was trying to pull it from her hands.

An eerie high-pitched shriek that hurt Isladora's ears came from the woman, and then the other two were grabbing the net and pulling her in! Isladora instinctively let go of the net, and all three fell back into the water.

They surfaced, smiling, holding their prize. "What a nice gift you have given us!" The blonde one cackled. She put the net around her hair. "Don't I look beautiful?"

"Give it to me," said the dark-haired woman, "it's not for your hair, it's to wear around your shoulders!" and she yanked it from her hands.

"No! It's perfect for my hair, give it back!" The blonde one shrieked.

"It's mine!" proclaimed the dark one. All three hissed and opened their mouths, which were full of sharp teeth like a shark. Isladora shrank back in fear. She couldn't believe she had thought them beautiful. Those teeth were terrifyingly angled and sharp. Isladora ran her hand over her arm where she had been bitten.

Isladora took perverse comfort in the realization that they didn't seem to want to leave the water so she felt brave enough to say, "The net is mine, and I need it to catch some fish to eat."

At first they appeared to consider her request, but that option soon dissolved as the red-haired one emitted another high-pitched scream, saying, "The fish are our children, you cannot have them!" Then she jumped out of the water with more speed than she looked capable of and snatched one of the fish Isladora had caught. Isladora let her take the fish, concerned that it really was her child. She shoved Isladora backwards as she dove back into the water with her fish.

The trout was most definitely not alive any longer. The creature took a huge bite of the trout with her razor-sharp teeth, tearing the flesh while she murmured, "Mmmmmm, delicious."

"That's your child and you are eating it?" Isladora was aghast.

In an uncultured rasp the creature snarled, "That's right human, we do what we want." She took another bite and then tossed the carcass away. "And we want to taste you, don't we girls?" The brown-haired one leapt from the water, too fast for Isladora to react, and grabbed her arm, pulling Isladora to the water. The creature was small but strong, but Isladora was bigger and stronger and the fish-woman began losing her grip. Seeing their prey about to gain the upper hand, the red-haired one jumped out and grabbed Isladora by the hair. Isladora lost her balance in the onslaught and fell as they dragged her to the water's edge.

They pulled her in and under the water; Air rushed from her lungs. Under the water they were much stronger and Isladora could see just how shark-like they were.

Sharks had one weakness, Isladora had read; they must swim to pass air through their gills. In her desperation for air, punching the gills became her one thought for survival. She supposed their gills must be on their neck, so she grabbed some hair to get her bearings and punched out hard. One let go, then Isladora punched and punched until they all released her. As Isladora kicked and swam upwards to the light, her chest felt like it was about to burst. She broke the surface, dragging air into her lungs, the fear of those shark teeth making her scramble to pull herself out, kicking her legs violently so they would not grab her again. Isladora raced to her only weapon, the metal stick, while the red-haired one climbed out of the water and was close behind.

Isladora gasped and coughed as her hands closed around the stick. The stick was under her so she didn't have time for a full swing. Thinking of it as a sword, she turned and thrust the stick straight at the fish-woman. The creature shrieked and stopped, her body impaled upon the stick, her hands grasping the stick and blackish-blue blood running down her chest. That's when Isladora saw that her stick was not a stick. Its metal had formed into a sharp blade, the blade of a long sword. *But that is impossible* she thought, *it is just a stick!* And with that thought, it became a stick again, leaving the fish-woman's body with a swooshing sound. As the creature collapsed to the floor, the blonde fish-woman grabbed her sister's arm and dragged her back into the water, and then they were gone.

Isladora had killed her! She dropped the stick to the floor. It didn't make sense; her mind could not work fast enough to catch up with what happened. She started to shake all over. She realized she was going into shock.

> *The main symptom of shock is low blood pressure. Other symptoms include rapid, shallow breathing; cold, clammy skin; rapid, weak pulse; dizziness, fainting, or weakness.*

Fainting! Oh, she could not do that! Those things would come back and drag her to her death. She had to slow her breathing and move further away from the water. As Isladora backed up, she could not seem to calm herself, she was going to hyperventilate. She had killed someone! Yes, she was defending her own life, but she had taken the life of a talking, breathing creature. Her mother would have been horrified!

"Calm down little one," Isladora heard in her mind. The ring glowed lightly. Like the pool. Her stomach clenched and she threw up the water she had swallowed. *"Pick up the stick,"* the ring said. *"We need to get out of here."* Isladora felt it warming on her finger. *"That's right, pick it up,"* it counseled. *"And pick up the fish."* It sounded so reasonable. Isladora just listened and did what it said. *"Come now, let us walk some and I will light the way."* It glowed brighter.

They continued to follow the only direction they could go for a time. Isladora trudged forward, not thinking, the ring silent but glowing. Her heart rate had slowed a little and she realized that she was mad. She was mad that those fish-women had tried to drown her, mad that they attacked and bit her! She looked at her arm and saw the bite wasn't that bad, but it was still a bite. She was mad that the thing was dead. Her intent had not been to kill her, just to stop her from trying to drown her. *"How dare those creatures!"* Isladora thought. Well, she had said she would learn to fight, but fight could mean kill, and kill she had, but she never thought it would have been today, nor in this manner.

"Okay, ring," she said out loud. "What is this stick?" She twirled it again in a circle. "I was thinking of thrusting it like a sword and it became a sword and killed that fish-woman!"

"She was not a woman, she was a water sprite," the ring spoke in her mind. *"And a cruel one at that. She was going to drown you and play with your dead body. I doubt they would have eaten you, but you never know with those creatures."*

Isladora gave a mental shudder but kept moving. She had heard of water sprites but thought they were a fictional creature like bed bugs or such.

"The escrima stick is made from a magically immersed metal, most likely before the Mage Wars by a skilled mage. I have seen similar weapons, permeable and changeable weapons in my days. It was probably crafted by a master." The ring was silent for a time and then, *"It appears to be just a dull metal stick; however, it can become what you will it to be within reason."* The ring continued, *"For instance, it cannot become more than it is, like a large boulder."*

"Or a tall ladder so I could climb out of this place," Isladora said with longing.

"Exactly."

Isladora thought this through and asked, "Do you mean if I think sharp, it becomes sharp, I think long and pointed, it becomes long and pointed?" Isladora tried it but nothing happened, it stayed a stick.

The ring gave a mental sigh. *"Yes, but you must be truly feeling it or it will not happen,"* it explained. *"As with any magical item, the price of controlling the magic is passion in the individual."*

Passion in the individual. Isladora had certainly been full of passion when it had changed to a sharp sword; the passion to live. "Okay, ring," she said to show she understood.

"My name is not 'Ring,'" it murmured.

"Many pardons," she paused. "We have not been formally introduced, I see," Isladora said with her best court manner. "I, sir, am Isladora, daughter of Princess Aceptye and King Thrace, who was killed in battle just a short while ago." She stopped and curtsied with her best royal training, her fingertips trailing the floor.

"Isladora, I am Meluha Crocus," he said formally. *"I am very old. I was born when the great dragons still roamed the earth and the skies."* He continued, *"I have been held captive in this cursed ring for longer than I can remember. I belonged to your mother most of her life and to many others before her."*

"Do you study the Way of the Heron, then?" Isladora asked, for that was the peaceful Way that her mother followed.

"Yes, Isladora, I have studied it, but I lost my Way long ago."

Isladora tried to ask more questions, but the ring, no… Meluha Crocus, would not answer.

Chapter 9: Keit and Ariah Fall in Love

Ariah could not wait to see Keit again; he knew what she was! A Draconian woman he had said. A Sssybarisss. "He ssaid I wasss sssstunning!" she murmured to herself. Ariah had so many pheromones running through her system from being near the wyverns that her body responded in new and wonderfully strange ways when she thought about Keit. If he knew that about her, she would be so embarrassed! What was wrong with her?

Ariah took great pains getting ready to meet Keit at the fence—it was vain and silly, but she couldn't help it. Her work was finished for the day, and she had nowhere to be until the next morning. She washed her hair with lemon juice and lavender and brushed it until it shone. She knew it was beautiful, even to humans. At the last minute she decided to wear a scarf over her head, her deep purple one, the one she kept for special occasions, although this would be her first special occasion. Her first date as the nomads called it, although hopefully Keit would not know that.

Keit was experienced in surveillance, and he used every skill he had to spy on her during the day. Never had he been so fascinated with someone. He watched her work, memorizing the way her body curved and moved with inhuman grace. She was a diligent worker, he had to give her that. Her betters just pointed and she got it done; no words were exchanged. Keit knew she was uncomfortable talking to people. When she began to get ready for their meeting, he left his surveillance to get cleaned up as well.

His hair slightly damp and smelling of aftershave, Keit arrived in time to watch her saunter to the fence. He was too mesmerized to do anything but watch the elegant way she moved.

Unaware that she was being observed and unaware of how attractive the flowing movements of her body were, Ariah saw that Keit wasn't at their meeting place. Her heart was saddened but she understood that no one would want to be seen with a freak like her. Still, she loved the wyverns and she stood in the setting sun to watch them eat. She may have been forgotten by the human, but now her date would be to study and treasure her favorite wyvern. She walked down the fence line towards the last cage, as she was particularly drawn to the smaller dark green one. He was torn up and missing a few teeth and claws, but something about him spoke of survival, and Ariah was drawn to that.

Json the wyvern hated his captivity and he hated that the Draconian woman was staring at him again, witnessing his imprisonment. He decided to put on a show, raising his great head and hissing at her, baring his teeth. Ariah responded by hissing back, and then embarrassed, she covered her mouth with her hand, looking around. Json thrashed his tail. Ariah removed her scarf and let her long hair blow in the breeze, arms extended. Json yanked against his chains. Ariah grabbed the fence and moved it back and forth to show him that she, too, hated his captivity.

Keit was totally in love watching Ariah with the wyvern; the two seemed to be in some primal dance or communication he could not under-stand. They were both such powerfully beautiful creatures, both captive to humans like him. That thought sickened him. When Ariah took off her scarf and Keit saw her hair uncovered for the first time, it took his breath away. Ariah stood proudly at the fence, shoulders back, her long hair blow-ing in the breeze. The sunset behind her paled in comparison to the colors of her body. She was glorious.

Ariah finally turned to leave. She had somehow known that Keit wouldn't come, and a tear fell from her eye and ran slowly down her cheek. Then she saw Keit, standing against a tree watching her and she froze, small butterflies twirling in her stomach, her scales hardening.

"I th...thought you weren't coming," Ariah told him breathlessly.

Keit approached her saying, "I'm sorry, it seems that watching you has become my favorite pastime." He smiled and his brown eyes danced with laughter, adding, "You, my dear, quite take my breath away."

"Breath away?" Ariah did not understand, and her senses were on over-load from his nearness.

"You are so beautiful Ariah, I cannot help but watch you and dream of you," he said.

She took a step back, nervous with him, "No one hassss sssaid I wassss beautiful before," Ariah said shyly, looking towards the ground.

Keit moved closer and slowly lifted her chin with his hand, raising her face to his. He saw the wet trail left by her tear and he gently wiped it away. "What is this?" he asked.

Json didn't want that man touching her. He let out a growling shriek when Keit raised Ariah's chin. Her scales responded to the glorious sound of her chosen wyvern and Ariah sighed, making a little mewling noise. Keit's reaction was similar, but not to the wyvern, to the strange and beauti-ful girl he wanted in his arms. He tried to get a hold on himself, it had been a long time since he'd been on a date with a woman, but not that long.

"I thought you weren't coming and my emotionsssss have been all a messs sssince I sssaw the wyvernssss." She gazed back towards her favorite dark green one. He was still watching her.

"It seems he thinks you are beautiful too." Keit looked at the wyvern. "They are possessive and intelligent creatures, you know."

"Thissss dark green one issss my favorite. Look at hisss eyessss, he hasss sssso much intelligencce and bravery." Ariah sighed, making another cooing noise. It reminded Keit of a dove. Ariah seemed shy of her noises, but he thought they were lovely, like a song.

"Come, I know a private place where we can sit and talk." Keit took Ariah's hand and led her away. They passed his tent, where he picked up a lantern and a blanket. They continued and then finally broke off that trail to climb another up into the mountain. Up and up they climbed; Keit worried that Ariah would get tired but she seemed to have even more strength and stamina than he had. He looked back to check on her, and while his breathing was labored, she was breathing quite normally. She tilted her head and smiled at him. Definitely glorious.

"Are you always this quiet?" Keit decided small talk might calm his nerves. Here he was, the 32-year-old captain of the guard, acting like a teenager. She completely undid him.

Finally, they reached a ledge and the view he wanted her to see. "Oh, it'ssss beautiful!" Ariah enthused, her forked tongue peeking out and wetting her lips. As far as Ariah could see were mountains and desert and a gorgeous full moon near the horizon. The moon was giant and orange; Ariah could see the seas upon its surface, a radiant moon.

Keit spread the blanket on the ground and lit the lantern, adjusting the flame to a small soft glow. "I don't even think we will need this lantern with a moon like that!" He took Ariah's hand and helped her sit on the blanket and then sat beside her.

This was the most amazing night of Ariah's life. The view was beautiful and Keit was extremely handsome. She wanted to lick his neck and breathe in his scent. She wasn't completely ignorant of what went on between a human man and woman; she lived in a camp and saw these things all the time. But she was a Draconian woman, and an inexperienced one at that.

Keit saw Ariah looking at his neck and chest and lower and he felt out of control again. He berated himself for his lack of restraint with her, but she aroused him that much and so with her he simply had none. He held still and let her see how much she turned him on; it wasn't like he could hide it at this point.

Ariah longed for this man, it was an experience she had never felt before. She had grown extremely wet between her legs, a wetness she did not understand. She could not let Keit see that, it would be too embarrassing. Keit leaned back on his elbows and she could see that his manhood was straining against his breeches. Ariah closed the distance and he lay back, pulling her on top of him.

Ariah got her wish and began licking his neck. Draconian women didn't really kiss, they tasted, but she didn't know that, she was going on instinct. She could smell Keit with her tongue, and she wanted to smell and taste all of him. Receptors on Ariah's tongue could pick up minuscule chemical particles, which she perceived as scent, sending information to her brain, which was currently overtaxed with his nearness.

Ariah longed to explore him with her sensory organ, it would tell her so much more about him.

Keit couldn't have stopped her; he was so far gone under the spell of this woman. Her hair fell upon his chest and he ran the silky strands between his fingers. When Ariah began unbuttoning his shirt, he let her. She moved the clothing out of her way and stared at his body. Then she began a thorough exploration. Her tongue was doing wonderful things, sending sensations all over his chest, torso, and abdomen. He was completely enraptured.

Ariah laid her great ears upon Keit's chest, listening to him breathe, to the rhythm of his heart, the music of his body. The sound of his voice as her ears were laid against his chest was a melody that went straight to her heart. "Thank you Keit, I needed to tasssste you."

Keit murmured, "Mmmmmmmm." Ariah's heart fluttered at the sound.

"I may need to do that to you again," she said as she caressed his chest and arms.

"Well come here and let me learn your body too." His hand started to drift towards Ariah's damp center. She could not let him see what her body was crazily doing! She started to panic as she grabbed his hands.

"No, oh no! Pleasssse jussst tell me about my home," Ariah begged.

Keit had no idea what was wrong with her, why she wouldn't let him reciprocate and explore her amazing body. He could feel her nervousness at the thought of him touching her, and he decided to let it go for now. Keit left his shirt open and let her place her head back on his chest. He could be patient for a little longer.

"I don't know much about Draconia and the Sybaris race," Keit began. "Draconia is north of here in the higher mountains. Travel there is only possible by flying, and so humans do not go there. Really not much is known about your race."

Ariah thought this over, saying, "And the wyvernssss, they are from there?"

"Oh yes, that is the natural home for the wyverns. The Draconian men are fierce warriors. Their women are too. They fly on the backs of the wyverns and are seen from time to time. Rarely do they attack anyone unless you come too close to their mountain range. They guard their borders zealously," Keit told her, stroking her hair.

"The wyverns have a natural homing sense, a beacon if you will, built into their very blood. Our first attempts at training them met failure. At first, we lost several of them and our riders because the wyverns just flew home when we tried to ride them. The only way a human can ride them is to drug them. The drug keeps them tamer and silences their homing beacon so they don't try to fly home."

"You drug them?" Ariah didn't like the thought of her dark green friend being drugged.

Keit explained, "Well, it's more like a supplement that suppresses their homing beacon and makes them more domestic." He played with her hair. "It doesn't hurt them in any way."

Ariah thought, doesn't hurt them, what did he know? To not be able to go home, to not be free was hurtful. No creature should experience captivity. Ariah had been a captive to humans almost her entire life! She realized that she had been foolish to come here with this man, her clumsy allure for him began to dissipate. She had gained new knowledge, so she owed him for that. Ariah wondered how she had been captured to begin with if her home was so difficult to reach.

"Pleassse take me back to camp Keit." Ariah sat up and helped him button his shirt. "I enjoyed our evening together very much."

Ariah had to go think. The wyverns, they knew how to go home. To Draconia. To her home. Ariah didn't know what she would find when she got there, but that was where she was going to go, and the dark green wyvern would take her there.

Chapter 10: Isladora and the King

Isladora's stomach grumbled. Would she ever be full again? Oh, how she longed for pastries, pancakes, and bread with plump fat raisins! She did have her two remaining fish and a package of meat mixture, which she needed for fish bait. She was not about to eat the trout raw like those horrid fish-women. Isladora had never built a fire in her life; her nursemaid and other servants had always taken care of that. She knew the pack contained a flint and steel, so she would just have to try to do it. She gathered branches and limbs, deep in thought about what she knew about making fires with flint.

> *Take the sharp edge of the flint and strike the fire steel at an acute angle. You are trying to shave small pieces of steel off the fire steel. The friction of shaving the metal off the fire steel heats the pieces to a molten state and creates sparks.*

Acute angle; she could do that, she thought. She found a good place for her attempt and bent down to arrange the sticks in a triangular pile. It took some doing, but she eventually made a spark. Realizing that her tinder was too large, she shaved off some pieces of bark and found small twigs and dried vines to ignite. After an hour she was exhausted, but she had a small fire going. She was faint with hunger by this time, her body ached, and her neck muscles were tense from working bent over.

Isladora needed a sharp stick to skewer the fish, and she didn't have any the right size left. She had stupidly burned the ones that would have worked getting the fire started. She cried out in anger and grabbed her metal stick to throw it when it turned into exactly the shape she needed for a spit. Fine. Good. *Passion*, she thought. She stabbed it through both fish, lest it change its mind and turn back into what it was. She propped the spike on a rock to turn.

The fish smelled so good while they cooked, although she thought it strange since she had never smelled anything before. Perhaps the mountain air was good for her sinuses. After some time, the skin was blackened but the fish was done. Isladora pulled the trout open and ate the entire first fish. She moaned in pleasure; it was by far the best meal of her life even though she burned her tongue at first.

She could have eaten the second fish, but instead wrapped it in a piece of oilcloth from the pack, keeping it for later. Then she fell into an exhausted sleep.

When Isladora woke she tried to change her stick into a spear. She thought about it with passion and once she got really pissed off, she could morph it. She was excited about her success. The spear head was extremely sharp and could easily hurt something. It would great for spearing fish, or fish-women, whatever the need may be. Isladora could scarcely believe that she'd had to kill the red-headed creature, but they had attacked with the intent to kill her, and she knew that she'd probably have to do it again. That thought both saddened her and filled her with a kind of dreadful anticipation whenever she thought about the Queen Mother being at the tip of that spear.

Isladora followed the river for several days, using her jerky bait, net, and spear to catch fish and cooking them on fires that she got better and better at building. Her sense of smell, so long absent it was almost forgotten, grew stronger, and she could smell the earthen floor now. She could smell when she was closer to the river again. Isladora learned what sticks and logs to pick up, which would burn the best. She spent a week waking, walking, eating fish, and drinking the water from the river. She knew sooner or later this subterranean river would leave the cavern and hopefully she would be free of this confinement. She craved and needed people to talk to, fresh air, and sunshine. The ring, Meluha Crocus, had been nothing but silent.

It must have been the morning of the twentieth day in the cavern when the ring began to glow and warm. "What is it?" Isladora whispered.

"I feel the presence of your father here," Meluha Crocus replied. *"I know it's impossible, but I feel him. I knew his great love for you and your mother."*

"My father is dead; he was killed in battle." Isladora reminded him, "We laid his body to rest, you know that Meluha Crocus, you were at the burial on my mother's finger!" She felt strange saying these things.

"That was not your true father."

Not her true father? Ridiculous! "King Thrace was my father. He raised me, my mother loved him!" Isladora was growing hysterical.

"No Isladora he was not. Your true father was Elijashen, The One True King." Meluha Crocus went on, *"Think, Isladora, why did your mother Aceptye and Thrace not have any children? It's because they never consummated their marriage. It was a marriage designed to keep you and your mother safe until Elijashen's return."*

Isladora was aghast. "Why didn't they tell me?" She shook her head in disbelief.

"*Your mother's name is not Aceptye. That is the name she took to disguise herself from the Queen Mother. Her true name is Anyumay, Queen Anyumay,*" Meluha Crocus calmly explained. "*Telling you would have been dangerous. They did not know what happened to Elijashen; he simply disappeared. You were barely walking when this happened. It was better to raise you thinking that your uncle was your father.*"

Isladora stopped to think this through. Well that explained the distance she had always felt from Thrace. She was mad that this stupid spirit ring knew even though she didn't. Thrace was never hateful, but he was never loving either. His attitude towards her had always baffled her and made her think she had done something wrong. Her mother and Thrace had simply been existing, pretending until The One True King could be found.

"And you feel him now?" Her father, her true father was Elijashen! A legendary warrior! The implications of that were starting to sink in. What would he think of his pudgy and spoiled little daughter? She reached down to cradle her stomach and realized a lot of it simply wasn't there any longer. She knew she had to tighten her belt to hold her pants up, but as she felt her body, Isladora realized that she was becoming lean!

"*Yes,*" the spirit responded. "*Keep going. It seems to be getting stronger as we go further.*"

They entered a larger cavern, and Meluha Crocus led her to the right side of the cave. They spent the entire morning searching. Finally, behind a boulder they found some dirt that was looser than the dirt around it. After several failures, Isladora finally angered herself enough to turn her stick into a small shovel of sorts and dug. She hit metal and worked it loose from the dirt, then held it up to the light. It was a small metal box, a cube maybe three inches on a side. She held her breath as she opened it. Inside the box was a beautiful orb, like a large marble with a crystallized substance floating inside of it.

The ring was glowing as bright as she had ever seen it. "*This is the spirit of Elijashen, The One True King. His spirit is trapped magically, much like I am. Isladora, meet your true father.*"

Holding the orb, Isladora sat down in the dirt, perplexed, overwhelmed, and scared. She stared at the orb for a long time, then resting her forehead upon it, she said aloud, "Father, can you hear me?"

The ring practically hummed, "*Isladora, he says yes he can hear you and that he loves you. He says that he is trapped and he needs your help. He says he can speak to the animals much like you can.*"

"It was more a mental telepathy and feeling I had with the animals, not true speech," Isladora exclaimed, "I didn't even know that anyone knew I could do that!"

"Elijashen says he had to learn to talk to the animals to send a message. Even a simple message to your mother Anyumay wasn't heard. He would try to tell her… I am alive… I am trapped, but she could not hear. So Elijashen learned to reach out to his horse and had him bring you here to find him."

Isladora was not used to her mother's true name of Anyumay so it took a little bit for her to work out the words in her mind. Her father sent the horse. No wonder Phoenix seemed drawn to her; he had been trying to communicate. Good God, she thought. "Phoenix?" She squeaked.

"Yes, and he sent the wolf."

"He bit me!" She was indignant.

"Be calm child, he says had to get you to enter the cave so that you could find him."

Isladora took a deep breath, "Hello, Father." She was so happy to not be alone, to be reunited with her father's spirit, and to have Meluha Crocus who could hear him. Tears ran down her face and she covered her cheeks with her hands, feeling the warmth of a newfound love cleanse her palms.

"Hello, brave girl," Meluha Crocus spoke for him. *"This orb contains my trapped spirit. My body is entombed in the family burial cave where you just buried my brother Thrace. You must place this orb near my body and then kill the one who entrapped me to break the curse."*

"It must have been the Queen Mother, she is Emperor Zhu's witch daughter. Father, she took over control of our kingdom." The implications were astounding. "Could I kill her?" Isladora questioned, "I have felt so much anger at this woman, the Queen Mother, that has ruled over and ruined our lives." Isladora thought that it would be easy for her to kill her if she only knew how. She couldn't think of anything that she wanted more than to see the Queen Mother dead, and that anticipatory dreadful feeling came to her again.

Meluha Crocus explained, *"Yes it was the Queen Mother, she's the only person with mage-like powers."* The ring glowed, *"He says to you, Isladora, my love, you are not ready. You are not strong enough to fight the evil woman. He says he will train you and it will demand every ounce of energy you have but with your help, you could reunite his spirit with his body and have him whole again."*

Isladora thought these words through. She was the daughter of Elijashen. He was going to train her to be one of his warriors, a warrior like Lepola. Elijashen, the One True King! "Anything you need, Father, although I have to tell you that the way out of here, it caved in," she explained. "I don't know if we will find another way out." Sighing, she got down on her knees and knelt in obeisance.

Meluha Crocus cautioned, *"I know about Zhu's evil daughter. Her mother was an evil spirit. She has black magic which she used to cunningly steal the throne, to drive people away from the fortress, even to influence the sages to write false histories. She is a mage trained from birth by her cruel father Zhu. She also knows the deathly logic of toxic poisons. She is immune to many of them from constant exposure over the years. She is lethal, and you are but a girl.*"

"I know Meluha, I felt her magic when she took my breath away from me before I fell off that cliff." Isladora was just a girl, but she was also the daughter of Elijashen. She questioned, "Why did Prince Thrace marry the Queen Mother as first wife and my mother as second? I grew up thinking he was my father."

Meluha Crocus spoke for Elijashen. "*Your father says, I know Isladora, and I am sorry. When I became trapped, they must have thought it best to pretend that Anyumay was a second wife and Prince Thrace must have made the Queen Mother his first wife to hold off war with Zhu until I could be found.*"

"That is why Thrace was called Regis King, because your body had never been found." Isladora knew that much.

Anyumay was a name her mother did not go by. Isladora had thought of it as a nickname for her of sorts, and she wasn't even sure how she knew that. "Her real name is Anyumay, Father? I was always taught it was Aceptye."

"*They must have changed her name to hide her true identity, Isladora, also to hide you, a royal heiress,*" my father explained through the ring. A mental sigh, "*We will find our way out of this cavern together my daughter.*"

Isladora hadn't even known her mother's true name. She was angry at the ignorant state they kept her in. She was sure that it was the Queen Mother that had Regis King Thrace killed. "Father, they were saying that Regis King Thrace's ride to the front of the battle line was a suicidal move," she told him. "When she tried to have me killed, the Queen Mother was trying to usurp power from your youngest brother, Prince Tonsaku."

"*We will begin your training now; time is of the utmost importance.*" The ring glowed even brighter, "*I am coming with you!*"

If Isladora had been duped all her life, how did she know that she wasn't being deceived now? "Wait!" She yelled. "How do I know that this is not a trick?" She was a fuming mass of confused adolescence, "How do I know this is my true father speaking and that these are not the words of Meluha Crocus?"

"*You do not know, Isladora. You must simply trust and survive.*" The ring went dark. Isladora felt lost without its light and admitted to herself that she probably hurt the spirit's feelings. She placed the orb back in its box and put it safely in her pack.

Maybe she was being manipulated, but they both had the same goal, to kill the Queen Mother. With their purpose aligned, Isladora needed their knowledge if she was going to stand up to her. Then God help Meluha Crocus if he deceived her; she thought she would bury him where no one would ever find him, even if she had to cut off her own finger to do it!

And so her training began. They stayed in the main cavern most days. Isladora did pushups and plyometrics every morning. They were difficult at first, her heart pounded, and her body felt heavy and ungainly. The first ten minutes of exercise felt deadly to her body, then after the first ten it was like her body was finally okay with the exertion and the exercise was easier. Isladora slowly learned that once her mind accepted the exercise, that was most of the battle. As the days went by, accepting the training got easier, and she even began to look forward to the feeling. She swam in the river against the flow. She only had her body weight to train with and so it was squats and lunges, sprints and jumps, pushups and sit-ups. At first she could only do a few, but as the days lengthened she could do an entire hour of plyometrics.

The pushups were the worst, but Isladora got stronger every day. Her father never made fun of her weakness; instead, he encouraged her and he built her up one muscle fiber at a time. After she achieved her core strength, they began martial arts training, basic kicks and punches. Without a sparring partner, Isladora had to rely on her mind envisioning the attack and performing it as real as possible.

Isladora found a weed growing on the side of the cave that she thought might be lambsquarter, but she wasn't sure. It grew in a small patch around the spot where direct sunlight could fall, spreading voraciously several feet outside the direct beams. Her body craved it with an intensity she found shocking. She wasn't sure if it was poison or not, so she rubbed some on her skin and waited. When nothing happened, she chewed on a leaf and then spit it out. It tasted bitter yet delicious, a little like spinach. When that was successful, she ate a small portion and waited some more. Eventually she ate a few leaves with her fish every day. Isladora knew from watching her mother that green plants were important to her diet, and her body responded to this new source of nutrition.

Finally, Isladora began to learn how to wield the stick most effectively. She learned to imbue passion into the stick to turn it into a stabbing point, to a cutting blade, to a small shield. The stick became her entire focus. It was a living, mystical, and magical thing in her hands. Under her father's tutelage, she learned the finer arts of war. She learned to bounce light off the surface of a shield to blind an attacker. She learned to use light reflection for camouflage.

She trained to her fullest ability. When she grew tired, she thought of the Queen Mother choking her with her magic, and this always gave her inner strength.

Chapter 11: Zhu's Stronghold

Aceptye did what she always did when she felt powerless; she stopped thinking about what was beyond her ability and focused on what she could influence. She missed being near her daughter, here it was all horse and man and dirt and blood. Aceptye wondered if Lepola was keeping Isladora out of harm's way and administering her magic-numbing drug. Without that drug, the Queen Mother would quickly realize Isladora was special and kill her.

As they rode, Aceptye tried to control her fear of what they were going to do to her. She thought back to Isladora's birth, how happy she and her husband had been then, when she had been called by her true name, Anyumay. She had lived in a small town a little west of the Juna stronghold where she practiced healing people through emotion therapy. She had fallen in love with King Elijashen upon sight when he and his men came for supplies. Her emotions had immediately wrapped themselves around the leader of the Juna tribe. In him, her emotions were anchored tight. Elijashen had told her later that her magic had entrapped his willing heart.

Anyumay wasn't royalty to most of the human race, but to the Juna royalty was defined in the moral standards of the individual. Because of her upbringing in the Way of the Heron and her work helping others overcome grief or fear, she was a jewel in the rough. Who would make a better queen than a woman whose essence strengthened her king? Elijashen was immediately taken with her and they were married. Isladora came exactly nine months after their wedding night. The Juna were elated for their royal couple. For Elijashen and Anyumay, there would be no greater love than the love they had for each other.

Aceptye was jolted from her reminiscing when she saw Zhu's stronghold on the horizon. They had traveled quickly to reach it; Aceptye had held on to her horse and tried not to fall off. The little animal was surprisingly fit and agile, and he had kept pace with the larger horses easily. He seemed to know her riding abilities and he kept her balanced on his back and safe.

The arrival at Zhu's stronghold was anti-climactic compared to Aceptye's fears. They took her from her horse, who she had secretly named Fashi, meaning *brave of heart* in the Juna tongue. The small scraggly horse was now her only friend there, and she silently bade him goodbye as they led her into the main entrance and then through a series of hallways, into a room that was to be her prison. Leaving Fashi made her more fearful; he was the only link to her home.

They led her to a room and then locked the heavy oak door from the outside, leaving her alone. One window looked out into a mature hawthorn tree, but the bars on the window were strong and unbreakable. The room contained a comfortable bed and a dresser that already contained clothing. A chamber pot sat in a corner, and Aceptye used it right away to her great relief; it had been humiliating to relieve herself in the presence of her captors, but they weren't about to let her out of their sight, even for that. They had jeered at her when Zhu scouted away from the main party and were utterly silent with eyes averted when he was around. That was even worse, however, because Zhu would watch her with his predator's eyes.

The room also contained a chair and table upon which was some fruit and a wooden pitcher of water with a wooden mug. There was no glass in the room, no mirrors, or anything that could be used as a weapon.

Aceptye poured herself some water and drank deeply. She figured if they wanted her dead she would be, and so she did not worry about poison, the weapon of choice for their cowardly race. Aceptye wandered over to the window and selected a leaf from the hawthorn tree, thanking it for being there, thanking it for its leaf. She chewed the leaf thoughtfully, and then she knelt upon the ground to pray.

> *Lithe body, compassionate heart, alert mind, lightness of being. No inner obstacles to impede my way.*
>
> *My intent moves from my body and my spirit, becoming emotions.*
>
> *Pure awareness becoming sensations, thoughts and feeling becoming strength. To form a silent resistance.*

Aceptye would use the Way of the Heron to endure her imprisonment. Without her ring on her finger, Aceptye had little magic. What little magic she did have was the ability to alter emotions, and so she altered hers to be one of steadfastness and bravery, thinking of the little shaggy horse. After a few hours she grew weary, and so she laid down on the bed and fell asleep.

Upon waking, the position of the sun through her window indicated it was probably midday. Without her ring's magic, Aceptye realized she'd better be careful altering her emotions. Apparently too much bravery led to incautiously sleeping all hours of the day amongst the enemy. She could still taste the hawthorn leaf, its life power ingested and mostly depleted, a thin line between being determined and arrogantly stubborn, an admonition to herself to be more careful.

Rising, Aceptye drank some more water and took care of her needs. Her hair was filthy, and she stank of fear, but she could do little about it. She was hungry and so ate two pieces of the fruit left on the table. She knew her magic fed not only on living plants but also on the nutrients in her body. She must maintain the proper balance of water and nutrition for her magic to be at its strongest. She was entirely lucky to be able to reach the leaves on the hawthorn tree; they would help.

A few hours later, she heard a key turning in the lock on her door. A female servant entered with a small curtsy and said, "Come with me."

Aceptye followed her, noting the guards outside her door that fell in step behind them. They were taking no chances with her then. Aceptye did not let her spirits fall; the extra security just made her more determined to find her way home.

The maid entered a bathing chamber and began removing Aceptye's clothing. Aceptye thought about stopping her, but they were alone, and she decided not to risk the burly guards making her cooperate.

The maid bathed her gently and thoroughly using cloths and brushes and soap that smelled of cinnamon spices. She rinsed her with warm water and then towel dried her. She put a robe over Aceptye's body and again said, "Come with me."

"Do you have a name?" Aceptye asked.

"Please miss, just come with me." Aceptye could feel the little maid's anxiety increase sharply, and she did not want to repay her kindness by making it worse. They passed back through the halls, Aceptye in her robe, the guards once again following, back to her room.

"I am to dress you for dinner tonight with his Highness," the maid said. "If you give me any trouble, the guards will be the ones dressing you and they aren't very good at hair like I am." The maid's attempt at humor surprised Aceptye.

"I understand," Aceptye laughed a little belatedly. "Please though, tell me your name."

The maid looked at her for a long time before saying gravely, "The servants do not have names here. Do not speak to me of this." Aceptye wondered what kind of people they were if the servants were treated thusly. With no name, they had no identity, a demoralizing tactic to be sure. Just one more way to keep people from joining together in a cause.

Aceptye knew very well the power of a name. With a change of name, her entire identity had been hidden. When Elijashen had been lost and Zhu's allies had captured their home, with a quick name change she became Aceptye, Thrace's timid wife. She had played the part well and aroused no suspicion, even when she was cast as second wife and Thrace married the Queen Mother as first wife to stave off further war with Zhu.

The maid was true to her word and styled Aceptye's hair in an elaborate coil that looked like a cinnamon snake. Aceptye imagined herself with fangs that could strike with speed and inject venom into Zhu but then stopped when she realized that it made her resemble the Queen Mother, Zhu's daughter. The reminder made her turn cold. She was about to have dinner with a sadist, one that cruelly poisoned his own daughter to make her the weapon she was. Aceptye realized she should be very frightened, and she was.

From the closet the maid retrieved a green silk gown that had four layers of varying shades of green. She helped Aceptye don it and tied the golden sash that crisscrossed in front of each breast and then around her waist. Aceptye looked down. She could see her nipples through the material. She exclaimed, "I cannot wear this!"

"You can, and you will my lady," the maid exclaimed. "It is much better to do as you are told the first time."

Aceptye was mortified; she could see through the material to every inch of her body! In her panic she began manipulating the maid's emotions, making her feel sorry for her so she would help her find something else. Aceptye opened a dresser drawer and saw that all the outfits were made of the same material, and all were see-through.

"I wish I could give you my clothes, my lady, but they are not fine enough. It is a great honor to dine with his Highness, and you are very beautiful. You have nothing to hide." The maid was gathering up the robe.

Aceptye wanted to blurt that only Elijashen had laid eyes on her body, but then they would know that she was in fact Queen Anyumay. She really had to get a hold on her emotions!

The guards came in, making sure that they looked down at the floor. Not once did they look at her semi-naked body; it was like on the road when Zhu was present. One of them said, "It is time."

As Aceptye walked through the halls, her hands crossed in front of her groin, embarrassed and mortified, she noticed that no one looked at her. Everyone they passed kept their gazes averted. It made her feel a little better, but not much. Aceptye reminded herself why she was here, what she must overcome to survive, to go home. She decided that she did want to live; she would do whatever it took to see her family again. She prayed as she walked.

> *The target of my strategies should not be the army of this stronghold, but the mind of the man who runs it. Fit in, adapt, conquer.*

Foolishly, Aceptye had not gathered another hawthorn leaf, so now she would have to rely only on her raw ability.

They entered Zhu's personal eating hall. It was much smaller than the main eating hall and more private for him.

"Ah, there you are my dear." Gone was the wild barbarian. Zhu's dress suit was immaculate, his hair neatly trimmed and slicked back, the ends held in a queue. He looked civilized. Deadly.

Aceptye kept her hands over her groin to hide her nakedness. "Please come sit and dine with me, Princess." He gestured for her to take a seat to his left. "No need to hide your beauty, come now and move your hands." Aceptye did as she was told; she would be pliant until it was time to strike. She sat as quickly as she was able.

The table was set for three more places. She had no way to cover her breasts, so their dinner partners would get quite a show. Aceptye wanted to cry, to scream, to run. She did none of these things; instead she formed a picture of her daughter Isladora in her mind.

"Bring in the others now that we are seated," Zhu ordered. The guards left and returned with three other women, dressed similarly to Aceptye in different and varied shades of silk. *So, Zhu is a collector of women*, Aceptye thought. She wondered if each was captured from another kingdom like she was. They were all great beauties, and all had the downward cast of the abused. Aceptye wondered how long they had been here. One looked worse than the others; she had bandages on her arms.

"Camille, I wish you to feed me today," Zhu ordered the one with the bandages. Camille got up as ordered and came around to sit on his lap. She began choosing morsels to feed him. "See, I knew you could be tamed my dear." The emotional anger coming from Camille was palpable, her eyes darting to the knife by Zhu's plate. Aceptye immediately used her magic to calm the woman.

"Princess, are you not hungry?" Zhu looked at Aceptye, malice in his eyes. "You will learn to bow to my every wish and fill my every need, just as these little jewels have." Aceptye took a bite, tasting nothing. Zhu gloated, "I have chosen these women from all over the world and given them a new life, the great honor of serving me."

Camille fed him a cherry, then as she reached for another it fell from the stem onto the floor. She looked at Zhu with real fear. "Now Camille, such a waste. I think I will need you in my chamber again this evening." Aceptye shuddered upon hearing that and looked to see Camille's response. From the hate boiling like strong embers in her eyes, she could tell the woman had not yet been completely beaten, but she meekly muttered, "Yes, my lord."

Aceptye could feel her fear; she could not imagine what had been done to the girl. The will to survive, to fight was nearly gone. Aceptye poured her strength and forbearance into the woman, trying to infuse some life back into her eyes, her heart.

Dinner finally ended, and the guards took her back to her room and locked her in. Aceptye prayed for Camille and she was shamefully grateful to not be the one in Zhu's chambers.

It wasn't until much later that night that Aceptye realized she should have manipulated Zhu's emotions to help the poor girl, it was Zhu's mind that she needed to attack. She sat down to plan.

Chapter 12: Ariah and Json

Json let out a vicious roar, baring his fangs and shooting steam from his nose, bashing his tail on the ground. He rose up to his full size, his wings spreading out then closing quickly against his back as he lunged at the fence.

"Hey there now!" one of the trainers yelled, jumping back from the cage. "I don't know what's gotten in to this one, he needs more of the drug!"

Json felt proud as the trainers that came to feed him shrunk back, frightened of him. Good. He was tired of her watching him in chains. He was meant to be free. Json hated the trainers for taking his freedom from him. He hated them more when the Draconian woman Ariah was there to bear witness.

Json forced himself to calm down, to appear somewhat docile. He did not want any more of the tranquilizer. Json made a pretense at eating the drug-laced mash so the trainers would go away. He waited until they left, then spat the substance through the fence to the other wyverns. He would wait for twilight when his woman fed him. The fresh meat that she brought him was healthier and delicious. The mash the humans fed him was awful, and the only reason any of the wyverns ate it was because there was nothing else and they were starving locked in their prison.

Json and the other wyverns knew the mash was drugged. They could understand every word the humans spoke, yet the humans seemed oblivious of their command of the human language. So when the dragoness named Ariah began bringing him all kinds of tender morsels, he ate them with relish. She whispered to him that she hand-picked the freshest meat and brought it just for him. She knew how much he needed to grow in strength, and she brought it every evening without fail.

His Draconian woman had made a small hole in the fence near the bottom which allowed her to get her hand and arm through. From there she could throw the meat chunks she brought for him where he could reach it, even with his chain. She never failed a throw, and once she began bringing him meat, she never forgot.

Evening arrived and she came. Ariah had stolen four chickens from the cook spits, and she hoped the portions would fill him up. "Hello, gorgeousssss," she said as she threw the first chunk in the air.

Json caught it in his teeth. It was half a chicken and as he crunched the bones, it was delicious. He liked his meat better raw, but it was still delicious. Json tried to tell her so. "I like this meat," he said in the wyvern tongue.

Ariah heard the chirps and croons her wyvern emitted, and she knew instinctively that he liked the chicken. Her body responded with the mewling noises; she couldn't control them when her wyvern made his. She wouldn't be able to bring many more chickens, as they were too hard to steal.

"In another week we will leave thissss placssse, you and I." Ariah threw another half of a chicken. "I don't know how to ride you, but I know we can do it."

Json tried talking to his dragoness but she didn't understand his language. How could that be so? Ariah whispered her longings to Json in the filthy human tongue, telling him to grow strong, that they would escape together. She did not understand when he spoke to her and Json wasn't sure why. She was a dragoness! She told him to kick the food the trainers brought into the next cage so they wouldn't know she was feeding him. She told him how the fresh meat would clear his mind so that he could find his way home. She told him how amazing he was, how magnificent. She told him they would go home together. Json tried to tell her she would need a saddle to stay on his back, but she could not understand him. He moaned with frustration.

Ariah could tell her wyvern was agitated. She threw him another piece. He finished the four chickens and Ariah said, "That issss all I could get." She added, "I will be back tomorrow. Grow ssssstrong."

Json was mortified to be fed by a woman. Women were taken care of by their males; the males were the hunters, not the other way around. Yet he knew the meat was fresh and didn't contain the mind-numbing poison of the trainer's mash.

Now that his mind was clearing from the drugs, Json's anger was palpable. He was angry that the freedom of hunting had been taken from him. Chasing and killing prey was a large part of a wyvern's life, as important as grooming and sunning. Json didn't even have full access to the sunlight; the mountain wall blocked it for most of the day. Now that he had stopped eating the drugged food, not having sun, not being free, not being able to hunt bothered him oh, so much more.

Json spotted the guard named Keit and he growled to warn Ariah. Her scales tightened instinctively with the warning.

"Hello, Ariah," Keit said. "You really shouldn't feed him, he is quite dangerous, you know."

"Oh, hi Keit!" Ariah was startled. She had been so distracted trying to figure out what had agitated her wyvern. "Pleasssse don't sssstop me from feeding him, I jusssst love to watch him eat," she begged.

"We've had this conversation before, Ariah. I could get in a lot of trouble for allowing this," Keit said. Ariah knew he was aware of the small hole in the fence.

Ariah sauntered up to him, "Can you sssspend sssssome time with me thissss evening Keit?" She ran her hand up his arm.

Keit knew he should tell her no, fix the fence, and be the guard he was supposed to be, but his heart raced every time she touched him. His nights were filled with dreams of what she might do with her tongue. He knew she had no happiness in her life and that when she fed the wyvern, she was content. Keit simply could not take that from her and risk ruining what he had with her. The wyvern she had chosen was a waste anyhow. He was small and his wing was partially torn. He could still fly but not with an armored man on his back.

Keit relented, "Of course I have time for you, come on." He took her hand and led her towards his tent. He would fix the fence some other day.

Json watched and listened to their conversation. Keit was so smitten with her, Json was disgusted when she touched Keit's arm. He knew Ariah was distracting Keit so that she could continue his meals. Json couldn't wait to get out of the cage and get his chains off. He was going to bite Keit's head off for daring to touch a dragoness. He growled low in his belly; his dragoness.

Ariah did not befriend this scarred war wyvern by feeding him scraps that the other wyverns did not get. Oh, he ate them, savored them, but he let her know it didn't matter. He hated her feeding him. Females did not provide sustenance, the males did. She didn't win his heart by never harassing and beating him the way the trainers did, he could care less about that too. She had mastered her fear of him, yet he didn't respect her for it. But at night, she came to his cage to watch him sleep, and this new thing made him feel… different about her.

Chapter 13: Isladora's Sparring Partner

Isladora's days were spent relentlessly going through her father's training exercises, described to her through the mental voice of Meluha Crocus. She was learning as fast as she could, pressing her mind and her body to each task, thinking each day about what the Queen Mother had done to her entire family. She used this anger, this drive to change her personality from the shy one who never quite knew what to say or do, the one who always withdrew too quickly when she imagined she was in the way.

She relived the moment in her mind again and again when her lungs were failing her as the Queen Mother gleefully constricted her airways with her awful magic. Isladora pictured turning her magic back upon the evil woman, and her demise. They trained one hour on and thirty minutes rest all day long with a two-hour rest for lunch. Isladora would collapse and fall asleep for a nap immediately after eating, waking charged and ready for more.

At night when she could not sleep her father talked to her about history and strategy, and she asked questions about all the things that she felt she should have known but through necessity had previously been hidden from her. Some he would answer, some he would not.

"Father, tell me about my nursemaid." Isladora grew morose thinking about her. "She could fight, she tried to save me from the Queen Mother's men." A tear fell. Then almost a whisper, "She fought them so I could get away."

"*Lepola is a warrior from the Juna tribe,*" her father began. "*The Juna tribe are my people; your people, Isladora. My father was the king of the Juna but we were a scattered tribe then and like all of us must, one day he passed away. When I married Anyumay, I wanted to find a way to bring us all together. The stronghold was full of dark magic and criminals. We took over the stronghold and built it to what it was before Emperor Zhu began to attack us.*"

He paused to think. "*The Juna are trained from adolescence in stealth, weapons, horses, and hand-to-hand combat. Our style is direct attack and linear power for the men. The women's style is similar but because of their size they must also learn how to redirect an opponent's energy and use their weight against them. They are fierce fighters, and Lepola was the most cunning of them all.*"

Her father's voice grew rigid and he added, "*Years ago, we were almost wiped out in a war with Zhu. It was a war we were not prepared to fight. They poisoned our water supply and our food supply, and some of us died slow painful deaths that we had no cure for. A year later, I was imprisoned by Zhu's daughter and her treachery."*

Meluha added, *"Then she cunningly took the throne with the threat of more war with Zhu. What is left of the Juna people are in hiding, building their numbers and training, always training."*

"I pray Lepola is still alive, Father." She wiped her face and nose. "I pray that she is still alive and back with the Juna." She paused to think, "The Juna have not been annihilated, like I was taught. Our people live!"

"Yes, our people were scattered. As for Lepola, I am sure she is alive Isladora, I'm sure she made it out," her father said. *"Now sleep, we must train again tomorrow."*

"Yes, Father." Isladora said. She fell asleep excited that she was Juna, that Lepola was true family! Someday she would make Lepola proud! Isladora had begun to feel like a warrior; the past month had certainly been a warrior's life for her. She had calluses on her hands and her feet. They had grown stronger and thick skinned. She could say the same thing for her mind and her heart; they were set on revenge.

It was early morning in the pre-dawn. Her father was attempting to train her instincts for war. *"Now Isladora, when the light flashes, I want you to take an evasive maneuver, then make a killing stab,"* he spoke through Meluha Crocus' magic.

The ring's light flashed, and Isladora jumped and turned the stick into a spear, driving it downward. At the next flash, she shoulder-rolled to the side and made the stick into a short sword, cutting upward. Another flash, and she dodged back and made the stick into a slender pike, driving forward, aiming for the throat. Isladora ran to the pile of rubble and boulders in the cave and turned her stick into a shield, matching the rubble to camouflage herself from view. She tried to imagine real enemies there, but only time would tell how she would react to an actual attacker. They continued practicing evasive maneuvers the remainder of the day.

The next day as Isladora was eating her breakfast fish, fish, and more fish, she felt troubled. She had run out of the lambsquarter and hadn't found another source. There were other plants, but upon inspection they were inedible. But this wasn't her true worry. She decided to speak up. "I need sparring partners, Father," she respectfully told him. "That is how all the king's men are trained; they sparred religiously every day!" Truth be told, she was frightened to say this, but her logical side knew it was a necessity, much like her body needing more than fish and water.

"I know daughter," She heard in her mind, *"but you have no sparring partners here and I have no body with which to train you."* The thought of sparring with her

father held her thoughts momentarily. Did one strike their king? She didn't know the answer to that. What an experience that would be, she thought! She thought about those horrible fish women, but she didn't know if she could find them again. She had traveled so far down this cavern. Plus, seeking out a smaller creature with intent to harm was not something she could do.

"I can make her a sparring partner," Meluha Crocus said. *"I can ensorcell that small boulder into a sparring creature. I will not be able to control it, only turn it on and off."*

"No Meluha Crocus, it is too dangerous for my daughter," her father ordered.

A sparring partner! "Yes, Father, you must let me try. The Queen Mother has trained all her life and she is my target," she reasoned. "Without actual partners, I won't stand a chance against her and you know it." Isladora thought about the Queen Mother's choking magic and her stomach quaked.

"Isladora you must control your fear of her," Meluha Crocus said.

The silence stretched for so long that Isladora was about to repeat her argument. Her father said with a sigh, *"Yes, tomorrow we will try. Meluha Crocus, cast your spell in the morning and Isladora will spar and learn."* She could hear the king in her father's words.

She slept and ate fish and drank water until it was time. Her training body needed clean fuel and rest and she knew it. Her body was becoming fit and her mind as sharp as a blade from the nutritious fish. Isladora loved it! She had not truly known how sick her body was from her overeating and sedentary lifestyle until now. Isladora truly felt closer to the Way of the Heron, to her God.

"Remember, I can only turn it on and off, I cannot control what it does, so be prepared," Meluha Crocus warned.

"My enemies will be the same, Meluha Crocus," she said.

"Push that small boulder on your left to the center of this area." He referred to the same boulder that Isladora pushed around the cave to strengthen her arms and legs. She did as Meluha Crocus asked, glorying in feeling her heart pump from the labor of pushing. Or maybe it was adrenaline; in a few moments this thing would try to hurt her.

Her father gave her one last word of advice. *"In a world in which many people are indecisive and overly cautious, speed will bring you untold power. Striking first, before your opponent has time to think or prepare, will make them emotional, unbalanced, and prone to error."*

The ring glowed and the rock shook, lengthening to become a short man-creature. It left its round shape as if it had been curled in the fetal position and opened until it was standing like a person. It had two short legs, two short arms, and no head. It turned towards Isladora, which was an odd sensation as it had no head or eyes, and she felt her heart pound for a different reason—fear. It would have no emotional imbalance; it was a rock.

When it stood it was only half her height, yet she was still frightened at the sight of it. It began running towards her, and Isladora froze in fear. When it got close to her, she tried to leap out of the way and ended up tripping on her own feet. It curled into a rock ball and crashed into her body. She felt her whole world explode; her mind went dark. Again, she was falling down the cliff away from the Queen Mother.

Isladora opened her eyes. "What happened?" She sat up and immediately regretted it.

"Your sparring partner knocked you out cold." She wasn't sure if she was talking to her father or Meluha Crocus.

"Oh." Isladora tried to stand and failed, feeling that concussive sensation again. She felt desolate and shaky. A single tear ran down her face.

"Where is the rock?" Isladora looked around for it, spotting it sitting in the middle of the area like some creepy nightmare.

"I turned it off." Definitely Meluha Crocus speaking.

Isladora brushed off her pants, noticing how old, torn, and awful they had become. "Father," she said shakily, "it has no emotions and therefore can make no emotional error."

"I know Isladora, bad advice," and he chuckled, or maybe Meluha Crocus did. So, her father was human and he could make a mistake.

"Perhaps a better maxim for this type of enemy would be that water is powerful because it follows the path of least resistance." Another warm chuckle, Isladora was almost sure it was her father's.

She closed her eyes and thought of her mother, how she gained strength from prayer and faith. Isladora had faith too; she prayed for strength. The prayer was difficult, as her mind would not calm remembering the pain of the rock creature slamming into her body. It took a long time. Finally, she pictured a black room, focused on her breathing, and then slowly calmed. She tried the prayer again, and this time she was successful.

Isladora searched her memory for strategies. She remembered how Lepola bent like a reed to avoid the blows of the men. She thought about catapult shot and how the only way to survive it was to move out of the way of its trajectory. She thought about fear and how as soon as she saw the creature, she should have been planning her defense. Isladora decided she would remove her emotions from the melee and focus on her strategy.

She thought about books she had read. From her text *Angular Momen-*

tum, Rolling and Torque, she knew that if the rock rolled, she needed to run uphill to slow it down. The cave did have an inclined side near the west end before it hit the river. If she could match its momentum, she could in fact roll with it and grab the thing. If it stayed on two legs, then she could use her martial arts and stick to fight it.

Isladora stood. "Wake it up. I am ready."

"No Isladora. You took a tough hit. You must rest and then we will continue tomorrow."

"I am ready!" She hit her chest, and exclaimed, "Wake it! I must carry my intentions to completion. I must become resolute."

"Very well." The ring began to glow and the rock slowly stood and turned towards her.

It immediately began to run at her again. Isladora turned and ran to the uphill side of the cave. Again, it changed to a ball but it slowed greatly when it hit the incline. She moved to the side and pushed it away with a front thrust kick using the bottom of her boot. The rock creature got stuck in some limbs and roots that grew into the cave.

Isladora could feel the ring get warmer on her finger in what felt like encouragement, so she took it as such.

She ran back to the flatter bottom where there were other rocks. The creature stood and worked its way from the limbs and roots. It turned towards her again and rolled downhill this time, becoming a fast ball of force. This time when it grew close, she jumped as high as she could—quite a good height thanks to all the plyometric drills her father and Meluha Crocus made her do—and it rolled under her, crashing into the other rocks.

As it untangled itself, Isladora ran towards the river, which was at a slight incline to where the creature was now. It ran towards her, changing into a ball again, and as it slowed on the incline Isladora sat and let it roll into her. She rolled backwards with it, using its force to roll her over, and as she rolled onto her back, she pushed it with her knees. She launched it into the river where, with a great splash, it sank. *Path of least resistance, hah!* She thought, rocks could not swim.

"Well done, Isladora!!" She didn't know if it was her father or Meluha Crocus speaking, but she didn't care. She had fought and won!

Isladora bowed respectfully. "Again please, Meluha Crocus. Make me another one." She let her anger and fears channel into a passionate martial power; she would not let fear control her.

For days they did this type of training, using bigger and smaller rock sparring partners. Isladora began using her magical escrima stick, and if she hit a killing target, by striking the heart, lungs, or stomach, the ring would shut it off.

Every time she won, she heard laughter in her head from the ring and she knew it was King Elijashen. She knew that laugh belonged to her father. Her father, who was training her with strength, dignity and, yes, laughter. It made her feel proud. It made her feel bigger than she had ever felt. This man believed in her, in her ability to free his trapped soul. No price was too high; there was no price that Isladora would not pay to hear that laughter again and again.

She had learned from being frozen in fear that first time. She trained her mind to handle the sight of the Queen Mother in battle. Isladora envisioned the woman at her worst and herself at her best, defeating her. She did this over and over; it became her mantra.

Isladora grew brave through these trials. Her whole world was to impress her father with her new skills, to hear his delighted laugh. That sound gave her strength; it took away the fear because hearing him laugh with each victory was her entire focus. Isladora realized that her prayer had been answered, and that night she knelt and said a prayer of true gratitude to God.

Chapter 14: Zhu's Dinner

A time would come. A time for release, revenge, and reward. Aceptye believed it with all her heart. It had been a long time since she had concentrated on manipulating someone's emotions, but this wasn't the first time. She had been at war before. Aceptye considered her goals. The first and foremost was freedom from Zhu; she must return to her daughter. The second was that her body not be violated. Her body had only known Elijashen, and that was precious to her beyond measure. Although she was married to his younger brother Thrace, it was in name only and for protection until Elijashen could be found. Aceptye would not believe that Elijashen was truly dead until she saw proof. Her body was only Elijashen's to command, and she prayed that would be true until her death. She did not belong to Zhu; she would never belong to Zhu. In this, Aceptye could control her heart and her mind, but Zhu, being stronger, could indeed control her body, and she hated that.

Aceptye thought about what sort of man Zhu was. He was impatient, temperamental, and accustomed to getting his way in all things. He would viciously take whatever he wanted from her. The bandages on Camille's arms at dinner were proof of that. Camille's fear of him had been palpable, and she seemed to be a strong and proud woman. Zhu was growing tired of conquering that one, and Aceptye knew that when Camille finally broke Zhu would turn his attention towards her. She must have a plan.

What Zhu seemed to enjoy the most was tearing down the woman's defiance and absorbing the woman's fear. He took pleasure in making women submit, and as long as they resisted he was entertained. The poor woman he was torturing right now was about done in. She had very little fight left.

Aceptye thought about the qualities Zhu lacked, empathy ranking right at the top. She decided she would pour empathy into his mind this evening. Perhaps expanding Zhu's capacity to feel Camille's fear and pain could move him to stop torturing her. Aceptye also decided that if Zhu made sexual advances towards her, she would infuse him with disgust for her body. If he didn't kill her, it might work. At least perhaps he would not be able to rape her.

As dinner time approached, Aceptye chose three leaves from the hawthorn tree to empower her magical strength. She hid them under the front sash of her gown. Ingested, they would boost her magic, as it fed from living things and green plants were the best.

For the millionth time, Aceptye wished she had her magical ring on her finger. She had taken off the ring when she meditated and prayed, as it interfered with her mind too much. The Queen Mother had taken her away during her daily hour of prayer, and it had been left on her nightstand. A foreboding chill swept over Aceptye; that ring in the hands of the Queen Mother could be devastating.

"Come my lady, it is time," her nameless maid said. The maid had artfully arranged her hair, piling it on top with soft curls tousling loose about her face. Aceptye looked like she was going to a ball, when in reality she was going to an insane dinner hosted by a madman.

The maid led her into the dining room, the guards following. Zhu was not yet present and Aceptye quickly took her seat. The two other women sat in silence with their heads bowed. The current favorite, Camille, came in slowly and sat gingerly, her arm at an odd angle to her body. She was obviously in a great deal of pain. Aceptye couldn't stifle the gasp that escaped her lips as she noticed that the arm was dislocated at the shoulder and on the other hand more than one finger was badly broken. The woman would be unable to use either arm to feed herself. Aceptye's fear of Zhu blossomed in her abdomen, and she felt very ill. She took one of the hawthorn leaves from her sash and chewed it slowly, forcing herself to remember her intent.

Zhu entered and placed a sharp knife in front of his favorite. "There you are my dear. Just pick it up and kill me with it!" Zhu laughed just as he had when he had made her arms and fingers useless.

"Yes ladies, Camille tried to stab me in my sleep last night. You would all do well to witness the result." Zhu spread his napkin in his lap like a true gentleman at a civilized court, smoothing the edges. "We cannot have such behavior in my kingdom."

Aceptye wanted to send strength to the woman, but she remembered her plan and instead focused on Zhu. She couldn't help with the pain anyway. For her magic to work she had to view the object of her emotions with love. Once that link was made, she could increase or decrease any emotion the person could experience. It was the Way of the Heron, strength through love.

The serving crew set plates down in front of them, some vegetables, potatoes, and meat in a brown sauce, along with loaves of bread and crocks of butter. None of the women at the table could take a bite knowing Camille was in so much pain and misery.

"Eat up ladies. I would hate for you to lose a finger or two!" Laughing at his own humor, Zhu dug into his plate with relish. He took a large bite of the crusty bread, the getting butter on his finger. He looked at Camille and licked it off his finger, wagging his eyebrows up and down.

"Eat. Now." He ordered.

Aceptye gazed at the cruel man and tried to picture him as one of God's creatures. She thought of him as a small child, before the world made him the sadistic man he was, and the link was made. Good. Aceptye picked up her fork and took a small bite, sending every bit of empathy she had into his mind.

Strange emotions floated in Zhu's head. He thought about how he had fallen from his horse once as a child and hurt his shoulder. He knew how much pain Camille must be in. He suddenly felt sorry for her, sorry that she could not eat. He also began to worry about the mental state of his other dinner partners. "Are you comfortable here, Aceptye?"

Aceptye wiped her mouth on her napkin to gain time to think before answering, "Why yes, Zhu, my chambers are lovely." She sipped her water and sent more empathy into Zhu.

Zhu's mind was at war; he could not tell if Aceptye was being sarcastic. The need to mentally challenge her was great. Yet the empathy he felt made him think about the others. "If you like I can show you the grounds later." He found himself offering like some nobleman host to an honored guest.

Any attention from him would be bad, but Aceptye had no choice. "Of course, I would be honored, Zhu," she agreed, looking demure and submissive. More empathy.

"See, Camille," Zhu spoke, "why can't you be mannered like Aceptye?" When she looked up with sorrowful eyes, something inside him shifted. What had he done to this poor woman?

Seeing the shift in his mind and fearing him, Camille quickly said, "Yes, your majesty."

"Okay Dru," he said to one of the other women, "you can feed her…" With relief, Dru came around the table to feed the broken woman.

"Please eat, Camille, it will give you strength," she whispered as she spooned a mouthful of broth and one small potato into her mouth. Camille opened her mouth automatically, her mind gone. She was but a fearful shell. Aceptye saw that one of her teeth was broken. Her concentration faltered at the sight of the jagged tooth.

Zhu suddenly realized he was being weak-minded. As he watched Dru feed Camille, he grew angry and disgusted. Camille tried to kill him; what did he care if she starved? And the sooner the better!

"Enough!" he yelled, pushing his chair back and drawing his sword. Dru fell back in fear, hitting the floor hard and crying out in pain. Camille just stared at him with that dead, blank stare.

Aceptye watched it as if it were in slow motion: his chair scraping back. Steel ringing as the sword was drawn from its scabbard. The dead look in Camille's eyes. The sword arcing across the table, barely missing the candelabra. Camille's head falling to the floor.

Aceptye was mortified. She was responsible for this girl's death! Feeling empathy made Zhu so angry that he lost control. Empathy made him want to release the girl from her pain, and to him that meant cutting her head off. In Camille's shoes though, Aceptye would have preferred death, her suffering had been so great. Aceptye did not want to imagine all the terrible things Zhu must have done to her.

"Now look what you made me do!" Zhu yelled at the corpse much like a spoiled and petulant child, but far, far more dangerous. "You ruined dinner!"

"You!" he pointed at the guard. "Bring some servant girls to my chambers. Now!" Zhu stormed out.

The guards didn't know what to do, but they knew better than to disobey. They took the three remaining women to the kitchens and sat them at the table. They grabbed two of the kitchen girls, both very young, and dragged them out the door. Neither girl screamed. One guard stood at the door to watch Aceptye, Dru, and the third woman.

The guard seemed more interested in what was going on in the other room, knowing they had little time, Aceptye asked Dru, "Where are you from, Dru?"

"I am from North Umbria," Dru answered. "It's North of the High County."

"I am from Timber Town," said the other woman, "east of North Umbria. My real name is Pislonna, but here I am called Princess Nishan. We were told to say we were royalty, that if Zhu did not believe us to be royals he would kill us immediately." She rubbed her face tiredly. "So we lied. I am really a housemaid and Dru is a merchant's daughter."

"We know you are true royalty," Dru told Aceptye. "No one will come looking for us." Dru looked back to where the guard stood. "Zhu is too dangerous," Dru continued. "But you, someone will come for you, a princess!"

Aceptye was saddened by the girls' plight. "How long have you been here?"

"For six months we have been here," Pislonna told her. "We were stolen by soldiers, brought here, and traded to Zhu for money, I do not know how much."

The girls were heartbreakingly hopeful when they asked Aceptye, "Will your tribe come for you? Do you have warriors?"

Aceptye would not be the destroyer of their hope, or hers. "Oh, I hope so, I hope that Prince Tonsaku knows to come find me here and free us all."

Chapter 15: Charming Keit

Ariah was pleased; her wyvern was growing stronger now that the drugs had left his system. The healthy meats she provided him gave his green scales a glorious sheen. Ariah knew it was getting harder for the wyvern to remain in captivity. The trainers had tried to tranquilize him twice now to calm him down. They had increased the drugs in his mash, but Json simply kicked it over to the other wyverns as soon as the guards left. If they stayed to watch him eat, he chewed but did not swallow. Json hated the pretense, it made him angry at the guards. It was also getting harder for Ariah to steal meat for him; her people had noticed the missing food and were keeping a more careful watch, though it appeared that they did not suspect her.

Json purred and chirped at her in their common language, asking Ariah when they would leave. Ariah did not remember their language, being with the humans since her youngling time. She had no idea that he was communicating with her, only that her body responded with mewling noises when he did. Ariah loved the way she felt around her wyvern. Her entire being was attuned to his; every movement and every gesture made her feel alive. She loved how her scales tightened when he was fierce, it made her want to scream out her joy.

Json was beyond frustrated trying to get her to understand that she needed a saddle or she would fall off when they made their escape. Json thrashed his head around, telling her one word. *Saddle.*

"What issss it, love?" Ariah tried to calm him with her voice. Ariah could swear he rolled his eyes at her.

Json looked at her and then at the tack shed. He said the word saddle again. Ariah did not understand, "You sssseem agitated today, are you feeling well?"

Json growled at her, tossing dirt and rocks at her with his back claws and looked again from her to the tack shed. Then again, a third time.

Ariah tried to figure it out. She looked over at the shed and then back at Json, and he nodded to her. He nodded! Keit had said they were intelligent, but Ariah thought like a dog, not like a person! Her wyvern was talking to her! Ariah approached the shed and peeked inside.

Inside were saddles, head pieces, and reins. Oh!

Ariah returned to her wyvern. "You are telling me we will need a ssssaddle!"

When Json nodded, closing his great eyes in agreement, she said, "Oh my!" Ariah was nearly undone with this ability to understand each other. She knelt upon the earth as a tear slid down her cheek. Looking up at him slowly, "Do you have a name, dear one?"

Json chirped his name for her. Ariah tried to make the sound, but she didn't have the muscles trained to pronounce it properly. Json shook his head. Then with precise letters, he wrote "JSON" in the dirt with his pointer claw.

"Jsssson," Ariah said with wonder. "You can write, you can understand me!" She stared into those intelligent eyes. "That issss a beautiful name, a name for a sssstrong warrior." Ariah smiled and tilted her head, saying, "And my name issss Ariah, but it wassss given to me by the humansssss. I do not remember my real name, nor my real home." She stood up, her shoulders naturally thrown back.

Json chirped that he would fly her there. That he knew how to travel to Draconia now that the drugs had worn off. Json told her they needed a plan to escape the cage, to escape to freedom in the sky. He had not flown in some time, but he was ready.

Ariah was completely charmed when Json tried to talk to her. She didn't understand a word of it, but he tilted his head much like she did when he chirped and carried on. When she spoke to him, he listened intently. Json was also an auditory being. Ariah had never known such attention and she loved it, loved him for it.

"I know you will take ussss home," Ariah told Json. "You will fly me on your great sssstrong back and take me to where there are othersss like me, like usss. We will be free, you and I."

Keit watched the exchange. He saw Ariah enter the tack shed, and that spelled trouble. His men were making suggestions that he had lost his mind with her and maybe they were right. He would put a stop to her feeding the wyvern. Keit knew it was why they were having trouble with this one. These wyverns were cunning and dangerous when they were not properly drugged. Keit hadn't been particularly worried about this wyvern, as he wasn't used for flight anyway. He was only used to fight the others when they became too aggressive. Keit decided he would spend time with her tonight and afterwards tell her she must not feed him again. Keit would then repair the fence and move on with his relationship with her. Her tongue pleased Keit in many ways, but he wanted all of her.

Json growled to warn Ariah that Keit was watching. He scrubbed the dirt where he had written the letters. Ariah looked up and saw Keit heading towards them. When she didn't offer her usual glorious smile, Keit grew jealous of her love for the wyvern and knew he must separate them now.

Keit reached her. "How are you today Ariah?" She looked guiltily up at him. She was not good at subterfuge.

"My men have noticed your attention for this wyvern, and I'm afraid I must stop your visits to him, especially no more feeding him." Keit spoke with his Captain's voice. When Ariah began to look angry, he softened his voice somewhat. "You know I have to follow orders Ariah; my hands are tied in this."

Ariah knew angering him would stop any chance of success they had. "I know Keit, I am jusssst sssso drawn to him, I sssimply cannot help it."

"Well drawn or not, you must stop your visits to the beast," Keit responded. "You don't have to stop your visits to me though." Keit chuckled, trying to sound charming.

Json growled deep in his throat, baring his fangs. He wanted to breathe fire and burn this man into nonexistence. He could, too. Without the drugs, his fire capability had returned; Json could feel it in his belly, his throat. He opened his mouth wide to spew it forth when Ariah saw and she quickly stepped between them.

"Of coursssse Keit, I'll do whatever you asssk of me," Ariah answered. "I know you are only trying to keep ussss all ssssafe."

Keit was relieved that she understood the wisdom in not being near the wyverns. "Can I see you tonight, Ariah?" He ran his fingers through his hair and looked at her with his rakish smile. "There's supposed to be another full moon." And boy did he have a wonderful memory of the last full moon.

"Yessss Keit, I would like that very much," Ariah lied. Anything to get him away from Json before things got worse.

"Great, tell green boy here goodbye for good and I'll see you later tonight," Keit told her as he turned away.

Ariah watched him leave, hating the power of men. Ariah also hated agreeing to meet Keit in front of Json, knowing that it upset her wyvern.

"Don't worry Jsssson," Ariah told him gently. "Tonight, I will sssssteal the keysss from him and we will be gone before firsssst light. Before the ssssun issss up, you will ssssspread thossse glorioussss wingssss."

Json purred to show his delight. He rose to his full height and pressed his chest out, sitting as regally as any king would do. He opened his wings to their full extension then knelt so his front claws could reach the earth.

He wrote one more word in the dirt before scrubbing it away as well, but Ariah had seen it. TONIGHT.

Chapter 16: Isladora Exits the Mountain

The smell of dead fish was overpowering. Isladora fought down a gag and covered her nose. The smell was so bad that she had to backtrack to where the air was clearer. She sat down and cradled her head in her hands trying to stop the feeling of nausea.

"What is it, Isladora?" her father said through the mental voice of Meluha Crocus.

"I smell something terrible." She battled with her queasy stomach. "It's like fish, but worse."

"Your senses are coming back to you then?" Meluha Crocus asked her.

Isladora was confused, "What do you mean, Father?" What did he mean that her senses were coming back?

"This is Meluha Crocus speaking now," the ring glowed. *"When you were a baby, your mother and others who are like her could feel the magic inside you. She was afraid that you would be taken from her when we were attacked."* He paused, then continued, *"When Elijashen could not be found, Anyumay was distraught and inconsolable. In her fear of losing you as well, she blocked your magic with a drug."*

Meluha Crocus paused for a moment, trying to find the right words to explain. He said, *"Magic and spirituality are closely related to nature. By giving you a poor diet of fats and sweets and the drug, your body would not be in the state of health most conducive to life and therefore magic. This ensured that what little magic you still had within you, you could not reach.*

Unfortunately, the drug also dulled your taste and smell."

"What magic do I have?" Isladora asked, cutting right to the quick.

"We do not know for sure, as we began blocking it when you were but a toddler." The ring glowed, so she assumed it was still Meluha Crocus speaking. *"Your mother has the ability to alter people's emotions."*

Isladora let out a small humph! "No wonder I couldn't fight with her." She sighed, "Every time I was angry or in the mood to fight with her, I have never been able to." She must have been manipulating her emotions.

The ring was not glowing, and with a laugh, her father said, *"Yes, she probably calmed you with her magic. She did that to me many, many times."*

Isladora was so mad, "You kept me a fat helpless thing; no wonder I was such an awkward kid!" Here she was, a warrior's daughter, and they had treated her badly, even poisoning her body to dull her magic ability.

Isladora didn't care what their reasons were, they should have told her long ago.

"It was your job to direct me!" She said in anger toward both her father and her absent mother. "Not keep me fat and stupid without even my basic senses in the dark!" She fumed, "No wonder I was such an easy target for the Queen Mother!" Isladora remembered the Queen Mother stealing her breath and falling pain-stricken off the cliff. Memories of the Queen Mother calling her fat and ridiculous also surfaced.

"We were all trying to protect you Isladora."

"Well you failed in that," she returned hotly. Isladora quickly admonished herself for behaving like a petulant child, but oh how angry she was at them. She loved her now-lean body, the strength she had gained. She loved training and fighting, it was now her way; she was a proud descendent of the Juna tribe. Isladora now knew where true happiness originated within her. It came from purpose, from inner drive. She wasn't just a lazy fat kid; she was a naturally driven person who needed outlets for those drives. Isladora had always felt so worthless before; she told her father this.

"But daughter, finding that drive isn't a once in a lifetime pursuit, it is an on-going purpose, for we do change with the tide." Her father continued, *"While you may resent it, your lazy upbringing allowed you to become learned. All the books, all the reading and tutoring, those were no mistake. It was to give you the power and brains behind the brawn you are now beginning to attain."*

"Yes, I suppose you are right Father," she conceded, still angry, but she could see his point. They had kept her unaware but well read. She could use her book smarts to outwit her enemies.

"We didn't make you anything, we have only begun to refine what is already there." He continued, *"It is this learning that allows you to see past your anger and acknowledge the wisdom in how we chose to protect you, to shape you, even while you do not agree."* Elijashen the King spoke here, not the father. The king continued, *"Focusing on negative feelings of the past can weigh you down and bring you misery. The past is immutable and unchangeable. You must make a conscious effort to force yourself to react in the present moment. Look to the future. Be ruthless with yourself in your training now. Use your studies to allow no static lines of defense in your strategy, making your plans and the future both fluid and mobile. If the wound still bleeds, you will not be strong until it closes."*

Isladora could see that he was right, that she must not focus on the past. She must focus on the present, and right now that was walking towards the worst smell she had ever encountered in her existence.

As they continued, the smell grew so bad that she had to tie a cloth around her nose and mouth. They were nearing the river. Isladora had never smelled such a smell of decay before. Looking for its source, she saw long hair and, *oh God*, a body. The river flowed quickly past, but the body had become lodged in the rocks in a small inlet.

Isladora scrambled to remove the cloth, as she was immediately sick. It wasn't just a body, it was the body of the fish-woman she had stabbed with her escrima blade. Her first kill.

She wiped her mouth and began to pray. She cried and prayed, blocking any words from her father or Meluha Crocus. "I did this," she whimpered, "I killed this creature." Isladora was both mortified and hysterical, rocking back and forth. She stayed that way for a long time, crying herself out and praying a nonsensical, constant stream of words.

After reason resurfaced she said, "We must bury her."

"No Isladora," spoke the glowing ring, *"she is of the water and should be buried in the water. Just free her body from the rocks and let it flow downstream and out to the ocean. It is the way of such water creatures."*

Isladora didn't question how he knew this, and she owed it to this creature to try to comply.

She changed her stick into a longer pole and wedged it under the boulder closest to her. Using another rock as a fulcrum, it took all her weight, but the rock finally gave and fell into the deeper part of the river. The body loosened, and with a final prayer, Isladora watched it enter the current and float downstream. She was morose and filled with grief.

They traveled in silence the rest of that day and the next. Isladora continued to look for the body, hoping it didn't get lodged somewhere else whenever they were close to the river. She never saw it again.

Then suddenly, like a dream, they saw a valley, finally, through an exit from the mountain ravine. The valley was small and green, and then the land was dry and flat as far as the eye could see. She saw trees, and they held fruit, cherries! Isladora ran to them and grabbed a handful, shoving them in her mouth. The flavor was intense, too sweet after such a bland diet. Isladora ate them anyway, barely taking the time to spit out the pits.

Isladora remembered her map of the world as she gazed over the valley at the land beyond. Only one place could be so dry and flat. The wastes of the Shadout Basin.

She slowed her chewing to speak, "Father." She cleared her throat from days of being unused. "We are on the wrong side of the mountain." They had emerged on the far side; the Juna stronghold was on the other side of this mountain range. The mountain rose in crags and sheer rock, no chance of climbing it.

"We will just have to find a pass," she whispered to herself. It was hopeless. Without food and water, she knew they would not make it very far. Without her father or Meluha Crocus answering her, she grew even more disheartened. They hadn't talked to her since she had sent the fish woman on to her watery grave.

Isladora needed to think, but this vast open space made her uncomfortable after being in the cavern for so long. She took more cherries and went back into the cave, her home of sorts. Isladora wasn't exactly sure how long she had been in the cave, but it had been more than a few months. Feeling hopeless, she laid down and fell asleep, her lips stained red.

When morning came, she tried again to speak to her father and again he did not answer. "Why have you left me?" She pulled at her hair, "You left me all alone in this place?" She yanked at the ring but it wouldn't come off. Isladora noticed the cherry juice stains on her fingertips. "I don't know where to go. Answer me damn you!" She yelled at no one.

"I am here, Isladora." her father answered, *"I have always been here."*

"But you wouldn't answer me!" Isladora cried.

"It was you, Isladora. You blocked us from answering you with your magic, in your grief," her father explained. *"If you had not, I would have told you to stop gorging yourself!"*

Isladora was scared, truly scared. She had not known that she used magic in isolating herself. She had grown up in isolation so that must be her comfort place, she thought. She was also ashamed of gorging herself on the cherries; it was too much like what she'd have done before.

"You don't have to be alone in your grief any longer," her father said. *"I will never leave your side again."*

"Big promises for someone who doesn't even have his body," Isladora tried to joke.

Her father was silent for a short time until finally he laughed, *"Yes daughter, you are right!"* Then more seriously he said, *"You have changed so much in a short time Isladora. You are a completely different person now. You are a warrior on the way to battle."*

Isladora didn't feel ready to go to battle. Just the sight of the creature she had killed made her fall to pieces. Maybe it would help if she saw these changes herself. She changed her escrima stick into a long flat oval, the metal gleaming like a mirror. She stood it against the wall and stepped back a few feet to look at her reflection.

What she saw amazed her. Gone was the pudgy little girl, and in her place was a stunning young woman. Even as dirty and worn as her clothes were, her legs were shapely and toned, her stomach flat, and her arms were muscular, though dirty. Her breasts hadn't gotten any larger, but they seemed larger with her newly toned body. The diet of nothing but fish, a few greens she had scavenged, and water had made her very lean. Her dark brown tresses had grown longer, some framing her face and the rest pulled back with a leather strip. She could see her cheekbones now that the pudginess was gone. Her full lips were still stained with cherry juice. As Isladora touched her face, she honestly didn't think that anyone would recognize her. One thing was for sure, she needed new clothes badly; hers had become threadbare and were falling off her lean hips.

Killing was a part of war. Isladora thought that when she killed the fish woman it was in self-defense, as she was trying to drown her. It was the creature's choice to attack and her choice to defend. The same would be said about the Queen Mother. She chose to attack her family, first imprisoning Elijashen, then killing Thrace. Isladora prayed her mother and Tonsaku were alive. Yes, it was the Queen Mother's choice to kill, and now it was her choice to seek revenge.

Isladora thought that if she had magic strong enough to stop Meluha Crocus from speaking, who knows what other magic she had whirling around inside of her. She could control the escrima stick with ease and shape it into anything she wanted. One thing was for sure, never again would she let people push her out of the way and into hiding.

Never again would she feed herself foods that were not beneficial to her body, a gift made by God. Isladora silently vowed that she would begin a lifetime pursuit of learning and training, nurturing her body and mind to the best of her ability.

But first, she thought, she had to rid the kingdom of the Queen Mother, and that meant finding a way home.

Chapter 17: Zhu's Visit

After Camille's beheading, there were no more dinners. Aceptye ate dinner alone in her room, thankful for the reprieve from Zhu and thankful they still allowed her food, albeit once a day. The food was bland and lacked nutrition, which affected her ability to alter emotions, including her own. Two moons had passed and Aceptye had grown forlorn. Her skin and hair became lusterless in her captivity, as lusterless as her heart without any hope.

She hated the demoralizing clothing. Every see-through garment was a direct blow to her moral standards and wearing it still unnerved her to the core. Having nothing else to wear left her feeling bereft and degraded. Many days she just sat with the bed sheet wrapped around her. Aceptye longed for her life back and spent a good portion of her time in prayer. She tried to stay strong and sat in the sun when it filtered through her window. She did calisthenics every day. In particularly weak moments, she picked a hawthorn leaf and ate it, but not many leaves were left that she could reach through her window.

Whenever the maid or guards opened her door, Aceptye practiced manipulating their emotions. When she used the hawthorn leaves first, her magic was always more powerful. She practiced maintaining her mental focus, whatever the circumstances, especially after inadvertently causing the death of Camille. Her cunning and magic were the only real weapons Aceptye had against Zhu. She tried to think deeper about the effect of certain emotions on his psyche. She now knew that pouring empathy into someone who simply did not feel it triggered frustration and then anger. Poor Camille.

Basic emotions of normal people were fairly easy to influence. Aceptye had been able to manipulate the guard to feel sad and happy within the same visit. It was the more complex combinations of emotions that she was working on now. Zhu was not what she would call a normal human being. He was ruthless and evil. Since Aceptye didn't know how to be ruthless and evil, she had to think things through before she caused other deaths, or her own.

The maid returned, this time to bathe her. It had been well over a week since she had been allowed to bathe, and she was happy at the chance for human interaction. Aceptye decided to try to manipulate the maid into telling her name. As they bathed, Aceptye poured truthfulness and openness into the maid. "I would really like to know your name," Aceptye sighed wistfully. "We spend a great deal of time together, you and I."

The maid opened her mouth to speak, but then closed it, stopping herself. "Princess, please do not ask me that, it is forbidden," the maid demurred. "Although I did have one once, it is not for us to use." She added more hot rocks to the water. Aceptye sank down further in the warm water. After days of not bathing, the water and attention felt wonderful. Aceptye added trust to the emotional cocktail she was sending to the maid.

"How long have you been here, then?" Aceptye asked.

"For most of my adult life," the maid answered, her deft fingers kneading Aceptye's shoulders and neck. "My father traded me to the keep in exchange for his debts." The maid sighed as she began washing Aceptye's hair with lavender and spice. "He did not want to trade me, as he needed me. My father is a farmer and could not pay his full rents to Emperor Zhu." The maid's hands worked their magic, massaging Aceptye's scalp. "While I am glad to be here, my father truly needed me at home; without me there I'm not sure how he is taking care of himself."

"I take it your mother passed away then?" Aceptye asked.

"I never knew my mother, and I don't know what happened to her." The maid poured clean water over Aceptye's head to rinse out the soap. "My father used to call me shortcake, but that is not my real name." The maid helped Aceptye to stand and then poured more water over her body for a final rinse and began to towel her dry. Aceptye kept sending the emotions.

"If you must know, my real name is Semmi, but I could lose my head for telling you that." Shocked at herself for telling Aceptye her name, the maid dropped the towel and held both hands over her mouth, her eyes wide and frightened.

Aceptye felt ashamed for practicing her magic on this dear creature and placing her in mortal danger; in the fortress of Zhu, all danger was mortal. She vowed that if she ever left this place, she would take Semmi with her and give her the best life she could. "I will never break your trust with me Semmi, this I promise you."

Fearful, knowing she had made a big mistake telling a prisoner her name, Semmi angrily hissed, "Do not use my name lady!" The maid accompanied her back to her room and left her with the guards.

Aceptye soon learned why she was allowed a bath when an hour later her door opened and Zhu entered her chamber for the first time since the fatal dinner. The maid followed him in, giving Aceptye a fearful warning look, then she made sure he was seated and poured him some wine she had brought on a tray. Semmi backed up and stood against the wall until he would need her again.

Zhu was wearing only dark pants and a white shirt that was open. A man like Zhu would come so dressed to her cell for only one reason, to gloat and to rape. His long dark hair was down, curly and wild about his face. Zhu was an immensely powerful man; every bit of him was chiseled muscle. "We have word that your Prince Tonsaku has gathered his men and is headed this way."

When he spoke this he saw hope blossom in Aceptye's face. Repulsed, he pinned Aceptye with his eyes, no mercy in their depths. His brow was heavy and lowered over his eyes in a permanent scowl. "When Tonsaku reaches the river and enters the Zoli Pass, my men will pick him off like the bothersome fly that he is." Zhu stretched his long legs out in front of him. "And you will already be ruined for him, just another one of my royal whores."

Aceptye used her magic first to calm herself. She was almost paralyzed with fear, visualizing Camille's head falling to the floor again and again. Aceptye did not want to be a broken woman like Camille. Camille had been all about resistance, and that did not work with Zhu.

She decided instead she would play to his ego. She took a calming breath and then spoke, "I have never seen a more powerful warrior than you my lord." Aceptye kept her gaze down. "I have no doubt that a youth like Tonsaku would be no match for you."

Zhu was taken aback by her acquiescence. He had expected her to put up something of a fight. Where was the fierce princess he had found in the forest? He decided to test this seeming acquiescence and ordered, "Take off your clothes, whore."

Aceptye knew she had no choice and kept thoughts of her daughter firm in her mind as she stood to remove her clothing. She was completely humiliated by his awful eyes and shaking with fear. Aceptye wished she had the strength of a man; she would kill him with her bare hands.

Aceptye used every bit of her magic to keep Zhu from feeling aroused. She infused boredom and distaste for her naked form.

Zhu looked at her body and it was beautiful, but somehow looking at her was not pleasing to him. She was too meek, that was it! He stood and struck her across the face, thinking a little blood might help get things moving along.

Aceptye's head snapped back and she fell to the side, blood trickling from her split lip. He stood up and grabbed her by the hair, "Please me, you high country filth!"

Aceptye sent loathing and disgust for her into his mind. As she slowly reached towards him, he pushed, shoving her away.

Zhu had no idea what was wrong with him. Arousal was never a problem, but when he looked at the beautiful princess, he felt the same way he would if her were looking at a smelly goat, or a doddering old grandmother. He grabbed the maid, looking for some semblance of sanity, at least as he perceived it. Aceptye tried to infuse the same emotions into him for Semmi, but without the power of a hawthorn leaf, her magic was drained.

As Zhu reached for the maid, Aceptye tried to grab his arm, but Zhu turned and backhanded her and she fell and hit the table, making her see stars for a moment and then she fell into black unconsciousness.

Aceptye became aware, intense pain in her head. She heard Semmi crying out, "Oh thank you, my lord!" Zhu shoved Semmi away, and she crashed to the ground, drawing great gulps of air into her lungs. Semmi was both crying and mystified that her lord would honor her so.

Zhu fastened his pants and left the room. He told the guard to take the maid to the infirmary. If she was pregnant then they would rejoice; if she was not, she would be killed. Zhu had strange views when it came to his seed.

Aceptye rushed past the guard and ran to Semmi's side. The maid's throat was bruised and red where he must have choked her. "Isn't he wonderful?" Semmi croaked.

Aceptye was shaking and crying, "Oh dear lord, no!" She tried to straighten Semmi's clothing. "You are bruised and your clothes are torn. Let me help you!"

"It is my honor," Semmi murmured as she smiled dreamily. "I have his seed inside me, the essence of the Emperor!" Semmi was overly excited, shaking all over from her near death from lack of oxygen, going into shock.

"Oh, I hope that it is true; I could be carrying his son!" Semmi touched her belly. "The son of Emperor Zhu!" Semmi laughed. "I will get to be housed with his other pregnant concubines!" Semmi would now be the one waited on and pampered, at least until they knew if she was pregnant. "Oh, thank you princess for helping me achieve this honor, thank you so much!"

Aceptye could do little, as the girl was completely enthralled with the treatment she had just received. She thought of it as a blessing, to be raped! What a crazy and horrible world this was. Tonsaku could not save her fast enough. Zhu had said that Tonsaku and his warriors were almost to the Zoli Pass. He was on his way.

As the guards came into the room to get the half-naked and bruised girl, Semmi told her, "You will be assigned another maid, princess."

"You have a name," Aceptye told her quietly.

"Do not speak it lady!" And like that, they were all gone, leaving her alone once again. Aceptye knelt naked and grieving in prayer and stayed that way for hours.

Chapter 18: Ariah Earns Their Freedom

Ariah went back to her tent to pack a small bag. She took only the things she would need to survive; she was somehow certain that these human things no longer belonged with her. She would wear her thickest pants, made of leather; they were supple and warm and would hide her unusual coloring. She stole a leather vest that was lined with fur, a knife that strapped to the thigh, and some rope from neighboring tents. Her meek, submissive behavior and the long years of loyal, unquestioning service worked in her favor now. Ariah wasn't watched around the campground, and stealing was quite easy; most trusted her like they would a camp dog.

The young dragoness was exhilarated that in a few short hours she would know what it was like to fly, to reach the clouds and see what the birds saw as they looked to the earth. She would learn these things and take her freedom back with Json, her beloved wyvern. She wondered how he would feel when she touched him. She could not wait to run her hands along his inky dark green scales and see if they felt like hers. She just knew that they would be soft and warm yet strong and hard for battle when the time came.

Her life had changed so much in just a few short weeks. She had learned where she was from and that there were others like her. Json knew how to get home. It was branded into his senses and into his blood. Ariah wondered if the people of Sybaris would welcome her or if they would be hostile to an outsider that couldn't even speak their language. It would be strange to see others like her after living with the nomads for as long as she could remember. Sybaris. That was what Keit had called her. A dragoness.

Ariah ate dinner, making sure she ate every bite, not knowing when her next meal would be. She was sad that she couldn't also feed Json, but she couldn't risk another visit.

For her visit with Keit, she decided to wear her normal clothes so she wouldn't make him suspicious. It was hard for her to spend time getting ready for a date she absolutely did not want to go on. Gone was the young woman that was infatuated with the Captain of the Guard. Still, she needed those keys and tried to dress the part. She would leave the pack and the leather clothing hidden in the tent she shared with two others and change into it later.

Ariah thought about leaving the nomads and realized there was no one she wanted to say goodbye to. She wandered aimlessly through the campground, silently saying goodbye to the life she had known and to ease her nerves.

Vald, one of their leaders, had left his vambraces on a table outside his tent. They were made of thick suede and leather. Ariah was drawn to them because they matched the dark green, almost black, of her wyvern. She quickly took them and returned to her tent. She uttered a sibilant hiss; she couldn't believe what a thief she had become. She told herself that it was okay to steal from her captors, as they had stolen her life and made her a slave. A slave with no friends and no hope. Json gave her hope, and that was a feeling she loved.

Ariah tried on the vambraces, sliding them onto her forearms and tying the leather ties to hold them in place. She flexed her forearms. She felt like a warrior with them on, and they would protect her forearms. They were beautifully tooled with a pattern stitched into the suede that she did not recognize, a bird of some sort rising in flames on the left one. In a few short hours, she too would be rising into the air on the back of her wyvern. With a sigh she took them off to get ready for her meeting with Keit. Keit, who was trying to separate her from the only creature on earth she had ever truly loved, her wyvern. He was no different from any of these humans.

Her plan was to get her unsuspecting admirer alone and take the ring of keys from his belt. Knowing she could not overpower him and not wanting to kill him, Ariah had taken a small bottle of wine and in it she added a strong sleeping draught they used for minor surgeries, also stolen from the healer's tent. Once he fell asleep, she would take the keys. Ariah had seen him open the cages before, so she knew those keys would work. Then she would wait until it was quiet and sneak out to free Json. Once they were airborne, no one could catch them. They would be free. With one last check to make sure her stolen things were hidden, Ariah left her tent.

Keit watched Ariah sauntering towards him, and again he was mesmerized by her gracefulness and the fluid way that she moved. He was sure she had no idea of the allure of her swaying hips on his body and mind. She looked to be deep in thought. She was almost upon him when she finally noticed him waiting there. "Oh, hi Keit," she breathed throatily, stopping before him.

Keit came close to her and reached up and took a strand of purple hair, running it through his fingers, "Beautiful as ever, Ariah." He took her hand, leading her back to the mountain path where they had watched the moon rise before.

Ariah followed silently behind him as he drew her along, noting with satisfaction the keys hooked to his belt. "Do you think the moon will be assss big asss it wassss lassst time?" She didn't really care but was trying to keep herself from focusing on the keys and giving away her intentions.

One thing she knew about these human men was that they were perceptive.

"What I remember about that night wasn't the size of the moon my dear, it was you," Keit answered. He could not wait to feel her tongue again; he had dreamed about it again and again, a mental litany. Obsession was a good word for it, he thought, and wondered what else that tongue might be capable of. He picked up his pace, pulling her along.

When the moon rose, at first it was dark orange, almost red like a blood moon. It was large and it would emit a lot of light as it rose into the sky, when she and Json were escaping.

Ariah hesitated. It would be better to leave on a darker night, but no, Json was expecting her. He had written 'tonight' in the dirt. Tonight it would be.

Ariah was having such a hard time focusing, her heart repeating Jssson, Jssson, Jssson with every step. Oh, why did men think they could hold other creatures captive? Why wasn't she free to choose her own path? Why was Json in a cage, beaten and before she came, drugged?

She could never love this human Keit. She was disgusted with herself that she had ever wanted to taste him. But then she hadn't known. She hadn't known that she wanted her freedom and that he held the key. She hadn't viewed him as a captor or the keeper of their prison. She did now. He was Json's enemy. He was her enemy. Her fangs began to protrude as she stared at the back of his neck. The sliding rocks under her boots hid her growl.

"What is running through that beautiful head of yours?" Keit smiled at her. "I don't think I've ever seen you this distracted. What's going on?" he queried.

"I am a little nervoussss tonight." Keit stopped and looked back at her. Ariah tilted her head and tried to look coquettishly at him, praying her fangs had retracted. "Being with you isss wonderful, and I jussst want to pleassse you." She placed her hand on his chest. "I brought ssssome wine for usss." She raised her other hand to show him the bottle.

"You did? Well then why don't we have some now?" Keit smiled back at her. She was adorable, he thought. Ariah uncorked the bottle and tipped it to her lips. She took none of it in her mouth but swallowed three times to make it look like she was drinking. She offered the bottle to Keit and he took a drink as well, matching her swallow for swallow. The pair continued to climb. Keit remarked, "That is really good stuff, I wouldn't have guessed that the nomads would have a good wine."

"Yessss, they do lovvvve their wine and trade offften for it," Ariah told him. "I think thisss wine came from the Dunssssabar grape fieldsss." Ariah demurred, "I fforgot to bring cupsssss with me, sssssorry."

"Dunsabar, wow that is a famous winery!" Keit commented as he took the bottle from her as they climbed. "No one needs cups for such a fine wine!" he said, trying to make the situation better so she would not be embarrassed.

They reached the place where they had stopped before and both sat down, Keit offering the bottle to Ariah. Ariah pretended to take another long drink, and Keit followed. "Delicious!" he said, "but not as delicious as you." He leaned over and began kissing her neck passionately. Ariah was immediately appalled and tried desperately to hide it. She felt like she was betraying Json. A snarling growl she could not stop curled up from her belly, and as Keit drew back in alarm at the sound, her scales hardened and the instinct to bite at his jugular warred inside her.

"Wow that climb must have gotten to me; I feel a little weird." Keit rubbed his hands over his face.

Ariah wanted to kill him! But no, she did not have a killer's heart. "Are you okay?" Ariah positioned herself a little behind him. "You do look a little ssstrange. Here, lie back and placcce your head in my lap." Ariah ran her fingers through his hair in an attempt to calm him, to calm herself. What was she thinking, wanting to bite his neck?

"Pleassse tell me again about the Ssssybarisss." When Keit didn't speak, Ariah ran her tongue over her fangs and focused on his neck. One bite, and he would bleed out; how she knew that she did not know. Keit had become fidgety, his legs twitching, and just when she began to panic that she would give in to her inner beast, he was out cold, snoring.

Thankful, Ariah wasted no time. She gently placed his head on the ground and took the keys from his belt. She hurried back down the mountain to rescue herself and her beloved. Ariah stopped at her tent quickly and donned the leather pants, her finest leather boots, and the fur-lined vest. She tied her hair back with another piece of leather and strapped the knife to the outside of her thigh. She tossed the rope and her small bag over her shoulder and lastly pulled the vambraces onto her forearms, tying them tight. To hide her hair, she pulled a black cap over her tresses. ·

Dressed in leathers and bound in darkness, ropes, and good intentions, she arrived and without remark unlocked the metal cage housing her loved one.

Chapter 19: Ariah and Json Take Flight

Ariah unlocked Json's cage, set her things on the floor, and ran back to the shed to get a bridle and saddle. As she searched the shed trying to find what she needed, she felt her heart hammer, pounding in anticipation. She returned with the items and hoped against hope she could figure out how to get them on her wyvern. She had saddled a horse before and she had watched the other trainers tack up their wyverns, so she thought she knew how.

Json had not moved even though the door to the cage was open. That's when Ariah noticed that he was chained to the floor. She thought it just as well; the nomads left their mounts tied up as they saddled them. She would unlock the manacle afterwards. "Okay Jsssson my lovvve," Ariah said as she approached with her hand outstretched, for he truly was intimidating. Ariah was somewhat afraid of his size and unsure of herself. He chirped a message to her, but she did not understand.

Json tried to tell her that no one would put a bit in his mouth. Ever. But the little dragoness did not understand. Json grabbed the bridle and reins in his teeth and yanked them away from her, tossing them noisily to the other side of the cage. Exasperated, Ariah ran and picked them up to try again. Snorting and chirping louder, he again tore them from her fingers. When she went to retrieve them again, he stopped her with his imposing head. Json shoved her back and shook his head back and forth to tell her "no" like the humans did. Instead, he shoved her towards the saddle and chirped again. Really, a dragoness that couldn't understand these simple things!

"Okay, okay, I get it! Ssssaddle only, then!" Json purred as Ariah finally understood. Thankful—at first she thought the wyvern had lost his mind or was wilder than she imagined.

Ariah grabbed the saddle and stood next to the wyvern. She was quite unsure, not knowing if he would reject that too. But no, he had told her she would need a saddle. She tossed it up onto his back just like the trainers did. As she moved around to his other side to grab the cinch, she ran her hands across his chest, finally feeling the warm leather sensation of his scales. They were much like hers, just bigger. She paused for a minute, closing her eyes and breathing in his scent. Ariah crooned to him; they were senseless sounds to her, but to Json they were a love song.

Ariah thought she heard something so she rushed to cinch up the saddle. Json knew it wasn't tight enough. He bent his long neck back and pulled the cinch tighter with his teeth, and Ariah quickly tied it off.

Now to unlock the manacle. Json was chained to the floor in the cage by a metal cuff linked to a chain that ran to a metal post in the ground. Keit's ring had three keys, and Ariah tried every one, but none opened the lock. Lights came on at the main barracks and an alert sounded. Json chirped and pushed Ariah towards the saddle. She climbed on his back, fitting her feet into the stirrups and buckling the saddle's straps around her legs and waist. Wyvern saddles were made so that the rider would not fall even if the wyvern flew upside down. She fastened the last buckle and then held on for dear life. Json tried to break the chain, pulling against it with all his might. The chain would not give. They could see the soldiers running down the hill towards them.

With a fiery roar Json blew a stream of deadly fire at the chain, until the metal glowed red hot.

Ariah gasped as her scales hardened. He pulled again, straining to be free when it finally broke, sending them crashing back against the cage. Dogs were barking now, and the soldiers would be upon them in seconds. Json launched from the cage. He began sprinting down the hill away from the soldiers. He spread his wings, and with a screech he jumped, pushing off the ground with his powerful legs, and they took flight. Ariah had never been on such a bucking object. She tightened her grip, closed her eyes, and stayed close to Json's back so she would not throw him off balance, trusting him to get them in the air. The climb was slow and rocky, but they were indeed airborne.

After months of captivity, Json's wings had grown weak. They were in bad shape anyway, riddled with tiny tears from the endless fighting. His wings strained against the force of the lift and the additional weight he carried. Json focused on climbing so they could fly out and away from the mountain cliff, and the task required all his finesse and concentration.

"Ariah!" Keit shouted from below. The drug must have worn off. Ariah looked down to see Keit with a longbow raised and an arrow pointed at them. He was going to shoot!

Keit drew back and released a warning shot that flew wide of Ariah and the wyvern. The wyvern banked to the left to miss the cliff side. Ariah, thinking that Keit simply missed, raised her arm in the air and shook her fist. A warrior's screech came bellowing out of her lungs, her scales tightening even harder in response. She shook her fist at Keit, yelling her victory over him.

Although with just a little more altitude Json would be able to fly away, he really wanted to swoop low, breathing fire over every human at the camp. Free from the drugs he had enough fire to kill them all easily. Except one. Keit. That one, he would bite off his head for daring to touch his dragoness. But Json could not risk their freedom; he could not risk making the climb a second time in his weakened state.

The dogs and wyverns below barked and roared, and the soldiers were trying to tranquilize the great beasts. Some of the wyverns attempted to breathe fire, but the drugs made it hopeless.

Keit had no choice, he had to stop them. It was his duty to do so and he would be court-martialed, perhaps even executed, if he let them get away. Keit's mind still swam with the drug she had given him. He couldn't believe she had tricked him. He should have seen it coming; the warning signs were there. His men were right, she did cloud his judgment. He raised the longbow and drew it back, praying that he would miss Ariah, fearing that he wouldn't. Keit's second arrow tore through the top of the wyvern's wing but he kept flying. Keit shot a third arrow just as they flew from his range.

Ariah felt a hot pain in her side and looked down to see an arrow protruding from her unscaled abdomen. She looked at Json's torn wing and wondered if his wing hurt this badly.

As they flew into the west, Json's homing beacon tried to lead him north, but he could not turn that direction with the holes in his wing. Json kept flying. He tried to fly straight, but his torn wings were slowly turning them west. In this great desert, he would have to keep flying as long as he could. It offered no cover.

Ariah could feel her energy waning as the blood flowed from her body. She felt very warm and sluggish. She sang a prayer of thankfulness for the freedom of her wyvern and for her own freedom. Json listened to her song and knew she was happy. As she laid her chest down on Json's neck to rest, she gazed at the ground below and felt the wind in her hair. She was flying! She had never felt so free, so alive. After some time, Ariah passed out strapped to Json's back, a peaceful smile of contentment on her face.

Json flew for a long time. He chirped to Ariah but she did not answer or move. Json knew she was wounded, and he feared that she was dead. Finally, he saw a mountain range ahead. He would try to land there. With his torn wing and months of captivity, he would be lucky to pull off a landing that didn't kill them both.

Ariah had not stirred at all. As they neared the mountains, Json chirped for her to hold on. With his torn wings he could not properly slow or control his landing. He crashed into the side of the mountain with his feet, breaking off pieces of rock and trees; debris flew everywhere.

Down he fell, tearing branches and limbs from trees. Finally, he hit the ground, taking most of the force with his forelimb and wing in order to protect Ariah. His forelimb fractured in half, and with a scream he slid and then ground to a halt.

Json laid there for some time. Ariah did not move. Json's forearm was broken and the bone protruded; he knew that he would never fly again. He looked back at Ariah, her beautiful form lifeless. He couldn't turn his head enough to remove the saddle with his teeth so he could tend to her body. He roared with an explosion of energy and danger, ferocity on a scale not meant to be in the realm of men. He would have no revenge against the cursed creatures; he would not make it home.

Json grieved for Ariah and himself the only way that a wyvern could, he began to sing his song of death, his chirps and croaks broadening into long vibrating notes that resonated down the mountain. His passionate lamentation filled air with his sorrow and mourning for the loss of Ariah, for the loss of his freedom a second time. When he finished, he laid his dark-skinned and weathered head down to await his own death, which would take a long, long time.

Chapter 20: Transformation

Isladora knew they were on the wrong side of the mountain. Once she left the cavern and ravine, she would have no more fish and no foreseeable water source. Her clothes were so threadbare they would provide little protection against the elements and in fact would be an embarrassment if she met any people. The river had disappeared underground, and she did not have a map. She knew she needed to go west, to the other side of the mountain, but she did not know if she would find a pass. She respected the mountain range now; its size and grandeur were humbling. She would have to choose a direction but based on her knowledge she felt that her selection would be no better than gambling, a toss of the dice.

East was nothing but the parched earth of the Shadout Basin. North, she saw a bend to the mountain but couldn't see past it. Isladora did know that this mountain range eventually led to the ocean in the north. South, the mountain range continued for as far as she could see. She decided to head north. Without food and water, she would likely quickly perish. She planned to catch and dry fish to store some food, but she only had one water skin, and when it ran out, death awaited. She must give in to the vast unknown, but she did not have to give up. Her goal was to end the Queen Mother, and she would think of only that. If she died in this wasteland, then so did any hope for her father and mother to be reunited. Her entire family would be wiped from the face of the planet. It was a chance she would have to take.

With these decisions made, she felt better. Having a purpose gave her hope. She walked to the edge of the cavern to say a prayer for guidance in the wilderness. She lifted her eyes to the sun and began her earnest prayer with a grateful heart, a smile on her lips.

"Look at Isladora, Meluha Crocus," her father said. *"God bless her. She remains calm and unperturbed, her head held high, a slight smile on her lips. The trials and tribulations of survival in this mountain have given her a nearly unshakable strength; she is a force to behold. My daughter."*

"Indeed," said Meluha Crocus, *"the daughter of a great king."*

As Isladora prayed for guidance, she began to hear the strangest sound. It echoed down the mountain and resonated deep inside her chest, bringing chills of fear to her spine. It sounded like a large creature singing deep in its throat. It scared her to death, raising goose bumps all over her skin. The sound went on and on. As she grew used to it and fear lessened its grip on her, it seemed like the sad song of grieving. Isladora wasn't sure what lived on the edge of the Shadout Basin, but after being alone with only mental companions for so long, she was curious enough to find out.

Isladora followed the edge of the mountain north, towards the sound. Rounding the bend, she saw all manner of debris littering the ground; large trees and pieces of the mountain wall had broken off and fallen. In the middle of the wreckage of trees, boulders, and rocks lay a large creature. As she grew closer Isladora could see a human-like figure strapped to a saddle of sorts on the back of the creature. The creature's eyes were closed as it sang. Isladora stayed out of sight, frightened of its large size. Eventually it finished its song and after that, simply passed out.

The beast seemed to be what Isladora knew from her books to be a wyvern. She had read that they were intelligent and fierce, not caring for humans at all. She also knew they had magic and that some could spew poisons and fire from their bellies. This wyvern was mysteriously beautiful and deadly looking; its claws alone could rip open any living creature.

Isladora watched them for more than an hour, but neither the wyvern nor its passenger showed sign of movement. She thought that they were both likely dead. She ventured closer, yet still no movement. She wanted to see if the rider was alive and needed help. She needed courage, and she recalled a specific moment from one of her favorite books when the hero was exploding with courage.

> He had fallen to the earth, not yet beaten by his foes but close. He would not lose heart; it just wasn't possible, for his father raised him to be unafraid. He would live through the horror of this ghoul and the next three after it. He stood and smiled, completely unafraid, daring the ghoul to try again.

Isladora tried to access what the hero had seen with his eyes as he fought the nasty ghoulish undead in the book. She heard with her ears and felt throughout her body the moment the hero stood and smiled. She thought of herself in action and at her best, letting the feeling of courage wash through her. She strode towards the wyvern like a warrior, a leader.

Isladora was close enough to touch them both, close enough to study the saddle straps and understand how to loosen them. The person was bent over and she couldn't see their face, only their back and legs. As she reached towards the first buckle, the great creature's eyes opened and looked straight at her, the wyvern's pupil enlarging as it focused on her. She froze in fear, her courage spent.

The beast studied her for a long time. Finally, it lifted its head from the ground chirping and gurgling. It waited for some time and then made the same sounds again. It was trying to talk to her.

"Meluha Crocus do you understand what it is saying?" Isladora asked in desperation. "Tell me now, I order you to do so!"

"Yes Isladora, I do understand. This is a male wyvern, as no female wyvern allows a rider. He wants your help." The ring glowed.

Her muscles loosened, "Tell him I will give it!" The beast was not going to hurt her.

The monster chirped again.

"He says he understands you, human," Meluha Crocus answered. Then as an afterthought he added, *"Do not order me again Isladora, I only speak to you because I want to."*

She had indeed ordered him. Yet, was she the only one who could not speak to anyone without Meluha Crocus' help? She immediately chastised herself for the thought and told herself to have a heart of gratefulness to Meluha Crocus that he could speak for her. "I am sorry, Meluha Crocus."

"Um, wyvern, what can I do to help you?" She asked with a gentler heart. She saw that his wing was broken and partially torn. The break looked horrible. It was his major limb that served as his arm and also attached his wing to his back. It had snapped in half.

He was chirping and gurgling again. Meluha Crocus translated, *"He says you must hurry. He needs you to build a large funeral pyre for Ariah, the biggest you can manage. She is the creature he is carrying. He needs you to build it right there between those two boulders. He bids you hurry."*

Ah, the creature was a woman and she was dead. Looking at the debris, she realized a human could not have survived the crash. The wyvern huffed and tossed his head, reminding her to hurry. She started to build the funeral pyre, a process that took her all morning and afternoon and every bit of her strength. She dragged the biggest logs she could to the bottom, thankful for the abundant debris. She collected every branch, every log, and built and built, leaving a cradle in the middle for the body. Isladora was exhausted and filthy, her hands cut from the branches and her arms bleeding from scratches.

Meluha Crocus told her, *"The wyvern says his name is Json. He thanks you and asks you to please hurry. He must light the fire as the sun sets. This is important. Now take her and clean her. She must have all the dirt and blood removed. He wants you to remove all of her clothing; she must not have anything man-made on her body."*

Isladora began to unbuckle the straps, noticing with a gasp that she was not human. She had fine, beautiful scales running up her arms. Once she was released from the saddle, Isladora strained to pull her off the wyvern and onto her shoulder. Isladora was reminded of Phoenix, the great warhorse who carried the dead Regis King, Thrace. How carefully he had stepped. His neck had been rigid, his haunches bulging. His hooves had made small furrows in the turf as he stretched the lines of his back to balance his load.

So Isladora did the same. She loaded the female over her shoulder, noticing the arrow protruding from her side. *Ah, so they have enemies like I do,* she thought. Isladora kept her legs bent and balanced and carefully placed each step, carrying the lady towards the cave and the water. "I will bring her back before the sun sets, Json. I can clean her at the river inside," she told the great beast.

Isladora entered the cave and laid her next to the river and began working quickly. She removed the lady's boots, knife, pants, and vest, noticing she the beautifully tooled vambraces on her forearms; Isladora thought that she must have been important to have them. Her beautiful scales ran down her legs too. Isladora had never seen such an amazing creature! When she removed her cap, Isladora gasped at the beauty of her red and purple tresses. She removed the leather tie holding her hair and then poured water over her with the water skin to wash away the dirt and the blood. Isladora brushed out her hair with her fingers, and then with a vicious yank, she pulled out the arrow and set it aside. She had to staunch the blood again and then clean up her torso.

This time she carried the lady in her arms and noted that she wasn't that heavy. She was a little smaller than Isladora. Still, she stepped carefully, balancing the load. Json was relieved to see her, chirping and carrying on. Isladora did not need Meluha Crocus to tell her that he was telling her to hurry.

Isladora placed her on the funeral pyre in the center and once more wiped away blood from the arrow wound. Json pulled himself from the debris and moved towards the pyre. Isladora backed away and stood at the entrance to the cavern.

She did not know what to expect, what he was going to do. When he began his magic by streaming green fire from his mouth, Isladora was moved to her very core. The green fire moved over the body, slowly curling it into the fetal position. Even her hair slowly transformed into a smooth mass lovingly placed around her body. The wyvern stopped and closed his eyes, emitting sounds in a language Isladora did not understand. Then he breathed lavender fire that sealed her in a clear glossy oval shell. Over the next thirty minutes as the sky changed colors, he breathed yellow, then orange, then red, and finally white hot. With each color change of the sky and the fire, the oval shrank in size. When it grew dark, he finished, and collapsed.

When the fire burned down, what was left of the body was an egg unlike any egg Isladora had ever seen. It was as large as her head, glossy, and almost effervescent with light green and lavender swirls. It was beautiful. The wyvern spoke, and her ring glowed as Meluha Crocus listened. When he was done speaking, the wyvern passed out, exhausted, on the ground.

Meluha Crocus told her, *"The wyvern said that you must take her to Draconia. She will have a chance for rebirth if the ruling clan decide it to be so. He thanked you for your help; if the sun had set on the day of her death, Ariah would have had no chance for rebirth. He told me that a male wyvern can make one egg in their lifetime. Json chose to do this for Ariah, but she must be taken to Draconia."* Meluha Crocus was silent for a time before saying, *"I would assume that he cannot take her himself because he cannot fly. To a wyvern, not being able to fly is to die, and so he awaits his death."*

"No, Meluha Crocus, he will take her to Draconia himself," Isladora declared. "We can fix his arm and his wing with your magic and my hands."

"You are not strong enough to hold the bones in place for that long. My magic can help heal but it cannot hold the bones in place Isladora," Meluha Crocus told her regretfully.

Chapter 21: Healing a Wyvern's Mind

Isladora slept little that night, restless, thinking about Json's forearm. The break was clean with no jagged edges, so it just needed to be held in place long enough to knit together. She thought of the bridge that had been built over the river near her home. The builders used segments of timber and bands of steel to attach the segments together. She felt she could do the same for Json's arm and stitch up the tear in his wing. She just had to find a way to band the two bone segments together.

When she woke, she saw the vambraces laying near her pack and they gave her an idea. She needed a strong brace, and nothing was stronger than the metal of her escrima stick. But to hold it in place, she would have to remain focused on it for the duration of healing so it wouldn't revert to a stick or tear his wing, which ran along the back of his forearm. Much like the laces on Ariah's vambraces, Isladora's mind must be the laces that would hold it together.

Not one to shy away from a challenge, she pictured what that brace would look like. It would be like a cast that was tight but didn't close fully where Json's wing met the forearm. She could make the edges curved and blunt around the wing to protect it from further damage. To test her theory, she practiced making the complex shape along the length of her leg, which was as about as long as Json's forearm. She practiced tightening it and holding it in place.

Later that morning she told Meluha Crocus about her idea. "So you see, my escrima stick can hold the bones in place. It is magical itself and strong enough!" She was determined to heal this great creature so he could take that poor Draconian woman home and see her reborn. Isladora knew that she could not make the trek to Draconia and even if she did, according to the books she had read, humans did not go to Draconia and survive; surely the wyvern knew that. "If we set the break, how long will it take the bone to heal?" She asked.

"Magical creatures like wyverns heal quickly, so I would say a few days," Meluha Crocus explained, alert and excited at the idea. *"If I can use my magic to speed it up, maybe in half that time, perhaps even faster."* With Meluha Crocus' magic and the wyvern's healing powers, she thought that they could do it, she just knew they could.

Isladora went to examine the egg. She carefully touched it to see if it would harm her. When nothing happened, she ran her hands over it and finally picked it up. The green and silver swirled around like a living thing covered in delicate glass. The egg was covered in ash but was still beautiful, full of swirling mists and sparkling mystery. When she took it into the cavern to clean it up, Json didn't even stir.

Isladora didn't want to dunk the egg in the river, as she might lose her hold and drop it to be lost forever in its depths. She picked up her metal stick and transformed it into a cradle and carefully set the egg on it. It took several waterskins full of water, but she gently and reverently washed it, amazed that Ariah was contained inside. As the ash washed away, the egg was even more mesmerizing. Just in case Ariah was aware, she told her how amazing the egg was to behold, she told her she would see her wyvern healthy so he could take her home, Isladora placed the cleaned egg gently on her pack.

Isladora caught and cooked fish, enough for three days, and placed water near where she would sit and concentrate on the wyvern's healing. Isladora planned to sit in the cave so she was out of the elements and wouldn't be distracted but where she could still see Json. While Isladora waited for the fish to cook, she cleaned Ariah's clothes in the river and hung them up to dry. She hoped that they would fit her; they would definitely solve her lack of clothing problem and just in time, too. Building the funeral pyre had torn what was left of her shirt to shreds, and her left breast was showing through the material.

When she had prepared everything, she approached the wyvern, who still hadn't stirred. "I'm going to try to pull your bones together and it's going to hurt," Isladora warned him. Json gave no response. She pulled his wing over a large boulder and then climbed up next to it. Isladora sat on the boulder and used her arms and legs to pull the bones apart and then together, making sure they had a good set. The wyvern's growl raised goose bumps on her arms, but she stayed on task. She changed the escrima stick into a long C-shaped metal brace, placed it over the break, and mentally tightened it. She checked to make sure the brace didn't pinch the wing. Already, she could feel the drain on her mind from keeping the metal's shape under that much pressure. Isladora moved to where she had laid out supplies for the next three days and sat down, closing her eyes and concentrating. At least the wyvern was keeping still and hadn't bellowed in pain.

"Okay Meluha, start your healing magic." Isladora whispered.

"I cannot," Meluha Crocus told her. *"He is stopping me!"*

Isladora couldn't even begin to fathom why the damn wyvern would do that. Without magical help, it would take at least three days. She tried her hardest to concentrate but after a few hours of the strain, she fell unconscious and the metal stick changed back into its natural form. The forearm broke back in two.

Isladora woke as the wyvern growled and hissed in pain. She shook her head to clear it then rose to collect the stick from the ground. "How… is he stopping you, Meluha?" She looked at the beast and exclaimed, "Why would you do such a thing! Why would you keep us from healing you with our magic?" The questions tumbled from her exhausted mind.

A mental sigh. *"Json does not have the will to live,"* Meluha Crocus explained. *"Without the will to live, his magic is inadvertently blocking mine. He could heal, but it would take longer than you can hold that stick in shape."*

"Then I will just have to concentrate for that long and keep the clamp in place." Isladora began softly crying, tears rolling down her cheeks, knowing very well that she could not hold it in place that long.

"No, you will not be able to. I am sorry, Isladora."

She was frustrated, crying from the strain and hopelessness she felt, her hopes dashed. When she pushed the wyvern's head with her foot, his eyes opened. "What is wrong with you—we are trying to help you heal?!"

Chirps and gurgles. Meluha Crocus translated, *"He says… go away human.."*

Isladora slumped down beside him and did what he did, she gave up. She cried and sat and slept and woke and sat some more. Isladora knew that synchrony and body language could be more powerful than the spoken word, so she lay beside him, trying to understand, and then slept until the next day dawned.

When Isladora woke she realized the mess they were in. She would be alone again because she would have to leave him here to die. Likely, she would die too in the mountain wilderness. Ariah would never make it to Draconia. In frustration, she stood and kicked his snout. "I never thought a dragon to be scared. Fight! Avenge her death! I will not take her to Draconia. They will kill me upon sight. I will fix you, you have to only allow the magic to run through your lousy good-for-nothing carcass!"

"He says no. Show the Draconians the egg, they will let you near," Json replied without remorse as Meluha Crocus translated.

"You know I cannot make that journey and you know I will die even if I do make it to Draconia. I need you to help me, and you are beholden to me to try!" Isladora was mad enough to kick him again. "I built that pyre for you, and I washed your friend. She would be gone forever if it weren't for me, so you owe me!" She screamed at him. "I don't know why you would spend your time to make that beautiful egg; you should have just let her pass from this earth if this is all the fight you have in you!"

Beautiful? Json lifted his head and looked to the ashes of what once was the pyre. *"Where is the egg? Show it to me."* A command.

Shocked, she didn't argue. She went into the cave to retrieve Ariah's egg. Isladora kept it secure against her body and walked carefully. As she came near, Json lifted his head to see her. Isladora didn't know what she expected him to do; she didn't know a wyvern could gasp, but he gasped, his eyes widening.

He raised his body using his other arm and got to his feet. As he gained his ground, he bowed so gracefully, and so low to the ground that Isladora thought him to be like the finest court gentleman. After a long pause he finally rose to his feet and began issuing orders. The ugly cur.

Json talked and Meluha Crocus translated, *"You must feed me and heal me, human."* He moved towards the cavern and entered the cave, settling down much like a cat near the river and taking a long drink. Isladora was so relieved to see him drinking and in the cavern, she wasn't even mad. She followed him and gently placed the egg back upon her pack where it would be safe, and then she hastened upriver where the fish were abundant. She caught almost a dozen of them, turning her stick into a long needle-like spear to string them on. She brought them back to the beast.

"This is all I have to eat," Isladora told him. "How do you like them cooked?" He growled and opened his great jaws. She tossed the first fish in and he swallowed it whole. By the time she got the fifth fish in his maw he began chewing, bones and all. He ate every fish. Isladora was starving too, so she sat and ate some of her cooked fish and drank some water as well.

When she was done eating, he began to stir again. He took his good arm and checked the sharpness of his claw, raking it against the rock floor and dunking it in the water, back and forth several times until it was clean and sharp and shiny. Then with a quick slice and more chirping language, he opened his chest at least twelve inches. Blue-black blood began to flow down his body. Isladora shrieked, "Why did you do that?!"

Meluha Crocus translated, *"He says to be quick and put the egg inside of his chest. He commands you to break a sharp bone from the spikes on his tail and sew it shut."* Isladora stood mortified, watching the blood rivulets creep down his body. *"Move, Isladora!"*

What an obnoxious beast! "No!" She yelled back at him. "The egg won't be safe in there; you will break it with your odious, inconsiderate, offending body!"

Json roared at that, the sound bouncing off the cave walls and hurting her ears. Okay, okay, Isladora thought, she might have gone too far, but this beast had pushed her to her breaking point. He roared again and then she roared back, too tired to care if he burned her alive. Then the beast snickered, or what could pass for a reptilian snicker. Bastard!

"He laughs at you Isladora, a puny human trying to protect what is his." He growled again, showing his fangs and tapping his large claw on the floor. *"He tells you that Sybaris eggs are strong, forged in magic and fire. Even with your magical stick you could not damage it. It will be safer inside his body than anywhere else, Isladora. He says his body and magic will protect the egg, and it will feed her what she needs and keep her strong. Bathed in his cells, his memories will become Ariah's memories as well."*

Isladora took her knife, tapping it on a rock too just so he would know that she acted on her own accord, not because he scared her. She went around to his tail to choose from the many sharp horns and spikes. Isladora selected the one that most resembled a large needle, and it had a hole in the center where she could pass string through. The hide was tough, but she cut it off at the base where his hide was softer, feeling no remorse at all. Json bled a little from that too. Good, she thought. She remembered that Lepola had a small rope in her pack. Isladora unraveled some of the rope into a smaller piece and cut off a length of it. Her nursemaid Lepola would not recognize this girl she had become; She didn't even recognize herself.

She took the egg, still carefully because the egg was beautiful, and carried it to him. Json's clawed hand helped guide her as Meluha Crocus translated his chirps, *"Place it large side down and push it to the left some."* As Isladora pushed it in and her hands became coated in the blue-black blood, the cells began sealing around it, making it secure. *"Good, he says. Now sew it up."*

Isladora rinsed off her hands in the river and began sewing him shut. The chirps went on and on while she stitched. When she was finished tying off the last knot, Meluha Crocus said, *"Json is torn in his feelings, perplexed and confused. He asks many questions like why would a royal Sybaris, the most precious of all creatures be living amongst humans, not even able to speak her own language? She had been enslaved in a life of servitude to humans, unaware of who she was. Even allowing a human male to touch her! This wyvern feels more protective anger than he has ever felt in his life, Isladora. He is now bound to this egg; she goes where he goes; he is her Deliverer. I think this translates to something like a parent but somehow more.*

"From what I can tell, Ariah is a royal creature stolen or lost at a young age. Json did not know that she was royal when he met her, or even when she flew upon his back, because she had no memory of her beginnings. Json explains that the egg is a royal egg. Only royal blood eggs have this coloring. Most Sybaris eggs are not beautiful, rather plain dark blue, almost black. Royal eggs are the most precious beings in Draconia, and they

are very rare, there hasn't been one in many centuries. Now he wants you to sew his wing and put your metal brace back on his forearm to fix the break. He also says for a human you are ingenious."

Ingenious. A compliment from the wretched beast. "Yes. I am." And with that, Isladora forgave him for some of his lack of manners and began sewing together the tears in his marvelous wings so he could return to a beautiful and winged life. Marvelous because they would be able to fly out of there. He had one large tear and several smaller ones. Isladora sewed them all, and then she slept. In the morning she fed herself and went to catch his breakfast.

Isladora returned with five fish. The ungrateful lout only said in his terse guttural tone, *"More fish, human, it's going to take a lot."* So much for manners, she thought, and with a huff went to provide for the beast.

Chapter 22: Fly Home

It was time to try to repair his broken forearm. Isladora had rested and felt up to the challenge. It was difficult this time to get his bones to set and hold them in place until she could apply the brace. Json had to help her with his one good arm, although he chirped like a lunatic. To keep herself from feeling ill about the horrible break, Isladora stayed angry. She told him that she did not want to hear a word until he learned to say thank you. Meluha Crocus translated none of what the creature said back to her, so she could only assume that a thank you was not forthcoming.

"You know, if you are going to be a royal Deliverer, you really should learn to converse without being condescending," Isladora told him. With much straining, they finally got the brace in place and Isladora sat to concentrate, holding it in shape and mentally squeezing it tight. Json stayed oddly quiet, much like he was in a trance. Meluha Crocus added his magic, and after almost two hours the healing was complete. It much easier this time around with the idiot beast cooperating.

"Isladora, you can remove the brace now. Json says to tell you, 'that will do, human. Get food.'"

Mentally drained, Isladora lost it, screaming, "You are welcome, lizard!"

Isladora decided she would be as rude and impudent to him as he was to her. She was sick of his demeaning attitude and she was so exhausted from holding the brace she couldn't think straight. Her mind felt strained and bent somehow. And now he wanted fish!

"No one deserves to be treated like you are treating me," she snapped. "I'm wearing myself out to help you, and I have been since I met you, and you treat me like filth! Enough!"

More chirping. Meluha Crocus translated, *"He says he hates humans and that you can't argue that humans shouldn't be wiped from the face of the earth. They are treacherous and unholy."*

"No, we aren't," Isladora answered angrily. "You are just a small-minded prejudiced thug."

"I am a thug? Who put you here, human? Certainly not a Draconian."

Isladora fell to her knees on the ground, exhausted and defeated. She couldn't reason with herself, much less him. She held her head in her hands until her breathing settled. She continued to take deep calming breaths. Isladora thought about what he had accused her race of; she rose to her feet and acquiesced, "You are right."

Her heart bled in anger as she thought of her nursemaid, her mother, her father, all attacked by humans wanting to take something that did not belong to them. "I *am* here because of humans."

She thought of the Queen Mother choking her with her foul magic, the pain of falling off the cliff, the devastation of her family, her home. All done by humans. "You are right Json, we are a faulted race."

Isladora didn't wait for his response. She went away, silent tears streaming down her face. She retreated further back into the cave, away from him, away from his truths. She found a place to lie down and fell into an exhausted sleep. She woke in the early dawn of the next day, disoriented, her head aching.

When she woke it was to the smell of perfectly roasted meat. As her stomach growled, she got up and ambled back to her camp. A quick look around the cavern showed her that Json was gone. Of course he would leave as soon as possible. Even though he frustrated her, being alone again made her scared and afraid, much like she was when the wolf chased her into the cave. She absentmindedly sat and rubbed her ankle where his jaws had clamped down, fresh tears flowing at being alone again. Isladora felt the pain of Json's absence like a tangible thing. She was tired of being alone. As the morning sun lengthened, she found that she missed him greatly.

Dejectedly, Isladora moved to the fire to eat. The meat was not fish and it was golden brown, crispy on the outside and tender on the inside. It had a nutty flavor, and after tasting the same charred fish she had cooked herself for months, it was like a glorious banquet. A gift. She smiled, Json had caught and cooked her food. Isladora decided she would take that as his thank you, and right then and there, between bites, forgave her only friend, who was now likely on his way to Draconia.

Isladora removed her clothes and bathed in the river. She washed away the loneliness, the dirt, and the tears. She was desperately trying to find her resolve, her strength to continue her journey. She dried herself with her old clothes and donned Ariah's leather pants. Isladora sighed; they fit perfectly, almost as if they were made for her. Her shirt fit and the vest closed up nicely, not too tight but concealing and snug around her growing breasts. Having new clothes made her feel special and knowing that they had belonged to a royal Draconian was even more special.

She sat down at the edge of the cavern, letting the wind dry her hair and ran her fingers through it, thinking about Ariah's stunning red and purple tresses. When they were dry, she used Ariah's leather hair tie to tie her own locks back. The leather boots fit nicely too, and Isladora strapped Ariah's knife to her thigh. Finally, she put on the beautiful vambraces. Isladora knew she would need to train in these new clothes and get used to them. The knife felt awkward and cumbersome on her thigh.

Isladora couldn't decide what to do right now, what path to take. She was just too sad now that she was alone again. When she felt ready, she would commit to a direction and leave, but it would not be today. Isladora practiced kicking, rolling, and modifying her stick into various weapons for several hours, always thinking of her strategy for facing the Queen Mother. The leather was so much better than her old clothing. It absorbed some of the impact and scrapes that she normally got from rolling. The vambraces made her forearms stronger, and she could hit harder with them on without worrying about damaging her forearms. She changed her stick into a short sword and balanced the edge against her vambrace, practicing blocking and counter-striking. The training made her think of her father, who she hadn't heard from in days. She went over to her pack to check the orb.

Suddenly, Isladora heard a great noise, flapping and sliding and scraping as her friend landed outside. He hadn't left, he was here! Her heart sang. She wasn't alone; he had come back! He chirped at her and she smiled.

"He was out flying to strengthen his wing Isladora," Meluha Crocus told her. *"Json is pleased that his bones are whole again. Though there is…"* Json stretched his wounded arm, *"lingering weakness. It will need to be strengthened with more flying."*

"Did you catch and cook this meat for me?" She had been ravenous and nothing had tasted better. Json blinked and nodded once.

"Oh thank you, it was perfectly roasted and delicious!" Isladora hadn't realized how wonderful it was to have someone do things for her. She was overly giddy; he came back! At the stronghold, people had waited on her hand and foot all her life. She hadn't even given a thought to the labor that was involved in feeding her. She had been a spoiled and overfed child. Even so, she missed Lepola with all her heart.

Isladora approached Json in Ariah's clothes, watching him for signs of anger. She grew somewhat self-conscious and stopped, looking down at Ariah's vest, using her hand to brush off some of the dirt from rolling on the ground.

"I know you loved Ariah, and that these are her clothes. But she was a warrior and so am I." She looked him in the eye. "You are right about humans. Even I am at war with some of my own race. We are deceptive and cunning and can be evil." She splayed her hands out in an appeal, "Yet, I need your help. My home is on the other side of these mountains and I do not know how to get to the other side. Please fly me home to my battle, to free my father, King Elijashen, from his imprisonment, and then you can take Ariah home." Isladora drew in a deep breath and said, "Please, my friend."

Those wyvern eyes stared at her, the black pupils enlarging and then shrinking back into the golden iris; they were quite beautiful. Finally, he blinked. *"Json says he can learn your memories. He wants to know what you know, see what you have seen, and then he will decide."*

Isladora thought that to be fair and admonished herself to be brave, to be stalwart and resolute. "Fair enough, how do we begin?" Json pointed his nose towards a large boulder so she sat upon it.

He lumbered to her and she became nervous. Everything inside of her wanted to back up, to retreat. He was so immense and intimidating, and while she had called him friend, she didn't yet trust him. And he was going to access her brain. What other choice did she have though?

Wandering around in the desert trying to find a mountain pass that may not exist was certain to bring about her demise. She knew she had to allow him this in order to have any chance of him agreeing to fly her over the mountain.

The hulking beast sat down close to her and wrapped his tail around her waist and up over her shoulder, supporting her back and holding her in place. His leathery skin felt softer than she thought it would, and it was warm.

"He says to be still, Isladora." He grasped her shoulder with his clawed hand and stuck one sharp claw into her neck, unerringly into her vein, and held it there. He breathed a fine mist over her and she fell unconscious.

Isladora's memories filtered into Json's mind. They were the memories of a lonely and neglected girl. He observed memories of an inquisitive mind that fed on books and knowledge and pastries in large and equal quantities. He saw her confusion about how the man she thought was her father, Thrace, treated her. He beheld her love for her nursemaid Lepola and perceived her love of her neglectful mother Aceptye. Because of the orb and Isladora's attachment to it, Json could see Elijashen's memories too. In those memories he witnessed a great kingdom that once was and could be again. The reign of the Juna.

The wyvern was moved by Isladora's memories. He felt her hatred for the Queen Mother and the pain she felt as she was suffocated and fell, and he knew this Queen Mother to be a frightful adversary for Isladora. Her fear of the Queen Mother started at a very young age; as a youngling she had thought the Queen Mother a witch who poisoned people. Json became aware of Zhu and his kingdom of evil. Isladora had been preparing herself to fight against these evil humans herself. She was going to try to wake her father from his ensorcelled sleep.

Json's mind reached out to the orb that held her father and realized that it was growing weak as Isladora moved further away from where he had been entrapped. She must hurry or she would lose her father for good. A father she didn't even know yet. She was fighting a worthy cause. Through these memories, Json learned the true nature of Isladora and her father Elijashen, and he found them to be good people. Json decided that would like to see Elijashen back on the throne, and he would like to see him establish a relationship with his daughter. Before he woke her, Json imparted some of his own wyvern memories to her, along with his language. He blew a strengthening and healing mist over her sleeping form and then he awakened her.

"I will fly you home to free Elijashen," Json told her as she woke up. "But we must hurry, Isladora. The orb that contains your father's essence has grown weaker as you have traveled away from where he was trapped. It needs to be united with his body, and then the source of the spell, the Queen Mother, must be killed to stop it."

"I can understand you now!" She said to him in awe. She spoke wyvern! Well, she understood wyvern; her throat couldn't make the sounds. "My father hasn't talked to me in days, and now I know why." Her heart sank in worry.

"Yes, he has lost the ability to communicate with you. I gave you some of my memories too."

Json could not believe he was helping this human, but he was moved by her plight. He still hated humans, but he did not hate Isladora. She had given of herself freely to him at great cost to herself. She was brave, standing up to a large, fire-breathing wyvern. He had changed and now he knew what had changed in him. He had watched Isladora praying and giving thanks to her God. He had watched her sing to regain her strength, a totally wyvern trait to Json. He'd fed and slept and waked, his body healed by her help. He now had the ability to deliver the royal creature he held within him. However bloody the mornings were to come, he had direction now, calmness and hope, because Isladora had healed him. Isladora helped him with his one and only creation, his egg, a private thing. Because of Isladora, he could take the egg home to be renewed. He could take the royal Sybaris home.

"Yes, I will fly you home, Isladora," he replied with a stiff nod.

"You said my name!" She exclaimed. She felt so whole, so refreshed, she wondered what he had done to her. "You gave me the gift of your memories. I know where you live, how to get there! I know where your other wyverns are trapped and held by humans trying to control and train them for battle!"

"Yes, we shared our memories," Json told her. "You will always carry the scar from it on your neck." Isladora reached up and felt her neck. Her fingers ran over a slightly raised pattern. "I will consider you as my one and only human friend; this scar marks you as a part of my clutch." He blinked and said, "You belong as a part of me."

A part of a powerful friend, indeed her life was changed for the better. "Amen," she said.

"Amen, indeed." Thinking of what this word meant to her he nodded his approval. "I'm going out to fly some more," he said as he lumbered towards the cavern entrance. "We need to leave tomorrow. We will rest and eat well tonight. Get ready, Isladora."

Her stomach clenched in apprehension. Tomorrow he would fly her home. She looked out towards the setting sun, a predatory cast to her gaze. Tomorrow she would defeat the Queen Mother and awaken her father or die trying.

Chapter 23: The Toll of Neglect

With tomorrow looming, her mind would not stop racing and she could not sleep. Her father's life was in her hands, and she was but a girl. Isladora kept thinking that on a night before a big event, most girls would want to converse with their mother. She really had no such desire, and that bothered her as she thought about her mother. Aceptye was beautiful and kind, but what did she really know about her? Isladora realized that she took care of her basic needs but that was where her care ended. She did not see to her education, only berated her when her head was in the clouds or she was lost in her books. She did not take Isladora on trips to help her understand the world. She did not groom her social skills. She didn't excite Isladora about her future by helping her make plans. She didn't seem to care how overweight she had grown. She didn't make sure she was physically trained so she could stand up for herself. She didn't worry about Isladora's lack of friends. Her mother had been.... detached from her. She had left her lacking in many areas that she would have to learn, was learning, by trial and error.

Now that her body was toned from a diet of survival, training, fish, and water, she felt completely different. Isladora never grew ravenously hungry like she used to when she ate pastries and other fatty and sugary foods all day. She was never sluggish and tired anymore. When she woke in the morning, she was filled with energy rather than a lethargic stupor. Her body moved fluidly and gracefully; it was hers to command. She was definitely healthier in this mountain range than she had ever been at the stronghold. Isladora thought of the dress that Lepola had helped her try on and thought that now it would hang from her lean body. Isladora felt powerful in a way that she had never felt, and with her new clean lifestyle she felt closer to God.

Isladora looked down at the ring the spirit of Meluha Crocus was trapped in. Her mother Aceptye had worn this ring every day. Had she talked to the spirit? He probably knew her more intimately than she did, Isladora thought jealously.

As her mind turned these things about this way and that, her fingers circled the ring. She turned the ring one way and then the other. Just out of curiosity, Isladora tried to remove it. It simply tightened when she tried to pull it off and relaxed when she stopped trying. "Meluha Crocus, I would like to talk about my mother," she told him.

He created a soft glow that cocooned her in light. *"You are restless tonight Isladora, but it is to be expected."*

"Did you talk with my mother like you do with me?" She was already angry just thinking about this possibility and realized that she was more than a little jealous that her mother could have relationships with others but not with her.

Peace, she told herself. She knew that jealousy was a two-headed monster, and that she felt insecure about her mother and angry because she was probably closer to Meluha Crocus than to her own daughter. Isladora thought that her self-worth should have come from her mother, it should have been built from her, but it had been sadly lacking. Isladora realized that she was both worried for her mother and apprehensive about meeting her again. She had changed. Her whole world was changed. How she had raised her was not okay, she thought. She had to redefine her self-image somehow before she went home. She was not that same little girl any longer.

"Meluha, I feel insecure about seeing my mother again," she told him. "I feel angry at her and at the same time, I have a deep hole inside where I miss her." She rubbed her arms. "It's causing me a great deal of confusion."

"Not to mention distraction. You cannot afford to be distracted tomorrow, Isladora. You are going into battle," he cautioned.

"I know I am. I just can't stop thinking about my mother. Did you know her well? Did you talk to her?"

"Yes, but I talked with her differently than I talk with you. She could not hear my words in her mind like you do. She could only sense emotions coming from me, because that is her magic," he explained.

"You couldn't speak words with her?" That was perplexing.

"No, and although I have puzzled upon it since meeting you, I'm not quite sure why I can with you. I feel depths of magical essence within you that are yet to be uncovered."

The fact that they hadn't been able to speak made Isladora think that they couldn't have been that close. Plus, now she knew she could do something that her mother could not. That lessened her jealousy somewhat. Then she felt bad for feeling that way about her mother. "I feel so sad, angry, and mad when I think of going home."

"Yes, you are insecure in your feelings for your parents. You did not know your true father, and you were brought up believing Thrace was your father instead of Elijashen," he reasoned.

The glowing continued, *"Your whole world, as you perceived it to be, has been overturned. During normal days, we all deal with insecurity. But during war, being inse-cure can get you killed. As you have recently learned, what is stable today may be broken or gone tomorrow. That is why we try to make ourselves better and more powerful. For protection, for security against our insecurity."*

Isladora had been making herself more powerful through survival in this mountain range. The wisdom and direction of Meluha Crocus and her father had also honed her skills. She rubbed Ariah's vambraces that covered her forearms.

"You are an amazing young lady, Isladora. Remember that whatever shaped you in the past has made you what you have now become. Your mother's guidance of your child-hood built a young lady that could handle the stress of what you have been through. Re-member that!" he encouraged.

When Isladora didn't answer, he forged on, *"Try to be forgiving of her, less judgmental. Think about why she may have dealt with you the way she did. You are her only child. Her husband was taken from her, maybe even killed. She still doesn't know where he is, only that he did not return, nor did they find his body. She had to raise you in waters swimming with sharks.*

"You are a royal princess, and that fact would be a liability to your conqueror; she had to hide your identity. Your mother Aceptye chose to hide you and disguise you by making you nondescript and bland. I think it was a smart thing she did. Her only pro-tection for you was your nursemaid, her husband's brothers, and making herself and you unnoticeable. Had she trained you for battle, they would have considered you a threat and you would likely already be dead."

Isladora could see the truth of his words. The Queen Mother would have had her killed when she first arrived. Her heart felt relief as under-standing dawned. Her mother did have a plan, a plan that showed great cunning and care for her daughter. "Yes, even I did not know that Thrace wasn't my father." Isladora thought it through. "I can see how she was pro-tecting me so that we could survive in that toxic environment."

Isladora thought about how she might have protected her own son or daughter if the roles were reversed, and she realized that her mother's way was indeed wise. The only other way would have been to flee. Her mother would not have left until she was certain her true husband was dead, that Isladora did know about her. She avoided taking Isladora to events and dinners as much as possible and she kept them sequestered as much as she could. She kept her from the sight of the Queen Mother by separating their rooms. She had Tonsaku give her access to as much learning as she could absorb in his library while making it seem forbidden and therefore enticing to Isladora. In this way, she made sure that her book learning was as much as she could absorb.

Meluha Crocus advised, *"Isladora, trying to view your mother in a bad way may seem like it raises you up, but really, every time you criticize her, you are also criticizing a quality you possess and are knocking yourself down. Instead, raise others up. Raise her up and raise yourself in the process."*

"Thank you, Meluha Crocus, for this new perception of my mother. Perhaps it wasn't true neglect, but planned neglect." Isladora laughed a little, but it was strained.

"Even now you are gaining as much information as you can. You already knew that you may be feeling insecure because you are dealing with uncertainty. You do not know what to expect when you arrive home, so you are making yourself stronger by gathering more information." He paused for a while, then slowly lessened the glow until it was dark again. *"I hope that with this knowledge you feel a little more in control. And Isladora, your mother would have done the same, you are very alike."*

Chapter 24: Up, Up, and Away

The next day dawned, and Json and Isladora ate their morning meal in reflective silence. Isladora knew that this would be her last meal of fish from this cavernous river, so she ate every bite with a meditative mind, thankful it had kept her alive. She also knew that this could be her last meal.

"The Queen Mother's poisons will still be dangerous to you in large doses," Json suddenly said. "You look worried," he told her, noting the red tinge to her eyes.

"How did you know she was a master in poisons…? Oh yes, you have my memories," Isladora answered her own question.

"Yes I do, and because of them I know how treacherous your adversary is. Before I woke you, I infused the wyvern memory of poison resistance into your cells. I healed what was torn and made your muscles a little stronger." Json spoke to her in his language, the structure of his mouth and vocal cords would not allow anything else. "I gave you the memory of flight and maybe a touch of wyvern fearlessness."

Isladora answered him in her language, as her vocal cords could not form his chirps and guttural sounds. "I did feel wonderful when I woke up, and now I know why, thank you!" She digested this new information. Wyvern fearlessness… hmm. "So the Queen Mother and I will be more evenly matched! What a godsend! Without her poisons, her blades will be the same as mine."

"Yes, Isladora, they will be sharp, hidden, and deadly," Json cautioned. "Help me with the saddle." Again, Json helped a female in distress try to tighten the cinch, and Isladora tied it off much like Ariah had. Json couldn't help but feel a little trepidation in attempting to carry another female and this time a more fragile human one. He must be careful.

Isladora spoke to him as they worked. "I know you miss Ariah, but without her death, you would have never known that she was a royal Sybaris. Now you can make right whatever wrong was caused to her." She patted his chest where the egg rested safely, learning memories of her race while she waited for rebirth. "Have you been in any battles, Json?"

The great tail jerked back and forth, "Not really. When we were taken by the raiders, a small group of us were in our southern feeding grounds hunting and taking our ease. The cowards drugged us, and we woke up in chains and cages. The food and water we had were also drugged, and that was how they kept me until Ariah came along."

"Well, any last words of advice then?" Isladora attempted a brave smile.

He showed a little fang and teeth, a wyvern smile, she supposed. "Yes," he said. "Distract your opponents' attention to the front, then attack them from the side, where they least expect it.

You are small but fast, so try not to fight head on. Bait your enemy into going out on a limb, exposing their weakness, and then rake them with fire from the side."

Isladora laughed, "I don't breathe fire, remember?" warming up to his game. "Or did you give me that memory too?"

"Of course not, your weak human throat would incinerate!" Json scoffed.

With wyvern eyes, he looked at the river, how it came around the bend seemingly at peace, then grew faster before it swept back under the ground. "Since you are too pathetic and feeble to breathe fire, my sage advice would be… as the ever-raging river flows, so must a warrior be."

It was time to get serious. Isladora thought of the Queen Mother's sneer as her magic constricted the air from her lungs. She pictured herself with a raging war cry, slicing the Queen Mother's head from her body. Isladora wanted to be reckless, head-on, powerful. Like a wild wyvern. Like a fast-flowing river.

She picked up Lepola's pack. It was dirty from the time in the caverns but still in great shape. She strapped it to her front, making sure her father's orb was well secured in the inner pocket. Isladora said a quick prayer over it that he was still hanging in there. She placed her escrima stick inside the pack with one end sticking out the top within easy reach. She had one water-skin full of water, and that was all her worldly belongings. Patting the knife strapped to her thigh, Isladora climbed into the saddle and strapped herself in with the buckles. "Whatever happens Json, thank you for taking me home! And for being my friend."

Flight was an incredible thing. After the sheer terror of the initial take-off, which consisted of Json running incredibly fast and jumping into the air, Isladora quite enjoyed it. Her stomach had been in her throat as they climbed, but once they were fully airborne it was an extraordinary experience.

Json's memories of flying that he had gifted to her made all the difference in the world; she balanced on his back, and she actually felt like she knew what she was doing. Json climbed higher and higher until they could see both sides of the mountain range. The trees and boulders looked small, and Isladora could see for miles. The Shadout Basin was an enormous wasteland, just as it was depicted in maps she had seen in her Uncle's library.

Json was definitely stronger now, fully healed, and taking to the wind like he was born to it. "Okay Isladora, which way is home?" he asked.

Isladora knew that her home was west and to the south, but she had no idea how far she had traveled north in this mountain and its ravine. "If you fly us back south down the mountain range, it should intersect with a large river flowing from the east, and that river will lead us close to my home. I should be able to recognize the landmarks," Isladora shouted to him.

The warhorse Phoenix had carried her on the day that the Queen Mother had attacked her. The horse had carried her from where she had lain bleeding and broken in the river all the way to the cave. In her semi-conscious state she had no idea how far the horse had taken her. She was hoping to recognize something.

They flew for a long time, landmarks came and went, and Isladora was beginning to think that she might have missed the river somehow when it finally came into sight. "There, Json! If we follow it to the west, my home is not far from here."

He banked and followed the river for a while until he recognized the cliff the Queen Mother had driven her from. What a heinous creature she was to do that to a scared little girl! Json chirped, and Isladora realized that he recognized it from her memories.

"Please take me to the sacred burial tombs, Json."

Json flew back to the north, using her memories as a map, towards the birch-covered red clay hills that led to the burial tomb. When they reached the destination, Json made a perfect landing right before the entrance to the burial cave. Isladora unstrapped herself from the saddle and half-climbed, half-slid down from his back.

As her feet touched the red earth, Isladora felt elated that she had made it home and that she did not die in that mountain range. She knelt and prayed, keeping one hand on her friend, this great beast.

Isladora stood and spoke to her wyvern friend, "God bless you, and God bless Ariah. I will pray every day for both of you." He lowered his head so that they were eye to eye. She framed his face with her hands and softly pressed her face against his. "You are a good friend Json, my first and only friend, and I love you for it." She touched his chest where Ariah was nestled safely and placed her hand over the egg. "Thank you for the warrior clothes, Ariah. I will endeavor to make you proud as I wear them." Isladora stepped back and checked her pack, stick, and knife and then she turned and entered the cave, worried for her father, as Json took flight for his own battle: the battle for Ariah's life.

Chapter 25: The Burial Chamber

Isladora descended into the burial tomb, down the narrow staircase, taking one of the many torches that lined the entrance and lighting it with the flint and steel that was on a shelf. Soaked with oil, the torch burned easily, so much easier to start than the fires she had to light in the mountain cave. She painfully remembered the last time she had taken these stairs with her mother, hand in hand as they descended together to lay Thrace to rest. She was a different person now. Her family had been under attack her entire life and now that she was aware of it, it was time to end the Queen Mother's reign.

Again, her eyes were drawn to the paintings on the wall, especially the one her mother had touched as they had left Thrace's funeral. That painting had stayed in her mind, disturbing her dreams. What a fierce face, one side of the face sleeping, the other awake and screaming for vengeance. Whoever it was, it was someone her mother had loved deeply.

All the kings and princes of the royal family had their own sarcophagus. Isladora easily found her father's and strained to push the heavy top open. Isladora panicked when she saw no body inside. She berated herself and then calmed down and looked inside, feeling around. She realized that the sarcophagus was not deep. Her fingers felt their way in the dark and discovered a false bottom, a wooden plank that hid what was underneath. Slowly she pulled up the wooden plank and gasped as she got her first glimpse of her true father and King, his body surrounded with magic.

Isladora noted with relief that there was no apparent decay of the body, and secondly that her father was very handsome. Although she couldn't see his chest moving with breath, his body simply looked asleep, and Isladora took that to mean that she wasn't too late to save him. The third thing she noted was that he *was* the man painted on the wall that her mother had so lovingly and longingly touched. Her heart swelled with pride. Isladora did the same thing her mother had done on the painting, she placed her hand on his cheek and closed her eyes, feeling a part of herself become whole again. Isladora opened her eyes and slowly whispered, "Hello, Father."

She was shaking with the huge responsibility placed on her shoulders. Her father hadn't told her exactly what to do with the orb, only to place it near his body and then kill the Queen Mother to release him from the spell.

Isladora took the orb from the box and placed it in the hollow of his throat; it seemed like a safe place. She could only hope that it was the right place.

Isladora whispered to her king, "I go now to free you Father. It is entirely possible that I might be the one to die, but so help me God, I will take her with me. The Queen Mother is vicious and has been trained for war from birth. But I am the daughter of a greater king and I will be the victor." She placed the plank back over his inert form and slid the lid shut.

Isladora couldn't help but wonder if this type of entrapment was what Meluha Crocus had endured. "Meluha Crocus, is this how you were entrapped?" What a horrible way to have to exist, she thought. "Could I find your body and break you free?"

A mental sigh. *"If it were only that easy, Isladora. My entrapment was done by a powerful mage a long time ago. The Queen Mother is but a minor witch in comparison. Unlike Elijashen, I do not know where my bones lie or if I can even be released. I should have already passed from this world; I do not know what holds me here."*

"Well, if we survive this, we will try to figure out how to set you free. No one should have their mind trapped in limbo," Isladora promised him.

"At least I have you to talk to, that is something I haven't had before. I had been silent with no one to hear me for an eternity it seems, so don't die!" he chuckled.

Isladora heard the true meaning in his words. "I would miss you too, Meluha Crocus."

She climbed back out of the burial tomb, dousing the torch in the dirt before its smoke and fire could be seen from the surface. It would be dark in a couple of hours, and she decided that she would get closer to the stronghold and do some surveillance before nightfall.

Isladora continued down the hill and left the trail, stepping as quietly as she could through the birch forest, heading towards the stronghold. This forest she knew well. She knew all the best hiding spots and where it was passable. As she grew closer, she could smell smoke and hear sounds of a battle. Staying in the cover of the trees, she crept forward, drawing her stick from her pack.

As Isladora emerged from the dense forest into view of the stronghold, she was not prepared for the scene before her. Smoke and fire were everywhere. Men and horses were screaming as a band of fierce tribesman attacked the stronghold. The Queen Mother's forces were holding them off, some from the battlements and some on the ground; men were both on foot and on horseback.

The sound of the fighting was unreal. The attackers were trying to gain entry through the stronghold gate. It was the only way inside unless they scaled the walls. The enemy leader shouted, "Shields!" as they formed a line

and rushed the wild men and women, stabbing under the shield cover as
they were taught. It seemed that the Queen Mother's men were winning,
pushing back the madmen, hacking and cutting them down. Suddenly, one
of the tribesmen galloped forward and through their line, shrieking like a
gutted horse. He half-fell, half-leapt from the back of his horse and in seconds turned the tide. Isladora realized that these warriors must be the Juna
tribe, her father's people! Lepola's people! She had help!

Where her rooms had been, smoke was streaming out the window
from the tar-pitched arrows hitting the curtains. She saw that all the windows with thick curtains had been set afire, causing confusion in the smoke.
Isladora hoped that such accuracy and planning meant that Lepola was
alive. Like Isladora, she had intimate knowledge of the stronghold; she had
been a trusted servant.

There would be no better time to breach the gate; the Juna warriors had
broken their line, and the Queen Mother's men were fighting on all sides.
Isladora sprinted towards the gate. One of the Queen Mother's cavalry saw
her making a run for it and he turned his horse to chase her down. Isladora
was exposed and out in the open with no place to hide. She ran as fast as
she could and turned sharply as he raised his sword to cut her down. The
horse whinnied and changed direction as the cavalry man gave a hard jerk
of the reins in pursuit of his prey. Isladora changed direction again and ran,
her feet slipping in the dirt and mud.

She looked back and saw that he was very close, she wasn't going to
make it. Suddenly an arrow appeared in the side of the soldier's neck and he
fell from horse. The horse's head turned as the man fell to the side and
the horse slowed as his neck was wrenched sideways, his hind quarters collapsing. The man tumbled off the other side and the horse righted himself.
She grabbed the bridle as the horse slid in confusion. Gathering the reins
tight so she could control the animal, she gripped the saddle horn and
swung up onto his back, still at a trot, something she used to practice just
for fun on her small pony, but now she had the strength to do it on a horse.

She bumped around and then finally gained her seat in the saddle and
then kicked the horse, reining him around to run pell-mell through the
stronghold gate. Isladora galloped to a smoldering tree where she knew she
could gain entrance through a window. She slowed the horse and tried to
get him to stop prancing so she could reach the limb. She held him as still
as she could and finally released the reins to scramble from his back into
the tree, balancing on its slippery smooth limbs until her arms locked
around the trunk. The horse bolted.

Another man saw this and ran to intercept her. As he tried to grab her foot, she moved it from his reach, changing her stick into a short sword and swiping it at his head. He blocked it with his shield. They fought back and forth. Isladora could not get past his shield, and he was gaining ground. She was not balanced and knew she had to get higher. He could not climb without dropping the shield, so higher she went. Sure enough, he threw the shield to the ground, and as he began to climb Isladora changed her short sword into a long spear and stabbed him through the throat before he could react to the sudden thrust. He fell, bleeding out on the ground. She had just made her second kill. Sick to her stomach but resolute, she climbed up and through the window, but this time she didn't retch. Maybe she was starting to think like a war wyvern.

The Queen Mother was not in her rooms, nor in the great hall. The stronghold was deserted; the men loyal to Thrace must have fled or been killed. What remained of the Queen Mother's men were out in the bailey and beyond the gate defending the stronghold from the Juna. Isladora ran through the main hall, thinking only of what she must do to set her father free, when she saw her nemesis through a window.

The Queen Mother was as beautiful as ever and dressed for battle. She wore the thick material of her fighting gi; it was black and belted at her waist. Her sword was on her back, and her poisoned knives were affixed in a strap across her chest. She was up on the flat roof of the second story overlooking the battle.

She had always been an intimidating woman and Isladora felt butterflies in her stomach, the same butterflies she got when the woman had come near her as a child. Isladora had grown up under her reign, and while Aceptye had hid her daughter most of the time, she had still been scared to death of her. She had always been so beautiful. So deadly. Isladora had not known then that she was the killer of her family. Now she did. She knew from her childhood the only two ways on or off that roof. There would be no surprising her.

Isladora thought of the countless people the Queen Mother had killed; she was such an evil woman. She was a hailstorm of shattered lives, and she had scattered Isladora's family to the wind without a second thought. King Elijashen's mind was trapped because of her. Isladora's childhood was stolen because of her. Aceptye and Lepola might be dead; Isladora grew hot with anger. She was going to kill the bitch! Her anger fed her confidence like a lightning bolt. Isladora ran through the halls and leapt through entrance to the roof.

The Queen Mother turned and looked at the young warrior before her. Isladora could see the confusion on her beautiful face, then recognition as she figured out who the young warrior was. She had marked her cheek for battle, probably the sigil of some spell or dark rite. The Queen Mother drew her sword, holding it with one hand in front of her. The wide sleeves of her war kimono tried to hide the fact that she was removing a poisoned dart to throw.

"Ah, Isladora, could that possibly be you?" her beautiful lips formed the words.

The ring was humming on her finger, but Isladora had silenced Meluha Crocus with her magic, fully concentrating on the task in front of her.

"Indeed, it is me. But I will not call you Queen Mother ever again," Isladora approached with a confident stride. "You will die for your crimes."

She shifted and turned her throwing arm into a better position, Isladora noted, knowing this from her father's training. The Queen Mother noticed her attention. "Where is the fat, stupid little girl Isladora?" Isladora felt her trying to constrict her airways with dark magic. The ring was at full glow and humming now; Meluha Crocus must be battling her magic with his own. Hah! "Too bad you missed your mother," she gloated. "I sent her to be one of my father's whores." She chuckled.

Isladora gasped and could only hope that her mother was still alive, as Zhu was one thousand times more evil than this woman, his daughter. "It is time for you to die," she forced through gritted teeth.

"Ha!" shouted the Queen Mother, throwing the dart, which struck Isladora in the shoulder. She threw another, and this one landed a little nearer to Isladora's heart. The darts stung like fire as they perforated her body. Isladora had to give her credit for accuracy, but the wyvern in her had been roused. She knew she had to stop the Queen Mother's ability to flee first and foremost. Thinking like a wyvern, Isladora turned her stick into a long whipping tail with a blade at the end and spun, sending the tail slicing through the Queen Mother's Achilles tendon. The Queen Mother shrieked in pain and dismay.

She grabbed her ankle. "Why aren't you dying, you little wretch?" she yelled. She pulled another dart from her sleeve and tasted the edge of it, satisfied that it was drenched in poison. This time when she threw it, Isladora changed her stick into a shield and it fell harmlessly to the stone roof.

"Because I am the daughter of Elijashen!" Isladora couldn't help shouting out her own triumph! Isladora pulled the darts from her shoulder and chest, throwing them on the ground. "Your poisons are nothing to me. You are nothing to me!" Oh, how she hated this woman.

"Impossible!" The evil queen yelled. Yet Isladora could see the realization of truth in her eyes.

Suddenly, Isladora was grabbed from behind in a bear hug and held by a man whose disgusting breath identified him, Malagard, the Queen Mother's lackey! Isladora's arms were trapped, so she moved her hips out of the way and slammed her fist into his groin. Her stick was in her other hand and as she moved her hips the other way, she made the stick become a thick war hammer and crashed it down on top of his foot. He bellowed in pain and let her go, just as the Queen Mother's throwing knife entered Isladora's upper thigh. The pain was excruciating as Isladora pulled it free and flung it away, watching as it went over the edge of the roof. Isladora could only hope that it had missed the large artery.

In the yard, the Juna were being driven back by several archers. They were in the open and exposed to the poisoned arrows. They had no protection from the poison like Isladora did, and it took its toll; they were dying upon contact. On the rooftop, it was just as grim, Isladora couldn't fight both Malagard and the Queen Mother; at those odds, she would lose. She ran away from Malagard, and the Queen Mother moved to intercept her, limping towards her with her sword at the ready. They cornered Isladora just as the Juna were cornered below.

Isladora changed her stick to a short sword, the weapon she was most comfortable with, when the Queen Mother attacked. Isladora parried her longer katana and countered furiously. The Queen Mother was vicious and excelled with her sword, even with her cut tendon. Malagard drew a long knife. Isladora saw the flash of it from where she could not block, but then suddenly Malagard was gone, slammed into the air by a spiked tail as Json flew in and hurled him over the edge, throwing him to the ground below. The Queen Mother's archers fired upon the large wyvern as he circled around, blowing a deadly stream of fire at them in his wyvern rage, killing them all and freeing the Juna warriors to advance. The Juna yelled glorious war cries at the wyvern, thankful that he had turned the tide and that he didn't seem to want to breathe his fiery doom upon them.

Isladora smiled at the Queen Mother, her own wyvern rage boiling inside her. Isladora increased her attacks, forcing the Queen Mother to lunge and turn on her bad leg. When she stumbled, Isladora was ready and her sword entered her evil heart. Everything around them seemed to still as they stared at each other, the moment seeming to hang in time. "Isladora, you fat thing," she wheezed as she slumped to the ground dead. Isladora had done it, she had killed her! She fell to her knees yelling, "Father!"

Her heart was filled with rejoicing over the victory, she was alive and her father would have his freedom from the Queen Mother's spell. Isladora watched as Json turned and flew away, she knew that he must. Oh, how it hurt to watch her friend leave.

Chapter 26: Elijashen

With the archers gone, the Juna quickly dispatched the rest of the Queen Mother's men. They showed no mercy and took no prisoners, they were all traitors and would not be spared.

Isladora limped down and out to the bailey and saw the most welcome sight. Phoenix, her father's and Thrace's great warhorse, nickered to her. He stood near the stairs where Isladora could easily slide upon his back. God had never made a more beautiful creature, she thought. Even after all she had been through, the horse simply took her breath away with his magnificence.

"Again, you carry me in my injuries, beautiful one." Isladora stoked his neck, leaning down to feel his mane against her face. The last time he had carried her, she had been semi-conscious and badly hurt.

"Isladora!" She looked up to see Lepola on the roof grinning at her, blood running down her temple.

"My father, Lepola, we must go to him!" Isladora yelled at her, gesturing to the tombs on top of the hill.

Lepola ran down and out of the keep to where Isladora sat on Phoenix's back. "My God Isladora, I can barely recognize you, you look like a Juna warrior!" She grabbed Isladora's leg, hugging it to her chest and nearly toppling her from the horse. "Your father is dead. We can go visit his tomb later; people need help here."

"You don't understand, Lepola. I mean Elijashen! King Elijashen! He is alive, I came here to save him. He is at the tomb. He is alive!" Isladora was crying and shaking, the adrenaline from her battle making her shaky.

The Juna around them heard his name. Suddenly his name was whispered everywhere. Could it be true?

Phoenix carried Isladora back up to the cave, and what was left of the Juna, including Lepola, followed her up the hill to the entrance of the burial tomb. There stood her father, her King, tall and proud, shoulders back, fierce, angry. The red blaze of the sunset lit his face and his broad shoulders. Isladora dismounted Phoenix, suddenly a shy, insecure little girl again. Would they have a relationship now? She wasn't sure where they would go from here, how she could get back the years they had lost. She wasn't even sure she could reconcile the voice that Meluha Crocus had relayed to her in the caverns and trained her with this man who was their King.

Isladora dismounted as they all knelt on the ground, paying homage to the greatest of all kings. King Elijashen was returned. They had rid the kingdom of Zhu's offspring. The Juna were united and the stronghold was theirs again.

Their legendary king scanned all their faces, taking in the blood, every cut, every scar, every one. He raised his hand to his heart in a warrior's greeting. The Juna answered, with their fist cupped in their hand, head bowed to honor him. When he spoke, his voice was a deep rumble, fierce and dark.

"Where is Anyumay?"

Part II—Ariah

Oh, lowly wind, Oh, earth and sea,
She was to love and be loved by me.

Here I lost my heart; I was torn apart,
by something more powerful, far greater than me.

~Meluha Crocus

Chapter 27: The Awakened King

The King gained consciousness in the dark space inside his own sarcophagus. It was dark, as he had known it would be, the smell dank and musty as he moved the plank of wood that had covered his hidden body. He rolled to his side, placing his forearm against the top of the tomb, pushing the lid away so he could sit up and climb out. His first thought was pride in his daughter, Isladora. She had done it! She had freed him from the Queen Mother's spell. That could only mean that the Queen Mother was dead and that her reign of deceit and terror had ended.

King Elijashen noted with relief that his body did not seem to have aged during the years of his entrapment. His muscle tone was good and he felt strong and alive, more rested than ever. He still had on the same leather pants and shirt he had worn when the Queen Mother entrapped him with her spell, separating his prescience from his body. As he gained his footing and slowly passed the other tombs in the royal crypt, he paused to kneel by his brother Thrace's tomb and said a prayer for his departed soul; he would miss him acutely. Thrace had been a strong fighter and the brothers had been close. However his brother had met his demise—Isladora had not said—Elijashen was certain that his daughter's suspicion was true and that the Queen Mother had been behind his murder. With relief he noted that Tonsaku's tomb was still empty. His last remaining brother might yet live.

Elijashen climbed up the stairs from the crypt. As he emerged into the fresh air, he breathed it deeply and reverently into his lungs. He would never take the simple act of breathing for granted again. The sun was setting, turning the sky a deep red-orange, and smoke was in the air. He looked down the hill towards the stronghold and saw people coming up the hill, and squinting, he rejoiced to see that they were *his* people. So few of them, still, he felt triumphant, seeing the Juna—some who had been in hiding—alive and ascending the mountain to gather around him. He could see the extreme fatigue on their faces from the battle they just fought. He studied each face, seeing the war etched there, and he silently vowed to care for each and every one until their lives were rebuilt in joy and peace.

King Elijashen's eyes alighted upon his daughter Isladora as she dismounted gingerly from his old warhorse, Phoenix; she was favoring her left leg where he saw a wound. She looked at him in wonder; they had developed a relationship of sorts when he was a spirit, but now here she was, father and daughter meeting in the flesh. He gazed upon her with his own eyes for the first time since she was a toddler. Isladora had dried blood on her chest and neck in addition to the wound on her leg, but she looked just as fierce as he had imagined she would as he gazed at her with human eyes. Isladora was a strong and beautiful young lady and his heart swelled with pride. He felt close to Isladora, having survived in the mountain range with her. By Isladora's side stood her protector and nursemaid, Juha Lepola. So, she had survived, of course, he thought, she wouldn't be a nursemaid any longer. Now she would be Isladora's training partner and part of her royal guard.

So many of his people were missing, but the King was glad to see Juho Saarela, his most intelligent advisor, standing with the men. Juho Nokela, his top general, with a nasty gash along the side of his face, faced him as well. Both were older men; they had come up together, reigned together, and survived together.

The people knelt in the setting sun, paying homage to their King, now returned. King Elijashen put his fist over his heart in a warrior's gesture. The Juna answered, still kneeling, pressing their fist into their hands, a warrior's tribute.

King Elijashen searched every face, but none were his beloved wife. He demanded, "Where is Anyumay?"

At first no one spoke. They all knew what they had to tell their King would cause him insurmountable grief. Finally, Juho Saarela cleared his throat and spoke, "She has been taken to Zhu, Sire. Tonsaku and his men have gone on a mission to save her, but they have not yet returned."

King Elijashen tried to process this information. Images of Zhu and his sneering face filtered through Elijashen's mind. No female should be in the clutches of Zhu! He collected women and toyed with them until he broke them in every way. The thought of the brute even touching his wife made his muscles clench; he felt his blood begin to boil and his stomach was pained as Elijashen threw his head back and let out a mighty roar. Elijashen's gentle wife, who followed the peaceful Way of the Heron, would be no match for the vicious barbarian. She would be better off dead.

Everyone was frozen, not knowing what to do—Elijashen was crazy in his agony. Upon hearing the deafening bellow of his King, Phoenix reared and trotted to King Elijashen as he was trained to do when hearing his master's shout. When Elijashen didn't mount, the warhorse shoved the King's chest hard with his entire forehead, breaking him from his grief. Phoenix blew fiercely out of his nostrils, pawed the ground, and then turned to his side so the King could mount.

The King scowled at the horse, anger emanating from him, but then reason returned. "You are right my friend; time is of the essence!" King Elijashen grabbed a handful of mane and swung himself up onto his back. Ever loyal, Phoenix had snapped him out of his temporary madness.

"Juho Saarela, you take back the stronghold and appoint people to positions there," King Elijashen commanded. "Juho Nokela, find four other brave men and get ready to ride; we go to save Anyumay."

"I am going with you, Father," Isladora told him.

At first the King was going to refuse, but Isladora had proven herself in battle. He was alive because of her bravery. If she was going to help lead these people, he had to show that he believed in her. "Of course you are, Isladora!" he exclaimed as he reached down, grabbed her arm, and swung her up behind him. As they rode towards the stronghold, he said, "Bring that wyvern of yours, too."

"He has gone on his own quest, Father; I doubt I will see him again." The wyvern mark Json had left on her neck began to burn when she said this and she raised her hand to touch it. Tears of exhaustion rolled down her cheeks.

When they reached the stronghold, the King continued to issue orders as he dismounted. "Saddle the horses, gather weapons and provisions, and let's get on the way. Get me at least one archer."

"Come sire, I have armor that will fit you, but I must caution you, my King," Juho Saarela told him, embracing his friend. "Ah, it is good to see you sire. Six warriors will be no match for the barbarian men." The older man sighed. "Tonsaku took a small regiment to free her and we have not heard from him. We fear that he is dead."

"*I* will be saving her, my friend, and killing Zhu, the cause of all our troubles," the King answered fiercely. In a softer voice laced with compassion he queried, "How many Juna are left, Saarela?"

"We are around sixty in number here, and another thirty or so women and children are still in hiding," Saarela answered. Elijashen was shocked by how few were left but he knew he could depend on Saarela to be good with numbers and true knowledge of his kingdom.

"Secure the stronghold and bring them all home," Elijashen ordered.

"Yes, Your Grace," Saarela told him, turning to leave, then he hesitated. "You ride to your death!" he dared call out to his King.

"No Saarela! I ride to my life!" he answered.

Isladora was so tired. It had been a long day, one that had begun on the back of her wyvern friend Json on the other side of the mountain range. Isladora had been in mortal combat and had been shot with poisoned darts and stabbed with a knife. Without the resistance to poison the wyvern had gifted her with, she would be dead. Without Meluha Crocus' protection from the Queen Mother's magic, she would be dead. With their help, she had rescued her father and now he trusted her to go to war to help rescue her mother. So much had changed, but she was weary to the bone.

Isladora ate the food Lepola brought her, hard boiled eggs, bread, and cheese, and she drank lots of water. Lepola bandaged her leg more carefully and put medicine on her other wounds, then gave her a root to chew that would dull the aches and pains. She was given a horse that was tacked up with food, water, and a sword. Isladora still had Lepola's pack strapped to her body, her magical escrima stick in her pack, and a ring on her finger that contained Meluha Crocus, the spirit of a powerful mage.

They saddled up and rode down the road into the darkening night. A few miles out, Elijashen knew Isladora would not be able to handle the night ride. He commanded them to stop and had her mount in front of him on Phoenix. For once she didn't argue and fell asleep immediately in his arms and slept like the dead.

It was wonderful cradling his daughter; he didn't ever want to let go. He could only pray that Anyumay was alive and that he could heal her mind from whatever Zhu had done to her, in this Isladora could help. All that mattered to him was to have Anyumay back. He held his daughter tighter and she sighed, her head falling to the side against his chest. King Elijashen looked down and saw the wyvern marking on her neck. It was shaped like a small wyvern, its body making an "S" shape. He frowned for a time, for he did not know the meaning of this mark.

It was a hard ride south. When the sun began to rise, they stopped for a quick meal and rested a few hours, allowing the horses to eat and drink. Isladora felt much more rested but her body hurt all over, so she chewed more of the root Lepola had given her. Then they were back in the saddle. By mid-day they were about a mile from the Zoli Pass, the one place they could easily be ambushed by Zhu's men. Elijashen sent his scout to check the area for ambush. While the scout was gone, they dismounted and rested again. The men were worn out too, and Elijashen felt a little guilty about pushing them so hard after a battle.

Isladora was finally revived enough to talk to Meluha Crocus. "Well, here we are again, and about to go into another battle. Are you with me?" she asked.

"*Yes, Isladora, I am here,*" the old spirit in the ring answered her. "*I pray your mother is alive and well, but you must be prepared for the worst.*"

Isladora hoped against all hope; she could not live without her mother.

She asked, "Can you feel her?"

"*No I cannot, but we are only connected when she wears this ring,*" the mage answered.

Isladora couldn't imagine giving the ring back to her mother, for she had grown close to Meluha Crocus and would feel empty without him. She decided she wouldn't think of that now. Right now, she would focus on saving her mother.

Chapter 28: Kingdom of Draconia

Json flew into the Draconian kingdom under the cover of night. He was close, in a few miles he would begin his ascent to the city of Sybaris which was in a higher elevation, and with his royal egg, he had to consider all his options. Json had been gone from Sybaris for many years and he had no knowledge of who ruled, what the laws were, or if he would be welcomed back into the flock. He had been a wyvern youngling when he was taken; he was a mature adult now. Besides that, he was carrying a rare and important creature within his chest. He shook his head in bewilderment, a royal Sybaris. It had been a very long time since the kingdom had a royal Sybaris, in the absence of one, they were governed by five ruling pairs of bonded wyverns and Sybaris. Json wondered if they still ruled.

Json thought back to the last time he had been home. It had been entering summertime, and he and his group of wyvern friends had descended to the lower hunting grounds to laze about and be a little wild. Capture by humans didn't even seem like a possibility; humans simply didn't pit themselves against the wyverns, they rarely even approached the mountainous kingdom. Still, he and all the youngling wyverns with him had been captured by the filthy creatures. The humans had drugged the water supply near their camp, making them easy targets. The drug made them sleep and they awoke in captivity, already loaded into carts, their limbs and mouths chained.

They were given regular doses of the drug through their nostrils along with another drug that dulled their vibrant scales and therefore their magic. When they could no longer spew fire or acid, they were taken to a human camp and caged. The humans believed they could domesticate them and train them to carry humans into war. Json shook his head in anger. *Never!*

The one good thing that came from being captured was finding Ariah. Ariah, a Draconian Sybaris who had miraculously been living with traders near the human camp. She fed Json fresh meat that had provided a source of nutrition and allowed the drugs to filter from his system. Free from the drugs, they had escaped from the human prison camp, but she had been killed by a human's arrow as they flew to their freedom. Not just any human, but the man who had been romancing her. Json growled; humans had absolutely no morals.

Before the sun set on the day of her death, Json had used his newly revived wyvern magic to crystallize her back into egg form to await rebirth. That egg now rode safely sewn inside of his chest. The magical process of creating her egg had imparted Json's memories to Ariah. Because Json had taken the memories of Isladora, a human girl, he also imparted the memories of the human girl and those of her father, King Elijashen. And because Isladora wore an enchanted ring on her finger that held the spirit of Meluha Crocus, who was once a mage, Ariah would have his memories as well. Needless to say, Ariah would have knowledge befitting royalty when she was reborn. This knowledge alone would make her powerful. Json hoped that she could handle the force of all those memories, for her life before had been a rough but simple existence.

He decided that it would be best to leave Ariah safe inside his chest while he reconnoitered. When the time came, he would remove her from his body and she could hatch. Unlike new eggs, she would be born at the age at which she died. He needed help; he didn't know how to hatch a Sybaris. He was not sure who he could trust in Draconia, and he needed to find out how she had become enslaved by humans in the first place.

The Draconians lived in homes high in the mountains where a vast forested plateau had formed. A large lake fed by meandering rivers provided plenty of cold freshwater and game for the Sybaris and the wyverns. The Sybaris built their homes on the plateau and at the base of the higher mountains. The wyverns preferred to live in the higher mountain range just above the plateau. Json patted his chest, "Well Ariah, we will wait until daylight and then fly up to the plateau, past the lake and the city and up into the great caves that house the other wyverns. Perhaps I can find help for us there."

Enough miles out to avoid being spotted, Json flew down into the trees and nestled out of sight to wait for dawn. Json slept lightly, attuned to any human activity. He woke to the delicious scent of a nearby deer, and his stomach rumbled. He had not eaten in days. Listening, he could smell the deer and hear it foraging through the leaves. Json slowly raised his head and in a moment spotted the deer, his pupils narrowing into hard focus. He tracked the deer with his eyes as it moved from plant to plant, aimlessly eating its fill. When the deer was close enough, Json lunged and killed it cleanly, having a filling breakfast. Belching somewhat carelessly, he let the meal settle and then eased from the trees and launched into the sky. He scanned for humans but found none. Except for Isladora, he considered all humans to be inexcusably nasty little things.

Json began his ascent up the mountainside. He had always loved returning to Draconia; it was a mystical and beautiful place, unique in the whole world. Up he climbed, finally reaching the plateau and the beautiful lake. Json flew across the water's vastness, letting his wings skim the surface as he always did. His heart was truly glad to be coming home. Never again would he be careless or underestimate the trickery of his enemy.

Json soared toward the city of Sybaris. He savored the view with the forest to one side and the meandering river that joined the lake. Everything was green and beautiful, truly nature's bounty. Up from the river the homes began. The Sybaris architecture was unlike anything built by humans. The homes were of all sizes but mostly the same shape. They were constructed of stone mined from the area: the bottom layer was the largest, built in a perfect square, the walls about ten feet tall. Each additional story was a smaller square. Most homes had at least two stories but some as many as six. Finally, the tops were built in a circular manner, made of the same stone. They resembled large upside-down funnels. The result was breathtaking, different-sized homes nestled in the forest trees, the larger homes towering above the trees. The biggest building was the Cystine Hall, where the Sybaris leaders and the wyvern leaders met to make decisions about their kingdom.

Json wondered which home Ariah had belonged to. She wouldn't remember, of course, having been with the humans for as long as she could recall. She didn't remember being taken from her home or being given to the nomadic traders that she was with when Json met her. Json wondered how a royal Sybaris could become the property of a human. It wasn't even possible! No human could come here; they didn't have wings. Someone must have stolen her.

Someone from Draconia. That thought chilled his blood.

Two wyverns flew up behind Json and chirped for him to continue onward past the city and up into the communal land governed by wyvern law. That was fine with Json because he was headed there anyway. They flanked him all the way in and landed beside him. Json stayed still and submissive, as he knew he must. They pushed up against him and smelled him all over. The wyvern sense of smell was tied to memory, and if he was part of their tribe their senses would tell them. As they sniffed around his chest area, Json wondered, could they smell Ariah? Did they know what he carried? If they killed him now, how would she hatch? If push came to shove, he would have to tell them that he was a Royal Deliverer, the carrier of a royal Sybaris egg sewn securely into his chest, but he would wait for the push.

The scout recognized that Json was a part of their flock, yet he could not identify some of the senses and smells he was picking up. He demanded, "Where have you been, pup?"

"It's a long story, really," Json sighed. "So long, in fact, that I would like to only tell it once to the Commander."

"And tell it you shall. Let's take him to Glock and get back in the air," the scout said as he lifted off to fly to Glock's quarters.

As Json followed the scouts, his mind was rushing. Glock was in charge? What had happened to the Commander? Glock was a large red and fierce wyvern; very few could best him in battle. He was a hard warrior, selfish and narcissistic; he would definitely not make a good leader for their flock. Not like the Commander. Json sensed treachery, and his protective instincts were on full alert for his precious cargo.

They entered the Commander's quarters, which had now evidently been assigned to Glock. They were situated high up on the mountain cliff and in the center of most of the other wyvern domiciles. From that vantage point, the leader could watch over most of the mountainside and the city of Sybaris below.

The wyverns maintained a symbiotic relationship with their half-human, half-wyvern Sybaris riders. The Sybaris provided the wyverns with an additional source of magic, making the wyverns stronger. Some wyverns fully bonded to a Sybaris if their magic was either complementary or additive and they were compatible. Other wyverns who couldn't bond could still sign contracts, usually a year in length, to be solely available for one Sybaris. No magic would be shared, but the wyvern and the Sybaris would be bound by the contract to each other. It was a system that worked and kept fights from breaking out over who rode what wyvern.

Wyverns and Sybaris of the same color were not allowed by law to bond because the magic synergy was too intense, too one-sided.

Json spied Glock in the back of his quarters looking over some large maps spread out on a stone table, and he was intimidated by Glock's deep red scales covering a large muscular body. Json had no idea how Glock's scales could be so vibrant. When Glock stood on his hind legs, he was taller than any of the other wyverns, something that would make ground fighting with him deadly. Json already knew that in the air he was agile for his large size and that he loved to fight.

Json knew real fear when those red eyes turned towards him. Glock seemed even bigger than he had been when he last saw him. Glock's nostrils flared as he sensed the air around Json. Json was probably half the size of Glock, and he wondered if this was how Isladora had felt when she had stood up to Json with her small human size. Taking a page from her book,

Json stood up straight and tall.

"I smell humans." Glock was not pleased, his brow furrowing.

Json said as calmly as he could, "I am ashamed to say that my friends and I were drugged and taken by humans when we were sleeping down in the lower range."

"Taken by humans?" Glock asked, his gaze transforming into a scowl.

"Yes, and the others are still being held in a human prison camp," Json explained. "I know where it is, and I can lead you there to free them."

"Hmmm," Glock grunted, glancing back at his maps. Json did not like that Glock seemed unsurprised by the news; instead, he seemed agitated.

"Where is the Commander?" Json ventured.

"I am the Commander now." Glock sharpened one claw on the stone table, not looking up. "The old Commander was relieved of duty, in a manner of speaking."

Json could see from Glock's armband that Glock was now bound to a deep red Sybaris, which could only mean the one named Solei. Solei was the mirror image of Glock in Sybaris form, his scales the deepest red of all the Sybaris. His face and muscular chest were mostly human, his back and legs were covered with scales. He had white-blonde hair and his scaled skin was a deep burgundy red. Solei could command the power of fire intensely. Overuse of combined magic had turned Glock's eyes and the skin around them red, so red they seemed to glow. Bonded to Glock, Solei's magic would make Glock extremely lethal.

"You will call me Commander, pup," he ordered.

Json knew that disputing him would mean death and so replied meekly, "Yes, Commander."

Another scout flew in, taking Glock's attention with an update. Json looked around the room, noting that it hadn't changed much since the Commander stayed here. The medicine and supply shelves were still here. He noted the large purple bulbs that only grew high in the mountain and were used to put wyverns to sleep during surgeries and to remove bondings. Json began to sense the danger he was now in. Humans could not have known how to make a drug strong enough to knock a wyvern out, much less dull their magic! They had to have been given the drug by a Draconian, perhaps the same Draconian wyvern and Sybaris that had removed the Commander. *Glock and Solei, it had to be!* And now they ruled? The kingdom of Draconia was in more trouble than he thought.

The scout flew off, bringing Glock's attention back to Json. "What were you doing so low in the hills?" Glock demanded. "How many are in human custody?"

"Five others were taken," he explained, but Json's heart was sinking fast. "Gumbo must have escaped or been killed, as he wasn't with us when we woke in chains." Gumbo was a fat and ungainly wyvern who wasn't very smart. If Glock had sold them out, dispensing with all the young male wyverns at once, he certainly wasn't going to bring the other five back.

"Yet you escaped and didn't rescue them? How convenient for you." Glock laughed a deep, guttural laugh.

"I came home to lead the rescue party," Json told him, even though it was mostly a lie. He came home to keep Ariah safe and to help her hatch, but he realized that anything he did to give her away would result in her destruction.

Glock laughed again. "You will stay here and be bonded," he ordered.

"What do you mean, be bonded? I haven't met the Sybaris I want to bond to." Json was growing more nervous; his wings itched to fly away from this madness.

"It's not a matter of choice. Under the new rules the governing body selects the bonds."

"New rules?" Json stammered.

"Now that I am in charge, we are more organized," Glock told him proudly. "You will report to the Cystine Hall tomorrow to be bonded, no arguments. Now be gone from my sight."

Chapter 29: Ariah's Confusion

Ariah's consciousness seemed to come and go like the wind; she felt like she was in a dream world where little made sense. She found she could talk, and hearing something in the void helped her focus enough to complete the thought. "I have lived five lives! My consciousness tells me this, but the lives are a muddled mass of flashing images that cause me great pain." She did not think anyone could hear her, but hearing her own voice was better than the awful silence. "These memories, they fight one another, battling for my attention, so I give in to them, but one is stronger than the others. I give in to him most, sometimes wanting to be him," she confided to no one.

At first the memories had been misty and vague and oftentimes frightened her. She talked through the visions and flashes that she couldn't seem to categorize. "I think the pull of his memories are dominant because he has lived longer—centuries." She flexed a little, "I feel drawn towards his anger and his pain, somehow wanting to help him as well as be him. I think I am supposed to remember to be me, but who cares about a simple slave girl?" Ariah tried to shift around in her egg and found that she could not.

"My own memories are nothing compared to his. My memories are about slaving around a human camp doing monotonous and lonely work in a dust-filled desert. *His* memories are of magic, wars, and romance. I have learned so much from his memories. Some of the things in his memories don't even exist any longer, they were that long ago. My favorite so far is of a large body of water called an ocean with great sea creatures and ships. The ships are like buildings that float upon the waters! I wonder sometimes if these places still exist." She closed her eyes tight.

When a vivid memory would come upon her in the before time, she would fight it. She would focus on who she was, on who she was supposed to be. It was painful, but Ariah would not let the memory claim her mind. Now she was learning to live with the pain and to welcome the memories, especially if they belonged to him. She began to greet the pain in her head like a friend, telling her another memory was coming. "Oh, let it be his!" She said aloud, embracing it.

She tells her unhearing Deliverer, "I become aware that I am standing on the deck of a ship. The salty spray, the call of the gulls, the smell of the sea, all enter my senses. I feel alive as the ship floats along the waves. I see we are close to land and I feel love in my heart, love for a woman named Mae Tarango that I am traveling towards."

*****

"Be aware now mates! Look alive!" She heard much yelling to get the ship ready to dock in the cove. Ariah saw that she had the hands of a human male as she stood at the wheel, steering it with her hands and her mind. This sea captain has mystical powers that control the wind and sea as he eases the ship into the bay for anchorage. The mates were not aware of his powers; they were simply happy to be working for him. Captain Crocus, they called him.

Now anchored, the Captain collected his things and went ashore. He had a collection of shells in his quarters, and as he touched their spires and knobs and admired their colors and textures, it came to Ariah that he is well-traveled. He knew each part of the world that they came from, their people, and their various languages.

He opened a tortoiseshell box and brought out a beautiful emerald and ruby ring that he purchased for Mae. He was shopping at a bazaar in the east when he came upon the ring in a junk tinker's shop.

Everything in the shop was useless, yet in the midst of the castoffs was this glorious ring. He purchased it from the vendor, a very old man with a knowing smile. When he took it to the metallurgist to have it cleaned, the metalsmith couldn't identify the metal, but nonetheless it was brilliantly made with golden strings interwoven into a beautiful pattern.

Ariah sees from his memories that he planned to ask his woman to marry him. He was a sea captain that could not be without his woman any longer. He could not wait to see Mae—he thought that loving her was like loving all the women of the world, she was that changeable. To him, her imagination was limitless, and her hands set him on fire. When he was with her, he tried to remember every touch, knowing that he had never felt this way with anyone else, afraid lest he forget. Captain Crocus loved this Mae and he vowed to never leave her side again.

As he left his cabin, his first mate Jasso Joel yelled, "All men have gone ashore Cap'n." At his Captain's nod he said, "I'll stay the first night, gun loaded and watch o'er the ship."

"You're a good first mate," he told him, and Jasso nodded. "That I am sir, now go get yer woman." He chuckled.

Captain Crocus didn't worry about the ship, Jasso was an excellent marksman with keen ears and an intelligent mind. Once in town, he entered Mae's home without knocking, and the smell of the food she prepared brought tears to his eyes. He had been away too long. He stood in the doorway closing his eyes, breathing it all in.

His body grew excited when he saw her. She squealed and ran towards him. She hugged him, and when her hand touched his back, even with clothing between them, his skin was alight with the wonder of how she made him feel. Just as she had always sensed, she knew what he needed. Between kisses, she drew a warm bath for him and eased him into it. She massaged his neck and then kissed him on the cheek and left him to bathe while she finished supper.

Supper was a mutton roast with small potatoes and carrots. He told her she was a fantastic cook, and she laughed and answered that yes, she knew. He felt he was in heaven, here with his love, his body nourished and clean, his heart waiting for what was to come next.

Sleeping with her was another dream in itself. The Captain was lost in her charms and her wonders until the wee hours of the morning. He realized as she lay her head to sleep in the crook of his arm that he had forgotten about the ring. He picked up her hand and played with her fingers, realizing, somewhat dumbfoundedly, that his beloved's third finger already wore a wedding band. His heart crushed as she drifted off.

*****

Ariah came out of the memory. She had to remind herself that she was Ariah. She said it to herself several times until she calmed. "I am Ariah... I am Ariah... I am safe inside my magical egg in my wyvern's chest. No harm can come to me. Json my Deliverer will protect me." She decided to rest until the next memory pain would come...it would be soon, for they seemed to come in waves, as if battling each other for attention, or survival.

Intense pain. Ariah's mind traveled into Isladora's memories, the human girl who helped Json save her life and create the egg that protects her. Ariah realized that through her she knows all about the human God, that He is amazing and powerful. Ariah also learned how to do summations, as Isladora's mind was a vessel in which arithmetic sailed on its journey. Ariah saw that she had the knowledge of sums and angles. She realized she knew countless calculations, like how to estimate volumes for common shapes like a cube or a cone. She experienced the true loneliness of a friendless little girl, just like she had been lonely in the trader's camp. Ariah wished that she could talk to Isladora, knowing that they could be the greatest of friends. Ariah fantasized what their friendship would be like and she craved it deeply.

Another flash of pain and the third memory surfaced, it was not to be left out or outdone by the other presences in her mind. Ariah could not control it or stop it. This was the memory of Elijashen, the King of the Juna tribe and Isladora's father....

*****

They were working on the south wall that day, fixing the holes where the wall had crumbled.

Someone had painted a beautiful mural on a portion of the wall. The mural was of a gorgeous countryside and a road traveled by three horsemen. The colors and use of the natural color of the stone were incredible. The king asked that the painter be found and brought to him.

He was not expecting the tattered and broken thing that knelt before him. Truly hideous, his body was malformed with large welts and bulges all over his skin. "Please stand," the king ordered, and the man rose to his feet with trouble. His face drooped on one side, his hair was matted and filthy. He smelled strongly and the king was immediately repulsed. He wondered if this was a joke. Nonetheless, he asked, "I am told you painted this mural, is this true?"

The man trembled with apprehension but answered in a well-spoken and eloquent manner, "Yes, Your Grace, I meant no offense. I wanted to create a thing of beauty in the rubble."

The king paused. "Indeed, you have, sir." He could plainly see that this source of talent was starving, in need of a bath and new clothing. "May I impose upon you to paint some murals in our new chapel, or are you otherwise employed?"

His eyes lit with surprise. "Truly, Your Majesty, to paint upon the chapel walls would be a dream come true," he said, bowing, though the motion was clearly painful for him.

The king told his men to take him to live in the back room of the chapel. There he would be comfortable while he worked. He was to be fed with the other staff, bathed and clothed, and provided with whatever supplies he needed. He was to be paid a stipend upon each completion.

Over the next year the hideous painter created murals in the chapel that were unbelievable to behold. The king's heart was touched as he saw a mural of himself on his warhorse's back, his sword raised in the air, defending his home. He had immortalized the king with features fierce and powerful.

The painters gift knew no bounds and the king realized with shame that he did not even know his name. The king visited him and learned that his name was Stefan. Stefan confided in the king about his great loneliness, how people were afraid of him and avoided him because of his deformities, keeping him from obtaining work. He feared that he would be forced back into poverty when his work in the chapel was done.

For days the king thought incessantly about Stefan's plight and prayed about it. Then he ran into Juha Conee, whose dog had a litter of the cutest pups. Full grown, they would be small. They were black wiry creatures with cute brown faces and soft curly hair.

When they grew old enough to be separated from their mother, the king brought a male pup to Stefan. The one working half of his face smiled, and the king knew then that this dog would change his life. He had the means to care for the dog now and he would no longer be alone. The pup grew and matured, never far from Stefan's side. The little dog ate with Stefan, watched him paint with rapt attention, and slept in the crook of his arm. Stefan trained the dog with manners befitting a fine gentleman.

As his time within the chapel neared its end, the king told him, "Now Stefan, I want you to try something thing for me. Take this dog with you to the market and see if people will approach you." Stefan was shy at first, so the king went with him the first trip out, creating quite a stir. Indeed, this broke the ice. Accompanied by his king, with the dog in his arms, people were drawn to him. As the king had hoped, focusing on the dog lessened people's fear of him and Stefan was able to speak to them. With the dog, he was no longer invisible. Instead of avoiding his hideous face with their gaze, they now looked at him and the well-cared-for dog. They spoke to him, often addressing the dog. When they heard Stefan's eloquent speech, they were taken by him as well. It was already well known that he was painting the murals in the chapel, and people began hiring him to do work.

*****

Ariah suddenly came out of the memory. Wrapped in her cocoon, she let herself lie dormant as she learned from these lives that had been gifted to her. Always, she would say the words, "I am Ariah."

Chapter 30: Zhu's Stronghold

The scout returned reporting of signs of a battle at Zoli Pass. "There were dead men sir, both Zhu's and ours," he reported. He had seen dead bodies littering the ground, and once he came to terms with his initial terror, a closer reconnoiter showed that the bodies were both Tonsaku's and Zhu's men. "Hoof prints showed horses leaving the area at a gallop, possibly as many as seven, and we saw no signs of men remaining in the immediate area."

"Good work scout, we will have about the same number of men then. Eyes sharp everyone, now mount up," King Elijashen ordered.

Elijashen had a feeling of dread in his gut that he would find his youngest brother Tonsaku dead in the Zoli Pass. The scout had not said and he hadn't asked. "Scout, you head to the Zhu's keep to see how many of his men are there. Stay out of sight."

With a slight nod the scout answered, "As you command, sire," then he reined his horse, kicking him into a canter.

The king and his Juna warriors rode for the pass at a slower pace, watching for trouble. The dirt road began to climb into an area that was both inhospitable and beautiful, a small canyon full of large boulders and granite rocks. The canyon terrain was impossible for a horse to travel and difficult for a man. It was striking country with granite boulders of all sizes and shapes interspersed with sparse shrubs and juniper. The canyon itself was a half-day's travel across, and the Zoli Pass was the only place where a road was cleared to pull carts and ride horses through.

The Juna were on high alert, their shields on their forearms for protection from arrows. A man could hide in hundreds of places near the pass. As they rode closer, the stench became overwhelming and the horses began to side-step in nervousness. There was no going around the pass with the horses. Bracing themselves for the worst, they rode through. The horses were careful not to step on the bodies, and Elijashen and Isladora were relieved that none of the bodies were Tonsaku's. Eight of the bodies were Zhu's men, and three were Juna.

Isladora said a prayer for the departed. "Will we take care of their bodies on the return trip Father?"

"Of course we will, Isladora," he answered.

Elijashen did not know how many men Tonsaku had taken with him, but from the signs on the ground, the scout thought that Tonsaku was in fast pursuit of Zhu's men as they had galloped away. Juho Saarela had told him that Tonsaku, as young as he was, was still a brilliant and well-read strategist, and Elijashen believed in his ability to outsmart the barbarians, although he admitted it could be Zhu and his men chasing after Tonsaku. Once through the pass, the trail forked and the pursuers had galloped east, while the track showed a lone rider had galloped south towards Zhu's stronghold, likely their Juna scout. Elijashen kicked his horse and headed towards the stronghold, where he prayed Anyumay was still alive.

As they galloped, Elijashen began issuing orders. "Isladora, when we get to the keep, you hang back until you get my signal, and then you help find Anyumay."

"Yes, Father," she said, relieved to let the men do what men do. She was still incredibly tired, for fighting off the Queen Mother's poisons had taken more from her than she'd expected. *Resistance is not immunity*, she thought.

"We will gallop in fast. You, archer, ride in behind us and find a place that you can do the most damage with your arrows, and stay out of sight."

"Yes, Sire," the archer said.

The scout was waiting on his horse to report to Elijashen at the last rise. "Sire, a few men are in the bailey, one in the tower." He tried to catch his breath, for he must have approached on foot. "Either the men are still gone or they are inside the buildings, but it looks fairly deserted to me."

"You have done well scout, let's take them fast and hard." Waiting for the scout to mount back up, Elijashen unsheathed his sword and then turned to race towards the gate.

As they galloped up to the opening of the keep, the archer took out the guard in the tower as he began alerting the men in the keep to their presence. They galloped and slid in the dust through the gate to find a handful of men, just like the scout had reported. Elijashen charged like a madman, his sword swinging through the air to decapitate one man on foot. His anger had no end, and God help them all if Anyumay was dead.

Witnessing his sudden rage, Isladora realized just how much she had to learn about her father the king.

Elijashen's men quickly dispatched the others. The king jumped from his horse and grabbed one of the dying men. "The women! Where are they kept?" Elijashen shook the man again, "Where are they?"

The dying man pointed to the left wing and passed out.

Elijashen screamed, "Anyumay!" He took off running, his men behind him, the archer left to watch their back and the gate. Isladora dismounted and ran along behind them. The men, realizing she followed, slowed to place her in the middle of them.

No guards were in the hall, and all the doors were shut and barred from the outside. Removing the first crossbar and throwing it across the hall, Elijashen entered the room to find a startled woman in red silks that left little to the imagination. "Do you know where Anyumay is?" King Elijashen asked her.

The startled woman hesitated, and when he moved towards her she backed up with her hands out, "No... no woman here is named Anyumay."

They entered two more doors and found two more women dressed in different colors. Elijashen thought that this must be Zhu's harem. Again, no one knew of a woman by that name. The women had followed the men out into the hall. Now released from their prison, they looked confused and not daring to believe they were finally saved.

"Father!" Isladora yelled as she finally caught up and heard what he was asking. "Mother did not go by that name. She used the name Aceptye to hide the fact that she was your wife. She's used that name for years."

"Yes, we do know Aceptye," said a brown-haired beauty, her pretty face marred with a spreading bruise about her eye, the white of her eye full of blood. "That door there." She pointed to the last door.

King Elijashen stopped in his tracks. Suddenly he was scared. What would he find when he opened the door? He feared for her health, both physical and mental. Zhu was a monster.

Elijashen had been trapped for more than a decade. Would she recognize him, still love him? She had pretended to be another man's wife, his brother Thrace, although in name only to keep herself and her daughter safe. Had she fallen in love with someone else?

Isladora saw trepidation passing across her father's face. She thought about the painting of King Elijashen on the wall in the tomb. Isladora remembered how her mother had lovingly caressed the fierce image. Isladora hadn't known at the time that the image was her father and she remembered being jealous of her mother's love as she fondly touched the image. On one side of the drawing, the artist captured the King in his sleep, and on the other side, he had been screaming a war-cry. Isladora had known then that her mother loved this man, and now she knew that the man was her father. She knew that her mother would always love her father and she told her King, "Go ahead, Father, Mother's love for you is endless, like the many stars."

King Elijashen looked at his brave daughter and took a deep breath. He

slowly took the bar from the door and set it down carefully. He slid the
door open and entered. There on the bed lay his beautiful wife, somewhat
older than the last time he saw her, sleeping. She looked gaunt and pale but
still beautiful. He noticed her steady breathing, and he let out the breath he
was holding. He sat on the bed and brushed her hair from her face as a tear
ran down his. He hadn't seen Anyumay for so long. She awoke, startled at
his touch, and he saw her eyes widen in fear. Her forehead was bruised, her
lower lip swollen. Her lips were cracked from dehydration. He would kill
that bastard Zhu! Then her eyes cleared and she smiled a dreamy smile. "Ah
my love, I dream of you again," she whispered softly, her hand reaching
towards his face.

Elijashen took her hand in his and brought it to his lips, slowly kissing
the back of her hand and then pressing it to his lips. "No, my love, I am
here. I've come to take you home."

Anyumay slowly sat up and placed her hands on both sides of his face.
Tears streamed unchecked as she felt him and realized that he was real. Her
husband was returned to her! She grabbed him in her arms and started crying, her body shaking with sobs. His men and his daughter watched until
her sobs were spent. She whispered, "But how?"

"It's a long story my love, and we are not safe here." He brushed the
tears from her cheek. "Zhu and his men are gone but they may come back.
We need to leave before we are outnumbered." Elijashen gently kissed her
lips just as he dreamed of doing so many times, not minding that they were
cracked. "Can you walk?"

"I have no clothes other than these." Anyumay looked down, her face
reddening in shame. Quickly, Elijashen took off his armor and then his shirt
and put it over her head. She pulled her arms through and then climbed
from the bed and stood on shaky legs, relieved to see that it covered most
of her, reaching down to the middle of her thighs. The king strapped his
armor back on and she helped buckle it, just as she had so many times,
hope blooming in her chest that had laid dormant for so many years. Her
arms encircled him. "I don't want to let you go," she said.

He pried her hands from around him and took her hand and they ran
from the room; his men and daughter were ready to go. Anyumay ran right
past her daughter without recognition, but Isladora was not hurt by this.
She knew how different she looked. She was no longer the pudgy, spoiled
little girl her mother had left at the stronghold; now she was a Juna warrior.
As they ran down the hall Anyumay yelled, "Women! Get to a horse and
ride with us. We will give you safe shelter in the High Country!"

Some of Zhu's men came around the corner at the noise, and Isladora took the knees out from under one of them with a sweep while the soldier behind her smashed his sword butt into his head. The other was run through. They ran on and out into the courtyard. Several more dead bodies lay where the archer had picked them off, changing his hiding place at random. They ran to their horses and Anyumay screamed, "I cannot leave without Fashi!"

"Who is Fashi?" Elijashen yelled back.

"My horse, I cannot leave without my horse!" She was crying and out of control of her usually calm emotions. She ran towards the stables. Elijashen ordered two of his men to the stables, his attention drawn to the women that followed her. Anyumay searched through the stalls until she found Fashi, her sturdy ugly mountain pony with a heart of gold.

"Are you sure, Lady, this horse?" the guard questioned. At her quick nod, he saddled him.

She grabbed the bridle that hung outside his stall door and handed it to the man. "Yes, I'm sure, hurry!" She nuzzled Fashi's nose, touching his biddable equine thoughts, calming hers. "There you are, my brave little warrior," she crooned to the horse.

Some horses were already tacked up and the women claimed three of them while Elijashen and the other men stood guard outside the stable door.

Elijashen didn't know what he had expected when his wife emerged with her mount into the daylight. She sat tall and regal on her squatty mountain pony like he was the finest royal equine. Elijashen's shirt hung on her body, and the green transparent clothing that Zhu had dressed her in peeked out. Her hair was a mess and her face was bruised and cut. She was glorious, and he could not stop smiling at her.

"Fall in!" he yelled, and as a group they galloped from the keep with Isladora at her mother's back, the men surrounding the women.

They exited the bailey and as they turned, Isladora looked up the road and her stomach lurched. At least fifteen of Zhu's men were mounted, weapons in hand but lowered toward the ground. "My king, look!" she cried.

Elijashen slowed his mount, trying to think quickly, for they were outnumbered and the rescued women were unarmored. Elijashen recognized the man mounted in front: he was Ascendi, Zhu's top warrior and a fierce fighter. As the Juna stopped in the middle of the road, the King of the Juna looked at his daughter, regretting that he had brought her here. He had six men, only five in heavy armor. The other was the archer, though he stood his ground bravely, an arrow nocked and ready. But worse, he had the women with him, and he felt equal parts rage and fear for them.

The bruised, brown-haired beauty moved her horse to the front and looked at one of the men. She spat in contempt and yelled, "Give me a sword and I will kill these dogs."

The man she was yelling at screamed in fury, for she was his whore to do with as he pleased. Who was she to shout at him? He charged at a gallop. He would rip her from her horse's back and teach her a lesson. Her horse shied but she kicked him and yanked his reins to keep him in control. With a look from Elijashen, the archer waited until the enemy approached to two horse-lengths from her and then he shot him through the neck. The ugly cur's body fell, sliding across the dusty ground, his sword clanking as his grip failed, his horse veering to miss her horse.

The archer yelled and pointed, "Your sword, milady!" She scrambled from her perch and grabbed the sword from the ground. She kicked the man's lifeless body and then ran back; handing the sword to the nearest man so she could pull herself back into the saddle. He reached down to help pull her up and with a shy smile handed the sword to her. It was completely foreign feeling in her hands. It was heavy, and she would somehow have to use two hands. She would rather die today then go back into that keep she thought, firming her grip.

"Elijashen!" Ascendi yelled at him. "Come forward!" Ascendi urged his mount towards them, leaving his men.

Elijashen moved his horse forward then turned back to his men. "There are thirteen of them, so that's two apiece. If they attack, you men spread out; you women stay behind the men. When they near you women, circle away and let the men handle the attack and strike from behind only. Archer, take out as many as you can."

The Juna, trained to act, put their fists on their hearts then readied for the attack. Isladora pulled the reins a little tighter in her hand. The horse, sensing her tension, pawed at the ground. It took intense concentration for her to channel her primal response as she watched her father head towards the enemy alone. The escrima stick in her hand elongated into a short sword, its edge sharp and deadly. Her horse reared.

Elijashen registered all the aspects of the coming fight with accelerated senses. The wind devils stirred the sand around his horse's hooves, churning like the devils in his heart.

Elijashen was not going to waste time talking to Ascendi; he knew him to be just as merciless as Zhu. A burst of wind spurred him towards his foe with a war cry.

Ascendi wasn't expecting Elijashen to charge, and his horse backed

away, making him lose precious time in beginning his own charge. Elijash-
en's horse slammed into his, causing Ascendi's horse to fall. Suddenly, Elijashen leapt through the air to attack Ascendi, who was rolling on the
ground trying to regain his feet.

Ascendi's men began their attack as soon as Elijashen charged. The Juna archer took out two of them before they got to close range. He was
nocking a third arrow when he was attacked from the side. The sword sliced
his drawing arm and he dropped his bow. Isladora was the closest and she
charged the man, her sword becoming a spear and impaling his eye. Isladora
moved to protect her mother, who dismounted and picked up the fallen
bow, scrambling to reach the arrows. "Mother!" she screamed, but her voice
was lost in the melee. Most of the Juna men were off their horses, locked in
hand-to-hand combat, their world transmuted into a blur of grappling and
kicking.

The archer was telling Anyumay what to do; he had been her instructor
at one time. His voice kept her calm as her hands shook placing the arrow.
Anyumay had no trouble pulling the bow back. She released the arrow into
the nearest barbarian, and it sunk deep into his thigh. The Juna man finished him off with his sword, quickly whirling to the barbarian fighting his
fellow Juna and stabbing him through the kidney. One of Zhu's men started towards Anyumay as she tried to nock another arrow, but her little horse
lunged for the man's neck, drawing blood as he spun and kicked the man in
his chest. The Juna men began to gain the upper hand by uniting against
each barbarian until only Ascendi and Elijashen were left fighting.

The Juna stood silently, their hearts in their throats as they watched Elijashen take a stunning blow to his jaw. Neither man had their sword any
longer, and they fought hand-to-hand. Elijashen staggered backwards, holding his jaw in his hand, bent over. Ascendi kicked him hard, and then again.

With a victorious laugh, Ascendi drew his knife from the sheath in his
boot and smiled an oily smile, his teeth amazingly clean compared to his
skin. He shifted the knife so that the blade was along his forearm, his favored position for knife fights.

He swung the blade in an arc, aiming for Elijashen's throat. At the last
second Elijashen blocked the attack with his forearms, grabbing the wrist
with one hand and smashing his fist into Ascendi's nose, hearing the bone
crunch. As Ascendi's head snapped back, Elijashen torqued his arm as he
spun him around, then reversing it into an elbow lock, taking Ascendi to the
ground. A stomp to the arm broke it at its bent angle, and the knife fell
from his hands. Elijashen picked up the knife and glanced back at his men
and women, relieved to see his wife and daughter still standing. As Ascendi

started to roll over and get back to his feet, Elijashen ended the evil general's life with a clean slice across the jugular.

The group headed home with one man dead, another wounded, and the archer too wounded to fight. As they rode back through the Zoli Pass, the men filled him in on the melee. King Elijashen had to admit the little pony had likely saved Anyumay's life. He looked over at the ugly beast with admiration; someone had taught that horse how to fight. He was just as fast as the war horses and he didn't seem to tire or stumble, while carefully keeping his novice rider centered on his back. As Elijashen looked at his wife and the tortured look on her face, his only regret was that *Emperor* Zhu, as he liked to call himself, would live another day. Having seen what passed for his "invincible fortress," Elijashen now realized Zhu was nothing more than a trumped-up bandit king whose only power came from his reputation.

Chapter 31: Cystine Hall Bonding

The next day, Json reported to the Cystine Hall early because he wasn't sure when the bondings took place. He entered the foyer and strolled up to the desk where an older Sybaris was reading. "Excuse me, I was told to come for bonding, is this the right place?"

The brown Sybaris sighed and put the book down, "Just at a good spot in the book you know, name please?"

"Json," he all but growled.

"Okay, got you down, now you sit and wait, and they'll come for you."

As Json perched in the front room, a large domed structure, he marveled at the immense columns that supported the Cystine Hall. It was said that magical earth creatures had helped put them in place. The hall was built large enough for even Glock to walk its corridors easily. A few Sybaris moved about the halls, but not as many as Json had expected, and he saw no other wyverns.

The main meeting room was at the back. Json knew that it was a large rectangular room with high ceilings and tables built for both the wyverns and the smaller Sybaris citizens. The governing board was made up of five pairs of bonded wyverns and Sybaris who had equal ruling powers. Together, they made decisions ranging from daily disputes to declaring war. It was a structure that had worked for many years.

As the hours passed, Json went through what he knew about the board members the last time he was here. The senior ruling pair had been the Commander and Aslay. The Commander was a white and black wyvern, one of the largest of their lot. His head, body, and wings were white, and his mane, feet, and the end of his arrow-shaped tail was black. He had two long golden horns that grew back towards his mane. He was chosen as their Commander because of his size, strength, and solid morals. He was bonded to Aslay, who had a human face, shoulders, and arms and silver scales that covered her legs, torso, and breasts. She had a full head of long blonde hair that was wavy and untamed. Aslay also had a military bearing and was fierce in battle. Together, they commanded the air. Json didn't know if they were alive any longer since Glock had told him the Commander had been "relieved of duty."

Json also remembered Arrington and Bedaiko. Arrington was a green

Sybaris with deep blue eyes. His green scales were larger than most and spaced farther apart. They ran across his forehead and framed his human face. His shoulders and back were covered in large scales and his was chest bare. He almost always wore coverings on his legs that resembled human pants. Json didn't care too much for Arrington. He always spoke with an arrogant manner, but he was known for his brilliant mind, creative problem solving, and his ability to render detail from memory. He was bonded to Bedaiko, a blue wyvern of medium build. Their colors weren't complementary to each other so the bonded pair shared no magic, but each had magic of their own. Green magic was like a wild card, it could be used for anything, but it wasn't predictable in its outcome and often did things it wasn't meant to. Blue magic could manipulate water.

Json had heard that bonding was a painful process, a melding of the minds. When the orderly looked up again from his book, he decided to ask him.

The orderly looked him up and down with gentle curiosity, "Yes, it is fairly painful and once a pair is bonded, the bond is inseparable until both beings wished it to be severed. You can only form one bond at a time."

Json was still perplexed about Glock and Solei, "Isn't it true that the law prevents same-colored Sybaris and wyverns from bonding to each other?" Json believed that the reason was that they could not become unbonded, even in death.

"It once was true, yes," the orderly wandered off, going about his duties with quiet grace.

Json remembered, it was thought that the strength of the same-color magic made the life span much shorter for the Sybaris. This was why Json was shocked to see Solei bonded to Glock. It would bring about an early death for Solei. When Json was taken, Glock had been bonded to Tunac, a yellow Sybaris who was old and near passing away. Perhaps she already had. Both Glock and Solei being deep red would be a deadly match.

Darkale and Abraxis, a blue and grey pair, and Toyah and Silverback, a purple and silver pair rounded out the ruling pairs. Json's thoughts were interrupted as he was called into the hall.

"You will enter now to be bonded," the court official told him, inclining his head.

Json noticed a Sybaris and another wyvern down the hall also get up and enter the main room ahead of him. Json followed, and as he passed through the door, his eyes fell upon Glock and Solei. Solei was no longer a young man; he had aged into mid-life at least. His eyes were blood-red and glowing, fissures and cracks running from the eye to the forehead. Solei was

still handsome with his white blonde hair that he kept short and his powerful body, but the magic was definitely taking its toll. Solei also wore a glowing red amulet around his neck, brimming with fire magic.

Json was intimidated being in the room with these powerful pairs. His
apprehension settled deep inside of him, all the while knowing he carried a
royal Sybaris in his chest that he must protect at any cost.

"The first bonding will be of the wyvern Gumbo and the Sybaris Rosetta," the official announced. "Please step forward."

Gumbo! He had been with the wyvern younglings when the humans
had captured them. Json wondered how Gumbo had escaped. Gumbo was
a large and ungainly wyvern, resembling a swollen bullfrog. He was green
all over, but his nose and pointy ears that stuck straight out were red. He
had large amounts of what looked like long hair that was made of thousands of tiny scales and wyvern skin. His wings were small for such a large
body; Json doubted that he could fly for long with a Sybaris on his back.
Rosetta was also a green Sybaris. Her entire body was covered in scales
except for half of her face. It was like her human side cut diagonally across
the upper part of her face. Her eyes were the same emerald green and she
had stunning red, very long hair.

"Excuse me, but this pair cannot be bonded; both are red and green!"
Json exclaimed. When Rosetta turned to look at Json in his outburst, Json
noticed that she was missing her arm; only a stump protruded from her
shoulder cap.

"Silence!" Glock roared. "One more outburst and you will be punished!"

The purple Sybaris that Json knew as Toyah spoke up. "Json, it is now
our law to bond same color pairs," she explained. "The risks are known and
completely agreed to by the pair." With a sigh, she said somberly, "Rosetta
is fully aware that this bonding may shorten her life span, but she has not
had a better offer in her lifetime with us and it is her choice." Toyah
paused. "Let us begin."

Json could see how much Rosetta wanted this bonding, it was in her
hopeful eyes and in the way she stepped forward first to receive the piercing. The bonding was performed by the exchange of blood induced to enter
the blood stream by magic. The orderly pierced Rosetta's forearm and
turned and pierced Gumbo's neck. Then Rosetta took a deep breath and
placed her bleeding arm over the wound on Gumbo's neck. Toyah and Silverback added the magic that would force the blood minerals to flow one
way and then the other in their bodies, forming the pair. Gumbo and Rosetta shrieked in pain but did not falter in holding steady for the blood to

transfer. After several minutes, the bonding was complete.

"Please demonstrate your bond," the orderly said.

Both were exhausted from the pain but they traded magic back and forth, her scales glowing brighter for an instant and then passing to the other half of the pair and flashing through his scales.

"Very good, the bonding stands," he remarked. "You will now be taken to another room for feeding and recovery. Please exit the door over there," he pointed. Json wondered what the pair's magic would be with the unpredictable green and the intense red. Time would tell.

The only unpaired being in the room now was a young Sybaris woman that had no scales at all. She sat quietly in the corner chair, her focus on Toyah. Json could tell the two knew each other, as Toyah tried to look reassuringly at the young Sybaris.

"Kaigen, please stand," stated the orderly.

When she stood, Json could see that she was indeed all human except for tattered wings that grew from her back. Her wings would not help her to fly, as they were only the structure of the wing and nothing else. She was a tragically beautiful and forlorn looking creature. She had long brown hair that was parted on the side and hung down into her face as if to provide a hiding place behind it if she chose. Her large brown eyes were doe-like and expressive. She wore a short brown leather and bone corset-dress that revealed much of her body. The same leather wrapped around her forearms and again as leather sandals on her feet. Most Sybaris chose to hide their human parts behind clothing; this young lady seemed to display her human skin proudly.

When Json stood before the ruling pairs, he began to understand. The bond mate they had chosen for him would make weak magic. The same color pairing of Gumbo and Rosetta showed that this administration didn't see them as a threat. Only those in power and some of the older pairs had beneficial bonds. Json knew that he and this Kaigen would make a weak bond. Without scales, Kaigen had no place to store magic for them. Json knew that magic was stored in the keratin scales of both wyvern and Sybaris; more scales equaled more magical stores.

Scales consisted of hard keratins that were transparent. The colors of the scale resulted from pigments in the inner layers of the skin rather than the scale material itself. Scales of all colors manifested in this manner except for blue and green. Blue coloring was caused by the different structure of those type of scales, and they diffracted light to give off a blue hue. If the inner skin was yellow and the structure was right, the scales would instead appear green. Json believed that this was why green scales gave off unpredictable magic because the structure under the scale could vary and be manipulated by the color of the skin. Json's own dark green to black scales meant that he had the structure to diffract light and that his inner skin was yellow to black.

Json now believed that Glock had killed the Commander. He also believed that he and his friends, the other younglings, had been betrayed and sold to the humans. He didn't for a second think that he was safe here. Without the younglings, Glock could not be threatened for his place on the governing board when they fully matured. Now Glock was slowly taking control from the remaining pairs. Json had no doubt that they would eventually be killed as well. Json could do little about that now, unfortunately. His main priority was keeping Ariah safe, and in order to do that, she must be kept secret until a circle of protection for her could be formed so she could hatch.

Json moved forward to be bonded to Kaigen. The orderly pierced Kaigen's forearm and then Json's neck. Toyah and Silverback moved forward to add the magic that would seal the bond. Json immediately roared as magical pain entered his body. It was a more intense pain than anything he had ever felt, like liquid fire running in his veins straight to his chest. Json clutched his chest where Ariah's egg was held, continuing to roar in pain. Kaigen was also screaming in pain, holding her forearm to Json's neck. Finally it ended, leaving both of them trembling. Json hoped that Glock didn't realize that he was trembling in fear.

Json was terrified because he knew he had formed a bond, but not with Kaigen. He was now bonded to Ariah! He looked at Kaigen in fear, his nostrils flaring, and he knew she had felt Ariah's presence and Json's bonding to Ariah. As soon as Kaigen spoke, Glock would know and kill him and his royal egg.

Again, the orderly gave a decisive nod and said, "Please demonstrate your bond."

Json knew that it was over. He would die fighting in this very room. He was no match for Glock, but he would not go out easily. Before he could shift into a fighting stance, Kaigen reached out and grabbed the side of his snout, looking him intently in the eye. Json could feel Toyah's full attention on him as well. Kaigen flexed her wing structure to full extension, and then they flashed slightly. Json, not knowing what was happening but being forced to trust in this strange Sybaris, reacted immediately by creating a pulsing glow in his dark green scales. He could feel Ariah's answering glow inside his body. Good, she was alive and well.

"Very good, the bonding stands," the orderly remarked, pointing the way to the door the first pair had left through.

Json couldn't believe it! Kaigen had pretended to be bonded to him, but for what reason? She had played them all false, somehow making it look like her wings shimmered with shared magic. Toyah looked at his chest where Ariah's egg was cradled and then she smiled at Json, turning away. Json followed Kaigen out the door and down the hall.

Chapter 32: Kaigen

Kaigen wasted no time in trying to establish the parameters of the false bonding. "I saved your tail back there," Kaigen said with reluctant heroism as they ate the manna provided for their bonding. Her wing structure twitched a little as Gumbo and Rosetta finished and left the room. She calmly selected another grain cake that had been infused with earth magic and nibbled off the corner.

"Yes, you did, and I appreciate it," Json told her, sticking the manna in his mouth. He still couldn't believe they had made it out of that room alive. Being in a room filled with creatures that could quickly end your life and trying to deceive them had been nerve wracking. As they ate, the manna began to heal their wounds, the earth magic repairing the tissues and strengthening the bond. Json wondered if the manna would affect Ariah where she rested inside him.

Kaigen took a bite and looked at him coquettishly. "Don't you mean you and your egg appreciate it?"

Json looked up with a low growl. So she did know! "Look, I know you risked your life pretending we were bonded. If Glock had noticed, we would all be dead." Json considered his words, making sure of them before saying, "I have to trust you. The egg I am carrying must be kept a secret until I can get help." Now he wasn't the only one who knew he was carrying the egg and this made him feel more panicky.

"Good, I'm aware of that and keeping your secret is no problem. All you have to do is fly me where I want to go." Kaigen smiled at him confidently. She looked down and her hair covered her eyes. Then she looked up and flicked her hair back with a shake of her head. She said firmly, "I want you to fly me to the steppes."

Json looked around, making sure no one heard her. When he saw that they were still alone in the room he said, "That is forbidden by treaty. Our kind are not allowed to go there, or has that changed too?"

"No it's still the law, but that is where I want to go." Kaigen sighed, and added, "You have a secret you want me to keep, so I think it is a fair trade."

Just then Toyah and Silverback entered the room. Json was jealous of the pair. They truly looked like they belonged together, and he envied their obvious comfort with one another. Json's attention was drawn to Silverback; he was a glorious wyvern. He was sleek and silver from head to tail and he moved his large body with a warrior's refinement. The under part of his wings and his belly were a deep purple, almost black. His wings were built for great speed, his body thin and lean. He had silver horns on top of his head and two more that came out the side of his head and curled towards his jaw. His regal bearing made him a striking creature. His silver tail ended in a diamond shape, the bone sharp and deadly. Silverback was extremely intelligent and one of the top officials in the country. Every wyvern alive worshipped Silverback.

Part of what made Silverback so regal was his dazzling bonded mate Toyah. The wyvern and Sybaris had been paired for as long as Json could remember. Everyone looked to the pair for wisdom and guidance; they were almost celebrities in Sybaris. Toyah's head and shoulders were bare like a human's. Her violet scales started at her shoulder and ran down both arms. The scales covered her breasts and the rest of her body. She had long dark brown hair that fell all the way to her buttocks, and two thin, spiral-shaped silver horns protruded from the top of her head. She had a kind but serious face, masking an intelligent mind.

"Well done today, congratulations on your pairing," Silverback said as they passed through.

Toyah placed one hand on Json as she passed and telepathically said, *"You will meet us at the north shore of the lake in two hours, Deliverer. Bring Kaigen. Tell no one."*

Json hadn't known that Toyah was capable of speaking mind to mind, but he wasn't surprised with such super-intelligent creatures. She had called him Deliverer; there was no doubt in his mind that she, too, knew about the egg. Json felt out of control. Both he and Kaigen stared as the pair left the room.

"Wow, isn't she great?" Kaigen exclaimed. "If I could be anyone, it would be her."

As they prepared to leave the room, Json gathered his scattered thoughts and wondered how he was going to get Kaigen on his back without telling her where they were going. As they left the building, he decided he would try directness. "Let us see how well you can fly," he told her. The governing pairs would expect that from them anyway. Json decided he would fly around with her until it was time and then fly back to the north shore of the lake.

Kaigen climbed on Json's back. The Sybaris did have saddles that they used for military exercises and battle, but most rode without them under normal conditions. In her awkwardness, Json wondered if Kaigen had ever flown before and asked, "Is this your first time to fly?"

"You know just because I have wing structure, that doesn't mean I can fly, you idiot." Kaigen was both defensive and proud, a bad mixture to get along with. Then, when Json didn't say anything, she amended in a slightly less belligerent voice, "Yes, it is my first time."

"Great," Json mumbled.

Once she was seated and holding onto the black spikes on his neck, Json started running and then lifted into the air. He started to fly out over the forest, but not long after they were airborne, Kaigen yelled, "Stop, please stop, I can't hold on!" Kaigen's wings, even though they were just the structure, pulled against the air, causing her pain and tearing her away from her seat on his back.

Json slowed, but the reduction in air flow wasn't enough to keep Kaigen from falling to the side. She was holding on with one arm and one leg, the other arm and leg flailing wildly. Json banked to the side she was falling from, and she screamed louder. He banked the other direction, and this tipped her to the top of his side, allowing her to pull herself back up and regain her seat. Her wings were still pulling against her back and she was crying, "Put me down, put me down!"

Json landed in a small clearing and Kaigen just sat on his back crying. "Are you all right, Kaigen? Are you hurt?" Json asked her, turning his head trying to see her.

"I... I think so," Kaigen said as she slid from his back.

"Here, turn around and let me see your wings," Json told her.

Kaigen turned and Json could see that the wing structure was still attached. "Can you open them wide like you did in the hall?" Kaigen turned and opened them to Json's obvious relief. Her defensiveness relaxed a little when she saw his reaction.

"It hurts, but I think they are okay," she said, wiping the tears from her cheeks.

Json didn't think she could ever fly on his back with her wing structure blowing against the wind flow like that. "Why don't you see if they can remove them?" he asked, but knowing it was a mistake as her face darkened the moment he uttered the words.

"Remove them, is that all you see when you look at them, you ugly wretch?!?" Kaigen turned away, her hair covering her face, dejected.

Json thought she was a touchy thing, wild and reclusive. He tried to repair the damage to their nascent relationship, saying, "No, well, I meant that if you can't use them to fly..." Json shut up when her shoulders began shaking because she was sobbing.

Finally, she looked up. "You think me weak, less powerful than you, right?" Her eyes grew stormy like a whorl of dead leaves.

Json knew he was more powerful than her. but that didn't seem a good thing to point out. "No, I didn't mean that," he finally said.

Kaigen stood straight and tall, lifting her head and closing her eyes, her hands open and pointing towards the ground. Her wings shimmered for a second, and then all hell seemed to break loose. Json heard a low rumble and then the earth started shaking. He felt off balance as a large fissure split the earth open, the crack running towards him. Json jumped back, prepared to take flight, when the crack stopped just at his feet.

"What on earth?" Json exclaimed.

Kaigen crossed her arms over her chest. "That's right, the power of the earth." She smiled in satisfaction and pride. "Earth magic."

Json was perplexed. What an extraordinary gift! "But you have no scales."

"Magic is contained in scales because they are keratin, not because they are scales! Keratin is in everything, you idiot, almost every living creature. In scales, hair, hooves, fins, bone. My wing structure is made of beta-keratins and holds more magic than all your blessed scales!" she told him heatedly.

"Your earth magic is impressive, Kaigen," he said. Json meant that, but he was also thinking what a disaster she could cause.

She closed her eyes again, and the earth rumbled as she healed the fissure she had made. Then she sat dejected upon the ground. "I know," she sighed. "It's still not going to help me fly with you to the steppes."

Json thought it wasn't going to help him fly her to meet Toyah and Silverback either. He said, "I have an idea. Stay here, I'll be right back." He took off running and flew towards the city. It took him some time to locate the leather tanner, and by the time he had gotten what he needed it was almost time for them to meet Toyah. Json flew quickly in his haste and thankfully found Kaigen exactly where he had left her.

Json had brought back a large piece of leather. He laid it out on the ground and cut off one long, narrow piece with his claw. He folded the leather in half and cut a hole in the center. "Now tuck your wings in close," he told Kaigen. He slid her head through the hole so that it made a large sleeveless shirt. Gathering her wings tight, he guided the leather around them snug and then tied the narrow strip around her body, making sure it didn't hurt her. "When we get back, we will have the tanner make something custom fitting, but until then this should do. Ready to test it out?" He didn't want to tell her they were late for an appointment she didn't know about.

"I'm scared, but yes I am ready," Kaigen told him. "I'm sorry I called you an idiot and tried to bury you in the ground."

Json chuckled, "Oh, I think if you wanted to bury me I would be blowing dirt from my nostrils now." His comment forced a soft throaty chuckle from her.

Again, she climbed on his back and Json ran and lifted off, going as slow as he could. He could feel her crouched low over his neck. When she didn't scream, he flew faster until they were flying the way they were meant to fly.

Kaigen was in awe of the scenery below. She had never known what it was like to fly, and she cried tears of joy, lovingly rubbing Json's neck. He smiled his wyvern smile; he definitely understood.

Json and Kaigen were a little late as they flew to the north shore of the lake. They skimmed along the bank, but neither Toyah nor Silverback were anywhere to be seen. On their second pass Json saw a flash in the trees, so he banked and landed despite being aware that it may be a trap. He needed allies too much not to risk it. They landed on the beach where he could see that under the cover of the large trees the pair stood waiting. Json's heart rate accelerated.

"Oh, that was wonderful!" Kaigen was babbling in her excitement of flight. "I can't believe that I finally flew for the first time, I can't wait to tell Von!" Then she noticed where Json was looking and she saw Toyah and Silverback. "What are they doing here?" Kaigen asked in fearful tones.

Json didn't want to explain what he didn't know, so he said nothing. Toyah gestured for them to come under the cover of the trees.

Chapter 33: Ariah's Mother

Ariah rode nestled in her egg safe beneath the layers of skin in Json's chest. She was curious about the feelings she felt. Audibly, she said, "I am bonded to Json. It is befitting, I think. He is my savior, my Deliverer, my only real friend, although we only knew each other a short time, both of us enslaved by humans. I'm not sure that I understand the full Draconian meaning of being bonded, but I know that we are and I now feel the magic flowing between us, the new magic of Json's blacks and greens combining with my reds and violets."

Ariah had sensed the danger Json felt and the presence of some of the others nearby during the bonding. She knew that he was afraid, and so she was also afraid also, and of her own people. This brought her grief. She had imagined many times what it would be like to find her people. "I know they are my people, even though I have never met them. These memories are so strange sometimes. The bonding process was painful as his blood moved to penetrate my shell and my blood raced to bond to his, guided by a third presence." Ariah paused in her telling, "When my shell began cracking, I thought I would die stuck here in Json's chest, but then the healing manna from the earth covered all the fissures in my shell. I think I am going to be fine. I haven't tried to use our combined magic. I don't understand it, and I don't want to hurt Json, and so I sit calmly in his chest, as disciplined as I can, lest I forget."

One thing excited Ariah beyond measure, surpassing all the grief she felt at fearing her own people, "I knew at the bonding that my mother was nearby. I felt her touch. She was better than all the pretend mothers I invented in my childhood. She was larger than life and oh, so powerful. Her name is Toyah. I rejoice in knowing this." Ariah laughed, "Around my mind flickered light containing all the emotion she ever felt for me. I pleaded with her to talk to me, here I am! Here I am! But she did not acknowledge me. Then, I could feel her love moving away from me. With my wyvern tongue I smelled the heat of her body, close to me, yet so far away. With my human skin I felt every tear she wept for me fall along my heart. With my scales, I felt her presence as she passed me by. My ears longed to hear her voice, no matter the words. I felt her close, with the part of my brain where you know something is true, yet it's too surreal to believe. Hear me, Mother! Then she was gone."

With her mother gone again, Ariah felt weak and alone. She reached out to Json through their bond to feel something, and his answering magic settled her. She started to feel intense pain as memories started to take over her mind again. To escape the pain she let them come, hoping they would be the memories of Captain Crocus, and they were.

*****

I fell asleep next to Mae, cradling her hand that wears someone else's wedding band. I have mixed emotions. I know Mae to be a faithful woman; why hadn't she waited for me? I had given her enough money that she wouldn't have to worry or work overly hard when I was away. Especially so she wouldn't be beholden to any man. The thought made my already over-heated blood boil.

I slept fitfully and wakened as soon as the sun beckoned to the day. Mae was curled on her side, her back to me. Normally I would pull her to me and make love to her again, but I just couldn't reach out to her. Instead, I got out of bed to dress and to leave.

She woke and joined me in the kitchen, where I sat dejected, looking for signs of a man in the house. I knew I was would kill him when I found him, and I couldn't bring myself to care.

She asked me what was wrong, knowing me like I knew my ship. I looked at her with deep sadness and she became fearful. She asked me if I am leaving her already. I told her that no, I had planned on never leaving her again. I told her that I was coming to take her to live with me in the islands where we would settle and retire from shipping in a beautiful house I had built for us.

I knew Mae would love the islands. The locals were peaceful and friendly, and I had plenty of goods stocked and a small plantation started. She would teach the islander children because the children would flock to her; she was that kind of woman. Mae could do things other people couldn't do because tolerance was rooted in her bones. Like travel with me on my ship; few women would do that and she would love the adventure. I looked at her ring and scowled deeper.

Then Mae started to giggle, and then laugh, and soon huge guffaws rolled from her like a woman possessed. I thought her a cruel creature at that moment, truly I did. When she could talk, done with her unladylike snorts, she showed me her ring. I scowled the most murderous scowl that my ship captain's face could form, the one I used when I didn't want my men to talk to me. How dare she! Being a ship's captain, I would lift her guffawing body over my shoulder and take her to sea and declare her divorced from the lout! And as soon as I could find a priest, I would take her as my wife. I stood up, as that was my plan of action.

Mae backed up a little when she saw the look on my face. She quickly explained that she wore the ring to show the world that she belongs to someone. And that that someone was an idiot beyond all other idiots. In short, me.

I sat there stupefied. Still scowling but feeling blessed, I picked her up over my shoulder anyway, to show her that I could, and she squealed in terror or delight, I know not which. I carried her into the bedroom, my scowl replaced with a claiming smile.

*****

Ariah emerged from the memory and felt relieved that no other memories were coming behind it. "Oh, to feel the love for another and have them love you back like the Captain and his woman! I want to hatch, I need to hatch!" Ariah felt vibrations of the earth, like an earthquake, so she vibrated her shell, hoping Json could set her free.

"Not now, Ariah!" Json said out loud. "It's not safe. I need to find a safe place for you. Please give me more time."

Ariah immediately stopped vibrating, but she felt cramped and claustrophobic. After some time, she felt her mother nearby again. "Mother!" She cried.

As Json and Kaigen walked under the cover of the trees, Kaigen asked, "Are we in trouble or something? I did what you asked of me."

"What are you talking about, Kaigen?" Json asked.

"Toyah told me that if I pretended to bond to you and fooled the others, that I would be able to fly with you." Her eyes looked at Json questioningly. "You didn't know?"

Json shook his head and looked at Toyah. "But how did you know that Kaigen and I wouldn't bond?" he asked.

"The egg in your chest is my daughter. I would know her presence anywhere," Toyah explained, her hands in a prayer of supplication for him to understand. "The moment you flew into Sybaris I felt her presence." Toyah spread her hands hoping Json would believe her. "I knew you would not be able to bond to anyone with the egg inside your body, you see, and I was afraid Glock would kill you both." Toyah's expression was at once full of hope, relief, and sadness. "We have searched and searched for her for years! Where did you find her?"

Json's stomach clenched; they knew about the egg! He chose to plead ignorance, even though he knew it would be fruitless. "What are you talking about?" Json needed more time, he needed to think.

Silverback came forward. "Wyvern to wyvern, Json, on my honor, you can trust us. Toyah speaks the truth."

Json wanted to believe, to have help. Who could protect Ariah more than her own mother? He wanted to believe, but she had already lost her once. He decided to be direct. "I found her enslaved to humans. How did you lose her in the first place?"

"To humans?" Toyah said, blinking in surprise. When Json nodded she spoke, "We were in a fierce battle. The birth process for us is half-human and half-wyvern. We carry an egg for nine months, go into labor like a human, and then we birth an egg that hatches immediately.

Since Silverback and I were lead generals, we were at the front even though I was near my time. Our front line started to fail. We knew if we didn't hold it, we would be finished. Silverback was very fast, so we thought we could get in and out with little danger to my egg. Silverback was hit in the head with flying debris and knocked unconscious. We fell through the air and crashed. The crash hurt me as well. I gave birth right there on the battlefield and passed out. When I woke up there was no sign of the egg, not even a piece of the shell, and no sign of the child."

Json knew a mother and her offspring were tightly linked by nature, and from what he was feeling from Ariah inside him, he now had no doubt that Toyah spoke the truth. He told them, "I found Ariah, which is her name, enslaved by the humans, but the truth is my friends and I were also enslaved by another group of humans and she rescued me." Json paused, and when there were no questions he continued, "Ariah was killed while we flew to our freedom. Before the sun set, I was able to create the egg so she could be reborn. I had her sewn inside my body to hide her, feed her, protect her, and now here we are."

"You were right to hide her from Glock," Silverback said. "Glock killed the Commander and ate his bonded Sybaris Aslay, thinking he would attain her magic."

Json was aghast and exclaimed, "He ate Aslay, he ate a Sybaris?" That was cannibalism! Silverback continued, "If you remember, Glock was bonded to the old yellow seer, Tunac? Oh, how she loved to ride around on her large red wyvern, knowing he was the most powerful. Glock hated it, hated her, but her magic made him strong. One night the old seer finally died, but before she died she told Glock that if he ingested her body, he would keep her magic. So he did it. And it worked."

Json could see how dangerous this could be for the entire Sybaris race; imagine their wyverns turning on them for their magic. He shuddered.

"With this idea in his mind, Glock fought and killed the Commander and then ate the Commander's bonded Sybaris Aslay alive," Toyah explained. "As you remember, she was a silver Sybaris. But this time, thankfully, he did not attain her magic. It seems you must be mutually bonded for life in order to gain magic this way."

Silverback added, "Glock has no care for Solei. He tricked him into a life bond. Every day Solei comes closer to dying and Glock could turn on him at any time, trying to gain his magic for himself."

Json nodded his understanding. "So, by bonding to a same color, it is for life and when Solei's life span is complete, Glock will gain his magic as well." Json was aghast, his mind reeling. He told them what he thought about the younglings, "I believe that Glock sold us to the humans and gave the humans the poison to knock us out, block our magic, and control us."

Silverback agreed. "Yes, I think so, too. With the young male wyverns gone it would be easier for Glock to maintain control. Glock must be destroyed before he destroys what's left of us, but he's become so powerful we don't know how."

Ariah started vibrating again and Json hissed, "Ariah, not now!" To Toyah he said, "You must help me find a safe pace. She is ready to hatch!"

Silverback said, "Now? Has it already been nine months?"

Toyah told them both, "A rebirth is not the same as a new birth. It is a second chance and a rare event. I've only known of one other in my life time."

Json grabbed his chest. "Well it is time!"

Toyah said, "Not here, let's take her back to our home. Follow me."

Chapter 34: Anyumay Comes Home

The Juna planned to ride all day and through the night to get back to the safety of the stronghold. When they reached the Zoli Pass, Elijashen pulled their provisions together and gave them to the scout, sending him to the east to try to find Tonsaku and his men. "Scout, you are to monitor them, get the logistics, and then come back for reinforcements." He wiped his face on his sleeve, "Zhu is still on the loose and he will have to be dealt with, but do not try to capture him by yourself, he's too dangerous for one man."

"I understand sire," he nodded in agreement as he stored the last of the provisions in his saddle bags.

There was no time for talk, just riding. Isladora was exhausted. She had no idea how the scout could continue like he did, he was quite amazing. Not knowing how she knew, she was sure he was young like she was.

"Father, what is the scout's name?" Isladora asked.

"I should know, but I do not, Isladora, I have a lot to catch up on." A terrible memory surfaced behind his eyes, "He is a good scout," the King said.

They rode toward home. As they entered the bailey, some men came out to take the tired horses. Coming home was bittersweet, for many people were missing that should have been there to greet them. Yet it was exciting to see the Juna families reunited in their home.

"Please rub the horses down, especially their legs; they rode hard and fast. Feed them well, and no one is to ride them for a few days," Elijashen ordered. "Take these women in and feed and give them clothing and rooms. They will shelter with us until we figure out where they came from and what must become of them." Anyumay wouldn't let anyone take her steed. She took him to the stable and cared for him herself, still in Elijashen's shirt and looking like a bedraggled waif. Elijashen was worried for her. She had never taken care of a horse before, but he knew it was her way of dealing with what had happened to her. They hadn't talked about it yet. They would talk about it when she was stronger.

Isladora also watched her mother work on the horse with worried interest. Anyumay was sequestered in her own mind and hadn't talked to anyone or even noticed that her daughter or the other women had ridden along with her group. She stood back in the shadows and watched her mother care for the little mountain pony. Her movements were awkward but loving and thorough as she cared for the beast. Finally, Anyumay tiredly entered the keep.

While they had been gone, Juho Saarela had assigned living quarters and temporary jobs to the Juna. There was both rejoicing when families were reunited and much grief for the departed. The deceased men and women had been given funeral rites and individual pyres. The air was still smoky.

Meals had been served all together in the big hall for simplicity, and Saarela hoped this would continue, as it gave everyone a much-needed sense of unity.

Anyumay was met by Juho Saarela, who said, "My Queen, please allow me to take you to your quarters." As he took her arm in his, Isladora followed behind them, drawn to her mother like a moth to a flame.

Anyumay was afraid to ask where her daughter was. She knew she must be dead. Instead, she said, "Take me to the chapel, please Saarela."

"Yes, Your Grace," he replied, and quietly led her to the chapel with Isladora following behind but out of sight. She wasn't ready to talk to her mother yet, but she also could not leave her side.

As her mother knelt in front of the beautiful image of heaven that Stefan had painted so many years ago, she stayed quietly behind her. It was her mother's favorite mural. It was a human, face lifted to the sky. You couldn't tell the gender or race of the human; it could be anyone. The face was lifted, receiving God's healing light. The light shown down from heaven onto the face, and in the clouds a tall figure rose, the suggestion of a presence. Right now, Anyumay needed that healing light. She didn't think she could go on without her daughter.

Anyumay prayed out loud. "It is not fair that I should live and my only living flesh die. I give you my life. I am so sorry. I protected her the only way I knew how, by hiding her, by hiding who she was, and now she is gone from me. I kept her weak when I should have made her strong. I hid her magic and dulled her senses with sugary foods and drugs. I would give my life to have her back again. To do it all over again."

Isladora was frozen by her mother's words. All the grief she had felt by being neglected as a child rose to the surface. Yet she could not stand to see her mother, who had survived the horrors of Zhu, suffer any longer. She spoke softly, "I am here, Mother."

Anyumay heard Isladora's voice and opened her eyes. Thinking it was Isladora's spirit talking to her, she slowly turned her head towards the voice.

When she saw the warrior woman who had ridden with them in their escape from Zhu, she was confused. As she looked closer, she recognized her daughter's eyes, and suddenly she knew that it was her. "Isladora, but how?" Slowly, Anyumay reached up to touch her daughter's face and then she was grabbing her and sobbing and holding her close saying, "Thank you Lord!" again and again.

Saarela let them reunite, touched by their gladness. Once they had spent their tears, he said, "Come ladies, baths have been prepared. If you will forgive my forwardness, you both smell like the goats in the pen." Hand in hand, Isladora and her mother laughed and followed Saarela.

The ladies bathed together and Anyumay could not believe that this svelte young woman was her daughter. Gone was the plump little girl and in her place was a woman of power, of strength. As they bathed, Isladora told her about some of the things that had happened since they had been separated. The trials in the mountain, the wyvern, killing the Queen Mother, the release of her father's trapped spirit.

"We are so, so lucky Isladora," her mother said. "We have survived so many things, and we have been given a second chance."

"Yes, Mother, and whatever Zhu did to you, we will heal together." Isladora looked at the bruises on her mother's body as they washed.

After a long silence, her mother said softly, "Zhu never got the chance to violate me." Then it was Anyumay's turn to tell her own story of being imprisoned with Zhu and his violence towards all creatures but especially those weaker than him. How she had used her magic to manipulate Zhu's emotions, rendering him unable to rape her. How he had tortured, raped, and even killed the other women that were imprisoned with her.

"You are clever, Mother, to have survived such a sadist. He will die for touching you," Isladora said surely and quietly, making Anyumay shiver. Her innocent daughter was gone.

At that moment, Anyumay saw her ring on Isladora's finger. "You are wearing my magical ring! May I have it?" Anyumay had missed the powers she had when she wore the ring. Her mind was still in turmoil at being held captive, and the ring had always made her feel powerful.

"No, she may not have the ring," Meluha Crocus said in Isladora's mind, the ring glowing hotly. *"I have chosen you, Isladora."*

Isladora tried to remove it, but it would not budge. "Mother, before I knew you were taken, I came to your room to find you. I was sitting on your bed and I saw your ring. I knew you were never without it and I grew afraid for you. I slid it on my finger then and it changed and tightened. I have not been able to remove it since then," Isladora explained.

"But you must. I need the magic in the ring," Anyumay told her. "It belongs to me."

"Hah! I belong to no one!" Meluha Crocus scoffed. The ring began glowing brighter.

Isladora ignored him. "Then you will have to cut off my finger because I cannot remove it." To Isladora it almost seemed like her mother was actually thinking about cutting off her finger.

"Tell her I have chosen you. Tell her!" Meluha Crocus warned.

"Meluha Crocus does not want the ring to be worn by you mother. He chooses me."

"Who is Meluha Crocus?"

"She doesn't know who you are, Meluha? How is this possible?" Isladora asked him.

Meluha Crocus answered, *"She cannot hear me speak like you can, remember."*

"Ah," Isladora said. "Mother, he is a mage whose spirit is trapped in this ring, much like Father's was entrapped in an orb." She continued, "I can talk to him and hear his voice in my head. He helped train me to fight. He protected me from the Queen Mother's magic. He has taught me many things about the world."

Anyumay was stunned. "The ring has a spirit mage trapped in it and you can talk to him? I do not believe you. It belongs to me, now give it to me!"

It was Isladora's turn to be stunned and somewhat hurt, for she had never lied to her mother. "I have never told you an untruth, Mother." Isladora began to dress in the leather pants and shirt that were brought for her. Maybe her mother was in a state of shock.

Meluha Crocus knew that Isladora was getting angry. *"Now Isladora, don't be angry. Your mother is losing a valuable tool and that is hard for her. I will tell you a story, please repeat it for me."*

With a sigh Isladora repeated the words that Meluha Crocus told her to her mother, "It was a warm spring day, and a man named Mateo was working on some repairs in the main hall. Mateo did excellent work but he was an older man, and he did the work at a slower pace, especially when it was hot. This frustrated the Queen Mother, who felt that everything should be done when she wanted it done. When he was nervous, he had trouble talking and either stuttered badly or couldn't even form the words. The Queen Mother wanted the old builder replaced with a younger man, so she told him the next time he stuttered he would be thrown out of the stronghold. Mateo didn't have anywhere to go, but he knew he couldn't control his fear of the Queen Mother. That's when you stepped in Mother. Any time Mateo had work to perform that might take him near the Queen Mother, you told him to come get you. You went with him and sat quietly to the side. When the Queen Mother would provoke him, you would magically calm his nerves and help him force the words out. This is one of many secrets that you never told anyone."

Anyumay stared at her daughter with wide eyes. "You could not know that."

"Of course not, Mother. Meluha Crocus told me the story to tell you. He says he can tell more if you still do not believe," Isladora said.

"No, please do not, I believe you." Anyumay exhaled with grief; she wanted that ring. But it was clear that the ring had chosen Isladora, and she forced herself to smile at her daughter despite her desire to have it.

As the days passed, Isladora fell into a new ritual at the stronghold. In the mornings she trained for battle with General Nokela. Then she rode out with her father to inspect their lands and help the few farmers they still had. She was quiet and worked, watched, and learned from him.

After lunch she studied with Juho Saarela and her mother, learning the finer arts and how to be a lady. Her mother always stared longingly at the ring, but she didn't mention it again. Some days she had riding lessons and once in a blue moon, strategy lessons with Juho Nokela, but these were rare.

Isladora's wyvern memories of flight and nesting had her climbing rock faces in any spare time she had. She just couldn't stop herself. It was in her blood.

Chapter 35: Tonsaku's Strategy

The scout preferred not to be called by his name, Tobin. The fewer who knew it the better. The young man known as Tobin was a nobody, but King Elijashen's scout, now he was somebody. Tobin didn't like that Isladora seemed to see through his ruse; she was too clever to be sure.

Tobin considered himself to be a master at subterfuge and disguise. He had spent most of his twenty-one years not standing out. Being raised by and hiding from a drunk father and an abusive older brother gave him many of the skills he relied on now. Tobin knew how to find food just about anywhere, he could track any creature, and he had been feeding himself for many years. He could hide in plain sight by blending into his surroundings, probably the first skill he had attained as a small child living in fear.

He did learn one thing from his drunkard father, he learned what not to be. He wanted his life to be opposite from his father's way of life in every way it could be, so he exercised religiously to hone his body and he ran every day. The running healed his mind; it was his therapy. He trained with the sword and the bow, the weapons of a true ranger, although he had never had lessons from a real ranger. Tobin had gotten into the Juna guard during the confusion in the battle with the Queen Mother. He dressed like a ranger, had the weapons of a ranger, and so they thought he was a ranger. Now that General Nokela was back at the keep, he hoped to learn weapons from a true expert.

Most people thought Tobin to be an older man when he kept his hood up. Tobin knew that a little slumping in the saddle and some dust on the face and hair could age a person years in people's minds. Tobin doubted that the king would have entrusted him with their lives if he knew Tobin's actual age or how he had learned his skills. Still, Tobin had done well, leading them safely through Zoli Pass and on to Zhu's stronghold. Of course, a lot of that was luck since Zhu and his top fighting men were out chasing or being chased by Tonsaku and his men. Now that Tobin was entrusted with finding Tonsaku and his men, he could not fail.

Tobin wished he had a sturdy mount like the mountain pony Queen Anyumay had taken from Zhu's stronghold. She had made a good choice in horse flesh, for even a novice could see that the pony was smart, he thought. The tall horse he was on now was built for speed, but he wouldn't be able to traverse the canyon and rocky hills like a true ranger's pony could. Tobin trotted through the Zoli Pass and decided that he would have to stick to the road for now or go on foot. He had no idea how far the trail Tonsaku and Zhu had left behind would take him, so he stayed on the road, urging the horse to greater speed as he tried to catch up.

As Tobin followed the tracks he could see where the next skirmish had taken place. When the road went around a bend and started to descend, he could plainly see where the horses had slid to a stop. He noted crushed plants; one horse must have fallen. Tobin dismounted and tied his horse to a scrub tree to get a closer look. Two more dead bodies, both killed by arrows, both Zhu's warriors. They were large men who would have been difficult to deal with in hand-to-hand combat. He looked for the archer's vantage point. Tobin was impressed as he went around a boulder on the other side of the road and found where the archer had lain in wait. He saw the holes in the ground where the archer had stood his arrows so he could fire them rapidly. Judging by the size of the footprints, Tobin guessed that the archer was about five feet eight inches tall. He was wearing the standard boots of the Juna. Tonsaku must have planted the archer there before the battle at Zoli Pass. Such strategy! He was picking off Zhu's larger force one by one. The archer's trail led away and finally turned back to the north, towards home. Without a horse, it would be a long trip.

Tobin made it back to his horse and kept following the hoofprints, which showed that the horses had resumed their hard gallop, the prints spread far apart and deep at the point. Tobin sat hunched in the saddle, making himself look like an old man while keeping an eye on the road ahead. The road descended again into a hilly area with grassy ravines and scrub brush. Some of the hoofprints galloped off the road and then were no more. Again, the scout dismounted to investigate. Nocking an arrow into his bow, he followed the prints to the edge of a small ravine. Upon closer inspection, he realized the ravine had been camouflaged to look like solid ground. If a horse came upon this at a canter, they would not have time to stop. At the bottom were two dead horses and bodies of Zhu's men. Score two more for Tonsaku. The scout could see hoofprints on the other side of the ravine that led back to the road and one set on this side that made it back.

With only two sets of hoofprints, and since none of the bodies had been Tonsaku or Zhu, Tobin didn't see how Tonsaku, who had just turned eighteen, could handle the much larger and battle-honed Zhu. Again, the prints showed the horses at a gallop. Tobin followed cautiously.

Ahead he saw a dead horse and two bodies littering the ground. One body was under the horse and another body lay to the side. Tobin dismounted and nocked another arrow while he crept quietly up to the first body. It was Zhu, the emperor of the immoral, dead with a crossbow dart between his open eyes. He had a sneer on his face even in death.

The second body was that of Tonsaku. His leg was trapped under the dead horse, a fatal slice to the horse's leg looked like it had bled out. As Tobin studied him, he noted that Zhu's sword had pinned Tonsaku's shoulder to the ground. In Tonsaku's lax right hand was a crossbow. Zhu must have been gloating and torturing Tonsaku, not knowing that Tonsaku had the crossbow looped around the saddle horn. Tonsaku must have surprised him and shot him between the eyes.

Tonsaku had been a brave young man Tobin thought; he would have been a good king.

With a gasp, Tobin realized that Tonsaku's chest was slowly rising and falling. He was still alive! Tobin ran to get water and eased some down the young warrior's throat. When that didn't wake him, he knew it wasn't a good sign. They were a day and a half's ride from home. Tobin made the decision to work quickly to try to save him.

Gathering supplies, Tobin quickly built a fire and placed his metal sword tip in the blaze. He unpacked bandages and rope.

Tobin tied the rope around the saddle horn of the dead horse and tightened the saddle as much as he could, then he tied the rope to his horse and pulled the dead animal over onto its other side. When the body thumped the ground, Tobin's horse was skittish, and again he wished for the little mountain pony. "Hold still, stupid!" he yelled at the horse.

Tonsaku's foot and lower leg looked twisted at an odd angle, but that could be dealt with later.

"I'm sorry, my prince, here we go!" He quickly pulled Zhu's sword from Tonsaku's shoulder then grabbed his own sword from the fire, cauterized the hole in his shoulder, and then rolled Tonsaku over and cauterized the one in back. There was a lot of blood on the ground. The smell of burning flesh gagged him, but he finished and then worked to get some more water down the prince's throat.

He picked up Tonsaku, glad he was not conscious, and after a few tries he set him on a large boulder. Tonsaku woke and tried to say something. "What, what did you say?" Tobin asked, leaning his ear towards Tonsaku.

"I said, take his head," Prince Tonsaku croaked and then passed out again.

With a grim face, Tobin did as the prince commanded, placing the head in a bag and hanging it from the saddle. Tonsaku spoke again, "No, tie the bag with Zhu's head around my neck." Tobin did again as he was commanded, then he got on the horse and pulled it alongside the boulder.

Tobin had to fight the horse and he strained, but he was finally able to drag Tonsaku off the boulder and onto the horse in front of him. Tonsaku's head lolled back against him, his hand touching the bag now hanging from his neck. Tobin shivered. He would never forget beheading a man, and his stomach churned at the fresh memory.

Tobin held his prince with one hand over Tonsaku's good shoulder and around his chest, the reins and saddle horn he held in the other. With both of them in the saddle's seat, Tobin had to sit up on the cantle, an uncomfortable position. He knew he had to get help for Tonsaku fast, but the horse's trot nearly unseated him with his burden. Finally, the horse broke into a steady canter and it was easier for him to hold Tonsaku in place.

Tobin didn't dare stop; he only hoped the horse built for running could run that long.

With extreme exhaustion, the trio ran through the night. King Elijashen's men spotted them a half-day's ride out. As soon as one of the men took Tonsaku, Tobin fell from his exhausted horse and passed out on the ground.

General Nokela took command, with help, lifting Tonsaku into the arms of one of his mounted men. "Get Tonsaku to the keep immediately!" The guard took off with him, three more following. Nokela pointed to his man who had the most horse experience, saying, "That horse needs to rest here or he's not going to make it. You stay with the animal and cool him down and water and feed it. Bring the horse tomorrow if he can finish his journey, and if he founders, be merciful and quick."

"Yes, commander!" the guardsman said, bowing in acknowledgement. He took the reins and led the sore-footed and exhausted horse off the road.

"You! Pick up that scout and get him home fast, he needs medical attention too!" Tobin was now the one being held, passed out against the man.

Chapter 36: The Royal Egg

Json kept telling Ariah, "Not now, not now!" But she knew that she could not stay in there forever. She had grown itchy with the need to expand.

Even though he couldn't hear her she said, "Json, please! I feel larger than life already, bursting with knowledge." She chastised herself to be patient. "Through my new memories I have led a good existence and I have also led a bad one. All in all, it is good; I have learned so much. Json, your memories remind me of the traditions of being a Sybaris, what it is like to be a wyvern, fierce and proud, and how to command the skies. Isladora's incessant book-learning makes my head expand like a scholar. Her fascination with someone's notes scribbled in the side pages made her favor books on strategies for war. Isladora's father, the King of the Juna, has taught me what it is like to be a wise and fair ruler." She vibrated again to tell Json she needs to hatch and the vibration instantly sent her back into Meluha Crocus' memories. The pain she feels seems less now, maybe she has grown accustomed to it, she thinks.

*****

My heart was glad. Mae accepted my proposal and wasted no time getting her affairs in order. She turned the home I had bought for her over to her friend, a mother with three children. By the time my men were ready to sail, Mae was too. Mae was overly excited about our plantation, what it looks like and what the indigenous people are like, and we talked until the wee hours of the morning every night, planning our new life together. I could not wait to show my love our new home.

A few days out to sea Mae took to sailing as she did to everything else, with grace and aplomb. She was accepted quickly by the crew, who treated her like their royal princess. She danced with the men on the deck and they took it in stride, loving her spirit as I did. With my magical powers, I guided the ship gently into the southbound current and we were truly under way to our new home, our sails unfurled, the sun warm on our skin, and smiles on our faces; our happiness was as tangible as the summer sun.

In the morning of the twenty-first day of our journey, the skies were red and the air felt charged with energy. My first mate Jasso Joel looked at me with dread and said, "Red in the mornin', sailors warnin', Cap'n."

By late afternoon we saw a great storm brewing in the east with giant billowing clouds and fierce lightning. I checked my maps and then turned the ship from the current to set us on a new course, towards a series of islands about five nautical miles away where we could put the vessel into a cove and avoid the worst of it. I ordered Mae to stay in our cabin, no matter what. The storm caught up to us anyway, and we brought in the sails, but it did nothing for us. In a few hours we were caught in waves so immense that the ship sounded as if it was breaking apart. I used all my magic to command the seas and the wind, but the storm was stronger than I, a tropical nightmare. Great waves crashed over us and I heard Mae screaming. Our cabin was full of water. She fell from the door and another great wave took her over the side.

I felt a moment of silence. Without her, there would be no life for me.

I ran and dove in after her, but she was already gone in the flailing seas. I commanded the sea to bring her to me with all my might, but like a fickle lover, it did not listen soon enough. I saw her white dress, and I had the currents push her to me. I took her in my arms, but I knew she was already gone...the last of my air was gone, too. My battered heart swelled with the rhythm of the sea and I held her tight in my arms, my teeth clenched in impotent fury and grief. It was so calm and silent under the surface compared to the hell that had been unleashed above. I focused on her beautiful hair, reaching out to encircle me. In a last-ditch effort to save myself from drowning, I cast my being outward with all my magic, even though I knew not to use my gift in such an unnatural manner. My spirit was captured into Mae's ring as my body died.

Our bodies stayed entwined, and we washed up on the beach of one of the islands. The locals eventually found us and dug us a grave for burial. The local islander, turned mortician, fancied the ring and took it from Mae's third finger. They buried us together as husband and wife with a marker that said only "Man and woman of the Sea."

I have entrapped myself in Mae's wedding ring but I don't care. Without Mae there is no life. I stayed with the islander for many years, but in time pirate raiders came and killed the villagers, pillaging and raping. My ring was taken by the blackest of souls, a pirate of absolutely no morals. As my feelings separated from the bones of my love, I found that even in my bodiless state my feelings were dark with anger and grief for what was stolen from me. I found that my heart was already black, though it proved to be a good match for my new bearer. Together we easily took over the South Seas.

*****

Ariah came out of the memory and she knew that she would be in tears if she were born already. She no longer wanted any more of Meluha Crocus' memories.

"Ariah, can you hear me?" Json asked. "I'm going to remove you from my chest."

Json cleaned his claw and then reopened his chest to gently remove her egg. Ariah found herself wishing that Isladora were there, even though Json would order her around and then make fun of her anger. She missed the little human girl who loved her enough to care for her dead body.

Ariah felt herself being lifted carefully, reverently, and cradled in Json's clawed hands.

Toyah, her mother, sang a song as she stitched Json's chest back together, and in moments he was healed. Toyah took the egg from Json, "You have done a wonderful service, Deliverer, bringing my daughter back to me. Anything you wish from me will be yours to command." Toyah smiled and said, "Let us wash off the blood and see what we have here."

Toyah rinsed the egg in running water, gasping and fumbling as she almost dropped the egg. "She's royal! This is a royal Sybaris egg!" All Sybaris eggs are black to dark blue, but not Ariah's egg, it is pearlescent, swirling purples and greens.

"Yes, that is why I hid her so fiercely; there has never been a royal egg during my lifetime," Json told Toyah. "How did you not know?" he demanded of her.

Toyah was enraptured, beyond speech for the moment, looking at the shell, turning it this way and that. "Remember when she was born, we were in a fierce battle. Silverback and I were knocked from the skies and rendered unconscious. When I woke there was no trace of her anywhere, no child, no shell, nothing." She turned and looked at Silverback, a tear of remembrance flowing freely down her beautiful face. "Now we know why there wasn't even a trace of shell, they hid everything from us!" Thoughts of that day traveled across her face and quickly turn to anger.

"To steal a royal Sybaris egg is unheard of, for they are to be our king or queen." She looked at Silverback shaking her head and trying to understand, "Who would do such a thing?"

"I don't know, Toyah, but they will die for it when we find out," Silverback said gravely.

All fingers pointed to Glock in Json's mind, but he kept his thoughts to himself. That was many years ago and it would be impossible to prove.

Toyah was frightened and said, "We must form a circle of protection around her before she hatches! We must keep her safe!"

Silverback nodded his head. "Indeed, she needs a Queen's Guard, and a strong one."

Toyah ran her hands through her hair. "Everyone is afraid of Glock. None of us have the power to control him now that he has grown so strong. The Commander was our best hope."

Kaigen had been silent all this time, but now she spoke. "You can always go to the Protectors."

Json gasped, "Go to the Protectors? They kill wyverns, Kaigen!"

Kaigen flipped her hair from her eyes and said, "The Protectors are here when balance needs to be restored. In history, the only time that they have killed wyverns was when the wyverns were mercilessly killing humans."

Silverback didn't like it either, but he said, "She is right, that is true. The Protectors haven't come from their lands in centuries. The last time they did was when the wyvern Sultay went crazy and started feasting on humans in their villages. We did nothing because we simply didn't care about it; we turned a blind eye to the humans' fate. When the Protectors came, they killed Sultay and left us with a grave warning."

"What warning was that?" Json asked.

"The wyvern skull on a pike near the Cystine Hall is the skull of Sultay. The Protectors left it there to remind us that killing humans would bring their wrath," Silverback explained. "We were told that to remove it would bring about our extinction."

Kaigen felt vindicated. "So you see, I am right. We should go to them for protection for Ariah."

Json didn't like her attitude. "You wanted to go to the steppes, where the Protectors live. Now you want us to contact them. What's in it for you, Kaigen?"

Kaigen looked incensed, "That's none of your business, wyvern!" She turned and walked away and out the door.

Json shook his head at her youthful tantrum. "No," Json said. "I will go rescue the other wyverns that are still trapped with the humans. If we could find the right Sybaris to form powerful bonds with, they can be her Queen's

Guard."

Silverback looked intrigued at the idea. "Yes Toyah, young wyverns are strong. If we form powerful bonds, they will be even stronger and we can stand up to Glock as a united force if need be."

Json said, "I will go rescue them and bring them to Toyah for bonding. When her guard is assembled, we will help Ariah hatch."

"What makes you think they will agree to be her guard?" Toyah asked.

"They are my friends, and I know them well. They have good morals and will hate that Glock has likely killed the Commander." Json's eyes narrowed. "That in itself is reason enough. When they see Ariah and realize that we have our first Sybaris Queen in centuries, they will protect her with their life. I am certain of this."

Silverback said, "I will go with you, Json." Json nodded and smiled. Silverback would put terror into those humans for sure.

Toyah said, "Go! Leave immediately and rescue your friends." Toyah held the egg to her chest. "I will be ready with Sybaris for the bonding, and we will perform the bonding here in our home." She pressed her face to the side of the egg, a mother reunited with her daughter. "What are the colors of your friends so that I can make the most powerful bonds I can?"

"You aren't going to make same color pair bondings are you?" Json believed that shortening the life of a Sybaris to gain power was an immoral exploitation of the Sybaris way of life.

Toyah was a mother bear, not willing to risk the life she now guarded, only to have it yanked from her once again. Insensibly she fell to her own interpretation, "Only if I have no other choice."

"We always have a choice, Toyah," Json reminded her. Toyah turned her purple-tinged eyes towards Json, narrowing them, trying to assess the threat. Backing down, Json said, "Very well, Andru is blue, Sokkur is brown, Masbiar is red, Setgra is purple, and Jayriz is yellow. Jayriz is a small and slender wyvern; he will need a smaller Sybaris rider."

Silverback looked at Json and said, "We will leave at dusk tonight. That is when Glock's scouts have their rotation. Hopefully by flying north we can avoid their notice."

Chapter 37: Tobin

King Elijashen was standing in the main hall puzzling over how to handle the distance he felt growing between him and his queen wife when Tonsaku was carried in with a flurry of men.

"Sire, Tonsaku is gravely injured! Where should we put him?" the leader asked with worry in his voice.

"Oh Tonsaku, thank God!" Anyumay exclaimed and then instantly began issuing orders. "You!" she yelled, pointing at one guard, "Go get the healer Juha Mumbai from the women's quarters!" She then pointed to the table. "Here, put Tonsaku here and go get clean water, linens, and build up that fire!"

Elijashen ran to his brother's side, both relieved that Tonsaku was still alive and that his wife had snapped out of her stupor. He knew he should be patient with her and that she had been tortured and starved and probably raped, but he had just wanted to shake her until she was his wife again. To do such a thing should have been unthinkable, but he had been helpless to find a way to aid her.

Tonsaku's wounds were severe. It looked like his shoulder had been stabbed through, though someone had burned the wound shut on both sides. His foot was rotated at a terrible angle with the bone pushing against the skin. His breathing was somewhat shallow but steady, and given his wounds, Anyumay was glad he was unconscious. She placed her head on his chest to listen to his heart and, satisfied that the beat was strong, she began checking each bone in his arms and legs. A large bag was looped on a rope around his neck, and Tonsaku had a firm grip around the top of the bag.

Anyumay started to remove the bag and Tonsaku stirred, opening his eyes, looking first at Anyumay and then at Elijashen. He didn't say anything, just reached weakly for Elijashen's hand. The king took his brother's hand in his. Tonsaku guided Elijashen's hand to the bag and closed it over the top, then placed his hand over his heart in the warrior's salute. Elijashen cut the cord around his neck and took the bag as Tonsaku passed out again.

The guard returned with Juha Mumbai, and the healer nearly leapt to Tonsaku's side, taking over command from the queen without a thought. The two women, working in concert, continued assessing the damages as

Anyumay reported what she had already found.

Elijashen slowly opened the bag and peered inside. Within, he saw the grisly trophy Tonsaku had carried home and his heart grew lighter somehow, for he had desired Zhu's head—though he'd meant to take it himself at the time—above nearly all things. He removed the head of Emperor Zhu and raised it up for the men to see with a wordless cry of triumph. Tonsaku had done it! He had outwitted the brutal and pitiless monster and laid him low.

The lifeless eyes stared down at all of them, no longer with the power to strike fear into his victims. "To Prince Tonsaku!" King Elijashen shouted. Though he was glad Zhu was dead, he struggled with the hatred and rage he'd generated toward him. It was festering inside of him but he had no outlet for it; one could not kill a man, even a monster, twice.

The men answered, "To Prince Tonsaku!"

Anyumay raised her head from her work, "Oh dear God, that's Zhu!" Anyumay was an emotional creature, a creature capable of altering others' emotions, but all she felt was a deep, dark hatred. It was so deep that she was incapable of helping her husband with his own overwhelming emotions. She stared at the lifeless thing, fury bubbling inside of her. She remembered when Zhu had beheaded one of the other women—she would never erase the memory of Camille's head falling to the floor, her mangled body, the lack of remorse in that monster's eyes.

"I killed him for you, my queen," Tonsaku whispered, bringing her attention back from her own wrathful feelings to the man hurting and broken on the table.

Anyumay closed her eyes with a prayer, struggling to regain some semblance of normalcy, of sanity. "Thank you, Tonsaku," she murmured. "I have no words to describe how unbelievably cruel he was, especially to women."

"Put it…" Tonsaku tried to lick his lips, but found no moisture. "…behind you." His eyes were half-glazed from the pain and blood loss, but they seemed to bore into her intently anyway.

Anyumay could see that Tonsaku was right. Her husband was frozen, staring at head of the man that he wanted vengeance from, already lifeless. "Elijashen, my husband," she spoke loudly so all in the hall would hear, "you must know…" then paused as she looked around at Elijashen's men. "You must all know that yes, Zhu shamed me. Yes, he struck me. Yes, he killed and tortured women in front of me to amuse himself and to break my will. But this I swear to you: I have only known one man, my true King Elijashen, for Zhu never violated my body. This I swear before you all."

Elijashen at first felt ashamed at the relief he felt, hearing these words from his beloved wife. The mere fact that she might have been raped had filled him with rage, and now that fell away from him like water streaming down the face of a mountain. Searching his own feelings, he found that his relief was not because she had remained unsullied—what did he care for that, save for how it would hurt her? No, his relief was because she had not endured the unendurable, that she did not have to heal from that violation. He took a deep, cleansing breath and gathered his fury and hatred, letting it drain away from him completely. In a calm voice, he ordered, "Put this head on the tallest pike you can find and stand it in the bailey where all can see the end of Emperor Zhu."

"Yes, Sire, your will be done!" The guards left to do his bidding, already murmuring to one another like old hens. He knew that before sundown, every member of his people would know of Zhu's death and Anyumay's declaration.

Anyumay came to him, placing her arms around her king. She had seen him let much of his rage go and was relieved to see it. She said, "He is dead. He is gone. Let us forget him and all his evil deeds."

Juha Mumbai interrupted brusquely, saying, "Anyumay, I need your help to hold these bones straight while I wrap the foot." As Anyumay moved to help, the healer added, "The wound will have to be reopened and cleaned, but whoever cauterized it saved his life. I don't see any other injuries, so if we can get him to eat and drink, he will be fine, though he may have a little limp once it's healed…time will tell on that."

"What about infection?" Elijashen asked. He had seen that take many men on campaign.

Juha Mumbai shook her head. "No, my King," she said. "We will clean the wound carefully and use all our skill to ensure that it will not set in. It is fortunate he was stabbed where he was and fortunate that he was brought to us so quickly."

Once the foot was straightened and wrapped, they moved Tonsaku to his room where Juha Mumbai continued to work on the puncture wound while Anyumay assisted as instructed, dribbling water down Tonsaku's throat when she had a chance for the remainder of the evening. As the sun set, she began giving him bone broth as well, and by that time his breathing was deeper. She'd managed to get a fair amount of water and an entire bowl of the broth down his throat, but now both women were completely exhausted. She called for someone to come to his room. Isladora had been waiting outside trying to be calm about her uncle's plight, and she answered the summons instantly, staying to watch over him so that Anyumay and

Juha Mumbai could go rest.

Isladora settled into a chair beside the bed. She brought a book about the history of the Juna, and she was so engrossed in its pages she didn't realize that Tonsaku had woken and was watching her. "Isladora, you have changed so much," Tonsaku whispered in wonder. "Where is the chubby little girl that came to steal my precious books?" His voice was hoarse and rough, but he managed a little grin and Isladora smiled back. God, she was beautiful, Tonsaku thought.

"I'm the same little girl, you see?" she said and held up the book with the smile still on her face.

Tonsaku slipped back into slumber for a time, and when he woke he wanted more water and food. Isladora went to the kitchens and brought back more bone broth. "Mother said only bone broth tonight; the marrow will help heal your body, replenish your blood."

Tonsaku sighed and said, "At least let me feed myself!"

Isladora laughed, "I promise, spoon feeding you is the last thing I want to do!" She handed him the bowl and he forwent the spoon to drink it straight from the bowl. She did end up having to help him, for he was too weak to hold it, but the Prince didn't seem to mind. "Tell me about the scout that found you, Tonsaku. Where is he? Who is he?"

"I don't know who he is," Tonsaku replied. "I was delirious when he found me, and I think he was almost as exhausted as I was. I know no more, for when we met my brother's men, they took me from him." Tonsaku sipped some water from a gourd bearing a hollow reed for a straw and asked, "Why the interest in the scout?"

Isladora couldn't name it. She shrugged and said, "I don't know, something about him bothers me."

"I always say to trust your feelings, and since you are like your mother and have strong perceptions about people, I would say that is as loud a warning bell as you need." Tonsaku yawned and started to stretch but stopped himself when pain shot through his shoulder. "I'm going to sleep for a while. Hopefully tomorrow I can bathe. I smell like a dead horse."

Isladora slept on the couch in his inner chamber in case he needed anything in the night. When she woke in the morning, Tonsaku was demanding food, not more of the broth. Isladora said, "Okay, okay, I will go get you some food even if I have to steal it!"

"That won't be necessary," her mother said as she entered the room with a plate of fruits, cured ham, and scrambled eggs. "I see we are doing much better today!" She still felt exhausted from the energy that she and the healer had put into Tonsaku's body, but it had been worth it, for her brother-in-law was clearly a lot better. "Start slow!" she ordered, and gently rapped his knuckles when he started to wolf a piece of the ham. "Slow! Or it's more broth!"

"Not more broth!" Tonsaku laughed and made himself eat more gingerly with a wink at Isladora.

Now that Anyumay was taking care of her uncle, Isladora left to find General Nokela. He knew just about everything as far as the fighting men were concerned, so hopefully he could tell her who the scout was. She wasn't able to find Nokela, but a quick look in the infirmary found the subject of her quest for information. Isladora entered the room quietly and stood watching him sleep. He was young, probably only a few years older than she was. This young man could not have the training to be a scout! The scouts were the most experienced of Nokela's men, not a man barely into his twenties! Isladora tried to fathom what else bothered her about him. Without the dust and dirt of the road and his cloak, he had a boyish face with a scar above his right eyebrow. He had dark brown hair that he kept short in front and down to his collar in the back, and his skin was brown from the sun. His muscles were well toned, though he was still slim. Why do I care about his muscles? Isladora wondered.

Tobin opened one eye, sensing he was not alone. For a moment, he thought his drunken father was looming over him in anger. He covered his head, ready for the attack, but it did not come.

"Easy now, scout. I'm not here to hurt you." Isladora wondered what battle he thought he woke to, although she admitted to herself that she would be alarmed waking with someone standing over her head. "Though I must confess, I don't think you're old enough to be a scout."

"I'm not frightened of you, you startled me," his voice rasped. "Are you going to rat me out?" Isladora considered this, saying, "That depends, are you a rat?"

Ignoring her question, he asked, "Did my horse make it?" The scout looked around the room. "I don't know, I can go find out," she said.

"Prince Tonsaku?"

"Yes, the Prince will be fine," Isladora told him. "I'm sure you will be well rewarded since you saved his life; he would have died out there. I myself am thankful to you, nameless scout. I love Prince Tonsaku like a brother." Her eyes glimmered for a moment, but she blinked away the tears before they could form.

"Is it true that you get to train with Nokela?" he asked, a little embarrassed to see the tears.

"Yes, I am honored to take private lessons with him," she replied. At his look, she added, "I know how fortunate that makes me; you don't have to say it aloud."

The scout began getting up. He wasn't injured, he was just exhausted and needed to rest and then he would be fine. Not to mention he needed to disguise himself as an older man again. Before he could leave, however, one of the King's Guard entered the room. "The king would like to have your report now, scout," he said with a scowl for the young man, and the word "scout" was said sarcastically. Tobin's face paled a little. He hadn't realized anyone but Princess Isladora had seen his true features until that moment.

Isladora followed him into the main room where the scout bravely approached her father, finally kneeling as he came before him.

"Rise, young man," Elijashen said. "I understand we have you to thank for the life of my only living brother, Prince Tonsaku." After a brief pause, the king continued, "Yet you deceived us, making us think you were a true ranger, an older and wiser man who could be trusted with the tasks I asked of you. Your youth and inexperience could have been a disaster."

"And yet it wasn't, Your Majesty," Tobin dared to point out.

"Silence, boy!" the king's advisor Juho Saarela yelled, scowling thunderously.

"Go easy, Saarela," the king advised and turned his attention back to the young man before him. "Where we thought he was a ranger, instead we see a boy. Here is a boy who is cunning and smart, but not battle tested. He is brave, but has not shown wisdom. He has shown initiative, yet demonstrated recklessness."

The king sighed heavily, fixing the young man with the full force of his stare. After a moment, he said, "Yet we must reward you for that cunning, bravery, and initiative. What is it you ask of me?"

Tobin did not falter or hesitate. A lifetime of abuse and making his own way had made him hungry and gave him the courage to speak boldly. "I would like the highland pony that Queen Anyumay rode back from Zhu's keep, Sire," he said.

King Elijashen looked to Anyumay, and seeing she did not object, nodded his head to the scout.

"I would also like martial training with General Nokela. I would like to join the private lessons he gives to Princess Isladora," Tobin continued without hesitating.

King Elijashen looked to Isladora, who nodded her head in agreement. "He is clearly someone who will never let someone tell him that he can't do a thing," she said. Besides, she thought, what else could she do? He had brought Tonsaku back to them.

"Finally, when I am battle ready and you have tested me, I want the title of King's Scout." Tobin issued his last request.

"My tests will not be easy," the king warned. "Many men do not survive them."

"I did not expect that they would be, my king," Tobin answered with a confidence he didn't really feel.

King Elijashen found he liked this brash and headstrong young man, though he let none of that show upon his face. "All that you have asked for, shall be done," said the king, looking to Nokela to confirm the order.

Tobin turned to leave, trying to bury inside the smile that had bloomed inside of his heart, at least until he was out of the hall. Then he was going to leap for joy! As he passed Isladora he quietly said, "My name is Tobin."

Behind him, he did not see the king and his general regarding him gravely and thoughtfully.

Chapter 38: Kaigen and Von

Kaigen was waiting for Json outside Toyah's home. "Before you go to rescue your friends, I need you to take me to the steppes," she said firmly.

"Why do you have such an interest in this forbidden place?" Json countered.

"We aren't going into the steppes," she hedged, "just near them. Look, do you want me to keep your secret or not? We had an agreement. My reasons are really no more your concern than your egg is mine." Kaigen checked that her leather wrapping was tied tightly and climbed on to Json's back.

Json was taken aback by her directness but decided he did not want to cause any further risk to Ariah with this petulant creature so he agreed, "Very well, I will fly you there now, but we must be back before dusk. I'm not going anywhere near the guardians, though." Json could see the sullenness and distrust flowing across Kaigen's face, but she didn't argue.

Json took off, Kaigen staying low to his back. She rode him more easily now that her tattered wing structure was furled and tucked away. Json flew northeast towards the steppes, and in about an hour he could see the great stone guardians rising from the sand. Just seeing them brought a chill to his blood, every instinct telling him that no wyvern should be here. The steppes were a desolate place, all desert sand and rock with little vegetation. The guardians were two immense statues built into each side of the hill pass that marked the only known entrance to the Protectors' territory.

Json regarded the statues, each of the giant stone heads were encased in armored helmets that covered the eyes and lower jaw. The mouth and nose were human in shape, the eyes empty hollows. Wings grew from the helmet where the ears would be on a Sybaris or a human. No one really knew what race the Protectors were, for they never mixed with other creatures and were only seen when extreme injustices needed to be balanced. Little else was known about them, save that they were both powerful and deadly.

"Bank to the right of the guardians and fly along the hill ridge for about a mile," Kaigen yelled to Json. Json turned and followed her directions, glad she wasn't going to try something stupid like enter the Protectors' land boundary. In about a mile they came upon a cabin with smoke rising from the chimney. "There! Land in that clearing near the house." Json reluctantly did as she bid him, calling up fire from his belly in case he needed to defend himself. Kaigen climbed from his back and approached the cottage. Json was puzzled when the cottage door opened and an old man stepped out.

"Who are you?" the old man shouted, pointing his knobby finger at them.

"It's Kaigen, sir," she spread her hands wide in a peaceful gesture. "Do you remember me? I am looking for Von; do you know where he is?" Kaigen nervously brushed her hair behind her ear.

"Don't try to trick me girl, as if my memory isn't pristine and sharp! We have never met before." The old man spat on the ground. "You want information from me, what did you bring me for trade?" Some of the spittle had stayed in his long unkempt grey beard that had yellowed with age. He pointed his walking stick at her. "Well, what did you bring?"

The old man had only a few teeth in his mouth, his skin was aged and wrinkled, and he had faint tattoo markings across his creased forehead. His eyes were milky grey and he had a large bulbous nose. He had no hair on the top of his head, but some hair still clung to the sides and grew into his long beard. His clothing, however, seemed fairly new and clean. Json looked around the area, noting a sharp axe and a pile of firewood, although no trees grew near the cabin. The place was well kept—more well-kept than a feeble, half-blind old man could manage—and he felt his scales harden, though he saw no threats.

Kaigen looked lost, feeling around her person, realizing she hadn't brought a single thing. Her face fell. "Please sir, I only want to speak to Von."

"I speak to no one without trade." He turned to go back inside, saying, "Go away!"

Frustrated, Kaigen felt around her person and realized that she had leather to trade. Desperately, she exclaimed, "I brought you leather for new sandals!"

"Kaigen, no!" Json exclaimed. "Without the leather covering you cannot fly back with me and it will be getting dark in a couple of hours."

"Please Json, we can give him a part of it, we have more than enough to cover my wings," she pleaded.

"Leather, let me see it!" The old man turned back towards them greedily.

Kaigen took off the leather wrapper and laid it out on the ground. The old man picked it up, running his hands over it. "Oh, this is fine leather, very fine leather; I will trade some of it for information."

Json lumbered forward and carefully using his claw, he trimmed off a piece big enough to make two pairs of sandals if the man were careful. The old man picked up the leather and held it to his face, rubbing it against his cheek and smelling it with deep satisfied breaths. He smiled his toothless smile and finally he spoke, "Von is not here." Then he headed towards the cottage with his prize.

"Wait! I need to see him, to speak with him." When the old man kept going, she exclaimed, "Please sir, we gave you what you needed!" Kaigen was almost in tears. Json began to puff up his chest to give a demonstration of fire.

The old man turned and looked back toward them. "Now, now, wyvern, no need for huffing and puffing, I am protected from your kind anyway," the old man said. To the girl he added, "I cannot tell you what I do not know. Von comes and goes as he pleases…but I haven't seen him in a few days, so he should show up soon if you want to wait." With that, he entered the cottage and closed the door.

"Who is this Von anyway, Kaigen? How did you know about this place?" Json questioned the tearful girl. "The old man said you and he had never met. Explain yourself."

"Don't talk to me as if you are my owner! I belong to myself," Kaigen said testily. "I saw Von in the forest one day, if you must know. He was hunting in our territory and I saw him and I thought that he was the most beautiful man I had ever seen!" Her eyes took on a dreamy look.

"So, you are infatuated with him." That explained a lot to Json, her need to see him and her peevish and demanding nature. "Is he your mate?"

Kaigen shook her head. "No! He doesn't even know that I exist," she admitted.

"How can that be so?"

"I told you, one day he was hunting and I saw him. I decided to follow him and I used my earth magic to disguise myself so he wouldn't see me. Several times he heard me and I quickly camouflaged myself. I am really good at it! I followed him from the forest all the way to this cottage where he brought meat to the old man. He sat and talked with him a while, he cut up some firewood, and then he left. I heard the old man call him Von."

"You haven't even talked to him?" Json raised one eyebrow.

Kaigen knelt on the ground. "Well, no I haven't, but I was going to today. I can't stop thinking about him."

"You know nothing about him! What if he is dangerous?" Json pointed out.

"Of course he is dangerous. He's a trained hunter. My earth magic is dangerous, you said so yourself! I can protect myself!" she proclaimed haughtily.

Json had no idea how to control this young female creature. With a deep sigh, he said, "Oh, Kaigen, you are so innocent; there are much more dangerous creatures in the world than you. What if he is a Protector, ever think about that?"

"Then what would he be doing out here, wyvern?" Kaigen was getting angry.

"He's right, you should listen," came a deep voice from behind them. Json's scales hardened and he readied his fire for attack, turning his body to see a man standing not ten feet from them, with Kaigen between the wyvern and the man. "I am a Protector and I assure you, I am quite dangerous."

Json tried to slip around Kaigen to see if he could get his body between them to protect her. He focused his power, calling up his fire, but the man only scoffed. "Your kind never learns. If you do that, wyvern," the man said, "I will end your life."

"No need for that, either of you!" Kaigen kept herself between them and said, "Hello Von. My name is Kaigen and I am truly glad to meet you." She daintily extended her hand.

With an annoyed sound, Json released the pent-up fire tension in his belly. Whether the stranger's threats were true or not, he couldn't attack with Kaigen in the way anyway. Her extended hand fell to her side when Von didn't take it, and mixed with her dejected look was the pouty one that annoyed Json so much.

Json glared at Von, trying to assess the risk. He had never met a Protector before and he wasn't sure what they were capable of. Von seemed human but bore telltale signs that he was not. He was a tall man with long dark hair and skin that was tan yet also had a pale shimmer.

His eyes were almost bronze colored, yet flickered with blue tones and his ears were a little pointed at the tips. His weaponry was unlike anything Json had seen before, composed of strange metals that gleamed in the sun.

His clothing was also made of materials that Json had never seen. They seemed to be made of metal but were close fitting like leather. The metal on his forearms, biceps, and chest was beautifully tooled. He had a red belt around his waist and a red cowl around his neck with strange markings. "We are sorry to intrude," the wyvern said at last. "Come on, Kaigen, let's leave while this one is willing to let us."

Kaigen was utterly smitten and was going nowhere if she could help it. "I saw you in the forest hunting, Von," she said breathlessly. "I followed you here but I meant no harm. Seeing you in the forest captivated me." She blushed upon this admission and covered her mouth. Where were these words coming from? To Kaigen, seeing him was like seeing a beautiful elk, majestic and glorious, enchanting.

Von saw that she was just a young girl. He relented a little and said, "It's all right, Kaigen. Your kind is drawn to us, to our power and charisma, like a moth to a flame. You simply cannot help feeling this way, but it is not real and you must fight it."

Kaigen was truly entranced by his nearness. With every part of her being she wanted to be with this man, his slave even. She moved a little closer to him, wanting to touch his skin, completely ignoring his words.

"Kaigen, the feelings you feel right now are not real, do not give in to them!" Von told her firmly. "You cannot touch my skin, it would harm you. This is one reason why Protectors do not mix with your race. Your kind cannot handle the emotions brought on by from being near us." He took a step back to match her hesitant step toward him.

"I just want to sit and talk to you, Von, get to know you. I assure you I am in control of myself," Kaigen said, looking around to consider where they were. "Does this cottage belong to you?" She would change the subject, if only to keep Von near.

"No, this cottage is outside the boundaries of the steppes where I live. It belongs to Seamis, the old man," Von answered.

Json commented, "Someone obviously cares for him. He could not heft that axe to cut his own wood, nor would he be strong enough to go get it. Why do you take care of this cantankerous old man?"

"You are perceptive," Von admitted. "He is my father and he has been exiled. His body ages as you have seen. If I didn't care for him, he would perish." Von sighed and rubbed his face. "Look, you need to get out of here. You should not be this close to the steppes." To Json, he said, "You should know that I saw the body of one of your kind, a large white wyvern. It lies nearby."

Json was aghast, blurting out, "You saw the Commander?"

"I don't know what he was called, but it is one of your kind. He is almost buried, only the crest of his back sticking out of the ground about three miles south of here. If you follow that ridge back to the forest you will find him," Von said.

"We must go, Kaigen!" Json exclaimed as he turned to face her. "If the Commander is indeed there, we need to see how he died. Get your wrap on, hurry!"

Kaigen felt something like a magnetic force pulling her heart towards Von, he attracted her strongly. She almost couldn't think beyond his presence, but she made herself listen to the wyvern. Mechanically, she picked up the leather and slid it over her head, tying it around her body. She climbed on Json's back and told Von, "I will see you again."

Von replied, "No, you will not. Do not come back here," although he knew it was not on her power to resist him and that she would not relinquish her pursuit.

Json flew off, marveling that they had met and talked with a Protector, a being that was an obscure idea, a myth. Kaigen wasn't even hanging on like she usually did; instead, she was dreamily swaying with the air currents and he had to be careful to bank slowly. They followed the ridge back to the forest. Blackened trees and torn earth indicated where a fight must have taken place. Json landed and began searching the area on foot. He almost missed seeing the Commander; the earth had all but swallowed him up.

"It's going to take a small army to dig his body out!" Json exclaimed.

Kaigen was finally emerging from her fog. "What? Oh! The Commander." Kaigen slid off Json and knelt where he was buried. "Let me take a look." Kaigen stuck her hands in the dirt and closed her eyes. Small vibrations pulsed around the area. Her eyes snapped open and she exclaimed, "He is alive, Json! He is trying to use the earth to heal himself. His skin is badly burned, and one side of his face is damaged." Kaigen placed one hand on the Commander's exposed back. "He knows we are here and he is glad we are friends."

Json shed some tears of relief, with the Commander back and Silverback and the small force of wyverns they were to rescue, they had a chance against Glock. "We have to go. Silverback is expecting us at dusk, but we cannot leave him here unprotected in this state."

"You go Json. Leave me here and I will care for him. I can help the earth heal him; you must let me try." Kaigen was crying too, her emotions were a mess from being near Von, yet she knew what this meant and it gave them both hope. "The earth will feed me, it always has." Kaigen looked at Json; all signs of her stubbornness and moodiness were gone. "I can protect myself and him, Json. If anyone comes within sight of us, I will bury them so deep no one will find their bones."

Json shivered that this chit of a girl had the power she did. He felt had had no other choice but to trust her motives. "Stay away from that Von. You heard what he said. You are only attracted to him because of his unnatural allure."

"Yes, I heard him, but that doesn't help what I feel in my heart," she replied sullenly.

Json didn't feel like that was an answer but he was running out of time.

"I will let the others know where you are. I'm convinced that Glock did this to the Commander, so if Glock comes here, promise me you will hide and not get involved."

Kaigen put a protective hand on the Commander. "I cannot make that promise, Json. Warrior to warrior, I will protect the Commander with my life."

Json nodded at her words, realizing she could say nothing else. Such was the code and way that they lived their lives, but he did find himself feeling a new respect for her that he had not had before.

"Go and rescue your friends. If the Commander can be healed, I will help him." Already, Kaigen was beginning to heal him, Json and Von all but forgotten.

Json was perplexed. Gone was the petulant infatuated girl and in her place a fierce warrior. Kaigen was a puzzle with interchangeable pieces.

Chapter 39: Isladora and Tobin

Despite the fact that she'd agreed, Isladora wasn't sure how she felt about sharing her private training time with General Nokela with Tobin. While she thought that Nokela was too easy on her when they were sparring, she had a feeling that Tobin would not be. Everything about him was hard and intense. He was like a lone spindly cactus growing out in the desert that somehow survived when nothing else did.

Today they would be learning about swordplay using the bokken, a wooden sword with no cutting edge. Nokela went over the proper method of handing the sword to another person. It was respectful to offer it upside down, with the handle to the right hand and with a slight bow while you looked them in the eye, then to lower your eyes demurely showing trust.

"Put your bokken in your training belt at your waist on the left side, blade upside down. Before each practice you kneel and bow like this." General Nokela demonstrated. "First, we kneel with the left knee, then the right knee, then sit all the way back with the tops of your feet on the ground. We sit this way until our mind has calmed and we think of nothing. Then place your left hand on the ground in front of you like this, then the right hand, forming a triangle with your fingers and thumbs. Then you bow, touching your head to your hands to signal you are ready." Nokela bowed then got back to his feet. "We begin each sword practice thusly."

What began as a prayerful and quiet moment soon turned into an exhausting practice of attack and counter-attack. Isladora's suspicion was right; Tobin did hit her harder than General Nokela had, often full force. Drawing back with a painful wince, she gritted her teeth and tried to keep up, deciding that she would not let this young upstart best her. Tobin came down hard with his overhead strike, and each time she blocked, raising her bokken horizontally above her head, the impact was jarring and painful to her arms. She could feel blisters forming on the palms of her hands.

"Now that you have learned how to block an overhead strike, our counter will be a diagonal strike. When your attacker is attacking with a diagonal strike you must either move or block it with your own diagonal strike, like so." Nokela demonstrated several times. "It is best to move and block at the same time, but that is a skill that will take time to master."

Nokela watched Tobin and Isladora cut and counter, back and forth for several minutes. "Now the two of you will spar using only the cuts I have taught you today. Whoever lets his opponent break through first will have the job of caring for the bokkens." Nokela looked at both of them, adding, "This may seem like a punishment, and it is. If we were using cutting blades, the outcome of your match would be that one of you would be badly hurt or dead. Now face off and begin."

Isladora didn't have time to get nervous; Tobin immediately began attacking with hard arm-numbing strikes. Isladora backed and moved, blocking and feeling her arms wear down quickly. He was so fast she couldn't get in any counterstrikes. She was completely on the defensive, and her arms were simply not strong enough to be faster than he was. Every time he struck, her muscles tensed to withstand the contact. Her muscles were locked tight and unable to release to counter. When he backed her to the wall and she ran out of space, his diagonal strike came crashing into her ribs and she cried out in pain and doubled over, holding her side. She thought she might throw up.

"Enough!" Nokela yelled. "Bow to each other, we must be respectful at all times." Isladora tried to straighten, but her ribs hurt badly. Still, she bowed to Tobin and he bowed in return. She felt embarrassment and hatred welling up inside of her chest, threatening to suffocate her.

"Now, face each other." Isladora didn't think she could even raise the bokken to defend herself. She wanted to throw it on the ground, but she was the daughter of the king and knew she could not. She turned and faced Tobin, her eyes seething with pent-up animosity. Her teeth were gritted and her lip curled slightly.

Nokela spoke, "I want you to look deeply at your partner's abdomen, their chest, and now their shoulders. I want you to view this sparring partner with fondness." At first Isladora thought she would choke on her revulsion for what Nokela was asking her to do. He waited patiently while she got herself under control and then he repeated the request a second time, speaking slowly.

"We must view our sparring partners with something akin to love. Without them we would have no opportunities for improvement or practice," General Nokela said. "Without practice, we would be no match when an enemy swordsman comes to hunt us down. Therefore, we must love our sparring partners for helping us to save our own life and the lives of those we love." Nokela went further in his lesson. "This is why we bow to each other. Part of the bow is to show respect, but the meaning is not just that we respect one another. It is to show our devotion to our way and to demonstrate thankfulness for the opportunities given to us by our opponent."

"Isladora, you will take that sanding stone and draw it down the wood of the bokken, shaving off the splinters you created by hitting your bokkens together. When you are done with that, you will take this rag and wipe this oil over the blade, from the hilt to the tip but not on the handle." Nokela showed her how to care for the bokken. "When you are finished, place it in its holder here on the wall, blade upside down, handle to your right."

"Yes, General," Isladora said and nodded that she understood. She felt overwhelmed. The general had taken her from abhorrence to a feeling of affection with but a few words. She was humbled by this great man who led others into battle. Her feelings for the general were intense, and at that moment she felt that she would obey and follow him to any war.

"I want all bokkens cared for in this manner. Isladora, you lost the match so you will care for all of them." He pointed to a large pile of bokkens. It would take her the rest of the day to finish them. Isladora felt tears welling up, but she held them back and did not let them fall.

"I understand, General. Thank you for the lesson." To her horror, Isladora's voice wavered a little. She picked up the sanding stone to begin on her bokken. Nokela left, probably glad to be rid of them and to go train real warriors. Wordlessly, Tobin picked up another sanding rock and sat down to help her. Isladora was thankful that he didn't talk to her. When the sun was setting, they finally finished. Had Tobin not helped her, she would have worked all night. Isladora's hands were blistered and sore and she was so hungry she went straight to the kitchen. When she tried to wash her hands, she cried out in pain but got through it. She took a flask of water and some bread and cheese back to her rooms.

Juha Lepola came to check on her while she was eating. She took one look at Isladora's face and didn't say a word. Lepola was a warrior, and she recognized the signs of a hard training day.

Wordlessly, she waited until Isladora was finished, then she took her hands and applied an ointment and wrapped them with gauze. "In the morning they will be better and the skin will eventually thicken." Lepola kissed Isladora on the top of her head and left the room. Isladora was too tired to cry, so she changed her clothes and climbed into bed and passed out.

The next morning before dawn, Lepola woke her, "Come now Isladora, get dressed in your training leathers and meet me in the stables."

Isladora gave a pout of mock annoyance. She felt like hell, her arms and shoulders ached, and her ribs were deeply bruised but she didn't think they were broken. She took a long drink of water and pulled on her training leathers. When she got to the stables, Lepola was waiting with two bokkens, one in her training belt and one in her hand. Isladora's stomach turned over. Lepola bowed to Isladora, handing her a bokken, upside down with the handle to her right just like General Nokela had taught her.

"What you will learn now, you won't learn from the men, who can prove to be difficult quarry," Lepola told her. "The men are strong, so they do not need to learn the ways of a woman's warfare." Lepola continued, "I will try to supplement your lessons so that you can become a better sparring partner for Tobin." At Isladora's ashamed look Lepola added, "It does not always have to come down to who is the stronger fighter; most times it can be who is smarter or more agile."

With that, Lepola taught Isladora how when the crushing overhead strike was coming down to first move a little bit out of the direct path of the blade on the balls of her feet and then instead of meeting force for force with a horizontal block, to angle the block down and away from her body at about a thirty degree angle. "This will cause his strike to continue on its downward trajectory, angled away from the original target. He will have to use an immense amount of strength to recoil it or lose time swinging it back around. This will give you the time you need to launch your own offense."

The two women practiced for a little while until Lepola said, "Come, let us eat breakfast."

"Thank you, Lepola. You have cared for me without thought for as long as I can remember," Isladora told her. Lepola had the supple muscles and scars of one born to fight and Isladora wondered how she had missed these signs when she was young and innocent.

"It was my duty and my honor, but it is more," Lepola told her. "You are like a daughter to me Isladora, the daughter I never had."

Chapter 40: Rescuing the Pack

Json and Silverback left at dusk to rescue the wyverns. They flew separately towards the north and met up where it was less likely they would run into Glock's scouts. "This way Silverback, to the Commander." Json led them northeast to fly over Kaigen and the Commander so that Silverback could see where they were located. He had told Silverback about finding the Commander's body and of leaving Kaigen to care for him with her earth magic. Then he told Silverback about the Protector and the old man.

Silverback took note of the location. "I can't believe he's alive!" Silverback said excitedly. "I am elated that the Commander is alive and hopefully can be healed, but I am worried about the presence of the Protector. That can't mean anything good for us wyverns," his face took on a grave expression.

They banked and flew back south to where human camp was located. As they neared, Json signaled for them to land on a high outcropping.

"What can you tell me about this human camp?" Silverback queried.

Json growled. "They kept us in cages that were in a line against a cliff wall. The wyverns are chained by their legs to a metal pole sunk deep into the ground. The drugs the humans gave us suppressed our magic, so they won't be able to use it until the drug has completely left their system, which will take a few days. The drugs also dull their homing beacon, so they won't be able to fly home without us. The humans have arrows with large heads; one tore through my wing as I escaped. Other than that, the humans are weak and pathetic." Json thought about Keit, the human guard who had shot and killed Ariah. "I would like to kill one human myself."

"We all know what can happen if we needlessly kill humans," Silverback cautioned. "And now you have actually seen and talked to a Protector, so we know they are still here even though we haven't seen them in many years. I understand your feelings about the humans, but we do not want to incite their wrath."

Json considered this. "I would like to think that in this case that the Protectors would be on our side. The humans captured and enslaved us. They fought us against each other for food while they made bets on the outcome. They tried to ride us and they poisoned our magic. One of them killed Ariah with an arrow. They deserve to die."

"Thankfully, your magic allowed you to save Ariah's life, Json. Just think, a royal Sybaris! I believe that a royal Sybaris is created when they are needed, and now when we free these wyverns and they become her guard, she can be reborn." Silverback puffed his chest with pride, looking in the direction of the human camp.

Json admired Silverback's sleek body and sharp mind, feeling pride that he was going to war with this wyvern.

"I'll do a quick flyover to gauge our direction of attack. At my speed and with my coloring, they won't be able to see me easily," Silverback told Json. "Stay here, I will be back in a flash."

Silverback was not gone long. When he came back, Json saw his normally regal face was masked in anguish. Json was taken aback by the myriad of emotions playing across Silverback's face and the message that they conveyed. "Json, I think another wyvern has beaten us here, except instead of just killing humans, he killed them all." Silverback closed his eyes as if he could erase the images. Opening them he spoke, "Everything is decimated in the camp, burned to a crisp. Only one wyvern has that much destructive power: Glock."

They took off, gliding down from their perch and flew over the human camp. The camp didn't look like Json remembered—there was that much destruction. Json could see the bodies of three of his friends still in their cages. He yelled at Silverback, "I left five wyverns, and I only see three bodies!" Json banked and landed near the cages. The stench was overwhelming but he saw no smoke or fires. "Glock must have ordered this done right after I made it back home," Json said in misery. "By coming home, I killed my friends."

"No, Json, never think that. Glock killed your friends."

Then from behind a structure they heard, "Json, is that you? Silverback?"

Json turned to see Jayriz, the smallest of their lot, a yellow wyvern. "Jayriz! How did you survive this?"

"I don't know. Glock did this. Glock and Solei," Jayriz told them. "When they arrived, we thought that we were being rescued, we were so elated, then they began raining wyvern fire down upon us as well as the humans. I wished with all my heart to vanish into invisibility and they never directly targeted me. I was burned a little, but it was as if they couldn't see me," Jayriz said in wonder. "Masbiar is alive but hurt badly. I moved him over there and have been trying to heal him, but my magic is too weak. I have barely managed to keep him alive."

Json knew Masbiar, being a red wyvern, could withstand more fire magic than the others. "Sokkur, Setaid, and Andru were all killed," Jayriz said as a golden tear rolled down his wyvern face. "I haven't been able to give their death rites yet; I have been conserving all my magic to save Masbiar. It is coming back to me without the drugs, but I haven't eaten in days and my magic is weak." Jayriz looked at Silverback with worshipful hope. "You can heal him easily, Silverback."

"Yes, show me where he is. Json, go find some fresh food for Jayriz if you can. We will need his strength." Silverback looked grievously at the charred remains of the young male wyverns. "Then we will give funeral rites to the others."

"Yes, Silverback," Json said as he ran to lift off to find some food.

Most of the cattle the humans kept for their own food had been destroyed, but a couple of stragglers were found in the desert, weak from hunger and thirst. Json killed one quickly and brought it back for Jayriz. Jayriz gladly ate the first fresh meat he had ingested in months. Json went back to find the other cow, knowing Masbiar would need nourishment as well.

All the wyverns had healing magic that could repair small damages. Rips and tears and broken bones could be easily mended, but burns took considerable strength and power to heal and rebuild because the tissue had to be created anew. Json and Jayriz watched as Silverback began to heal Masbiar's burns. He started at the tip of his tail and worked his way down the body, grafting new red skin and recreating one scale at a time. Masbiar was silent and still, but Json could see the tension leave his face now that he was under the care of friends.

Json left to build a pyre for his other friends that weren't so lucky. He used pieces of the destroyed buildings and couldn't help but think about the time that Isladora had built a pyre for Ariah so that he could use his wyvern magic to create her egg. It had taken her all day because she was a small human. It took Json only a few hours to build one much larger. Once he was done building the pyre, he and Jayriz gathered what was left of the bodies of their friends.

Sadly, they were still chained to the poles in their cages, but Json severed them angrily with a burst of acid fire from his belly. They placed the bodies carefully on the pyre and waited for Silverback. Json couldn't believe his friends were gone, and even worse, he couldn't believe that Glock would do this terrible thing. No wyvern should rise against another, but Glock had grown powerful and it had changed him. Now he was killing freely, wyvern and Sybaris alike. He must be stopped.

While they waited for Silverback, Json used his own magic to help heal the scrapes and burns on Jayriz. Jayriz was already stronger, and they took turns watching and sleeping overnight. In the morning, Masbiar was almost healed enough to fly home.

Silverback and Masbiar shared the cow Json had killed. When they were finished, Silverback said, "Let us light the pyre and send our friends off." The four wyverns stood around the pyre, three singing their deep-throated death song, one silent. Each song was different but formed a melody of sorts. When they were finished, all but Masbiar shot a stream of fire, igniting the pyre as they said their last farewell to their friends.

They returned to their makeshift camp, and as Silverback continued to work on healing Masbiar, Json told the two survivors all that had happened since he and Ariah had fled the human camp.

"So we are to become Ariah's guard?" Jayriz asked.

"It is Queen Ariah, and yes we will all be her Royal Guard," Silverback corrected. "Glock will try to kill her as soon as he finds out about her existence. She must be guarded."

"Glock must die for his crimes against Draconia," Json said vehemently. "He has even turned on the Sybaris. He killed and ate the Commander's bonded Sybaris!"

Masbiar and Jayriz were aghast. Jayriz said, "Glock will try to kill us when he finds out we live, but are the four of us strong enough?"

"Maybe five of us. It is my greatest hope that the Commander can also be healed," Silverback said. "The Commander no longer has a bonded mate, however, so if he lives, we must help him form a bond." Silverback looked at Masbiar and Jayriz and said, "Toyah is looking for bond mates for both of you. We plan to fly back in secrecy and form your bonds to make your magic stronger for the fight ahead. I'm afraid they will not be of your choosing, but I hope that you will accept this task as part of Queen Ariah's Royal Guard."

"It would be my honor," said Jayriz. "I never imagined that I would see a royal Sybaris. To be a part of her circle of protection is above anything I thought I could accomplish."

"Yes, we will make a good team, we always have," Json reminded him.

Masbiar remained silent. He had not spoken since they found him. Silverback was worried that somehow his mind had been damaged in addition to the grievous wounds he'd suffered.

Some birds flew overhead. Back home, Masbiar liked to observe the birds, as they were so similar to wyverns. He was fascinated with the migrating species and puzzled about what made them migrate; it was not something that wyverns did. He particularly liked flocks and how they shifted direction at the same time, with little individuality, all part of a much bigger thing. Guarding the Queen would be a much bigger thing.

"We are a flock," Masbiar said suddenly.

All three wyverns turned their heads to stare when Masbiar spoke, but his attention was still on the birds. Silverback and Json were relieved to hear him speak. Silverback decided that he would take the statement as Masbiar's acquiescence. They would need his red fire magic to win against Glock's much stronger red fire magic.

Chapter 41: Meluha Crocus' Memories

Toyah was obsessed with the royal egg. She held it gently in her purple scaled arms, all the while humming songs. She talked to her daughter about the kingdom and the state of affairs they found themselves in now.

"I hear you Mother," Ariah said but Toyah couldn't hear her. "You are making plans for us, and I find you to be wise but not in control of your emotions." The perils of having such a disciplined mind, Ariah thought. "They say that when a mother loses a child that something gets lost in the mother, something that is difficult for them to move forward from." Ariah sighed, "Now that you have me back, you are too overprotective, and I fear for your life now. Your judgement seems somewhat skewed."

Toyah's apprentice, a young Sybaris named Sully, came into the room unannounced, startling Toyah. "Sully!" She almost dropped the egg as she tried to hide it from his view. "What are you doing here? You frightened me."

"I always come here at this time." He looked at her like she'd gone crazy.

"Yes, yes, forgive me," she said hastily as she hid the egg in a stack of bags. "I've just been cleaning up in here."

"Would you like me to come back?" he asked, and then Toyah remembered her decision.

"No, please stay. I want to talk to you about a possible bonding," she demurred. She looked over Sully's features, noticing his large scales. He was almost fully scaled, everywhere but his stomach area and eyes. His indigo hair was always caught up in a severe topknot. His indigo color gave him the ability to alter perceptions.

"Glock won't allow any of the remaining wyverns to bond," he pointed out.

"Glock isn't aware of all the wyverns. We know where Jayriz was taken. He is being rescued by Silverback, and when they return, I want you to bond with him."

"Are we going to war against Glock?" Sully asked. "It's a little too late for that now that the Commander is gone."

Toyah ignored this statement. "If you remember, Jayriz is a yellow wyvern and he commands the power of intellect and visions. Together the two of you can help guard against Glock; your combined magic will be a mental nightmare." She rubbed her hands, imagining her planning coming to fruition.

Toyah was excited now, oblivious to Sully's reaction as she schemed. "Imagine Glock driven crazy by things that he can only see in his mind. It is my hope that your combined magic will be able to implant terrible visions in his psyche and distract him while others take him out."

Sully was not convinced. "Guard what against Glock?"

Toyah brought the egg out for him to see. Sully gasped. Toyah knew it was dangerous, but she decided that she must trust Sully with her life and that of her daughter's. "My daughter has been found."

Sully's eyes widened at seeing the rare royal egg, and he lowered himself to one knee and bowed. Toyah smiled as he rose, thinking that she made the right choice to trust in her friend.

She explained, "We all know the stories of what life was like when Draconia was ruled by a monarchy. There was peace and harmony. It wasn't necessary to bond Sybaris to wyverns in order to gain magic. It abounded freely."

Toyah smiled and the moment passed. Ariah was drawn away by more memories, but they were not of the time she had been witnessing, nor even of wyverns. She no longer experienced the memories of King Elijashen, Isladora, or even Json.

To gain control over the memories, she spoke to herself, "I think it is because their life spans are shorter and I have lived them all, they were wide open to me. However, I am fighting a losing battle with the memories of Meluha Crocus." Her memory shield wasn't strong enough.

"His lifetime spans so many years, and after Mae Tarango died and he lost his body, most of the memories are of lives lived with depravity, greed, and corruption. Once his spirit was trapped in the ring, he attached himself first to the pirate, then to a corrupt politician, and then over many years to other people, both good and bad, but I am sad to say, mostly bad."

"For a long time, he was attached to no one and he lived in silence and loneliness. I do not like these memories and I do not want them. It becomes a struggle to remember who I am and what my own morals are so that I do not become like him. I know that I am affected by my environment and so I fear that the sins of his bearers will stain me. I fear that his memories of loneliness will drive me insane. This is why I battle his memories. I fight to reach the memories of who he was before Mae Tarango died, when he was whole and a good person."

With no one to hear her, she continued, "I have grown strong enough to force the memories, but they seem to be locked, a lock that my mind is incapable of opening or understanding. I sense that Meluha Crocus is a creature far more advanced than I."

Ariah bore down on the memory, trying to force the timeline that she wanted. The pain was intense but she had learned to ignore a great deal of pain in order to solve this mystery.

Finally, she broke through the barrier and saw Meluha Crocus surrounded by the most beautiful creatures she had ever witnessed. They were part human, part supernatural beings. She immediately perceived that she was not meant to see these creatures, even in memory. Their skin glistened with an unnatural glow, and some of them stood near him in discussion while others levitated without wings. They moved with grace and speed that was stunning to Ariah.

"These creatures argue, and I begin to understand that Meluha Crocus has been cast out. Exiled. The creatures have stripped him of his rank and bound his hands. He is both ashamed and unmoving. The levitating creatures seem to be sentinels; they have a bluish light surrounding them. They lift him and set him down gently at a set of large gates. The gates open, and he is unbound and told to go. They hold silvery swords in case he attempts to stay. They are sad, but final. With great resignation, Meluha Crocus turns and walks through the gates, and they slam shut. He keeps walking and finally passes through the last large barrier to his home. He takes one last look back, and I am chilled by what he sees in this memory. He looks back and sees two large statues built into each side of the hill pass, giant stone heads encased in armored helmets that cover the eyes and lower jaw. The guardians. And then I understand." Oh, how Ariah wished her mother could hear her.

"Mother, Meluha Crocus is a Protector, an exiled Protector, but a Protector. He is one of the immortals. At any time he could have taken on the body of another, even Isladora, but he has chosen to stay trapped in the ring. Perhaps for penance? Or perhaps he does not realize he has the power to escape."

Ariah thinks of the human girl, Isladora. She wonders if she is in danger from wearing the ring containing Meluha Crocus' spirit. He has lain dormant for years, existing only as a spirit, but his memories tell Ariah that can change at any time.

"I want to know more, but I cannot unlock any more memories. They are forbidden to me." Finally, Ariah sleeps, rough and unguided in her egg.

Chapter 42: Kaigen and the Commander

"Commander?" Kaigen gently asked.

A tiny bit of movement stirred the dirt and the Commander raised part of his head, one eye, to gaze at her. "Ah, it is you, Kaigen," he said, his tone wistful.

Interpreting his tone as disappointment, Kaigen was taken aback. "Well, sorry to disappoint you," she said angrily. Then, truly seeing his burned face for the first time, she felt bad for being rude. The Commander had been a beautiful and rare white wyvern before Glock tried to kill him. He hadn't spoken to her often—in truth, she usually avoided the wyverns—but the few times, he had not been unkind.

The Commander responded, "I am not disappointed to see you. I just thought you were my earth friends."

Earth friends? Kaigen wondered. "You feel them too?"

The Commander answered, "Yes, at first I just sensed that I wasn't alone, then after a while they came and sat with me for a time. They are not here now; they have burrowed away into their caves and underground passageways. They raised rich compost and minerals around me and they gave me magic so I could breathe in the dirt. Although I never actually saw one of them, their magic dulled the great fire pain I suffered."

Kaigen had never seen one of the earth creatures either, but she knew that they were intelligent and numerous. "I'm going to try to heal you, Commander. We need you to be whole."

The Commander went on as if she never spoke, "Did you know they can create their own sunlight? Fascinating creatures, really. You have earth magic, Kaigen. A great deal of it, I understand. If you stay here with me and be still, they will return. They are easily startled, so you must not move much."

Kaigen could not get him to pay attention to what was going on in the wyvern world. She told him about the royal egg.

"A royal egg? Now that is something!" He was silent so long Kaigen thought he was asleep. "You are right, she must be protected. Well, try to heal me if you must, but I cannot say I will be disappointed if you fail. I want to stay with these simple creatures and acquaint myself with their culture. They want me. They need me desperately, but for what I do not know.

I feel almost spiritual towards them, like a father of sorts," the Commander told her.

Most of the Commander's skin was badly burned, leaving no scales except for the ones on the crest of his back. "Hold still, Commander, I'm going to try to create a new scale on your back, right next to these." Kaigen sank one hand into the earth to begin gathering the minerals together, but she could not find the amount of keratin she needed. Keratin, a structural protein, was the key material that made up the outer layer of a scale. The soil contained an abundance of calcium carbonate, but all she managed to create was a small hard shell in the place where the scale would be. It was much larger than a scale, and it looked like the inside of a clam shell, pearlescent and hard.

Kaigen cried out in failure. She just did not have the material or the skills to recreate his beautiful white skin and scales.

"Our first duty is to cover the naked skin, to protect it from the elements, which you have done," the Commander told her. "The question I must ask of you is what makes you who you are?"

"What do you mean, Commander?" Kaigen asked.

"Must you adorn yourself with beauty to be who you are?"

When she shook her head, he said, "No? Then I needn't, either."

Kaigen sighed. "I have created you something that resembles a shell, Commander, not a scale."

"True beauty will not be found by our eyes. They deceive us. They make us believe things that do not matter. True beauty is not just what we see, but also what we feel, here in nature, with the earth. If you must cover me, the shell you created is perfect. I want coverings that will help me burrow in the earth and feel its loving soil. It is a new adventure that I must embark upon. I want to see these benevolent earth creatures and win their trust so that I might thank them for my life."

Kaigen sighed and said, "You will look like a freak, even more than I do, Commander."

"The finest blooms in nature need the utmost care, so treat me thusly. I do not want scales. A hard shell will do." The Commander pointed painfully with his snout and said, "There—see that beetle? A smooth carapace like he has that will glide through the ground is what I want. In place of my ruined hands, I want pincers that will cleave the ground so I can burrow." Then, realizing what she had just said about herself, he added, "You are a beautiful girl, Kaigen. Where does this hatred of yourself come from?"

Kaigen flared her skeleton wings and said angrily, "I have wings that cannot fly! Instead, they help me command the earth…how backwards is

that? I have a boyfriend that will not notice me. In fact, he told me to stay
away from him. I cannot make him see me without beauty."

"If this is true, then he is not the man for you," the Commander pointed out. "Who is this callous boyfriend anyway?"

Kaigen breathed out a long breath. "Oh, he is a Protector from the
steppes, but he doesn't like me."

"A Protector, are you sure?"

"Yes, he told me that he was. His father has been exiled and he lives
not far from here. Von, that's his name, leaves the steppes to care for the
old man."

"We cannot be near the Protectors; nor can we trust them with their
supernatural powers," the Commander warned.

Thinking of his strong shoulders and chiseled jaw, Kaigen said, "I
would do anything for Von."

The Commander laughed. "You see? You are already in his power."

"Yes, he told me that but I don't care. I want to be with him," Kaigen
said willfully.

The Commander left it alone; he knew she wouldn't listen. "If you cannot make scales and heal my wings, I am of no use in the fight against
Glock. Rob the earth of its minerals to prepare my shelter; I will go live a
life of simplicity. I do not need a place in the Cystine Hall or to be a leader
of Draconia. I wish to shift myself and take a turn to the earth where I feel
I am needed. Do your work, Kaigen."

Kaigen began the exhausting labor of creating a carapace that would
move in the dirt and protect the Commander's skin as it healed. She used
the beetle for her design but made the carapace of a series of movable parts
and connections. She rested in the earth when she grew tired, and it fed her,
keeping her strong. What keratin monomers she could find she assembled
into bundles to form intermediate filaments, which were tough and would
form strong connective tissues for the carapace parts.

Little did she know that Von watched the entire process, nor did she
know he was as fascinated with her as she was with him. This obstinate little girl was quite the scientist and creator, he thought. She had rattled his
semi-peaceful life. Her healing powers were comparable to those of a
shaman Protector. And she was like a smoldering volcano, a warning not to
be ignored in female creatures.

It sounded like things were pretty bad in the wyvern world, Von
thought. He decided he was going to investigate this Glock creature that
was killing his own kind in order to rule. This was just the kind of thing
Protectors existed to watch for.

When Kaigen finished, she sat back in the earth and gazed at her creation. The Commander could definitely not pass for a wyvern now, yet he was beautiful in his own way. He had a white and brown pearlescent carapace that began at his snout and went all the way back to the end of his tail. He had the basic shape of a wyvern but looked like a centipede, or the tail of a lobster. He had pincers that could open for picking up things or close for digging. What looked like fingers proved to be fiercely hooked claws. Those claws, when dug into the ground, would help pull his body through the earth.

Kaigen could already feel the magic filling his new structures as they fused. The Commander had air magic before; Kaigen wondered if that would change with the new colors of his carapace.

"Well, see how it feels, Commander," Kaigen told him.

He smiled. The pain was entirely gone! Kaigen had taken him from the brink of death to a new life. Thinking about the earth creatures, he said, "Come on Kaigen, you can ride on my back and we will look for a safe place for me to try to burrow."

"I know! We can go visit Von's father and you can burrow in the sand dunes near his place. Nothing lives out there." The Commander knew she just wanted to see this Von, but after what she had done for him, he would deny her nothing in his power to give.

Kaigen climbed on the Commander's back, and after a time they reached the sand dunes. "I feel great, Kaigen. The structures you have built are conducive to magic. Now, let us see how they burrow." Kaigen climbed down from his carapace and the Commander dove into the sand, disappearing at once.

When he came back up, Kaigen said, "How did you disappear so quickly? It didn't even look like you had to dig."

Commander laughed. "I didn't, it seems I still have my command of air magic and I used it to do the digging for me. My air magic aids in the digging and made it easy to traverse under the sand. What was my air magic has somehow become a kind of air-earth magic, though not like yours."

"That is amazing!" Kaigen laughed.

Kaigen had made a hole in the first small shell piece that she had made for the Commander and strung it on a leather cord she cut from her wrap. She rode on the Commander's back to Von's father's house, but she didn't knock or call out to the old man. She simply left the necklace as a gift, hanging it from the doorknob. Von floated nearby, still hidden, watching her. He thought that Sybaris were truly curious creatures. When she left, he took the necklace and strung it upon his neck.

When they got back to camp where the Commander's body had been buried, Kaigen and the Commander sat still for a long time, hoping the earth creatures would come. In the morning, Silverback, Json, Jayriz, and Masbiar flew into the clearing.

"Whoa!" Jayriz exclaimed upon seeing the Commander. "What happened to you?!?"

The Commander stood tall, letting the sun reflect from his carapace. "I am of the earth now."

Silverback didn't know what the Commander meant by that, but got straight to the point. He declared, "We need you Commander. We have a royal Queen to protect."

"So I hear. I cannot fly, Silverback, but perhaps I can be of help on the ground or under it," the white-shelled creature said.

"Well, we thought we would be a force of eight. Instead we are a force of five, and one of us cannot fly. I don't see how we are going to be able to stop Glock, but perhaps we can get the other two ruling pairs, Arrington and Bedaiko and Darkale and Abraxis, to join us." Silverback began planning.

"Don't forget Gumbo and Rosetta, too," Json said. "Every being helps."

"Indeed they do, my young friend," Silverback whispered. Still, he prayed it would be enough, for he had seen firsthand the power that Glock now wielded.

Chapter 43: Tobin and Isladora

For three weeks Isladora and Tobin continued the bokken lessons with General Nokela. Juha Lepola's supplemental lessons helped Isladora immensely. She still could not beat Tobin, but she was improving with her swordsmanship and not taking as many blows.

She became a student of two masters, General Nokela and Lepola. Really, it was all about movement, and most of her training with Lepola was how to move away from the blow just enough to avoid injury. It was humbling to spar Lepola and see how easily she avoided Isladora's strikes, yet at an angle that her own strikes were still effective. Isladora hoped to gain these skills, but it was frustrating.

"At first, the student has no technique," Lepola told her. "Then, after many repetitions, the student learns technique. After using this technique in thousands of ways, from the left, from the right, while jumping, while landing, while breathing, then the student will develop non-technique."

"Non-technique?" Isladora questioned her.

"Yes, non-technique is technique without thought or mind, and it is what we strive for," Lepola instructed her student. "You must enter a state of mind without mind, thinking without thinking. You must leave your fear behind. In this state, the mind is not occupied by thought or emotion and so it is open to everything. Most people cannot understand this until they have reached mastery."

Isladora was confused. "Then how will I understand it?"

"You will know when you arrive. The first time I experienced it in combat I was elated. Everything seemed easy; I could out-think my opponent and my body felt in tune with all the nature, light, and sounds around it." Lepola quietly added, "I think that is how it feels to be a Protector."

Isladora was intrigued. Some of the oldest books mentioned them, but in the most hushed and reverent tones. "The magical race? Are they real?"

"Yes, they are real, and deadly." Lepola's face grew serious. "When you reach non-technique, you will be able to rely not on what you think should be the next move, but what your trained natural reaction is. Your mind will be working at a high speed, but with no intention, plan, or direction."

Isladora nodded her head in understanding of the concept, even though she had no idea how to reach the non-technique state of mind. "And this happens through repetition?"

"Yes, but so many repetitions that people often give up long before mastery."

Isladora grew serious. She said quietly, "I will not give up."

"No Princess, you will not," Lepola agreed. It was no mere sophistry; the former nursemaid had seen what Isladora had already accomplished and knew she had the potential for much more.

Tobin and Isladora began free sparring under the direction of Nokela. Free sparring meant anything goes, but no broken bones or deep cuts. These were the most painful and humiliating days of Isladora's life. She had grown up spoiled, fat, and soft. Tobin had grown up in full survival mode with his drunk father and mean older brothers. She couldn't catch up to Tobin's mental state; his mind was honed for survival. Isladora could beat him to the punch with her hands though, and when they fought empty-handed, it felt good to be faster at something.

King Elijashen needed General Nokela to go on a mission, so he was called away for an unknown amount of time. While he was gone, he wanted Tobin and Isladora to join the morning sessions with the fighting men and women. He felt that they were ready.

On the first day, Isladora learned that while Tobin had been a difficult opponent, she had been much, much safer with him. He had control over his body that some of the other men didn't seem to have, or care to have. Lepola scolded the men when Isladora took a nasty kick to her jaw and couldn't chew solid food for week. After that, the men began calling her Princess instead of her given name. They said it in a derogatory manner and Isladora hated it.

When it was time to pair up, the men avoided partnering with Isladora. She had to ask people to spar with her and usually that meant getting paired with beginners or large men that no one else wanted to pair with.

The women were crueler than the men, it seemed; they were competitive and freakishly strong. During grappling matches, Isladora fought to survive but oftentimes got choked or had to submit. One of the men, Jeremy, who seemed to dislike Isladora the most, would seek her out for abuse. She avoided him when she could, but he was crafty.

"Grab a new partner, and this time we will start standing!" the trainer yelled. "Your job is to take the person to the ground and submit them."

Isladora's stomach rolled over when Jeremy came to face off with her. When the trainer yelled go, Jeremy tried to do a double leg takedown on her but Isladora sprawled and fought it off. He rolled to his back but he had Isladora's wrist and he pulled her towards him, swinging one leg up around her neck and sealing the triangle choke with his other leg. She was still on her feet but her arm and throat were caught in the vise grip of Jeremy's legs. She started to black out as the oxygen flow to her brain was closed off by the choke. She tapped in submission, but Jeremy didn't let go. The next thing she knew, Lepola was trying to wake her up. At first Isladora was confused at Lepola's concern.

"What are you doing here?" Isladora asked, looking around and seeing that everyone was looking at her.

"You got choked out. I saw you tap, but Jeremy didn't let go. I came to see if you are all right," Lepola told her.

"I'm fine!" Isladora scrambled to her feet. The men laughed and she blushed furiously. She looked up at Jeremy and saw the predatory look in his eyes and it made her feel ill.

Jeremy pushed her arm. "Way to go, *Princess*," he sneered.

"Enough, Jeremy!" yelled the trainer, giving him a dark look.

Jeremy's torment of her was ceaseless. Later that day he made his way near her again and low enough so that only she could hear he said, "Princess want to wrestle?" He taunted her, wagging his eyebrows up and down and grabbing his crotch where no one else could see. Isladora shoved him hard, her hands exploding on his chest and knocking him back several feet.

"Shut your mouth, Jeremy, you are nothing but an unmannered pig!" Isladora was disgusted with him and at her limit. "Touch me again and I will kill you."

"Why wait? Let's meet outside later and have it out, just you and I," he taunted her.

Isladora was fuming. She would not take his abuse any longer. She would bring her escrima stick and end this now. "Just name the place and time, you honorless dog," she replied.

"Outside in the yard, by the large oak tree, after class." He gently slapped her face. "It'll be fun," he said, licking his lips. He could easily choke her out and then do whatever he wanted to her with no one the wiser.

Suddenly Tobin yelled, "Hey Jeremy, mind coming over here a minute?" Isladora was relieved to get away from him. She would either put him in his place or die trying because she could not endure his harassment any longer.

Jeremy sauntered over to Tobin and the next thing Isladora knew, Tobin threw a punch at Jeremy's face that knocked him out cold! The big man was standing one moment and then falling to the ground the next. Tobin apparently couldn't take any more of Jeremy's abuse either, and no way would he let Isladora meet this guy alone, even if that meant losing his place here. Tobin knew the rules, and if you broke them you were out.

The trainer saw the entire exchange and as Tobin reached to start packing up his things, the trainer began to clap, slowly at first and then with more vigor. The other men began clapping as well.

When Jeremy woke up, he was escorted out by the trainer in an unspoken and unanimous decision by the men.

The trainer told the lout, "If you try to return here or are seen anywhere near the stronghold, you will be imprisoned and turned over to King Elijashen. With a full report of the circumstances of your banishment, I will add."

Jeremy paled; he knew what conclusion the fearsome king would reach and what his reaction would be afterward.

Isladora felt so many emotions. She felt like she was one of them now, accepted. They were all supposed to take care of each other. She felt good towards her training hall for not turning a blind eye to her plight, but mostly she felt love towards Tobin for being her defender. She was elated.

After class she couldn't contain herself any longer. Her elation, combined with the wyvern memories Json had given to her, made her want to fly, to soar upon the wind. She couldn't fly like he could, but she could climb! She took off running for the mountain. Tobin saw her and mistook her running off for grief. He followed, but couldn't quite catch her.

She began to climb the mountain wall, completely fearless, part of the wyvern now. The wyvern mark burned on her neck as she climbed and climbed, finding footholds wherever she could.

While climbing, she lowered the barrier between her fears and Json's wyvern memories, feeling each new rush of memories and awareness. Reaching the top, her breathing steadied.

Behind the princess, climbing higher and higher, Tobin followed, but he was getting quite scared. The climb was dangerous and they were high enough now that a fall would mean certain death. Her courage had kept her going, but his was failing him.

Isladora looked out over the horizon, her reward for the climb. Then she noticed Tobin climbing after her. She held her breath while he made it the last twenty feet. She grabbed his hand and helped pull him up onto her shelf.

"Are you crazy?" she asked him.

"Me? You are the one climbing this cliff wall, I'm just following! I thought you needed a friend." He was breathing hard with the exertion as he sat down next to her. They sat in silence as Jeremy's breathing slowed.

"Thank you for what you did back there. I would have fought him, to the death even, but you saved me, Tobin. That guy is more like one of Zhu's men than one of us." She could think of no stronger condemnation.

Tobin wiped the sweat from his tanned face. "None of us liked him and the way he treated you. Princess or not, it was inexcusable."

"Well, I owe you one," she told him. They gazed out at the view for a long time.

After a while Tobin said, "It was nothing." He smiled at her, noting her beauty. They sat in peace for a while longer, comfortable in the silence together as only training partners could be. She really had no idea how beautiful she was, he thought, her dark hair clinging in wet tendrils to her graceful neck. Her pulse was beating alongside her wyvern mark. "I do want one thing."

She saw him looking at her in a new way. Isladora could feel her face flush as her hormones kicked in with a vengeance. "What is that?" she whispered.

Tobin looked at her mouth and licked his lips. He took a deep breath and murmured, "A kiss."

A kiss? Isladora looked at him for a long time. He was handsome, she supposed, his brown hair falling over his forehead, partly covering his serious and fierce brown eyes. The way he protected her and the way he fought with her, always pushing her to her limit but keeping her safe. She knew that now. She had always been safe sparring with him.

She leaned over, and what began as a light caress of her lips turned into a much deeper thing. She should have known it would. Tobin was a multi-faceted young man, but the strongest facet was that he was direct. He was a man who was extremely brave and who knew what he wanted. The kiss deepened yet remained gentle, and it rocked her to her core. She was not prepared for the feelings of desire she felt from the kiss. Her heartbeat accelerated and she felt a pulling sensation deep in her heart towards him.

Isladora's ring began to grow warm around her finger, bringing her back to her senses. Her body screamed for more, but she was able to break off the kiss. She raised her hands to her lips, taking in a deep breath. The kiss was her first, and it was perfect. Her analytical mind said that no living thing is perfect, science told her that. Her emotional state seemed to be taking over though. "Wow," was all she could say. Isladora began the perilous descent down the cliff side in a trance, trusting in her wyvern-granted sense of heights to keep her from falling.

Later, in her own rooms she decided to talk to Meluha Crocus. "I still feel all dreamy inside, Meluha. I was so taken in by Tobin's kiss; I would have allowed him any liberties!"

"*I know, Isladora. Luckily you have me to knock some sense into your brain!*" The spirit scoffed.

"When is this feeling going to go away? I can't have these feelings in training."

"*You should have thought of that before you let the young cur kiss you. He knew better than to ask that of a princess!*"

Isladora closed her eyes, remembering every detail of the kiss. "Well, it seemed a simple trade. I didn't know what was going to happen, he quite…."

"*Took your breath away, I know. Look, I loved once and it was the most wonderful thing in the world, to love and be loved by her. But she was taken from me. Just like that she was gone and I was powerless to bring her back to me. I have never loved again. I have never gotten over the hurt. I truly wish I had never loved her. You would do good to remember that what we love can easily be taken from us.*"

"Oh Meluha, that is so sad. I will remember."

Chapter 44: Choosing Sybaris for Bonding

Jayriz, Masbiar, Silverback, Json, and Kaigen flew back towards Toyah's home, taking the northern route to avoid Glock's scouts. The Commander dug into the ground and was gone, seeking the caves and the creatures that beckoned to him below the earth's surface.

Silverback introduced Jayriz and Masbiar to Toyah. Toyah was extremely glad to see them, saying, "Where are the other wyverns you told me about?"

Json lowered his head. "The human camp was attacked by Glock maybe a day or two after I arrived home," he growled angrily. "Jayriz and Masbiar were the only survivors."

Toyah let this information sink in, then looked at Silverback and said, "We must act quickly then, so we can surprise Glock with an attack. We won't be able to hide the new bondings for long." She brushed her long hair away from her face and touched her silver horns in thought. "Silverback, you and Json formulate a plan for our attack, and I will help bond Sully to Jayriz."

"Who will be the bonded mate for Masbiar?" Json asked, still worried she would try to bond same color pairings.

"When it came to selection, I trusted no other Sybaris with the knowledge of our Queen," Toyah said, then looked over at Kaigen. "No one, except Kaigen."

Kaigen was surprised. "But I'm supposed to be pretending to be bonded to Json…" she stammered.

"It won't matter anyway, Kaigen, once we attack," Silverback pointed out.

"That is true…" Kaigen acquiesced, flipping her brown hair from her eyes. "Whatever I can do to help, I'll do." Json smiled at her bravery. Maybe she was maturing after all.

Toyah told them, "I enlisted the help of Rosetta and Gumbo but I was afraid to ask the other two ruling pairs. They are too close to Glock and I really don't know which side they will choose."

Json snarled, "I have never liked Arrington."

Silverback said, "He just takes some getting used to. Believe me, he is a brilliant strategist and it's to our detriment that we can't have him here with us now." Silverback moved toward the other room, saying over his shoulder, "Come on, Json. Let us see what kind of strategists we can be."

Toyah began the bonding ritual of Sully and Jayriz, an indigo Sybaris and a yellow wyvern, and knowing the need for secrecy, neither cried out in their pain. "I wasn't able to steal the healing manna from the Cystine Hall, so your strength will come back more slowly," she told them. "Can you demonstrate your combined magic? I believe that Jayriz's control over intellect and visions paired with Sully's ability to alter perceptions will be powerful."

Jayriz and Sully traded magic back and forth for several minutes. Suddenly, Toyah and Kaigen could see enormous butterflies of various shapes and colors darting around the room.

Toyah watched as a beautiful blue butterfly grazed her upper arm as it flew by. "I hope that your combined magic will be able to implant terrible visions in Glock's mind to distract him while the others take him out. These butterflies are beautiful, but can they be terrible?"

Suddenly, the butterflies grew fangs and hissed, trying to bite Kaigen and Toyah. Kaigen screamed.

"Enough!" Toyah yelled, and the images vanished. "That was an effective demonstration, Sully and Jayriz!" Her laughter filled the room with their success.

"Please go and join Silverback and Json in the planning. If you give them a demonstration of your powers, please warn them first! We don't want to risk another scream!"

"Yes, Toyah," Sully answered, proud of himself and his wyvern.

Kaigen asked, "Don't you think Darkale and Abraxis need to be told and at our side when we attack?"

"I just can't risk going near the Cystine Hall. If Glock were to see, he will know I have been using bonding magic and that something is up," Toyah told her. "It is my hope that when we attack that Darkale and Abraxis and Arrington and his wyvern Bedaiko will come to our aid."

Kaigen gave voice to both of their fears. "What if they come to Glock's aid instead?"

Toyah sighed. "Then this will be a short coup, and my daughter, our Queen, will not be protected, and we will all likely be killed." A look of fierce determination stole over Toyah's face. "Come, Kaigen, it is time to bond you to Masbiar and see what earth and fire magic can do when combined."

When the red wyvern made no move to come forward, Kaigen asked, "Masbiar, are you ready?" He didn't speak or even look at them, but he did lumber forward.

The bonding began, and immediately Kaigen could tell Masbiar's mind was damaged. Toyah attempted to infuse them with the bonding magic, but it was if someone had sealed Masbiar off. Toyah tried to open the lock in his mind to discover what he feared so they could bond. Masbiar, a creature of fire, began to burn as Toyah probed. At first the fire covered just his head, and then it crept down his neck to where Kaigen was holding her arm for the bonding. Kaigen cried out. Her earth magic immediately protected her from burning, but the heat was intense. Finally, Toyah broke through the mental barrier. The memories of Glock burning him had completely consumed Masbiar's mind. Toyah saw that Masbiar had fought back with his own stream of fire, but in the end, he hadn't been strong enough and Glock's stream slowly wore his down. Out-battled, and the slow gloating way Glock had overrun his magic had left a deep streak of anger which Masbiar fed in alarming intensity. He had one thought: vengeance. Toyah could feel that he was jealous that Glock had Solei, a red Sybaris, and he had Kaigen, a silly brown creature with no scales. Toyah could see that Masbiar had no control over his anger, and that was dangerous.

Toyah matched his anger with her own. "You are a fool to dismiss Kaigen's earth magic! Earth and fire means lava, but you are too foolish to think of the possibilities of your bonding. Lava will be thicker and stronger than Glock's fire stream," Toyah pointed out.

Masbiar paused in his burning to listen.

"We will have to go to the steppes to practice our magic, Toyah," Kaigen told her, ignoring Masbiar's troubles.

"Why is it always the steppes with you, Kaigen?" Toyah queried.

"It's a desolate place and no one goes there. If we are going to be throwing lava around it is the only place we can do that without notice." Kaigen smiled coquettishly at Toyah and said, "And if we happen to see Von, well that is just an added bonus."

"Well go and practice, but do not be seen," Toyah ordered.

Masbiar continued to calm down, and Kaigen nodded at Toyah. "Can you fly us there, Masbiar?" Kaigen asked him.

Masbiar finally spoke, his voice gravelly and strange, "I can, and I will."

Kaigen looked at Toyah. Truth be told, she was a little worried about his control over his emotions. He might fly straight to Glock and try to kill him, which was definitely not something Kaigen wanted to risk, but Toyah didn't seem to be worried about Masbiar's rage or what it might do to Kaigen. She was already planning the next step, hatching her daughter.

Chapter 45: Hatchling

Ariah talked into the great void of her nothingness environment, "My mother wants me to hatch now, and while I am ready, I am not the same being that I once was. Gone is the lost Sybaris girl who didn't even know the name of her own race. I spent my life living with the traveling nomads. They never mistreated me, but I was a slave. I lived with people, but I didn't have any family or friends. When I was traveling with them, never once did I question how wrong it was to be kept as a slave. I was ignorant about it because I grew up as a slave. It was a way of life to me. Now that I have lived parts of all these other lives through memories, I know how wrong it is. Shame on those humans for keeping me thusly. I wonder if they knew where I came from, how they found me. Maybe I will ask them someday. I will ask them from the back of my great wyvern and see if they think me a slave then."

Time passed. "I no longer feel like I once did. I feel like a queen. I feel responsibility towards my people and I want to rule. I know the type of queen that I want to be and with my human memories and protector memories and wyvern memories, I will be unique; a royal Sybaris who has had a slave background. I will never allow slaves in my kingdom."

"I know that we have a battle ahead of us and we may be destroyed. I hear my mother and the others making plans, and I am ready to meet my Royal Guard. They will protect me, and I will protect them. We will become a network of sorts, a family with extraordinary preternatural skills. I wonder about this Glock and Solei and how powerful they have become. It is against our laws, the laws my mother has been teaching me about, to bond with a same color wyvern. Glock's bond will end Solei's life early, and when he is used up, Glock will consume him like he did his first bonded mistress and gain his powers. This flesh-eating is against every law that we hold dear. It turns our civilization upside down, worse than slavery, into one of savagery. The damage that has already been done to Solei we will not be able to undo. He will have to be destroyed along with Glock, if he still lives."

"How is this hatching going to work, Toyah?" Json asked. "I created her egg through magic; the magic formed and shaped and fitted her into the shell."

"I honestly don't know Json; we've never had a royal egg or even a rebirth in my time," Toyah answered him. "Young Sybaris come out small and grow as you know, but she was formed as a mature Sybaris with male wyvern magic. I couldn't find anything in the history books, no references as to how we go about helping her hatch."

Ariah whispered to no one, "Most of my guard is gathered around me. They have high expectations, I know. My bonded wyvern Json, Toyah and Silverback, and Sully and Jayriz are all here. Kaigen and Masbiar are out testing their combined magic. I feel proud of them, and now they expect something from me but I do not know how to begin."

"Ariah," Json said, "I remember feeling you vibrate when you were in my chest. Remember, you vibrated intensely when Kaigen was shaking the earth. Try that now." The egg began to shake and quiver. "That's good, Ariah, try to break through." Json knew that his magic had placed her in the shell; his magic may be needed to get Ariah out.

Ariah tried to break through the egg shell, but it didn't seem to give and she began to panic. Feeling her panic through their bond, suddenly Json began singing again, a deep-throated song. A fissure appeared in the egg.

"It's working, Json, keep singing! Oh, my daughter!" Toyah was overcome with emotion.

As Json continued to sing, more fissures appeared in her shell until the pieces cracked in half, spilling her out in a mess of amniotic fluid. Json never wavered in his song, once he began it, his paternal instincts took over and he remained steadfast. His magic began to straighten and fill her limbs, first her legs and then her arms. His eyes were closed and his magic curled around her, helping her to sit and then to stand. Ariah was taller than she had been. The fluids began to leave her skin and her hair began to dry and fan out around her shoulders in soft waves. Her muscles expanded, and they were bigger than they had been. Finally, her eyes began to clear fully of their haze. Json stopped singing and slowly opened his wyvern eyes.

What stood in front of Json was not what he expected. Ariah did not look like the girl that had helped him escape from the human camp. Ariah looked like a warrior goddess ready for battle. She was tall, her long legs muscular and tight. Her face had matured, and her eyes glowed with amber light. She still had violet to red scales like she had before, but now golden scales highlighted her arms and torso. Her long hair, which once was violet to red, now also had gold streaks. It fell riotously about her face.

She took in a deep breath, filling her lungs. She looked down to where the arrow had taken her life; not even a scar remained. She looked around the room, finding Json, and she smiled, "You did it my friend, you saved me, and you brought me back."

Json and the others were speechless in her glory; all of them, including her mother, knelt upon the ground, tears in their eyes.

"Please rise and swear fealty to me," Ariah spoke the words that she knew she must. One by one they swore to protect her, to be reliable and steadfast. The first of her guard.

"I swear to you, as my supplicants and as my Royal Guard to protect you with my life, to give my life in service of Draconia." Even though the Queen was not yet clothed, she had no shyness—everything about her was bold. "I swear to be a fair and upright ruler, depending on my advisors but ruling by my own decisions. You will be my Royal Guard, and together we will make this kingdom a safe place." Ariah gazed at all of them, her eyes finally resting upon her mother. Oh, she thought, how beautiful her mother was! She went to her and hugged her. Toyah held her daughter for the first time and they wept together. Silverback approached and nestled his large neck and head around both of them while the others left the room, giving them privacy.

Chapter 46: First Kiss

"Isladora, it was just a kiss." Isladora had been acting weird since Tobin had asked for a kiss, and he just wanted her to act normal again. Isladora sped up her attack, grabbing Tobin into an arm drag to get behind him and wrapping her arm around his throat. She sealed the choke by grabbing her bicep and began pushing his head forward to finish it off. Tobin thought about taking it to the ground to escape her hold but he didn't want to further anger her. When Tobin tapped in submission, she didn't immediately let go until Meluha Crocus lit up her finger as a reminder. She released Tobin, panting.

"It's not his fault that you kissed him back, Isladora," she heard in her mind. Isladora had no clue how to handle her emotions. Every time she thought about the kiss she got flustered. She needed time away from Tobin to think, but at the same time she didn't want to be away from him.

Tobin took her hands in his. "Look at me." When she did he said, "Let's just forget that it happened, okay?" Isladora didn't want to forget; she wanted to experience it again. She looked down at his mouth, wetting her lips. Tobin's body reacted immediately, but he knew that now was not the time or the place. She felt rejected when he looked away. The kiss must not have meant as much to him as it had to her. Tears welled in her eyes. When he saw her tears it wrenched his heart. "Isladora, please talk to me about it. I didn't mean to make you feel bad."

Isladora was used to bottling up her emotions; she wasn't used to discussing them. "You... you kissed me, and now you act like it was no big deal." She went on, "You act like we were doing something normal...like eating or sparring." She rubbed her lips. "To me, it was earth-shattering, and now nothing seems normal, and I almost hate you for the feelings you made me have when to you it is nothing!" She turned to run, but Tobin was ready and grabbed her arm, stopping her flight.

Tobin loved Isladora, of that he had no doubt. Training alongside her every day was the most bittersweet thing he had experienced in his twenty-one years. She was everything to him; she was beautiful and brave, even when she wanted to blast holes in his hide. Her intellect outshone some of the scholars he had learned from since he had been at the stronghold. Being near her had become as needful as breathing. But he had to admit that he had changed things when he asked her for the kiss. He knew the rules of their society. He knew he wasn't supposed to touch her that way. All he wanted was to be with her and if that meant as training partners only then he would have to adapt. But he would be honest. "It wasn't 'nothing' to me, Isladora. Kissing you was everything I have ever wanted in life all rolled up into a single moment," Tobin told her earnestly. He sighed, running his hand over his face. "But I want things back the way they were before I asked for the kiss. I had no right. You are a princess, for God's sake!" He knew he was not in the league of men that King Elijashen would want for her. Isladora searched his eyes and saw his honesty shining through. Her heart did a curious little flip.

"Tobin!" It was General Nokela. "Tobin, ah there you are. Come, King Elijashen needs you immediately."

Tobin knew what this was about. Dirty sons of drunken fathers did not kiss royal princesses. He was done for. Yet, he told himself as he marched towards his doom, it was a price he would gladly pay to have felt her lips against his. He cleaned himself up the best he could and then left for the royal hall, Isladora following curiously behind.

Tobin knelt before the king, wondering if he would take his head off right then and there. "Rise, Tobin." Tobin got to his feet and felt real fear when King Elijashen stood as well and said, "It is time for you to be test-ed." This was it then, the end of twenty-one years by the kiss of a royal princess. Definitely worth it, he thought.

"Tobin, this is Suguru and Pislonna," King Elijashen said. Tobin saw an old man and one of the young women that had been rescued from Zhu's stronghold. "You and Suguru will deliver Pislonna safely back to her home in Timber Town. Suguru will take care of her needs on the trail, and you will provide game and protection. I want you to leave immediately." Tobin looked at the old man again, noting that he looked like an old drunk. He tried to hide his disappointment. Escorting this woman to her home was a far cry from what he wanted to do, to become King's Scout.

Pislonna spoke up, her voice sultry and sweet, "Oh, such a handsome escort. I shall feel safe under his care." Pislonna smiled sweetly at Tobin. Isladora was not prepared for the wild streak of jealousy that flooded her body. Pislonna was beautiful and feminine. Her long curly blonde hair fell all the way to her waist, and she had a beautiful mouth and a curvaceous body.

She was everything Isladora was not, and right now Tobin was staring at Pislonna. Isladora was all but forgotten already. Isladora's hand came to rest on the handle of her knife as her eyes narrowed at Tobin, and if she had been carrying her escrima stick, she might not have been able to stay her own hand.

King Elijashen noted his daughter's envy but made no sign. Instead, he said, "Isladora, you will come with me. We are thinking about building another wing to the stronghold and I need your head with figures." Isladora's eyes were drawn back to her father and she struggled with her emotions. They felt wild, like a wyvern. Her eyes dilated. "Go to my chambers, Isladora, I will meet you there," said the king firmly.

Isladora took one last look at Tobin and he gazed back at her, his hands spreading wide. He wanted to take Isladora in his arms and tell her that she was the only girl for him. The differences in the two women were night and day. Isladora was tanned and toned from training, her clothes were leather, her hair was pulled back from her face and still damp from this morning's training. She was every bit the girl of Tobin's dreams, and now she was mad at him and he would have to leave her that way. Isladora left to await her father.

King Elijashen spoke again, "Tobin, after you deliver Pislonna to her family, I have a special duty for you on the way back."

Ah, so this would be the real test Tobin thought excitedly.

"I want you to capture the man known as the Fox; he lives in the wooded area southwest of Timber Town."

"The Fox?" Tobin asked. "How will I know him?"

The king explained, "He lives by himself and he goes by that name. No one knows much about him, I'm afraid, but he does have a special sword that I can describe to you. He is crafty and dangerous. I want him brought back to me alive. I have important questions that I need to ask him, so do not seriously harm him."

"Yes sir, I understand. What is special about this sword?"

The king nodded. "The sword's name is Kitsune. It was forged by a master mage and is said to have magic imbued in its steel. It never tarnishes. The tsuba is made from a black metal and is patterned with a golden fox." Tobin knew that the tsuba was the sword guard that kept other blades from sliding down the sword and slicing the hand. The king continued, "The menuki, which is an ornament found under the handle wrap on the sword, is also a fox crafted from a large ruby. It is worth a king's ransom."

King Elijashen smiled, quite the rogue. "Bring the Fox to me; this is your test." The king placed his fist over his heart in a warrior's gesture.

"Yes, King Elijashen!" Tobin bowed with his fist in his hand, the warrior's salute of obeisance.

King Elijashen entered his chambers to find a pouty daughter. He ignored her attitude and said, "I want to add a new wing to the stronghold. You are to help me design this as if you wanted it for your own family."

King Elijashen got out some preliminary drawings. Even in her maddened state, her analytical side took over as she looked at the sketches. They were crude drawings, but Isladora could picture the air flow from the main entrance.

"As you can see, I have marked out the space but no detail as to the shape and size of the rooms. I want you to design this for a large family, say a husband and wife and several children." King Elijashen smiled at her. "Work out the details with Prince Tonsaku. He has nothing better to do than lay around healing anyway."

"Yes, Father," Isladora said. "What is this wing to be for?"

He admired how his daughter always went straight to the point. "For your future family. It is time you married."

So he did know about the kiss! But no, he couldn't have known; they were on top of a mountain wall when it happened. "Have you chosen someone for me?"

"Yes, as a matter of fact we have. He is from another tribe, but he will be brought to us soon." He ignored the hurt look on her face.

Thinking of Tobin, Isladora said, "I will not marry him." The King answered, "Yes, Isladora, you will."

Later that night, she lay in her bed hugging the pillow and pretending it was Tobin. She cried a little at the unfairness of her life, yet she knew her responsibility to the kingdom. She tried to picture loving another man, but only Tobin's beautiful and strong face came to her mind. He had left without saying goodbye, but she knew he had no choice. The thought of Tobin traveling with the curvaceous Pislonna for the three days it would take them to reach Timber Town made Isladora resentful. Isladora forcibly put her emotions to the side; instead, she dug through her intellect and recognized that these feelings of desire were pulling her away from the desires of her family. She was a royal princess and it was her duty to marry and have offspring, not fall in love with the first man who kissed her like a silly schoolgirl. She would move on and continue down her path, and she would only allow thoughts of their shared kiss to intrude upon her when she lay down at night. Then she would allow herself to remember everything.

Chapter 47: The Fox

Tobin, Pislonna, and Suguru headed out for Timber Town. Tobin wanted to tell Isladora goodbye, but there was no time. Pislonna wasn't a very good rider, so they chose a large gentle plow horse for her mount. Tobin rode Fashi, his little mountain pony, and Suguru rode an older mare, a blood bay with black socks. Suguru stayed alongside Pislonna in case she had trouble.

The first night they would camp in the open, for there were no towns or lodging nearby. Pislonna chatted incessantly about this and that, and Tobin tried to be a gentleman, but her endless prattle left him craving the watchful silence of Isladora. Anyone could sneak up on them with her distracting prattle. Tobin loved how he and Isladora could be together all day and not say a word to each other. He realized how attached he had grown to being near her.

When the day grew long, Tobin scouted ahead and chose a clearing that was off the trail a bit. He groomed Fashi and tethered him to a grassy spot, made sure Suguru and Pislonna were safely settled, and finally headed off to find some game. They didn't need the meat; they had plenty of hard bread, apples, and cheese, but he needed to get away for a while and to make sure there were no other people lurking about.

Tobin returned later to Suguru and Pislonna sitting comfortably by a small fire talking quietly together. Pislonna's face was animated and Suguru seemed to truly be enjoying listening to her. Tobin admitted to himself that she was a beautiful woman and he was glad she had survived her captivity with Zhu. Tobin noted with gratitude that the horses had been tethered correctly and fed some oats; perhaps Suguru wasn't that bad after all. He took an apple to Fashi, who chomped it down like a glutton. Tobin laughed at the little horse.

"There you are, Tobin, come sit and talk with us!" Pislonna called, scooting over on her log and making room for him. Tobin suppressed a groan and did as she bid, noting how her breasts strained against the fabric barely holding them in.

"Weren't lucky enough to find us some game, were you?" the old man pointed his finger at him. When Tobin shook his head, Suguru said, "Here, have a swig of this," and offered Tobin a flask.

Tobin took it from him and smelled it; it was some kind of fermented whisky. Disgusted, Tobin shook his head and gave it back. "That will corrode your brain, old man."

"What, you don't drink?" Suguru laughed at him. "What kind of man doesn't drink? Maybe you're too young still?"

Tobin scowled at Suguru. "Rot your innards if you like, old man, but keep your filthy spirits away from me." The smell had immediately brought back horrible memories of his father. It was uncanny how smells could recall the strongest memories. Tobin now battled the beat of his troubled heart.

"Tobin…" Pislonna smiled at him. "Such a strange name. Are you married?"

Tobin wished he could say that he was married so she would leave him alone. "No, I'm not married, but my heart belongs to another." They broke the bread and Tobin ate in silence while Suguru and Pislonna talked about Timber Town. Suguru eventually went to his mat and rolled up in his blanket away from them to go to sleep.

Pislonna placed her hand on Tobin's leg suggestively. "Your heart may belong to another but your body is here with me." She smiled at him, reaching up to touch his face.

Tobin shied away from her hands and said, "My body is no longer mine to command, as it belongs to her as well." He stalked into the forest. Tobin found a tree and leaned against it, glad to be away from the cloying scent of Pislonna's heavy perfumes. He stayed alert most of the night and kept watch, only lightly dozing, as a scout should. He thought about the Fox and how he might capture him. That night he had strange dreams of chasing a real fox.

After another two days of uneventful travel, the trio finally rode into Timber Town, and Tobin left Suguru and Pislonna at the home of her family. He didn't wait to see the reunion; Pislonna had Suguru to ease the way back. Tobin went to find a hotel and get some supper, a bath, and a good night's sleep before he went after the Fox. His stench alone would alert the Fox of his presence.

He settled Fashi in the hotel's stables, brushing him down and rubbing his legs. Then he went to get a room. The hotel fed him some stew with large chunks of carrots and potatoes. Tobin guessed that the meat might possibly be from a cow, but whatever it was it was hearty and tender. He drank some apple cider, watered down the way he liked it, and chewed on a crust of bread while he looked around. Most of the patrons seemed like good people. When the waitress returned he asked her about the Fox, but she hadn't heard of him. Tobin went to the bathhouse and cleaned up and then slept soundly until dawn.

Tobin saddled Fashi and left early the next morning. Fashi checked his pockets for apples and was disappointed to find none. They followed the road back towards home and then turned southwest on the road that would take him to the thickest part of the forest where King Elijashen had told him to begin looking for the Fox. Tobin and Fashi rode systematically through the forest for several days looking for signs of human habitation. So far, they hadn't even come across a deserted camp site. Tobin began to worry that the king had given him poor intelligence.

Despite his worry, Tobin was proud of his little horse. Fashi moved quietly and on alert. When Tobin stopped to listen, Fashi listened also. The horse seemed to enjoy the hunt as much as Tobin did. The mountain pony's hearing was astute, his ears would turn towards a sound but he never turned his head. A large head movement could alert prey or predator to their location. Fashi was a true ranger's pony, and Tobin wondered who had trained him. Tobin could nock an arrow and then guide the pony through the forest with only the pressure of his legs. Fashi was sensitive to the slightest pressure. If Tobin wanted Fashi to speed up, he didn't even have to kick him, just lean forward in the saddle.

As they traveled further south, they came across a stream where Tobin made camp and caught some fish. While roasting the fish over the fire, Tobin took out his knife to cut some cheese when he heard Fashi nicker. Tobin was immediately on alert; he knew the pony had sharp hearing. Tobin unsheathed his sword, never far from his side, and when he looked around in alarm, he saw a dirty old thing staring back at him. He couldn't tell the gender or the size of the person, as they were covered head to toe in a cloak that was the same colors as the forest. The person could have been watching Tobin for hours with that kind of camouflage. The face was covered, and all Tobin could see were two brown eyes. The person pointed at the fish.

"Ah, you want some dinner?" Tobin decided to pretend friendship to learn more about this foe. He re-sheathed his sword but kept it in his hand.

When the person nodded once, Tobin said, "Help yourself," backing up several feet and sitting down to eat his own fish. As the person approached the fire, Tobin decided that the person must be male. He was just too large to be a woman.

The person chose a large fish and sat on a stump on the opposite side of the clearing from Tobin. He carried a sword on his back, and as he sat down he took it off and set it against the tree. Tobin also set his sword down to lean against the log he was sitting on. Tobin noted that the sword was still easily within the man's reach, and so was his. Tobin began eating his fish while studying this odd man. The stranger unhooked his face covering to eat but kept his head turned away so Tobin still could not see his face. The pair ate in silence.

The setting sun broke through the bottoms of the trees, and the light reflected off something red, shining a red prism on the forest floor. Tobin followed the beam back to the sword. He realized it was the red ruby menuki shining through the wrap! He was eating fish with the Fox! Tobin's eyes widened and his heart accelerated. He jumped to his feet to charge the man when suddenly he couldn't see or breathe. Smoke surrounded Tobin. He bent over coughing, his eyes watering, and he stumbled over to the other side of the clearing where the air was clearer. When he could see and breathe again, the Fox was gone.

Tobin searched the area, but he could find no discernable prints to follow. When he returned to his fire, the rest of the fish were gone. He had been bested by the Fox, and he felt somewhat foolish, but tomorrow was another day and he would hunt the man down.

Tobin hunted the Fox for several days. He could find a few tracks but not much else. When he half-fell into a hole that had been covered with forest debris, Tobin realized that the Fox was playing with him. As he got back to his feet, Tobin saw some wild garlic. Gathering it up, he began to plan. He decided to go back to the beginning and repeat the only thing he knew would bring out the Fox—his appetite. Tobin caught and cooked some more fish, taking his time preparing the meat. He seasoned them with the wild garlic, placing several large bulbs in the center of the fish. The smell would travel for miles, but that was what he wanted, sort of like ringing the dinner bell.

Sure enough, it worked; Fashi nickered again, not in alarm but in greeting. If Tobin didn't know better, he would say that the horse recognized the Fox.

"I know you're there. Come out and have some fish. It's delicious," Tobin said, taking a large bite of his. "Mmmmm." This time Tobin had his bow and arrow ready, cleverly disguised in the small wood pile by the fire. When the Fox entered the clearing, Tobin noted that his cloak was very high quality and his boots were made of thick leather with no heel. No wonder his adversary didn't leave marks on the ground. This time, the Fox did not take his sword from his back but instead stood leaning against the tree, enjoying his fish. He still hid his face in the hood of the cloak, but Tobin could see a clean-shaven jawline. Not what he expected for a forest man. Finishing his fish, Tobin slowly reached down to put his plate on the ground then quickly picked up the bow and nocked an arrow toward the Fox. The Fox turned and within seconds was behind the big tree. Tobin had already let fly, but his arrow thunked into wood. The Fox took off, zigzagging through the trees. Tobin shot two more arrows at him, but the Fox was too quick and Tobin lost him. As he retrieved his arrows he noted with satisfaction that one arrow had hit the Fox's cloak and torn a long strip from it.

Gathering his trophy, Tobin went back to his camp to find that again the remaining fish were gone. Truly incensed now, Tobin tied the strip of cloak around his head. This was getting serious.

The next day, an arrow whizzed by Tobin's head and buried itself in the tree. When Tobin looked up he saw the Fox on a horse, galloping away. Tobin broke camp and mounted Fashi. If the Fox were on horseback, he would be easy to trail. For several days Tobin tracked the Fox, only gaining sight of him once. They were headed south towards the stronghold. In another day they would be back out of the forest, and that would be Tobin's last chance for camouflage.

Tobin knew he had to get ahead of the Fox. Apologizing to Fashi, he backtracked to the road and rode at a full-out gallop until they reached the edge of the forest. Tobin turned back to the northwest and followed the line of trees, looking for a vantage point. He found a large boulder where he could see quite a ways in both directions but would be hidden by the boulder. He sat and waited, estimating the time it would take for the Fox to travel and hoping he hadn't changed directions.

Finally, he saw the Fox carefully approaching the tree line. He was within arrow distance, but the king wanted him alive for questioning. If Tobin had to shoot, he would shoot the horse first. As the Fox and his horse cleared the trees, Tobin made himself known, an arrow aimed not at the Fox, but instead to kill the horse. "I don't want to kill your horse, but I will if you don't do what I tell you to."

The Fox was genuinely surprised to see Tobin; he was about to set his own trap when Tobin had outsmarted him. The Fox raised his hands, steering the animal with his legs.

"Ride towards the road," Tobin ordered him.

The Fox complied, turning his horse, and Tobin followed behind, arrow nocked and ready. "I'm taking you back to the Juna stronghold. King Elijashen has questions for you." Tobin continued to ride behind the Fox. "If you try to flee, your horse will die and you can walk. And if you try to run after that, you will die." They rode this way for a few hours, when to

Tobin's vast relief the stronghold came into sight. As he steered the Fox into the bailey, armed men came and took the Fox from his horse. They removed his weapons and then brought him inside to the king.

Chapter 48: The Fox and the King

Isladora and Tonsaku had just about finished designing the new wing. From the inner courts, large windows could be opened to let in natural light and air. The main bedrooms would be first, then the children's rooms with the bathrooms on the other side of the hall in between. A cistern would be placed on the roof where water could be pumped and held. The largest room was reserved for Isladora's future library and council chamber. She planned on helping to rule the kingdom as she learned to manage things, and this would be the focus of her family life.

Tonsaku looked at Isladora. She was bent over the table studying the calculations they just made. Her body had changed drastically in the last year, and as protective as she was, she would make a fine mother. Now that the pudginess was gone, he could see the delicate and beautiful features of her mother's clan. "Do you know this man you are supposed to marry?"

Isladora looked up, a scowl marking her beautiful face. She said flatly, "No, I don't even know his name, and I don't care, really." She looked at Tonsaku's foot, still healing from his battle with Zhu. "Have you ever been in love, Tonsaku?"

"With every barmaid in the land!" he smiled and teased her. When he saw that she was serious he added, "No, not really. Are you in love, Isladora?" She refused to answer, but when she blushed Tonsaku decided that she was in love, but with whom? The only person she spent a lot of time with was the drunkard's son, Tobin. "You're in love with Tobin?" Tonsaku was incredulous. "Oh, your father will never allow that!" Tonsaku was too smart for his own good; she should have known that he would figure it out.

Isladora ran from the room in tears. Tonsaku didn't even know Tobin! She ran outside, her inner wyvern calling her to climb. In the bailey the king's men were checking a cloaked man for weapons. She skidded to a halt. Tobin sat on his mount with an arrow pointed at the man. Her heart reacted strongly. This must be the Fox, Isladora thought. Tobin had done it, he had captured the Fox!

Her anger evaporated and Isladora's heart beat hard. She was so glad to see Tobin; she had been torn with jealousy watching him ride off with the enchanting Pislonna. She entered the hall behind Tobin and the men.

Isladora now knew that being a dutiful daughter and Princess to the

kingdom was no match for her love for Tobin. She could never love or
touch another man intimately. She would renounce her throne; there was
no other way. Tobin would become King's Scout. She knew that with his
talent and drive he would eventually achieve this goal he had set. She would
leave the stronghold rather than embarrass her family.

King Elijashen was watching the wild emotions flitting across his
daughter's face as they brought the man known as the Fox to him. She was
head-over-heels in love with Tobin, of that the king had no doubt, and she
was distraught at her future. It was time to wipe that look from her face, he
thought, but first was men's business.

The men brought the Fox to the dais and he knelt on the floor, his
head hanging down. "Bring me Kitsune," the king ordered.

One of the men brought the sword to him. King Elijashen handled the
sword reverently, running his hand over the red menuki and laying the
sword across his lap to stare at the Fox. The Fox did not look up; he continued to stare at the ground, defeated. The king stood and drew the blade
from the scabbard, making an unearthly noise as the ensorcelled metal was
released. Tobin thought surely he would ask the Fox questions before he
cut his head off. The king made a few cuts in the air, testing the weight of
the blade, and then he said, "You will stand, Fox." They all watched as the
Fox got nimbly to his feet.

To Tobin's confusion, the king bowed and handed the sword to the
Fox. A live blade, all the Fox had to do was cut and the king would be hurt
badly or dead! Tobin moved forward and began to draw back his bow to
stop this madness. This man was a skilled killer! Then the Fox and the king
embraced, laughing together, halting Tobin in his tracks. To Tobin's relief,
the Fox re-sheathed Kitsune.

The king began questioning the Fox. Tobin could only make out a few
words. The king's men stood relaxed, completely unconcerned that their
king was near a trained killer. The two men talked for some time, and Tobin
was confused. He looked at Isladora, but she, too, was confused. She
looked so sad that Tobin wanted to hold her in his arms. He knew it would
be hard to get her in his arms, but once he did, he knew she would relax
and let him care for her.

Just when Tobin thought he couldn't watch the two men talking any
longer without knowing what was going on, the king spoke. "Tobin, please
come here. You too, Isladora."

As the young people approached the king, they looked at each other
trying to assess what was happening. "Neither of you will speak until I am
done talking, is this understood?"

Perplexed but ever respectful of their king, both uttered their acquiescence.

"Tobin, your quick action saved my brother Tonsaku's life," the king began. "You could have asked for money, but instead you asked for investments in your future here. General Nokela and I have kept a close watch on all that you do, even outside of the training hall." At this, the king looked at Isladora and back at Tobin. "Through your daily actions, you have become one of the tribe. You train physically and you are intensely trying to catch up in your studies."

It was all Tobin could do to think straight. He had brought the king the Fox; this was supposed to be about his scouting abilities.

"Pay attention, Tobin," the king remonstrated. "You demonstrated your faithfulness when Pislonna threw herself at you camping in the woods." At this, Isladora's eyes narrowed. "You do not drink any alcohol, and being the son of a drunk, that is a good thing. In fact, even goaded by another man, you chose not to imbibe." The king continued, "You have demonstrated your care for others, and of your mount Fashi. You have demonstrated that you can live off the land and provide for those in your charge. I also hear that you are quite the cook!"

The king let his words sink in, and he asked Tobin, "Have you any questions for me?"

"How is this a scout's test?" Tobin asked.

"I wasn't testing you to be a King's Scout, young man," the king said. "General Nokela and I both agree that we still have some work to do with your scouting abilities." At this, the Fox began peeling what looked to be wax from his face and Tobin gasped to see that the Fox was General Nokela!

"General Nokela, you are the Fox?" Tobin asked, incredulous.

"Yes, indeed. I am not just a general, I can also be a master of disguises, boy. I am also Suguru, who went with you to take Pislonna home," General Nokela said.

"No, Tobin, this test was not about you being King's Scout. This test was to see if you should have the honor of being able to court my daughter, Isladora," the king said.

Tobin tried to grasp all that had happened; it was happening too quickly. Suguru, the old drunk, the Fox, and General Nokela were the same man. They had all been testing him! "Pislonna was in on this too?" Tobin asked. He was too stunned to realize the last thing the king had said.

"Yes, she was aware of her part to play in seeing if you were faithful. She would have gone on with it too if you had agreed to her charms," General Nokela said with a throaty chuckle.

As the king smiled at Isladora, Isladora looked back at her father in wonder, speechless.

Suddenly, Tobin realized that he was being given permission to court Isladora. Maybe even marry her! His heart leapt; it almost felt like it was leaving his chest.

He took Isadora's hand and gently kissed the top. Then he turned and knelt, unable to hide his smile, and answered, "Yes, my king."

"Tobin, you may rise. General Nokela will be taking you on a mission during which he will teach you all that he knows about being a master scout. Isladora, you will stay here and ride with me to the west fields. It seems they have a problem with beetles."

"Yes, Father," she said with a huge smile of genuine affection and respect on her face. Her heart was soaring as well! Her father made it his business to know everything going on in her life and he loved her enough to make sure the path she was on was a good one. "What about this man you were bringing here for me to marry?"

Watching Tobin retreat, the king said, "That man is already here, but whether or not you choose to marry him will be up to you." Isladora smiled, understanding it was her choice. The king sighed. "That is, if he survives General Nokela's training."

Tobin was still coming to grips with the fact that he had been traveling with and hunting his mentor General Nokela. He had shot three arrows at him. He could have killed him! Tobin had no doubt that the king had been aware of him and Isladora's budding attraction for each other. Maybe the king was even aware that he had kissed the princess.

As Tobin and General Nokela walked away, Tobin thought about the day the Fox had shot an arrow from more than 100 yards, purposely missing his head but close enough Tobin could feel the wind from the arrow's passage. He turned to Nokela and said, "So if I had failed these tests, I wouldn't have made it back with the Fox...I wouldn't have made it back at all, am I right?"

General Nokela looked at Tobin so seriously that chills ran down his spine. "No, you wouldn't have made it back."

Chapter 49: Glock Calls a Meeting

"Call another meeting of the governing board," Glock commanded, looking through the ceiling windows of the Cystine Hall. "Tomorrow, here, at the usual time."

The bonded pair Abraxis and Darkale looked at each other with dread. "And what shall we say the meeting is about?" Darkale asked, his voice echoing in the large hallway, although he thought he knew already.

Glock glared at Darkale. "This meeting is confidential. I will tell you what it's about at the beginning of the meeting. Now announce it."

Darkale knew if he didn't do what Glock asked that Glock would put him in the pits like he had done to Arrington and Bedaiko. Poor Arrington, Darkale thought, his impeccable appearance was a part of his armor and who he was. He would certainly be filthy down there.

Glock had imprisoned them because he feared they were plotting against him. Glock would kill Arrington and maybe his wyvern, too. Darkale went to raise the flag to call the meeting for the next day as Glock watched over his shoulder. He had to find a way to warn the others that they were walking into what he believed was a trap.

As Glock watched he said, "Remove that face covering, Darkale, I don't like it." Darkale was a blue Sybaris and his entire body was pleasing to look at by Sybaris standards, just the right amount of human skin and wyvern scales, all a brilliant blue. His eyes were light blue and often dazzled others with their icy intensity, a sharp contrast to his dark brown to black hair. But his lower jaw was a gruesome mess of half-wyvern, half-human features. Darkale preferred to keep it covered.

Abraxis, his bonded wyvern, growled and spoke up, knowing how much that would bother Darkale. "I don't think that's a good idea, Glock. It tends to frighten others."

Glock immediately hissed and roared, the echo in the archway deafening. Abraxis roared back in reaction. Abraxis had the most frightening wyvern mouth of all of them, and he knew it. His longer and wider snout contained rows of lethally sharp teeth.

Glock loved to see Abraxis' jaw, it thrilled him every time. "Back off, pup, or I'll put you in the pits with Arrington and Bedaiko," Glock warned as he spit a stream of fire that landed on Abraxis' chest. Abraxis was a grey

wyvern and his magic was that of cold and ice. He immediately countered
the fire burning into his skin with ice. Banishing them to the pits wasn't
part of Glock's plan for them, yet, so he backed off. "Keep your covering,
Darkale; however, one should not hide one's true self."

Darkale searched through Glock's words for the hidden meaning. If
anyone had been hiding their true self, it was Glock. Glock had killed and
eaten the old Sybaris he was bonded to and gained her magic. He must have
sold the missing young wyverns to the humans. That Darkale had done
nothing to stop him made him disgusted with his own weakness. Glock had
killed the Commander and eaten the Commander's Sybaris alive as a test to
see if he would gain her magic. The test had failed, and she was dead. Glock
was sucking the life from his own bonded mate, Solei, and he would turn
on him soon and eat him too, absorbing Solei's fire magic through their
bond. Now Glock planned to kill Toyah and Silverback, he was sure of it.
Darkale had not seen Toyah and Silverback in some time, but he must find
a way to warn them.

Darkale knew that even if Toyah and Silverback aided him and Abraxis
that the four of them weren't nearly strong enough to control Glock. He
had grown too powerful. Darkale didn't know anyone who was strong
enough.

Glock watched Darkale and Abraxis leave the hall. He ordered one of
his two loyal scouts to follow them. The pair went down one street and
then another, obviously looking for someone. When they came to Solis
Square, a place where all the bonded pairs liked to hang out, they noticed
the newly paired Rosetta and Gumbo and went over to speak to them.

When Gumbo looked up and saw Abraxis and Darkale staring at him, he
almost wet himself. No one wanted the attention of the ruling pairs; it
was always a bad thing. They always pushed the bonded pairs to make more
of themselves, to do more, learn more. Gumbo was large and lazy, and he
loved being that way. He didn't want anyone pushing him, except maybe
Rosetta. Now her, he loved.

"What's wrong, Gumbo?" Rosetta could feel his anxiety sharpen. She
followed his gaze and her eyes linked with Darkale's ice blue ones. "Oh,"
she said. Gumbo and Rosetta were a same-color newly-bonded wyvern and
Sybaris, both largely green with red coloration. In Rosetta's case it was her
fiery hair, and for Gumbo, the red was in crimson streaks across his neck.
Green was wild card magic; it would intensify things and sometimes have
strange outcomes. The pair had discovered that they had a powerful magic
together that no one else had. They had been practicing trying to build a
small fire, and when it got out of control, their combined magic had saved

them by teleporting them away. They had been practicing this teleportation ever since. Sometimes they would end up where they wanted to be by thinking of that place together. But if they weren't thinking of the exact same place, the magic could teleport them anywhere. The real trouble was that Gumbo's mind was on the simple side and he easily lost focus.

As Abraxis and Darkale headed towards them, Gumbo panicked and they teleported a street away.

"Sheesh, Gumbo! Why did you do that?" Rosetta yelled at him. "Now they know what we can do!"

Gumbo's nose began to turn a deep red. "Gumbo don't mean to. I sorry Rosetta, don't be mad," Gumbo pouted in his way, his large chin and throat blowing up like a frog's.

Rosetta knew how sensitive Gumbo could be, so she immediately consoled him. "It's all right, sweetling. I'm sure we can explain our rudeness to Darkale." She looked up and saw them turn the corner, approaching them once more. "Oh dear, now Gumbo just relax and let's be friendly." She placed her dainty hand on Gumbo's shoulder and smiled at Darkale, "Hi Darkale, how are you today sir?" Gumbo backed up a few feet.

"Easy now, Gumbo, we just came to say hello," Abraxis told him.

Gumbo took in Abraxis' frightening teeth and how awfully big he was. "You not say hello, you want something," Gumbo told Abraxis suspiciously.

"Well, yes we do, as a matter of fact. How did you get so smart, Gumbo?" Darkale asked him. Gumbo didn't like this at all. "Gumbo knows," was all the chubby wyvern said in return.

Rosetta was almost rendered speechless by the mysterious Darkale. His raven black hair and gorgeous body made every woman want to peek under his face covering. She remembered her manners, though. "What can we help you with, sir?"

Darkale smiled at her then remembered if she could see his smile, she would run away screaming for sure. "Well, now that we see you can teleport, this might not be as dangerous as we thought. That's amazing by the way."

"What do you mean?" asked Rosetta.

Darkale told Rosetta of his fears, about calling a meeting and that when Toyah and Silverback answered the call in the morning, he feared they would be killed or imprisoned by Glock.

"You can teleport to Toyah's home and warn them, and no one will be the wiser."

"Well, yes we could try, but the problem is we have never seen the inside of her home so we can't visualize it. If both of us visualize something different, we could end up anywhere," Rosetta explained.

Abraxis was impatient. "Can't you visualize the outside of her home and then knock on the door?"

Rosetta felt foolish. "Yes, of course we can." With one look at Gumbo, the pair vanished.

Abraxis and Darkale waited for hours but the pair never returned. "We can only hope for the best now and be prepared if the message doesn't reach Toyah and Silverback."

Glock's scout left to report everything to his commander, Glock.

Chapter 50: Rosetta's Warning

Ariah shrieked as Json carried her through the sky. The wind blew through her hair and she felt more alive than she had ever felt before. Json smiled and executed a wide winding climb and then he began a dive straight down, only to swoop up and climb again. "Your balance and riding ability impress me!" Json shouted.

"It's the memories that give me the edge," she smiled ruefully as he climbed, master of the air.

He couldn't help but remember the one other time she had ridden on his back. After she had released him from his human prison, they had both been shot by arrows. He belatedly searched the skies for trouble.

Ariah was thinking the same thing, remembering how it felt to die and how Json must have felt with her still strapped to the saddle on his back. "Thank you for saving my life and giving me a second chance Json. I will never forget what you have done for me, for our race." Json was proud to be bonded to their reborn Queen, he would gladly die for her. Seeing the skies were safe for now, she laughed again as Json twirled, the pair frolicking in the breeze.

Json's black coloring tempered the magic of his dark green coloring, and while he didn't have any magical skills of his own, he was a strong catalyst for Ariah's magic. Ariah was just beginning to figure out what her magic was. She was exploring everything right now. Her coloring was violet, red, and gold. She could produce and throw a small fireball. As Json spun, the sun glittered off the golden scales that ran across her shoulders and down her arms, marking her as royalty. She was glorious, and she was his bonded partner. Her strongest magic seemed to come from her many purple scales, the magic of perception. Ariah's perceptions were growing at a rapid pace. Her senses picked up colors, scents, and sounds long before anyone else. She could tell who was nearby without seeing them. She could see things at far greater distances.

Her knowledge and attention were highly focused. No one in Draconia had the knowledge that Ariah had. Her natal memories consisted of five lifetimes and scores of cultural diversity and kingdoms: her own lifetime and those of Json, King Elijashen, Isladora, and Meluha Crocus.

Ariah looked down and saw her mother Toyah waving her in. Ariah tapped Json on his shoulder and pointed. Json nodded and flew back, landing near Toyah. "What is it, Mother?" Ariah asked. Her hair was windblown, and she was smiling ear to ear.

"I see you can fly very well daughter," Toyah remarked. As Json raised his brows at her, she shrugged and smiled, knowing her offspring's riding ability was excellent, almost equal to her own.

"My Queen, we have decided that when we challenge Glock that we need to be far away from the city," Toyah said, thinking about how radiant her daughter was with her golden scales and golden streaks in her hair. "We want to minimize injury and destruction of all we hold dear, as we know it will be a bloody fight."

Ariah jumped down from Json's back. "Yes, Mother, you're right."

Toyah knew the longer they waited the more time Glock would have to figure out how many of them would stand against him. They needed to act immediately, before Glock learned of their royal Sybaris. Toyah was about to ask them to come in to plan how to get Glock away from the city when Ariah charged her, tackling her mother to the ground.

Json yelled, "Ariah!" at the same time her mother grunted in pain, hitting the ground hard. Suddenly, a large green and red wyvern appeared right where Toyah had been standing, carrying a young Sybaris.

Ariah got to her feet and bent, offering her mother a hand. "I'm sorry, Mother, I felt them coming and I didn't know what else to do."

Toyah looked at Gumbo. "I'm glad you did. I would have been crushed!" Toyah dusted the twigs and dirt from her palms. "Gumbo and Rosetta, what on earth are you doing here?"

Rosetta started to cry. She looked up to Toyah as her role model, and now she had almost hurt her. "Oh, I knew we shouldn't try this!" Her words came out in spurts. "We've come to warn you, Toyah. Darkale made us. Our magic is new, and we have trouble controlling it. Sometimes we think the same thing. But your house. We haven't been here. Only passed by."

The others came from Toyah's house to see what was going on. When Rosetta saw them all glaring at her, she ran and hid behind Gumbo, her one arm around his neck. Gumbo growled at them, his red-streaked neck puffing up to show that he meant to protect her.

The poor Sybaris wasn't making sense, and Ariah could perceive her horror at almost hurting Toyah. Worse, Gumbo looked like he was going to burst. "Everything is all right, Gumbo," Ariah spoke gently and turned to his bondmate. "Rosetta is your name? A beautiful name indeed, especially with those long locks of red hair." Ariah approached them slowly, extending her golden arms out to demonstrate peace.

Rosetta saw the gold. The meaning did not sink in immediately. Rosetta only knew about gold scales from history books where she had seen a picture of a king, once in his golden glory, and she asked quietly, "Are you a Royal?"

Gumbo was already bowing when Ariah said, "Yes, I am your Queen, but do not be frightened. I am loyal to you and all you believe in. Do you accept me?"

Rosetta knelt; she knew this was a blessing for all of them. She said, "Oh, yes. I accept you, my Queen." Rosetta got to her feet, her eyes wide and fearful, but her fear was not aimed at Ariah. "We were sent here to warn you not to answer the summons to come to the Cystine Hall tomorrow, Toyah. Darkale and Abraxis think that Glock is going to try to kill you and Silverback!"

Ariah had closed her eyes. She opened them and stared at her mother. "Glock already knows, Mother. We must find our place to make our stand. He is on his way!"

Toyah didn't question how her daughter and Queen knew this. "Let us get to the steppes like Kaigen suggested. It is a wasteland and there will be less destruction. We will hide at the edge of the forest and try to surprise him."

Five bonded pairs would stand against Glock and Solei. Toyah and Silverback gathered with them in the forest, all eyes on the direction Glock should come from. They really only had one pair with tested offensive power, Kaigen and Masbiar with their lava. Json and Ariah could make a small fireball, but that would be no match against the power of Glock. The others had defensive powers. They spoke quickly, making their battle plans.

"Listen to me," said Ariah. "Through Isladora and Meluha Crocus' memories, I have learned a lot about battle strategy and as your Queen you have all sworn to follow my orders, but I ask that you trust in the battle knowledge I have gained." When no one spoke to challenge her, Ariah turned to Kaigen. "Kaigen, I want you to send a signal through the ground and see if you can reach the Commander and his earth creatures. Tell them we need help."

"Gumbo and Rosetta, if one of us gets in trouble, you teleport in and bring the wounded back here. You are not to engage the enemy. Rosetta nodded, her face intense and showing her mercurial spirit as her fiery hair glowed to match Gumbo's coloring.

Silverback and Toyah, your gift is air and speed. You fly to meet Glock and let him chase you towards us here. Once Glock enters the area, Jayriz and Sully will use their magic to place terrible visions in Glock's head to confuse him. Once that happens, Masbiar and Kaigen will blast Glock with their lava while Json and I hit him from above with our fireballs."

"As your Queen's Guard, I must speak. You can't go into battle, you are royalty!" Toyah said, ever protective of the daughter she must not lose a second time.

"If we do not win this battle, Glock will kill me anyway, Mother," Ariah pointed out.

Kaigen thought about the Queen's orders and then pointed, saying, "Bring Glock to that ridge, Toyah. Masbiar and I can make the thickest lava from where the desert joins the ridge."

Ariah placed her hand on Json's neck. "All or nothing, my friends," Ariah said, mimicking the tone inflection of Meluha Crocus, capturing the nuances of his battle tone exactly. She just hoped that it inspired them as much as it had inspired her.

Chapter 51: Battle with Glock

Kaigen knelt and put both hands flat on the ground. She sent a series of magical pulses into the ground, but other than that she did not know how to communicate with the Commander, who could be who knows where as he traveled under the ground. Now that Kaigen knew other creatures lived down there, she was afraid to send too much of a shockwave. The Commander was more like a large worm now than a wyvern, but at least Kaigen's earth magic had been able to heal him.

Toyah and Silverback left immediately to intercept Glock while the others moved into position. They had all agreed that Glock and Solei had to die, and possibly the other wyverns that Glock used as scouts. There would be no turning back from this course. They would protect their Queen and their way of life. Glock was a direct threat to all they held dear.

Jayriz and Sully had settled into the branches of one of the large trees that bordered the ridge. It would take fifteen Sybaris with their arms spread wide to circle around the trunk of the tree they nestled in. The tree was so large that even with Jayriz's yellow coloring they would be hidden from view and close enough to Glock to send visions of terror into his mind. Rosetta and Gumbo were also hidden in the trees, ready to transport the injured to safety.

"How I know which tree to teleport to?" The stocky Gumbo muttered as they followed the others into position. "They all look same Rosetta, can't tell apart."

Rosetta knew Gumbo was right, if they thought of different places, it could mean disaster.

"Gumbo, see those large statues in the distance?" Rosetta pointed to the steppes as his eyes followed. "Our new plan is to teleport any injured straight to the guardians of the steppes, those large concrete statues." She knew that they marked the entrance to the home of the Protectors, but it was easy to visualize, and under battle stress it would be a good place for Gumbo to envisage.

"Okay, Rosetta." Gumbo was relieved, that would be easy to picture in his mind.

Kaigen and Masbiar had prepared a large pit of lava on the far side of the ridge. If things went as planned, Glock wouldn't see it until it was too late. Although Kaigen and Masbiar had worked together to create the lava, Masbiar still wouldn't speak and Kaigen worried that his mind wasn't completely stable. The lava they could create would be devastating, a natural disaster to be sure; she only hoped Masbiar could hold it together when he saw Glock. The young wyvern harbored hatred for the one who slaughtered his friends.

Json and Ariah circled high above, hopefully higher than Glock would see, as his attention should be fixed on Silverback, flying at mid-altitiude. They would blast him with fireballs from above at the same time Kaigen and Masbiar blasted him from below with lava.

Silverback and Toyah made it all the way back to the city without encountering Glock. *"Do you think we should go to the Cystine Hall?"* Toyah spoke mind-to-mind with Silverback.

"Too dangerous to go there. If we land we may become trapped, and we are only faster in the air," Silverback answered. "Let's fly past his quarters and see if we can locate him."

"Keep your eyes sharp!" Toyah sent. As they neared the mountainside where Glock's quarters were, they banked and slowed a bit, deciding to circle back around for another pass.

From nowhere came an intense inferno as Glock attacked from an angle, singeing Toyah's hair and skin. Silverback tipped to the side to protect her with his thicker skin, and he increased his speed. The chase was on.

"Are you all right?" Silverback sent.

Toyah reached up to feel that most of her was hair gone and the skin on her left side was burned. Glock was a true monster. "Yes, just fly, my friend, sleek and fast as you can." She leaned down low on his back and looked back. What she saw took her breath away and made her lose hope.

Glock had changed. He was bigger, his color a deep blood red. His chest was wider and covered with a gold metal plate. Solei wasn't riding on his back—Glock must have killed and eaten his bonded mate to gain his fire magic! Glock's eyes were red and glowing; his entire body was an inferno. Dark spikes had grown all over his body. He was a ball of burning fire. He was faster, too, keeping up with them. One wrong turn and he could spray his fiery power all over them. Toyah was in a panic. Glock would kill them all! Her daughter, their Queen, was going to die.

"Stay with the plan, Toyah," Silverback commanded. *"Stay the course! None of us can afford to lose focus."* They both felt a blast of fire as Glock tried to reach them with his white-hot torrent.

Sully saw the heat trails in the air before he could see them approaching. "Get ready!" he shouted to Jayriz. They worked together to create an image of an entire army of wyverns hovering in the air and raining fire back at Glock. It wouldn't take him long to recognize it was an illusion, but hopefully by then he would be buried in Kaigen's lava pit.

As Glock chased Silverback, he easily gained on him, laughing because Silverback was no longer the fastest in the sky. Silverback had always been so proud of that, and now Glock would take that away from him. Glock flew over the ridge and slowed, startled by a vast army of wyverns. He banked from chasing Silverback and prepared to engage the nearest threat. He blew a flood of deadly fire through the entire line with purposeful triumph. He had never killed this many before! When nothing happened and the fire went straight through them unchecked, he flew directly towards them, bracing for the impact. When they didn't collide, he realized it was an illusion. Suddenly, he was attacked from above with fireballs, as Json and Ariah flew in to drive him downward. Glock shifted elevation, flying lower to the ground to assess the threat when a large stream of lava erupted from the ground, reaching into the sky and engulfing him completely. He plunged directly into a pit of lava.

The Queen's Guard cheered in triumph as the large wyvern sank in the lava pit. Json and Ariah held back their fireballs and circled above the pit. It was eerily quiet; there was no sign of the horrible beast.

Then suddenly, the entire pit exploded, lava shooting straight up in a giant blast. Json avoided most of the spray, but they were both singed with the small bits. In the pit was a laughing Glock. "Best bath I've had in years!" he shouted, though Json thought he might be faking a lack of injury. Even if the heat hadn't burned him, the lava was immensely heavy, and being struck by several tons of rock had to have wounded the mad wyvern.

Abruptly Glock's eyes narrowed. "Masbiar, I thought you were dead!" More deep laughter in his belly. "Came back for more, did you?" He laughed as Masbiar growled. "You are no match for me. Come and join me, and I'll make you my first student." As Glock climbed out of the pit, they could see that his body was not burned at all by the lava. Fire and earth were the Queen's Guard's only weapons, and he seemed immune to fire.

Masbiar had gone insane and Kaigen knew it. She struggled to unstrap herself from the battle harness as Masbiar considered his next action. Kaigen knew their magic together was stronger. Without her, all Masbiar had in his arsenal was a fire spray nowhere near the strength of the lava blast they could produce together, but the wyvern wasn't listening to reason and she had no choice. Kaigen got the straps free and jumped from Masbiar's back just as Masbiar launched his fire stream at Glock. Masbiar's mind had returned to the human camp where he had defended his life against Glock's fire. Glock fired back, just as he had then, his much larger stream closing the gap fast.

"Masbiar!" Kaigen screamed, but it was no use. She could do nothing but flee. Her body couldn't handle the intense heat these wyverns were creating. Glock's stream quickly overpowered Masbiar's and the combined stream hit his body, killing the smaller red wyvern as he burned up.

Glock stopped firing, a vicious gleam in his horrible red eyes. Those eyes then turned on Kaigen, and his chest expanded for his next kill. Kaigen would not go without a fight. She closed her eyes, hands pointing to the ground. The earth began to shake and rumble, then a crevice opened under Glock's body. He fell into the chasm she created, and then she buried him whole with rock.

The rocks continued to shake, but this time it wasn't Kaigen. Ariah yelled at her from above, "Kaigen! Get to safety! Run!" Kaigen turned and ran, her tattered wings making escape awkward.

Glock scrambled from the rock pile. His skin had been torn across his face and his left eye had been damaged. He was furious. He spotted Kaigen immediately and fired at her. She fell to the side, but the fire caught her tattered wing. She rolled to put it out, then got up and tried to run again, but Glock had gotten himself untangled from the rocks and landed near her, hitting her with his tail and knocking her into the air. Gumbo and Rosetta teleported from the safety of the tree and grabbed her in mid-air. All three of them disappeared.

The pair transported Kaigen to the safety of the steppes and laid her on the ground. Kaigen cried out in pain. She was conscious, but her ribs and chest had been crushed. "Oh my, Kaigen!" Rosetta began crying. "Okay. Okay, just hold on now." She looked at Gumbo hopelessly. "We will be back to help you. Come on now, be strong."

Kaigen was having trouble breathing. They had no choice but to leave her and get back to the fight; both were in tears, not used to the violence. They were frightened, but they transported back to the tree.

Glock looked up to see Json and Ariah circling and he took off running and leapt into the air. Silverback landed and told Toyah to dismount. "The only weapon we have now is our strength, and I can't fight with him with you on my back. You will be killed immediately." Toyah didn't argue. That was her daughter! She unstrapped herself and jumped from his back.

"Go save my daughter! Go save our kingdom!" Toyah yelled at him. The magical pairings they had made were for times of peace; they were not equipped for this war creature.

Glock and Json circled each other. "I knew I should have killed you when you flew home that day," Glock told Json. "Look at the trouble you've caused."

Json and Ariah knew they were defenseless. Json also knew that Gumbo and Rosetta wouldn't be able to transport him, he was too big. But they could transport Ariah if he could get her unstrapped from his body. He knew Ariah wouldn't go willingly.

Ariah knew they had only one defense left. She spread her golden arms and let them sparkle in the sun, showing Glock that she was a royal Sybaris.

Glock saw her golden scales. They were real golden scales, not the fake gold like he had strapped on his body. For a moment he toyed with the thought of bonding to her and then eating her to see if he would gain her royal status. He knew now that it didn't work that way, however. There had never been a golden wyvern, only the Sybaris had ever been born royalty.

Ariah yelled, her voice one of authority, "I command you to stop this, Glock!" She held her arms out, pointing at him. "As your Queen, I order you to the ground!"

Glock knew that royalty must be obeyed; it was in his genes to obey. Then he looked at his golden chest and the gold he had placed over his claws and how strong he was compared to her pathetically weak frame, and he knew that if the gods were going to choose royalty, he should be their choice. He was stronger than them all, he always had been. And he was smarter than them all.

Look how easy it had been to kill the Commander and take over the kingdom.

Json had been waiting for his attack. He looked at Gumbo and Rosetta to make sure they were watching and circled wider to approach the trees. When Glock fired upon Ariah, Json turned his belly to the fire, something that was against the nature of any animal, and he let the fire burn away the cinch for the saddle. The saddle broke free and Ariah fell. Glock flew to intercept her, his gaping jaws wide. He was going to eat her. Silverback came flying out of nowhere and slammed into Glock's enormous body. Json attacked as well, slamming into Glock, both wyverns dragging him back to the earth. Gumbo and Rosetta burst from the trees, grabbed Ariah's falling body, and transported their Queen to safety.

Ariah was shaken when she suddenly appeared at the steppes. She saw Kaigen lying unmoving and ran to her. "Go back and get my mother!" Ariah yelled at Rosetta and Gumbo. They disappeared and reappeared a few moments later with Toyah.

"Json and Silverback are all alone with that monster!" Ariah cried out as her mother knelt on the ground to try to heal Kaigen.

"My injuries are too bad, aren't they?" Kaigen gasped as she whispered to Toyah. Seeing the look of distress on Toyah's face she said, "I'm going to die here in the steppes."

"Hush now," Toyah said, but she knew Kaigen spoke the truth. Her broken body would not be mended.

"I want to be buried here, near the guardians," Kaigen told them, her breathing labored. When they didn't answer she repeated, "Bury me here. I have no family and it is my dying wish." Kaigen wanted to see Von one more time; that was her true dying wish. But if she couldn't do that, then she would be buried near him.

"We are your family, Kaigen," Ariah told her. "We will bury you here if it is your wish."

"Thank you, my Queen," she gasped as her eyes closed. She wheezed, trying to draw breath into her crushed lungs.

Ariah began to pray as she had learned from Isladora's memories. She prayed to the one Creator, falling to her knees and praying that His will be done. Ariah knew that Isladora's God was all powerful and that He had a plan and a purpose to bring peace, prosperity, and stability to the earth. Glock was not a part of that plan. He was evil, and this fight was about good versus evil.

She prayed in earnest as white foam spittle tinged with blood dribbled from Kaigen's open mouth.

*****

Silverback and Json crashed to the ground with Glock, and a terrible fight ensued. Silverback held onto Glock's mouth, holding it shut as Json tried to bite through his neck. As the trio grappled, Json blew his acid stream at Glock's exposed belly. Glock's armored tail swung, knocking Json to the side, and within seconds, Glock was able to free himself from Silverback's grip. He bit into Silverback's exposed neck; Silverback was smooth and sleek and had no spikes to stop the bite. Json slammed into Glock again, but it was too late for Silverback. Glock then slammed Json against the rocks, where he lay unmoving.

Glock jumped back into the sky and began to search the ground for Ariah. There could be only one royal, and that was him. After he killed her, he would go back to Sybaris and declare himself royal. He was a little surprised that he hadn't thought of that himself, that it took seeing a royal

Sybaris to remember that he could be a king. He could be anything he wanted to be. No one was strong enough to stop him. He let out a victorious roar.

Glock saw the reflection of light against gold first. The three pathetic Sybaris were completely defenseless against him, and he landed, deciding to revel at their pitiful state. Too bad he had no pity. He had stopped burning when he landed, but he was still a terrifying beast to behold. He now had a jagged cut across his left eye and he glowed with evil and hate. His teeth still dripped Silverback's blood.

Kaigen opened her eyes to see the nightmare that put her in her death throes. Glock's attention was on their Queen, and Toyah had shoved herself in front of her daughter. Nearby was a large boulder, and with her last piece of life force, Kaigen hurled it at Glock. It crashed into his side, but all it did was anger him.

As he drew in breath to rain lethal fire at them, the ground began to shake. Suddenly, the Commander emerged, shielding the three sybaris from the worst of the fire. The blasting flame continued on and on, but the Commander's thick carapace deflected the heat.

The Commander had no way to attack, so it was just a matter of time before he could no longer protect them from Glock. Sooner or later, Glock would reach the Sybaris and then it would be over.

A flash of white appeared out of nowhere, a man. His glittering armor was white. He had a white shield and a white sword, and his cape trailed behind him. His face was partially hidden by a hood, and what little could be seen was covered by a mask. He was incredibly fast as he rocketed across the sky. He swept in with his sword held high to attack Glock, drawing the power-mad wyvern's attention away from the Sybaris and stopping the stream of fire.

As Glock roared and lurched toward the intruder, the flying man arced up in a circle and then suddenly down, his sword slicing through the neck of the great beast in a single deadly stroke.

Ariah watched as her prayers were answered and Glock's bloody crimson head tumbled to the ground, the dreadful eye staring and vacant. It was done. A prayer and an answer, she marveled.

The man landed and sheathed his sword. He ignored Ariah and Toyah and strode straight to Kaigen. The Commander backed away to give him room. The man moved his hands along her body and her caved-in ribs snapped back into place. Her lungs began to fill with air. He produced a flask of a liquid substance and dribbled a little into her mouth.

The liquid running down her cheek roused her, the trickle finding its way to the hollow of her throat. Kaigen opened her eyes, and when her vision cleared she was startled to see that the kind hands belonged to a masked face. She could breathe again; *This must be the next life*, she thought. He moved her hair where it covered her face and cupped her cheek. "Who are you?" she whispered.

All at once others like him streamed from between the guardians. Some came on foot, some flew, but they all approached with blinding speed. "The Protectors," Ariah said. They looked just like the creatures she saw in Meluha Crocus' memories. She bowed immediately. Toyah followed suit, dropping to one knee, her head bent towards the ground.

The Protectors hadn't ventured outside of their territory in a long time. They flew out to the other wounded, healing them as they found them. One Protector landed near Toyah and wordlessly began to heal her burns. Her scalp became whole again and her hair grew back.

Kaigen noticed that the other protectors weren't masked. She could see their skin glistening like diamonds in the sunlight. "Von?"

Von removed his mask, and his beauty threatened to once again take her breath away. "You wanted to see me so much, that you would be buried in this awful wasteland?" he asked Kaigen, smiling a small smile.

"Oh, yes." Kaigen breathed as she smiled back.

Chapter 52: The Protectors

The Protectors healed the wyverns and Sybaris alike. There would be scars, both physical and mental, but the body could be healed. Sadly, Masbiar was beyond their restorative skills. The Protectors were willing enough to heal but they did not like to bring creatures back from the dead. It often went wrong, and it was against their customs.

Silverback and Kaigen had taken the most damage. The bite to Silverback's neck would have been fatal and he had almost bled out on the ground. The Protectors healed the wound, and while Silverback would be weak until his body could replace the lost fluid, he would live. Json's bones were repaired where he had been thrown against the rocks, and the burns on his stomach were healed. The Protectors did not utter a word.

Two Protectors stood next to the Commander. "What are they doing?" Toyah asked.

Ariah watched as they examined the Commander, touching here and there along his carapace. "They are discussing the Commander," Ariah told her mother.

Finally, one of them spoke, his voice taking on a note of forced briskness, "Who did this work?" He pointed to the Commander.

"What do you mean, work?" Ariah questioned.

"This used to be a wyvern, did it not?" The strange man requested of them.

"Yes, he once was, our lead wyvern actually. The Commander was gravely injured and Kaigen healed him with her earth magic the best she could," Ariah told them as Von and Kaigen approached.

The Commander didn't like being discussed where he couldn't hear them and he turned to lumber closer. Kaigen looked at him as he settled near. "The Commander was the most beautiful of all our wyverns," she said. She took a deep breath and forced a neutral tone as she continued, "He was white and black. I couldn't seem to make the color he once was. His pale pink color and his segmented carapace are very different. I think I made him look more like an armored worm, but he asked for this. As you can see, his once beautiful wyvern claws are now pincers for digging and tunneling."

"I did this work, as you have called it, with my earth magic," Kaigen mused. "I could not regrow his scales, so I made him as he asked me to."

The Protector turned to look at the Commander for confirmation. The Commander said, "Yes, I am exactly as I want to be. I am needed below the surface for greater things," his voice colored by a reluctant humor.

The Protector did not smile but turned to look at another Protector, clearly displeased, but said, "As you will." His white teeth flashed as he added, "We do not have a problem with what she made you, Commander, the design is brilliant, and we wish to know where her knowledge originates."

Ariah tried to restrain an unladylike snort. She did not like his interest in Kaigen, but they had just saved their lives. "In that case, we would be honored to have all of you for dinner at our meeting place, the Cystine Hall, to show our appreciation to you for saving our lives." Ariah looked at Kaigen, who was attached to Von, her arm threaded through his. "I'm sure Kaigen would be glad to tell you more at that time?"

"Can Von be there? I would like to tell you very much, but only if Von is there." Kaigen always got right to the point with her direct manner. Von looked uncomfortable as the eldest Protector scrutinized him.

"How does she know your name?" the elder Protector asked Von.

Von shifted uncomfortably, knowing he was caught. "I have been taking care of my exiled father. I know it is against the rules, but he has grown old and he needs me. If this means that I too shall be exiled, then it shall be."

As if in an answer to a question, Von looked at the eldest of the Protectors and nodded. The elder said, nodding towards his counterpart and Von, "The three of us will come to your Hall tomorrow at dusk." Then, as if some silent horn had blown, the Protectors left, passing back between the guardians to their home, some walking, some floating.

Kaigen did not want Von to be in trouble. "Do you not see how wonderful he is?" Kaigen asked. "Tell them Commander, tell them how wonderful Von is."

The Commander sat in silence until the Protectors left. "I don't know anything about them, Kaigen, but if I were you, I would be wary of their interest in your knowledge," the Commander told her. "We don't know anything about them, and you saw today how easily they destroyed Glock after we couldn't handle him."

"Von would never let them hurt me," she said, her eyes narrowing.

"Ah Kaigen, don't be a fool, we can all be blinded by love. Von may be exiled now simply because you know his name," warned the Commander. "They are a hard race and not to be trifled with."

They made their way back to their homes, exhausted and hungry but

thankful. All of them felt the loss of Masbiar. Ariah was silent and thoughtful about her new faith in Isladora's God. She had asked and He had provided. One of Isladora's favorite passages had been, "I sought the Lord,
and he answered me; he delivered me from all my fears." Now that mantra
had been passed to Ariah, who was still reeling from her first spiritual experience.

As they flew home, Silverback and Json decided that the safest place
for their Queen to make her home was on the mountainside close to the
wyverns, and so they all landed there. Toyah argued, "She is Sybaris, she
needs the comforts of the Sybaris. She cannot fly. Every time she wishes to
go somewhere, you would have to carry her down the mountain."

Json piped up. "I know I don't even need to say this, but I will gladly
carry her."

Toyah was incensed. "You are missing my point. Look, I know we
were attacked by Glock, but he was the only wyvern like him. There is no
need to keep Ariah out of reach of her people."

Silverback cautioned, "We still haven't found his scouts, and we don't
know where Darkale, Abraxis, Arrington, and Bedaiko stand."

Json growled, "The scouts better be far from here. The Queen needs to
be close to her subjects. I say give her…"

Ariah interrupted them all, saying, "I appreciate all of you trying to look
out for me, but I already researched this and thought this through. I wish to
be housed in the Royal Court. It was built for royalty. It is above the city
but within easy distance and it is right below the first level of wyvern caves.
Its walls are thick and Json tells me about secret passageways that lead
through the mountain."

Shaking his head, dirt and wyvern blood dried in the lines of his face,
Silverback cautioned, "It is haunted, my Queen. No one goes there."

Ariah was not to be sidetracked. "Regardless, it is where you will take
me now."

Toyah gave a soft grunt, "We won't be able to find servants willing to
live there."

"I will find people to work for me for pay, or do without." Ariah remembered her time as a slave with no future. "No longer will there be any
unpaid servants, nor slaves, I forbid it."

"I will be with her; that will become my home as well," Json proclaimed, making Ariah smile in an unalloyed flicker of joy.

Toyah finally spoke, "I will bring you some clothes to wear for our
meeting with the Protectors tomorrow, until you can have suitable attire
made. I will also make sure the preparations for the dinner with the Protec-

tors are under way." She could already picture the gown her daughter would wear, one fit for the Queen she was. "Silverback, you and I must go to the pits and see if Arrington and Bedaiko are still incarcerated, do you feel up to it?"

Silverback gave a soft grunt, "No, but they would come for us, I think." He actually wasn't sure what Arrington would do.

Ariah was so proud of her mother and the way she handled things. "Thank you, Mother."

Toyah climbed on Silverback and they took off, headed for the pits. Neither of them spoke; they didn't know what they would find.

The pits were large holes in the ground covered with metal grates. Before Glock began imprisoning his own people, they hadn't been used for anything. Silverback landed near one of the smaller pits. The area was silent and foreboding, and the stench was almost unbearable. Toyah looked at Silverback with apprehension, not knowing what they would find that could smell that bad. Silverback tentatively called out to the wyvern, "Bedaiko?" They approached the only pit that was held closed with a pin and Silverback removed it.

Toyah called out, "Arrington?"

Suddenly, a tiny wyvern flew out of the hole through the grate. He flew through Toyah's long hair and then began attacking Silverback, trying to drive him back by fluttering around his head and pecking at his eyes.

"Whoa, there!" Silverback tried to defend himself without hurting the tiny creature. "We are friends of Bedaiko. We are here to help!" Silverback protested. The creature stopped and flew back down into the grate. Silverback slowly raised the pit door, letting it fall to the side. When they looked into the pit, Bedaiko was curled up on his side and Arrington was unconscious or dead, held in the circle of the wyvern's body. Bedaiko closed his eyes against the sudden flood of light.

"Lower me down with your tail," Toyah said grimly. She grabbed Silverback's tail and he slowly lowered her into the pit. She had no room to stand so she knelt on Bedaiko's body to see if Arrington was alive. The dove-sized wyvern had flown to sit on Bedaiko's side, near Arrington's prone body. Toyah checked his pulse—it was there, but faint. She was shocked to see the proud Arrington, who always dressed to perfection, looking and smelling like death. They were covered in muck and slime. The pit was too small, and they were covered in their own waste.

Bedaiko spoke, his voice sounded gravelly and unused, "Our little friend has kept us alive. He brought us the bonding manna and water, but he is so small he could not carry much through the grate. I tried to keep

Arrington's body out of the waste as much as I could. Arrington hasn't woken since last night, and I fear for his life." The little friend chirped in agreement.

Toyah was nauseous from the stench and now it covered her hands and arms as well. Toyah looked at Silverback, and he curled his tail around her arm and held on to her. She closed her eyes and placed her hands on Arrington, sending her perceptive magic into Arrington's body. "You did well my friend, but he is dehydrated and sick from the waste. We must get him out of here and to the doctor."

"I cannot stand up without crushing him. Silverback will have to lift him," Bedaiko said. Toyah realized that he must have not moved from this position in a long while.

Silverback wrapped his long tail around Arrington as Toyah lifted him by the arms, his head falling back. She helped balance him as Silverback lifted him from the hole. He gently placed him on the ground and then lifted Toyah out. She was filthy and lost control of herself as the nausea overwhelmed her. When she threw up on the ground, she was careful not to wipe her mouth with her dirty hands.

"Bedaiko, try to jump out, we will move back." Silverback lifted Arrington again, drawing his body away from the pit. Bedaiko hadn't used his muscles in weeks, but after several attempts, he cleared the side of the pit. Wyverns were much hardier than their Sybaris counterparts, but the time in the pit had definitely taken a terrible toll on him. His scales were dull and his muscles were weak. And he was filthy.

Silverback thought he could carry both Toyah and Arrington. He asked, "Bedaiko, can you lift Arrington onto my back, then Toyah can hold on to him? Do you think you can fly? I can carry these two if you can fly yourself to the hall."

Bedaiko loaded his bonded partner onto Silverback and Toyah climbed on behind Arrington to hold him. Bedaiko leapt into the air. It was rough going but he could maintain his own weight in the air. "I'll be right back," he said. They watched as the blue wyvern flew off towards the lake.

A few minutes later he came back, obviously having plunged into the lake to wash off the muck. He still needed a thorough cleansing, but most of the waste debris was gone. "I saw Darkale and Abraxis at the side of the lake. Darkale looked hurt," Bedaiko told Silverback.

Silverback leapt into the air. The take-off was tricky, but they managed it. Toyah tried hard to hold her breath but the stench from Arrington still got to her until they were under way. The breeze helped. She couldn't fathom the horror that being in that pit must have been.

They delivered Arrington to the infirmary and Bedaiko went to get cleansed. The wyverns had a large bathing chamber and paid Sybaris servants to help them scrub. Toyah left Arrington with the nursing staff and went to bathe herself. Silverback decided to fly to the lake to see what Darkale and Abraxis were up to. He still wasn't quite sure where the ruling pair had stood with Glock, although they had sent Gumbo and Rosetta with a warning.

As Silverback circled over the lake, he could see signs of a battle. Trees had been crushed and spattered with acid that one of Glock's scouts could spew. Darkale was a blue Sybaris who could control water and Abraxis was a grey wyvern who could control the cold.

Together, they were powerful enough to make ice with a water source near. Silverback thought he knew what happened, but he flew down to make sure.

"Is it safe to assume that you made scout ice-cubes?" Silverback approached Abraxis warily. This close to a large body of water was a dangerous place to be with this pair.

"Yes, my friend." The mighty Abraxis muttered, "Darkale and I decided to take them out before Glock returned, but now we are in no shape to fight...Darkale is caught in a nightmare." Abraxis was distraught with worry.

Silverback looked at Darkale's prone form; his eyes were closed and moving in a fast twitch. The second scout's magic was that of waking dreams, or nightmares if he so chose, and he had obviously attacked Darkale. Abraxis added, "When Glock gets back, we will all be dead. You should leave here."

"Glock is dead," Silverback said gladly.

Abraxis turned his snout towards Silverback in surprise. "How can that be?" he whispered. Silverback told him about the battle, about the Protectors, the new Queen, and the upcoming dinner.

Abraxis shed a tear that immediately turned to ice, "We are freed," his words accompanied by the clacking together of his rows of teeth.

Silverback felt his own tears well up. "Yes. The scouts are dead?"

"Quite," another clack of teeth. "We froze them in ice and wedged them under large boulders at the bottom to drown. We have been here for hours, long enough for the wyverns to run out of air," Abraxis said.

Silverback looked out over the middle of the lake. "Why hasn't the nightmare been broken?" With the nightmare scout dead, Darkale should have woken up.

Abraxis shook his head. "I don't know. Help me load him on my back and we will fly him home."

Chapter 53: Darkale

Darkale was taken to the infirmary, his fearsome large grey wyvern Abraxis beside him. The pair made the Sybaris nurses nervous, one with his large vicious teeth, the other who was so hideous that he kept part of his face hidden. Abraxis, also known for his intelligent mind, intimidated both visually and intellectually. He snapped at the nurses, gnashing his rows of teeth, demanding the best care for his bonded colleague.

"Sir, we can take care of him better without you threatening us," Chablis, the head doctor calmly told Abraxis. When he didn't back off she said, "You don't frighten me, so just go sit over there if you can't be useful." Chablis pointed to the far corner. She was used to taking charge and used to the high emotional state one could be in when someone you loved was badly hurt.

Abraxis growled and stared at the stunning pink Sybaris but did as she bid. He ambled to the far corner to sit and watch. He knew if Darkale were awake, he would be mortified that Chablis could see his face, but the covering had been lost in the battle.

The wyvern/human mixture of the Sybaris race was a beautiful thing to the inhabitants of Draconia; each one of the Sybaris was unique. No one was sure how their race began, the DNA fusion that created both scales and the human skin; the scales were of all shapes, colors, and sizes. So was the magic. Darkale was a particularly handsome Sybaris everywhere but his mouth. His blackish brown hair with dark blue hues fell in waves around his face. His ice blue scales covered his muscular torso and arms. Diamond-shaped scales framed his forehead, stopping just above his eyebrows. The most beautiful feature though, were his eyes. They were framed by black eyebrows and black eyelids. His eyes were both striking and mysterious. When he was awake and animated, his eyebrows arched in a manner that made him look stately. Darkale and Abraxis had been part of the ruling pairs for a long time, their intelligence widely used for planning and building. Darkale also taught engineering principles to the young Sybaris, but socially he was a recluse. That had to do with the rest of his face.

Most Sybaris had never seen Darkale's mouth; he kept it hidden under a mask. He had been hatched with a mouth that was half human and half wyvern, a freak of nature for the Sybaris. A feature was typically either all wyvern or all human, not half of each. Darkale had human lips and sharp wyvern teeth.

Chablis lovingly checked all of Darkale's body. She had known him for many years, and they passed each other in the hall almost daily, but to her regret, he simply did not notice her. "Well, Abraxis, I don't see that his body is injured. We need a yellow Sybaris or wyvern to consult with on intellect and visions. He is caught in a memory dream. That scout of Glock's is the only one I know, can you go find him?"

"That scout is who put him in this state and he's dead, we killed him. Have you not heard that Glock is dead?" With that statement, the entire infirmary stopped what they were doing and looked up. They all froze, then smiled quietly. They immediately went back to work like the highly trained staff they were.

Toyah, having bathed, returned to check on Arrington and Darkale. "Yes, Glock and his two scouts are dead," she affirmed. She told Chablis about the battle and the Protectors while the beautiful doctor worked.

Arrington was beginning to come around, the fluids and manna they were pumping into him doing the trick. Bedaiko had returned to the infirmary, now cleansed, and he, too, was receiving the healing manna, his tiny blue wyvern not leaving his side. "I've decided to call him Manna, since he is the only reason that we are alive."

"I didn't know that wyverns could be so small. Where did you find him?" one of the nurses asked Bedaiko.

"He just flew into the pits and brought us what manna and water he could carry. He kept us alive in that horrible place," Bedaiko told her.

Toyah saw the way Chablis didn't leave Darkale's side. She saw the way the doctor lovingly touched his cheek and chest every time she checked on him. The doctor was in love, but Toyah had known that. They all worked together in the Cystine Hall and the doctor's attraction to him over the years was apparent to everyone but Darkale.

"The problem is, we need a yellow Sybaris or wyvern to help guide his mind back home," Chablis told Toyah as she adjusted the blankets around Darkale.

"There's Jayriz," Toyah told her. At the doctor's puzzled look, Toyah added, "He was one of the young male wyverns that was captured by the humans and held in the human camp."

"How could a wyvern be captured by a human?" Chablis wondered aloud. Toyah told her, "Glock gave the purple cone flowers to the humans."

"But those flowers are for surgeries only, they are dangerous! The wyverns could have been killed!" Chablis was outraged.

"That was what Glock was hoping; anyway, he didn't care. He wanted the young male wyverns gone so they couldn't challenge him."

Chablis agreed. "It is good that we are free from him. Please go get Jayriz and we will see if we can wake Darkale from his dream sleep."

Toyah left and returned with Jayriz. He was a smaller yellow wyvern, his head was pointed like an arrow, and his horns pointed straight back, making him look slim. His wings were transparent and more fragile than scaled wings. "How may I assist, doctor?" he asked politely.

Chablis took him over to Darkale. She didn't like the way Jayriz avoided looking at Darkale's mouth, but at least he didn't grimace. "He is caught in a dream created by another yellow wyvern that is now dead."

Jayriz laid his clawed appendage upon Darkale's head, he then closed his eyes and began to enter Darkale's mind. Darkale was in a dream loop and he was aware of it, but he just didn't care. The dream cycle began when he was a young Sybaris. He and his best friend played together every day. They ran through the forest, swam in the lake, and studied the stars and their books together. Darkale loved her deeply. She never looked at his mouth in the strange way that others did; she didn't seem to see his mouth at all. For years they grew closer and closer, and Darkale knew that they were destined to be together forever. As they grew older, Darkale wanted to show his deepening affection for her. Other Sybaris their age kissed, but he knew that it wasn't possible for him to kiss her with his ugly mouth. He made plans to take her on a hike around the lake, and then he would hold her hand and tell her how he felt.

He decided to surprise her. When he came around the corner of her home, he saw her with another male. Her back was pressed against the wall of her home as they kissed. He ran to her and grabbed the male, throwing him to the ground. He immediately summoned water from the nearby well and doused the male, driving him further back. The boy was sputtering and his friend was screaming for him to stop.

"What are you doing? Stop it!" She began crying and calling up her own magic to defend the boy. When Darkale realized that she meant to use her magic on him, he stopped the flow of water and bent over, breathing hard.

"Are you crazy?" she yelled at Darkale.

"He was pressing you up against the wall and kissing you!" Darkale yelled back, his ugly teeth flashing. The boy got to his feet and ran around the side of the house; he didn't want anything to do with these crazy creatures.

"I wanted him to kiss me, stupid, and now you've ruined everything!"

"You are my girlfriend, not his!" Darkale was fuming.

"I would never be your girlfriend! Do you hear me, you freak? Never!" She ran into the house.

Darkale did not talk to her again. He began isolating himself. Her rejection had hurt him to the core. He continued this isolation for so long that it became a lonely habit. He poured himself into his studies, becoming the best student, and he never reached out to another female Sybaris. His horrible face was not something a female could overcome. He began wearing the mask when he went out in public. His intelligent mind led him to eventually become one of the ruling pairs.

Then the dream went back to Glock. Glock, who was always trying to make him remove the face covering. Glock used his weakness to isolate Darkale further from the others, to keep him under his control. Now, Darkale just didn't care anymore. He no longer wanted to live.

Jayriz opened his eyes. "He can come out of the dream state any time he wants to. He has lost the will to live, to continue. He believes that because of his face that he is unlovable, and he no longer wants to live his segregated life. It seems rejection by a close friend at a young age took its toll on the male we see today."

Chablis looked at the others shyly and said, "Tell him that I wish to be with him, that I always have. To me, he is the most beautiful male in Draconia."

"I cannot speak to him in his mind, the dream state blocks my magic. I am sorry, doctor," Jayriz said and turned to leave.

Arrington woke and was taken home. The others left.

The doctor was alone with her patient. She talked to him long into the night. She told him about her feelings for him. She touched his mouth, wondering at this thing that had ruined his life. It really wasn't bad at all, just different. He was an amazing man with a gorgeous body and mind. She told him that. The doctor knew that rejection at a young age could be hard to overcome. She asked him to try. She held him. He did not respond.

She began yelling at him for ignoring her. She yelled at him at how long she had waited for him to even notice her. That right under his eyes, she had always loved him. He didn't have to be alone, he chose to be alone. She fell onto his chest crying. Finally, she sat up and slapped him hard. Then horrified that she, a doctor, had struck one of her patients, and an unconscious one at that, she turned and held her head in her hands.

She felt a hand tentatively touch her shoulder. She turned in disbelief to look at him. His ice blue eyes bored into her soul and butterflies erupted in her stomach. He captivated her.

"You have always loved me?" he asked her, but he already knew it was true. He had felt her attention all these years, but he was too scared to reach out towards it. He knew she watched him every day, he even knew she was interested in him. The trust he now felt came from years of watching her never take another male proved her loyalty to him, her want of him. He was ready to trust one more time. The doctor said nothing; she leaned down and gently kissed his mouth, careful to avoid the razor-sharp teeth.

Chapter 54: Dinner

Toyah excelled at making elaborate plans on short notice. After a healing rest, she went straight to the Cystine Hall the next morning. She wasn't sure what beings of light ate for dinner, so she ordered a variety of fruit and vegetable dishes to be served along with some fish from the lake. She knew keeping things simple would be the best way.

The servants went about cleaning the hall. They did excellent work on their own, and Toyah wasn't worried about their ability to make a good impression. She could not remember a time when the Protectors had graced their hall. It was truly a historic occasion, and everyone was feeling the festive mood.

Arrington was much better this morning and would be coming to meet the Protectors and his Queen. It was quite a momentous day for the government of Draconia. Only three ruling pairs remained: Toyah and Silverback, Arrington and Bedaiko, and Darkale and Abraxis. Now that they had a Queen, he knew that things would change.

The ruling pairs met early that afternoon with Ariah. Arrington, always the skeptic, did not believe it until he saw her golden scales for the first time. His eyes alighted upon her. Never had he seen such a glorious sight as her golden scales! The trauma of all he had been through and the hope that she represented brought him to his knees in tears. Every protective instinct he had was drawn towards her. Json stood proudly at her side looking very much like a war wyvern. Ariah was dressed in a sleeveless yellow gown with a simple circlet of gold around her forehead.

Arrington, Bedaiko, Darkale, and Abraxis immediately swore fealty to her, and she to them.

Queen Ariah spoke, "I would like to maintain the same ruling pair system that we have always had in place. It has worked for years and what is not broken does not need to be fixed. You will all be equal advisors just as you have always been. Json and I will be the fourth pair, but what I rule upon as Queen of Draconia shall be. I promise to never take my position for granted and to never make an important decision without hearing and weighing your input. Your thoughts are important to me, and I have a lot of learning to do." Ariah let this sink in, then she continued, "I have the wisdom and memories of three different races, and because of these memories

I feel that we may need to be more involved with the world."

The others looked surprised at this, but none of them grumbled. "Actually, Majesty, if I may speak? I've been saying that for years." Arrington smiled at her, his manner charming. "We have many interesting items we could trade if we came down from our mountain."

Ariah smiled at him. "I have heard how ingenious you are Arrington," and he blushed at her compliment. "I look forward to many discussions and new directions with you."

"One thing is for certain, we are riding the winds of change," Silverback observed.

After a long discussion, the ruling pairs left to get ready for the dinner that evening with the Protectors. Word had traveled fast, first about Glock's death and then about the visit from the mysterious Protectors. The entire city held an air of festivity but also an air of foreboding. A single Protector had killed Glock with one strike, so they were obviously extremely dangerous, and no one really knew where the Protectors stood on anything. It had been too long since the two races had met, but at least they were coming to dinner peacefully and not to invade.

The servants, paid now because of their new queen, had done wonders with the hall. Everything was clean and spotless. The lighting from the chandeliers cast a soft glow upon the dinner table, which was set simply with golden plates and white linens. The wyverns had all been to the baths and their scales shone in the light as they mingled with each other at one end of the room. Every moment was more treasured, more precious having been through what they had suffered.

Arrington arrived in his formal wear, looking dapper but a little thin. Darkale was in his usual dark blue to black attire, his face covering in place. On his arm was the beautiful doctor, Chablis, her pink hair styled in an elaborate coil at the top of her head. They made a stunning couple, and Toyah was glad to see that Darkale's eyes were smiling. Toyah had left her long brown hair cascading down her back. She wore a lavender velvet gown that accentuated her curves, her swirled silver horns shining from her head. The gown that she had lent Ariah was royal red with gold patterns on the bodice and down the train. Ariah left her hair down and the gold strands sparkled in the soft light. Kaigen was still healing from the battle, but she arrived in a silver and blue gown. Even with her tattered wings she was quite beautiful, Ariah thought. When the appointed time came, the three Protectors suddenly appeared.

Kaigen was the first to notice them and she gasped with surprise, bringing the others' attention to their guests. The Protectors were all dressed in white with a red sash around their waists. Their skin seemed to glisten as if with microscopic diamonds. They each carried a variety of weapons that they placed slowly and calmly on a table by the door. They also had strange metal pieces that circled their upper arms. Ariah did not like that they brought weapons to dinner.

As if reading her mind, the female Protector spoke, "Not to worry, Queen Ariah, they are gifts."

"Hello, Von," Kaigen said shyly.

Von smiled back at her and then warily looked at the Elder. "Hello, Kaigen. How are you feeling?"

"I'm just perfect now that you are here."

Toyah knew she had to stop this nonsense. "Please, if you all would like to have a seat, we can get started with the meal."

The servants brought out each course, and Toyah was relieved to see that the Protectors enjoyed most of it. They made small talk, asking about the customs and traditions in Draconia until dinner was cleared away.

"What of the customs where you come from?" Ariah queried. "Do you call your home the steppes, like we do, or does it have a name?"

All attempts to learn about the Protectors were cleverly but politely evaded. Ariah realized that while the Sybaris and wyverns had been answering freely, these people were not.

Ariah tried again. "Do you have given names, or are you just called Elder? Is this your wife, and does she have a name?"

The Elder had grown agitated with Ariah's questioning. He ignored her queries and stated, "Now to get down to the reasons why we are here. The first is Kaigen's magic." He looked at Kaigen, who was startled, as she had been completely focused on Von. "How did you learn to design the carapace you made for the Commander?"

Kaigen did not like the way he spoke to her and she leaned closer to Von. "I told you already, sir, I did not learn it anywhere. It is simply in my head." She was young but she was sure she was being treated with contempt.

"A design that brilliant doesn't just 'come from your head,' child, it comes from years of training and long practice in the art of bioengineering," the Elder instructed, using a word none of them had heard. "Who are your parents, then?"

"I never knew my parents, if you must know!" Kaigen, who was already a high-strung, emotional girl, was getting upset.

Toyah stepped into the conversation. "Kaigen was found by the lake as a child. She just appeared one day and we took her in and raised her as one of us. We knew early on that she had a lot of earth magic, so we taught her to control it so she wouldn't hurt anyone." Toyah looked at the young girl lovingly. "She has knowledge about magical things without explanation, as she has never had formal training or schooling on the matters that she knows about. It is just a part of who she is. A brilliant young female."

"Ah, but you agree that she is not Sybaris?" the Elder's female counterpart asked.

"No, she does not seem to be Sybaris, as she doesn't have a scale on her body," Toyah answered cautiously. "Yet we did successfully bond her to Masbiar so I think we could say she is a unique Sybaris."

The female Protector said bluntly, "We want to take her home with us for testing."

"Absolutely not!" Queen Ariah stated flatly, her hand slamming down on the table. "She is not an experiment!"

Kaigen was growing frightened. She knew they could take her if they wanted to. "Von, you aren't going to let them take me, are you?"

Von looked at the Elder and his partner and squared his shoulders. He said gravely, "No, I will not."

The Elder was shocked at Von's protectiveness towards Kaigen, but he quickly schooled his features to hide his surprise. "We will discuss this at a later date, Von." He cleared his throat. "This brings me to the second reason we are here." He looked at Queen Ariah, "You have grown complacent, which always makes room for evil. With no rules, evil can easily find a foothold. You should always remain true to your standards, checking them over and over for outliers. If you find an outlier, you must study the cause."

"Are you referring to Glock?" Toyah asked.

"Silence. Listen. Learn. To govern is to be guided by more than just whim and sentiment. You cannot vacillate in your view of what is right and wrong. Your view of what evil is must remain unchanged. Without this moral direction you are lost at sea with no compass to guide you." The Elder paused to look at each of them. Finally, his unnatural blue-tinged eyes gazed sharply at Ariah. "All of you knew that Glock was not honorable, yet you left him in a position of power and turned the other cheek when he stepped out of line."

In the silence he grew even bolder. "Your failure as queen to oust this predator is why we have had to involve ourselves again with your race." He looked disgusted as he continued, "You allowed this evil creature to grow strong in your midst. You should have destroyed him long before he ate his own bondmate and took her magic for himself. You should have stopped him then. You are a failure as a queen."

Ariah was not alarmed by his assertions. She calmly spoke, "You judge me as a failure even though you just met me. I say to you that you are too quick to judge, for you have not bothered to learn anything of us before you passed your unfair judgement. Yes, it is true that Glock's evil was allowed to grow unchecked, but you are not correct that I am a failure as a queen. I wasn't here at that time. I was reborn a short time ago." Ariah could feel her growing magic circle her belly and her heart as she stood, her golden scales flashing in the light. "You will not be welcome here if you arrive as a judge unwilling to listen to the facts."

The Elder was intrigued as he looked at his partner. "Please sit, Queen Ariah, and we will listen," said the Elder's counterpart. Ariah felt like they were manipulating their emotions but she wasn't sure. "How is it that you were reborn?"

Toyah told them, "We have not had a royal Sybaris born to us for centuries. Ariah, my daughter, was taken from us during a battle. She was raised with the humans. We do not know who stole her from us, and we did not know at that time that she was royal. She grew up as a slave to humankind. Json and Ariah found each other and escaped their human captivity together. She was killed with an arrow as they fled the human camp. Json used his wyvern magic to enfold her back into egg form to be reborn, something a male wyvern can do once in his lifetime. When Json saw the egg he had created, he realized that she was royalty and he brought her home to us. Glock had already taken control of Draconia by then."

The Protector said, "We can sense truths and see patterns that you cannot. It is possible that I could tell who stole her from you." He looked at Toyah. "Would you like me to try? There may still be evil lurking in your kingdom."

"I would like to know who." Toyah looked at Silverback for acquiescence. "Will this hurt or change my daughter in any way?"

"No, it will not."

Ariah was torn; she did not trust the Protectors. They seemed to her to be selfish and judgmental. If Von, who was one of their own, wasn't there to stop them, they would have taken Kaigen against her wishes. "Von, do you think that we should allow him to access to our memories?"

Von shifted uncomfortably, looking to the Elder. Finally he confirmed, "No harm will come to you, Queen Ariah."

Ariah weighed the options. It would be important to know who was treacherous enough to steal a royal egg. Von had not given his thoughts on the matter, only told her it would not harm her.

Taking some words from the life of Meluha Crocus, Ariah said philosophically, "Ah, it matters not. Whatever will be, will be."

The Elder's eyes snapped up hearing those words. "It is quite strange that you would say that. My brother used to say this all the time. Never mind, let us stay to the issue at hand. We believe we can help you if you will open your memories to us. If you prefer, we can start with Toyah?"

Toyah opened her mind to the Elder as he laid his hands upon her head, avoiding her silver horns. The Protector relived the battle, but he could only see what Toyah could and found no evidence as to who took her newly born egg. "I am sorry. I cannot see who took the egg. Shall we try Silverback's memories instead?"

Silverback answered, "I was unconscious when we fell from the sky, and I don't see how that will help."

"That is true. Queen Ariah, may I?"

Ariah wasn't sure why she felt so protective of her memories. She felt like she was endangering King Elijashen, Isladora, and Meluha Crocus. "No, I don't think so, Elder. My memories are mine to keep."

"I'm not going to take them from you, just listening in, so to speak," he told her, looking at his counterpart and nodding.

The female Protector closed her eyes and suddenly they were all in a trance-like state, unable to move or speak. The Elder approached Queen Ariah and Von said flatly, "I will have no part of this. What you two are doing is wrong." Silently, he added to them, "*You must know that going against free will is not what we are about. We should have their trust. Our powers increase our obligation to serve them well, not exercise our powers to their detriment. You are abusing their trust by not using restraint, pushing us into a course that is against the interest of our beliefs and theirs.*"

"I am your leader, you have little choice, Von. Kneel." As he spoke the command, Von was forced to kneel upon the ground. The Elder placed his hands on Ariah's head. Silently he said to Von, "*She spoke words of my childhood. I must know, Von. Surely you understand.*"

As the Protector dug through Ariah's memories, he learned about her life and how she came to be whom and what she was. Her first memories were with the humans, so they must have taken her from the battlefield when her mother and Silverback fell from the sky. He learned of the great stores of magic that she had that would continue to grow over time. She would be a great queen; of that he had no doubt. He learned the memories of King Elijashen of the High County and his daughter Isladora. As he came across the memories of Meluha Crocus he was shocked to the core. His exiled brother yet lived! He plowed through every memory with a fine-tooth comb and then made a second run, making sure he missed nothing.

When he was finished, he released the Sybaris and their wyverns. Queen Ariah was ready for war when the Protector released her mind and the others from stasis. Her magic felt like it was eating her from the inside as she expanded it to circle the Protectors. She would kill this callous being!

The Elder looked at Von and his female counterpart. "My brother lives. Call him home." Then the Protectors disappeared, Kaigen along with them.

Chapter 55: The Ring

Isladora jumped as Meluha Crocus made the ring glow brighter than it had ever glowed before. It heated to almost burning on Isladora's finger, forcing her to cry out. He told her, *"I want you to take the ring off, right now! I think they are calling me back!"*

Isladora questioned, "Who? Who is calling you back?"

"The Protectors, my race. If they call me while I am on your finger, you will have no choice but to obey their call. Take the ring off right now!"

Isladora would not lose her connection to her beloved friend. "I will not. You are my friend, and where you need to go, I will take you."

Meluha Crocus was furious. *"You silly girl, they cannot call me back without someone to carry me. Take off the ring!"* He made the metal burn her skin and she screamed, but still she did not comply.

"This is why I lay dormant for a thousand years until they stopped calling me. I do not want to go back. They will destroy me. Somehow they found out I'm still alive."

Isladora was panting and holding her hand. "How many years has it been? A lot can change, even for someone immortal like you." She drew in some gulps of air, trying to catch her breath. She looked down at her hand, relieved to see that her skin was fine.

His magic was so powerful, and others were like him. "Meluha, you cannot go on living as a spirit trapped in a ring. Don't you want to walk again, be your own person? Maybe they can help you?" Isladora reasoned.

A mental sigh. *"I would like to breathe again,"* he admitted.

"What are you afraid of, then? If they kill you, then you will no longer have to live without love. Look at you, standing all day like a captain's wife pacing her widow's walk."

"You will likely be killed by them, Isladora, or worse," Meluha Crocus warned.

The call came again, stronger this time, and this time, Isladora could only obey. She went to get her weapons ready and to write a note. The call could not be ignored, but it would not put her in immediate danger or risk her ability to carry him home.

In the morning, Tobin found a note from Isladora. He made a thorough search of the stronghold. She had taken her weapons and Phoenix, the king's horse, who Tobin knew she was attuned to. Her note said only: *Meluha and I have been called to Issedones.*

He ran to tell the king. No matter what the king ordered, Tobin already had his own plans. Tobin loved that girl and he would use every skill he had to track her and bring her back to his arms.

Part III—Meluha Crocus

Chapter 56: The Call of Issedones

Issedones. The word echoed in Isladora's mind. The name of Meluha Crocus' mysterious homeland was an unending litany that would not release her from its grip. She cursed as she tried to think of something else, anything else: her own home, those she loved, anything from her own life. The need to get to this place called Issedones was growing in her mind like a creeping black mold. Its influence was taking over a part of her will with each passing day, and Isladora knew she was losing her own identity to the fuzzy darkness.

The always-faithful Phoenix picked his way through the forest, his hooves churning up pine needles and the dark, rich loam. The pine trees, so unlike the trees of the forests near her home, would normally be a source of beauty to Isladora, but now they only seemed oppressive, prickly, and sticky. Everything around her was damp from a recent rain, and the mist rising from the forest floor intensified the ethereal pounding in her head.

Isladora felt more disheartened than she ever had in her whole life—more even than the worst days of the Queen Mother's cruelty—and she let go of Phoenix's reins and let her hands rest on his mane, winding her fingers through his black tresses, allowing their connection to anchor and comfort her. She heard a bird land in a tree, and turning, she looked up to see him puff out his ochre chest and ruffle his feathers. She tried to breathe in his beauty and continue her fight against the summoning spell's power. She reached her left hand up to her neck and felt the wyvern mark, felt it grow warm under her fingertips as she thought of Json. She grounded herself thinking of her strong friends, Phoenix the warhorse and Json the wyvern, until the maddening reverberation let go of her mind.

The ring on her finger glowed warmly. *"That was very good, Isladora, you must maintain control of your psyche. We have to find some help for you. The Protector's magic is just too strong; you cannot keep up this pace. As it calls you to my home, you will die if someone doesn't feed you and make you rest."* The ancient spirit was careful not to say the name Issedones to her; the last time he'd done that, it had produced unfortunate consequences.

Isladora sighed. She was utterly exhausted. Her head was raw from fighting the magical pull on her mind and her body from the long, unending ride to her destination. It had proved impossible for her to rest for any length of time before the call would return stronger than before. "Meluha, you and I have been friends for a long time; you will take care of me," she said wearily, almost dreamily. The long lack of sleep was taking a terrible toll on her once-strong will.

"Be reasonable, Isladora!" The mage snapped at her. *"I have no hands to feed you with, no legs with which to find food; I cannot take care of you while I'm stuck here in this ring!"* Meluha Crocus was growing angry with her absurdity but tried to reign in his words. Badgering the girl won't do any good, he reminded himself once again.

"Nonsense, you made the rock in the cave attack me so I could practice sparring, remember?" She smiled a little at the memory. "You can do anything with your magic."

Meluha sighed at her naivety. *"Once that was true, but I cannot command food to appear in any case, or stop you from walking this horse to its death."*

Isladora ignored him. "Won't it be great to walk again, Meluha?" Isladora was almost delusional from the exhaustion. "I can't wait to look at you, person to person, eye to eye." Isladora's head slumped towards her chest; just sitting up straight had become a burden. Her auburn hair felt heavy and thick on her damp neck. She reached her hand and felt the knife at her waist. When they stopped she would cut it all off, and what a relief it would be, she thought.

Meluha Crocus tried to reason with her—for the umpteenth time that same day, *"Isladora, we must stop and hunt for food. Phoenix is too loud—he's a war-horse, not a scouting pony. We will never find a food source if you don't stop to hunt while you still have the strength."*

Isladora rubbed her tired eyes and forehead. "I just can't think enough to hunt. The pressure in my mind is so intense it numbs my senses."

Meluha Crocus realized that if that was true, she was lost; without the strength to hunt, she would continue to weaken until she died. *"The ring, take it off now, Isladora!"* He commanded.

Isladora looked at her finger where the ring glowed with his anger. "I tried to take it off a week ago, remember? I cannot," she reminded him. "It burns when I try to move it past my knuckle. It's too painful, I can't stand it."

Isladora looked down at the ring and said, "I'm sorry I'm so stubborn and that I didn't listen to you." A tear fell down her cheek. "I meant to tell you that you were right, that I should have taken the ring off when you told me to, but I didn't want to lose our connection." Another tear fell and she wiped it away, her grimy hands leaving a stain on her cheek. "I foolishly thought that I could help you. Now I will die, and your ring will never be found in this never-ending forest." Her hollow stomach rolled with nausea as she fought off panic and despair. "Please forgive me, Meluha."

Although they had no food, there was plenty of water, as they had been following a small stream for several days. Isladora and Meluha Crocus were certain there were fish in the stream, but the young woman was in no shape to try to catch any. At least they didn't have to add dehydration to her list of woes.

The trio had been traveling east by northeast for about two moon cycles. Although she'd taken a large bundle of dried rations, Isladora's food supply had run out over a week ago, and the nonstop pace had stolen her strength one bit at a time like a thief in the night. Phoenix had plenty of tree bark in the forest and grass that grew next to the stream where the sun broke through and he was faring much better than Isladora, but he too was weary and his head slumped towards the ground as he carefully chose his steps.

If only she had listened and had taken the ring containing the spirit of Meluha Crocus off the moment he had felt the Protectors calling him home! Then they might have been able to control how and when she took him home. The only problem with that idea was that she didn't know where Issedones was.

As much as she hated it, she needed the magic summoning her or she would not know how to find it, and according to Meluha Crocus, no human knew where it was, or could even get there. If Isladora was honest with herself, in her desire to help Meluha, she had chosen for Meluha to go home regardless of how he felt. Now they both would pay the price.

Meluha himself was torn about going home. If he were going to escape this ring, he felt that home was the only place that could happen. Moreover, he longed to see the great city again. He had not forgotten, Issedones was a marvelous place, built from magic, full of wondrous architecture, canals, and streets. Building in Issedones was by permit only; lead architects on any project, large or small, had to be the best in their class. No building could have the same design, and every design was approved by the Elder himself. It had been mandated centuries ago that each building had to be constructed of the same materials and enhanced with frost, the source of the Protectors' magic. Superficially resembling natural frost, though it could take on several different colors, the mineral was concentrated magic. Magic so potent, in fact, that only the most skilled Protectors could directly shape and mold it.

The frost created glowing veins in the rock walls of the buildings, and the effect crafted an entire city that glowed in beautiful color. Over the years, competition to create bigger and better buildings led to an ever-higher demand for frost, and the Protectorate Guild of Science spent most of their energies achieving better drilling methods to reach deeper and richer sources of frost underground.

All roads leading into Issedones were protected with magical wards that kept out all manner of creatures—and exiled Protectors like himself, of course. Meluha wasn't sure what was going to happen to them once they reached the wards; he could not pass them when he had a humanoid frame. Perhaps as a spirit bound into the ring, he could, or perhaps they were waiting for him and would lower them once he arrived. *Or perhaps they mean only to destroy the ring once I am home*, he thought grimly.

Meluha thought about the days preceding his exile. He had been one of their top researchers. His team had discovered a technology that was a leap forward in frost drilling techniques. Using the new technique, the Protectors would be able to reach rich pockets of frost potential they hadn't previously dreamed of. His whole team had been excited, working around the clock to make the devices ready.

The center of the new method was a magic-infused rotary drill bit that could penetrate the hard rock that concealed the frost potential. They had tried diamond-impregnated bits before that, but the diamonds would wear away unevenly, causing the hole to become unstable; the magic would prevent wear on the tiny diamonds entirely.

For the test hole, they chose a young Protector named Aslog as the operator. Aslog's main aptitude was earth magic, and with that talent he could locate the target deposit and guide the drill bit to stay aimed true.

Soon after they hit the first deep target, a vast underground store of the highest grade frost they had ever gathered, Meluha and his team had also discovered that the frost was part of a cycle of life for creatures that lived under the ground.

They named the creatures Annites, and after some preliminary studies they ascertained that the creatures were intelligent, living in underground structures they built in the earth. The discovery of these deep-earth creatures had astonished the Protectors. They had never before considered the possibility of ill effects from mining the frost.

Meluha ordered part of his team to study these creatures, who observed that they moved to protect the frost from the intruding drill equipment. Based on this evidence, the group determined that the creatures and the frost were somehow closely related. They knew that mining the frost was damaging the Annites' environment, but they weren't sure to what extent.

When Meluha brought their findings to the Elder, Vernondiander commanded him to stop wasting their drilling efforts on studying them. Faced with a moral decision, Meluha and his team persisted, determined to examine the effects of drilling on the Annites. At his personal order, they ceased the drilling program. When his brother, the Elder, found out, Meluha was exiled and cut off from the frost.

Over the years of his exile, his skin, which had once glistened with frost, had dulled, and his eyes had faded to what he now suspected was his natural brown instead of the shining silver-blue brought on by the frost in his blood. He lost his sharp vision, his keen hearing, and his ability to float through the air.

Meluha Crocus had at first remained near his home, but eventually decided that he looked more human than Protector, so he went to live with them.

Now he was returning to face the misdeeds of a man whose every action was towards gaining greater power. Meluha knew that his brother could be charming. Vernondiander would first appear as the best of men; he often fooled others into thinking that he was looking out for their well-being, and the power of his magic coupled with his charm made gaining his attention so wonderful that one wanted to bask in it. It would only be much later, if at all, when his victims would realize he robbed them of whatever he had coveted.

Meluha had drawn the line at causing unknown harm to the newly discovered Annites; to his brother, these creatures were of no importance; only obtaining more frost mattered, and he would have it no matter the cost to lesser beings.

The long centuries of exile and then imprisonment in the ring had salved over much of the anguish Meluha had suffered from his betrayal and banishment from Issedones. Time had clouded his grief, diminishing it to something that Meluha examined only on occasion.

Long ago, he had realized he'd been a fool to think that his work was important to his brother. Or that he was. Vernondiander was only interested in the power he could attain from the frost; he would eradicate anything and anyone who stood in his way. Here in this dark green forest of pine and birch trees, heading toward the place of his birth, his ancient memories assaulted him, warning him of the great danger to himself and to Isladora. He had to find a way to protect her from his brother's avarice, for he had no illusions that he was summoned simply because Vernondiander missed his brother at long last.

No, the Elder had need of him, and Meluha felt sure it had something to do with frost production. His brother's action to summon him home had tasted somehow of desperation.

Despite the power of the call on Isladora, Meluha did not feel defeated, for he had met men even worse than his brother—some even made Vernon seem like a saint—and he knew that such men could be defeated. He had once been a master sage, and he would find a way to keep Isladora alive and away from Vernondiander, the self-styled Elder of the Protectors.

The next day, Isladora rode slumped over in the saddle, staying on the back of her warhorse only because the war saddle was designed to help keep her there. She knew that she needed to keep watch for danger, but she just couldn't keep her eyes open. Her mind ached and pounded with the unending call…Issedones…Issedones…Issedones. She was reaching a point where she truly didn't care if she died; she just wanted it to cease.

She was completely unconscious by late afternoon, and without being told to stop, Phoenix continued through the forest. The warhorse meandered along, despite no guidance from the princess.

Isladora did not stir during the long ride through the night-black forest and as the dew was leaving her mark on the early morning world, Isladora fell senselessly from Phoenix's back onto the wet ground and rolled halfway into the underbrush. Fortunately, she fell on the pine needle-covered floor and not onto a rock or stump.

The ring's spirit could feel her weak breathing. The connection to her was still strong, but nothing he did could wake her. He tried to command the horse to help her, but Phoenix did not respond. He bent his weary head to eat some grass; he too was exhausted from their nonstop journey. The horse ate his fill and then he lay down near Isladora, falling asleep almost immediately.

Meluha had been fighting an almost unknown sensation—panic—through the long day and into the night, trying to focus on considering his options. In the morning, the horse at first was unwilling to rise, but then he scrambled to his feet, shaking hard enough to throw dew in all directions. After that, Phoenix seemed much better and he foraged near the area where Isladora lay.

His grazing fulfilled, the horse strode back toward his rider, gently nudging her back with his nose. Isladora moaned and tried to sit up but couldn't find the strength to raise her torso more than a few inches. She lay back down and began to cry softly.

She had battled the Queen Mother, she had ridden a war wyvern, she had climbed a cliff wall, and even received her first kiss, but she did not know how to defeat this exhaustion. After she cried herself out, she was left only with the incessant pounding of Issedones…Issedones…Issedones. To stop it she thought about the kiss she'd shared with Tobin. She played the kiss over in her mind again and again, finding comfort in the memory of the passion she'd felt. She focused on the reminiscence, staving off her panic, but though she could push back the repetition of the summons, it didn't help her regain her strength. She allowed the exhaustion to claim her again, knowing that she would likely not be able to awaken again. She was going to die.

After a few hours of trying to command the horse mind-to-mind as he would a human, Meluha realized he'd have to try something else. Instead of words or thoughts, he sent a feeling of panic into the animal and the urge to race home. He created a large burst from the dirt, like an explosion, spraying debris all around Phoenix's legs and the great warhorse took off like a shot. Meluha rejoiced, hoping that someone could trail him back to this glen and find her body before it was too late.

To be attached to her while her human body died and returned to the earth would be a punishment unlike any other he had endured, including losing his love, Mae Tarango. At least when his love had died, Meluha's human body had died with her, his spirit cast into this strange ring he had bought at a bazaar for their marriage. To exist on Isladora's young finger as she turned back into dust would be a prison that even his brother would dread.

Chapter 57: Tobin

Fashi slowed and then halted in the forest, alerting Tobin to a rabbit foraging in the ferns. Tobin sighted and released, his arrow cleanly killing the rabbit. As another rabbit ran off, Tobin drew another arrow and released. "Good work, Fashi," Tobin climbed down from the gelding's back, giving his furry neck a pat. "We'll make a quick fire tonight and have some fresh meat for a couple of days."

Fashi nudged his back. "And yes, an apple for you my friend," he said in a grudging tone, then laughed. Tobin retrieved the arrows and cleaned them, and then field dressed the two rabbits and placed them in his game pouch. " I probably would have spotted the rabbits myself you know, but I think you are the better game hunter Fashi."

Tobin had been following what he hoped were Phoenix's tracks for weeks, trying to close the gap between him and Isladora. She was traveling at such a speed that Tobin wasn't sure how she was doing it. Tobin had not seen the king's men since he left the stronghold, but he knew they were out searching for Isladora too. Tobin had not waited for the king's orders; he had gathered his horse and equipment and headed out. Phoenix turned his left foreleg when he walked; leaving a distinct mark in the mud and dirt, so Tobin was confident that he was on the right track, though the inevitable fear that he was following some other rider haunted him in the middle of the night.

The tracks showed the warhorse's hoof marks in the pine mulch and dirt, with no sign of a campfire or bedroll. Tobin knew that no one could keep up such a pace, and he feared she would drive herself and her steed to death if she didn't slow down. He also feared that some kind of foul magic was at work on the girl that he loved, for he knew that she was smart enough not to push herself this way.

Tobin pulled a small cotton handkerchief from under his belt and brought it to his face. It had long since lost Isladora's smell, but he imagined her scent anyway. She had dropped the handkerchief one day and Tobin had kept it instead of returning it to her just to have a part of her close by. Isladora had embroidered small green wyvern shapes on it, and Tobin rubbed the thread between his fingers, remembering the day he'd seen the real creature.

The wyvern Json had been a thrilling and amazing spectacle in their battle against the Queen Mother. Tobin would never forget the large dark green body coming from nowhere to knock Malagard off the roof. The power of the wyvern's shriek had made every combatant across the battle-field stop momentarily to look up in awe. It was the wyvern and his deadly fire that had turned the tide against the Queen Mother's men; it was be-cause of him the Juna were the victors. Isladora was fortunate to have a powerful friend like that.

Tobin smelled the handkerchief again and put it back under his belt. He knew that he loved her now; his heart followed her wherever she went. She was unlike any of the other women at the stronghold. Some women were dainty and some were warriors—Isladora could be both. What drew him the most though was her mind. She was already very learned, and her thirst for knowledge was unquenchable. With her, Tobin knew he would never become stagnant. He would love her and learn with her and they would grow together. But that was all at risk now, and he was scared nearly out of his wits.

Tobin kept on, urging Fashi to quicken his pace. Near dark he made camp, built a fire, spitted the rabbits, and cooked them, remembering to bring Fashi his apple. Fashi took his time, taking small bites from the apple proffered in Tobin's hand. When Fashi was finished, Tobin rinsed the sticky mess from his hands in the stream and stretched his muscles, tired from the days of riding. Before he was a king's man, he had possessed little muscle; he had been all protruding collar bones and ribs. With the constant nutrition he now received, he had grown into his man-body, but now those muscles demanded a constant supply of meat and his skill with the bow and Fashi's help ensured he had it. Tobin knew he was in the best shape of his twenty-three years, and he thought that he might need every bit of his strength in the days to come.

The next day Tobin lost the trail, so he continued in the same general direction, looking for signs. He could make no sense as to why she would leave the stream, why she wasn't making camps or looking for game or oth-er sources of water. He had only been traveling close to the stream thinking she would do the same, but it had cost him the trail and he was afraid he'd have to lose time doubling back to try to pick it up again.

In the mid-afternoon, Tobin and Fashi emerged from the woods into a valley with knee-high yellow grasses blowing in the wind. Tobin's heart sank as he saw the valley; tracking her in this grass would be next to impossible. Just at that moment, Fashi quietly grunted in warning and came to an immediate halt. Tobin knew that the horse was trained not to move so that it was harder for an enemy to spot them.

Tobin held still too, then slowly nocked an arrow and strained to see or hear what was alarming his horse. He turned his head slowly towards the direction Fashi had turned one ear. Moments later, Tobin heard what Fashi's sensitive ears had picked up: a large animal crashing through the forest at a run. Tobin drew back and aimed his arrow towards the noise; underneath, he could feel Fashi's muscles bunching, ready to move.

Suddenly, Phoenix burst from the forest headlong, sticks and pine needles caught in his mane, bridle, and saddle. The stallion's eyes were wild and he ran like his tail was on fire. Tobin's heart seemed to stop, for Isladora was not on the horse's back. He felt a hollow pain in his stomach that spread into waves of nausea at the sight and the fear that she was lying unhorsed somewhere all alone.

Alone and with that damn ring, he thought. Phoenix was too far away for Fashi to catch with his shorter legs and the panic-stricken warhorse ignored Tobin's shrill whistle. Gods, what could panic *Phoenix* like that? Tobin wondered as he nudged Fashi with his knees and they galloped into the forest at an angle to pick up the signs of the warhorse's passage. At least it'll be easy to follow his backtrail, he thought.

Night came with no moon, so Tobin was forced to stop and rest. He fed Fashi and ate some of the rabbit. He slept little, cursing the lack of light. In the thick pine trees, false dawn was too dark to try to track, and he cursed the delay. Isladora could be bleeding her last somewhere, and he was helpless.

Finally, the light grew strong enough that he could follow Phoenix's crashing path again and he had Fashi set a gait that would eat up the miles and still leave him steady enough to shoot. He hadn't seen any blood, but one explanation for her losing her saddle was that she'd been ambushed by enemies unknown, so he rode with his entire nervous system as taut as a bowstring and with an arrow nocked and one more in his string hand.

Tobin had just noticed that the tracks had changed when Fashi alerted him again with a low whicker. Ahead of him were the deep grooves where Phoenix's hooves had dug in to take off and a large hole in the ground that looked like some monster had burst from the earth itself, scattering debris in a great circle. Whatever that was, it had to be what had scared Phoenix, but no other animal or human tracks littered the forest floor.

He dismounted Fashi to investigate, giving the horse a soft pat on the neck, and then he saw what Fashi had noticed. A leather-clad leg and soft-booted foot lay sticking out of some low bushes, and his blood pounded as he recognized it. *Dear Lord, let her be alive*, he thought as his heart pounded, and he rushed to Isladora's side. A quick check showed that she was unconscious but breathing and he said a quick prayer of thankfulness.

Tobin checked her carefully all over; he could see no bruising or bleeding, but her normal healthy color was but a pale shade of grey. He felt her head for lumps but found none. She had some bites on her skin from insects and she was far thinner than when he'd seen her last, though her lips weren't cracked from dehydration. He could tell by her gaunt look that she hadn't eaten anything substantial in some time. Tobin got his canteen and a clean bandage and poured some water onto the corner of it. He squeezed a few drops of water into her mouth, and she reflexively swallowed it.

He then dared to pour a small stream of water into her mouth directly from the canteen and Isladora sputtered as she gagged a little on the water, coming awake weakly coughing as she cleared her throat of the water.

When she stopped coughing, Isladora realized that she was being supported by a strong arm. She slowed her breathing and then fought to turn her head—seemingly made of solid lead, it was so heavy—to see what manner of man it was through the haze of her weakened vision. It was Tobin! When she saw his face staring down at her with his concern writ large on his broad features, she made a mewling sound, somewhere between a sob and a whimper. Tobin reached out to touch her face and she weakly reached for his hand and held it to her face to begin weeping in earnest.

Tobin made shushing sounds, gathering her close, and as he held her tight, he breathed another prayer of thankfulness. She was weak and would be some time recovering her strength, but she was alive! That was all that mattered, and his own tears fell on her long dark hair as he held her.

"Tobin…" Isladora's voice was hoarse and rough, but she managed to croak, "Thank God it's you… I … I didn't understand, I didn't know, and now I'm going to die here. At least I'm not going to die alone." She pressed her aching head against him and continued to sob.

Tobin fought through his shock at the defeat and despair in her voice. He'd seen this woman face down the Queen Mother and her poisons without fear, and she was ready to give up? "Nonsense," Tobin told her gently, rocking her back and forth. "I'm, here now and there will be no dying on this day. Buck up now my girl! Where is my brave and haughty friend?"

The princess moaned, saying, "The ring, it's calling me to Is…" She cut off the word with a harsh shake of her head that threatened to plunge her back into darkness, snapping her mouth shut so hard her teeth clacked. "It's calling me onward. The pull of the ring on my mind, Tobin, it's too strong. I simply cannot bear it any longer. Please just kill me; I can't stand its echoes in my head." Isladora wept in his arms, curling into a ball.

Tobin saw that her face was etched with pain and soothed her, brushing back her hair. He had been right, foul magic was at work upon her. "You are my life Isladora, ever and always. I will never harm you in any way," Tobin looked at the damned ring, "but I will harm those doing this to you." He reached to pull the ring off her finger, but when he pulled she screamed and curled tighter into a fetal position.

She sobbed some more, holding her head. "It cannot be removed Tobin. I don't even know if it can be cut from my body, but maybe we should try." She held her hand toward him.

"Cut your finger off?" Tobin was aghast. "But how will you shoot a bow?" Gently laying her head down, Tobin went to his saddlebags and dug through his pack to find the medical kit all warriors were given for their field packs. Inside was a root that was useful for relieving pain and the dried leaves of a plant that would sedate her somewhat. He decided to give her both. Tobin made her a makeshift pallet using his bedroll and carried her to it, lying her down gently and brushing debris from her tangled hair, then dug a small pit and built a fire and headed to the stream to fill his pot.

He stripped the meat off the bones of one of the cooked rabbits, placed the bones in the pot, and set it to boil. The marrow would be nourishing to her starved body, and in her condition, she wouldn't be able to keep anything more substantial down. In a smaller pot he boiled water and added the root and the leaves to make a tisane. He wasn't sure how strong to make the herbal tea, so he began with a small amount. He looked at his patient. She was curled into a ball, still holding her head.

When the bones grew soft, he broke them open to release the marrow and continued to boil them, all the while thinking of what he was going to do about this spirit in the ring that had Isladora so entrapped. Isladora had said that once the spirit in the ring had been a person—a male person. Tobin scowled and thought if he could get that ring from her finger, he would fling it to the bottom of the deepest pit. *If that spirit was alive, I'd challenge him to the death on the spot!* he thought. *What kind of man puts a young woman in this much peril? An evil man to be sure!*

Tobin let the bone broth cool as he gave Isladora a little more water. She was able to drink it without gagging, which he took as a good sign. Still, as she moaned and cried, Tobin felt his heart wrenching in two. "Isladora, I have put a root for pain and one to sedate you in this tea. I need you to drink the entire thing," he said as he held her head up and tipped the cup to her lips. "Come on now, this will help."

Slowly, Isladora drank the tea, not even caring about the bitter, horrible taste if it gave her some relief. Tobin waited to see if anything came back up, and then had her drink as much of the bone broth as she could. Finally, she closed her eyes and thrashed around for a while. Eventually she fell into a deep sleep, her face free from signs of pain, her breathing deep and even. It was a small degree of improvement, and his heart unwound just a little to see it.

He took care of Fashi, rubbing him down, and then he ate some of the rabbit meat, added some logs to the fire, and covered her with a blanket to wait out the night. In the middle of the night when she began thrashing again, he gave her more tea and the rest of the bone broth. He held her in his arms, afraid she would flail into the fire pit. He picked up her hand and looked at the ring, the firelight dancing off its strange metal. Tobin did not like her connection to this mage, and he scowled at it but didn't try to re-move it again, lest he cause her more harm.

In the morning, Isladora woke to a familiar and beloved smell—Tobin. The scout always smelled of forest and horse and leather, but she'd already discovered it was her favorite scent in the world. Her head lay against To-bin's chest and she took stock of herself.

She could feel the compulsion to get up and move towards Issedones, but the aching, pounding horridness she had felt was now a dull pain and a foggy sense of intent; she attributed the weakening of the spell to the drugs he'd fed her, but some part of her believed that Tobin's presence had helped, too.

She smiled into his chest. She was alive. She felt weak but both happy and safe as well. Moreover, she felt Tobin's love for her; it was not just that he'd come looking for her, but how he'd cared for her, and how fiercely he wanted to protect her. She breathed in his scent and felt her body respond to his, though even that felt different through the drug haze. She blushed, but that didn't stop her from sliding her arms around him and holding on tight. Tobin was awake—had been for some time—but he feigned sleep, enjoying the feel of her clinging to him. When she nuzzled into his chest and breathed deeply, his body came alive as well, and he was faced with a choice. He could stop feigning sleep, or he could let her feel exactly how alive he'd become. He decided to shift position, his face several shades darker than usual.

Feeling him stir, Isladora was the first to speak. "Our first night togeth-er and I don't remember a thing," she rasped jokingly, then turned even redder.

"How are you feeling?" Tobin asked as he stroked her hair; the tresses that had escaped her braid were soft and silky in his callused fingers.

"You came for me," Isladora smiled. She tried to sit up and he helped her, reaching out to slide one of the bags from Fashi's saddle behind her to prop her there. It had the side effect of letting him hide the most obvious sign of his attraction until he could get it under control.

"Your father and his men are out searching, too," Tobin told her as he stood up. "I lost your trail a few days ago, but then I saw Phoenix burst from the forest and followed his tracks back to you." The ring began to glow and Tobin knew she was having a mental conversation with the spirit of the ring. He grew angry but tried to keep any sign of it from reaching his face.

Isladora began to unwind her tangled hair. "Meluha said that when I fell from the horse, he used magic to create an explosion to make Phoenix run because he couldn't do anything else to help me." She shrugged as if to say what else could he have done, but that didn't satisfy the scout.

Tobin scowled at her, thinking that of course the mage couldn't help her; he got her into this mess in the first place. Choosing his words carefully, he said firmly, "Tell this Meluha that I want him out of your head."

"He can hear you, Tobin, you just can't hear him," Isladora explained. She grimaced slightly, then started to stand and he helped her up, steadying her with his arms. Isladora continued, looking around, blushing again, "I need some, ah, privacy please." She felt like her bladder was about to burst.

Tobin led her into the forest and after looking around for any dangers, took a few steps away to let do her business. "I don't know how you can have privacy with this mage attached to you," he muttered before he could stop himself. Kicking himself internally and feeling like a jealous ass, he added more softly, "Call if you need me, I won't be far."

Tobin was putting the last of his rabbit meat on a rock for them to share when she came out from the bushes. This was the first time he'd seen her standing, and it was clear that she'd lost a fair amount of weight and the dark circles under her eyes looked like angry bruises. Still, his heartbeat quickened to see her, just like it always did. "Well, let's get this thing off you, my girl," he told her.

"I cannot take it off, Tobin," she said calmly. "And even if I could, I wouldn't. I want to take him home to... the place."

"Last night you were begging me to cut your finger off!" Tobin exclaimed standing and crossing his arms. "Is it so you can meet him as a man? Is that it?" He kicked the pine needles off to the side as he fumed. "You're in love with him, aren't you?" Tobin turned his back to her, his hands clenched into fists. He wanted to hurt something. Fashi nickered, and he scowled at the little horse, saying, "I will not calm down—you stay out of this." Tobin turned back to the campfire and jabbed a stick through the meat and thrust it at her. "Here is your portion."

Isladora didn't have the strength to appease Tobin's jealousy; she slumped down to the ground and reached for the stick, tasting the first real food she had in days. She knew to eat it slowly and sighed sadly as she chewed and watched Tobin angrily gather up his gear.

"That young man is quite taken with you, Isladora," Meluha told her as she chewed. *"Thank God he showed up; you were nearly beyond help."* Meluha shuddered in his mind at the thought of her dying; he didn't want to say it.

"Are you thanking my God, Meluha?" She asked by way of reply. The thought of her Lord, even in passing, somehow infused her with renewed purpose. The ring didn't answer, for Meluha Crocus found himself confused about the matter.

Isladora watched as Tobin began boiling more of the tea to give her as they traveled. In his anger he pinched off a larger portion of the sedation herb. He was distracted, making a mental checklist of his belongings as General Nokela had taught him. He was going to have to hunt for some more game before they could leave.

"Meluha says that's too much, Tobin," Isladora warned him. "He says that the herb is henbane. That amount is enough for Fashi." Isladora smiled as she listened to Meluha. "He says one-quarter of that pinch for the size of the pot you have. Too much, and I could sicken and die."

Tobin was furious, being ordered around by His Highness, the Lord High Wizard. She sure didn't smile at him that way when they talked. He listened to the directions grudgingly and said sarcastically, "Tell his brilliance thank you," as he bowed mockingly.

"Meluha says you are the brilliant one for thinking of the tea. With it I will be able to continue," she complimented him warmly, even though Meluha didn't say it.

Tobin seethed some more, "No, I changed my mind, Isladora. Tell His Highness that he is a jackass." Tobin grimaced, "Better yet, tell him you belong to me and I want him out of your mind and off of your body."

Meluha chuckled and told Isladora, *"I agree with the whelp."*

Isladora smiled inside, knowing Tobin's jealousy was because he loved her. She stopped herself from replying, knowing Tobin was in no condition to listen to reason, so she wisely chose to stay quiet.

Chapter 58: Vernondiander

Vernondiander stared at the creature in the small black cage as he ate his dinner. About one-eighth the size of his palm, it was the biggest one they had found yet. It must be centuries old, as most of these creatures were almost microscopic. Pitiful creatures really, he thought. The creature had curled up into as small a ball as he could. Vernondiander knew they were sensitive to light and couldn't live above ground for more than a few days. In order to see the creature, he had to cover it in red dye and place it in a dark box.

He had already learned that without soil and rock to shelter them and draw nutrients from, they withered and died. The last creature he had studied, he added soil to the cage, and it did keep the creature alive a little longer, but not by much. No matter, he had had an endless supply of these creatures to study now that they had found a way to extract them.

He cracked open the shellfish he was eating, enjoying the way the shell contained the meat but did not attach to it. The creatures also seemed to have a delicate shell-like material in the underside of their exoskeletons. He wondered if the shell-like material played a role in how they manufactured the frost from the mica. He wondered if the creatures would taste similar to the tender meat, and if they would give him stronger magic when ingested. Of course, they might be poisonous as well, he thought, deciding to postpone tasting them for another time.

"Elder, would you like more shellfish?" the serving woman asked, floating into the room. Vernondiander scowled at her. He did not like to see the servants practice levitation in his presence; it made them seem too regal, somehow. He thought about replacing her, but then he would have to train another, and she did perform her duties excellently. She smiled at him, and the Elder noted that his serving woman had grown powerful too, a consequence of being near him and therefore being near so much frost. Her hair and eyes were tinted like his, silvery-blue. Other Protectors' eyes were silver, and they had a silvery mica frost to their skin. That thought made him wish once again that he had a way to disguise his access to more powerful frost, but he didn't as of yet.

She stared politely at him, awaiting an answer. Snapping out of his distraction, Vernondiander said, "No, no, Elsbeth." He sucked some meat from the shell, going back to pondering the organism. Suddenly he said, "Elsbeth, take some of these shells and place them in the cage with the creature."

"Last time I opened her cage, she bit me!" Elsbeth exclaimed, looking in trepidation at the girl known as Kaigen. The girl glared back from her much larger enclosure.

"No, no," Vernondiander said irritably. "The Annite, the pitiful little ball." He waved a claw of the shellfish to point at the small cage sitting on the dining table in front of him. "They never move. You will be quite safe, my dear." He pushed the plate of leftover shells towards her.

Elsbeth selected a few small pieces of shell, working to keep the serene smile on her face that she knew the Elder required, and took them to the cage. She slowly opened the cage and placed the shells on the top of the soil.

"No, no, put the shells closer to it," he sighed with impatience, his eyes gleaming with faint traceries of blue fire, though Elsbeth's back was turned and she didn't see the loss of control that signaled.

Elsbeth moved the soil around so she could see the creature, carefully keeping all signs of her distaste for the act from marring her features. She began placing the shells next to it when she noticed that it had begun to turn grey. Lowering her voice, she said, "I think it is dead, Elder." She poked its body lightly with the shell and got no response.

"Well, go to the lab and tell them to get me another," Vernondiander ordered crossly. "There's no shortage of them, after all."

Kaigen struck the crystalline walls of her cage hard enough to make them ring, mindless of the bruises she'd have from the impact. "You sick... beast!" Kaigen's violent movement and outburst made Elsbeth jump several feet off the ground; her magic kept her floating, the Elder frowned. "The Annites are intelligent living beings, killing them is just like killing one of your fellow Protectors!" She paused for emphasis, "They cannot live above ground!" Kaigen slapped helplessly at the clear walls of her larger cage, as she had many times since she was brought here.

He looked at Kaigen, noting her scowl and her dirty face. She reminded him of his brother, always meddling, always trying to rescue things. "I told you, Kaigen, all you have to do is aid me in my research and I will not bring another creature up from the ground," he explained as he fixed his penetrating gaze on her, a kind smile on his handsome face. The oddly-made Sybaris—if that was what she truly was, and he had doubts—was highly resistant to that gaze, though that hadn't been true at first.

Kaigen gritted her teeth and growled, "As soon as you release me, I will send you into a fissure so deep that even the Annites will never find your body!" Elsbeth backed away from her.

Her violent manner of addressing him always shocked him. No one in Issedones dared to challenge him so any longer. He had long ago rid himself of anyone who chose to go against him, and the examples of their exiles, or worse, served to keep the rest of the Protectors in line. He began to lift a finger to magically punish her, but then he simply laughed, replying in a precise, almost sympathetic tone, "Listen to her Elsbeth, she thinks she is the one in control here. Well, if she won't cooperate, we could at least use her anger to deepen our drilling plan." When no one laughed at his joke, the Elder rubbed his chin and sighed. "Bring in Von. I think we shall raise the stakes."

Elsbeth bowed and left just as Logistician Trugard entered the room, his dark grey uniform spotless as usual. The insignia of his office gleamed in gold on his chest. "Ah Trugard, I hope it's good news for me today."

Trugard's high office was usually tasked with planning and carrying out the maneuvers of military forces as well as the logistical support to supply them. He was quite peeved to be using them to keep dibs on a mere human girl, but he knew to keep his face utterly neutral. The Elder made it quite clear that it was Trugard's personal duty to track the human girl and the ring bound Meluha Crocus' as they journeyed to Issedones.

Trugard stopped in front of Vernondiander, noting the dead creature and the pile of shells with a disgust that he carefully did not allow to reach his face or his eyes. "Sir, the pace you have set has already almost killed the human girl that carries the ring. She lost her horse and nearly died. A Juna scout named Tobin has found her and is nursing her back to health. He has herbs that are helping her deal with the pull of the calling, so I think she might recover."

"Where are they?" The Elder demanded, caring little whether Isladora lived or died, other than it would be necessary to send someone to fetch the ring. He was impatient to have Meluha Crocus back in Issedones, but until now, he'd been content to have the human pawn bear him as far as she could.

Trugard shifted his weight to the other leg and admonished himself to be still. "Almost to the northeast edge of the Berrelian Forest, Elder."

Vernondiander slammed his hand down. "Humans are so slow," he said in disgust. He rose and hovered over to gaze at the map on his desk. Trugard noted the Elder's new robe, a garment interwoven with so much frost it was deep blue in color. Vernondiander, noticing his perusal, smiled at the officer, his lips curling arrogantly. "Shoot me with your weapon, Trugard."

"What, Elder?" Trugard asked doubtfully, though his hand went to the frost-based weapon at his hip. The rod of frost-infused glass could shoot bursts of electrical energy as potent as the spells of the strongest mages. Before these weapons were manufactured, only such wizards could generate bolts of electrical energy. The new weapons stored the frost's power and channeled it into an electrical charge strong enough to kill. Even someone like the Elder had no defense against such a bolt.

"You heard me, shoot me," Vernondiander said firmly. "I want you to see how amazing this robe really is." He pulled it closed over his middle and positioned himself for the shot.

With a shrug, Trugard drew his weapon, aimed, and fired, the meter-long bolt of pure electrical energy directed by his mind at the Elder's chest. The bolt disappeared into the fabric right over the Elder's heart, where the material glowed and then turned a deeper blue. He watched in wonder as the robe stored the power, Trugard thoughts turned grim, wondering what the Elder could do with the energy.

Vernondiander noted the dead aim with a smile and patted his chest. He exclaimed, "You shot to kill, I see! A man after my own heart!" Then he laughed a merry laugh. "Yes, quite the new material, eh, Trugard?" He laughed again before turning his attention back to the map "Now, I want you to place the human girl on a new route. Take her through the Silver Road… I presume you know it?" The Elder referred to the underground road that was actually a network of old mines. He raised an interrogatory eyebrow to see if Trugard was following his train of thought and with the Logistician's nod, continued, "That will shorten her travel time, taking her through the mountains instead of over them."

"Elder, you know traces of frost or other elements may remain there," Trugard cautioned as he sheathed his weapon. "What if she becomes imbued with magic?" He knew the Elder wouldn't care about other considerations, like whether the human girl would fall into a pit or suffer a cave-in. He'd just order the other Protectors to go retrieve her corpse.

Vernondiander scoffed, "So what? We have finer elements and stronger magic here. We'll put her in a box, like Kaigen, here." The Elder looked at Kaigen and seemed to come to some sort of decision. "That will be all, Logistician."

"Yes sir, it will be done." He saluted and turned and left the room.

"Now, Kaigen," he pressed his lips together and tapped them with his fore finger. "You don't like it when I torture you, obviously, but I think to break your will might require killing you." A cunning smile slowly bloomed on the Elder's face and he adjusted his robe. "And you don't like it when I kill the Annites, but yet you do not cooperate in order to stop me. So the question really is, what resource do I have to gain your cooperation?" He smiled at her kindly and his frost-changed blue eyes twinkled at her.

Fear ravaged Kaigen with that smile. It was the same kind smile he had on his face when he tortured her. "You have nothing!" Kaigen spat at him as her insides turned to liquid. He'd already said a name that both knew had special meaning to her.

"Ah, my dear, that is where you are wrong." The Elder looked quite pleased with himself. "Come in, Von."

Kaigen's horror grew as Von entered the room. She hadn't seen him since the dinner party when the Elder had forcibly taken her from her home with the Draconians. She froze at first, not wanting him to see her caged like an animal. In a moment, realizing that she had nowhere to hide, she stood tall and forced her chin up.

Von did not wear a uniform like Trugard. Instead, he wore a strange flowing tunic and pants that were tucked into leather soft-soled boots. The tunic was white and grey in color with a black and red belt. He had metal on his upper and lower arms; his sword he carried on his back. She noted his powerful body under the white garments he wore. He was absolutely gorgeous, and she mentally shrunk in her cage, covered in filth as she was.

Von quickly scanned the room. "Kaigen?" His hand immediately went up to grasp the necklace she had made for his father and he had taken. Von was shocked to see the state the proud young girl was in. She had filth all over her, her hair was matted, and her skin, especially her hands, looked bruised in several areas. Her tattered wings had grown even more ragged.

Von looked at the Elder in disbelief. "You said no harm would come to her!"

"Yes, well, I underestimated how stubborn she would be," the Elder said calmly and changed his stance to stand with feet apart, his hands hidden by sleeves, but his arms were pointed towards the ground. Von saw him change his posture and immediately grew wary. It was the stance a Protector used when gathering their stores of magic. "Actually, that is why I need your help, Von, it seems you may be the only thing she cares enough about to gain her cooperation."

Suddenly, and far faster than he'd expected, Von was hit with a blinding light that made him cry out in pain. He raised his arms to shield himself and deflected the majority of the energy. He left the ground, circling Vernondiander to hurl bolt after bolt of lightning at the Elder. Every bolt harmlessly dissolved into the Elder's robe, deepening its blue wherever it touched.

Von's attempt to aim a bolt at his foe's uncovered head was in vain; the older Protector simply raised his sleeve and absorbed the strike.

Von was reeling both physically and mentally from the unexpected on-slaught; the Elder had grown strong and was now immune to Von's own strikes! Von began to tire and he hit the floor hard, rolling. Vernondiander kept up the painful torrent until Von lay completely still. He stopped the stream of power and looked at Kaigen, her face twisted in pure horror, tears streaming down her dirty face. "Tell me you will cooperate, Kaigen, or Von will die."

Kaigen yelled as the Elder raised his hands for another volley. Von had not moved from where he fell. To her worried eyes, he looked like he might already be dead. "Stop, stop, I yield, just stop it!" she cried.

"Well then, wonderful!" The Elder ceased gathering another surge of power. He clapped his hands together happily. Over his shoulder, he sarcas-tically added, "Sorry about that Von, all in the call of science you know!"

Using a crystal on his desk, Vernondiander called for the city guard. When they arrived they looked in confusion at Von. He was their captain, and they followed him with a deep respect born of decades of service to the Protectors. "Restrain his power and then take him to the healer. When she's done with him, put him in a cell on the upper floor."

The guards were bewildered; Von was not only an officer of the guard, but until now, had always been one of Vernondiander's favorites. They gen-tly picked him up under the arms and dragged him from the room. Kaigen wept seeing Von fully unconscious, his head lolling from side to side. On his chest Kaigen caught a glimpse of the necklace she had left on the door-knob of his father's house; he must have taken it and kept it. Her heart turned over in her chest seeing the necklace against his bronze skin. Maybe he did care for her after all! Her hatred for the Elder increased sharply, and so did her resolve.

"Now, that's better, Kaigen, I have so many questions. With your assis-tance, let us see what new heights of science our new relationship can take! Elsbeth!" the Elder cried, summoning his serving woman.

Elsbeth came into the room, and Vernondiander was glad to see that she was walking this time, though he pretended not to notice. Good, he thought, everyone needed a little cowing now and then. "Put the magic re-straint on her. It will be painful, but it will keep her from using her earth magic." Elsbeth knew how painful the strange metal could be. The metal was magically sealed around the neck, a collar of sorts. It effectively blocked magic, as Kaigen would soon learn. Elsbeth had been exposed to the col-lar's effects during the Elder's experimentation with the method. "Take

Kaigen under guard and get her cleaned up and fed." He looked askance at Kaigen and seeing her lust for retribution written on her face he said, "If you do not cooperate, girl, I will have Von killed immediately," then turned back to Elsbeth as if he hadn't paused. "I want her kept near the drilling lab but ward her rooms so she cannot leave."

"Yes, Elder, by your decree," Elsbeth whispered, glad she wasn't the center of his attention this time. She knew she'd risked his ire by hovering into the room and given what he'd just done to Von— effortlessly done to Von—she realized now how dangerous that was.

Chapter 59: Meluha Crocus and the Protectors

The small party started out again just before dawn, with Isladora riding Fashi and Fashi following Tobin. *"He adjusted the amount of the henbane in the tisane, it should be just the perfect strength to give you some relief from the summoning spell, but it shouldn't make you too drowsy,"* Meluha told her. Her health and her mood had improved immensely. Tobin's, however, had not; he was surly and jealous, even as he took care of her needs. Isladora felt the tension in Tobin but she also detected an undercurrent of unease in Meluha's thoughts.

Meluha understood Tobin's feelings towards him. When Isladora fell from Phoenix's back to lay lifeless in the forest debris, becoming weaker and Meluha powerless to help her, he felt the same way towards himself. He was thankful that Tobin found her in time; the lad was a good tracker.

Meluha could feel the Protectors pulling her towards the Silver Roads. The roads ran underground and were unsafe, but for the first time since the calling had begun, he had hope. If they could find enough elemental minerals, especially frost, Isladora could become stronger, like a Protector. Once the frost was infused throughout her body, she would be able to access her own magic and Meluha could instruct her how to defend herself. Moreover, the spirit himself would be empowered by feeding from her magical energy and he could help to keep her safe.

"Isladora, I want you to repeat what I am going to say to Tobin," Meluha told her as they rode. *"This change in direction means that the Protectors are calling us towards the Silver Roads, the mica mines that travel through the mountains. This will shorten our travel time, so my brother must be becoming impatient."* Isladora repeated the words, keeping her reaction to "my brother" in check for the moment.

Meluha paused for a moment to think when Tobin said, "No one has gone into those mines for decades. They're full of ghosts and those few who have entered never come back."

Meluha continued on, ignoring Tobin's comment for the moment. *"It is a closely guarded secret for our kind,"* he began, *"that the mica is somehow transformed by small creatures we termed the Annites into a magical substance that we Protectors call frost. We have been mining it from them for centuries, and it gives us magical powers and extraordinarily long life spans. Any person, in fact, will develop magical powers if they get enough frost in their system."*

Meluha paused as Isladora reiterated the dialog to Tobin, who for the first time looked at the ring with something other than malice. The scowl he had worn the last few days became thoughtful. "So we can become magical?" Tobin asked. "To have powers like your people?"

"Yes, you, Isladora, even Fashi here," Meluha replied to Tobin through Isladora. *"The babes born in the frost are extremely powerful, and my brother and I were ones such as this. You cannot become as strong as we are, but you will gain strength and I can help you learn the magical arts."*

"Much like our training in these mountains before," Isladora said with a shudder. This did not sound like the gentle, natural magic that her mother could perform with a sufficient supply of fresh leaves or flower petals, but something somehow harsher, more dangerous.

"Well, yes, like before, but magical training is very different than physical training. You and Tobin are both clever students, so you will be able to learn quickly."

Isladora tried to quell her fears and have an open mind. "Tobin, he says that magical training will be different," Isladora told the young man. "I am used to the physical training now, I enjoy it so much, I can't even believe that once it was difficult for me. I was a chubby and weak thing before."

Tobin turned and looked at her, "Yes, and you have been lax in your training, but now that you feel better, we must keep up our sparring. But that wasn't why you brought that up, is it?"

Isladora sighed and shook her head. She felt better but the tisane made her groggy and she felt weak. "You are right about the sparring, Tobin. The more we practice the more ready we will be for whatever comes. But I meant that at first, the physical training was more like dying than living. My muscles were weak and my mind could not command my body as I wanted it to. The Protectors have had years, decades, even longer perhaps, to practice."

"Yes, Isladora, you grasp the truth of it, and it will be hard at first."

Tobin scoffed, "They shouldn't even be called Protectors anyway; they're more like cold-blooded killers." Tobin ran his hand down to the knife at his waist. "They only protect their own way of life. They aren't watchmen for the races, and if indeed they are called such, it is only because they protect the source of their own magic."

"The search for frost has become a power in and of itself, but it wasn't always like that. This turning point in thinking was brought on by the greedy nature of my brother, Vernondiander," Meluha explained. *"I was a scientist…"* He paused for nearly a minute, then continued, *"I am a scientist. My brother is avaricious, but he is no scientist, though he commands their efforts. And he has made a grievous error in judg-*

ment by choosing the Silver Roads. It will be difficult, especially at first, but I know how quickly you both learn; I have witnessed it! With access to the frost and other elemental minerals, we will have a chance. Vernondiander is far too much of an egotist—nay, a narcissist!—and he will be too arrogant to suspect that you might emerge from the Silver Roads a threat."

Isladora sighed, telling Tobin what he said and then adding, "It always seems that the world is at war, creatures fighting each other for control over things that truly do not matter." She placed her hand on her heart. "Do you believe in God, Meluha?"

Meluha was taken aback by her reference to faith, and not knowing what to say, he fell silent. His thoughts about her God were confused, but since he had met Isladora and her mother, Anyumay, he had been moved by their strong belief. He had to admit that every time Isladora had prayed, her prayers had been answered. He liked the thought of a loving deity watching over their affairs. As Isladora had fought through her many trials, Meluha had found his faith responding to hers, growing through her charitable disposition and her unwavering belief. He found that he did believe, but despite his great age and experience, he didn't really know how to discuss it with her.

Tobin reached up to check that the girth was tight then rested his hand on her calf. "What did you mean about control, Isladora?" he asked.

Her hand tightened on the saddle horn in response to his touch, her mouth forming a smile, "It is our souls that ultimately matter, not the physical self that contains our soul." Isladora taught from what she'd learned, both from reading the extensive libraries of the kingdom and from her experiences. "Look at Meluha, he doesn't even have a body, so he must share in the body he is attached to, but he still has thoughts and dreams. That is a proof of the existence of our souls. In turn, that we have souls tells us that we are meant to live forever, beyond this body." She paused, gathering her thoughts. "While religion gives us hope, our souls are in a constant battle with the needs and wants of our bodies." Isladora turned Meluha's ring around and around as she tried to find her words.

"We fight over material things because our bodies can't help but crave more control. Even when we have all that we need, our physical self can try to force us to reach for more." Thinking back to when she was a spoiled little girl, she said, "We gorge ourselves on food when we know people are dying from starvation, for example. It is only when our soul craves that which the body craves that we begin wanting more than we need. Carried to an extreme, as I think it was with the Queen Mother and Emperor Zhu...I think that's how the great injustices of the world are born. We must guard ourselves from giving into this craving for more, for the body is selfish, and therefore it's a constant battle within us."

The group grew silent for a time, then Isladora continued, playing with Fashi's mane as she talked. "You remember when we were in Zhu's stronghold?" she asked and Tobin nodded. "The suffering was great. You could see the effects of power hunger in the terrible fear of the women, the desolate rooms, the parched land, the broken walls, even the ferocity and evil of the men who served Zhu."

Tobin was confused and said so. "So you are saying that if we could live outside our bodies, we would see how foolish we are?" he asked, scratching his head.

At least he's too focused to remember to be jealous, Isladora thought, not unkindly.

Meluha chuckled, *"I am outside my body and still foolish. The reality of flesh and bone still drives my desires."*

She laughed at both of them. "Yes, I suppose so," Isladora said without repeating Meluha's comment, for she hadn't been speaking of his peculiar state.

Her eyes grew distant, remembering one of the memories from her childhood, "I slept next to a barnyard once when I was very young. The artisans were painting our wing of the stronghold, so we had to make our beds in the barn. I heard a terrible screeching that awoke me in a terror, so I fled from my bed and ran to my uncle Tonsaku, who often comforted me when I was scared. The sun was just rising, and he smiled and laughed at me, picked me up, and said, 'It's just a chicken laying an egg, Isladora, the same terrible eggs you eat for breakfast.'

"At my dumbfounded look, he said, 'Come, let us go find this terrifying beast.' We walked out into the barnyard, and there on a plank of wood sat a single egg. But as we watched, the startled hen jumped from the plank and the egg began to roll until it fell and burst open upon the ground. And then the most astonishing thing happened: all the fowl, the ducks, and also the rest of the chickens, ran towards the fallen egg! The duck reached it first, his head diving towards the ground and turning his beak sideways so he could lap up the yolk from the ground before the other birds could reach it. Seconds later, the chickens swarmed and fought over the contents of the egg until every bit of it was gone."

Isladora paused, looking at Tobin, "The duck, I understood, eating the broken egg of one of the hens, but the chickens fighting over every drop of the egg's contents horrified me. All they cared about was stealing the sustenance, the power, if you will, of the egg, even though it had been laid by one of them." She shook her head. "My point is that hens didn't normally fight each other over anything, but even with their little brains they knew the sustenance of the yolk was powerful."

Tobin didn't seem to catch her meaning, so she tried a different tact, saying, "Don't you see, the yolk and the birds, especially the chickens, it's like the frost and the Elder. Nothing matters but the bright substance that gives him power. Surrounded by it, it's become all he wants, and he will do anything regardless of consequences to get more and more."

This was why Tobin loved Isladora so much. She understood the deeper meaning in everything she had learned and experienced in her life. He knew that fowl had to be carefully managed and cared for or they would turn cannibal, but he'd never have thought to draw the analogy toward the Elder and the rest of the Protectors. This other way of looking at things challenged all that was related to his world, his more limited and focused understanding of things; he'd never cared much about anything save what he needed to learn to become a good scout.

It dawned on him that to be a good prince, if he succeeded in winning Isladora's hand, he might need to learn to see things in a totally different way. "You are wise beyond your years, my Isladora," Tobin told her when she was done with her story. "I don't see how knowing this helps us, but it's an interesting idea." They fell silent then, each lost in their own thoughts as they traveled on. By mid-morning they came to a place where the stream thickened into a lake. Tobin immediately halted and set about catching some fish to eat, ordering baths for everyone.

As the humans took care of their bodies, Meluha thought back to when he was more human than Protector. Without the frost, his body had slowly turned back to its native, mortal state and he had aged, albeit much slower than his fellow humans. As his body had rid itself of its desire to acquire frost—Isladora was right, in that the Protectors wanted a steady supply of the substance—he fell in love with a human girl, his Mae. In a way, his ability to love Mae was again proof that Isladora was correct.

He had decided to ask Mae to be his wife, and he remembered finding the perfect ring in a bazaar in a seaport where his ship had docked to trade cargoes. He found it in a tinker's shop, a ring to symbolize their union with one another. He knew now that he was drawn to that ring because it alone in all the wares that tinker had for sale was made of metals from in his homeland.

He had never questioned this, merely found himself so glad to see it that he had to have it, though at the time he thought only of how magnificent it would look on his beloved's hand. But now he wasn't so sure that it was a random happenstance. *Did Vernondiander arrange for that ring to find me, somehow?* Meluha Crocus wondered, and the moment he thought it, he realized it had to be true.

Some random ring, even one made from frost-imbued elements, would never have been able to entrap him, and he cursed himself for not realizing it before: his brother had not been satisfied with exile, he'd used the ring to entrap his magically vulnerable brother. *Why didn't I consider this before?* he wondered, cursing his foolishness for believing the ring had possessed some intrinsic, but natural, property that had caught his spirit.

He remembered the storm that had risen far faster than any natural weather. The unnatural storm had blown in on his ship—carrying not only Meluha and his crew, but his new bride as well—and it had been both merciless and untamable despite the power he retained. All his efforts had failed to calm the water, and it had capsized the ship in its terrible ravening fury, drowning Meluha, his crew, and his beloved Mae.

As he'd drowned—not one of his favorite memories—he remembered hurling himself into the ring on Mae's finger in a last-ditch effort to save himself. *But why did I even think of doing that?* Meluha thought, realizing it was something he'd never have done normally. *The ring drew me to it somehow, subtly but powerfully, and just as mercilessly as the sea and storm. But it wasn't the sea's mercy that was lacking, was it, Meluha? It was Vernondiander's hand at work.*

He had believed that he was out of Vernondiander's reach, living as he was in the human world, but he'd been wrong. *He must have meant to recover the ring from the bottom of the sea, not realizing that our bodies would travel in the currents,* Meluha thought, *so he lost me. He's powerful, but he's ignorant of anything outside of the city—and frost, of course—and that's something we might be able to exploit if we're clever enough.*

Meluha, in his arrogance, had believed he could control the wind and the seas when the storm arose; he'd never even thought that the storm was a method of attack. *By wind and sea, Vernondiander murdered my Mae along with me and my men!* he thought. For years, Meluha thought being trapped in the ring was his penance for not being able to protect his wife from the unruly storm. In his grief he had not cared, and not caring, he had not wondered how it had come to pass.

But he did care now, because Isladora's very life depended upon it, and Tobin's now that he was with her. Meluha knew that the scout would stay with Isladora and face whatever came, no matter how dangerous or terrible. The Protectors had sent a call to him a few decades after his imprisonment; he'd felt it for many years, centuries in fact, but ignored it until it had faded away. The imprisonment in the ring had prevented that call from influencing his actions, but the one the princess labored under was very different.

Maybe I don't have the power to escape the ring, but I do know how to make Isladora stronger, and to teach her the secrets I still keep, to safeguard her from the Protectors. He found he no longer truly considered himself one of them, but as one of their best researchers, he knew things about the elemental minerals that Vernondiander did not. He knew that the frost in the Silver Roads would make Isladora and Tobin powerful, but that alone would not be enough to face his brother, for he had no doubt that the Elder was so immersed in frost by now that even the other Protectors would not dare provoke him.

He could not wait to begin their training, but first they had to locate what they needed. Humans—even ones as exceptional as Aceptye and Isladora—didn't have enough innate magic to stand against even the weakest of the Protectors.

Once again, Meluha found himself thinking of Isladora's God. He wanted to say a prayer to Him, but he didn't know where to begin. *No, I'm afraid to begin*, he thought, *for I have much to answer for in my long existence. How could He accept me, with all the evils I've done or aided?* He had been worn by many men with black hearts, and he'd surrendered to his own rage at Mae's death and, he had to admit, his own. He'd helped such men conquer their fellows and subjugate them; he'd become a dark kingmaker in his ring prison, and he feared Isladora's God would never forgive him those crimes.

He knew these questions and feelings were signs of his blossoming faith, but instead of feeling strength from it like Isladora obviously did, instead he was terrified. *How can faith turn a man into a coward afraid to ask for help?* he thought, and he felt lost, as he had for so long.

Just before dusk the next day, they reached a hill that rose above a bend in the river. They looked down upon a town in the shadows of the mountain range on the other side of the river, and saw there was a ford just below the curve would allow them to cross over, for Isladora's course now led her across and then away from the river.

When she told him that they would need to leave the river, Tobin stopped to fill the water skins while Fashi drank his fill of the crisp, clear water. As they walked, leading Fashi behind him, Isladora told Tobin about the Silver Roads, about their training, and about the frost. He seemed to take it all in stride, interested mostly in the possibility of being able to defend themselves—he thought of it in terms of defending Isladora—from the Protectors.

Tobin decided to stop at the town to see what supplies could be had. "I'm going into town to get supplies. I won't be able to get much, but I have a couple silver pieces," he stepped back to the pony to retrieve them from his pack.

Isladora took a smaller pouch from the pack Lepola had given her that she wore strapped to her back. "Here, I have some coin as well." Isladora handed him all the gold and silver pieces she had, dumping them into his cupped palm.

Tobin whistled. "Where on earth did you get such a fortune?" he asked as the heavy gold coins landed in his hand. There was a lot of silver, but even one of the gold coins was worth more than all the silver ones together, and he counted six…no, seven! of the gold ones. It was wealth beyond anything he'd ever seen.

"Well it shouldn't be that surprising; I am a princess after all!" she smiled, straightening her shoulders to stand eye-to-eye with him with a haughty look that dissolved into a laugh as Tobin's expression soured. She surrounded his coin-filled hand with her hands, and her voice was level and serious as she added, "I'm also the woman you've been sparring with for months and the scared young woman who fought against Zhu with you. That I am the daughter of Elijashen the King is important, but it is not all of who I am."

Tobin nodded; that she was the daughter of the king of his people was something he tended to forget the longer he was around her. For a moment he'd fallen back on the doubts and fears of the drunkard's son he was, knowing he wasn't good enough for her. Her words had helped him shake that feeling, but he knew it was something he'd have to find a way to overcome. He knew he was more than that drunkard's son, much more, but it was hard to break the chains of his past.

He sighed as he pocketed the coins and took a long loop of rope from Fashi's saddle. "Isladora, I'm going to have to tie you to that tree over there out of the way." As Isladora's eyes rounded, he added, "It's for your own good. What if the pull of the Protectors makes you leave without me?"

She nodded roughly, seeing the sense in it. After telling her he'd be back quickly, Tobin left Isladora bound to a tree with only Fashi to guard her. It felt strange as he tied her, but if it kept her from entering those caves alone, she would do anything. She inhaled his scent as he worked to tie her, a smell she would never tire of. Isladora gazed longingly at Tobin's backside as he walked away from her. He had grown to be quite a man, and she loved how he protected and worried about her.

Meluha Crocus agreed that tying her made sense, but silently he worried that something would happen to Tobin and she would be vulnerable. He knew that Tobin had weighed her safety carefully; the scout did not want to risk the pull making her run off without him into that mine.

True to his word, the little horse that had once borne her mother Anyumay guarded her as well as any guard dog would have done. Isladora was not quite sure if he was guarding her from leaving, or from strangers coming. He was constantly alert and watchful. When she fiddled with the knot, Fashi grunted and pawed the ground, and when she stopped, he would nod his head in obvious approval.

Isladora and Meluha both thought it uncanny, the little pony's intelligence, each unaware of the other's thoughts.

Fashi nickered as Tobin returned to the clearing with his supplies. He had medicine, foodstuffs, rope, water skins, oats for the horse, a chisel and hammer, and a bundle of torches that he set upon the ground. "Ah, Fashi, a job well done!" Tobin exclaimed as he fed the little gelding an apple, which Fashi accepted as his just due. It struck Isladora that Tobin looked like a servant offering a tithe to his king, though to Tobin it seemed nothing of the sort, of course. He waited patiently for Fashi to savor the treat.

Isladora chuckled affectionately at the little horse and his rider. Then she cleared her throat. "Um, you can untie me now," she said just a little pointedly.

Tobin looked up without tilting his head and regarded her through his bangs. "Nah, I just thought I'd leave you there a bit longer and steal a kiss," he smiled. He'd smiled before, many times, but something about this one made Isladora shiver a little. It wasn't predatory, that smile, but something somehow like it. Not threatening, exactly, but full of both possibility and promise.

Isladora blushed, at his smile more than his words, and whispered, "You don't have to tie me up to kiss me."

Tobin slowly stood and prowled over to her, untying the rope gently and pressing her body firmly to the tree with his. He ran the tip of his nose up the side of her neck, making her shiver in delight. He cupped her face and lightly ran his thumb across her lips. After looking deep into her eyes, he slowly closed his eyes and pressed his lips to hers. It didn't take long for the kiss to deepen, her hands traveling over Tobin's chest and back.

"Ow!" she suddenly yelled, pushing Tobin away from her and grabbing her hand.

"You are a princess, Isladora, and an unmarried one at that. Control yourself!" Meluha admonished.

Tobin knew it was the ring that had startled her. "Someday old man, we are going to meet face to face," Tobin said in anger. Isladora walked some distance away, fighting for control over her racing heart.

"Tell the cur, indeed, we will," Meluha told Isladora, but she kept her mouth shut, her mouth that had just been deliciously kissed a second time!

She put her hands to her lips and smiled as they got under way. She was mad at Meluha for interrupting, but grateful, too, for he was right. *There would be time for that sort of thing once we are married*, she thought with another blush.

A few days later, as the small party stood outside of the entrance to the abandoned mines, Isladora had a moment of hesitation, remembering the trials she had survived in this very mountain range, though far to the south of here. She stopped and said a quiet prayer, and then like the brave woman Meluha knew her to be, she entered the mountain towards the Silver Roads.

"Isladora, what did you say in your prayer?" Meluha asked, curious.

"First, I praised God for all he created—the heavens and the earth—then I asked for forgiveness of my sins. I prayed that He grant me safety from evil and guidance for our steps, and I reaffirmed my faith in His promise of life everlasting." Knowing her friend as she did, she knew what was bothering him. "Take time to talk to God and He will talk to you, Meluha. All you need to do is allow your soul to listen, and then you will have something special, something sacred in your life."

Even though her words comforted him deep inside, Meluha was still too afraid to pray. He feared that his prayers would be answered with wrath instead of weal. And if so, he believed, it would be no more than he deserved.

At first, the mines showed signs of human activity. Timbers and old rusty tools highlighted where the locals had once tried to extract copper and silver from these tunnels, but they also found more than one location where the roof had fallen in on their inexpert efforts. A skeletal arm reached hopelessly from one pile in the torchlight. They ignored the side tunnels, led unerringly deeper into the mountain by the compulsion spell, and for the first few days, the way was easy enough, though without the spell, they might have become hopelessly lost. The amazing thing to Isladora and Tobin was that the floor was smooth, for the most part clear of obstacles, and while the grade could be steep in places, it was nothing they couldn't handle. Tobin found the condition of the "Silver Roads," as the ring's spirit had called them, a fortunate thing, for he did not want to leave Fashi behind.

When they first began to see the silver dust, it was beautiful, yet left them with an ominous feeling. Meluha had seen many of these mica dust caverns, all frost mined and removed. Many humans thought that the dust was from the washed-out bones of long dead miners, but he knew it for what it was—crushed mica. They would soon be covered in it and look like ghosts themselves. Meluha hoped to find a deep shaft. The deeper the mine shaft, the more likely they would be able to find an untapped vein of frost. He knew the signs to look for in the rock, and he taught them to her and she in turn taught them to Tobin. Fashi didn't seem to mind the closed in walls of the mine, it was big enough for the mining donkeys, so it was big enough for him.

"Isladora, I want to tell you about my brother, Vernondiander," Meluha said to her. *"Vernondiander calls himself The Elder. It was a self-granted title, but he was one of the oldest of us, so at the time, we didn't challenge it.*

"Over many years he gained power and status, but so slowly that by the time we all realized that he was in control, he had built a city and a government with himself as the center. Everyone simply accepted it as how it was, and admittedly, his ability in organization and the administration of the government was unmatched."

Meluha sighed, lost for a moment in a memory, before continuing, *"His ability to administer the government is aided by the fact that he's utterly charming when he wants to be. Even when he's at his worst, his demeanor can be totally pleasant and polite. I've seen him kill, in fact, with a congenial smile on his lips, with his eyes seeming to show nothing but gentleness, but that was much later.*

"We never dreamed that this beautiful apple would be rotten at the core; we were all pleased to do his bidding because we thought he wanted what was best for all of us. And in many ways, it was, for the city expanded into the most beautiful place on earth, Isladora." His mental "voice" was full of regret, and she knew it was because he had been denied Issedones' beauty for so long.

The ring-bound spirit was silent for a short time, but then spoke again. *"He considers himself to be our king and he believes he's a gentleman and an intellectual, wiser by far than anyone else among us. He had access—later, we realized, gave himself access—to the purest frost, and that made him the most powerful Protector by far. And once he gained enough of an edge over the rest of us to feel secure in his power...that was when we began to learn that he had no boundaries."*

Meluha's tone became angry as he spoke. *"He crosses all personal lines because he does not seem to recognize that others are separate from him. He views all living things as an extension of himself and expects everyone to do his bidding without question. When a person does not comply, he considers it an attack on his superiority, and he quickly rids himself of this person using any way available to him. Even by killing.*

"In my case, I suppose he felt some sort of pity since I am his brother, and he ordered me exiled instead of killed. He prefers to keep the people that are close to him in a subservient position where resistance would be difficult or even impossible. He fully exploits any living creature without regard for their feelings or interests; they merely exist as a part of his needs and are expected to live up to those expectations."

He knew there was more to tell, especially in regard to Vernondiander's power, but she needed an understanding of the power of the elemental minerals before he could describe that to her. *"I am telling you this so you can understand that you have no purpose to him other than delivering me to Issedones. Once that happens, he might allow you to go your own way, but more likely, he will consider you a nuisance to be rid of, and he may strike out at you. We must be ready to deal with that and have a plan to get you to safety, no matter what happens to me."*

Isladora told him that she understood, but he knew that until she had fully experienced his brother's power and unending arrogance, she would not truly understand the many facets of danger that she faced. Vernondiander was demented and broken, full of malignant self-love, and more terrible by far than even the Queen Mother and her dark emperor father had been.

Meluha told her, *"Until we can find the materials I need and see what magical wards you are able to conjure, I will not know what defenses to put in place. It has been many years since I have had access to frost or any other mineral, but rest assured that I was one of the best frost exploration scientists, and I have high hopes."*

"I have confidence in you, Meluha," she said earnestly.

Chapter 60: Commander

The tiny earth creature rode with him. She had made a home on what used to be his snout, and although he couldn't see her shape, he could see her attempts to communicate with him—small flashes of light. At first they had been barely noticeable, but somehow she had increased the radiance so he could easily see her signals now.

The Commander admitted to himself that he didn't really know that it was a she, but the creature was temperamental and abrupt like the female wyverns. He would bet his last meal that the little flashes of light belonged to a girl. They had developed a code they each understood for left and right, up and down, so they could traverse the underground world. That was simply based on trial and error and how agitated she grew when he didn't go the way she wanted him to. "You're a bossy little thing really," he told her affectionately. "Since we cannot exchange names formally, I have decided to call you Nim. I hope this meets with your approval."

She pulsed with a warm glow, which he assumed meant that she was pleased. He had already learned that when she was agitated, she gave off sharp bright pulses of blue light.

Nim had taken him through tunnels filled with loosened dirt that emerged from time to time into caverns. The magic the creatures had given him allowed him to breathe and burrow freely in the earth. He could absorb the minerals for sustenance, but he still felt claustrophobic with so much dirt and pressure around him. It took him traveling some distance to realize that the loosened dirt was similar to roads and the caverns were like empty cities. In the first cavern they had entered, Nim seemed to go crazy, flashing wildly, and he had stopped moving, trying to comprehend what she wanted. Finally, he understood that he could crush structures if he didn't stay on the path she indicated. He could see large pockets of glowing blue running along one wall that went on for as far as he could see, he assumed it was their source of light down here. He enjoyed the caverns; it gave him a break from the heaviness and made him feel less likely to panic. Truly at times the weight of it all had crushed his spirit entirely.

He fretted about going deeper, yet they traveled on, "Nim I want you to know that I was a glorious creature of the air once, now here I am burrowing as far down in the ground as I had soared in the skies." It was difficult for him to not feel confined. The passageways of pliable abutting up to hard rock were dark and, he admitted to himself, more than a little eerie.

Like the midst of a gentle rain, Nim's pulsing light was the only thing that relieved him from pure blindness as they burrowed. She seemed to sense when he felt anxiety from the dark and she would reassure him by glowing warmly, matching the beating of his heart to slow it. They reached another cavern and he surprised her with a laugh, saying, "Oh what a relief!" This cavern was filled with the blue glowing veins, and he realized that it was the same material Nim used to communicate with him. The Commander's carapace was changing as it reacted to the substance. His shell was becoming more pliable, almost like the skin and scales he had before, and he felt great stores of magic growing in him. Each day, it became easier to manipulate the dirt when they traveled, and along with the minerals in the soil, the blue substance made him feel powerful.

"What is this blue mineral Nim?" He wondered. He had been a magically powerful wyvern before Glock had burned him nearly to death; but this was different. He remembered how difficult it had been to control his power as a youngling, and he knew that what he'd learned then might not work with this new magic. He must be careful, but he had always been a relentlessly optimistic creature.

Onward they trekked, the big armored wyvern following Nim's cues, obeying her commands with an amused feeling of indulgence. It wasn't as if he had something else to do or somewhere else to go, after all.

The tunnel they were passing through was much smaller than the others, and he could feel the dirt pressing on and around him. As it continued to shrink in size he used his battle training to help him stay calm as he focused on Nim's light. His pincers were now scraping over bare rock, but Nim urged him on, her light flashing vehemently in energized conversation.

The tunnel narrowed further, and his pincers could no longer move him through. The dirt had become mostly rock, and he could not grasp to pull himself forward. He felt chills and then heat all over his body as he became more frightened. He tried to back out of the tunnel and found himself truly stuck. He yelled, "Nim, you forced me into a tunnel too small!"

He panicked at first, but then he became aware that Nim was not alone. Although he could not see them, he could feel small creatures working madly to free him. After several hours, they finally loosened the rock enough that he could slowly back out of the tunnel. He was grateful, but his trust in the creatures had faltered. They wanted him to continue down a different road, but instead he sat in the cavern for several hours feeling the heavy weight of stone over his head. He felt oppressed, unnerved, and trapped.

His gaze shifted to the furiously blinking creature on his nose, "Look Nim, I'm not moving. You got me stuck in there."

Nim glowed for a long time then flashed the signal for "move left." Then she repeated it.

The Commander understood the flashes and told her again, "I'm going to sit here and maybe even figure out how to go back to the surface."

This time Nim flashed hotly, small short bursts of anger pouring from her. She flashed the signal for him to move left again. The Commander looked to his left and sighed. He really had no choice; he could never find the surface without her help anyway. As soon as he began moving the way she wanted, he could feel her satisfaction.

She led him into another part of the cavern near pools of blue glowing water. She led him right up to the water and told him to stop.

He lowered his head slowly, giving her plenty of time to flash a warning if he wasn't supposed to drink it. He slowly tasted the water—it felt cool on his tongue and was slightly sweet. "Oh wow, this is very good," he murmured, taking a deeper drink and Nim pulsed warmly, her signal that she was pleased with him. A volley of warmth spread through him from his groin to his chest, and he suddenly felt as if he could float, though he was afraid to try.

He closed his eyes and was surprised to see images. No…not images, a map. A map of the underground roads and caverns, hundreds of them. The Commander knew and understood maps from his decades of service as the wyverns' battle commander, and he studied it carefully. He somehow knew which mark indicated the cavern they were in, and from there, an understanding blossomed of where he was in the underground network.

He also found that he understood more of Nim's intent, that she realized she'd erred by getting him stuck and that they were now giving him this power to navigate underground, or even to rise back to the surface if he wished. But he could also tell that she wanted him to proceed to a place with a tremendous source of the blue mineral; it was where she'd tried to lead him when he'd gotten stuck.

The knowledge he now had meant that he neither needed Nim's guidance or aid any longer, and he knew that the little creatures had chosen to trust that he would stay after being granted this freedom. He smiled at Nim, "That's quite some water, isn't it?" She seemed to flash in agreement.

"I have the map now, behind my eyes," he said. "I thank you for it, Nim." Having his orientation back, knowing where passages that were large enough for him were, and having a method to get back to the surface any time he chose restored his self-assurance. They were taking a desperate gamble and he knew it. "I see on the map that you were leading me to a certain place, and I will continue to follow you, my small friends."

Nim glowed warmly again, then indicated for him to drink again and rest. The Commander did as she requested, amazed at how much easier it was to understand her now as he settled down to sleep. As he slept, the little creatures continued to work on his carapace and scales, though he didn't know what their objective was. What he did know was that each time he awoke after their "treatments," as he'd come to think of them, he felt more like the wyvern he used to be.

A wyvern without wings, yes, for what was left of them was sealed underneath the carapace that Kaigen had created for him, but still strong and powerful, and he wondered what need Nim and her people had for such a creature as he.

They stayed in this cavern for some time, drinking the cool blue liquid and resting. It was hard for the Commander to tell time down here; he could perceive no day or night. A day or two, at most, they'd stayed in the cavern, though he admitted he could have slept longer without knowing it.

Nim was trying to communicate with him again, but this time it was something more complicated, and his deeper grasp of her meaning proved insufficient. He stayed still and tried to figure out what the little creatures wanted, but it was just a collection of flashes of blue light, echoes by more points of light here and there throughout the cavern.

"I know you're frustrated creatures of the earth. I am also frustrated," his gaze returned to Nim. "I know you need my help, our communications are getting better, but it is more like knowing what you are feeling, not what you are thinking." He understood that they gave him the knowledge of the map for a reason and they had much more he needed to know. The map itself was proof that they were intelligent, perhaps advanced, beings. They had healed his wyvern hands, and now he could slide the carapace pincers forward for digging and then slide them back to use his wyvern hands and claws when needed.

After a while, Nim stopped trying to tell him the new information; he could tell she was disappointed but not angry with him, and he was glad.

Finally, they indicated it was time to move and began a downward trajectory towards the large blue mineral source. He had learned the scale of the map, and he estimated that it would take several days to reach their destination. As they went deeper, he began to feel heavier and he worried the pressure would become too intense. When he became jumpy and unnerved, they would lead him to another dark blue pool and he would drink and feel the pressure equalize inside.

With the blue substance, the Commander's burned skin rarely bothered him now and he didn't need to rest as much. He felt a sensation like worker bees all over him, repairing and cleaning, but he could see nothing. He knew they had gone very deep, and though he had no way to determine it, it must have been more than a mile deep and many miles laterally.

They finally emerged into a cavern where they fed him even darker blue water and he rested, trying to keep his claustrophobic panic at bay, for despite the wide cavern he felt the press of the millions of tons of rock above him. He fell into a deep sleep, and when he woke up, he found thousands of little black and dark red creatures all over and around him, although he didn't feel any of their weight.

He jumped up and roared in fright at these new creatures, and dozens of them poured from him on every side.

Nim's flashes were incredibly fast now, bright and insistent, and she succeeded at getting his attention before he moved side to side and crushed any of the little creatures. When he stilled, she was "silent" again, waiting. He tried to focus on the tip of his nostril where she rode and found that he could see far more clearly, especially close-up, than he'd ever seen. Then he realized that he could now see Nim's body as well!

Chapter 61: Mezzi

The healer named Chablis shook her head at the young Sybaris. "Mezzi, it's simply foolish for you to be up in the clouds with those female wyverns. They are extremely dangerous." Chablis continued to suture her back where the skin had torn. "One day they are going to kill you, and no one will be the wiser because you live alone up there."

"Look, if I could stitch up my own back, I wouldn't be bothering you," Mezzi told the doctor in her typically aloof fashion. Mezzi was a healer in her own right, but she couldn't reach the tear in her back, so she had come down to Sybaris to get help.

"You aren't bothering me, stop being so foolish," Chablis told her. "I am worried about you. This isn't the first time you've been hurt by the she-wyverns." She finished the suture and neatly cut the string. "You will have to come back down in a week to get these out. Or maybe I will get one of the male wyverns to fly me up so I can see what you're up to."

"No, no! Don't bring a male wyvern right now. Mating season is almost upon us," Mezzi cautioned, returning the doctor's gaze with a small smile.

Chablis laughed, what a mess that would be! "Well, in that case, if you don't make it back down here to get the stitches removed, I will go to the governing board and tell them to ground you."

Mezzi knew it wasn't a real threat. "Chablis, healing is your life." She looked at the doctor in earnest, "What if I told you that I was going to take that from you, wouldn't you feel threatened?" Mezzi tried to make her understand.

"Yes, of course, but I am not in any danger," Chablis reasoned, brushing a strand of pink hair behind her ear.

Mezzi told her, "Neither am I. I understand these female wyverns, and I have been healing their injuries for several years now. I just got too close, too quickly. I will be more careful."

"Still, I wish we could communicate some way so I know that you are well," Chablis said as she turned to the sink to scrub her hands. "Aren't you lonely up there?"

Mezzi placed her hand on the doctor's back. "I know you worry about me. I'll start coming down once a moon cycle and we can sup together, okay?"

Chablis looked over her shoulder at the young Sybaris, giving her an arch look. She said sternly, "I'm still going to discuss your back injury with Darkale."

"I know you don't keep anything from him anyway; you two are thick as wolves," Mezzi replied and laughed, thinking of the dark and mysterious male Sybaris whose lower jaw was so frightening that he kept it covered. He and the doctor were madly in love and they made a stunning couple, at least as long as he covered his maw. She wondered how Chablis felt about that but decided it would be rude to ask.

"Do be careful. Here is some ointment to keep on the abrasions until they heal." Chablis shook her head, handing the medicine to her and saying, "You really are impossible, you know."

Changing the subject, Mezzi said, "I can only pay you with wyvern claws. I hope that's all right." Mezzi went to grab her backpack.

"Of course! I was hoping you would bring some!" Chablis could barely hide her excitement as Mezzi pulled six claw pieces from her bag and handed them to the doctor. The claws of the female wyverns in actuality were the outer edge of the claw that they shed relatively infrequently as they grew in new, longer ones, and they held a variety of healing properties that could be extracted.

"These are valuable and I do need them," Chablis said. The doctor grabbed her jar, pulling some coins from it. "Here, I'll pay you for the rest of them and then you can buy some supplies. I'm sure you need something up there in the wild blue yonder."

Mezzi took the coins and placed them in her pouch. She smiled and thanked the doctor, "I'll see you soon, I promise." Then she left. The doctor watched the cute sway of her hips and the sensuous way she moved her tail. Shaking her head, she thought that girl would attract quite a few males if she stayed down in the city for too long. She was a brave girl, Chablis thought, living alone up there, and she had barely batted an eye when the doctor had sewn her back shut.

Mezzi knew that she had some nasty abrasions in addition to the contusion, but she was so close to being able to climb on the back of her favorite wyvern, Sunny. Although no one had ever ridden a female wyvern, Mezzi knew she would be the first to tame one. She thought about Sunny's temperament and sighed. She had her work cut out for her.

Mezzi was fairly short for a Sybaris. She had cyan hair that she kept in two messy buns on top of her head. She had the pink scales of a healer, like Chablis, on the right side of her forehead, just over her eye up to her hairline. The pink scales continued on her left forearm and then began at her buttocks and ran down her right leg. Cyan scales wrapped her lower abdomen, both of her upper arms, and up her back to her neck. The cyan magic allowed her to levitate for short amounts of time. She used it to slow her falls and to jump high. Her most glorious feature, she knew, was her wyvern tail. No other Sybaris that she knew of had a tail. She waved it in the air as she thought about Sunny. Her tail was her strongest appendage, and she used it to wrap around limbs and for balance when she was high up in the mountains and trees where the female wyverns lived. It had saved her more than once from falling to a painful death. Her tail had cyan scales from beginning to end, and the same cyan-colored hair she had on her head was also on the tip of her tail.

To protect her body from harm, she wore brown leather pants and tunic. Her leather pouch was normally strapped to her back, but it always slid around and she couldn't get anything from it easily when she was treating an injured wyvern. Of course, right now it was far too painful to sling it that way anyhow, so maybe she could think of an alternative.

Her tunic was ripped in the back, thanks to Sunny, so Mezzi headed for the tanner's shop to get a new shirt. At least it wasn't her pants, she thought. Those were custom made because of her tail and would cost more than she could afford to replace.

Mezzi entered the shop and took a deep breath, loving the smell of leather. She picked up the closest item, a pair of gloves, and brought them to her face, inhaling the scent. She smiled and turned the gloves over in her hand and then slowly tried one on. It fit perfectly; she flexed her hand and made a fist, pulling the strap on the back tight to her wrist. She would need gloves like these to ride Sunny.

"May I help you?" The shopkeeper asked her.

"Yes, I came in for a new tunic; do you have one that might fit?" Mezzi extended her arms.

The shopkeeper nodded, "Surely a pretty young Sybaris like you would prefer finer materials?"

Mezzi smiled at him, "I assure you, leather is fine." She figured he was flattering her in order to make more sales; it never occurred to her that she was truly striking, but she'd been a late bloomer and in her adolescence she'd definitely been the ugly duckling. Now she was a swan, and a beautiful one at that.

"Ok, how about one of these?" he asked, pointing to three tunics. After carefully studying each one, Mezzi chose the one that would closely match her brown pants. It had crème-colored leather at the shoulders tied across the front.

She held up the gloves on her hands and asked, "I would like these gloves, too. How much are they?" "Three coins for the shirt, two for the gloves," he told her with a smile.

Mezzi's eye caught upon a fancy tooled belt that had a pouch made of tough leather, and she gasped. The opening folded over and had clever metal snaps to keep the flap shut and a second belt at the bottom of the pouch that strapped around the thigh. It would be secure, easy to get tools from, and the contents would stay in even when she was inverted. "How much for this pouch and belt?" she asked him hopefully, turning it over in her hands. "Wherever did you get this? It's fantastic!"

The shopkeeper beamed at her, pleased to finally have someone interested in it. He explained, "I got the idea from some human traders that had crossbow holsters strapped to their leg, but no one's seemed interested in it yet, except for you. How about three more coins, then, eight in all?" He knew he could have asked three times as much, given the excitement in her eyes, but he found that he wanted her to have it. He justified it to himself that if the other Sybaris saw her wearing it, they might want one as well.

Mezzi smiled at him with glee and eagerly handed him the coins. She slipped behind the privacy screen to quickly don the shirt, wincing as she pulled on the stitches despite her caution. She then strapped the belt around her waist and then secured the smaller belt about her thigh. She was so excited about it that she almost forgot to grab her gloves and old shirt. She could make something from the shirt—bandage ties if nothing else—and living alone, she had learned not to waste anything.

She posed for the shopkeeper with her new pouch and he clapped lightly in approval. She smiled back at him, unaware that he'd been appreciating her appearance more than the way the pouch rode on her thigh, and then moved into the general store side of his establishment. There, she purchased some thick twine and more purple bulbs to make the sedation medicine as well as some vegetables that she couldn't grow at her garden's altitude. Finally, she saw a beautiful purple orb made of solid glass, and for no other reason than she could afford to, she bought it as well.

The storekeeper watched her leave, his eyes never leaving her glorious tail. "I didn't haggle at all," he realized with a chuckle. "That's quite an amazing Sybaris, and I don't think she even knows it!"

Mezzi saw Silverback heading towards the Cystine Hall, his slick silver scales flashing in the sun. She ran to catch up. "Hi, Silverback! How have you been?"

Silverback stopped and turned his long neck to look at her. "Ah, Mezzi, hello!" he greeted her. "I've been good, thank you. We have all been busy reorganizing things with Queen Ariah."

"Is she as amazing as I've heard?" Mezzi knew that Ariah was a true royal, with golden scales. She had seen her flying on her fleet green wyvern, Json, but hadn't had the opportunity to meet her yet.

Silverback showed his teeth, a wyvern smile. "You should come to the Hall and meet her yourself."

Mezzi felt too nervous to go to the Hall. "Ah, well, maybe. I wondered, I mean… I meant to ask you, when will mating time begin this year?"

Silverback shuddered as he smiled—it was a time that male wyverns looked forward to but dreaded as well. "Right after the next full moon, I do believe," he told her. The male wyverns lived in the lower mountain range, closer to the city of Sybaris, and they helped defend and rule Draconia.

The female wyverns were just as intelligent, but were too wild to become bonded or ridden. They had a social order of their own, but declined—violently, usually—to be civilized. No Sybaris ever bonded to a female wyvern; only the males made bonded pairs. It was said that if the she-wyverns ever went to war, it would be like a tide of destruction and as unstoppable as a hurricane.

"The next full moon, eh?" she said. "I better get busy. Thanks, Silverback!" She began to move away.

"Want me to give you a lift back to your home?" Silverback asked her. "I mean, I know you can levitate, but I can take you a whole lot faster, you know." He winked at her.

"Wow! Would you mind?" Her smile grew from ear to ear.

Silverback was the sleekest and fastest wyvern in all of Draconia. It took the females a long time to catch him, which was a good thing for Silverback; the lucky she-wyvern was usually too tired to hurt him much in the catching. "Let me go get a saddle for you."

Mezzi waved her hand, "I absolutely don't need that. Remember where I work!"

"Yes, but you don't try to ride them, or do you?" he asked as he tilted his head to the side.

Silverback was so intuitive, she thought. Too intuitive. "Not yet I don't, but I know I could!" Mezzi dissembled, trying to make it sound like a joke, but she had a feeling Silverback saw right through her. Silverback lowered his body to the ground and she scrambled on his back, using her tail to hang on, her thigh pouch and backpack, worn in front for the moment, bulging with her purchases.

"Up, up, and away, hang on!" the silver wyvern called to her. Silverback trotted and then gently leaped into the air, the wind immediately catching his silver wings.

"Woohoo!" Mezzi cried out, loving every second of it. As she centered her weight, she extended her tail straight out behind her, just like his, letting it slide in the slipstream and further stabilize her perch. Up they climbed, out of the city and past the caverns the male wyverns lived in.

He changed direction and pointed to the haunted place that had once been the old palace, saying, "Queen Ariah and Json live there." She wanted to ask about it, but she didn't want to yell. He took her out over the lake because he knew she would love it. Then he changed direction again and climbed to the higher mountain range until he saw the familiar small plateau with its sprinkling of a few small trees.

Mezzi pointed it out to him, shouting, "There!"

Silverback nodded his head and descended to land. A brown dog came from nowhere, barking madly at the huge wyvern, hackles up and fangs bared. The wyvern didn't think that expression was a smile like it was for wyverns; it looked rather more like it was stretching its lips out of the way to take a large bite from his leg, not that it could have done serious damage through his armored scales.

"Hush, Unsu!" Mezzi yelled, and to Silverback's surprise, the dog quieted.

"What kind of animal is that?" Silverback asked as he looked at the furry brown creature that was so obviously protective of Mezzi and her place.

"I'm not sure. The humans' word for them is 'dog,' and he is loyal," she said, pulling some dried meat from her pack and tossing it down to him. The animal made short work of the morsel, though he didn't take his eyes off the imposing wyvern. "So... this is my home."

Silverback noted the neat cave built into the side of the hill and the well-tended garden with herbs and plants bearing vegetation of all kinds.

"You better get out of here before Sunny smells you!" Mezzi warned him and laughed, thinking of the great chase last mating season. "Thank you for the lift, Silverback, I won't forget the favor!" She watched as he took off, laughing as he cautiously searched the skies for signs of Sunny or any of the other she-wyverns.

Mezzi stood for a long time after Silverback left. The dog whined and she aimlessly stroked his head and the soft spot behind his ears. Chablis had asked if she were lonely up here. Looking up, she observed a young she-wyvern alternately soaring and tumbling through the air, learning to gauge the wind. The underside of her wings were silky and smooth and she executed a beautiful fall, turning over and over then recovering and regaining her altitude. She appeared to be alone, content with only the wind and the sky for companions. Yet, Mezzi thought with a smile, it was not alone, and neither was she.

She was refreshed by the sight of the wyvern; perhaps she, too, was enjoying being watched by the Sybaris healer while showing off. Mezzi wasn't sure what being lonely felt like, but what she felt when she was up here wasn't it.

Mating time was a busy time for her. The male wyverns traveled up to the mating grounds once a year to mate. The females were somewhat calmer and gentler during this time, but they were a far cry from safe. If a female chose the same mate as another female, a fight would ensue until one of them gave up, and if both were particularly stubborn and they were fairly well-matched, the fight could be to the death.

Unlike birds and mammals, wyvern females chased the males at mating time, and singular wyverns treated the flight and chase differently. The males set the pattern: they could give in easily if the closest wyvern appealed to them, or they could strive to escape. She knew that many of the males enjoyed the chase almost as much as the joining.

Mezzi carefully placed the purple bulb flower on her medicine shelf. It was much easier to work on the wyverns' injuries with sedation. Later, she would prepare some of the sedative to that she could coat her cloth-tipped blow darts. She was quite adept at blowing them into a wounded she-wyvern's nostril without the risk of injury a steel-tipped dart would represent.

At the doses she used, the wyvern would sleep lightly for a short time, usually long enough for her to see to their needs without worrying about being bitten or scorched. When the young wyverns of either gender hatched, they were strong and wild and they often hurt themselves falling and fighting, just being wyvern young. Mezzi was there to patch them up when it was too much for their overprotective mothers to tend; she often had to sedate the parent, as well.

And when all that was done, she would definitely ride Sunny. The female wyvern just didn't know it yet.

Chapter 62: Sybaris

Silverback flew towards the center of the city for a meeting of the ruling pairs. As he surveyed the ground from his aerial view, he noted that Sybaris had really blossomed and changed under Queen Ariah. The streets were clean, the land was prospering, and commerce was definitely in an upward trend as the market had grown. Having a royal Sybaris made the Draconians proud, and now that Glock was gone from their governmental system, the ruling pairs could conduct their meetings with ease.

More was accomplished than it had in a long time. The ruling pairs all missed Solei and felt sorry for his death at the hands of his bond-mate Glock, but the destruction of Glock had been a good thing for all of Draconia. He had been difficult to deal with and cunning in his pursuit of power. Silverback shook his head; problems always arose when someone took more than their share.

Silverback slowed and landed, extending his silver wings gracefully for the drop, in front of the Cystine Hall. He was a little late, and his Sybaris bonded pair Toyah would already be inside. He imagined she might also be more than a little peeved at him. He hurried through the main door and down the hall to the meeting room, favoring Queen Ariah with an overly florid bow as he took his place next to Toyah.

Arrington noted his arrival, tilting his green head in obvious amusement. "Ah, Silverback, at least it wasn't me that was late this time." Silverback noted that even Arrington's arrogance had toned down some after all that had happened to them. Arrington and Bedaiko had been locked in a pit by Glock, and Arrington had been nearly dead when they found and rescued them.

As she always did, Queen Ariah stood and the ruling pairs stood with her. "A moment of silence please. Let us take a moment to reflect on the importance of the decisions we make, a moment to be thankful for our history." They were all proud of their Queen, who was once enslaved to humans. Reborn as a warrior, muscular and strong, her hair long and flowing with mostly red tresses and some purple and gold. Queen Ariah dressed in the fine clothes befitting a queen, but she had demanded that they be suitable for flying and battle. She wanted no one to doubt that she would fight to the death for their beliefs.

The tailor had cut the cloth so that her golden scales could be seen, and the metalsmith had created lightweight metal armor that covered her un-scaled torso and shoulders. Her human face had filled out; she was a wom-an now, not a young girl. Her full lips and high cheekbones made her regal and equal in beauty to her mother, Toyah.

The bonded ruling pairs opened their eyes, still standing, and looked at one another: Queen Ariah and Json, Arrington and Bedaiko, Silverback and Toyah, and Darkale and Abraxis. Queen Ariah and Json had taken the place of the Commander and Aslay. Two empty places remained where Glock and Solei used to reside.

"I want to call this meeting to order," Arrington began as he was the meeting's Chairman. "Our first order of business is that the domiciles of some Sybaris are getting closer and closer to the shores of the lake." It was true, the gardens and orchards were somehow getting planted closer every year.

Darkale spoke, his lower jaw covered as usual. "The lake should belong to everyone. I propose to pass a rule that will preserve the land around it, with no settling allowed within one mile of the shoreline." While Darkale's demeanor had gentled since he and Chablis had begun their courtship, his ice blue eyes were still direct and piercing. "Abraxis and I did a flyover, and two farms have already staked out land within that mile." He pushed his black hair off his forehead. "I believe we are all in agreement on this ruling. Does anyone disagree?" When no one did he added, "I will post a notice immediately, and Abraxis and I will visit the encroachers in person to ex-plain."

"Well, that will definitely terrify them into obedience!" Arrington joked. He wasn't sure whose teeth were more terrifying, Darkale's or his fierce wyvern Abraxis.

Json spoke before the easily-provoked Darkale or Abraxis could re-spond to Arrington's taunt. "Very good, Darkale. It's a good solution," and was pleased to see both of the pair relax at his praise. As the Queen's wy-vern, Json had more authority than his relative youth would normally bring, and so far he'd shown a talent for diplomacy that Ariah hadn't foreseen.

"Let me see, next on our agenda is an application for a new bonding," Json announced and then turned toward the court orderly, a Sybaris named Damarn. "Please bring in Cassian and Petrus." Damarn nodded and depart-ed to get the wyvern and Sybaris in question.

The ruling pairs had not formed a new bond since the battle with Glock. The fact that they were considering one now meant to all of them that the kingdom of Draconia was healing. Four pairs of heads turned expectantly towards the door as a young male Sybaris entered the room followed by his chosen wyvern. The young male was dressed in black leather pants and tunic. His hair was long and brown, and he wore it straight back and tied in a neat queue. He had large white scales that also grew from his scalp and were swept back in neat rows like he'd trained his hair to do. The wyvern Cassian was mostly dark green to black like Json, but he had a long snout and dark blue scales on his forehead and down his back. The green was unpredictable and the black brought balance; both were a catalyst for power. Blue scales meant water magic.

The wyvern spoke, bowing before the Queen, "Your Majesty, it is an honor to meet you. My name is Cassian and I seek permission to be bonded to the white Sybaris Petrus."

According to tradition, the Sybaris requested the bond, not the wyvern. Queen Ariah was curious as to why Cassian was representing them both, but she said only, "I see." She glanced at Json both to gauge his reaction and to give him a cue to take over.

"Cassian, you are requesting the bond?" Json queried, his tone free of any judgment for the odd procedure, but clearly curious.

"Yes, Json." Cassian bowed respectfully to the war wyvern, "It is my desire to trade with the humans now that the law has been changed. To do so, I need a fellow Sybaris to help ease the way, as they are closer to the humans than we are."

"Ah," Json answered, returning his gaze. "Might we inquire as to what you will trade?"

"Well, all sorts of things," Cassian told him, surprised by the question. "Think of me as a merchant. I will buy things here to trade down there, sort of an aid to the sale, and of course hopefully gain some profit from it."

Queen Ariah asked, "Petrus have you other scales upon your body? And if so, what are the colors?"

Petrus began to remove his tunic, but then thought better of it. "May I remove my shirt so I can show you, Your Majesty?" he asked. When the Queen nodded, he removed his shirt. Petrus' torso was fully scaled with white scales of various shapes; the scales were pearlescent and breathtaking. "These white scales are also present on my legs, and I have no other colors."

Queen Ariah smiled in appreciation of the scales. "Your scales are very beautiful, and why ever would you hide them under all this black leather?" Most Sybaris wore clothes designed to accentuate and accent their scales.

Before Petrus could answer, Darkale asked, "And what magic power do they command?"

Petrus scowled, struggling to master his features before the ruling council. He couldn't keep his unhappiness from his voice. "I hide them because they are useless. I can purify things, clean things, and sometimes protect them."

"Why, that is something to be proud of, not hide!" Darkale exclaimed, surprised at Petrus' reaction. "Chablis, our healer, would put you to work immediately!"

Petrus angrily shoved his arms into his jacket sleeves. "I would trade them for red scales any day," he said morosely.

"The power to build, cleanse, and protect are by far greater powers than the ability to destroy with fire," Queen Ariah said, thinking of the destruction Glock had rained down upon their race only a short few months before.

"Forgive me my Queen, but you yourself have red scales. Are you saying that you would trade me?" Cassian growled at his friend and Petrus bowed immediately, then looked up to see how much trouble he was in for speaking out so.

The Queen took no offense to the young and impetuous Sybaris, though she was perplexed by his reaction. "I am what I am, Petrus, and you are what you are. Your gift is extremely important, and your scales are the most beautiful scales I have had the pleasure to look upon. I approve this bonding and I hope that you would speak to Chablis, our healer, and see what use she has of you. We will perform the bonding at the next full moon."

She rose and added, "Do try to be proud of who you are, Petrus. It will make all of us stronger for it." With that, she dismissed them both.

Cassian and Petrus bowed and left the room, and the ruling pairs sat quietly for a few moments to consider what Petrus had said. Each of them wondered what the source of his resentment was.

Darkale broke the silence, and all seven heads turned to hear what he had to say. "I have something I would like to discuss. Since we mentioned Chablis, I want to tell you that she has shown concern for Mezzi living in the highlands by herself. Mezzi came down with her back torn open badly enough that our healer had to stitch it back up. Chablis thinks that Mezzi might be intending to try to tame one of the female wyverns."

Silverback nodded his head, "I just returned from giving Mezzi a ride back up to her home and she joked about being able to harness Sunny. At first, I thought that she was probably teasing, but she had a gleam in her eye, and then she tried to make light of it…too much so, if you catch my meaning."

"Female wyverns are not for riding," Abraxis said firmly in his gravelly voice, and Bedaiko concurred. "Only a foolish Sybaris would attempt such a thing." Everyone knew how foolhardy it would be to try to tame a female.

"Does anyone really know this Mezzi well?" Queen Ariah asked.

Arrington replied, "No, she stays in the highlands by herself. The female wyverns allow it because she cares for their young when they're hurt—she's a healer. She has been known to care for the grown females too, but they allow her close only when they are badly wounded and even then, she has to sedate them to keep them from lashing out at her. If I had to guess, I'd say Chablis has had the most contact with her."

Silverback added, "She has a brown furry creature, very small, that makes a lot of noise. She called it a 'dog,' a human word."

The Queen nodded her head and smiled. "They had dogs in the human camp where I was a slave; I always got along well with them. However did she get a dog up that high, though?"

"Well, I never thought to ask her that," Silverback said, blinking. Such a creature could not climb up to Mezzi's plateau; there was no trail or path, just sheer cliffs.

When everyone stayed quiet for some time, Arrington said, "We have one final thing to discuss. Have any of you had any success in your attempts to find Kaigen?"

Ariah and Json had made several attempts themselves at locating Kaigen. "We have searched all around the entrance to the Protector's home," Json told them. "When we fly between the large stone heads, we see nothing for miles and miles. We think that they have wards that hide the real entrance and perhaps lead you to fly in circles without realizing it."

Arrington harrumphed. "I have been studying the metal in the swords that were given to us by the Protectors when they came and took Kaigen. They have a strange reaction to magic of any kind, and I think that I can use them to find the wards' key spells...possibly even disrupt them."

Json praised him, "Why that's brilliant, Arrington! Of course, let us know how we can help. The longer Kaigen is with them, the shorter are her chances for survival. We all know how, um... reckless she can be. I fear she will not last long with them, and we owe it to her to rescue her." He hoped Ariah could contain her temper if they weren't able to rescue her. His rider was passionate about protecting her subjects, as befit the warrior queen she was, and if the Protectors harmed Kaigen in addition to kidnapping her, Json worried what Ariah's reaction might be.

Chapter 63: Kaigen

Elsbeth placed the collar around Kaigen's neck. Kaigen thought about biting her again just to hear her squeal, but she knew the only way out was to make a plan and execute it. She was of no use to anyone locked in a cage that her earth magic could not penetrate, although she had tried. She did show her incisors to Elsbeth so she would know she was thinking about it.

Elsbeth looked at the dirty girl and sighed, "I'm not your enemy," she told her. She led her from the room and down the hall to a bathing room. Elsbeth turned on the water, and Kaigen was amazed to see water coming from a pipe so that you could stand under it and clean yourself. She touched the water and found that it was warm!

"What a marvel." Kaigen said, looking at Elsbeth, at once forgetting her anger.

"Yes, one of many we have here." Elsbeth was all business, still not trusting the girl not to bite her. Handing her a towel, she said, "You can dry off with this, and here is some soap to get clean." She pointed at the collar. "I was trained with one of those collars. If you attempt any earth magic or try to remove it from your neck, you will feel intense pain." She hesitated, then continued, "I know how long you have been without bathing, so take as long as you need. I will be out here." She looked at Kaigen's leather clothing. "I can try to have your clothes cleaned, but they are pretty ruined." She pointed to a stack of clothing. "These are the standard clothes of a lab assistant, which is where you will be working if you continue to cooperate."

Kaigen noted the clothing and nodded her head. Her cooperation must begin now. "Thank you, Elsbeth. I am sorry I bit you." As Elsbeth looked at her with relief and compassion, Kaigen found to her surprise that she really was more than a little sorry; she doubted Elsbeth had any more choice in serving Vernondiander than she did.

Kaigen stepped into the bathing area, and Elsbeth drew a short curtain around it so she would have privacy. The warm water felt incredible. Kaigen lathered and rinsed herself three times, paying close attention to her cuts and her nails where filth had gathered. She stood under the warm stream as long as she dared and then dried herself off, donning the undergarments then the light brown pants. She stared at the white camisole and shirt and the matching longer coat, not quite understanding how they went on. At her helplessness, anger quickly resurfaced at the degrading treatment she had received in the cage, but she tamped it back down.

Elsbeth stood up from the chair she had been sitting on. "All the clothing has been altered to allow for your wing structure, if you will allow me to help." She helped Kaigen slide on the tight camisole and then put her arms through the sleeves of the shirt. "You put your arms in and then fasten the snaps closed." Elsbeth helped with the shirt and then the lab coat. It fit nicely, snug around her wings. Kaigen marveled at the snaps but was too proud to ask about them. She also wondered how long they had been waiting for her cooperation if they already had clothing like this made. Kaigen felt the softness of the material, noting it felt similar to what Von wore. Thinking about Von and that he may be suffering caused a pang deep inside her belly. Just like each article of clothing, she mentally donned a layer of deception for her battle for freedom and to rescue Von. Her sole purpose was to rescue him, and together maybe they could stop Vernondiander.

She squared her shoulders and followed Elsbeth from the bathing room. Elsbeth led her through corridors and up several flights of marble stairs. Kaigen gazed around in wonder—the structure was elegant; nothing in Sybaris could come close to this architecture. The floors and ceilings came together flawlessly as if they were created that way. As she climbed a spiral staircase, she ran her hands along the marble wall, feeling the coolness of the stone. Streaks of blue were imbued in the marble; the faint blue lines were almost like the veins of a living entity, although she knew it was just stone.

Elsbeth entered a large room and gestured gracefully. "This is one of our drilling labs." Kaigen looked around at the equipment, large metal devices she had never seen before, in wonder. Metal steps led up to a platform with even more strange machines. Several tables were littered with charts and colored maps. "The men over there are drilling scientists, and the woman is a ground scientist." Kaigen noted the men and the woman all wore similar lab coats. "Your job here will be to use your earth magic and help them determine the route they will take to locate frost under the ground. I really don't know much more than that."

Elsbeth stiffened as one of the women sauntered over to them. Kaigen noted that Elsbeth's lips had reflexively tightened, though her tone was neutral, "Ah, Sigrida, how are you these days?"

Sigrida was petite and slender. She ran her hand up Elsbeth's arm and Elsbeth stiffened but didn't try to pull her arm away. Sigrida's burgundy red hair was pushed straight back and the sides of her head were shaved. Colored mica dust in several shades of grey coated her eyelids, making them seem shiny and seductive. Her eyelashes were long and dark, adding to the effect.

"Why so formal, El?" Sigrida patted her on the back, letting her hand linger and smiling knowingly at Kaigen. "El here is always so uptight, aren't you El? I can help you with that any time you like, you know!" She laughed, the sound a little like music, but Kaigen's trepidation only grew as Elsbeth groaned slightly at Sigrida's words.

"No, thank you, Sigrida," the Elder's assistant said flatly. Elsbeth managed to pull away from Sigrida's touch without looking too much like she was fleeing, and put some distance between herself and the scientist, concealing her distress by gesturing at the captive. "This is Kaigen. She has agreed to help you in locating the frost."

"Business, business. Always so serious with you," Sigrida said with a sigh of regret. She turned to look at Kaigen. "So Kaigen, Vernondiander has high hopes for you!"

Kaigen looked down at the floor, not wanting to be the center of attention for this petite creature that somehow seemed to dominate the entire room. Her provocative posture and sensuous voice were weapons, not simply something she was.

"What, do you not talk?" Sigrida prodded her with a finger. Kaigen slowly raised her eyes, her anger and turmoil visible in her glare. Despite the fact Kaigen wore an inhibitor collar, Sigrida decided discretion was the better part of valor. In a much more businesslike tone, she tried a different tack. "Vernondiander has asked that I explain to you what we are trying to accomplish here," Sigrida waved her hand at the machinery. "I am sorry that I cannot take your collar off, precious girl. The Elder's orders are that it is to be removed only when he is here personally, you see."

Elsbeth interrupted her. "She is to sleep in the magically sealed room and stay with you at all other times." She pointed at the door. "The guards will remain outside the drilling room and take her there when you are finished each day." Elsbeth looked at Kaigen. "Your reward for cooperating will be to eat dinner with Von. Vernondiander intends to dine with you also, his way of ensuring your continued teamwork."

Kaigen nodded her head in acquiescence, relieved to hear that Von must be okay if they were to sup together. To protect Von she would become pliant, all the while planning the destruction of Vernondiander and his entire city. She watched as Elsbeth floated from the room and then considered Sigrida. She would grow close to this strange female scientist; she would win her trust first, and Vernondiander's. Then, when she could, she would strike. She turned and smiled at Sigrida. "Where do we begin?"

Sigrida was taken aback at the girl's words and sudden change of attitude. Her eyes narrowed as she studied Kaigen, again pursing her full lips. Kaigen remained still, seeming at ease, as the woman studied her. Sigrida reached towards her and checked that the constraining collar was indeed tight in place, and then she checked that the guards were watching them closely. Only then did she take Kaigen's hand and lead her to a nearby table.

The table held a large map that looked like a surface depiction, and the underground world was presented with various colors to show the different rock properties. Sigrida pointed at the highest point on the map. "We draw maps based on characteristics within the rock unit, things like the type of rock we find under the ground: sand, limestone, shale, granite." Her fingers flitted along, pointing out features. "We look for fossils and sedimentary structures that are typical of those that we have found near frost before, to help us zone-in on our drilling target. Without a magically gifted operator like you," she added, "we have to rely on what science tells us."

Sigrida took her to another table where other maps were spread out. "These are seismic maps. With your earth magic you can send magical pulses into the ground and our equipment will be able to pick up the returning vibrations to map the larger veins of frost."

Kaigen was interested in the seismic drawings but not for the reasons Sigrida thought. "You are going to let me send pulses into the ground?" she asked, touching the collar questioningly.

"Why, of course. That is but one of the ways you will be helping us," Sigrida said, then led the taller woman over to a table of rock samples and cuttings. "These come straight from the drilling site and also give us an idea of what type of rock we are dealing with."

She pointed to a black metal device that stood on the end of the table, away from the larger samples. "This is a microscope. When you look in it, it helps to see things that are too tiny for the eye to see; hence, we call them microscopic." Sigrida demonstrated by looking through the eyepiece. "Here, you look. Don't close your other eye," she instructed. "Just let it rest unfocused on whatever is in front of you; let your other eye become dominant. If you find you can't do that, switch eyes."

Kaigen found it easy to do as Sigrida instructed and was rewarded by a view of rock she'd never even considered possible. She was mesmerized as she studied the tiny, thinly sliced piece of rock on the slide. She could see the different grains and minerals and realized that she could identify them. Inside the microscope, the tiny mineral fragments looked like large rocks and crystals, and she could see a translucent purplish-grey structure that looked like a hand. Her breathing halted, her heart pounding.

Kaigen looked away from the eyepieces. She already knew what it was, for she had a good sense of the creatures of the underground. With trepidation she asked anyway, "What is this purple thing, at the top left?"

Sigrida looked into the eyepiece then made a tutting noise. "Oh, that is just a piece of an Annite! You have a good eye for this, Kaigen! Finding an Annite in a rock sample is a good thing. They are always present when we are near a source of frost."

Kaigen tried hard to hide her disgust and knew she was failing miserably. She tried to look back into the microscope to disguise her thoughts, but she saw the tiny arm again and tears formed. She felt overwhelmed by her anger, too much rage to contain despite her best efforts. Her face heated up and her neck began to ache as her magic tried to escape. The collar was giving her a warning sensation, but she was too angry to heed it.

Sigrida was watching Kaigen battle her anger. "Control your temper at once, Kaigen!" she ordered. When Kaigen turned her anger towards Sigrida, she just smiled snidely. "You can't do anything to me with your magic while you're chained up like a pet monkey!" She laughed heartily and derisively, though her glance back toward the guards belied her fear of the other woman.

Kaigen tried to use her magic to hurl some of the rock at Sigrida and the guards, but the effort triggered the collar's own magic. The pain from the device drove her to her knees and she could not help but cry out in agony. It hurt more than anything she'd ever felt before, more than she could have imagined something could hurt.

"What's the matter, little monkey?" Sigrid demanded, laughing even louder.

Kaigen's only answer was to lunge to her feet and charge the conceited Protector. There was nothing wrong with her hands and legs, and she would wipe that smile from Sigrida's face!

The Protector's laughter ceased and her eyes took on a cruelty that reminded Kaigen of Glock. With a flick of her wrist, Sigrida's magic threw Kaigen through the air until her body slammed against the wall. Kaigen's head snapped back to strike the wall, making her see stars. Her body fell to the ground and curled into a ball in response to the pain. But instead of fearing the pain, she welcomed it.

The pain was a gift, she knew, for it helped her close off the grief and sorrow she felt for the poor Annites. These people obviously did not care if Annites were killed in job lots if the process produced more of what they called frost. Kaigen knew the Annites were not only intelligent but kind and gentle as well, for they had healed the Commander's terrible wounds while she'd watched. The Protectors used frost for everything: it enhanced their magic, and their bodies and their city were infused with it. Even their clothing was coated in it. God only knew how many of the poor creatures had been slaughtered over the years.

"Poor monkey," Sigrida said without a shred of pity as she walked away to talk to one of the other scientists in the room.

Kaigen fought to get herself under control. She wondered what would make these Protectors feel that their lives mattered so much more than others, for she literally could not understand it. They had taken her forcibly from her home just so they could gobble up more frost. She would fight to free Von; she would fight for the Annites. She would cooperate fully until her moment came, and then she would shatter this place into fragments until everything and everyone in it was dust.

Sigrida headed back towards her, stopping to look down at the girl at her feet. She spoke as if nothing had happened, as if Kaigen's suffering was so far beneath her that it—and Kaigen—were utterly unimportant. "I want you to spend the rest of today studying the seismic maps. They were the best we had since we lost the last operator, but they are not near close enough to the area we are researching now. In the morning, we will take you to the field above our new drill site and you will send some pulses down so we can gather new seismic data."

Sigrida looked at Kaigen seriously. "We must stay ahead of the other drilling teams, and now that we have you, that should be easy!" Sigrida laughed and turned away. As Kaigen regarded Sigrida's back, she imagined that the other woman's deep burgundy hair was colored with the blood of the Annites.

Chapter 64: Silver Roads

"Isladora, you are supposed to be looking for signs of frost," Meluha admonished the girl. She had been watching Tobin, studying him, noting the way he leaned to pause to study the wall, how he stood, how much he had filled out. Her job was to carry the torch, seated upon Fashi's back to light the mine tunnels as they progressed. Every day without fail Tobin would make the tisane for her to drink, and while she could still feel the pull of the Protector's summons, it wasn't overwhelming.

"Oh, sorry, yes," Isladora said as she snapped her attention back to the task at hand, but after another mile or so she was back to watching Tobin's hands as they grazed along the wall, feeling the temperature of the rock, seeking the light blue veins. Isladora thought about those same hands traveling along her body, holding her close for another kiss. She could not wait for his attention to be on her again so she could bask in it.

"Meluha," she said through their mind connection so Tobin couldn't hear, *"these feelings I have, it almost feels like it's consuming me, like what the Protector's pull was doing to my mind before Tobin made the tisane for me, but in a pleasant way."*

Meluha laughed. *"Hormones are a strong thing, maybe one of the strongest connections in nature. You already have strong feelings of love for Tobin; it is only natural that you feel physical desire for him as well."* He paused and then added, *"You should probably drink some more of the concoction soon."* He tried to recall what long-term dosing with henbane did to its user, but couldn't remember. He suspected it wasn't good, but what choice did they have?

Tobin stopped and using his pick and hammer, he broke a chunk of rock from the wall. He held it closer to the light, and then shaking his head, tossed it on the ground. Fashi stopped when he got near his master, touching Tobin's back with his nose. Tobin turned and patted Fashi's neck and then continued down the mine.

Isladora watched him leave, jealous that he patted the horse and didn't even say a word to her. She didn't even have to really direct Fashi; the little horse and his master were connected like a chain. *"Well, I definitely feel it, it's hard to think about much else."* Isladora adjusted her grip on the torch, transferring it carefully to her other hand. She wasn't sure how Fashi felt about fire and she didn't want to spook him.

"It is my job to remind you that you must wait until marriage, princess or not. It is the way of your people," Meluha reasoned with her.

"It's not just the way of my people; it is the way of all people, Meluha." She adjusted the torch back to her dominant hand. *"We are meant to cleave to one person and follow the protection and love of a family. God has said as much."*

They continued in silence for some time until Tobin stopped for a repast. As she ate, Isladora thought about familial love and duty and realized that it was important to her. *"What if we die?"* She asked Meluha, watching Tobin eat.

Meluha sighed. *"There is that,"* he admitted, understanding instantly what she meant. If either or both of the young lovers died before consummating their feelings, they'd never have the chance.

"Did you wait with Mae Tarango?" Isladora asked quietly.

So many questions, he thought, realizing she was searching for a justification. *"She and I were married,"* he answered, but knew that was insufficient. *"We didn't wait until then, but it wasn't the practice of her people. There was no dishonor in lying with her before the actual ceremony."* He was surprised to find himself able to talk of his dead wife without pain.

Tobin was enjoying his dried fish and Fashi his oats, loving the way they could sit in silence together and be comfortable like a family. Meluha had told him that before they created the deeper drilling methods, the frost miners would tunnel horizontally from the bottom of their prospect shaft to follow the frost along the surface of the bedrock. Some of the mine was reinforced with timber supports, but for the most part the shaft was only rock and old cave-ins that could possibly block their passage through.

Isladora continued, watching Tobin as she ate, *"You stopped waiting when you knew in your hearts that you were going to marry, did you not? Why should I be different?"* Again, her meaning was crystal clear: she meant to marry Tobin, Elijashen's approval and permission or no.

Tobin choked on his fish and coughed once, trying to clear the piece from his windpipe.

Meluha tried not to get frustrated with her. Choosing his words carefully, thinking of all he'd heard among the Juna in the years Isladora and Anyumay had worn his ring, he said, *"Let me speak as a father to his daughter, since your father is so far away."* He could see the immediate impact his words had. *"I can see that your heart is filled with this young man, and his with you, but you and Tobin must consider the possibility that you could become with child. Being compelled to journey to a hostile land where enemies await is not the right environment for a child to grow."*

She swallowed hard but didn't argue. *"You must think of this un-conceived child and put its needs first, Isladora. For most, it is enough to think only of the basic needs of a newborn, that it be fed and kept safe from predators, but you have read enough to know that is not all a child will need. It takes an entire family, a whole community, to raise a child in security, and the stronger the family, the more likely the child will grow not only strong, but strongly moral. That is the reason why your people require marriage before pursuing the physical side of love, not to deny the lovers what they desire."*

Isladora thought about her own lonely childhood and about what a child born among the Protectors might face and conceded the point to him. *"I do know these things, Meluha Crocus, for I have heard my mother offer advice to young lovers before. I don't know why I'm questioning these things; I know that God's law is to honor one's family, and if I act on my love with Tobin, I will not be following God's law. It is His expectation, Meluha, to put family first, and that means that marriage and fidelity are far more important than they first appear."*

His mental "voice" was sympathetic, *"You question them because your hormones are making you crazy. That is natural law, not your God's law, and I know that you are strong enough to overcome the one to follow the other. Besides, your hormones are making me crazy, too,"* he joked. *"I am glad you are willing to reason this out and understand why you must wait; I did not want to have to magically restrain you for your own good."*

Isladora scowled. *"You can do that?"* she demanded. She really didn't like the sound of that.

Meluha answered dryly, *"Yes, but Tobin would not like the effect on his, ah... manhood, as your people say."*

"You'd do something like that to him? You can't be serious!" She didn't find that idea funny at all, and she twisted the ring as if to try removing it. To cover her consternation, she busied herself with cleaning up after their meal, her movements angry despite her attempts to calm herself.

"On the contrary, Isladora, I would never kid about such a serious matter," he said in his most compassionate tone. *"But I care about you and the things you care about—or should care about, at least, and I would do as I implied."*

She looked at Tobin, who had sensed Isladora was upset about something and was looking a question at her. She shook her head, indicating he should stay put. *"You wouldn't,"* she said, almost a growl.

"You have my word, my young friend, that I would," he said dourly. *"I would not kill him, but injure him? Yes, I would."*

They packed up and got moving again. This time Isladora led Fashi, choosing to walk. Perhaps the exercise would keep her anger—and her hormones—in check. And after a time of marching at a severe pace, enough to get her blood pumping from the exertion, she found that it did help.

Less than an hour after their meal break, Tobin stopped. "Hey, what about this one?" he asked, pointing at a darker blue vein in the wall. "Isladora, ask Meluha about this one." When she didn't answer he looked back at her and found her angrily stalking along behind him, glaring down at the ground. She yanked her gaze up to his face, blushing a red that looked only ruddier by the torchlight.

Before he could stop himself, he demanded, "What?!? Are you two talking about me?" He immediately wished he'd thought better of it and turned back toward the wall.

Isladora cleared her throat, "He says that vein is promising, and you should, ah...look for the next offshoot." Tobin shook his head and began following the line of the vein along the mineshaft wall.

After a time, Isladora managed to calm herself down, and decided to talk to the ring spirit again. *"Have you forgiven your people, Meluha?"* Isladora inquired.

Meluha considered this. He no longer felt anger towards his brother; he only knew that he must be stopped from harming Isladora and Tobin. It was true, his people had chosen not to stand up for him, but they, too, had suffered under Vernondiander. *"Yes, I have forgiven them,"* he said at last.

Isladora smiled. *"That's good. God's word teaches that we must forgive others from our heart. My faith says that if we can do this, then God in turn will forgive us for the evils we do. Compared to that forgiveness, whatever wrongs are done to us are but a trifle, are they not? I believe God forgives me all the time, even when I do not realize that I have done wrong in His eyes."*

"Yes, I have heard that," Meluha said, though he found it difficult to believe that God could and would forgive his crimes. *"I spent many years in this ring with a priest, and while he battled with his own morals, it still allowed me to spend time with other believers. I learned a great deal about holy writings, including the concept of eternal life, but I didn't actually believe in any of it."*

"It's good that you question, Meluha," she said. *"God gave us our minds, and He expects us to use them to contemplate His many mysteries. I struggle to understand many of them, but not the one you named. Life eternal is our greatest hope."* Isladora felt warm inside talking of this. *"When this mere flesh that is my body dies and withers away, I will not perish, and neither will you, Meluha, if you but believe."*

Tobin exclaimed ahead of them, "Finally!" He had grown tired of the enclosed feeling of the mines. The shaft had turned ahead of them, opening into a central room with old torches along the wall; Isladora gladly lit a few of them after struggling a bit to get them burning, for the fuel was long dried and she had to wait for the cloth-wrapped wood to catch. There were old mine carts that were broken and useless, but it was easy to imagine men working there. Another passageway went on to the right, sloping steeply upward and then narrowing.

"There, Isladora. Tell Tobin to follow that tunnel." The tunnel led to a cave-in with a hole in the ground that was big enough for a single person. Tobin dropped a rock down the hole, and by the sound of the rock landing, he gauged it about ten to fifteen feet deep.

"Meluha says it used to be a shaft where they would bring rock up to the surface. If we are lucky, we might find some fragments of frost. He wants you to tie the rope securely around your waist and let Fashi and I lower you down," Isladora explained, taking the rope from the saddle bag.

Tobin growled his agreement and pulled a fresh torch from his saddle, lighting it from hers. He dropped it down the shaft, praying it wasn't wet below and that it would stay lit. He didn't really want to listen to the old man, as he had begun thinking of Meluha, but he couldn't very well send Isladora into the hole. They placed a blanket along the edge so the rope would easily slide and not become frayed. Tobin tied a large loop in the rope and then tied the other end to Fashi's saddle about twenty feet back from the hole. "Once I am lowered enough, I'll use the loop as a seat, so my hands are free to use the pick and hammer if the frost is in the walls of the shaft."

"What if you fall?" Isladora checked the knot again and resisted the urge to grab him and hold him. She had no fear of going down the hole herself—she had conquered her fear of such things when she had passed through the mountain with Meluha Crocus—but she didn't know how well Tobin was taking it.

Tobin winked at her, mistaking her fear for a desire not to go down the hole herself. "All right, Fashi, now don't drop me and I'll give you an apple later." To Isladora he said, "Tell him to stand or to back up. Those are the commands he knows well." Tobin started to pull against the rope and the little horse shook his head and neck and snorted, but he adjusted for a better angle.

Tobin made sure Fashi could hold the line tight, and then he went over the edge, inching down the rope and then putting his legs through the loop to sit when he got in far enough in. "OK, lower slowly," he called.

The horse calmly moved forward, keeping the rope tense. "Easy now, Fashi, nice and slow," Isladora told him, mostly to calm her own nerves. Despite the torch at the bottom, to her the hole seemed as black as night. The rope slid down as she guided the horse forward.

"OK, stop here!" Tobin yelled.

"Whoa, Fashi, stand." The little horse braced his legs against the weight of his master.

Tobin called out, his voice echoing a little, "Bring your torch over the hole, but be careful. I don't want you to fall in here—there are jagged rocks down below, and *something's* moving among them." Isladora shivered and inched towards the hole with the torch.

Tobin's head was about ten feet below her, and as soon as he could see, he immediately began hammering, then moving, then hammering some more. It was difficult to get purchase on the smooth shaft wall and properly aim his blows; he wasn't a trained miner. He was trying to find something blue, but it was dark and hard to tell what color the rock was. Meluha had told him when he hit it with the pick and hammer, it would make a softer sound than did the rock, closer to the sound it would make if he hit saddle leather.

Suddenly, the edge of the shaft supporting the weight of the rope crumbled and fell down on and past Tobin, who yelled out in pain and surprise. He began coughing as the dust flew everywhere about him. Fashi nervously stomped and started backing up. Isladora had fallen backward in surprise, losing the torch, and she scrambled to her feet to grab Fashi's reins. "Stand, Fashi!" she said firmly, keeping herself from yelling at the pony, knowing that would only startle him.

"Tobin!" she called, and the torch chose that same moment to sputter out and die. Isladora coughed, too, as the lighter particles in the dust swirled around them all, and Fashi blew out to clear his own nostrils. In the eerie silence and darkness Isladora's heart pounded as she wondered what had happened to Tobin. She clung to Fashi's neck to steady herself more than anything else, and it seemed like a year passed in a few seconds' time.

"I'm OK!" Tobin managed to say through some rough coughing. The dust was settling, and he had managed to get Isladora's handkerchief tied about his mouth so he could breathe more normally. The woman and horse above him didn't have that problem, because not nearly as much dust had come up to their level. She steadied the horse, who'd looked like he would follow Tobin's voice, petting his neck and crooning to him softly. "Isladora, bring the light! I said I'm fine, Isladora!"

"I don't want to leave the horse. What if he spooks?" Isladora's ring began to glow, giving her a little light to see with.

Tobin was glad she couldn't see his exasperation. "That little horse can't be spooked, he's fine. Come on, get a torch lit and get over here." Tobin did not like hanging in the hole in the dark. He imagined every type of spider he had ever known crawling all over him.

Isladora found their flint and relit the torch after some effort, still coughing the dust from her lungs. Fashi's eyes were wide, but he stayed still and kept the rope tight. She and Fashi were dusted with the white powder, but Isladora imagined it must cover Tobin from head to toe. Checking Fashi one last time—who seemed much calmer now with some light—she shone the light down to Tobin. The blanket had fallen in when the rock face had collapsed and she couldn't see it anywhere; the torch Tobin had dropped must have been smothered by the rocks or the blanket. She carefully looked down, not sure what she was going to see, but there was Tobin's dust-covered smiling face holding up a fist-sized chunk of brilliant blue stone that glimmered and refracted the light in a thousand different ways. It had to be frost.

"Oh, my," she whispered.

"Here, take it and have Fashi back up when I'm ready," he warned her then tossed the chunk up and out of the shaft where she was able to catch it. Tobin began to ease himself from the loop, bracing his feet against the other wall, which was still smooth. He looked ghostly, covered in the fine mica powder; in the faint light cast by the torch down the shaft, he looked more like a ghost than a person.

When Isladora caught the rock with her free hand, the blue crystalline side was facing away from her; she'd caught it by the sedimentary rock it was embedded in. She turned it over, and as soon as the frost touched her skin, the ring began glowing brightly enough to light the entire cave. "Whoa!" She exclaimed, talking to herself more than Fashi. "I guess we don't need the torch any longer!" She tossed the torch to the ground and approached Fashi, telling him to back up at Tobin's signal.

The saddle was shifting sideways with Tobin's weight and the angle the horse was tugging, so she set the frost down and helped pull. The horse nickered when he saw Tobin's head, obviously relieved to see his master coming back. He was smart enough not to go down a hole in the ground and seemed to be wondering why Tobin wasn't.

Tobin scrambled from the hole, his muscles aching from the effort. He coiled the rope and placed it back in Fashi's saddlebag after knocking off what dust he could. "Wow, that light is bright!" He loosened Fashi's cinch and righted the saddle, then tightened it back up.

Isladora had picked the brilliant blue stone back up. "Yes, Meluha's magic is stronger now, I can feel it!" She smiled at Tobin, laughing out loud at the wonder of it.

Her laughter was like a thousand songs playing at once inside of him. He walked over to her, smiling back, and kissed her full on her dust-covered lips. "Even covered in dirt, you taste wonderful," he told her.

Chapter 65: Seismic and the Frost

The Elder and ground scientist Sigrida sat at a long table in the drilling lab. On the extended glass table were neatly arranged documents, thick folders of analysis work, and maps that Sigrida pointed to as she informed The Elder of her findings. "I assembled this information over the last month or so and I think we have our drilling target. But to be certain, we need dependable seismic readings," she said dryly. Their attempts up to now had not been successful. She pointed out markers on one of the maps. "I would like to have Kaigen set off some low-level pulses of energy at these designated places, and with her sensitivity, she should also be able to help us refine our ability to interpret the return signals.

"None of the seismic maps we have reach deep enough to get a reliable look at the structures underground, despite having some rock samples to refine the mathematics," she said with a sigh. "And quite frankly, without some kind of advancement in interpretation, even signals that reach deeper aren't going to help us." Sigrida smoothed her shirtwaist and sat up straighter, looking at the Elder with cool eyes. She was careful to fully vet any information that reached the Elder, double- and triple-checking the results before passing them on. He was not very understanding of mistakes, and her late, not-lamented predecessor had not been as careful.

Vernondiander didn't really understand much of her presentation, although as usual she'd done an excellent job in the summary to give him a grasp of what she was talking about. He endured the ground science part of the presentations largely because Sigrida was quite attractive. He especially enjoyed her curves and had not failed to take note of the way her pert breasts strained at her current outfit. Oh, true, she was a competent scientist—though not in league with his brother, he thought sardonically—but he'd allowed her promotion for reasons that had nothing to do with her proficiency.

The Elder sat back and touched his hand to his mouth, toying with the thought of taking her back to his rooms now. He let her see the interest in his eyes—eyes that only showed what their owner wanted them to; it was one of his best weapons. When she apparently declined to rise to the bait, he straightened his pose and dragged his attention back to the matter at hand. He decided to ask some pointed questions. "Why, exactly, do we need to generate more seismic maps?" he asked, his kindly voice sounding utterly reasonable. "I brought you Kaigen; is she not enough to ensure you will hit our target?"

Careful, Sigrida, she thought. She knew that his temper was always just under the surface, and he could go from kind to cruel without warning. "Her abilities will no doubt help a great deal, Elder," she explained, picking her words with a caution born of experience. She decided the Elder didn't need to know who it was that showed her the microscope. "And normally, I would say that her senses would be all we need, but as she was touring the lab, she was introduced to the microscope."

"And that matters because?" Vernondiander asked with a touch of impatience.

"She saw an Annite's remains in the microscope lens. She apparently had some prior knowledge of the creatures," she said, which was somewhat self-serving but also true, "and her reaction was quite strongly negative. I'm not sure what she would do if we asked her to guide the drill bit into a large source of them." She didn't have to explain that a large source of the Annites would also be a large source of frost; that much, Vernondiander knew well enough. "So, if she helps us to extract better seismic maps first, a later refusal to cooperate will at least leave us with them." She blinked slowly at him, "I plan to avoid mentioning the little fact that I can use better seismic maps to find the frost myself, of course," she said, one lip curling in amusement.

He didn't really want to see any more delays in the production of frost, and this approach of Sigrida's would not be as quick as having the earth-powerful girl simply direct the drill. The Elder did not know what had happened to the drilling apparatus in the current hole, for word had not reached Issedones of that little disaster yet.

However, he saw Sigrida's point that if they had to end up destroying Kaigen (and Von, if that proved necessary), they would still have something to show for it. "Very good, Sigrida," he smiled broadly, and though the smile reached his eyes, she knew better than to trust in that. "This is why you remain in a position of great responsibility, this kind of forward planning." The threat underneath, which she didn't need to be reminded of, was that he could remove her easily. "The boughs that bear the most fruit hover lowest to the ground my dear!"

"Come see me later in my quarters," his tone betraying his lascivious intent. "I will have the artisans cut one of these robes for your... figure." He brushed his hand sensually down the side of his blue frost-infused robe. "It's not dyed, as I'm sure you already noticed—it has the ability to absorb directed magical energy and store it for later use." He meant hostilely directed magical energy, she was sure.

She usually could school her features almost as well as the Elder, but her eyes widened at the implications of such a magical achievement. The Protectors could create magical energy—for some, quite a lot of it—but no process ever discovered was able to store it as the Annites somehow did through their innate natures.

He smiled to see her reaction; he was adept at finding what people wanted and providing it to them, so long as it didn't prevent him from getting what he wanted, of course. He knew that she would come to him that evening and that she would surrender to his advances, if he still wanted her when she arrived. He would have to think about whether she'd be easier to control if they became involved, or harder, for unlike most of his conquests, Sigrida was accustomed to being the manipulator in a relationship.

"For now, we will follow your plan in regard to the use of Kaigen's talent," he rose from his seat and straightened his robe. "Let us gather Von and the girl and head out into the field. I presume you have already located the sites where you want her to send the pulses?"

She didn't like the idea of Von being brought along; she knew what had happened with Von before, and the only reason for the Elder to bring him was to harm him again if Kaigen didn't cooperate. She didn't know Von that well, but he was easy on the eye and she didn't mean him any harm. *Well, the little brat knows that he'll do it without hesitation,* she thought. *It'll be her fault if she brings the Elder's wrath down on Von.*

She smiled at the man who ruled the Protectors. "Of course, Elder," she said respectfully. "We have already placed the devices that will record the returning impulses; we just need her to send them down farther than we can reliably send them ourselves. I will ready Kaigen and meet you at the platform."

"I need not tell you that she is to know nothing of why we have her do these things?" the Elder asked semi-rhetorically.

Sigrida knew a command when she heard one, however it was phrased. "As you command," Sigrida rose and bowed her head. Leaving Kaigen too ignorant, however, would compromise the effectiveness of her efforts, and her agile mind considered how best to follow the intent of the Elder's command. The Elder didn't return her nod as he left to make his own preparations and to arrange for Von to be brought along, but that was nothing new. Sigrida went to the sealed room on the far side of the laboratory to fetch the girl.

Kaigen stood near the window of her prison, looking out at the lands below. She had seen the Elder enter the room and her anger had risen, but every time she tried to call her earth magic, the collar made her neck ache, or worse if she pressed it.

Through the lens of her experiences, Sigrida thought she looked rather sad and pathetic, not as she was in fact: dangerous. The scientist knew that if Kaigen did allow herself to become angry enough to refuse to help, despite her precautions earlier to spread the blame around, it would likely be Sigrida who would lose her head over it, not Kaigen. Sigrida, after all, was replaceable; the girl looking out the window was unique.

I need to tell her something that will make sure she keeps herself under control, she thought, tapping her fingernail on her pert, upturned nose. "Kaigen, I have good news for you." The younger woman looked at her askance. "You will get to see Von today." Kaigen was unable to conceal her immediate joy at that idea, though it was quickly clouded with concern; she knew that the Elder thought of Von only as a lever to force her to do as he wanted. "We are all headed out into the field—several spots in the mountains, I mean." She watched Kaigen's eyes as she told her the destination but saw no sign that she'd try to take advantage of being outside to try to escape.

I can't trust that, the scientist thought, *but I think she hasn't figured out how she plans to escape yet. She'll be a good little girl until she thinks she has the advantage, or at least an opening, and then all hell will break loose.* Sigrida carefully checked the neck restraint was still tight and that Kaigen hadn't managed to find some way to weaken it. As they reached the entryway to the drilling laboratory, she motioned to the guards and they placed another set of magical restraints on Kaigen's wrists, securing them together.

Kaigen was happy that she would be able to see Von, but she also knew she needed to steel herself. At least this time she wasn't covered in filth, even if she was manacled and collared. She was, in fact, overwhelmed by many different emotions, each powerful in its own stead. Joy that she would see Von was coupled with relief that he wasn't dead from the Elder's cruel attack. But the joy and relief were joined by apprehension and fear, for Von wasn't being brought just so she could see the Protector she loved. No, the Elder wanted Von there because he could hurt him and in so doing, hurt her.

Somehow, she had to convince the Protectors, perhaps even Von, that she was cooperating fully, for with the restraints in place, she was helpless and she knew it. *Von will think worse of me,* she thought sadly. *He will think I'm weak and timid and that I've given up already because I'm not worthy to be near him.* She knew, however, that she had no choice.

Sigrida led Kaigen and her guards from the building and onto a large metal square, like the base of a room, but without walls. They stood in the center of a large engraved circle edged with symbols that Kaigen couldn't read and waited.

"This platform is how we will travel to the first site," Sigrida explained. "The Elder will use his magic to transport us to another pad there. It's easier to start directly in the center of a plate, though not strictly necessary."

Her face grew serious. "Do not fight the magic, Kaigen," she said gravely. "If you do, you will feel pain, and in some extreme cases, cause internal injuries. Just breathe normally and try to think of something pleasant. The experience is unpleasant even when you don't fight it, but it will last only a few seconds at most."

Kaigen thought about how the Protectors had magically appeared in the Draconian city of Sybaris. "I understand Sigrida. Thank you for the warning." Kaigen gave the scientist a faint smile, not having to pretend that she was afraid. She couldn't manage to summon a brighter smile, but thought Sigrida wouldn't trust it anyhow, so it didn't matter. "Sigrida, can any Protector travel this way? And must they always use the pads?"

Sigrida laughed inside at the several levels of ignorance Kaigen betrayed with her question but fought to keep it from her eyes. "We are powerful, but we are not gods, Kaigen," she said patiently. "We must have the metal as a point of reference to address our magic." Seeing Kaigen's confusion, she explained further. "We can reach out to the metal, and it will give us a signal, if you will, but not like a flag or column of smoke; the signal is magical. If we traveled without focusing on one of these manufactured metal points, we could wind up anywhere and be lost for a long time." She didn't feel any need to tell the girl that most Protectors couldn't manage the transport magic even with the pads, nor that without the reference plates, the most likely outcome was death.

Sigrida's explanation made Kaigen's mind race. If the Protectors had suddenly appeared in her home town and then disappeared again when they kidnapped her, there must be a metal reference point in Sybaris, maybe even several. That meant that she might be closer to home than she thought! Most of Sybaris was constructed from stone mined from the area; the only metal structure she could think of was the fountain in front of the Cystine Hall. She tried to remember the history of the fountain, but she never had paid much attention to those things and so she didn't know.

She cast her mind back to the day the Protectors had come to dinner as welcome guests of Draconia's ruling pairs—guests that had betrayed her queen's hospitality, invaded the queen's mind, and kidnapped Kaigen—but she fought her irate feelings back. Time for that later, not now, she admonished herself. They had ended up here on this very spot, she remembered now, the female with Vernondiander dragging her into the building to her left to be thrown into that clear-walled cage in Vernondiander's quarters. She had to find a way to ask Von about the fountain without being overheard.

The Elder and Von, escorted by two more guards flanking him to either side, left the building and approached the pad. Kaigen sighed in relief, a small keening sound leaving her body. Von looked much better now, but he had the ensorcelled metal on his neck, wrists, and ankles, along with a chain between his feet to keep him from running. He was in chains, but he was alive, and the sight of him affected her as it always did, with a longing too strong for words.

At the same time, Von saw Kaigen standing on the pad with Sigrida and the guards, and his shoulders rose as he took a deep breath and let it out in relief. *Thank the heavens, she's unhurt!* he thought. He saw that they let her get clean and dressed. He was deeply ashamed of his people's treatment of her, but at the moment he could do nothing. The Elder had always been powerful, but with that new robe of his, he could have any amount of magic stored up to turn against them. He knew he'd have to be patient and wait for an opportunity to escape with Kaigen.

Kaigen blushed as she saw Von's reaction to her, and she tried to distract herself from the perfection of his features and his body by searching for the necklace and the shell she had made for his father. She could see the leather cord on one side of his shirt; he must have tucked it inside. His strong jaw was clenched, and his long dark hair was clean but she thought it might be a little longer, touching his shoulders in the back. *Have we been captives that long?* she wondered with a mental shake of her head. She didn't think so, unless the Protectors had done something to her time sense. She decided that the Protectors' hair must grow faster than hers.

They had removed all his protective armor from his body, but he still looked like a powerful man. He stared at her with his intense greyish-blue eyes and he seemed angrier than anything else. And well he should be, she thought. She was angry, too, after all. But while he was free to demonstrate his anger, she wasn't, and she allowed her gladness in seeing him to show.

She had a part to play, but she hid her rage at the other Protectors beneath that veneer of gladness and worry. The two of them were not finished yet! It was difficult; seeing Von made the world brighter somehow, and her life worth living, and she wanted to dance in joy at the same time she wanted to claw the Elder's eyes out. Being near him again made all things seem possible. He nourished her in some unknown way, as if she'd been dying of thirst and starving, and now she could dine on his presence.

I will see him released or die trying, she vowed silently. *I will deceive all of these arrogant fools and when the time is right, I shall strike.* She and Von would cast away their fetters and depart Issedones together instead of living caged like beasts under a cruel master's dominion.

Vernondiander was in a good mood, excited about the prospect of finding the frost and unmindful of the undercurrents flowing within and between Kaigen and Von. "Are all of you ready?" he asked Sigrida and the guards. "Hold still, Kaigen, and don't fight the transport or you will regret it. You don't want your insides to be as tattered as your wings, do you?" The Elder raised his arms, and in one moment the group was standing in the city, and in the next they were out in a wasteland with rock, scrub brush, dust, and wind. They stood on a metal plate like the one they had left, although this one was undecorated.

Kaigen had felt nothing in the transport process, although she could tell two of the guards looked queasy. Feeling nothing was both better and worse: she didn't feel the nausea that some of the Protectors were feeling, but neither had she felt any part of Vernondiander's magic. She had no idea how to make the platforms work and she strained to keep from gnashing her teeth in frustration.

The Elder motioned Kaigen and Von to stay put and moved a short distance away with Sigrida. "Where did you set the receivers?" he asked her quietly, for none of Sigrida's engineers were in evidence. He could see the transmission area from which Kaigen would send her first set of pulses marked off a few hundred yards into the wasteland.

"We placed ten of them at varying distances from where Kaigen will send her energy pulses," Sigrida replied, trying to gauge how much detail the Elder wanted and decided he was too impatient for that. "The engineers picked the distances; I just chose the geological area. I could summon one if you want a more detailed explanation?" Sigrida answered with a little trepidation; you never knew when the Elder's impatience would become cruelty.

He shook his head, turning back to Kaigen and gesturing her to join them. "Kaigen, what Sigrida and I want you to do is to send pulses of earth magic down into the earth from that flagged area," he explained condescendingly. "Nothing too big, mind you. We don't want to damage any of the structures underground, only to understand them better, my dear." He added, "Do I need to mention what will transpire for Von if you do not cooperate fully?"

Kaigen shook her head timidly, "How will I be able to help you with my earth magic while I wear this collar?"

Vernondiander smiled broadly at her, showing his perfect teeth, and his eyes sparkled with pleasure at her submissive attitude. "We will remove the bindings while you work your magic for us," he nodded at a guard. He waited patiently while the other Protector removed her wrist manacles and then her collar, but Von could see his hands were held straight down.

Kaigen doesn't know that's how we gather our power to attack! Von thought and prayed that his friend wouldn't choose this moment to attack. The Elder was ready for any attempt on her part to harm him.

Von didn't know what else the Elder was ready for, and when the collar was loosened but before the hated thing was off her neck, the Elder gestured at him and Von doubled over in pain, crying out despite his best attempt at remaining silent. "Remember the consequences if you defy me, Kaigen," the Elder warned with that too-sweet voice. The most chilling thing about him, Kaigen realized, was that his eyes still sparkled with kindness. "Before you can even begin to hurt me, Von will be dead, I assure you."

Von looked up towards Kaigen and gave an almost-imperceptible shake of his head. He knew that if she tried to save him now they would both die. "It's okay, Kaigen… I'm… go." He mouthed at her, and then allowed his head to slump down as he gasped for breath. He thought, go do your work. Our only hope is that he tires of your services and then will release me. He wanted to tell her this, but he dared not say anything.

The Elder was pleased to see his assumption that hurting Von would command the little creature's obedience was correct. His assumptions, after all, usually were. "Well, carry on, my dear! No time to waste!"

Hiding her sadness, disgust, and anger, Kaigen looked to Sigrida for direction.

Sigrida led her out into the wasteland to the markers where the engineers wanted the pulses to originate. Kaigen was tempted to flick a rock out of her way with her magic, but that would not serve her intent in remaining placid and docile until the right moment. When they stopped, Kaigen looked back—she could barely see Von, but he was still kneeling, still in pain. Mindful of the need to deceive Sigrida as well as the Elder, Kaigen said in a meek voice, "Von isn't too hurt, is he?"

Sigrida considered lying, but she didn't trust this sudden cooperation. "I really have no idea if your lover is hurt or not," she said in her most contemptuous voice, but Kaigen didn't turn her angry eyes on her, instead wringing her hands and staring at Von.

"Pay attention, Kaigen," Sigrida snapped, and the captive yanked her gaze from Von and onto her. "Use the smallest pulses of energy that you can at first. I will ask you to increase them slowly until you reach the upper strength we need, and then you must stop releasing them completely when I tell you to. Do you understand?" Kaigen nodded and then looked back at Von despondently. Sigrida sighed; she didn't have time for this foolish infatuation, but she had to concede the Elder had hit the nail on the head by using Von against her. She added more gently, "It won't take long and then I'm sure the Elder will release him." She suspected that wasn't the case, but that wouldn't help get Kaigen to do what they wanted. "Von is strong, he'll be all right."

"If you say so, Sigrida," Kaigen said glumly in that same small tone. She looked at Von one last time and then examined the ground. She moved to a clay-rich spot with fewer rocks inside the markers. She knelt in the dirt and began to draw power from the ground. She felt the earth as if it were her parent holding her in their arms, and she also felt its almost unlimited potential for destruction. She closed her eyes, fighting the urge to let loose and destroy them all, because even if she somehow made the earth swallow the Elder in an instant—and she doubted she could do it that quickly—she had no way to protect Von.

She tried to focus on the ground and her magic and not on her love for Von, because thinking of him only reminded her why she was furious at the Elder, and this was not the time for anger and precipitate action. This was the time for gentleness and submission.

She breathed in and out several times and then dug her hands down under the surface until they were covered with the reddish-brown earth. She began slowly releasing pulses into the ground, feeling them reflect off the subsurface structures. As Sigrida had bid, she slowly increased the intensity and the pulses traveled deeper. Kaigen knew from her own experiences that these types of pulses wouldn't damage the structures even if she increased her power level significantly, but it was clear the Protector scientists didn't fully understand that. It was pleasing to find that they weren't all-knowing, even though it was something relatively minor.

Keeping her eyes closed, Kaigen focused her mind to examine the reflections to discern what the Protectors wanted. The return echoes from her pulses were chaotic and sounded and resounded in patterns different from what she sent, and she realized that she wasn't in the ideal place to extract information from the echoes. But that means Sigrida isn't, either, Kaigen thought. There must be others positioned elsewhere, where a better set of return echoes can be felt.

Sigrida was excited when one of her engineers over the next ridge raised a prearranged flag to signal that the receivers had begun picking up the signals and that her cleverly-designed machines were gathering the returning echoes of Kaigen's earth magic. These data would in turn allow them to begin mapping the depth and structure of the underground region that held the Elder's interest.

Not needing the Protector's devices and despite being in a less than ideal listening position, Kaigen's senses told her where the veins of frost were; slightly to the east was a large deep source. She increased the intensity of her pulses again, turning her "listening" towards that area. She began to perceive veins of softer rock and large hollow spaces, but it was impossible to discern true detail. She increased the intensity once more, and Sigrida shouted, "Enough!"

Kaigen stopped and stood fighting back tears, the earth falling from her hands, because she knew what the Protectors would learn from their analysis of her pulses. *I will avenge the Annites, too*, she reminded herself, and though her eyes were misty when she looked back at Von still kneeling on the platform, no tears fell.

Sigrida stepped quickly over to Kaigen and slid the collar around her neck, locking it in place. "You did well, Kaigen. The Elder will be pleased, and the two of you are that much closer to being released." It wasn't precisely what she'd implied in her earlier reassurances, but Kaigen only nodded obediently, turning her chin up obligingly so Sigrida could more easily fasten the device.

The guards were helping Von struggle to his feet, and Kaigen felt defeated. The Elder had won and gotten what he wanted, and she was no closer to finding a way to fight back. If she waited too long, she knew they would kill countless Annites in addition to the danger to her and Von, and she hung her head as they rejoined Von and the Elder on the platform.

The Elder smiled at Von, almost giddy with the success of Kaigen's directed earth power. Even he, and even through the platform, had felt the return pulses from the girl's power. And though he lacked the understanding necessary to make use of them, he knew Sigrida and her people didn't. He clapped Von affectionately on the back.

Von looked into the Elder's dark blue eyes, seeing for the first time the depth of his arrogance and lack of care for anyone or anything else beyond himself. His intellect was a self-important one, and his feelings were well-worn into channels of desire for more and more powerful sources of magical energy. Vernondiander, Von realized, loved only himself, and that self-love had grown until it was a malignancy that beggared imagination. He shivered inside, wondering how they could possibly fight this magically powerful enemy who was empty inside.

Chapter 66: Oh, Spirit

Finding the chunk of frost in the mine shaft and the simple lack of darkness restored their hope and belief that this whole thing could turn in their favor. Darkness had been the bane of this domain as torches were not the best source of illumination in the best of conditions. Down in the depths of the mine, torches had cast a tiny circle of light compared to the magical light emanating from Isladora's ring.

Tobin and Isladora were reenergized and talked elatedly as they traveled the Silver Roads. The two humans and the horse were covered in mica dust, but there was no help for it until they passed through the mountain to the other side where Meluha had said they would find a river. "How long is this road, Meluha?" Tobin enquired. "How long until we pass through?"

Meluha was surprised that Tobin spoke directly to him. *"It is about a week's travel to pass through. We've traveled some of that already, so I would guess another three or four days,"* Meluha told Isladora and she repeated it to Tobin. *"Remember that you need time to train, so we may not want to reemerge on the surface for a time."* They hadn't decided where the best place to train would be, and Meluha Crocus hoped they'd be able to find some other elemental minerals.

The road eventually widened and then forked. The right fork dead-ended into what almost looked like an old miner's supply store. "No one uses this; the wood looks like it will crumble," Tobin said. He checked the planks that made up the sidewalk and they seemed solid enough, "but we can sleep here and at least be a little out of the dust."

"Oh, thank goodness!" Isladora was exhausted and her head had begun hurting again. She sat down on the rough planks and rested her head on her knees.

Tobin had forgotten to give her the tisane; he nudged her with his boot and then guiltily handed her the canteen. Tobin unsaddled and unbridled Fashi, rubbed him down, and gave him some water, then filled his feeding bag with oats and secured it to his halter so he could eat. Tobin built a small fire and put some potatoes and dried meat in the pot to cook, then he took out their bed rolls and set them on either side of the fire. Isladora looked at her bedroll longingly.

"Time to train, my dear; let us knock some of that dust from your pretty locks," Tobin teased her, taking his sword from the scabbard tied to the saddle.

"I lost my sword when I lost Phoenix," she said dejectedly. "And my head hurts. No training for me tonight."

"You *will* train, Juna warrior," Tobin said levelly. "You must remember what General Nokela said: 'Never forego your training; treat it like the precious commodity it is, and remember always that it can save your life.' My interpretation of that is that you'd better take this sword from me, or you're going to be pretty bruised in a few minutes." He lunged at her, stabbing in the spontaneity of true combat. She moved to the side, rolling as he knew she would, and Tobin swung the flat of the blade around expertly, slapping her on the behind.

She scowled at him in fierce anger, her headache forcing tense lines of ire on her face. He smacked her again, making dust fly everywhere, and he coupled that with a laugh, provoking her. She drew her metal escrima stick from the pack attached to her front. The pair had never sparred with it. It was magical and Tobin knew that she could change it into any shape she wanted to—he stopped smiling because he wasn't sure how he felt about that. Would she be able to control it, or would it strike with killing force?

She was too mad to think about such things, and spat, "What's the matter, Tobin, cat got your tongue?" She launched an attack of her own, and now Tobin was the one battling with his sword and scrambling not to be struck. The escrima stick seemed made of flashing liquid metal as she manipulated it with her mind. One moment it was a stick, the next a short sword, then a short spear—and her ability to change its shape was faster than he'd expected.

Tobin's attention narrowed to the fight, his mind reaching a place that he truly loved, an inner serenity despite the frenzy of his motions. His cognizance was filled only with the sounds of his own breath, the shuffle of their feet in the dust. Tobin relaxed his breathing, even as he sped up his defenses so he could get in a counterattack. Isladora went to block his horizontal strike, changing her short spear into a small shield at the last moment and surprising him. His sword strike's energy was repulsed with a mighty crash and his grip on the handle slipped, the sword flying from his hands to clatter on the ground ten feet away. Isladora leapt forward and smashed the shield against Tobin's chest, mica dust splashed away from his body in a rewarding cloud. With the exertion of the fight, especially with her the victor, she found she was no longer mad and stopped to laugh at the hilarity of all the dust, her shield changing once again into a stick.

Still laughing, Tobin charged her and tackled her to the ground, making sure his body landed first as they rolled across the dusty floor. He stopped the roll and held her down. One arm was stuck underneath him and the other he held to the ground next to her head. She struggled for a time, then stilled as she looked into his eyes. He released her arm and began to draw in the silver dust that rested on her face, the Juna symbol for the heart, and he traced it over both cheeks and three times on her forehead.

Tobin's stomach chose that moment to growl loudly, and he looked at her sheepishly; they both burst out laughing.

Wordlessly, he stood up and pulled her up. The tisane and getting her blood moving had lessened her headache. She sat on the wood planks again while Tobin dished out their food. Tobin handed her a bowl with a whole potato and small chunks of meat. Her mouth watered; she was starving.

They ate every bite and drank the broth. Stomach satisfied, she asked, "What about our magical training, Meluha? Now that we have the frost, can we begin to learn?" Tobin turned his head towards her as she asked the question, his eyes intent upon the ring.

Meluha spoke, *"In the magical arts, we merge energy with our spirit, and breathing is the key, specifically the inhalation and exhalation. Over time, this act becomes thoughtless and we can call our magic as easily as blinking an eye."* Meluha stopped to gather his words as Isladora repeated them for Tobin. *"The intricate act of building of the magic is accomplished during the inhale, execution during the mid-breath, and release and manifestation begins in exhale. Pressing down against the diaphragm creates more strength in the flow that extends outward from the body."*

Isladora nodded in understanding. "What you describe is much like General Nokela's teaching about taking a hit. If we hold our breath when the blow arrives, more of the force will be transmitted internally and the pain more intense. When we learned to breathe out when taking a blow, the damaging energy was sent outward and away from our vital organs."

"Yes, the technique is similar, the breathing out the general described. But it's the breathing in that will begin to generate the magic," Meluha said, then added, *"A regulating chant before the inhale can help the beginner."*

Tobin crossed his arms with a stern frown on his brow, "I'm not chanting like some weird monk."

"Wait... Tobin, you heard me?" Meluha exclaimed in surprise.

"Yes I did, old man," he said with a teeth-baring grin at Isladora. "I have been able to hear both of you since shortly after we entered the Silver Roads." Isladora's face lit up like a flame as she realized he'd probably heard a lot more than she'd intended, embarrassed that he might have heard their earlier conversation about his manhood.

Tobin relented; teasing her to a point was all well and good, but he loved her too much to truly be cruel. "Oh, don't feel too awful, Isladora! At least I know you feel as strongly towards me as I do to you." Her face relaxed a little, the dust covering her face hiding her blushing glow, but she found she was speechless anyway.

Meluha asked Tobin, *"Where is the frost?"*

Tobin patted his shirt front where it was tucked into his pants. "I stuck it down my shirt for safekeeping."

Meluha didn't know any Protector who could have stood having that much frost touching them directly. *"The frost itself, it's touching your skin?"* he asked in wonder, and when Tobin nodded, asked, *"It hasn't burned you? Well, that is a wonder... could this frost be impure? Let us hope it's not too impure to have eliminated its strength, but unless we find more elemental minerals, it's what we have.*

"Nevertheless, we must begin, and the first step is to determine if your magic is either offensive or defensive, as most beings have either one or the other. It is extremely rare to have both."

Isladora was excited. "You have offensive magic, right Meluha?" she asked. "That's how you were able to command the sea and the air, wasn't it?"

"That's right, Isladora," he answered. *"Now sit facing each other and join hands."* Tobin began to shake his head no but Meluha added, his tone full of amusement, *"Come now, Tobin, don't balk. With your hands joined, with you in contact with the ring's metal, I might be able to contain the magic if you lose control of it. I doubt you want to toss a bolt of lightning at Fashi, for example."* At the spirit's words, Tobin sat quickly, knowing he needed to gain such a power, but not wanting to endanger Isladora or Fashi.

The pair sat facing each other, their legs bent and feet crossed. They reached and joined hands, hers palm up and Tobin's palm down, the representation of the masculine and the feminine in the Juna philosophy, and without knowing it was so, among the Protectors as well.

"Now, keep your eyes open but visualize a shining ball of light in your mind," the spirit said. *"Empty your lungs of the air you now have, then breathe in as you see your ball growing brighter and fuller. Hold your breath. Good, just like that. Now exhale while imagining that the ball is releasing its light."*

Both of them exhaled, and when nothing materialized Tobin asked, "What was supposed to happen?"

"That's just it, we don't know yet. You will sit here and repeat this process until something magical comes streaming forth, even if it takes a thousand attempts," Meluha said. *"I caution you that this training will be more draining, physically and mentally, than anything you have experienced as yet.*

However, you are both strong, so do not be afraid of failure. Instead, focus on the ball of light. Go on now, try again."

They sat for a long time, breathing in and out, until Isladora's already-exhausted mind began to wander. Fashi had grown sleepy, and he had long ago knelt and lay down to doze. Isladora banished the concept of the ball of light from her mind, instead focusing on her love for Tobin and her love for Meluha. She visualized pouring her love into them, knowing love was limitless and she could give it freely and forever. Her religion, reinforced by her family's teachings, taught that of all things, love remained endless and eternal.

She had closed her eyes so she couldn't see it, but a kind of glow began to build around them until they were inside her sphere of light. It was, and was not real, and didn't betray its presence to her through her eyelids, but when she heard Tobin gasp she opened her eyes to gaze in wonder at the brightness all about them. It was like she and Tobin were in a small white dome. Then, to their side, they sensed a third presence. She breathed in deeply again, held the breath, and focused as she released it. As she did so, the presence began to move towards them and seemed to solidify somewhat.

Isladora began to tremble. Although she had never seen this face before, she knew exactly who it was. "Meluha! Oh, I.... I can see you! You are here, Meluha!" Her mouth gaped open as she stared at his translucent form.

Meluha looked at her in astonishment, then spread his hands out towards her. "What were you thinking about when you created this magic Isladora?" he asked. Fashi's ears flicked at the sound of an unknown voice; the horse could hear him, too.

Isladora's beautiful eyes were large with wonder. "I was thinking that we are commanded by God to love one another. I was focusing on the love I feel for you and for Tobin." She ignored Tobin's scowl. "Lord, help us to let go," she began to pray. "Help us trust in you, Lord God, with all our heart, all our soul, all our mind." Words tumbled from Isladora's lips and though her magic faltered as she split her concentration between spell and prayer, she felt Meluha's magic joining hers and sustaining it.

Meluha said softly, awe in his voice, "You have linked your magic to the love you feel for us, Isladora. Your magic manifests itself in a spiritual way, I should have guessed." He came closer and knelt beside them.

She opened her eyes and marveled at him. His ghostly apparition appeared in the form of a middle-aged human, roughly the same age as her father. His dark brown hair was parted on the side and pulled back into a queue. He was dressed much like the sea captain he used to be with a dark green and brown coat and cloth tied at his neck. He wore a saber that made no noise as he moved and knelt. This must have been what he looked like when he and his wife were killed in the sea. Isladora found herself feeling deeply concerned for his eternal soul.

She tried to touch his face, but her hand passed through him. She laid her hand in her lap and spoke. "Your soul," she began, then continued, "Do you not see, Meluha, you already know the source of eternal life. Trust in the Lord God. Trust in His love, and let go of yourself. Let go and be at peace."

Meluha shook his head, looked down towards the ground, and sighed. Suddenly he lifted his eyes towards her and smiled, and she smiled gently back at the lines forming about his eyes. How could he tell this young girl with her faith burning so bright it could do this…how could he explain to her what this meant to him, but that he could not accept it. He said, "It's not that simple, my dear. I cannot let go. With or without me, you will still be called to Issedones. I am needed now more than ever, and this time, I will be there." Somehow, when he said the name of the city, it didn't invoke the compulsion.

At his words, emotion swept over Isladora and she lost the serenity that gave her control over the magic. Without a sound, without fading, the light suddenly disappeared and with it Meluha's form vanished as well, leaving her gasping and cold. With a tremendous sobbing intake of breath, she released Tobin's hands. In the next moment, a wave of exhaustion overcame her, and she started to fall to her side unconscious.

Tobin eased her down to the ground, arranging her legs and cradling her head. "Old man?" he asked, shock at Isladora's demonstration of power mixing with concern over her condition.

"She's just asleep, Tobin," Meluha told him, his voice once again spiritual. *"We will keep working on your magic, as these things take time; you should get some rest as well. All too soon, we will have to exit the mines and begin our journey to the Horn."* Inside the ring once again, the spirit was far more shocked than Tobin. He had felt the world about him! The grit of the ground, the smell of the horse, the sound of his friends' voices!

And he felt heartbroken, because he knew that if he had done as Isladora had urged him to, he could have, in that moment, that perfect moment, let go of himself. He *could* have given himself over to God's mercy, come what may, and now he had turned his back upon it! Now, perhaps, he would never be free, for would He offer such mercy again? His fear told him no, speaking far more loudly than his heart, which whispered, *"Yes."* The quiet, still voice of Isladora's God.

Ignorant of the turmoil going through Meluha's mind, Tobin struggled to his feet, more exhausted himself than he expected. He wanted to ask about the Horn, he wanted to question Meluha's intentions towards Islado-ra, he wanted the spirit to manifest again so he could take a swing at him! But he was too tired for any of that; it even took him a few tries to pick up Isladora and carry her to her pallet.

The scout tucked her in and kissed her temple. "You're always the first across the finish line, beautiful girl," he said gently, proud of his love for what she'd made occur. He had felt the power moving, and he knew he'd be able to figure out this magic business—this magic crap, he thought ir-reverently—but right now he could barely hold his eyes open. Thank God we're relatively safe from predators in these mines, he thought. In the shape he and Isladora were in, he doubted they could defend themselves. Tobin rolled up into his bedroll alongside Isladora's and was soon fast asleep.

Chapter 67: Townspeople

The next morning, Tobin woke to the smell of simmering meat. He rolled to a sitting position to see what Isladora was cooking. She had made a hash with the potatoes and some of the dried meat and the heavenly smell turned his stomach into a growling lion. "How'd you get the potatoes grated like that?" he asked.

She looked over at him. She had been deep in thought and no words came to her mind, so she simply held up her escrima stick. The end of it changed into a grating tool like the palace kitchens had, and then reverted to its normal form.

"Mmmph," he grunted and then quietly sat back so he could watch her work. She had a scowl on her face, and it was clear that whatever she was thinking about was more than troublesome.

Before he could say anything, Fashi saw that he was awake and pawed the ground. Tobin moved to get up and feed him. "I know, I know, the apple is always first," he said affectionately to the pony, plucking a small crabapple—Fashi loved that super-sour fruit— and some oats from his supplies. He took a bite, fighting off the pucker from the intense sourness, and then fed the rest to Fashi. He then attached the feed sack to his halter and began to brush him down. When dust went everywhere, he decided to just brush the area where the saddle would sit. He picked up each hoof and checked for sharp rocks, glancing over to Isladora to see that she was still deep in thought.

Isladora made two heaping plates of food and held his out to him. Tobin set down his grooming tools and took the plate. He knew better than to rush her in telling him what had disturbed her so.

"I believe he is a ghost," Isladora said, her eyes were wide and haunted by the thought. Ghosts were extremely difficult to break free from their haunts; most people simply abandoned a place rather than try to deal with them, and they could be dangerous.

"Nonsense, we already know his story," Tobin told her. "He is trapped in that ring."

Isladora shook her head. "No, he thinks he is trapped in that ring," she replied. "I think that his violent death and his regret have caused him to become a ghost." She was silent for a time, eating mechanically and not tasting the food. After a while, she met Tobin's eyes and said somberly, "We must help release his soul."

Tobin was nonplussed. "Only he can do that, Isladora, a person's soul is their own responsibility." Freedom of choice, freedom of will, and a personal relationship with God were all foundations of the Juna philosophy.

Meluha interrupted them. *"I am trapped in here. Don't you think I would know if I could leave?"* he demanded with an exasperated sigh. Meluha wished he had her faith, her belief, but he didn't even know how to pray! Instead he said, *"Today we should be able to rise to the level of the final leg of the Silver Roads, and from there find the exit."*

Isladora began to gather their things and put out the fire. She knew that even religious men stumbled from time to time because they were not able to perceive that God's existence transcended their human state. Human life was pervaded with foibles and weaknesses, the human endeavor of man apart from God was the true test. Meluha Crocus was the antithesis of religious, and she knew he was in pain because he wanted to believe. She prayed that God would show him the way.

They packed up the supplies and began walking the Silver Roads in silence, their steps muffled in the mica dust. The creaking of the saddle became their marching song. It was easy to think that they were all spectral like Meluha's form had been; the mica dust and the eerie blue frost light leant themselves to the illusion.

Two days later, they came upon an abandoned mining supply zone. Meluha said, *"Just up ahead is the exit, we are close now."* They marched on, finally rounding a bend and then gasped, as they could see that the mouth of the cave had fallen in. Some sunlight filtered through and they put their fingers in the sun beam, breathing a sigh of relief, even Fashi nickered.

"Meluha can you move those boulders like you moved the rocks before?" Isladora asked.

Meluha chose the rocks at the top of the cave-in and used his magic to push them outwards. *"There, I think I can move enough rocks for you to be able to climb out over the fall-in."*

Tobin looked at Fashi. "What about Fashi?" he demanded. "He cannot climb that pile and I'm not leaving him here."

Meluha considered the animal. He'd grown fond of the incredibly bright pony as well. *"I hate to think about leaving him, but if I try to move more of it, I risk bringing down the whole ceiling."*

Tobin was torn between his devotion to Fashi and to Isladora.

Isladora's calm voice spoke. "We aren't leaving him, Meluha Crocus. Be careful, certainly, but make a path for his hooves."

Fashi knew they were talking about him and he grew nervous and nickered again. Tobin fought back a shudder, he knew he couldn't leave this horse and he admired Isladora's bravery and compassion. He drew comfort as he patted the pony's neck absentmindedly.

Meluha began moving the rocks, one at a time and carefully until they had a path through, but the rocks kept shifting and the stone above creaked menacingly. *"This won't hold for long. You must go now, quickly!"* Meluha exclaimed, focusing all his will on reinforcing his work.

Tobin went first, holding Isladora's hand in one hand and Fashi's lead rope in his other hand. They were only halfway through the blockage when one of the larger rocks began to slide, deceptively slowly in the first moment, and then dozens of rocks were cascading down upon them. Fashi panicked as they struck his fetlocks and he shot forward, the rope burning Tobin's hand as the pony rushed ahead, pulling it from his grip.

With a terrible crash and an explosion of more mica dust, part of the cavern roof smashed down, burying Tobin and Isladora completely. Tobin clutched Isladora tightly to him and something within him flared to life, igniting in shades of amber, ochre, and gold. The power surrounded them in a protective bubble beneath the countless tons of rock. His strained eyes were striking, tiny daubs of green flecked in with the brown as his magic held the stones from crushing them.

She looked at Tobin's pained face, "How long can you hold this?" Isladora wondered. Even a wyvern's strength couldn't have carried the weight of stone above them. A little stronger, "Hold Tobin!"

"He will have to hold it long enough," Meluha said grimly, reaching his power out to push the rocks ahead of them aside one after another as quickly as he could. Her ruthless command gave him strength where kindness would have done him in. Tobin was shaking, pale, and cold to the touch by the time the two of them staggered out of the cave-in and into the afternoon sunlight.

"Tobin, you saved us!" Isladora exclaimed, hugging him tightly and surreptitiously holding him up at the same time, because his legs were shaking.

He gave her a brilliant smile and said, "I guess I did!" before collapsing to the ground, the princess helping him reach a sitting position. An unharmed if dust-covered Fashi looked at them both from the edge of the tree line beside the road. He shook and dust flew out in a great white cloud, making him sneeze. Tobin and Isladora laughed together at the pony's antics.

Meluha told them, *"Up ahead should be a river. You will probably have to wash everything to get rid of the mica dust."* They were all glad to feel the sun on their faces and backs after the dank darkness of the Silver Roads, they sat basking in it, in no hurry to move. Even the spirit had felt the effects of the long days in near-darkness.

The river's course had moved several hundred yards since Meluha had last seen it, but it was very much alive, a deep and gently moving dark blue beauty. They meandered along its banks, taking in its peace and serenity. The roots of the trees on the bank stretched out into it and Tobin set his fishing snares, knowing they would be full when he returned. They walked a little farther along to a sandy shoreline that would be perfect for bathing with tree limbs to hang their clothes to dry.

Fashi took a long drink and then moved to the grass and began eating the lush blades. Tobin followed him to unsaddle and unbridle him knowing he wouldn't run off and told him, "You'll be last to bathe, you wretch," and then he patted him on his dusty flank watching him continue his grazing.

They took turns bathing, taking off each article of clothing and cleaning the dirt and grime from it. Tobin gave Isladora plenty of privacy, going further down the river to bathe but close enough to hear if she cried out. She hummed to herself, happy at being clean, and she wrapped herself in her blanket as she waited to fully dry. Tobin just wandered around in his braies while their outer clothes dried on flat rocks and tree limbs. They built a fire and Tobin went back upriver to check his snares. He returned with three fat fish, already field dressed and spitted on sticks that he placed over the fire. She laughed at the sight of him in his boots and underwear.

He blushed but otherwise ignored the laugh, secretly pleased she was watching him, no matter how he was dressed. He got out his pot to make some more tisane for his girl, then went to bathe Fashi. Tobin looped a rope around his neck and took him towards the river. "Let's get you clean," he told him. The horse responded by laying down on his back and rolling in the soft loam that lay near the riverbank. By the time he rose, he was covered in wet mud. Tobin jumped back as Fashi stood and shook, slinging mud with a satisfied look. Nothing like a good roll in the mud!

Tobin led Fashi into the river where the current was a little stronger and rinsed him off, letting the river flow smoothly around his withers. Tobin led him deeper until his back was under water, rubbing and splashing water on his head and neck. Leading him from the river, he left him to graze and then sat down to check the fish. They were crispy on the outside but perfectly done when he pushed the fish open on the plate. He handed it to Isladora, who said a prayer of thanks and then began to eat. Isladora felt better than she had in days, now that she was clean and almost dry. The fish was delicious.

Meluha waited for them to finish eating before he told them about the next leg of their journey. When their leathers were almost dry, Tobin took a stiff bristled brush and brushed the leather in long swift strokes so it would remain supple for fighting as he listened.

"The town is called Horn because of its history," Meluha said. *"Many, many years ago the wyverns and humans coexisted and often traded goods. The wyverns live high up in the mountain ranges of Draconia. The mountain cliff offers no way for anyone without the power of flight to reach Draconia, so the metalsmiths created a giant horn to call the wyverns when they wanted to trade."*

The ancient spirit's voice was a warning as he continued, *"We will have to be careful because the wyverns and humans are enemies now. The townspeople are not going to stand idly by and let us blow the horn."*

"Then how are we going to blow it? Surely we will have to blow it several times for the wyverns to hear," Isladora asked, though her heart was beating faster with the thought of drawing wyverns down from the mountains. She touched the mark on her neck, which warmed under her touch.

Meluha said they would have to blow it repeatedly. *"The horn is kept in the middle of a small fort,"* he described. *"We will have to sneak into the fort and find a way to call the wyverns without being caught. Wyverns have extremely sharp hearing but we will have to sound it over and over until they come. The townspeople will try to stop you, for they are afraid of the wyverns now. And if the horn's been destroyed since the older days, I'm not sure what course we will take."*

They dressed and packed up their supplies, heading into the town of Horn. When they reached the main road, they were glad to see people going from place to place after the loneliness of the Silver Roads. The other travelers weren't well dressed, but they weren't paupers either; they looked like hard-working, rough stock. Meluha told them a little more about the town. *"This town grew because of the river that widens and then flows to the sea. They provide lumber downstream and they also have a mill to grind wheat farmed in the area that gets transported to other places."* Tobin could see that the lumberjacks were thick-muscled men.

They noted an inn and decided to check into a room so they could leave their supplies. Tobin rented them a room for ten days and unloaded their camping supplies while Isladora stayed with Fashi. He came out of the inn and told her, "Let's go take a look at the horn and then come back to eat. Something smells delicious."

They could see the fort walls—they were the highest thing in the town so it was easy to find. They approached the fort gates, disappointed to see they were locked. A tall building across the street had a second story roof, so Tobin left Isladora and Fashi and climbed up to look over the fort wall.

He could see the horn in the center. It didn't seem to be guarded by anything but the fort walls.

Isladora was watching Tobin climb when she felt a meaty hand on her arm. "Your purse if you please, little girl," a strangely accented voice said. She was assaulted with foul breath as a large man turned her to face him. In a split second her hand was on her escrima stick, but he grabbed her arm to prevent her from drawing it. Fashi bared his teeth and lunged for the man's neck, while Isladora shoved both hands on his chest. The man flew back, landing hard against the ground.

He reached up and felt his neck and his hand came away slick with blood. He yelled, "Stupid wench!" and got back to his feet. Isladora drew her stick, still her only weapon since Phoenix had run off. The magical metal took the shape of her favored short sword in her hands. Noting the clumsiness of the man as he struggled to rise, she whirled and grabbed the saddle horn with her left hand and swung up on Fashi's back, not bothering to gather the reins from where they rested on the saddle horn, knowing Fashi responded to other signals.

Giving him one of them with her knees, Fashi lunged forward suddenly, charging at the man and Isladora raised her sword, ready to slash if an opening came. The would-be robber heaved himself back out of her reach, and Fashi stopped suddenly enough to raise his hindquarters, turning in the air, the intelligent little pony angling his maneuver to leave his hooves aimed directly at the man's belly.

Fashi's powerful legs drove his hooves into the man's stomach like twin sledgehammers, hurling the man back and onto the ground with a heavy thump. The blow rendered the man insensate and he slid back until his head touched the stone wall of the building, motionless.

Tobin had seen the scuffle from the rooftop and dropped to the ground ready to fight, breathing hard. He was so grateful that Isladora was no weak courtier who had never seen combat; his love could defend herself, though that didn't make him feel any less like kicking the man's ribs in.

Isladora dismounted and turned to face the little horse squarely. She said crossly, "Fashi, you're such a pig! You could let someone else have some of the fun!" She rubbed him across the ears the way he liked to show him she wasn't that mad at him, but with the danger no longer looming, the pony already looked bored. "Who does he think he is, a one-horse army?" Isladora asked Tobin, exasperated. The man had actually touched her and made demands of her, and she'd wanted to deal with the affront herself.

Tobin shrugged. "He's battle trained Isladora. It's what he's trained to do, and worth every apple on the planet." Taking a quick look at the unconscious man, Tobin produced an apple for the little warrior, crooning to him as he scratched his furry head. "Come on, let's get out of here before captain charming wakes up."

As they walked, Tobin told her, "Tonight we will get some sleep in a real bed and have that delicious smelling meal. In the early hours before dawn, we will scale the fort wall and blow the horn. I think I can keep the people away with my new magic skills while you operate the thing." He hoped he wasn't being overconfident, but he didn't see another way to keep guards away from Isladora and the horn while she blew it.

They took Fashi to the stable closest to the inn. The stable was run by a father and his young son, who both seemed to be good people. Tobin said, "I'd like to stable my horse here for some time, I'm not sure how long, but I want him to have the best care you can offer."

The stable master smiled, "Of course, we have plenty of room for him. It will be one-tenth silver per week of full care." The man's eyes widened when Tobin at first produced ten silver coins, far more than the man had asked for, then changed his mind and slipped a worn gold coin from the pouch.

"This is for his care until our return, however long that may be," Tobin said as he set the heavy coin in the stable master's palm and the astounded man could only nod his head in agreement. Tobin then handed the man a rolled-up scroll with the mark of the house of Juna on the seal. "If we do not make it back, this letter will tell the king's stable master to pay you another gold coin for his return to the palace, for he is beloved not only of me, but also of Queen Anyumay of the Juna. The King's gratitude will be great."

"For a gold doublet," the stable master exclaimed, using the local term for a gold coin of that size, "he can live with us in our home like the prince of horses for the rest of his life!" He laughed merrily, hugging his young son to him.

Tobin was glad to see the stableman's reaction, and added, "I'm sure you don't want the tax collectors coming by to collect their due, so you should probably use your new fortune cautiously, no?" He didn't want to draw attention to the fact that Isladora's coins made them tremendously wealthy. Even among the Juna was an occasional thief, but out there in what he considered less civilized places, he supposed they were as thick as flies.

The stable master's expression became serious. "Not just the tax men, but others'll like to take the whole of it, not just a share." He swore, "With God as my witness, my family and I will care for your little friend until your return. And if you have not returned in a year, we will take him to your queen ourselves."

Tobin nodded. "This horse has been battle trained by King Elijashen's best horse masters, and he won't allow anyone but me or the young lady to ride him." He received a nod of understanding from the stable master and his son both. "He will allow you to place a pack on his back, so he can ease your travels, but don't try to mount."

The man and his son both knelt low, touching Tobin's boot in a gesture the scout had never seen, but was clearly a sign of their respect for him and their fidelity to their oath to him. Tobin smiled, ruffled the hair on the boy's head, and stood, leaving Fashi in their hands. He wished he didn't have to leave the stout, loyal little war pony behind, but if they succeeded in calling the wyverns, they couldn't carry Fashi.

The inn was serving mutton stew with thick slices of buttered bread. Isladora and Tobin feasted shamelessly on the first hearty food they'd had in a long time, washing it down with watered ale. They trudged to their room and Tobin fell upon the bed. Before joining him, Isladora knelt to pray for Fashi's care, for their safe journey, and for Meluha to find peace. Afterward, they fell asleep immediately; Isladora cradled protectively in Tobin's arms.

Meluha watched over them all night as he always did, not needing to sleep. Isladora was an unexpected marvel in his life. He thought again about praying, but in the end he could not find the words. One of the Protectors' beliefs was that existence was more than the relatively short physical life they all lived; even Protectors were children compared to the mountains.

He had to believe in something after death, or else his love Mae's paltry thirty short years would mean nothing. He found comfort in the idea that her soul continued in a realm that he could not yet fathom but perhaps he could join. Even if he was troubled with his faith, Isladora's calm convictions were a source of strength for him. He would say that his meeting Isladora was fate and destiny, but he knew that she would say that it was God's will, because all things come from Him and back to Him in the end. He so very badly wanted to believe that.

Chapter 68: Sigrida

Back at the lab, Sigrida and her team whooped and hollered, their excitement overflowing as they celebrated the clearest seismic readings they had ever produced. The readings verified what they had postulated, and they all knew that they would be richly rewarded by the Elder, to the point of opulence in fact. Vernondiander would be immensely pleased with them for having found such a rich source of frost. The scientists talked excitedly with each other, setting up a plan to begin retargeting the drilling operations the next day, almost forgetting about Kaigen now that she'd accomplished their objectives for them.

Even better news was that they would be able to shift the angle of drilling in the current pilot hole; they wouldn't have to start a new surface penetration. It wasn't a particularly complex job to do so, as they'd long ago refined their technique for spudding into the rock, but it took time and engineering finesse.

"I knew we were close!" the young drilling operations engineer exclaimed, his face jubilant.

Sigrida, however, had more experience than him in cracking this particular kind of egg and she knew that it wasn't yet time to count the chickens. "Close isn't good enough to recover the frost, men," she reminded them. "And we would have come up empty again if we had continued to follow our original drilling plan," she added somberly, pointing to the map that showed the path of the bit. With their revised seismic data, they could all see that the shaft would have missed the frost deposit by more than a hundred yards to the southwest.

All of them knew what the Elder's reaction to that unfortunate circumstance would have been.

Sigrida knew their challenges weren't over, either. Although it would save a lot of time, the task of deviating a hole at such an acute angle from the original course would be difficult in the best of circumstances. Without Kaigen's active guidance, she believed, it would be extremely risky, though her engineers seemed to think they could work out the new vector without her. The ground scientist was experienced—and honest—enough to realize that without Kaigen's earth magic telling them the precise trajectory to take, they could still miss the frost-bearing formation.

Two thousand feet was all that separated them from this new deposit, and on the surface that was trivial. All Vernondiander's praise and rewards would only begin when they'd begun actually pumping the frost up to the surface, so for now two thousand feet might as well have been two thousand miles.

Kaigen felt sick listening to them praise each other and wax poetic over what they'd do with the rewards to come. She glanced over at the microscope and thought about the Annites. She knew that if the Protectors were successful, many thousands more of them would be killed and it would be because of her actions. She walked over to the window and sat on the floor, pulling her knees up to her chin, looking out, her heart troubled, her neck aching. She quietly began to cry, not only for herself and Von, but for the poor defenseless Annites.

Sigrida watched the girl stare dejectedly out the corner window. "That's enough celebrating in my laboratory," she said to her scientists and engineers, keeping her tone light so they didn't think she was yelling at them. "You may all go home early and celebrate with your families and friends. I'll finish up here." The other Protectors weren't about to look at gift horse in the mouth, and they excitedly tidied up their workspaces and started to leave as a large group. "We will make an early start in the morning," she added to them as they left, "so don't get carried away."

As she finished her work for the day, Sigrida found herself sympathizing with Kaigen, although she was mistaken as to the reason. It would never occur to her that Kaigen's sorrows encompassed the Annites' plight—her tears must be for Von's plight. Sigrida sighed and approached the girl, wondering how to help her. She wanted Kaigen to be her friend—the reverse certainly wasn't going to be true, of course—so that they'd be able to work together more effectively, and safely.

With Kaigen believing herself free among the Protectors, without the shadow of the Elder's threats toward Von…in fact, Sigrida thought, tapping her nose with a fingertip, Von free to visit her any time he wanted to might be more of a motivation than he is now. The scientist knew that together she and the girl could tap more and richer sources of frost, and Sigrida's career would have limitless bounds.

But Kaigen needed to trust her and to feel obligated toward her. Sigrida didn't know why her instincts made her wary of even touching the girl. True, she was explosive at times, but now she'd proven to be vulnerable and lonely. *I need to overcome my wariness around her*, Sigrida thought, *and to do something that will indebt her to me*. Checking that Kaigen's guards were near she said kindly, "You did well today, Kaigen," taking a seat in a chair near her and patting one for her to sit upon.

The girl got up and sat in the proffered chair. Kaigen wanted nothing more than to scream at Sigrida, nothing more than perhaps crushing the lead researcher beneath tons of rocks, but she remained outwardly timid, sitting down uncomfortably beside her captor. "Thank you, Sigrida," she said, "but do you know how Von is? He was still limping…" Her arms trembled with the urge to strangle Sigrida, and she used that physical reaction to make it seem that she was love-sotted, wringing her shaking hands in her lap. Her jaw ached from clenching her teeth whenever her mouth closed.

Sigrida could see that Kaigen had changed for the better, and the blindness imparted by her knowledge that the Protectors were far superior to all other races prevented her from looking at the young woman objectively. Instead, Sigrida's mood improved significantly and she thought only about how to deepen the bond between Kaigen and herself. "I have an appointment to see the Elder shortly, and I'm going to be gone for a number of hours," she said, and she could see Kaigen trying to figure out why she was saying that. "While I am gone, I can arrange to leave you in Von's cell. Would you like that?"

Bullseye! Sigridia thought, seeing Kaigen's eyes snap to her face, a range of emotions—most strongly, Sigrida was sure, desire—flashed through the captive's eyes and face in moments. "Don't get too excited," she cautioned her. "A guard is posted outside, and you will remain locked in, but you'll be able to be with him for a while.

"If you continue to cooperate with us to the best of your ability," she added, "I'm sure we can arrange similar visits in the future." *The girl is so addicted to Von's mere presence, she'll soon forget about everything else*, the scientist thought cunningly, though years of dealing with Vernondiander prevented any of that cunning from reaching her compassionate-seeming eyes.

Kaigen was elated—though not for the reasons Sigrida thought—and excitedly made a show of keeping herself calm as possible. "I would love that, Sigrida," she said a little breathlessly, not at all faked, because she was elated at the prospect of having time relatively alone with Von. "Do you think I can have a little while to prepare myself?" She pointed at her dusty clothes and disheveled, wind-blown hair.

She needed information from Von to plan their escape, and a chance like this was beyond her wildest dreams. And, she admitted to herself, *I really do want to see him*. Her heart leapt when he was near, and she wanted to nothing but stare at him for hours on end, but she had other things to do before she would be free to let her infatuation have reign over her actions. For Von's own good as well as hers and the Annites, they must figure out a way to stop the Protectors' mining operations.

Sigrida laughed brightly at the young girl's eagerness to see Von and her vanity in wanting to look her best. She opened the enclosure door and pointed to the laboratory sinks. "You may wash your face there and use the brushes to remove the dust. I don't have time before my appointment to procure a change of clothes, but we can make the best of what we have." That little twinge of instinctual fear kept Sigrida out of arm's reach, but Kaigen just bowed her head gratefully and approached the bench.

The cool water felt good on her tear-swollen eyes and dirty face. She rinsed the dust from her hair standing over the sink, being careful not to wet her clothes to make mud of the dust. She looked at the cakes of soap by the faucet and asked Sigrida. "Do you think this will harm my hair?"

"It's not ideal, little one," she replied, "but once or twice won't hurt you. I'll arrange for proper supplies to be brought to you over the next few days."

Kaigen nodded and lathered her hair to give it the first wash since the bath several days ago. *What will I say to Von?* she wondered. *We need to make plans, but he was disappointed to see me cooperating so eagerly with the Elder and Sigrida.* She knew she'd have to overcome that first, and that she'd have to be careful not to let the guards see her true feelings.

Sigrida went to the accompanying deep-bottomed sink and washed her own hands thoroughly. "It must be a tradition among women all the way back to antiquity," she said sweetly to Kaigen. "Washing and preening before seeing one's man." She didn't particularly want to go to the Elder, but she also didn't want to risk missing a chance to not only examine the magic of the Elder's robe but also to receive one of her own. It might even be worth the price of submitting to his lechery, she thought as she dried her hands carefully with one of the many lab towels. But first, she had to talk the guards into acceding to her request to leave Kaigen with Von in his cell.

She knew that would be fairly easy, since Kaigen's guard was infatuated with her beauty, prestige, and wealth. This guard usually watched her, rather than his charge, whenever he thought he could get away with it, and she knew that he was lonely, for long stretches of duty time prevented most guards from any real social time. She'd already hinted that she found him attractive—and he was—and she didn't think it would be too hard to convince him.

Sigrida locked the laboratory doors behind them and nodded to the guard that she and Kaigen were ready. He locked the bracelets of the wrist restraints onto the prisoner; they were connected by an eighteen-inch chain to give her some freedom of movement, unlike the ones Von had worn, which were locked together by only three links.

The guard, Pol, had been on duty for a long time and he was looking forward to time in the barracks, putting his feet up and enjoying the effervescent beer that had become his favored drink over the last few years.

To Pol's shock and pleasant surprise, Sigrida fell back to take his arm as they walked. He smiled down at her, wondering what she intended, but not complaining. She was from time to time familiar with her underlings—though Pol thought the rumors of her sexual appetite were probably embellished by the telling—and now seemed to be one of those times. He thought about how the day had gone, with the Elder being satisfied as the biggest plus, and smiled as he thought that Sigrida leaning into him was quite a good finish. Well, that and the upcoming beer.

Sigrida's fingers traced along the unarmored sleeve of his arm and he looked down at her in question. "Pol," she said, hoping she'd remembered his name correctly, "I think Kaigen here has earned a reward for her efforts." Before he could reply, she continued, her fingernails raising goose bumps below the cloth of his uniform tunic. "And I think that you deserve one as well."

Their course, which Sigrida had subtly directed despite hanging onto Pol's arm, had led them to the higher security cell block where Von was imprisoned. Before Pol could speak, she put a finger to his lip gently, "I would like Kaigen to have the opportunity to visit Von for a few hours, while I keep my appointment with the Elder. I would be grateful, and I was hoping that afterwards we could spend some time alone together."

Even Pol wasn't besotted enough to agree that easily, but found himself saying, "I don't think that will be a problem, Sigrida, so long as we leave their restraints on while she's in the cell. I see no harm."

"I was hoping you would say that, Pol!" she said, smiling broadly at him. To Pol's surprise, she also produced four chits. These would allow him to draw currency from the treasury, in a fixed amount, from Sigrida's personal accounts. The amount was generous, but Pol knew the wealthy scientist could certainly afford it. "A token of my appreciation, until later Pol."

Kaigen watched the entire proceedings in a mild state of shock. She hadn't realized that Sigrida hadn't arranged for the visit with Von ahead of time and was amazed at how easily she'd manipulated the guard. Doing this had to be at least somewhat risky for Sigrida, as she would face the Elder's wrath if something went wrong. Kaigen still hated Sigrida but realized that there might be more to the woman than she thought.

Pol carefully checked Kaigen's restraints, especially the magic-inhibiting collar, one final time then knocked on Von's door before inserting his cell key. He opened the door slightly to see Von sitting on the one piece of furniture he had in the cell, his bed. "Good evening, Von," he said respectfully to his former captain. "Kaigen is being permitted to visit you, but we will need to put your other restraints back on. Is that acceptable?"

Von didn't answer but held his wrists out. Pol gestured for the women to remain outside, taking the restraints that hung outside Von's door from the hook and entering the room. Von allowed the guard to fasten them on, all the while remaining silent and staring straight ahead. Pol said, "You've been granted three hours, after which I will take her back to her cell. If you try to take advantage of this in any way, it will go poorly for you both." Pol felt more than a little uncomfortable threatening his former commander, but "goes poorly" would be a dire understatement if the Elder's wishes were thwarted. For all of them.

Ushering in a nervous-looking Kaigen, he left and locked the door to the cell behind them. Von sat silently for almost a minute before he spoke. "So, I see that you've decided to help them." Von's first words to her; they hurt more than she'd been expecting.

She stood by the door, not coming farther into the room. She had expected this coldness, and he'd maintained since she first met him that he didn't want her affections, if only because it could be harmful to her. It still felt like someone had slid a knife into her belly. "Actually, Von," she said softly, "I am biding my time until I can figure out how to destroy them. The Elder will kill you if I do not aid him, and we both know he won't stop there. He brought me here; what's to stop him from bringing everyone I love in Sybaris here, one by one, and killing them as well? I can't risk that, so for now I cooperate. I don't know another way."

Von blinked, shaking his head in surprise. *She's not the helpless victim you thought, is she Von?* he rebuked himself, seeing that she had matured during this ordeal. He could see that she wasn't looking at him with that almost hallucinating dreaminess she'd used to before, though it was clear that she longed to cross over to him. The Kaigen he knew had been quick to anger, haughty and arrogant, almost as flighty as a bird; this girl before him was both calm and calculating. *She's learned a lot from Sigrida, it seems,* he thought ironically, though he knew that Kaigen was nothing like the manipulative chief scientist.

Von found that he liked this new Kaigen. He liked her quite a lot, in fact. Through her imprisonment and torment, she had transformed from a small but gorgeous waif of a girl into something else entirely. Something still beautiful—*funny how I never noticed how beautiful before*, he thought—but also hard and capable.

Remember your manners, you oaf, Von reminded himself. "Please sit down, Kaigen," he said, sliding to the head of the bed to leave her to foot to sit on. "I would offer you some refreshments, but I'm afraid the larder's a bit bare." He didn't quite smile, but his tone was far lighter than it had been a moment ago.

Kaigen's heart leapt, and she shyly sat near him on the bed. The change from his judging tone somehow felt like a huge weight had been removed from her shoulders, though she hadn't been aware of it until that moment. She realized also that the infatuation she'd once possessed had changed, as well. I'm in love with this man, she thought, realizing that before she'd only thought she was in love with Von.

He wasn't the cold Protector that he pretended to be in order to drive her away. She could desire that creature's touch, its nearness, but she might as well love a statue as love such a one as that. Here was a man who risked exile or death, depending on the Elder's mood, to care for his exiled and aging father. Here was a Protector powerful enough to end Glock's miserable life with a single stroke of his sword.

But most importantly, here was a man that obviously cared for her far more than he'd been willing to admit. She should have realized that days ago, when she'd seen that he bore the necklace she herself had crafted as a gift for his cantankerous and taciturn old father. Kaigen had left it hanging on the old man's doorknob, but she guessed that Von had found it first and kept it. She could see its cord, made of carefully wound leather that she'd made to carry it, still peeking from the back of his shirt.

I love him, she thought, and he loves me, too, I think. She sat across from him on the bed and just watched him for a while.

"I shouldn't have assumed you were that weak," he said by way of apology. He noticed what she was gazing at and pulled the shell medallion out from under his shirt. He held it cupped in his hand. "I never thanked you for this."

"It was a gift for your father," she said archly.

"Well, if I see him, I will give it back," Von replied stiffly, then saw the twinkle in her eyes and the smile on her face.

She laughed. "No, Von, it means the world to me that you wear it. When you saw me in that damned transparent cage that day, I was almost beyond hope. When I realized how filthy I was, how disgusting, for an instant I had truly given up. But then I saw what you wore on your neck, and it all changed. I felt I had a reason to live. Seeing you wear my gift gave me strength."

"You didn't need me to give you strength. You are strength itself," he chuckled. He thought back to the day that she made the necklace. "I was hidden, you know, when you made this." She shook her head, for she hadn't known that. "I watched you make the shell, but I also watched how you healed the wyvern, the Commander, by creating a whole carapace made of it to cover his burned flesh.

"I'd never seen anyone who wasn't a trained Protector able to direct such a feat of magic," he said, "and it was humbling to see you do it. Before that, I admit, I thought you were just an infatuated little wisp of a girl, perhaps a touch arrogant." She flushed a little at his characterization of her, despite the kindness in his voice. "There you were, hopelessly infatuated with someone you had to have thought of as an angel, but when I witnessed what you did with your power, I realized you were more than that.

"Even if I didn't admit it to myself until much later," he added, then sighed and let the shell rest against his chest. "Anyhow, when I saw you make this from your creation for the Commander, I decided I had to have it." He didn't apologize for "stealing" her gift for his father, and he'd have done it regardless.

Kaigen realized that being with him in the cell wasn't what she needed. She needed to have a chance to develop a relationship with this man, to have a chance for some kind of life together. The details were going to be messy, him a Protector and theoretically immortal while she was…well, whatever she was. She knew she wasn't Sybaris, but neither she nor they nor the wyverns had known what she was. And to have a chance at figuring any of that out, she thought fretfully, we must escape.

She drew a great breath and let it out, changing the subject. "Now, Von," how do we get out of here?" She looked around his cell, but this one was even stronger than her enclosure in the lab. There were no windows, though the ceiling had a dull glow for illumination, so at least it wasn't dark. The only way out, barring her earth magic, was through the locked and guarded door.

"We can't, Kaigen," Von said, lowering his head into his hands. "Vernondiander has grown too powerful to stop, and we would be killed." *And I got you into this,* Von thought in anguish. *You'll serve the Elder's insane needs, or you'll die. He'll never let you go.*

Kaigen shook her head firmly seeing the defeated look on his face and took Von's hand in hers. The contact made her feel giddy, some of the old glamour affecting her, but she wasn't overcome by it. "Look at me, Von. Together we will find a way to stop him. At first, I meant to destroy the whole city," she said gravely and matter-of-factly, and his eyes lit up in alarm, "but now I realize that most of your people are as helpless as I am."

Von could see in her eyes that she meant what she'd said, that she'd have brought Issedones down into cataclysm if she'd been able. He suppressed a shiver and said, "You don't comprehend the danger, Kaigen. The Elder was powerful before, dangerously so, but now he has gained the ability to store magical energy in his robe. In a magical battle, he can outlast the best of us; you saw what he did to me and I was fighting back as hard as I could. I had as little chance against him as a fly…his magic is far too strong."

Kaigen looked down towards the floor in thought, hair falling to cover half her face; Von longed to brush it back but restrained himself. "The blue robe does make the Elder very powerful," she conceded. "But what happens when it's full?" she asked.

"When what is full?" he asked in a momentary confusion. "Oh, the robe?" He thought about that, drawing on everything he'd ever been taught about magical power. "I don't know, but if we were able to flood the robe with magical energy. I don't know if it has a limit, though."

"Von, it is a law of nature that everything has a limit," she said. "The robe makes him powerful, but in the end, it is like a pitcher…no, like a barrel, a sealed barrel! It must be, or the magic would fade away as it evaporated. And if you overfill a barrel, it will burst, and I think that would turn that robe of his into a weapon against him, not a shield to protect him, don't you agree?" Her lips pressed together as she thought about what she'd just proposed.

This one's even more dangerous than I believed, Von thought with a chill coupled with something warmer. He was attracted to her amazing intelligence; one would have to think twice about crossing her. *The Elder doesn't know what he's let in the front door,* he thought.

She shifted a little on the bed then said, "I'm curious about these metal transport platforms and the method of using them. You Protectors were able to transport directly to Sybaris, weren't you? And that means that there's one of those metal panels in the city. It's the fountain outside the Cystine Hall, or under it anyway, isn't it?"

Again, he was impressed with her keen mind, not to mention her powers of observation. "Yes, Kaigen," he affirmed. "The fountain was a gift from the Protectors to your two races, the Sybaris and the wyverns, I mean. Other fountains and similar metal 'artwork' have been placed in many key places throughout the world, and we can use any of them for transport."

"My personal favorite," Von told her, "and I will take you there some time, is a stone ridge that looks out over the Rubian Sea. I love to sit on the rock face, warm from the heat of the day, and watch the sea and the sea life on the shores below. In the colder part of the year, slick brown seals migrate there to bathe, play, battle for mates, and to bear and rear their younglings. Such a noise they make, you can hear it from the cliff top!

"And when the sun is setting?" he continued, his eyes seeing his memories of the place. "The cliff faces south and it's on a point, so to the west, the thousand colors of the sunset are displayed in all their glorious shades. At that time, a feeling of peace comes over me, such that I've rarely felt.

Sometimes I sleep on the cliff, just so I can see the sunrise as well and greet the new day."

Her eyes had grown dreamy watching him talk. "That does sound amazing," she said, picturing the scene as he described it to her, although she didn't know what a "seal" was. Some kind of eel, perhaps?

Despite not knowing what a seal was, she could picture the entire scene, knowing that exploring the Rubian Sea with Von and seeing other wonders of the world was something that could be hers.

But first things first, she reminded herself. It was all moot if they could not defeat the Elder. Still, it would be good to have an escape plan. "Can you teach me how they work?" she asked.

Kaigen's mind never seems to settle, Von thought, always seeking answers. He leaned his head to the side. "It's not quite that simple," he said. "We warded the transport plates, so only someone who knows the keys to the magical wards can use them to transport people. I'm one of them, and it would be a huge undertaking to change the wards, so the key in my mind probably still works.

"Also, it's something that can only be taught by doing," he added. "We are tested for the potential, but the way I learned it—the only way to learn it—is to be with someone else when it is done and see how they did it." He hoped she believed him, for it was the truth. Knowing her determination and the impetuousness he'd seen from her in the past, she would only get hurt or killed if she tried to use the transport platforms alone. He decided to change the subject.

"Tell me something of your youth, Kaigen," he said.

He doesn't trust me with the knowledge; Kaigen thought at first but she didn't take offense. Trust was something earned, and something earned slowly. She grew to trust Json and Queen Ariah amazingly quickly, she supposed, but the circumstances had been different, and they were her people not these mysterious "Protectors."

"I don't remember my parents," she told him. "I don't remember where I am from; my earliest memories were of Draconia and the Sybaris and wyverns. They told me that I was a foundling, and despite what you saw of Glock, the people of Draconia do not have lying natures. They raised me as a Sybaris and they all treated me as one of their own."

She told Von the tale of learning to fly on Json's back, of the wing coverlet he'd made for her to keep her wings from being pulled off—or from pulling her off. She spoke of her long friendship with the Commander and of how horrified he was when they found him burned and nearly dead from Glock's tender mercies.

Von was charmed by her soft-spoken voice, and somehow he knew that her smiles were just for him, not something that she gave freely to anyone else. He watched her and thought that when she laughed, he felt elation like he'd never felt. He had been with women from time to time in his life, but he'd never married one of them; none of them had been the one. Being near her felt somehow like he was being bathed in light; it was a different sensation than any he was used to.

Am I falling in love with this mortal girl? he wondered, amazed at himself, but honest enough to admit it was possible. The gulf between them was vast: he was a military man, chosen from the youngest of the Protectors, but he was still already several centuries old, and provided he wasn't banished from Issedones for his defiance of the Elder, he'd live uncounted centuries more. Kaigen, whatever she truly was, would not.

When the guard politely knocked on the door, they both startled at the sound. Neither believed that three hours could possibly have passed, and they longed to keep talking all night. The cell door opened. "Forgive the intrusion, Von," the guard Pol said. "It is time for Kaigen to return to her own cell." His manner was polite, and he smiled at them both, but neither prisoner failed to notice his eyes carefully examining each of their bindings.

I didn't even try to loosen her collar, Von realized. *I wasn't this distracted when I was young and had my first crush!*

"Thank you, Pol," Von said and they both stood, Von's arms fixed in front of him because of the design of the shackles. His hands were gripped into fists, but he made them relax. The last thing he wanted to do was to alarm the guard; they would at least curtail these visits, which would be bad. But they might also take additional precautions, and their situation was desperate enough.

Von leaned down and kissed Kaigen gently on the forehead. "Sleep well, my young friend. Your visit helped pass the time, and I hope we can do this again soon." They were hardly the words of a lover to his love and probably seemed quite fraternal, even paternal, to the guards, but Kaigen knew what he really meant and reveled in the kiss, chaste as it had been. "Until I see you again."

Kaigen's lips narrowed and her eyes looked for a moment like she'd do something rash, whether that was a rush forward to kiss him properly or a suicidal dash at one of the guards, he didn't know, but she restrained herself and simply nodded. "I would love to see this place you described," she said, staring at his lips and then letting the side of her face that didn't face the guards curl up knowingly.

Von thought, *I will kiss you on the cliff top over the Rubian Sea, little woman,* and was shocked by his own romanticism.

Kaigen studied his face, as if to memorize every feature, then squared her shoulders and nodded to the guard that she was ready to go. *I will find a way to have a true kiss from you, Von,* she thought, and as she walked beside Pol, her back was tall and straight and her eyes were bright.

Chapter 69: Sunny and the Horn

The day had finally arrived, Sunny thought as she soared along the breeze, her golden wings gliding along the updraft. Breeding day was arguably the most important time of all for the wyvern race. It wasn't just the finding of a mate, she knew, but a time for the renewal of their species, as it had been since the before time, before they developed intelligence and joined with the Sybaris. The chronicle of memories passed down from mother to daughter-egg remembered the before time fuzzily, but the memories were there. It was something the male wyverns could never understand, but they didn't need to.

Sunny flew to her favorite place to watch the sun rise, a high mountain peak where she could look over the nests of her flock of females. Six of the adults would be mating this year. Others still had young to care for, and they would not feel the call to the sky when the moment came upon them.

This was fortunate, for the fledglings needed looking after for at least another year before they could fly. Some were still too young, although she suspected there might be a seventh from among the younger ones who would feel the pull. She would, or she would not; it wasn't like the Sybaris, who chose when to mate or not to mate. The call to mate was as inexorable as the dawn.

At least with only six this season they would have plenty of males to choose from and hopefully no fighting, she thought. Even so, Mezzi was well supplied and skilled and could patch them up unless it truly got out of hand.

The thought of Mezzi spurred her to action and Sunny leapt from her perch and dove downward along the sheer side of the cliff. She then opened her amber-hued wings and allowed them to catch enough air to start leveling out, eventually turning the plummeting dive into a slowly descending glide. Sunny drifted towards the plain where Mezzi lived and saw her running and frolicking with two of the younglings that couldn't fly yet; their mothers, ever wary and wild, rested where the tree line met the cliff, where they could get into the air instantly if they needed to.

Mezzi's small creature, what she called a "dog," was out in front of the younglings. Unsu's sleek brown body stretched out as they raced along the banks of the stream. Downstream, it was a dangerous thing, that stream,

plunging down in a long waterfall to the forest below, but here near Mezzi's
home it was placid. Close on Unsu's heels was the white wyvern Jalall, lop-
ing along in a playful canter and making the high buzzing sound that was
the laughter of wyvern children.

Mezzi herself was running fast and laughing, her tail undulating behind
her in the breeze of her passage. She was staying ahead of the younglings
like Unsu, until one of them, the black youngling named Rio, got close
enough to try to nip at her tail. Sunny loved all the wyvern younglings, but
she felt pity for Rio. The solid black fledgling had been born without any
wings and he would never leave the ground under his own power. Mezzi
had befriended him and lately he had spent most of his time in the area near
her home, often sleeping near her doorstep.

Sunny flew up from behind them and then soared over them with her
wings wide, shrieking her wyvern song to the glee of the younglings and to
Mezzi's great delight.

"Sunny!" Mezzi called as she flew by. The foursome came to a pell-mell
halt laughing, barking, chirping, and breathing hard. Sunny was such a beautiful wyvern, Mezzi thought.

Sunny was one of the largest wyverns of all, golden-hued. Her head was
shaped in a way that gave her a regal look, her horns angling straight back
with diamond-shaped tips running down her neck. Mezzi loved all the
fierce she-wyverns, but she was drawn to Sunny most of all.

"Unsu, you are one fast little beast!" Mezzi bent over panting. The animal barked at Mezzi and hopped and hopped, circling around her with a
bark, already wanting to run again. Rio nudged him—gently, Sunny noted—away and circled Mezzi protectively with his neck. "It's okay, Rio, he's
just playing," Mezzi said as she placed her hand on the young black wyvern's head.

Sunny did a wingover to reverse her course, making Mezzi's breath
catch at the grace and power that she displayed. Her landing was flawless
and she transitioned from flight to a quick walk smoothly as she neared the
others. "Hello, Mezzi!" She said. "I'm sure I don't have to tell you what day
this is, but I wanted to make extra certain you were ready."

Mezzi gently scratched Rio's head in the softer spot just above his eye,
making the young male trill softly in pleasure. "Yes Sunny," the healer replied. "I have plenty of sedative prepared and I had more than enough
claws to sell that I'm fully stocked up on my medical supplies. I'm as ready
as I'll ever be."

Sunny gestured with her snout. "I regret that you were so injured that
you had to descend for attention." She did not say that she regretted hurt-

ing Mezzi, only that she'd done worse than she intended.

Mezzi cocked her head side to side, chuckling. "Chablis does good work, and I knew better than to try to climb on your back."

"It is forbidden and even more so, you know how I will react," Sunny said, shaking her huge head side to side, "yet you try anyway. We are all too wild for that. We cannot forget the chronicle memories, like it is with the males below."

Mezzi knew what Sunny would say, but she would also never give up her dream to ride on that golden back. "It doesn't have to be forbidden," she insisted gently.

The golden wyvern opened her maw to answer when suddenly a strange sound echoed through the mountainside. All of them froze, their scales hardening instinctively. The sound was foreign to Mezzi's ears, and to Sunny's. Sunny searched her memories, looking back into the chronicle for a few moments. The sound came again. "That sound hasn't been heard in hundreds of years or more!" she said, her voice trembling from rage, "Why today of all days?!"

At Mezzi's dumbfounded look, Sunny growled. "It is the Horn," Sunny's bulk and purposeful aggression made an impressive sight, "The humans! They are going to ruin the day! The nerve of those wretched little creatures!"

Mezzi moved closer to the great head. She said, "Sunny, wait, what do you mean? I do not understand!"

Given the battle reaction that the horn's song had created, it was unwise for Mezzi to block any wyvern's path, but a she-wyvern more than most. Sunny scowled at her and nudged her with her massive head and the healer stumbled backwards, tripped by Rio's protective presence.

Rio instantly lunged at Sunny to try to protect Mezzi. As Mezzi tried to keep herself from landing wound-first—fortunately, her tail helped prevent this—Rio's little throat bellowed a challenge at Sunny and he attacked.

Mezzi yelled, "Rio, no! Oh, Sunny don't hurt him!" Sunny threw the young male to the ground and then held him down effortlessly. Unsu was now barking his head off and Mezzi ran to pick him up, afraid Sunny would fry him.

"You will learn control, little frog," Sunny told Rio, using her pet name for the male, as he struggled. Her voice was gruff, but it held no rage, and Mezzi relaxed a little. Ignoring Rio's struggles beneath her massive claws, Sunny turned her large head toward Mezzi and told her, "We used to be friendlier with the humans. We would trade with them and sometimes even eat with them." Rio thrashed again under her, not yet ready to give up, and

Sunny just held him down harder, her claws digging into his neck until he stilled. "Our ruling pairs and especially Arrington and Bedaiko want to establish relationships with them again, but to my knowledge we have not yet succeeded."

"What does that have to do with that sound?" Mezzi asked her; concerned for Rio but realizing that the youngling had overstepped his bounds by, oh, a few wyvern-lengths, and that he needed to learn that the adult females were dangerous.

"The humans have no wings, no magical powers, and therefore no way to climb up to where we live," Sunny explained, gesturing around the mountain-scape with her tail. "So, when they wanted or needed us, they would blow on a great horn. It was so large that the sound could reach even up here in the tops of the mountain chain.

"When we heard it, we would fly down to see what they wanted," Sunny said. "Someone is blowing that horn now, but I can't believe any of those townsfolk would have the courage to do so." She released some of the pressure on Rio's forelimbs and relaxed the claws at his neck. "I'm going to let you up Rio. If you attack me again, I'm going to really hurt you."

When Sunny let him up, he didn't say anything to her, just crept over to Mezzi and lay in front of her, glowering at the she-wyvern towering over them both. It was ridiculous, given their size disparity, but it was obvious he would attack again if he felt Mezzi was in danger. Mezzi put a now-quieter Unsu down and hugged Rio's head to her chest, telling him he was brave, but that he shouldn't do such things.

Sunny laughed. "That crazy wyvern must love you a lot Mezzi!" she said, then her head snapped in the direction of the town. Whoever it was, they were blowing the horn again and with that sound, the females would be distracted. Some of them might not rise to the mating flight, while others might be enraged enough to harm each other or the male wyverns pursuing them. It was her responsibility to ensure the success of breeding day and she said angrily, "This has to stop. I'm going to fly down there and melt that horn!" Sunny was furious and spread her wings to take off.

"Take me with you Sunny!" Mezzi cried. "You shouldn't fly down there alone, and you know it! You don't know what's happening, what they will do. They might shoot arrows at you!"

"That would be their last mistake," Sunny said coldly. She looked Mezzi in the eye. "You will never ride me; it is *forbidden*." Sunny jumped into the air, her powerful wingbeats lifting her vertically and Mezzi had to lean in against the wind of it.

"It is forbidden only because it's forbidden, not for a good reason!"

Mezzi yelled back, angry and hurt. "The stupid law is just tradition, and you can change it if you want to!"

The horn sounded again, hardening the scales on Sunny's neck still further. Her nostrils flared and she snorted. She gained height and began her flight towards the human town, her anger making her yellow scales glow with yellow fire. To her knowledge, the Draconians had made no contact with the humans for many years. Well, she was about to make contact with them, that was certain, and they were going to regret ruining breeding day.

Although she had the power of levitation, Mezzi simply couldn't fly fast like wyverns could, and so she climbed on Rio's back in desperation. "Run, Rio!" she cried. "Run as fast as you can, we must stop her!" Mezzi pointed the direction she wanted to go, and Rio took off, leaving Unsu far behind as the young wyvern picked up speed.

Far faster than she could have run, especially with her back still in stiches, Rio ran Mezzi to the edge of the cliff-side that she used to reach the city of Sybaris below. She had to tell the others! Sunny didn't understand that the humans were clever and had tools far deadlier than mere arrows. She was flying into danger alone. Mezzi jumped off Rio's back, patting his neck and telling him to stay.

Normally, she would descend slowly using her levitation power, but she cursed as she realized she had no time. Pulling back away from the cliff edge, she ran with all her might and leapt into the empty air, plummeting down toward the forest below. Rio cried out to her, his buzzing roar already fading into the wind, but thankfully he didn't follow her off the cliff.

She used her tail to aim her impromptu flight toward the city, but that wouldn't keep her from being impaled on the trees, of course. *I hope I can slow my fall,* Mezzi thought as the trees started growing nearer. She'd never used her levitation to arrest her fall before, and she wasn't exactly sure she could, but she focused on the power of her cyan scales and her fall slowed and then she was in controlled motion.

She heard the faint sound of the horn again and cursed again. Even with her drop from the heights, Sunny would no doubt reach the human camp long before she would be able to rouse the ruling pairs and get help to her.

Sunny's anger grew as she flew, made more intense by the resounding horn. By the time she saw the human town, she was a flying inferno, her wrath causing her belly to heat with liquid fire. The horn sounded again, and she zeroed in on it with her vision, as sharp as any eagle's eyes. She adjusted her course and flew straight towards it.

Isladora took a deep breath and blew the Horn once again. The instru-

ment was a monstrous contraption made of brass, though somehow it
wasn't all covered in verdigris, nearly as big as Json had been. The first time
she had blown it, she had been amazed at how loud it was when it reverber-
ated off the mountains, and this was probably the last one she could manage, since Tobin's strength was obviously flagging and he wouldn't be able
to keep the townsfolk at bay much longer. She rejoiced when she saw the
bright yellow wyvern flying towards them because they were almost out of
time.

"I see one Tobin, it's working! Once the wyvern arrives, we can convince the townsfolk everything's fine," she told him, she was looking forward to seeing one of Json's brood.

The Protectors' pull had led them to the town, but Meluha had led
them up to the Horn. Unfortunately, the entire town had been built around
the Horn, for it was the centerpiece of their history. Meluha had explained
that calling down the wyverns was the only way he knew to get them up to
the lands controlled by the Protectors; his tone had made his annoyance at
his people's lack of planning in regard to helping Isladora reach them plain.

However, horses and wyverns did not get along, unless the horse was in
a wyvern's stomach, so they'd been forced to leave Fashi behind. She was
glad that the stableman had been of good stock, and that the little horse
would be looked after if they never returned. They had eaten at the inn after
making their arrangements and then waited until dark to climb the fort; despite it having been originally built as a fortification, its defenses had been
allowed to crumble, and it was easy for both of the trained warriors to as-
cend to the Horn's platform.

It had taken them until mid-morning to figure out how to make the
Horn sound—it required an application of will rather than simply an air
supply—and as they'd both expected, once the townspeople heard it, they
had quickly reacted. First, they'd surrounded the fort, demanding the two
come down and stop all the foolishness, but when Isladora and Tobin
hadn't immediately complied, they'd started beating down the barred door.

This time, the fortress' age had worked against them, and the door
hadn't withstood the men's efforts for long. They'd swarmed inside to
climb to the roof, but there they had met Tobin's magic, blocking the only
stairwell to the roof with a field of amber energy. That had frustrated them
for a time, but then they'd started climbing the ill-maintained walls and Tobin had been forced to join Isladora by the Horn.

His shimmering sphere of amber, ochre, and gold colors surrounded
them now, and it had easily cast aside the crossbow bolts and spears the
men had hurled at them, but it wasn't going to last. He was running out of

strength to keep up the barrier, and they had so angered the crowd that the consequences would be dire if they reached them.

The arrival of the golden wyvern changed all that, and the townspeople yelled out in alarm when they saw its form racing directly toward the Horn. Suddenly, it was no longer a priority to capture, or kill, Isladora and Tobin; getting away from the fort was.

Isladora grew a little nervous when she saw that the wyvern was not Json, but that blossomed into fear as she saw the much larger yellow wyvern was in a state of rage, its scales burning with coruscating energy. The wyvern flew over the town, screaming an ear-piercing shriek, and the townsfolk redoubled their efforts to abandon the fort and to find a place to hide.

The wyvern banked sharply and dove in at them, opening its maw to spew yellow fire onto the wooden fort and the Horn. Isladora swallowed hard and ducked, but Tobin's magic held against the liquid fire that poured over and about them. Isladora could see the strain on Tobin's face as he battled to maintain his focus, and Isladora didn't think that he could withstand another attack. Another flame strike like this one, and they'd roast alive!

Isladora didn't understand; Meluha had told her that this was how to call the wyverns in peace, and now this one was trying to kill them!

Sunny was perplexed; her fire had set the entire fort ablaze, but somehow had not touched the two humans or the blasted Horn. The Horn that still stood. The Horn that could still be blown to disturb her sisters and daughters in their mating flight! But through her rage came ancient memory. Humans did not have the power to protect themselves from wyvern fire, only Protectors did, and that thought quenched her next measure of chaos.

But Protectors didn't use the Horn; they had no need of such a thing since they could fly to the wyverns. She looked more carefully at the humans, her sharp eyes bringing their images to her through the flickering shield in great detail.

Isladora didn't know what to do while she watched Tobin shaking on his knees, his eyes closed, his palms up and open as he concentrated on his power. Below and around them, the fort was ablaze, and it wouldn't be long, she knew, for the old wood to collapse under them, plunging them into destruction no matter what the wyvern did.

Touching the mark on her neck, she began shouting at the top of her lungs at the wyvern. The odd sounds coming from Isladora's throat were nothing a human should have been able to make, and they meant nothing to Tobin. But Json had gifted her with the ability to speak the wyvern tongue when he needed her help to save Queen Ariah's life, and now Isladora used that ability desperately. Json's mark was hot and visibly glowing as she focused all her attention and will on the yellow wyvern.

Tobin didn't understand and wondered if the imminent immolation and the sudden ferocious attack by someone she'd thought would be friendly had driven Isladora mad when he'd heard the strange guttural chirps, shrieks, and growls.

But to Sunny, those sounds were not strange, they were language. Her sharp hearing picked out some of the words. "Peace" and "help" and "Json" were what the she-wyvern could pick out of the roaring of the flames. How would a human know how to speak the wyvern tongue? How would their little mammalian throats be able to even make the sounds? She circled to look for danger and seeing none, landed next to the shimmering amber ball that surrounded the humans. She was in no danger from the burning building.

The flames cast a malevolent glow on her scowling face, and her eyes burned with amber fire. "How is it that you can speak to me?" she demanded. "Answer me!"

Isladora was frightened of this much larger wyvern—it was many times bigger than Json!—but she remembered that Json had acted like a bully, too, when she had first met him. As she'd done then, she stood her ground now. "I am a friend and battle companion of Json," she yelled, turning her head and holding her hair to show Json's wyvern mark glowing with power on her neck. "He told me that if I ever needed help, I could come to him. You must take us to him, please, because we need his help!" Sunny snarled at the very idea of carrying humans and Isladora added, "I am also a friend of Ariah. I helped Json make the pyre for her."

That brought Sunny up short, and she spat, "It is Queen Ariah, human," but the words were merely stalling for time. This human knew Json and her Queen? She aided Json in making the royal egg? Her mind reeled, for if this were true, then Sunny had no choice, no choice at all. The symbiosis between the wyverns and the Sybaris was vital to the wellbeing of both races, and part of that relationship meant that the Sybaris queen was the wyvern's queen as well.

I must honor the mark on her neck and investigate further, she thought, glancing down at the creaking building. And if they die, I cannot do that. It would be easy enough to destroy them later if the girl was lying, after all, and she snorted at Isladora. "What is it you require of me, who claims friendship with our queen?"

The big wyvern didn't acknowledge the friendship, only the claim of it, and Isladora swallowed the lump in her throat. "I need you to take us to Json and Queen Ariah," she said.

Sunny snorted again, more like a growl. "How is that you have Protector magic but cannot fly?" she demanded. "Or step between places?" she added as her ancestors' memories yielded more information.

"Tell her that you are not a full Protector Isladora," Meluha said.

Isladora did not know what the wyvern meant about stepping between places, but she did as Meluha bid, saying, "I am not a full Protector, and I cannot make it up the mountain to Sybaris without your help."

Sunny, however, had heard the voice of Meluha Crocus, and her senses felt the magic of his speech. She also knew that many humans were tricksters, and her eyes narrowed suspiciously. "You have a mage with you, Isladora," she said, her mouth making the human name sound much more sibilant. "Where is he? I cannot see him." She slowly inhaled as she waited for the answer, preparing subtly to breathe fire at them again.

Isladora realized that Sunny had heard Meluha's voice, since she had not used her name, and she raised her hand to show Sunny the ring. "The mage is trapped in this ring, and he is the reason for our journey. I cannot remove it, and through it, he is summoned to Iss..." she stumbled over the name, "the Protectors' homeland." The language of the wyverns wasn't up to saying Issedones, and she was glad it couldn't, because the last thing she needed now was the distraction of the call flaring up.

She'd learned to ignore it, but it was still hard to endure. "I need your help to reach it."

Sunny huffed, glaring at the wyvern mark that she made her honorbound to obey this little human's request, and she let out her fire breath slowly. "I will not take you to the Protectors' city," she said, knowing she couldn't easily say the name anyway, although she knew it from the stored memories, "but I will get you to Json and Queen Ariah."

But I won't carry you, Sunny thought stubbornly. She recognized that she had caused this building to burn underneath them, and she gathered them all up in her great wing inside the sphere that the male "not full Protector" human was maintaining. She lifted them all up, Horn and its pedestal included, effortlessly and handed them down to the ground below.

Tobin's magic field went out almost the instant they reached the ground, and the two humans had to scramble to keep the Horn from falling on them. *Good!* Sunny thought. *Maybe it's broken now and they can't blow it anymore and disrupt our lives!*

Now that she wasn't enraged anymore, the she-wyvern could reason, and she realized Mezzi was probably bringing more wyverns. Male wyverns, who would give them the use of their backs. In the meantime, she would guard these odd little not-Protectors from the humans if they dared to poke their noses back out of their homes.

The fortress chose that moment to collapse, and embers leapt into the sky to join the column of smoke. Isladora dragged Tobin back from the holocaust and the two of them sat down against a building across the street. Fortunately, the town had never built directly against the fortress walls, so the fire looked like it wasn't going to spread, but the building was going to be a complete loss. To Isladora's eyes, the Horn looked okay, though its bell might be bent.

Silverback saw the column of smoke and feared the worst, but he saw two humans sitting opposite from Sunny, watching her as she watched them, and glided in for a landing. Large as he was, Sunny dwarfed him, and he cocked his head at the she-wyvern for an explanation. She only snorted and looked away, which didn't really surprise him, and so he turned to the humans. He didn't speak their tongue, but maybe they could communicate somehow… His thoughts broke off as the woman spoke in the wyvern tongue, and he knew who this had to be, though he'd never met her. This was Isladora, the one who'd saved them all by helping Json.

"Hello," Isladora said. "I am Isladora and this is Tobin, and we must speak to Json and Queen Ariah." She was trembling, waiting for this new wyvern to attack her, too, but her voice showed no sign of her tremors.

"Then climb aboard my back, Isladora and Tobin," Silverback said politely, lowering himself to allow them to climb aboard. He turned his long neck so he could watch them, waiting to see if he needed to instruct them, but Isladora had been taught to fly by Json, and now she directed Tobin how to sit, what he could hold onto, and what he should leave alone. Tobin was obviously exhausted, so Isladora resolutely put him in front of her so she could hold onto him.

In fact, I think this young man is too exhausted to be afraid of me, or Sunny, or the thought of flying, the wise old wyvern thought. When he was sure Isladora was ready, he turned down the street—by now, the townsfolk were peeping from their windows at the two beautiful but deadly wyverns—and ran forward, taking off as gently as he could.

Isladora steadied Tobin, who slumped over semi-conscious as Silverback climbed, shifting her balance expertly as the wyvern banked, quickly joined in his flight by Sunny, who flew above and behind him to keep an eye on the no-doubt treacherous humans.

Despite Tobin's exhaustion and the other thousand things she had to worry about, Isladora exulted in flying again. She gripped her love fiercely, helping keep their centers of mass at the proper position as the wyvern carried them higher. She looked back down to see the ruined fort, the Horn laying on its side, still gleaming bright in the sunlight despite its hasty repositioning, and the townspeople all streaming from cover to gawk at the wyverns flying them away.

They would have a lot of explaining to do when they stopped back in to pick up Fashi.

Chapter 70: Annites

Exposure to the dark liquid had caused a number of changes within the Commander. He had become quite strong, but not just physically—his senses were fine tuned to his environment in a way they had never been before. He could taste the different minerals in the rock, and with his sense of smell he could assess temperature change as the rocks warmed and cooled. He was beginning to understand the nature of the minerals and how they were a part of the geological processes that surrounded him.

He glanced down to where Nim was grooming herself on his snout, finding peace in her repetitive movements. The symbiotic relationship that the Annites had with the earth was complex and he did not understand much of it yet, but he wanted to. The blue substance they created was addictively powerful. It had changed his eyesight and he could see minute details; for the first time, he thought he might be able to get used to staying deep under the surface.

Nim had created a series of cylindrical cells, elegant tubes that were adhered to his snout that she stayed in most of the time. She had constructed the tubes with the opening towards his eye so that when they tunneled through the dirt, they remained intact. They reminded him of the homes that mud daubers built, but much more intricate.

"Nim, that's some construction work you've done." She paused in her ablutions and her tiny arm waved at him. As her head turned and his eye focused, he marveled at the dense silver hairs that covered her tiny face.

"We should reach that big lake on the map today, right?" She nodded her head yes, something she had learned from watching him. They had been steadily moving towards the lake on the map and they were getting close. The Commander was hopeful that he would begin to grasp the nature of their problem when they arrived. She waved her arm indicating the direction of travel and he laughed, "All right, let's get started then."

He traveled forward with excitement. He was more than ready to comprehend what it was that they needed him for. After some time, he knew they had reached their goal as his eyes alighted upon the small lake of sky-blue water. Annites played along the shores and frolicked in the lake, going about their lives. He even saw some of them laying tiny eggs. Nim, who normally never left him, climbed down and moved off towards the water.

Soon, she also began laying eggs, sighing in relief, and then she dove under the water and was gone.

He stayed there for several days, watching the Annites, patiently waiting for Nim's return. He couldn't tell the little things apart, so he would just have to wait until she appeared on his snout. Some would come and lay on him, climbing up to the top of his back and head, but none of them approached her little home. The Commander enjoyed the opportunity to do nothing more than rest. He was a soldier, and he knew that whatever was to come, he'd have little chance to get rest soon enough.

When Nim finally did appear, she was deep blue in color and somewhat larger. The Commander was extremely glad to see her. "Nim, I thought you left me for good!" When she didn't respond he asked, "The blue water is like a placenta?" At her look of confusion, he said, "It is like a container that holds and nourishes your eggs?" She flashed her signal for yes.

She tapped her head, which was her indication to consult the map. The Commander dutifully closed his eyes and focused his cerebral vision until he could see the map in his mind. Nim showed him the cavern they were in, the lake, and another empty cavern that was close to the lake and slightly deeper.

"You want me to go there?" She flashed the signal for no three times, and he laughed. "Okay, so we are not going there but you want me to know that it is important?" Nim nodded her head yes. She pointed to her eyes and then to the lake. "I have been watching the lake," he told her. She kept giving him the signal to stay where he was and to watch the lake.

Suddenly, they heard a loud sound and a fissure opened. The water in the lake began rushing into the hole. The Commander started to get up, but Nim flashed hotly for him to stay still. He saw that all the Annites were sitting at the edge of the lake watching, too. None were in the water and they were excited but not panicked. He settled back down to watch.

The lake drained most of its liquid and he could see that the bottom was smooth and tilted towards the hole. The Annites moved as a group, thousands of them, to push the remaining eggs into the hole, and then they sealed the hole using dirt and thicker blue minerals. It was an impressive feat done with a level of coordination that rocked him to the core. Nim tapped her head again and he dutifully closed his eyes as she asked him to. The map had changed. The blue lake was gone, but he could see that the water and eggs were now stored in the lower cavern. "The eggs, they are safe in this place?" Nim glowed warmly, nodding her assent. "So you somehow make the liquid and lay your eggs in the lake and then you funnel them into a sealed area. Then what happens, do the eggs hatch?"

Nim tapped her head again and he closed his eyes. He could see a similar blue egg store on the map that was glowing brighter than the rest. "Ah, you want us to travel to this place because I will be able to see the eggs that are ready to hatch?" She nodded her head then flashed the signal for rest. The Commander closed his eyes again, noting another line on the map that went all the way to the surface. He opened his eyes to ask Nim about it, but she had already retreated into her den. He looked around to see that most of the other Annites had gone to their homes and the cavern was once again quiet.

He lay down and tried to sleep. The Annites that usually settled around him looked grateful; they were tired too. They used to annoy him, but he had gotten used to their constant presence. Every day they cleaned him, healed him, and now they protected him when he slept, not that he was sure how such tiny things could actually protect him from a physical threat large enough to endanger him. He wasn't sure how he had gained such honor among these beings, for they were showing him their entire way of life, stressing to him especially how they were part of a much bigger ecosystem.

When the Annites woke they began his daily grooming. When that was complete, Nim had him travel on to see the last stage where the Annites hatched. Nim located him near the far end of the cavern this time. There were many holes in the cavern wall, and he could see large pieces of the wall had broken off and fallen to the cavern floor. Inside the rock, he could see veins of hardened blue matter. As he watched, another hole opened up and several new Annites tumbled out to the ground.

"Did these just hatch, Nim?" When she nodded her head yes, he continued. "They are full grown like you were when I met you," he observed. "Now you are bigger, so every time you lay eggs, you grow in size?" She nodded and he pointed to the fallen debris. "And the veins in the rock are the trails they made when they traveled out of the rock." He was silent for a moment and then said, "That means all the veins we have passed must have at one time been Annites hatching and making their way back to the group."

Nim raised her little hands in the air as if saying, "Tada!"

As she led him on, he began to feel faint vibrations in the rock. The tremors started so small he thought he was imagining it. When debris began to fall on his head he asked, "What's happening, Nim?" She had retreated into her little burrow. The noise steadily grew louder and the vibrations stronger. He stopped moving in fear, but Nim came out to order him to continue on, then she went back into her hole. The debris falling on his head was annoying to him but would be deadly if it hit Nim. He looked at the far wall off in the distance. The Annites had surrounded it like they were trying to hold it together, standing on each other trying to shore up the wall. Some were being crushed by falling debris.

The Commander quickly went to the wall to help them brace it, trying to not crush the tiny creatures. His now-healed wyvern hands could feel the vibrations, and he moved along the wall to where they were the strongest. The rock there had begun to get hotter. When the Commander closed his eyes to concentrate on the map, he could see the long line he had spotted yesterday that started at the surface was now entering the hatching ground. Suddenly, a spinning metal contraption began to break though the rock formation; its destructive force destroying all that was in its path. He could hear the creatures for the first time—they were collectively screaming, he could see their light pulses everywhere.

He realized that he must act to save them. "Nim, hang tight!" He yelled. "Move out of the way, Annites!" They scrambled out of his way, and the Commander began punching the rock, digging his way to the source of the vibration. Suddenly, the rock face crumbled, knocking him backwards, and the sharp metal broke through, flaying eggs and new hatchlings. The Commander jumped back to keep from being torn to pieces. The blades were spinning too fast for him to grab, and when the device hit the blue, it easily cut into the softer substance. Finally it stopped, leaving an eerie silence.

The Commander could see that the metal was a drill bit, but then it changed somehow, the end became porous—or perhaps some kind of plug was withdrawn, the Commander thought—and they heard a new sound as thick tubes slid down from the base of the bit and into the blue vein of the formation. They heard a slurping sound as the line began to drain the blue elements, taking the substance back to the surface. At this, the Annites started screaming again, spurring him into action. He climbed higher, sliding back and scrambling for purchase to climb to where he could grab the end of the pipe, but it was far stronger than iron and he couldn't budge it.

Instead, he closed his maw around the tubes that extruded from the end of the pipe, crushing one with his teeth; two of his teeth broke in the process, for even the tubes were immensely strong, but the flow in that tube stopped almost completely. Moments later, the draining of the blue came to an abrupt halt in sudden silence. He heard great cheers as the Annites rejoiced in the victory, but the Commander knew that this was but a small victory in what was going to be a much greater struggle. There was intelligence, an inimical intelligence, behind this drilling tool and the extraction tubes, and they would not give up their prize so easily.

He closed his eyes and again traced this line all the way to the surface. Someone on the surface had a lot of explaining to do. He decided that if they could drain the blue substance without a thought for the Annites' well-being, then he would send fire up the tubes, all the way to the surface if he could push his flames that hard.

"I want you all to get back out of the way. You too, Nim," he said gently, though a hardness in his eyes belied his calm words. The little Annite stuck her head out of her den. "Yes Nim, you too. I'm going to send fire up the other tubes, maybe ruin the tool completely, and that's going to take as much power as I can muster. I don't want you burned." In fact, he'd never unleashed the full fury of his flames, even in battle. With a huff, she scrambled down.

When the Commander was sure the little creatures were out of harm's way, he gathered the partially flexible tubes into a bunch, except the crushed one, into his mouth and blew liquid fire into them. As they melted, he advanced to blow fire up the hollow center of the drilling apparatus. When he consulted his mental map, he was disappointed to see that his liquid fire had not made it anywhere near the surface, but the intense heat had at least ruined the extraction tubes. This particular tool would not harm the Annites again, and the Commander felt pleased.

Even if the enemy had more tools, it would take them a lot of time to clear the wreckage and run another tool down the shaft. He wondered if he could collapse the hole, or somehow make it unstable. That was something he'd have to think about.

The Annites wanted the Commander to rest in a pool of their healing waters while they celebrated the victory, but he'd seen another red-limned line to the south. "Take me to the other place where this is happening," he said to Nim, and after a few moments, she and her little friends led him to another chamber.

This one made his heart ache, for it was nearly devoid of any of the rich blue light that the Annites created in their intricate and magical life cycle. The tubes were sucking a lot of air, but as he watched, they greedily sucked up the few remnants that were left. Remnants that were young Annites, and the Commander's shell gleamed with white fire as his anger rose. He set Nim safely aside and then plunged across the bowl that had once been filled with a lake, in turn once filled with cavorting Annites, and gathered up the flexible, prehensile tubes near the tip of the drill pipe. With a white-hot burst of flame, he severed them clean, and then he blew once again up that pipe, straining himself even more than he'd done the first time, until he was sure the pipe was ruined.

Now he could rest, and Nim led him back to the previous chamber. A great celebration was held that night. The Commander sat in a pool of their healing waters while the creatures bathed him and fed him the only way they could. It was an odd victory feast for a veteran wyvern warrior, but he didn't mind at all. Nim came out of her den and he asked her, "This battle isn't really an underground battle, is it?" Nim shook her head no as he spoke, tapping her head so they could consult the map. His eyes narrowed in focus and he gasped as she showed him hundreds of drilling lines that ran from the surface into now-empty hatchling stores. This one-sided war had been going on for a long time. A tear left his eye as he realized the full impact to their underground world. There weren't many stores remaining.

"I'm going to have to go back to the surface to stop whoever is doing this to you," he said grimly, his voice trembling a little at the devastation. Nim looked sad; she had grown attached to the Commander. "You can't go up into the light, can you Nim?" Sadly, she shook her head no. "Well, I will take care of whoever is attacking you, and after I engineer their downfall, I will return to visit you." The Commander wasn't sure, but he thought that what looked like her mouth had smiled. He smiled back, returning her warm gaze, but he knew that he might not survive to return to the tiny creatures' world. He was prepared to face that, but he vowed that whoever these surface dwellers were, they were about to feel the grit of a true marksman.

Chapter 71: Blown Away

Pol and his best friend, a guard named Koss, locked a dreamy and seemingly peaceful Kaigen into her chamber for the night as they both sighed in relief. They'd made it through the day, and it's "irregularities," both intact and undiscovered, which was even better. Pol had convinced Koss to help him take Kaigen back to her cell for a share of the chits. Koss knew that Sigrida had conspired with Pol to allow the prisoners to be together, and Pol had shared the chits and the knowledge with Koss but they both knew that Sigrida wouldn't bear the brunt of the discipline if someone had spotted and reported them. No, it would be the two guards who would suffer.

The two friends headed back toward the barracks. Pol sighed again, thinking of Sigrida. She was a beautiful woman and she'd been quite affectionate with him, so he dared to imagine that he could win her heart for more than just a single night. He swung the keys about his finger and whistled a jaunty tune as he sauntered down the hall, and Koss rolled his eyes as he followed a step behind. He silently thought that his friend was a fool, knowing that Sigrida was far above a mere guard's station, she wasn't likely to lower herself to Pol's level no matter what she had said.

They had almost reached the barracks when the ground heaved and the building shook. The magically powered lights flickered and then stabilized as vibrations rattled the windows in their panes. A moment later, a huge explosion rocked the night, glaring a bright incandescent cerulean blue in the darkness. Both guards threw themselves to the floor, covering their heads against falling debris, and despite the fact that the explosion was over at the drill site and not within the city itself, the shockwave struck hard, exploding glass and knocking smaller features off the buildings to rain down to the ground.

Another explosion followed, and then another, shocks hammering at Issedones, until finally they stopped. The guards ran to look out the window and saw that the nearest drilling site was engulfed in an inferno of azure flames. The adjacent buildings were half flattened, and the guards flinched to think about how many Protectors had just died. They could only shake their heads to try to clear the fuzzy distress from their minds, and then their training kicked in and they began hurrying toward the exit to help contain whatever attack this was.

Sigrida met them as she came wheeling around the corner, coming face to face with the guards. "Where is Kaigen?" she screamed at Pol. "Did Kaigen cause this? Or Von? Where are they?" she demanded, grabbing at the Pol's tabard.

The other guard said, "Kaigen is in the laboratory, ma'am!" Pol grabbed her hands to remove them from his uniform. He appreciated the chief scientist's beauty as much as the next man, but he was damned if he was going to let her manhandle him! "It couldn't have been her; her magical restraints are secure!"

Sigrida calmed a little. If Kaigen was in her enclosure and the collar was on her neck, she couldn't have caused the explosion. If the girl's earth magic had done it, the Elder would have probably killed Sigrida, no matter what her reason was for having allowed her and Von time together.

She allowed the guard to gently push her back and looked out the window to see the blue-tinged flames fading to amethyst as the smoke billowed up from the wreckage. She put her palm over her mouth, so many had been against drilling this close to Issedones.

This is unconceivable! she thought, and her mind reeled. She knew that the frost, and especially the liquid medium that contained it, could become explosive when heated to certain temperatures and pressures, but drilling and pumping conditions were nowhere near those levels of heat or force. And she knew that once frost began burning, they would have no choice but to let it continue to flare until the pressure dropped enough to seal it off.

She was immensely relieved that they hadn't had time to fill all the receiving tanks yet, or the explosion might have set them off too.

Emergency engineering crews and members of the guard were already arriving at the site to contain the flames and to try to protect the nearby buildings with shields of power. Others began searching through the wreckage to look for survivors, but she knew the night crew was likely all dead, given the force of the initial explosion.

Sigrida's attention was snatched from the window and she flinched when she heard the Elder's roar.

He flew around the corner and she saw him contemplate blowing the door to Kaigen's cell open, but instead he landed and yelled at the guard. "Open that door immediately! I'm going to kill that little wretch for what she's done!"

The guard's face was pale; the Elder's eyes showed little sanity and a whole lot of blue fire, and he only nodded and began unlocking the door, fumbling with the key in his haste.

"It wasn't her, Elder!" Sigrida yelled, daring the Elder's wrath, but with this disaster their need for Kaigen was ten times what it had been just an hour before. "She is in her cell, and the collar is secure about her neck!" By now the guard had the door open, and she took the chance of grabbing the Elder's arm and threw her hand up to point at Kaigen, who was standing at the window of her cell to try to see what was happening. She was self-evidently still restrained and magically helpless.

Sigrida wouldn't have dared touch him normally, but they'd just spent several hours together—it had required her to submit to his advances, to get her own robe, though she still carried it wrapped in silk ribbon—and she felt that preserving Kaigen was worth the risk.

The Elder's stormy eyes didn't register Sigrida or the fact that the enclosure and collar were secure; he saw only the loss of the frost. "I don't know how in the skies above and earth below she did this, but she will pay!" Another explosion rocked the building, and Sigrida, the guards, and Kaigen all recoiled, but the Elder's wrath insulated him from the shock.

I've got to stop this, Sigrida thought, and tried to get his attention again, but that proved to be a mistake. Vernondiander's power reached out and batted the scientist and both guards back against the corridor wall as if they'd been made of paper, and then pressed them against the surface until all three cried out in pain. He let them drop to the floor and said, "Get that little heathen wretch and bring her to my chambers." He flew back the way he'd come, and Sigrida pulled herself to her feet.

"He's gone utterly mad," she whispered.

The Elder stormed into the drilling engineers' headquarters, where the staff had gathered to try to determine what had just happened. They all paled as he flew through the open doorway, but he ignored almost all of them.

"Show me the drilling history," he ordered. He didn't understand the tool the engineers used to record drilling conditions, but he knew how to read the output. The panel of pale green stone glowed for a moment, and then figures appeared. One was a representation of the current status of the drilling apparatus itself, and its schematic was covered in slashes of lurid red showing damage to various components. *In fact*, the Elder thought viciously, *I can't see anything that isn't red!*

The lead engineer touched the side of the panel, unable to keep his hands from shaking, and the device displayed events backward in time. The various magical sensors placed throughout the wellhead, the drill machinery, and in the pipe and extraction tubing showed the explosion happening in reverse, the parts gathering themselves back together and then plunging down the well. The other engineers had gathered to watch, albeit at a careful distance from the Elder, and as the record of the pressure and temperature changes throughout the entire enterprise scrolled past, one of them dared to speak.

"Elder, this destruction came from below, from the end of the pipe," he said. "Flow terminated in tube four, upon which the pumping system automatically stopped."

"Why did it stop?" the Elder demanded, glaring at the man but still listening.

"Stopping the pump is a safety precaution," the man said unflinchingly, "intended to prevent damage to the pump or tubing if a blockage occurs. It's a safety measure…"

"Does that look safe to you?!" the Elder nearly screamed at them, pointing toward the still-burning flames that had been the wellhead.

"It is intended, Elder," one of the others said, clearing his nervous throat, "to prevent something like this from happening. As Indal said, it came from below. It didn't originate at the surface." And the surface, the engineer knew, was where the Protectors facing the Elders were. If it didn't come from the surface, none of them could be at fault, or at least that was his hope.

"I can see that, you idiot," Vernondiander said harshly. "How could it have come from below?" He wasn't yelling anymore, but the engineers still took a collective step back from him, not that a few more feet would have protected them.

Trying to appear confident and un-cowed, the engineer adjusted the device and said, "Here, Elder, look at this readout. The temperature rise began at the far end of the well, although pressure didn't build until about a thousand feet below the surface. At that point, the frost still in the tubing must have ignited, sending the temperature skyrocketing as the reaction traveled back up the line. The explosion occurred as soon as the molten frost touched the air."

The Elder turned those uncanny blue eyes on him. "So, you're telling me that liquid fire exists down below and somehow traveled up the line, obliterating what was about to be one of our greatest achievements?" He turned to face the man fully, his arms reaching towards the floor in the stance to build magical power, although he wasn't doing so; he just felt like threatening the engineer, who had gone weak in the knees. "So how is it that this miraculous liquid fire has never shown up before?"

"I have no explanation at this time, Elder," he managed to croak. "Forgive my ignorance, but we will work on this without rest, I assure you, until we have the answers you require."

Before the Elder could reply, whether by words or power, Sigrida entered the room with Kaigen and her two guards in tow, neck and wrist restraints in place. Kaigen was shocked by the power of the conflagration outside the window, shining up in an almost-vertical line into the sky now that the second emergency response team had used magic to channel it upward. She was mesmerized by its destructive force; she could feel the heat and hear the azure flames roaring in an uncontrolled frost burn.

At that moment, the display device flickered and then showed another drill apparatus schematic, this one for the southern site. It was an older site that was no longer producing large amounts of frost—hence the need for a new, more potent source—but was still in operation. As the pressure and temperature values soared, everyone present could only watch in horror as the same sequence of events, save the initial loss of pressure on one line and the stoppage of the flow, unfolded.

"No!!!" the Elder screamed, and before he stopped screaming, the ground heaved again as the shockwave traveled through the bedrock at six times the speed of sound in air. All eyes turned south as one, and the actinic flash of a new explosion appeared over the site, this one bigger than the first.

They were still pumping, Sigrida thought in horror, *and the storage cylinders are too close for this kind of disaster!*

The storage tanks were in fact far too close, and this set of secondary explosions hammered the entire city with shocks transmitted through the ground with far greater effect than the newer site's destruction. Those, however, were relatively mild compared to the surface explosions, and destruction spread in all directions. The only saving grace was that the southern site was far enough from Issedones itself to limit damage to the city and its people, but the blasts cracked the ground open in a set of massive craters, leaving little hope for survivors at the site.

The Elder was motionless, staring out the southern window, when a bloody and dirty worker arrived, held up by the Elder's servant Elsbeth. By the color of his clothes, he was a worker at the new drill site. How he'd managed to survive, Sigrida couldn't begin to fathom, but he stood as straight as he could to report. "Elder, the rig is a complete loss. The pipe and the extraction lines are all completely destroyed, and we will have to build a completely new rig before we can begin again."

The Elder didn't seem to hear him, but neither did he interrupt, so the man continued, "The storage tanks were almost empty, and at this site, far enough back that they weren't completely destroyed. We'll have to replace a third of them, but…" He broke off, unmindful of the blood dripping down his temple.

"I was thrown clear of the destruction and was able to control my velocity before I was crushed against a building, Elder," the man explained. "I then transported here as soon as possible to report."

When the Elder didn't respond, he cleared his throat and continued. He was too dazed to notice how still everyone stood, in terror of Vernondiander's reaction once his odd stillness ended. "I could see bodies around the rig site for hundreds of yards, and I don't believe anyone else survived. The events transpired far too quickly to react; after the pumps kicked off because of the loss of flow in one tube, it was mere moments before the pressure and temperature kick started.

"We had no warning, Elder," he added, inhaling raggedly as some of the horror began to penetrate his shock. "No one else at the central site survived, but some of them might be trapped in the outer buildings. They need help, Elder, please!"

"There is *nothing* left!" Vernondiander yelled suddenly, pushing the wounded man away from him and turning to the engineers. "I need frost production resumed immediately; do you hear me? I need that frost!" The room was deathly silent, even the field worker stunned into utter silence, but the Elder had no care for any of them. And no one spoke, each of them far too afraid of what the powerful man would do.

He's a monster, Sigrida realized, though she didn't dare move, much less speak. *We should be sending teams out to look for survivors, to evaluate damage to structures, to see if the shocks have damaged domiciles and businesses, but all he cares about is the frost and his own power*, she thought.

Kaigen was aware of what the others were saying, but her attention was riveted to the destruction outside. She could see that the response team's efforts to contain the first fire had been disrupted by the second set of explosions, and now that fire had spread to some of the downwind buildings. Try as she might, she couldn't hold back a small peaceful smile of hope.

I should feel sorry for this man and for the people who have just died, but whether the Protectors realize this or not, this is war, she thought. *A few dozen died tonight, but how many thousands, tens of thousands, millions, of the Annites have been destroyed by their greed for frost?* She didn't know how, but it was clear the Annites had found a way to fight back! She was incredibly delighted. However they'd done it, the Annites had stopped the drilling and she would not be responsible for Annite deaths.

She glanced at the Elder's trembling form and realized that this victory was only temporary. The Protector city-state reeled from this disaster, but their resources were tremendous, and they'd soon enough devise a way to protect against whatever the Annites did. That thought wiped the smile from her face.

Vernondiander's fury was even more incandescent than the frost flames outside. Someone was going to pay dearly for this attack on him! It never occurred to him that this was an attack on his community; all he cared about was his own well-being, and that was married indelibly to the frost supply. Despite his near-fugue state of rage, he hadn't failed to notice the gratified look on Kaigen's face as the blue light of the drill site flames danced on her face.

In an instant, he gathered power and then brought it down upon her head and shoulders. She crumpled to the ground screaming, and Kaigen's body and wings were crushed under the massive force he brought to bear on her helpless form.

"Stop!" Sigrida cried, "Stop, Elder! She is necessary to our…" She changed tack. "She can restore the frost flow, Elder! Stop, please Vernon!" It was a dire risk to try to intervene at all, and doubly so to use the "pet" name he'd had her use during their love-play while they were in public, but she could think of nothing else.

Kaigen instinctively tried to fight back with her earth magic, remembering the collar too late, and her agony increased as her neck burned and magical pain that felt like flames shot through her nervous system. The agony of the collar was redoubled by the pressure flattening her onto the ground, and her wings felt worse than when she'd first flown with Json, like they were being ripped from her back. She tried to roll behind a desk to escape Vernondiander's line of sight, but she was pinned under the power of his insane rage and couldn't move. Kaigen had never felt so much pain in her life! And then she felt nothing.

The Elder looked around at the stunned faces as he released the girl from his power. "You will all pay dearly if the frost supply is not restored immediately! Anything less is treason!" he yelled at them, and then his power whipped him into flight and out the door.

Sigrida ran to Kaigen's side. She didn't seem to be breathing and her wings were a crumpled mess of broken tissue and bone. The medical building's too far away, she thought in horror. "You," she said to one of the relief guards, not that she'd ever learned their names, "pick her up gently and bring her to my laboratory. It's the strongest place in the building, and it will have the least damage."

She turned to Pol, "You, go fetch Von from his cell," she snapped.

"He's a healer and he might be able to save her. Hurry, man! This girl is our best chance to get frost production going again, and if she dies, we're all doomed!" That shocked the man from his stupor, and he ran off to retrieve his former captain from his cell.

They'll have to remove his inhibitors for him to heal her, she thought as she ran alongside the first guard. *I hope that other idiot is smart enough to bring Von's guards, too. And if she's beyond his abilities, what the hell can we do?*

Without her earth magic, the process of redesigning the drills to withstand fire and pressure and then building a new rig would mean weeks if not months before they could restore even a trickle of frost. She was their only hope to salve the Elder's madness.

Pol arrived at Von's cell and found it unguarded. The others must have gone to help with the fires, he thought, but he knew time was of the essence, so he took the keys from where they hung and opened the door in haste. He didn't care if the Elder punished or even killed him for letting Von out; he'd seen the monster behind those shining blue eyes and he didn't really care what the Elder thought. Fear would come later, he knew, and he'd no doubt begin bowing and scraping again, but at this moment, he didn't care.

He approached Von and began removing his restraints. "Kaigen is badly hurt, sir," he said as he worked to release Von. "She's in Sigrida's lab, and I think she's not breathing." His hands were shaking as he fumbled with the final restraint.

Von said coolly, "You must calm yourself. You cannot bring me to help her if you keep fumbling. Take a deep breath, Pol." Unlike the Elder, Von knew the names of all the guards.

Pol nodded and did as Von commanded, fitting the small key to the collar lock and helping him slide it over his head. "The central and southern drill sites are totally destroyed," he explained as they ran toward Sigrida's lab. Von could fly, unlike Pol, but his magic was still confounded by the aftereffects of the collar. "The closer drilling lab was flattened, too, but the engineering and ground science labs are intact. I think it might have been sabotage; the engineers certainly don't have a clue how it could have happened."

"How was Kaigen injured?" Von asked as they ran, his heart threatening to leap from his throat in his fear. *She can't be dead!* he thought.

Pol swallowed, but at a glare from Von, he said, "The Elder blamed it on her, even though Sigrida had proof that she couldn't have done it. He crushed her with his magic, and I don't know if even your abilities will be enough, sir."

Von didn't answer but ran faster toward the woman he now realized that he loved.

They entered Sigrida's laboratory. The lead scientist had placed the young girl on her bed in the enclosure, though the door was open and its anti-magic properties weren't engaged. *Just a little while ago,* Sigrida thought, *we were all celebrating our successes, and now…* She nodded to Von as he ran in, gesturing at Kaigen's tilted-back head. "We cleared her air passage enough that she's breathing, but it's shallow and I can barely feel her pulse."

Von ran to Kaigen's side and gently placed his hands on her chest as he knelt beside the bed. He closed his eyes and began to repair the most life-threatening of the damage done by Vernondiander's rage-fueled power. "You must take off her collar. It's interfering with my efforts to repair her neck," he lied, but added truthfully, "She has healing magic as well, and I may be able to trigger it to help me if she's free."

Sigrida hesitated for a few moments, and then looked at Pol. "Do as he says," she ordered. "We must save her." *By the First Protectors, do I actually care about this little thing's life?* she wondered. In many ways, that was more shocking to her than anything that had happened this night.

With steady hands, the guard unlocked the restraint and helped Von lift it off Kaigen's head, trying not to endanger her spine any further. Von carefully cradled her head and neck with the crook of his arm and placed his other hand over her head. The worst of the damage, his healing talent informed him, was the ruptured blood vessels in her brain. The damage to her throat and thorax was severe as well and would kill her if left unhealed, but the immediate threat was the bleeding in her cranial cavity.

He began to breathe deeply, permeating his healing magic into her body. Her chest continued its weak motion as her body struggled to breathe through the partially crushed larynx, and her heart kept beating. Once he relieved the pressure on her brain, he began working on her damaged throat as well as strengthening her feeble pulse. Her chest began to rise and fall more deeply, and he was satisfied that the worst life-threatening injuries were stable.

He grimaced at her wings. "I don't think I can salvage these wings," he whispered. "I'm going to have to remove them."

Kaigen opened her eyes, then gasped for breath and coughed. Sigrida brought her some water from the lab sink, but Kaigen just looked at the cup and closed her eyes in pain; she tried to talk and coughed again. "Von," she rasped, and he had to place his ear at her mouth so he could hear. "I need them."

"They are too damaged, Kaigen," he said gravely. "I can't repair them."

She nodded in understanding, but said, "Can't fly...anyhow. They're my magic..." She was fading into unconsciousness, "Can't lose them..."

Von thought furiously, then reached into his shirt and brought out the shell that she had formed when he watched her heal the white wyvern. He gently rolled her onto her stomach, hoping he'd evaluated her spine properly, and then held out a hand, pointing at Pol's blade. The guard handed it over without question.

He slit the back of her shirt and let the material fall to the side. All three of the other Protectors gasped when they saw the damage the Elder had done to her wing structures. They were crumpled and broken. Von closed his eyes and reached his magic towards her shattered wings. He pictured the smoothness of the shell, and as magic flowed from the center of his power, love poured from the center of his soul. He thought of kissing her again, of them standing on the shores of the sea, and then he pictured Kaigen's wings as those of a beautiful butterfly attached to the skin of her back, rather than as the separate gangly things they had been before.

The damaged structure began conforming to his wishes and slowly fused onto the skin of her back. She cried out in pain, but he did not falter, and to Von's surprise, Sigrida knelt and took Kaigen's hands. She had little healing talent, but she used what she had, and she reached out to take a share of Kaigen's anguish into herself, suffering through a share of the agony while Von worked.

When Von finished, he lay his head down beside Kaigen's, face to face, and she opened her eyes so she could see him. Von reached out and brushed the hair from her cheek and smiled weakly at her as she smiled at him. "Did you do it?" she whispered. "Did you save them?" She was too weak to even think of feeling for her magic.

"Oh, yes," he answered. "Their structure is part of your back now, so you won't need that leather get-up to fly anymore."

Kaigen realized that Sigrida was holding one of her hands, and she looked up at her in surprise. Sigrida hastily tried to let go of her hand and stand, but Kaigen motioned for it back. "Thank you, Sigrida. I could feel you absorb some of the pain."

Sigrida nodded weakly, squeezing her hand, and then finished standing. From her vantage, she could see Kaigen's back, and she gasped.

Kaigen felt dejected; she knew she must have ugly scarring to have provoked such a reaction. Would Von love her if she was horribly disfigured?

"Oh, Kaigen," Sigrida said, tears glittering in her eyes. "It's so beautiful." Kaigen blinked.

"It's... beautiful?" Kaigen asked breathlessly.

"You've always been beautiful," Von said as he smiled. "Do you feel any pain?" He nodded in satisfaction when Kaigen shook her head no.

"What do I look like?" she asked.

"It's become similar to butterfly wings," Sigrida said, reaching out to touch the raised surface as gently as she could. "It's like a mosaic made of tiny little scale-like shells, but it's you, not something attached. Those delicate wings you once had are now a beautiful butterfly on your back. They are so thin you should be able to lay on your back now!"

Von said, "They're shells because I was thinking of shells, but they look a lot like Sybaris scales, too."

Kaigen had always wanted to roll onto her back, something her wing structure had never allowed, and she did so now, albeit cautiously. "Ah," she breathed. "I've always wanted to lie on my back and look at the stars." She stared at the ceiling wistfully, imagining them. Suddenly the room went dark and stars twinkled up above on the ceiling as Von's magic brought her wish to life.

They sat silently for a long time in the star-speckled darkness.

In the dark, Sigrida broke the silence. "We must kill him before he kills us," she said coldly to the others present. "When he finds out that we saved her, he may kill us. We must strike now, or it will be too late." But it was too late; the Elder's guards, accompanied by the man himself, strode quickly into the room.

The Elder took in the scene and said in the kindest voice anyone had ever heard, "Put restraints on the traitors, then take them to the Arena and lock them in a cage. We'll feed them all to the Tigerell."

Chapter 72: The Commander

As he dug his way back to the central hub of the Annites, the Commander cursed the lost time and lives. If he had been quicker to understand the nature of the Annites' crisis, he would have been able to save more of them. If only they could actually talk to each other, he thought, he would have figured out what to do more quickly.

According to the cerebral map, no more active egg stores were in immediate danger from above, but he knew that the first site could all too easily be reached again now that the nemesis knew where it was. "Well Nim, we stopped the attack, and now I need to travel to the surface and see who is responsible for these atrocities," he told her as she nodded.

"Whoever they are, they have powerful magic and technology." He clenched his clawed fist, "These are no amateurs; they've been drawing the minerals up for quite a span based on the number of those empty shafts." He shuddered to think how many millions, perhaps billions, of Annites had perished over those years. "All life is precious, dear Nim, whether tiny or huge. Now off with you, you cannot go where I am headed." She climbed down, patting his snout once.

He flexed his shoulders and turned to leave, beginning the journey back to the surface. The Annites had been so diligent in their healing of him that he could feel something like his wings under his carapace; they itched to break free, though he couldn't do it while he was tunneling upward. His body wasn't completely mended, and now that he was going away from that sweet blue liquid, the Annites would no longer be able to soothe his pains. Pain, however, was a warrior's portion, and now that he was at war, he found that he had no fear of it.

After a time, however, he realized that it wasn't pain, exactly, that he was feeling. He itched all over, much like he felt when he was going into the molting process that was part of the wyvern lifecycle throughout their growth phases. It felt sort of like when the Annites had repaired the damaged teeth; they felt as good as new now, but they'd itched like this during the healing.

It was no surprise that he already missed his little passenger Nim, and he felt lonely here under all this rock and pressure without her. Her presence had given him a navigational confidence that he wasn't feeling now, and he missed her soft glow. As he burrowed steadily upward, he had a sudden additional realization. Nim had showed him that they couldn't withstand the surface environment, and that meant that the swarms of invisible Annites who had come to the surface to heal him when Glock had incinerated his skin and scales had likely not survived to return to their native depths.

By all that is sacred, he thought, stunned into immobility. They had given their lives to save his, and it was apparent to him now why they'd done so. They'd died in great numbers so that he could save the rest of their community from the threat, whoever they were.

It was humbling, what they had gone through to heal his ravaged body, and it gave him a burning need to give back. His anger at whoever was responsible had doubled and redoubled again, and he began digging steadily and rapidly upward toward the surface location of the third oldest of the drilling holes, which lay several dozen miles by his estimation from the two newer sites he'd damaged. He didn't want to emerge in the middle of the enemy without having a chance to plan his attack. Even at the pace his great digging claws could attain, it was still days to reach the surface, for the Annites had drawn him very deep indeed.

He began humming the melody of an old war hymn. "Mmmm-o, aaaah-o, mmmm-o, deeee-o," he sang in his throat as he moved along. On the second day he could feel distant vibrations in the earth when he pressed his head against solid stone. They weren't like any natural sounds and they were continuous.

They've started doing something to get their operation back into swing, he thought. He thought about cutting over to the new location, but a solid expanse of stone—sort of like an underground mountain—lay between him and the new sounds.

His mental map was still with him, and he located the fastest course around to reach the location of the new shaft. "Hrmph," he grunted, positioning himself below its path to wait for it to pierce through.

He'd already determined the melting point of the drill pipe metal, the hard way, and his flame was ready. In moments of the penetration, the drill bit and several dozen yards of pipe attached to it became a solid lump of molten slag, and he snorted in amusement as the operators above tried to pull it back up the shaft. "Good luck with that," he muttered out loud, for the remains of the assembly were now wider than the shaft.

He moved away, putting in some distance before he rested, as reaching it in time to intercept it had taken a lot of his strength. He closed his eyes and was surprised to see how close to the surface he now was. Why, that last drill pipe had only been a few hundred feet below the surface! Now that the deep earth wasn't pressing in on him, he found that somehow, paradoxically, he missed the pressing feeling, or more likely he just missed Nim.

The itching was driving him mad, so he bent to open his carapace segments up a little, using his clawed appendages to pull out a small cylinder similar to Nim's house on his nose. It was sealed on both ends and filled with the blue minerals his little friends had packed in the hollow between his segments.

He crunched through the shell of the cylinder and ate the contents contentedly. He immediately felt stronger and more stable, the itching eased a little, and his exhaustion faded as if it had never been. He hummed some more, trying not to get frustrated as he had to backtrack twice because of large formations; his map was not accurate this close to the surface, but that didn't bother him. He was a patient wyvern. A wyvern at war.

He moved along under the earth, pretending that Nim was bossing him around; his imagination was not much comfort to him, but it helped. He slept twice more before he reached the surface, consuming doses of the minerals. He had traveled away from the drilling lines into a kind of null zone between all of them, and he burst up through the soil, breathing the air of the surface world for the first time for what seemed like a lifetime. He dragged himself easily from the earth and then sat quietly, trying to get his bearings. It was nighttime and he could tell he was at roughly the same latitude from the stars, but he didn't recognize the surrounding wasteland. Nothing stirred as far as his eyes could see, and he settled down to contemplate.

He woke as the sun rose, rejoicing in the earth's beauty and surface life. Although he missed Nim and her people terribly, underground life had been a difficult adjustment for him, and the sun felt glorious. When the sun hit his carapace, however, the itching became a scratching, crawling torture, first his snout and then his arms, until his entire body prickled and burned. He rubbed his snout at first on a tree, but it collapsed quickly under the force, so he sidled up to boulders and rubbed his snout, his neck, his arms, even his back against the largest rocks to try to alleviate the terrible itching.

He couldn't scratch fast enough. His carapace began shedding in chunks as he rolled, cracking along his back and freeing his wing-arms. He rolled to his feet and opened the wings slowly. It was painful; he was definitely in something like a full molt. Where the old skin had sloughed off, his new skin and scales glistened in the sun. They were like they had been before his battle with Glock, some black as lodestone, some white as snow but now covered in the tiny spheres the Annites had on their bodies.

He checked his snout and arms; they were also covered in the tiny spheres. He turned his arm and hands this way and that, and depending on the angle of the spheres, the light reflections rendered him invisible. He realized that he was like a butterfly emerging from its chrysalis, and further, the loss of his carapace meant that he would be unable to return to the Annites. Nim and the others must have known, he realized, even planned it this way.

All the time that he thought they were grooming him they had been hard at work making new scales and wings that could be invisible with a simple change in scale angle. Despite the highly uncomfortable molting-like feeling, he mercilessly forced himself to practice shifting his scales and the spheres until he could make his entire body invisible, for he didn't know how long it would take for the drillers to start a fourth hole. For all he knew, they had an endless supply of the machinery they needed to do their reprehensible work.

His torso and main body were once again white, while his snout, hands, feet, and tail were black. He was as he once was when he helped rule Draconia, a glorious white wyvern! He let out a deafening roar. The digging and tunneling had made him larger and physically powerful.

Later that day he began to test his new wings until he was comfortable with taking off. He ran and picked up speed, flapping his wings as he jumped into the air, gliding like he had before. The repaired, or perhaps new, wings worked well, but his muscles lacked tone and he didn't stay aloft for long. Nonetheless, he was able to identify landmarks so he could at least reference his movements to his starting point. Despite the painful muscles, it felt wonderful to fly.

He rested again, knowing that he couldn't afford to do so much longer but needing the ability to fly to find his objective. He made himself invisible and took off again, flying towards the lines of smoke he saw rising on the horizon. As he climbed, the horizon fell away, and he estimated the smoke originated about eight miles from where he'd surfaced.

When he caught sight of the city, his heart fell. The beautiful architecture could only mean one thing: it belonged to the Protectors. He flew higher to soar over the city and saw the destruction he had caused to a cluster of structures, and to the north evidence of an even greater catastrophe. He wondered why that was, since that northern pipe had barely been siphoning, while the first one had been tapping an abundance of the mineral-laden fluids before he'd intervened.

If this is a Protector city, he thought, *then I'm not far from the Steppes. And if this enemy of my friends turns out to be the Protectors, I'm going to need help.* Now that he realized where he must be, he angled to the southeast to fly back home. He passed over some fields and smelled something like the Annites' mineral in the steam rising from large metal tanks scattered about the fields like artificial trees. Some of them were open at the tops, and inside was the mineral and the fluid. It was an entire field of storage tanks. The Protectors had found a way to contain the Annites' dead offspring as magical energy!

He growled as he soared over them. *I will ask them once, he thought. If they knew about Nim's people, if they knew they were slaughtering them by the millions, I will kill them. I will kill them all.* But first, he knew, he'd have to go home for reinforcements.

As he flew past the mountains where the she-wyverns lived, the Commander remained invisible. One never knew what mood they'd be in, and sometimes they objected to males invading their space. A closer look revealed he needn't have bothered for that reason, though he was glad he'd remained invisible. *What are the odds I'd return home on the day of mating?* he wondered.

The chase was almost done, save for two pairs whose males hadn't quite given up yet, and he could see other pairs in the process of mating or nesting. It took days, usually, until the she-wyvern was satisfied that a nice, defensible, and stable nest had been created. During that time, the she-wyverns were almost sweet, he remembered, and loving to their mates. But soon after? The smart male watched for the signs and was prepared to leave as soon as he was not wanted.

The less sharp males came home with wounds.

When he was younger, the red color in a breeding female's neck would have gotten his blood pumping, but he found he had no interest in mating now. He was still affected by it though, and his blood sang with the promise of a new generation of wyverns.

He flew into Sybaris cautiously. He had been gone since Glock's destruction and he hoped that things were better under Queen Ariah, but he didn't know for sure. As he approached, he saw Sunny and Silverback, the latter with two Sybaris on his back. Something odd must be happening, he thought, for Sunny should be up at the she-wyverns' roosts making sure any wounded got proper care, not escorting Silverback.

The duo of wyverns flew straight to the Cystine Hall and landed, and as he approached, he could see that the two figures climbing down off Silverback weren't Sybaris at all. They were humans! What were humans doing in Draconia? He chose to remain unseen, gliding into a gentle landing so that he wouldn't be observed.

Sunny wanted to return to the roost, but her duty was not discharged yet. "At least I didn't have to allow the humans to ride me," she murmured with a grateful look at Silverback, who had never minded riders. Even he seemed taken aback to have humans on his back, however.

The Commander crept along invisibly behind them; the sounds of his movement masked by the many sounds of the center of the city.

"Do not speak until you are given leave," Sunny snapped at Isladora and Tobin, but the point was somewhat lost because Isladora had to translate for her companion. Sunny snorted angrily; this was intolerable!

The door to the main meeting room the ruling pairs used was closed so Sunny knocked and then looked over her shoulder to give the humans a dirty look and bare her fangs, daring them to move. Her dislike for them was obvious. The ruling pairs called for them to enter and she opened the door and lumbered into the room, followed by the humans and Silverback, who had remained silent most of the time.

All eyes were upon her, for a she-wyvern entering the Cystine Hall was unusual. "Stop here," she ordered the humans, putting up a claw to get the point across to Tobin. They both stopped, standing quietly as instructed. Tobin was still exhausted, but he was at least standing on his own two feet.

Mezzi, she could see, was talking to the ruling pairs. She had come to explain what she'd experienced; the sounding of the Horn and Sunny's disappearance, and Queen Ariah had immediately sent Silverback after Sunny in case she needed help. He was, by far, the fastest wyvern, and could catch up to her. After that, she'd remained to discuss what else they should plan to do about the unexpected call of the Horn.

When the Queen, Json, and Mezzi spotted the humans, their conversation ceased. The only thing that would have shocked Mezzi more than seeing humans in the Cystine Hall would have been if they'd been on Sunny's back.

"Sunny, mother of many, I greet and welcome you," Ariah said formally.

"Ariah, Queen of the Sybaris, Queen of the wyverns, mother of us all, I thank you," Sunny said just as formally. She knew the customs of the Sybaris and the male wyverns, even if she hadn't partaken of them before. It felt strange to be inside, and she longed to return to the skies.

Json was surprised to see Isladora and took a step towards her. "Isladora?"

After getting over the astonishment of the humans Ariah added, "I see that you bear Mae's ring still upon your hand, so I greet and welcome Meluha Crocus as well, if he is still within it. Who is your companion?"

Sunny was flabbergasted and she blinked several times to make sure she wasn't hallucinating. Did the Queen of the Sybaris just welcome a human to court by name? *Oh, by the First Scale,* she thought, *the little creature was telling the truth!* Her instincts warred with her mind, as it always was on the day of breeding. She was suddenly very, very glad that she hadn't succeeded in incinerating the two humans, and she now wondered what the queen would have to say about destroying the human's fortress.

Meluha Crocus was even more stunned than Sunny. How could the Sybaris queen know Mae's name? Or about him? It was impossible!

"Queen Ariah, thank you for your welcome," Isladora said. "I greet you and the war wyvern Json. We did not blow the Horn lightly, for we have dire need of your aid. Meluha Crocus also thanks you for your welcome, and his need is also great. My companion is Tobin, a scout of the Juna, and my betrothed." She took Tobin's hand shyly as she said the last.

Ariah had changed so much! She seemed similar to the dead Sybaris girl that Isladora had helped wash and prepare for Json's pyre, but this creature! This golden creature was much larger than Ariah's corpse had been, far more muscular, and one did not have to be Sybaris to sense her authority. This was a queen, and Isladora knelt in homage to her, followed quickly by a still-confused Tobin.

"Please rise, Princess Isladora," Ariah said. "You bear my bond-mate's mark, so be welcome here, now and always."

"You will find," added Bedaiko, "that you have the gratitude of our entire nation, once word spreads of your arrival. You made it possible for our Queen to be brought to us, and your kindness to Json and Ariah saved us all from a terrible fate."

"My betrothed does not speak Draconian, Your Majesty," Isladora said. "May I have your leave to translate for him?" Ariah nodded and then waited patiently along with her people—with the possible exception of Sunny—while she brought Tobin up to date.

Once she was done, Ariah said, "I never met you, Isladora, but my experience in the egg, and within Json, allowed me access to his memories and because you bear the wyvern mark, access to yours as well. This is how I know that it is Mae's ring you wear, and that Meluha Crocus is within it. And it is how I know your father and the evil that befell him. That makes me feel like I know you both, though I of course do not. But knowing these things or not, I never had an opportunity to thank you for my life. It pleases me that we meet."

Json smiled his wyvern smile, making Tobin nervous until Isladora explained that it was like a dog's "smile." "I admit that I have missed you, annoying little human girl," he said, and his grin widened. He'd deliberately used the sullen tone he'd used when they first met, but she knew he was only kidding her.

Isladora took that as her cue to move on to business. "I need your help, Json," she said. "I am magically bound to travel to Issedones." She held up the ring, fighting off the ringing of the city's name in her head, and as she did, she glanced at her forearms, sheathed in the vambraces she had taken from Queen Ariah's corpse. "I, uh, still have your vambraces, Your Majesty," she said, blushing.

Queen Ariah laughed. "I am glad they serve you well," she said brightly. "Please keep them; I stole them anyway, when I was a slave to you humans."

That was the opening Abraxis was waiting for, and he hissed. "Why would we help a human?" He scoffed. "They have no honor."

Ariah said evenly, "You do not know of which you speak, Abraxis."

Json rose up and faced his fellow council member. "Whether most do or most do not, this human does, Abraxis. You can see that she bears my mark. She is under my protection."

Once Isladora translated for him, Tobin found he was vastly relieved to hear that. *I hope her mark extends to me as well*, he thought, and tried to focus on looking stoic and brave. That wasn't easy while standing in a room with six wyverns, each far bigger than the largest horse.

"Lord Abraxis," Isladora said, hoping he'd consider the title a form of respect. "I understand your attitude, for many of my race are selfish and do not follow the basic rules of human kindness given to us by God. But do not judge us all harshly because of a few who have turned down a dark path." The long-nosed and dangerous-looking wyvern didn't respond but did look away uncomfortably. He could not help but remember that even the wyverns had turned out to have a few that had, as she had said, turned down a dark path.

She turned to Json. "Do you remember Meluha Crocus, the mage trapped in this ring?" she asked, holding her ring up for all to see. Ariah had already said she'd recognized his ring, or more properly, his wife's ring, but Isladora said it for the benefit of the others. "He is being called home by the Protectors and I am taking him. I must take him, for their call is irresistible."

Darkale said, "Perhaps your coming is fortuitous, Princess Isladora. You see, we must also go to Issedones, but for war. They have kidnapped one of ours." Abraxis growled at Darkale's words, he'd always loved Kaigen. "They came here claiming peace and then stole one of ours right in front of us after forcibly invading our queen's mind." That brought a growl from everyone present, including Sunny.

"Please, we have discussed this," Ariah said firmly. "What happened to me was unfortunate, but I don't care about that crime. What I care about is getting Kaigen back safely and to ensure that they cannot do anything like that to us again."

While the others grudgingly agreed, Isladora knew they did care, and she didn't think the Protectors knew what they'd done by assaulting their queen in that way. Ariah added, "We have been trying to plan how to bring her back."

"Ask them why, Isladora," Meluha said.

"Meluha Crocus wants me to ask you, why do you think they kidnapped this Kaigen?"

Toyah answered, "They took her because she has powerful earth magic, but they did not explain why this was important." Silverback's bond-mate rose and came to stand by him. "And frankly, we do not care why they want her, only that we get her back."

"My brother is going to use her to help find frost," Meluha warned.

"The Elder of the Protectors is the brother of the mage trapped in this ring," Isladora announced, prompting growls from several of the wyverns and Sybaris. "He says that the Elder will use Kaigen's earth magic to find what they call frost, the magical element of the Protector race."

"Well, it seems that we both need something from the other," Silverback said, nudging his Sybaris bond-mate affectionately. "We need to break through the Protectors' wards so we can rescue Kaigen, and you need us to take you."

So far, the Draconians had been unsuccessful in lifting, or even clearly perceiving, the wards around the Protectors' lands to rescue Kaigen. "Yes, if this brother of the Elder will agree to help us break through the wards, we will take you," Arrington said, his dislike for Meluha's relationship to the Elder not affecting his willingness to work with him. Kaigen had been a captive of the Protectors for far too long. She may not even still be alive.

Sunny was trying to be patient, but she found that she was growing more and more agitated. It suddenly dawned on her why: her mating urge was rising, something that hadn't happened in years. She tried hard to quash the feelings and focus on the conversation. She had no feelings for these ruling pairs, so she didn't know why she suddenly felt so impassioned.

Ignorant of the sudden turmoil boiling in Sunny's veins, Isladora said, "We agree, and we thank you. Any aid we can offer you in recovering Kaigen, we will gladly give in return." That was a heavy burden, she knew, to add to the load she was already carrying, but honor required her to offer.

"What's in this for you, human?" Darkale wondered darkly.

"Meluha Crocus is my friend. He helped our tribe in our battle, and along with Json he helped me defeat the evil Queen Mother," Isladora said, squaring her shoulders to the masked Sybaris. "I must help him for all the aid he has offered. I must also try to see him released from his captivity. I would see him escape this prison so that his spirit may be released to move on to whatever is next.

"I must also aid my friend Json, as I am aided by him," she added, "for we will always remain friends. The Juna do not abandon friends, even when the danger is great."

Queen Ariah had this girl's memories, so she knew that Isladora spoke the truth, at least as she believed it. She wondered if Isladora was in danger from the spirit, for he had done much wrong in his life. It appeared that he might have changed in the long centuries of imprisonment in the ring, but those memories…they told Queen Ariah that he was capable of much evil. "Does Meluha Crocus now believe in your God?" she asked. If he had found something to believe in, he might be less dangerous to Isladora.

After the princess translated, Tobin placed his hand on her shoulder to remind her to be cautious in her response, but she simply said, "My God is the creator of the heavens and the earth and everything in it; he is therefore your God, too, Your Majesty."

Queen Ariah, to the surprise of her council, seemed to take this quite seriously. What did wyverns and Sybaris care about some human god? they were all wondering. "How could we know this God, that my memories say we cannot converse with, or even see?" Her tone was not disrespectful, only questioning.

The young human girl had the faith of a priest and it shone like a beacon in the night, if only those with her could see it. From the wellspring of that faith, she smiled confidently and said, "It is not a matter of knowing, but of faith, Your Majesty. When we think of God, our minds cannot encompass all that He is. Just as looking at a single scale cannot encompass all that a Sybaris or a wyvern is.

"We can see the beauty of the scale and imagine what the whole creature might be like, but we lack the perspective to see the whole. God is like this, for we can see the beauty in His creations, feel part of His love for us in the love we feel for—and from—the people in our lives, but the whole? He is so far beyond us that we can only express the concept in fragmentary ways," she continued, her face animated and her eyes bright as she spoke.

"Understanding the whole is a journey throughout life," she said. "It is a journey whose end transcends life into death, in fact, for we are eternal and once free of this body that withers and dies," she touched her arm, "we may gain the perspective we lack." Speaking of God with the Draconians filled her heart but also made her worry that she would not see her friend Meluha Crocus in eternity. Her expression turned somber. "I regret to tell you, Your Majesty, that Meluha struggles with this and has not found his faith yet. He tries, however, and he seeks, and that is a very important step."

"Merely seeking is important?" Bedaiko asked, his tone thoughtful.

"Oh, yes!" Isladora said earnestly. "The dark men and women I have met, and fought, in my life are the ones who do not seek God. Even one who already believes can make mistakes, can even cause harm when we forget what we are taught, but the ones who turn their backs completely and do not even think of God in passing? Their evil can shake the world, and such evil was nearly the end of the Juna people."

Sunny was feeling more and more uncomfortable; her breathing was becoming labored. Silverback saw the red begin to climb up Sunny's neck and became alarmed. "The breeding time has come upon you, Sunny!" he exclaimed. She was, in fact, too deep into the cycle to climb up to the breeding grounds.

"You must choose one of the wyverns here, quickly!" Queen Ariah said. It was dangerous for the breeding instinct to remain unfulfilled, for the red coloration was a heat not dissimilar to the wyvern's molten fire, and if it rose too far, a she-wyvern could literally incinerate herself.

"I know, my queen," Sunny rasped, struggling to stay rational, because self-immolation was only one aspect of the danger. An unsatisfied female was liable to go berserk and destroy anything and anyone near her. "I have no… pull… toward any of them, however."

The wyverns and Sybaris were all confused, for she wouldn't have this reaction, this strongly, without a compatible mate in her presence. Sunny had only ever mated with the Commander, disdaining any other wyvern's touch, and although Silverback was the fastest of the wyverns, she'd maneuvered and clawed at him a number of times; only the white Commander was allowed to catch her. But he was gone.

"I know I sound crazy," she said with deep embarrassment, "but I can… smell my true mate. I feel that the Commander is here." She lowered her head in shame, knowing her words, truthful though they were, marked her as having gone mad. Mezzi cried out and ran to her dangerous friend and touched her massive head with her left hand, running the other down Sunny's warm neck, trying desperately to think of something in the healing lore that might help her.

Isladora didn't know how to react to these mating rites of the wyverns and didn't know whether "noticing" it would give offense. She was also ignorant of the true seriousness of Sunny's predicament, so she continued, "Meluha says to tell you that his brother, the Elder of the Protectors, must be stopped. We must unite before he grows so powerful that none of us can stop him." Isladora was not ignorant, however, of Sunny's plight, for it was clear that the she-wyvern was suffering, and she longed to offer some words of comfort; she simply didn't know enough about wyvern culture to do so.

The Commander completely understood the danger Sunny was in and decided it was time to act. To the amazement of everyone present—Tobin's reaction was to put a hand on his blade, though he was wise enough not to draw it—the Commander released his invisibility and appeared in the room, not only healed but even larger and stronger than he had been when he lead the ruling council!

Sunny's head snapped around and the red color pulsed in time with her pounding heart. She half hissed, half snarled, gurgling in her throat. He was *here*! She wasn't insane, or she'd gone so insane that she was visually hallucinating, but she was certain it was no delusion. *Her mate was here!*

Knowing there was little time, the Commander addressed the silent, shocked group, saying, "This human princess is right. This Protector has found a way to store blue minerals that he mines from underground. But it is not just minerals; it is made from the bodies of tiny but intelligent underground creatures called Annites. He has killed millions of them collecting this magical mineral over time, and they are in desperate straits."

The Commander looked at Sunny with both pride and trepidation. His pride was born of the fact that the powerful she-wyvern—by far, the most powerful of all the wyverns, in fact—had always wanted him for her mate. The trepidation was because there was no time for a mating flight, and that very power could tear him to shreds if she reacted violently. It will be worth it if she tears me to ribbons, he thought with a soft smile, but I really hope she doesn't. "I am here, Sunny."

With her last ounce of control, she gently nudged Mezzi, Isladora, and Tobin out of harm's way; even that "gentle" nudge tossed them onto their backsides, though Mezzi skidded along upright because of her tail. The Sybaris swarmed over the tables and dragged the three further back because no one knew what the distressed she-wyvern would do.

At that moment, Sunny's neck flared to a deep red, and all the Draconians present knew that now her reason was gone, and she was now a being of pure instinct. Her entire existence had narrowed to the call that nature had placed in her genes for the survival of her race, and that narrow focus was directed at the Commander. She must catch him!

In an instant, however, the Commander shot away, taking advantage of the head start created by having hovered near the entrance. He ran from the hall and then mighty beats of his newly healed wings pulled him away from the ground. He knew that however wonderful the mating dance would be, how beautiful Sunny was to him in this precious moment, that he and Sunny would destroy the room, and perhaps the entire Cystine Hall, if he didn't lead them away from it.

Sunny roared in protest, whirling her body about and moving faster than Isladora and Tobin would have believed possible for a wyvern on the ground. In her haste, her leg tore one of the great doors partially off its hinges as she scrabbled for purchase to leap forward. The golden she-wyvern roared again and in a single wingbeat was ten feet off the ground, then flapping madly to climb and pursue him, all semblance of control completely gone.

For a long moment, everyone present in the hall was too stunned to move. The wyverns and Sybaris were shocked because the Commander had materialized from thin air, and the humans were shocked because of the immense violence Sunny had shown, for the doors were stout and would have withstood a battering ram. Finally, Arrington broke the silence with a laugh. "Meeting adjourned!" he said, and they all laughed, even Tobin, for though he didn't understand the words, Arrington's tone had been expressively sardonic.

After they settled down somewhat, Ariah said, "I rejoice that the Commander has returned to us, and we have much to discuss, but Arrington is right; we must adjourn until he can return to us again." Surprising Tobin, she switched to the human tongue. "You, scout of the Juna and betrothed of Isladora, look like you're about to drop from exhaustion. You will be given quarters where you may rest, bathe, and be refreshed, and we will speak again in the morning." She glanced up toward the skies with a happy but also amused smile. "Perhaps late in the morning, when she's done with him."

Chapter 73: Ruling Pairs

Tobin found himself even more surprised than a moment ago, and that was saying something. Ariah had called him betrothed of Isladora, and that could only mean that Isladora had told the Draconians that he was. His heart sang, even while he wondered what the king's reaction would be to that revelation, and to a head of state at that.

Darkale gently let Mezzi go and said to Isladora, "When the Commander comes back, we can develop our strategy to get into Issedones, but as Her Majesty said, that won't be until tomorrow." Darkale considered Isladora and Tobin, who had not yet spoken; both were clearly distracted by Mezzi's long wyvern tail. He cleared his throat. "What do humans eat, anyway?"

Abraxis swung his large tail around in irritation and grumbled, "Who cares what humans eat, feed them offal." He'd spoken softly, not really caring if anyone heard, that is, until the queen turned on him.

"Enough of that, Abraxis," she said commandingly. "I care. More than that, I know exactly what humans eat because feeding them used to be my job." She didn't repeat that it was her job as a slave; they all knew what she had been in her previous life and reminding them of it would only raise tensions.

She felt that she needed to make this a point and her golden scales glistened as she allowed her annoyance to show. "If I can care for and about them as your Queen, then I think that it would be well for you to think carefully about that," she admonished. "Darkale, will you and Chablis take Tobin and Isladora to your home and feed them properly, then give them a place to sleep?" Darkale nodded his assent without the signs of dislike that his bond-mate had shown. "Thank you. We will meet back here in the third hour of the morning."

Ariah had another reason for asking the masked Sybaris to house the humans. Darkale and Chablis lived the closest to the Cystine Hall because Chablis was their medical practitioner. The Sybaris had built her a large home with many comforts, connected directly to the city's sanatorium so that she could reach her patients without delay. The rare visitor to Sybaris usually stayed there because it was convenient, and the vivacious and friendly Chablis enjoyed having guests. Now that she and Darkale were a couple, he lived there as well, though he was still getting used to the concept of visitors.

Darkale looked at Tobin, remembering how the young man had reacted to the Commander's appearance by touching his sword. He lifted his mask to one side gnashing his wyvern teeth to frighten him, and then put it back in place and said, "Come with me; you'll be perfectly safe," patiently waiting for Isladora to translate.

Tobin had recovered a lot of his poise, and he bowed, covering the shock of seeing those teeth and said, "We, um, thank you for your hospitality, Darkale." He mispronounced the name, but he got close. "I look forward to meeting Chablis."

Darkale waited for the translation and then laughed at Tobin's attempt at good manners, slapping him on the back, his blue scales flashing in the light.

Deciding she didn't really care if she was breaking protocol, Isladora approached and hugged Queen Ariah, who returned the hug willingly. "I thought your egg was beautiful when Json created it, but its loveliness was nothing compared to your beauty and magnificence now," she said. "Your people are fortunate beyond words, that you could be reborn." She touched Json's snout and smiled.

Json smiled his wyvern smile back at her, and once again recalling their verbal sparring when they first met, he said some of the few words he'd learned to say from the human tongue, "Ssstupid human." He nudged her gently with his snout to make sure Tobin knew he was joking.

Isladora smiled even more widely and replied, "Hateful wyvern," leaning into the comforting massiveness of her friend. Even though he was on the small side for a wyvern, he still dwarfed her.

They all departed for the evening. As the couples approached Darkale and Chablis' home, they saw blood spots on the ground outside the sanatorium's entrance and the light was on. "Looks like something happened," Darkale said.

"I'll go and see. It is mating day you know," Chablis told Darkale. "You take our guests on inside, I'll call if I need help."

Tobin and Darkale started towards the door, but Isladora followed Chablis into the infirmary. Darkale shrugged his shoulders and gestured for Tobin to follow him. Isladora had experience with first aid, including triage if necessary, that General Nokela taught her.

Chablis was too distracted to notice at first that the human had entered along with her. It was breeding day and Mezzi hadn't been up in the highlands, so Chablis had been expecting a wounded wyvern to be in the massive area reserved for them. But it wasn't a wyvern. It was Petrus, the white-scaled Sybaris they had recently bonded to the wyvern Cassian. Blood dripped down his arms and on the side of his head; he was unconscious lying on the examining table. Obviously, someone had brought him here.

Chablis' face was grim as she focused on stopping the severe bleeding; she hadn't had time to cut his clothes off, and she knew there were other wounds that she needed to check, so she was relieved Darkale had followed her. "I need you to get…" she started but then realized it was Isladora and her jaw snapped shut.

"We need to get his clothes cut off," Isladora said confidently in the wyvern tongue. "Where are the shears?"

Blinking hard, she extended a hand toward the table where she kept the tools of her trade, watching motionlessly as the strange mammal girl confidently selected the special rounded shears that would allow cutting away the clothes without risking further injury. As she began cutting away the blood-soaked cloth with a gentle touch, the pink-scaled healer shook herself from her trance.

"We will have to sew this wound shut," she said to her new helper. "The vein has been nicked, and I can hold the blood back if you can stitch?" Isladora nodded, motioning over to continue cutting off the clothes. She quickly but thoroughly washed her hands in the sink, then selected fine thread from the prepared needles and returned to the wounded Sybaris.

"That makes this much easier," she said as she watched the blood pull back away from the small tear in the vein. She'd had to sew veins and even minor arteries shut while one of the warriors pinched off the blood flow. That was not only painful, but could do more damage if the wounds were extensive enough.

"He's got another nasty gash where the scales meet the skin," Chablis told her. "I think it missed the femoral artery, but it might also be nicked." If that had gone, the Sybaris would already be dead.

"We will examine it carefully when we are done here," she said to Isladora, knowing it could wait. "Until then, please keep looking for more injuries, but also keep an eye on that gash." She nodded once and kept working.

"I will make Petrus' body absorb the stitches later," the Sybaris healer said, "so you can close up the flesh above the vein."

Isladora nodded, selecting another, larger needle from the stock, and while Chablis sealed the leaking vein she began sewing the surface wound together with neat and even stitches.

"I am grateful for your help," Chablis told her. "I could have used more magic to save him, but that would leave me weakened if anyone else needs assistance. On the day of breeding, many injuries are common."

"It helps to have a second pair of hands," Chablis said. "It's why I wished Mezzi lived here in the city instead of on the heights, but then she's closer to the younglings if they get hurt, so it goes both ways."

"Mezzi is also a healer?" Isladora asked. They hadn't spoken, only introduced.

Chablis nodded. "It's the pink scales," she explained. "They're a sign of healing magic." She pursed her lips, examining her patient with her magical senses as well as her eyes. "I dislike how much blood he's lost. I'm going to give him some, but it may mean I need more help later if I am drained too much." She raised an eyebrow at Isladora, who nodded solemnly. Chablis nodded her head sharply back and then closed her eyes as she touched Petrus' neck. Isladora was mesmerized as Chablis closed her eyes and used her healing magic to transfer some of her own blood to the patient. His color richened and he relaxed into a deep sleep, while Chablis' color became a touch more pallid.

"Wow," Isladora whispered. If the Juna could learn to do that so many lives might be saved when they would have been lost.

Suddenly, a wyvern came charging into the room, startling them. "Oh, thank you!" Cassian, Petrus' bond-mate, exclaimed. "How is he? Is he going to be all right?" The big wyvern was almost dancing side to side in his agitation, and he hadn't registered that a human was present. "I ran to find you after I laid him here; I thought I was going to lose him!"

"He's fine, Cassian, see?" Chablis said, pulling an errant strand of her pink hair back behind her ear; the rest was bound into the tidy bun she always wore. "But what did this to him?"

Cassian let out a low growl, "Humans," and there couldn't have been a worse time for his eyes to finally register Isladora. His growl deepened and his jaw opened to reveal his deadly teeth.

Isladora backed up and Chablis quickly said, "Petrus would be in much worse shape without this human's help!" That made Cassian blink, noticing the blood all over her hands and arms, just as it was on Chablis'. "This human is also under the protection of Queen Ariah, so you will not harm her in any event. Where were you that a human could get close enough to you to harm you?"

"I'll tell you," Cassian said indignantly. He wasn't in a threatening posture anymore, but his eyes burned as he looked not at Chablis but instead at the human. "We went to make a peaceful trade with the humans in Horn town. We've already made two successful and profitable trips, so we didn't expect any danger, but when I touched down, they attacked us without warning!"

"I'm afraid that might be my doing, Chablis," Isladora said quietly, as the Draconians turned to stare at her. "We broke into the fort in Horn town and started blowing the Horn so you would hear us and come down. The townspeople were afraid and tried to stop us, but Tobin was able to hold them back long enough for Sunny to arrive."

"Sunny?" Cassian said, and Isladora's next words were no surprise to him at all. On the day of breeding, Sunny would be more like an elemental force than a wyvern.

Isladora nodded. "When Sunny arrived, she was so angry she glowed like the sun, and in her first pass, she set the entire fort ablaze. She would have killed us, too, if Tobin's magic hadn't been enough to hold her liquid fire at bay. The townspeople must believe the wyverns have gone to war with them." Her voice was full of regret.

Chablis shook her head. "You could not have known that it is forbidden—and dangerous—to blow that Horn on the day of breeding," she said. "In fact, you could not have known that it was breeding day. This new problem is a situation for the ruling pairs and will have to wait."

She turned to the wyvern. "Cassian, are you hurt?" He shook his head; it was clear the crossbow bolts had bounced off his hardened scales, though to Isladora, Petrus' wounds were eerily similar to those of Ariah when she and Json had escaped the humans. "You will stay here tonight and help us keep watch over your bond-mate. Call me when he wakes, but you must keep him still or he'll re-injure himself.

"Now, we need to finish working on him, so please step back, my friend."

Cassian lumbered around to sit on his haunches and worriedly watched as Chablis and Isladora finished examining and patching him up. When they had things under control, Chablis and Isladora finished dressing the wounds and cleaned up, dropping the used tools in a large pot of boiling water to cleanse them. Isladora belatedly started to worry about the often-hot-tempered Tobin being left alone with Darkale.

When they entered the common room, Darkale's mask was off and he and Tobin were talking in the human tongue like old friends and drinking the Sybaris version of beer, which was green and lacked effervescence but smelled hoppy and yeasty just like beer in Juna.

"Where did you learn the human tongue?" Chablis asked, surprised.

"Glock apparently, and purely by accident, mind you, could occasionally do something right," Darkale said in the Sybaris tongue with a wide, fang-brandishing grin. "He sent me to spy on the humans many times, and I didn't mind because it kept me by myself. Well, by myself and Abraxis, I mean. I learned their language by listening to them and practiced it with Petrus. Is he going to be all right?"

Chablis smiled and nodded, leading Isladora over to the table. As soon as the princess saw the breads, fruits, and vegetables, her stomach growled. She blushed, for it seemed louder than Cassian's growl had been, and Chablis laughed. "So much like a wyvern," she teased and laughed again as Isladora's blush deepened.

"Come make a plate," she said. "Darkale will probably eat later, as he doesn't like being watched…" She stopped as she realized that her lover hadn't just been drinking with Tobin but eating with him as well.

"I started out trying to intimidate him with my teeth," Darkale admitted, "and he responded by asking me how effective they were in a fight. One thing led to another, and, well, here we are." He grinned—Isladora admitted, it was a frightful grin—and popped a sweet tomato into his mouth.

"You are betrothed," Darkale said politely. "Does that mean that you would prefer separate chambers?"

Tobin and Isladora both blushed now, and Tobin shook his head. "Princess Isladora and I are not yet married but we have been traveling together for a long time," he said. "If it will not break a custom of yours for unmarried couples to sleep in the same room, we can manage it." Isladora was dead on her feet and her head had started to thrum again with the call; she needed more tisane.

Isladora translated for Chablis, who said, "Oh, no! We go where our heart tells us, and when we select our mates we do not marry as humans do. We have no need of such ceremony, for we mate for life." She smiled and took Darkale's hand, clearly happy beyond measure that she could.

The strikingly pink doctor added, "You may have the room opposite the tree painting, down that hall," she told the humans. "The bath chamber is adjacent and should be stocked with everything you need." She had heard of this concept of marriage, but it was not done among the Draconians. The she-wyverns often had favorites, or even exclusive partners, like Sunny and the Commander, but they could also choose different mates each year if that was where their passions took them.

The Sybaris were less driven by their hormonal cycles, and for them selecting a mate was a serious thing to be considered carefully. Even Glock had not tried to force mating pairs on the Sybaris, though Darkale and

Chablis suspected he would have eventually done so, simply because he wanted to control every detail of the Draconians' lives.

The humans' ritual, though, appealed to Chablis. It was a way to mark the event of joining throughout the Sybaris community, and she decided to ask Isladora more about it later.

At the appointed hour the next morning, the ruling pairs met with Tobin and Isladora at the Cystine Hall. It was another hour before the Commander arrived, battered and bruised from his encounter with Sunny but looking satisfied. At the queen's gesture, he took his old position at the place of honor, which had been vacant since Glock has usurped the council.

Sitting next to the small, empty chair of his bond-mate, reminded him of his lost friend Aslay. He still couldn't believe that Glock hadn't just killed her, but had eaten her. And the monstrous Glock had eaten her alive, right in front of the burned and helpless Commander. He couldn't think of a worse way to die. The Commander would grieve for her for a long time to come, but he tried to put aside the memory for now with a big sigh.

The entire world was better off with Glock dead, though he'd only been defeated by the intercession of the Protectors. Von had flown down and severed Glock's fiery red head from his body in a single sword stroke, and that had saved Ariah and her companions, for the battle had been going poorly. Von's help was a point in the Protectors' favor, but the Elder's actions were ten thousand points against them, so far as the Commander was concerned. The Commander didn't know if most of the Protectors were evil or good, but he planned to find out.

I will destroy them all if they laid waste to the Annites purposefully; he thought as he settled into his spot. He sat up tall, his large white-scaled head and black mane at a cocky angle, his golden eyes and horns shining in the morning light.

"So, I see she caught you," teased Silverback. "Your smile is going to break your jaw open."

The Commander was too experienced with Silverback's jesting the day after the mating flight to be embarrassed. "It is good to be home from my underground travels," he said, his eyes gleaming, and it had been good to renew his passion with the ever-volatile Sunny, in his eyes the most beautiful wyvern ever.

The Commander became much more serious as he began to tell them all about the Annites, how they lived, and that Kaigen's earth magic could sense them too. He told them about the great stores of blue minerals that the Annites made when they procreated and how the Protectors were drilling into these stores and killing droves of them and how few of the Annite chambers were left. "There might be more Annites elsewhere under the world, but there may not be," he concluded. "If not, they are about to be driven to extinction by the drilling."

Tobin found himself grateful to Meluha Crocus, to his personal annoyance, because the spirit, taking advantage of the fact that he could hear his spirit voice, was translating for him.

Isladora explained, "Meluha wants me to tell you that the blue substance is referred to as "frost" by the Protectors. They have been mining it for hundreds of years, and it is the source of much of their power."

"Do they know that this mining is killing the Annites?" Toyah asked. The Commander's head snapped around so fast to look at Isladora that she was forced to take a step back in alarm.

"Apologies," the Commander rumbled, forcing himself to settle back down.

Isladora swallowed and nodded. "Meluha says that he discovered the Annites existed a long time ago," she explained. "He refused to continue drilling operations until they understood the nature of the creatures and what effect their drilling would have on their environment, and when he did so, his brother had him stripped of rank and exiled. He hasn't been to his homeland since, so he doesn't know what they do and do not know about the Annites.

"My suspicion is that any inquiries into the creatures is harshly discouraged," she added.

Queen Ariah held up one of the magical weapons the Protectors had left when they stole Kaigen. She said, "We were hoping to use these to help us force our way past the wards, but so far we have been unsuccessful." It had only made sense, to use Protector magic against Protector magic.

"Isladora, pick one of them up," Meluha urged, and she asked to hold one.

Ariah handed Isladora a sword as she reached for it and she held it in both hands, then nodded as she listened to the spirit's voice. "Meluha says he doesn't detect any magic that would aid you. Instead, the weapons are able to act as transport beacons the Protectors can use."

Arrington did not like the thought that the Protectors' gifts were instead some kind of traps. His green-scaled face and emerald eyes darkened and he demanded, "Explain what you mean by transport!"

"The Protectors appeared to you from thin air, did they not?" Isladora asked at Meluha's prompting.

"Yes, we were standing at the entrance to the Cystine Hall when they appeared suddenly to keep their dinner appointment," Json said.

Isladora's face scrunched up as she tried to understand and explain, "The metal in the artifacts they left with you allows certain Protectors to use their magic to transport themselves and others instantaneously from place to place. They use this type of metal as a homing beacon."

Beacon was a word the wyverns knew well. "So like Gumbo and Rosetta, they have the magic to transport. For Gumbo and Rosetta, as long as they have seen the place they are transporting to, they don't get lost. For the Protectors, it is the signature in a certain kind of metal?" Json asked Isladora.

Arrington was as crestfallen and angry. "So the weapons cannot help us break the wards, then," he growled.

"No, but Meluha says the wards twist one's perceptions such that you are forced to travel back the way you came," Isladora said. "Any time you near the entrance to their lands, a device built into or near the warning statues senses your approach and triggers the magic. One simply never sees what is beyond and ends up turned around. But it is like the shell of an egg, so if your Rosetta and Gumbo can transport across it, they should be able to damage the device so the rest of you can fly through."

"That won't work. As they have never seen the other side, they cannot transport to it. They would be lost, at best, if they tried," Toyah said thinking of Gumbo's simple mind. "And it is possible to transport into an object, like a mountain, which would kill them both."

"The devices only engage when they perceive a target?" the Commander asked, and Isladora nodded. "Remember, I can now become invisible."

"Of course," Abraxis said, conking his head on the wall to rattle his brains into working. "You appeared from nowhere, even though you were well inside the hall. How were you able to do that?" Abraxis' gravelly voice could have been interpreted as hostile, but the Commander knew it was just his way of speaking.

"The Annites gave me many gifts, none greater than their friendship, but they coated my scales with tiny spheres that reflect and refract light. I can shift these to make me nearly completely invisible." After he spoke, the Commander suddenly vanished. He then moved about the room, and as he did, they could occasionally catch a glimpse of part of him or a kind of shimmer in the air as the light was not diffracted perfectly around him.

"Outside and without knowing what to look for, I think you would be completely invisible," Ariah said in wonder. "What great friends were these Annites, to give you such a gift."

"Meluha says that even though the invisibility is not perfect, it should be enough to fool the ward device," Isladora said. "Once the Commander is inside the ward shell, he can destroy the device." She turned to the Commander, still invisible, although she was addressing his hindquarters instead of his head. "The device looks like a small rectangular box of black stone, either built into the back of the warning heads or near them somewhere."

Resisting the impulse to glance at Tobin, Isladora said, "If I can somehow ride hidden with you, Commander, Meluha can help us locate it quickly so you can destroy it." She winced as Meluha translated her words faithfully.

"You mean if *we* can ride, don't you?" Tobin exclaimed, glaring at her.

"He says that I will be in little danger," Isladora said soothingly. "The ward isn't an army of guards with crossbows waiting for a target; it is a magical device with a singular purpose. Once the Commander destroys it, you can all come charging through and join us."

"Which brings us to our objectives once we are inside," Ariah said, and Isladora nodded. "We have a number of different tasks, including rescuing Kaigen."

The Commander nodded. "That is of course critically important, but I must find a way to stop this frost drilling permanently. Kaigen, I am sure, would agree with me, that her life is not as important as millions of Annites. They are not just magical; they are intelligent and kind."

Isladora nodded, listening for a moment to Meluha Crocus. She sighed and nodded to him, then said, "Meluha says that your objective is our objective, Commander, and I must agree with him. To stop the drilling will require destruction of the Elder, for so long as he lives, he would never allow the drilling to end. Vernondiander, the Elder I mean, has grown utterly dependent upon the frost for the magical power and ability to dominate the other Protectors. His brother's magic is also what calls me to bear the ring there, and even now calls me. If Tobin had not helped me and brewed a tincture that deadened the magical call upon my mind, I would be dead of exhaustion in the wilderness.

"We do not know what the Elder wants from Meluha after all the ages of his imprisonment, but he believes that his brother has need of his knowledge of frost production. I don't know what will happen when we get to their city or what the summoning call will try to force me to do."

Silverback said, "I understand the Commander's desires and they are important. But to me, Kaigen is the most important objective, for she is a part of Draconia's family. We will do anything necessary to retrieve her, even if the result is all-out war with the Protectors." The Draconians all nodded their heads in agreement with Silverback's words. Kaigen had been stolen from them against her will, a crime punishable by wyvern fire.

The Commander said, "It may be that all our objectives merge, but it may also be that they are in opposition. I will focus on the frost production facilities, and the rest of you must search for Kaigen and retrieve her."

"And anyone who resists either of those efforts?" Abraxis added with a deep basso growl, "Burn."

Chapter 74: The Arena

The Draconians and the two humans landed on the ridge overlooking the entrance to the Protectors' domain. In the distance, the large concrete heads rose from the sand where the wards kept the true gate beyond hidden, negating all previous attempts to rescue Kaigen.

To everyone's surprise, Sunny and five of her largest she-wyverns had descended to the city as they prepared to depart, saying, "Queen Ariah, we know that Draconia goes to war with the Protectors, and we cannot imagine a more dangerous adversary. We stand with you."

Queen Ariah had been stunned at first but quickly recovered, bowing gratefully to the six she-wyverns. "We will have need to coordinate with you," she said, wondering how to broach a subject that the she-wyverns felt quite strongly about.

Sunny had simply nodded, staring straight at Mezzi. "We know this," she said gravely. "It is why we accept that we must pair up with Sybaris." She lowered her wing to the healer who'd been pursuing her for so long. "And I know who I want on my back."

The leader of the she-wyverns had bristled and growled as Mezzi climbed aboard, but once the Sybaris was properly perched on her back, she managed to stop herself. "You get what you always wanted anyhow, it seems," she said to Mezzi, and then reached her head around to nudge her gently. Mezzi had simply clung to her lower jaw, speechless.

Now, Mezzi sat on Sunny's back, an expression of joy and love seeming permanently fixed on her face. Tobin rode on Abraxis behind his friend Darkale, while Isladora rode on the Commander's back. Tobin was more than a little intimidated by the rough, gruff Abraxis, and he hoped he could remember what Isladora taught him about what he could hang onto and what might offend his mount. Abraxis, to him, looked like he'd rather eat him than allow him on his back.

The Commander looked around. He had been defeated by Glock and almost killed in a forest a little south from here, and Glock had met his own death in this valley. The scars of that battle remained on the ground.

Queen Ariah perused the remnants of the lava pit they had created to ensnare Glock and asked Json, "Will we always be at war?"

Json glanced back at his bond-mate, "It depends on our leadership. If they are power hungry and unsatisfied, jealous over the possessions of another, we will always be at war."

Isladora heard them and said, "That is our true test here. Our bodies house our souls and what the body may need to survive sometimes overrides what our soul knows is not necessary. Hence, the craving for things we should not take because they belong to another."

Ariah nodded. As a former slave, she knew what it felt like to be controlled by another. Now Kaigen was a slave. "All right Isladora, time to try to break through the wards," Queen Ariah ordered.

Meluha told Isladora, *"Remember to stay hidden along the very top of his back. As long as the warding device cannot sense motion, it won't be triggered."* She looked back at Tobin. He placed his fist on his heart, and she responded in kind. Oh, how she loved him! And how he'd hated to let her ride alone on the Commander's back, but the fact was that both of them could not have remained hidden from the ward device, while Isladora could alone.

"I understand, my friend." She settled herself and began to prepare for their task, envisioning successfully finding and destroying the warding device.

Json said, "Good luck, brave human girl." He knew her mental preparation was what helped keep her calm, something her father, the King of the Juna, had taught her. He sent good thoughts for luck as the Commander ran and then leapt into the air with Isladora hanging on as if she were born to it.

Isladora had never seen statues as large as the giant heads that stood as sentries. She was intimidated by their sheer magnitude and how little she knew about the Protectors; she didn't know what to expect. *How did one build statues this large, anyway,* she wondered.

She laid out flat along the Commander's back, and as they neared, he shifted his scales and became invisible. She could feel the ripple of his muscles and the warmth of his scales against her cheek. She held tight and tried to remain calm despite the inescapable sensation that she was simply hurling along in the empty air. They had determined that she could only be seen from above; from below they would both be invisible, blocked from view by the Commander's body and his Annite-granted trick of the light.

After they flew between the heads, if she or Meluha Crocus spotted the location of the device, she was to tap left or right on the Commander's shoulder, fast for land or once for a slight adjustment in that direction. She swallowed as the empty eyes of the giant heads stared at her.

"There!" Meluha said. *"The mound behind the right-hand statue! See how it doesn't quite match the color of the sand?"*

Isladora tapped once on the Commander's right shoulder, and he angled his body towards the direction she indicated. As they got closer, she tapped several times quickly, telling him to land. The Commander's sharp vision picked up on the different look of the small sand dune. He landed and Isladora yelled, "The sand dune is fake! Can you punch a hole in it?"

"Hang on!" The Commander shouted back, then gathered himself to jump with a huge flap of his wings. In the chase with Sunny—what a wild flight that had been!—he'd discovered just how strong the new wings were, and he used them to rise up and then pound hard on the dune, grabbing with his much larger back claws, digging into the fake dune, crushing in a part of it as he flapped his wings to keep his balance.

Sand and dust flew all around them and Isladora leaned way over and turned her face into the crook of her armpit to cover her mouth and nose, clenching her eyes tightly shut. She didn't dare let go with her hands. As soon as the Commander lowered to the ground, Isladora leapt from his back and entered the hole he had made. She saw the black stone box immediately and tried to drag it back toward the Commander, but it was too heavy.

She produced the escrima stick and willed it to become a looped cable around the box, and then handed the end to the Commander's foreclaw. "It's too heavy," she explained, and he simply nodded and tugged, dragging the hundreds of pounds of stone box as if it was made of paper.

"Stand back while I crush it!" the Commander warned her. She nodded and drew herself and her escrima stick well back behind the huge wyvern's body. The Commander raised the box and then smashed it down, stone splinters flying in every direction as it was crushed under the might of his strength. An explosion of blue-white energy played across his massive head, and he cried out in pain. "Aaargh!" Isladora lost sight of him in the dust as he collapsed to the ground beside the remains of the box.

As the dust settled around them, they looked around for the enemy, waiting for someone to appear and challenge them.

"It's not an alarm Isladora," Meluha told her, *"the wards are a mirage device, the Protectors will not be alerted to our presence yet."* She relayed the information to the Commander, so he left her to fly back and get the others. In the silence she bent her knee and tried to calm her racing heart.

When Tobin saw the Commander returning without Isladora he panicked. "She's fine, Tobin," the Commander told them, "come, the wards have been destroyed."

In Issedones, however, Trugard rushed into the Elder's quarters. The Logistician was quite agitated—it had been an exciting few days—but he tried to report calmly. Perhaps this bit of good news would distract the Elder from his glowering and dangerous mood. "The girl and your brother have reached the Steppes, Elder. At first, she entered the gateway, but now she's moving back toward the site of the wyvern's squabble."

Vernondiander jumped up, his black mood dispelled in an instant. With a great smile on his face and a sparkle in his eyes, he clasped the Logistician's hand in both of his and squeezed. "Excellent news, Trugard!" he exclaimed and summoned the two guards waiting outside his door.

He had a metal transport plate in his room and he fairly leapt upon it with the guards scrambling after him. "You too, Trugard, quickly!" he said, scowling at the dolt. He transported them to the metal plate the Protectors had placed under the ground directly beneath the two heads and materialized right in front of Isladora.

Isladora screamed in fright and scrambled backward, stumbling as she overcame her forward momentum. She backed away from the four Protectors, but Meluha cautioned her strongly, *"Careful, Isladora. The one with the blue robe is my brother. You must not anger him. Stall for time. Until the wyverns get here, you have no chance against them."*

Isladora didn't really need Meluha to tell her that this was the Elder; she could see the similarities to Meluha's ghost, in the face.

Moreover, the Elder stood and looked like a prince, his beautiful blue robe of an incredible richness, and underneath it, more rich clothes were adorned with metal fittings. Even his boots, in a style she'd never seen before, were something rare and rich.

"So, you made it here at last," Vernondiander said to her. "I cannot tell you how long I have waited to be reunited with my beloved brother." His voice was kind and gentle, reminding her of her Uncle Tonsaku, and his eyes seemed to sparkle with even more kindness. Knowing what she did of him, however, she knew that was all a veneer of civility to hide the ugliness beneath. She stood holding her hand on her heart.

"Elder, how did she pass through the ward?" the Logistician asked, peering about him.

The Elder dismissed the question with a snort. "The summoning spell led her through it, obviously," he gestured Isladora to join the Protectors where they stood, unbeknownst to her, atop the buried transport platform. "Were you not paying attention when I told you it would?"

Although Trugard knew very well he had not, and was fully educated on what the summoning spell could and could not do, said nothing. Crossing the Elder, even when something so inconvenient as the truth was involved, could be dangerous.

"Let's go," the Elder said, gesturing at her impatiently, and Meluha Crocus warned her to move, so she joined them. "Take her arms." The guards took her arms, holding her still in their iron grips. She thought about fighting, but Meluha was still warning her not to, so she stood still as they wanted.

"If you resist the transport magic in any way," Trugard warned her, "it will be at best painful and at worst, deadly."

"He tells you the truth, Isladora, don't move!" Meluha agreed insistently. Isladora began to feel cold all over but she held still, trusting in Meluha, as the Elder transported them straight to the Arena. When they materialized, Isladora was shaking in reaction to the magic. *"If you had tried to flee or attack during the transport phase, you would have been badly injured or destroyed."* Isladora thought she was going to throw up. Her stomach roiled and she grabbed at her abdomen and tried to kneel on the ground, but the guards held her roughly erect.

Vernondiander looked at the ring on Isladora's finger. "Ah, I see my brother's spirit is still with you! What a marvelous day! It has been such a long time, Meluha, such a long time. Welcome to the Arena. It was built for sporting competitions, but I think I've discovered a better use for it, as I'm sure you'll agree." He gestured for them to take in the construction around them.

Isladora's innards were calming down after the transport, the nauseous feeling leaving as quickly as it came, and she looked around at the most incredible edifice she had ever seen. As he said, they were in the center of an arena, surrounded by a twenty-foot-tall wall of marbled stone with intricately carved columns every twenty yards. These rose up high into the roofless sky, as if they held up some kind of ceiling, though she didn't see one.

Thousands of people could be seated here, and the retaining wall was sheer and impossible to climb without a grappling hook. Six double doors were spaced about the oval arena, each fifteen feet tall, and she guessed that someone or something would enter through them, but they were all sealed shut.

At the far end of the sandy Arena floor was yet another column, seemingly haven risen from below, and she heard a roar from that direction that made her hair stand on end in fear. Chained to the column was a large striped cat like a tiger, but this one was six feet tall at the shoulder and must have weighed two tons, all rippling muscle.

Near the column but well out of the pacing creature's reach was a large cage containing five people. Three of them seemed to be standing protectively around the other two, smaller figures.

"As you can see, my pet is very hungry," the Elder gloated. "Very soon now, we shall let him have his meal."

One of the two smaller people stepped forward to the edge of the cage. She was a beautiful lady with striking red hair, and she called out to him. "You don't have to do this, Vernondiander," she pleaded, opening her hands in supplication. "Please, let us go!"

"Oh, beautiful Sigrida," the Elder said sadly, and Isladora could almost believe that he was sincere, "you have betrayed my trust, freeing Von and healing Kaigen against not just my wishes, but my own actions. No, Sigrida, as much as I love your sharp mind—and those lovely curves—you all will die. These two guards have betrayed their oaths, so they shall die with you."

"What about Kaigen?" Sigrida asked. "With the two of us working together, we can find you more frost, you know that! More frost than you could ever have dreamed of!" She knew that she couldn't win Von, or even the poor guards, a reprieve, but maybe she could save Kaigen.

He strolled closer to the cage, though well outside of the cat's reach, Isladora noted. "No," he said with that same kindly smile and tone. "I have decided that I have other plans for Kaigen. You four will die for betraying me, but she will have a high honor!"

Von and Sigrida quailed to think of what the Elder could mean. "What do you mean, Elder?" Kaigen demanded.

"Your body and all its powerful earth magic will now house the spirit of my brother. I am going to force Meluha's spirit from the ring into you, and I am afraid," he said with a kindly twinkle in his eye, "that you will simply cease to exist. Your body will become that of my long, lost brother, though I suppose I'll have to call him my sister from now on." He laughed, returning to Isladora, readying his magic as he did so.

"Now, my dear child," he said in his kindly, most beneficent voice, "give me the ring."

Kaigen's eyes went wide with fright and she grabbed Von's arm in terror. He couldn't put his arms around her because of the restraints the Elder's guards had placed upon him, but he leaned his head against hers.

"Captain," Pol whispered, "they didn't search me. I have a set of keys in my belt pouch."

"Quickly, the restraints!" Von exclaimed and held up his hands to bring the locks into Pol's reach. Pol unlocked but did not remove the restraints. If the Elder or his men realized what they were doing, they'd put a stop to it, but fortunately, the cage had been placed on the opposite side of the long end of the Arena sands and the distance worked in their favor.

Von said softly to his fellow captives, "This will be our only chance;

even together we cannot defeat him directly. But I believe his robe that stores magical energy has a finite limit. We must all blast Vernondiander with every ounce of our magic and pray it's enough to overwhelm the robe's capacity. If we do, it will explode like an overpressured beer barrel!" He smiled sadly at Kaigen, for it had been her idea and her analogy, but he needed the guards to believe in him and to strike when he signaled them; if they knew it was Kaigen's idea, they would doubt.

Across the sands, noting the activity in the cage but drawing no attention to it, Isladora looked calmly into Vernondiander's blue eyes. "I cannot remove it. Don't you think I have tried?"

"Bah!" the Elder said. "I have released the summoning spell, foolish girl! You can take it off, and you will do so now!"

Isladora tried to remove the ring but it would no more budge than it had before.

While the Elder's attention was focused on retrieving Meluha's ring, Von tried the keys on the cage door, but none of them fit. "Hide me removing the collar," Kaigen said, and the three men stood obligingly in front of her. The cage door was metal, she thought, and metal is of the earth! Her earth magic corroded the metal as if ten thousand years of oxidation had worked upon it, and the lock fell to pieces. Impressed at her ingenuity, Von quietly slid the cage door ajar, and while the tiger-like creature hissed at him, none of the others had noticed yet.

Isladora tugged on the ring to show him that it was stuck.

The Elder shook his head and said, "Meluha, let the girl go, or I will kill her and remove it from her burned corpse." At once, the ring widened and loosened and fell to the ground.

The Elder stepped past her to pluck up the ring, but then turned and struck her with his magic anyway. Her body flew through the air away from him, and she landed less than five feet from the Tigrell. The creature took at defensive swipe at her, but her still form didn't seem like much of a challenge, so he just crouched and hissed.

The Elder smiled and picked up the ring. Meluha felt himself being drawn from the only world he'd known for a thousand years as the Elder's unearthly power forced his spirit to leave the ring. And why could he not? He'd created the thing to entrap his brother in the first place!

With a final magical tug, the Elder succeeded in extracting his brother's spirit from the ring, then he hurled the spirit toward Kaigen. *If I reach the child, the magic will displace her spirit*, Meluha thought as he flew. He couldn't stop himself, but he remembered what one of his instructors had taught him about magic.

"Magic, Meluha," the man had said at the time, "is the alteration of natural physics to achieve a desired effect. It can break physical laws, but it follows natural laws of its own." Meluha knew that he couldn't stop his spirit's momentum, but he could alter it and quite possibly kill several birds with one stone, for the Tigrell was overcoming its surprise and beginning to sniff toward Isladora's motionless form.

As he heard the Tigrell's roar, he diverted himself hard, with every bit of will he could muster, toward that sound. He entered the tiger's body and the beast went crazy, twisting this way and that as it tried to fight off something it couldn't comprehend.

Isladora regained consciousness at the rattling of the Tigrell's chain, and she felt her friend's spirit had somehow entered the beast. "Meluha!" she croaked, but she heard no answer.

Inside the Tigrell, Meluha's spirit clashed violently with the animal mind of the wild creature. Its primal terror and fear tried to fight him off, and because the Elder's magic had been intended to eject a sentient mind from Kaigen's head, it hadn't just tossed the Tigrell's spirit, such as it was, free of the body. The Tigrell in its madness looked for a physical enemy to rend and tear, and the only one in range of its chain was Isladora. It bounded toward her, claws fully extended and teeth flashing in the sunlight. Before she could pull out of its way, it knocked her down hard, where she lay supine once again.

Vernondiander laughed uproariously. "Oh, you were always the clever one!" he exclaimed. "And what a fine animal you will be, brother!" It didn't matter; he'd just extract Meluha's spirit from the beast and inject it into the girl as he'd intended, but it was hilarious to watch his brother struggle.

The Tigrell's primal fear had flooded its body with adrenaline and now it snapped the chain as it ran away from the column that its dim mind had associated with the danger. It leapt up the wall, but the heavy chain prevented it from reaching the top, and it fell back to the sandy floor of the Arena. This made the Elder laugh even harder.

Suddenly, the Tigrell went utterly still and the shook its head. "Excellent, brother!" the Elder called to it. "You're in control of the cat now!" As the tiger turned to bound towards him with blood in its eye, Vernondiander raised a hand, hurling it all the way to the far side of the Arena. "Oh, please, Meluha, be reasonable! You have no chance to resist my power in the body of a dumb beast!"

Sigrida, Von, and Kaigen aimed their magical powers at the robe while the two guards ran at the Elder; they hadn't had enough access to frost to have the power to throw lightning, but they were capable of breaking the older man's neck if they could reach him. The three streams of magic made the robe turn from sky blue to ultramarine as it soaked in their magic, unfortunately providing more to the Elder, but they had no other plan.

He unleashed a blistering torrent of power at the two guards, and their screams were mercifully cut short as he incinerated them, laughing maniacally all the while. He turned that blistering stream at Kaigen, and though she cried out in pain, she didn't stop her assault. He pushed harder, forcing her to direct her stream of magic at his, and his dark blue pushed at her earth-toned energy, drawing it closer and closer to her, where it would annihilate her.

Before he could finish her—a sure sign of his madness, for he needed her earth magic to restore the flow of frost—he heard the war scream of wyverns as they arrived over the coliseum, a full dozen of them with riders astride. The Elder temporarily halted his attack in disbelief, allowing the magic streams from the three on the ground to strike his robe as he considered this new danger. Wyverns in Issedones! He allowed the magic to flow into his robe, after all, more power would only be an advantage if he had to fry the wyverns, too.

As the Tigrell headed towards the people on the ground, first in a crouch and then building its speed, Sunny, out in front, flew to intercept the beast as it ran, grabbing it with her claws and tossing it into the wall. It fell, lifeless, to the sand, blood flowing from its mouth. Silverback raced towards Kaigen and she yelled, "Aim your magic towards the Elder, help us!" A wild melee of magic erupted from the ground and Vernondiander fired back, aiming at Von's stream which had begun to weaken.

Silverback shrieked and commanded his air magics towards Vernondiander. Abraxis and Darkale hit him with ice, and the five airborne female wyverns, drawing on their chronicle memories to focus their powers far more accurately than the males, struck the Elder's defenses together. The Elder's magic began to falter as his robe finally hit its limit. It exploded in an arc, an ice-blue waving surge of power.

It reached the eastern seats behind and nearest him first, and that entire side of the Arena was crushed to powder by the expanding sphere of power. The shockwave it created knocked the wyverns from the air, where they rained down on stadium seating and beyond the wall, struggling to control their falls to preserve their riders. Tobin clung for dear life as Sunny hit the wall, shielding his frail human body with her own.

As the dust cleared, Tobin was stunned but he clamored from Sunny's back and fell into the dirt. He stood shakily, his eyes taking in the scene and looking for the one thing that was everything to him. He sucked in a breath as he saw her body lying lifeless in the dirt. He ran across the coliseum sands to Isladora and turned her over, but her chest wasn't moving. His love was no longer breathing. "Oh God, please no!" he cried. "No!"

*****

Isladora was dreaming. She dreamed that she strolled through a forest of beautiful trees. It was neither warm nor cold, and it was misty and surreal. She thought of her grandmother for some reason, and started to look for her. She was going to speak to Meluha, tell him about her grandmother, but she suddenly felt the absence of Mae's ring. She looked down, her hand oddly empty without it.

She realized she could see through her hand to some degree, and she waved it in front of herself in wonder. Another hand reached out to take hers gently, and she knew that hand, for it had belonged to her grandmother. Her thoughts were disjointed, somewhere between reality and memories, and she held warmly to her grandmother's hand. She looked up to her face and saw her smile.

"Meluha," she said in the mental voice she'd used to talk to the spirit, *"this is my grandmother! I remember her touch; it was soft as a whispered lullaby, but she could be as strong as a steel plow. She furrowed our lives; she helped us grow; she taught us to reach for ourselves towards the sun. I can't remember a time in my youngest days when her love wasn't constantly surrounding me."*

Then out loud, "I never thanked her for that," Isladora said sadly. "I took it for granted, and then one day she was gone, and I never got to tell her. For a time, especially after Father disappeared, nothing kept my young thoughts fertile and productive like those that she had always cultivated." She wondered where Meluha was; he was always around.

"Ah, there you are," said Meluha. He was also translucent, glowing like he had the one time she had seen his body back on the Silver Roads. She took in his flattering ship captain's garb; he was very handsome. *"Come, it is not time for you to be here, come with me."* He took her other hand and led her through the forest. Slowly, she realized that they were not alone. Other spirits moved near them. She looked up and saw her grandmother smile at her. There was a soft glow of white light up ahead and Meluha stopped.

"Your faith has saved me, my dear, dear friend Isladora," he said. *"My chains are broken, and I am free, but now you must go back to the light."* He pushed her a little and pointed for her to go.

She did as he bade her, for who could argue with that winsome smile, she thought as she approached the light. She started to feel heavy and her feet felt like she was dragging through wet sand. She turned to look at him. His arm was around a beautiful woman and they were smiling at each other. *Ah, that must be his Mae Tarango*, she thought. *His beloved wife who died in the sea so long ago.*

"Goodbye Isladora," he said. *"And know that in the end, I did ask God for His forgiveness and His love, and for that bounty I will always remember you."* He turned and retreated into the forest, his arm around his beautiful Mae.

Pain was all she felt now, the hot sun, the dirt as she coughed and breathed dusty air into her lungs. Von's healing magic was working upon her and she coughed again and choked, her ribs snapping back into place. Tobin was holding her firmly. "Oh, thank God," he exclaimed as she took a breath, and the another, tears running freely down his grimy soot-covered face. "That's my girl, take another breath." Tobin was crying and rocking her gently back and forth.

She opened her eyes and looked at up at him. "Your face is dirty," she said weakly with a teasing smile.

"I know," he said, bending down to kiss her anyway. "I thought I'd lost you," he breathed against her hair.

"I was right here," she whispered. "I'm not going anywhere." It was all she could say, she felt so weak.

She whispered, "Goodbye, Meluha."

Chapter 75: On Ceremony

Abraxis was the first to recover from the aftershock of having his well-armored hide blasted from the air. He arched his neck to see that Darkale was bleeding from one ear but otherwise conscious and angry. Abraxis growled at his bonded friend. Nothing of the Elder remained, just a huge crater where he once stood.

"Kaigen," Darkale whispered, finding and reattaching his mask. Abraxis looked to where Kaigen had been standing and saw a large pit, not realizing that she'd created it to shield them from the blast.

Abraxis stamped heavily to the pit, the ground shaking under his feet, and looked down to see two Protectors and Kaigen. Von looked up at the large wyvern and slowly reached to draw his sword from his back but his hand met thin air. Too late, he remembered that he had no weapons. Abraxis roared at him, ready to reach down with his frightening maw and snap up Von and then the female Protector.

Von reflexively began to draw any magic he might have left into his hands, but Kaigen yelled at him, "No, Abraxis! Von!" Her tone carried "you idiots" quite clearly. "Von, Abraxis is family!" she said and looked up. "Abraxis, I'd appreciate it if you would help us up out of here and not to eat my friends."

Abraxis snorted and released a little puff of grey into the air. His raspy voice boomed. "What happened to your wings?" he demanded.

"Are you going to worry about my wings, which never flew me any-where anyway," she said impatiently back to him, "or are you going to lift us out of this pit?" Kaigen had made the pit when the explosion went off to protect herself, Sigrida, and Von, and now they were stuck down in it, too exhausted to get themselves out. "Well?"

Abraxis made a chirping gurgling growl. *Kaigen, still bossy as ever,* he thought, but he turned and lowered his tail so they could climb out. Von and Sigrida let Kaigen go first; they didn't trust the deadly wyvern and figured that Kaigen could intercede for them better if she went first.

"Oh, I didn't realize their skin would be so soft," Sigrida said as she half-climbed and Von half-pushed her up out of the pit.

"Who are you calling soft?" Abraxis growled. He liked to fight anyway and was still looking for a reason to bite the Protectors' heads off. Von reached for Kaigen, and Abraxis' head snapped around at the pit.

"Enough!" Kaigen said sternly. It was almost funny to see her standing arms akimbo facing down the huge wyvern, and the Commander started laughing as he landed on the sands, for it reminded him of Nim. She said, "Von, *my dear and true friend*, this is Abraxis and his bonded mate Darkale." Von looked up to see the wyvern's Sybaris rider now peering over the edge of the pit. Seeing the rider did little to calm his fears, as the handsome Sybaris with his masked face looked like a worthy opponent, but he nodded politely at him.

"And this is my friend Sigrida," she said, putting an arm around the lead scientist's shoulders protectively. "I will be cross if any of you eat, burn, or shred either of them!" When Von finally climbed from the pit, he stood near Kaigen but didn't put his arm around her, and her heart twisted a little in her chest. She sighed; she was weary from trying to earn his love, and if fighting together wasn't enough, what would be?

The other Draconians had come to stand with their little group, the she-wyverns hanging back so their instincts didn't end up snapping a Protector's head off anyway. "Where are your wings?" Json asked.

"The Elder turned his magic on me and crushed them. They were damaged beyond repair, but Von healed me," she explained, and then her eyes sparkled and she exclaimed, "And look what he made of them!" Kaigen took off her shirt and turned around to show them her back, her long brown hair drawn forward over her breasts. The Draconians gasped in surprise: her entire back was covered in a beautiful pattern of swirly scales.

"Wow, that's really beautiful, Kaigen," Json told her truthfully, and the queen murmured her agreement.

"I know," Kaigen said as she smiled. "And the best part is, I can sleep on my back now and wear normal clothes!"

Von found that he didn't particularly like her standing here half-naked before all these others, and he said, "Speaking of which, let's cover you now, if you don't mind?" He gently took the shirt from her and helped her put it back on.

That's interesting, Queen Ariah thought, seeing that the man was jealous. Behind her, the she-wyverns looked knowingly at each other; they'd seen it, too.

"Come on Kaigen, let's go home now," Silverback said with his own special smile for the girl.

Toyah gestured to the spot behind her on her bond-mate's back. "You can ride with us," she couldn't stop smiling at the girl who was like a daughter to her.

Kaigen turned to look at Von, her eyes shining with all the hope she had in her heart. She couldn't breathe and her heart was pounding so hard she thought her ribs would burst.

I'm not about to let her fly out of my life, Von thought. He saw that longing look that had once so annoyed him. He said, "With the Elder gone we have a unique chance for renewal. Not just a change of reign over our city and government of Issedones, but that of our relationships with other king-doms." He took Kaigen's hand in his and looked over at the Sybaris queen. "I have grown to love this girl with all my heart. I want to have the oppor-tunity to know and love her family as well."

I think I can fly, wings or no! Kaigen thought, her heart hammering even harder now that Von had announced his love before her family…and those two humans, she added to herself. She could figure out what they were do-ing here later; in that moment, every hope Kaigen had ever held of being truly in love, and of having someone to love her, was in bright focus.

Von glanced at Abraxis, but at least the heavy beast didn't growl. "Let our love for each other be the first connection of our two kingdoms," the Protector said.

Sigrida said, "You do not know our customs, Draconians and humans, so I will explain." She smiled at Von and Kaigen and her heart soared at the girl's obvious happiness after so much suffering. Who thought that Sigrida could care about someone else? "A vow to or by a Protector, is a sacred covenant. He has given her his heart, and if she accepts it, the next step would be a life-bonding."

She looked around at the Draconians. "Who speaks for this girl?" she asked.

At first no one spoke up, and Kaigen's heart fell. She really didn't have a mother or a father; the Draconians had found her and taken her in. They weren't even sure what race she was, in fact, so there was no one to speak for her. As her face began fell and her eyes misted over, the queen quickly stepped forward.

"I do," Queen Ariah said. "Json does. We all do, for she is a daughter and sister to us all." The Draconians all nodded and stepped even closer to form a circle around Kaigen, though the she-wyverns still kept their dis-tance.

That wasn't exactly the Protectors' custom, but Von ignored any con-sternation to simply kneel before them all. "If she agrees, I ask your permis-sion to bind my life to Kaigen's, from now until the end of our lives." He looked back and up at Kaigen and smiled at her. He was who he was, and he still had enough arrogance to know that she wouldn't refuse; she was deeply in love with him, after all. No, to Von this was simply a formality, a declaration of his commitment to her, because he knew that they still needed to learn to fully trust one another.

Kaigen nodded happily and he stood and embraced her, kissing her chastely on the cheek. "On the cliffs of the Rubian Sea, remember?" he breathed into her ear, and she shuddered and blushed bright red to the laughter and joy of her family.

"You're so going to pay for that," she said, but only clung tighter to his strong, sweet embrace, tears of joy falling down her cheeks. He was hers to hold.

Suddenly a deep-throated song began in the throat of Json and then the harmony was matched by the other wyverns until they all were singing. The melody floated around them and echoed off what was left of the Arena's walls. Kaigen whispered to Von, "This is the song of a permanent pairing, so their answer is yes." Von smiled, thinking what a beautiful tribute it was, and he held on to her as the reverberation echoed in his chest and sealed their oath.

When the wyverns finished Von said, "Come, my new friends, we must tell my countrymen that everything has changed, and Sigrida and I will arrange a feast to celebrate this first joining of our two nations. Much is left to be determined, and I can only speak for myself, but I like this new beginning very much indeed."

He's still arrogant, Queen Ariah thought, but he's also changed. She nodded in approval. "Certain things, like the destruction of the Annites, we will not compromise upon," she said warningly, "but you are right in that we seem to be making a good beginning." She led her subjects and the two humans from the shattered Arena, led by the two Protectors and Von's new bride.

Twelve large wyverns, five bonded mates, seven other Sybaris, Kaigen, and two humans made quite a procession as they walked down the streets of Issedones, and the Protectors all came out to see. The senior Protectors cautiously approached and then began talking to Von. They knew that the Elder was dead, and they wanted to know what Von thought they should do.

Von realized that none of the Protectors, quite possibly including himself, had any idea how to govern in the absence of the Elder's iron-tight control. At least as the head of the military he had some experience, and he could already tell he was going to have the senior Protectors' support. None of them wanted anything to do with stepping into Vernondiander's shoes; the evil despot had threatened and even crushed any thought of leadership from all of the, it would take time to recover from that.

Von knew that most of the Protectors were decent enough people, if only because the Elder killed anyone remotely like him, he thought sardonically. But however it had happened, only the Elder had become so overwhelmingly obsessed with power. He would also have lumped Sigrida and her lust for ever-higher status and wealth in with the same lot, but the chief scientist had revealed depths that none of them had guessed. *And my guess is that no one's more surprised to learn that than her,* he thought and chuckled softly.

"My first act, I think," he said to Kaigen, though he knew the others around him were listening, "is to bring my father home." The other Protectors, to a roll of Sigrida's eyes, all agreed that yes, yes, that sounded like an excellent idea. *I'm going to have to teach them how to argue with me, I can tell,* thought Von.

He turned to two of the senior Protectors at random. "Yamil, could you please fly ahead and bring word to the remaining administration to meet us at the park? Ghyl, would you please arrange for guards and porters to go out into the Steppes and bring my father home? He will be, I think, quite happy to find that Vernondiander is dead."

"Yes, of course!" they exclaimed in unison, and Ghyl added, "It's an honor to serve you, Von."

Definitely going to have to teach them how to argue, he thought, but only bowed formally to them. "My thanks, gentlemen," he said and watched as the two men flew off on their errands.

Von laughed and told Kaigen, "Whoever he ends up sending is going to have quite a tough time with that cantankerous old man!" Kaigen laughed too, she had met Seamus and knew firsthand how ornery he was.

Von looked at Isladora, who was walking with Tobin's arm around her. Tobin was asking her about Meluha.

"He is at peace now, Tobin," Isladora said with a bittersweet smile. "You should know, since the two of you were never on good terms, that it was Meluha who led me back to the light." She noticed Von listening and she smiled shyly at the beautiful Protector. Tobin tightened his hold on her, scowling at the other man.

Von laughed and said wryly. "My new partner, I think, would bury me deep if I even looked at another woman." He laughed as Tobin's face turned red and the proud young scout cleared his throat.

"He's going to have to work on that jealousy," Sunny said to the Commander as they walked side by side.

"Didn't you almost kill Virixia when she nearly caught me that one year?" her mate asked affectionately. Sunny had *not* been amused to have competition for the Commander's affections, and Virixia had paid painfully for her temerity.

"That's completely different," Sunny said and sniffed. The Commander only laughed and nudged her head lovingly. It was still close enough to their mating flight that he could even get away with it with his hide intact.

They reached the center of town, a massive circular park with giant cottonwood trees that could provide shade, even for the wyverns. More of the townsfolk had joined in the parade, curious about the wyverns and seeing Von released from his incarceration, and the news that they were free from the Elder's rule spread outward from the center like blue wyvern fire.

"This is the best I can do for your friends, Kaigen, since the Arena was destroyed. The pillars allowed us to shade the entire place if we wanted to, but that magic's gone now. All the rest of our buildings are just too small for them," Von told her, hoping he wasn't offering offense.

"This will be perfect," Queen Ariah said to him, having overheard. "It is quite beautiful and fitting for wyvern and Sybaris both." She didn't trust that their problems were done, but the young queen wanted peace between them if possible. It was hard to believe that all this evil, pain, and loss had been the result of one man, and she intended to keep her eyes, and those of her bond-mate Json, wide open as they negotiated for the future.

The Protectors involved in administering the various departments of the government—though all at the whim of the Elder—came out of their various buildings as they'd been summoned, and Von gathered them around to address them. "As you have probably ascertained, the Elder has been destroyed," he said. He'd been tempted to tell them that the Elder had destroyed himself, which was in some ways true, but he decided that he'd begin always by giving and expecting the truth.

At first, there was shock and consternation, then smiles and hopeful looks, and then shock and consternation again. "Who will direct us?" the chief metallurgist asked plaintively.

"Von has experience leading the guard," Sigrida said with a curling half smile. She gave them three, perhaps four seconds, before they jumped on that idea, but she honestly couldn't think of a better candidate.

"Yes, Von, you must direct us!" they quickly agreed. "All hail Elder Von!"

"Stop!" Von shouted. "First, Vernondiander claimed that title for himself long ago, and it has too many evil connotations. Second, I am newly bound to Kaigen." They were taken aback at this, for to announce such a thing publicly was to make it true by affirmation.

He smiled, that was going to take some getting used to. "I will retain command of the guard, but I think a more rounded form of government should suffice until we figure this out. I expect we can all meet to advise one another on the matters of our own departments until we have time to determine a permanent system of governance."

Sigrida couldn't decide if she wanted to hug Von or kill him on the spot. The prestige of leading the Protectors was a high honor, even if no one had held it for a thousand years but the Elder, but she could already see that it was going to be a monumental pain to try to get people thinking for themselves again.

Not one of them had a thing to say, but the lower-level administrators and general population that were in a position to hear it seemed to think that was a wise policy. None of them wanted another Elder.

"Now," Von said, "we must celebrate our new union with the Draconians under Queen Ariah. Please spread the word that we will have a feast here in the park in celebration!" After some argument as to which department was paying for, Sigrida divided the cost by the size of their relative budgets, and they all went away happy.

Once tables had been delivered and arranged and then loaded down with food and drink, the wyverns seated themselves in the grass next to the table where the Sybaris sat. Seeing the huge beasts curled up and clearly enjoying themselves, the Protectors began to relax and began to ask dozens of questions about their way of life and their kingdom.

The Commander lumbered over to Sigrida, Von, and Kaigen and said, "I am happy for you both, and I recognize that this is a first and important step in our nations' futures, but I am here for a grave reason."

Sigrida nodded seriously, and she and Von squared off to face the extremely serious wyvern. "Surely there is nothing we cannot overcome together," Sigrida said.

"Alas, this may be one that we cannot," the Commander said darkly, "for I expect us to disagree deeply on the matter."

Von was disappointed they would have trouble so soon, though he wondered what it was. Sigrida, on the other hand, simply said, "I cannot decide that until I hear what it is, Commander."

"This frost that you mine," the Commander said, growing angry despite trying to remain calm. "Are you aware that the process by which you retrieve it is killing thousands upon thousands of intelligent creatures?" The Commander puffed up, his anger making him grow hot just thinking about the careless destruction of the Annites' entire way of life.

Von and Sigrida looked at each other. Von said, "The frost is something that we have grown dependent on, it is true. It is the source of our magical powers. But I did not know intelligent creatures were involved. Is this true, Sigrida?"

Thinking about the little arms and legs she had seen in the microscope, at first Kaigen was afraid Sigrida was going to lie. Sigrida only took a deep breath and said without flinching, "It is true that the Annites are killed during the frost mining, Von." His face grew horrified, and they could both feel the waves of heat rolling off the Commander. "We have known about the Annites for a long time, as soon as we learned to stain the rock samples and observe them under the microscope."

Von's look was stricken, "But why, Sigrida?"

"What we didn't know," Sigrida continued, "was that they were intelligent. I believe, now, that the Elder knew, given his stance on certain lines of research. He quashed any attempt to investigate the Annites by anyone but himself."

Elsbeth had been hovering nearby, lost without the Elder's affairs to look after, and she interjected herself into the conversation. "I believe your suspicion is correct, Sigrida," she said without her usual malice for the female scientist. "He started having living ones brought to him, and he was experimenting with ways to keep them alive on the surface. He discouraged anyone from inquiring what he was after, including me, but I think that he recognized they were intelligent."

Sigrida nodded. "He wouldn't care if it was Protectors being killed," and at the Commander's growl, quickly turned to him. "No, I'm not discounting the importance of the Annites, Commander. I mean that to him, all other living things were merely tools, a means to an end. Whatever his whim was for the moment, we had to provide," she added, shifting uncomfortably as she thought about their night of lovemaking. *I submitted to him for a stupid robe*, she thought, *and now I learn it was stained with the blood of sentient beings*. She felt sick.

She shook herself. This was too important to bother with her own feelings. "As I said," she continued, "the Elder didn't care. A long time ago we mined the light blue frost, remember Von? There were no traces of the creatures in it."

"Well, that would be right," the Commander said. "Those would have come from the old breeding grounds they had abandoned—once their offspring hatch from the egg form, they leave the protection of the blue and do not use it again."

Sigrida nodded and sighed deeply. "Yes, well, when our drilling stumbled upon the darker blue frost and Vernondiander realized how powerful it was, everything changed. I think that's when he went from merely obsessive to tyrant, in fact. Anyone who dared to interfere with his desire for the darker, richer frost was killed or exiled, even his own brother, Meluha Crocus." She smoothed her shirt front uncomfortably. "As our understanding of ground science increased, we became good at detecting where these stores could be, what underground structures represented the richest supplies."

She looked woeful as she looked into the angry wyvern's eyes. "Once we developed microscopes and staining techniques, we could see the tiny bodies in the lens, but we were more afraid of the Elder than we were of killing these creatures. We did not know that they were intelligent, but that's hardly any kind of excuse."

"You did not care to know," the Commander agreed, heat rolling from his mouth as he spoke. "Hear me well, Sigrida. It stops, immediately. Not tomorrow, now. Not one single more Annite will be harmed by your people."

Von started to speak and Sigrida held up her hand. "One moment," she said, rising and looking through the crowd. "Beni!" she called out, and a man in the robes of the engineering division ran up.

"Yes, Sigrida?"

"All efforts to restore drilling operations are suspended immediately," she said. "Until we determine a method of finding stores of frost that are guaranteed to be free of Annites, that we are certain will not harm any of them, they will remain suspended."

"B-but Sigrida," Beni objected, swallowing hard when he heard the Commander's low growl, "how will we provide enough frost for everyone?"

Sigrida's eyes were cold. "If we do not find methods to return to the non-Annitious frost," she said, "we won't." Beni paled and she relented slightly. "However, the Elder's reserves will be used to make up the difference until we restore safe production. And all research into concentrated uses of frost will be halted to ensure the supply lasts as long as possible."

Beni nodded, relieved. Frost withdrawal would hit the weakest Protectors the hardest, and like Von's father and Meluha Crocus, they would start to age first. But the more powerful Protectors would probably resent it the most because their powers relied on constant exposure to new frost. "That seems wise, Sigrida," he agreed and left to convey her instructions.

"That gives us perhaps a year to find new sources, Commander," Sigrida said. "Perhaps eighteen months if we begin rationing what we've already mined. Do you have a way of communicating with the Annites, to ensure that we can direct our exploration away from their active homes?"

As an afterthought, she quickly added, "And to ensure they don't care about us taking the light blue frost from their old ones?"

"You know, the light blue stores will grow in number over time as the Annites heal and their community grows large again," the Commander offered.

Von only realized his mouth was hanging open when a chuckling Kaigen closed it. He'd never guessed Sigrida would so readily agree to such a thing!

The Commander answered, "Yes, I know they care little for their old homes, so the light blue stores should be fine, but without Kaigen's approval, there will be no drilling. Her earth magic can sense where to drill that will not harm them, true Kaigen?"

"Yes, that is true," Kaigen said and turned to her new friend Sigrida. "It looks like you were telling the Elder the truth, Sigrida. We will make a champion team!"

The four races, including the humans, enjoyed the rest of the day, getting to know one another. The she-wyverns departed immediately, returning to their roosts. They were too dangerous to stay near all these little flammable people, especially the ones who were pregnant and were already feeling overprotective of the fertilized eggs in their bellies.

But the male wyverns, the Sybaris, and the humans agreed that before the humans and the Draconians departed Issedones they would create and enact a temporary treaty so they would have a document of mutual prosperity to build their blossoming trust with one another. It was a start.

The document outlined how the governments of the Juna, the Draconians, and the Protectors would cooperate with one another in their efforts to establish and maintain a new order of mutual prosperity. They hoped that the hostility of the people of Horn could be assuaged and that the attack could be forgiven, even if Draconia had to make restitution, and that their agreements with Juna could be extended to other human lands as well.

They agreed that the welfare of all concerned would be the forefront. Overuse or hoarding of power would not be tolerated, whether it was humans enslaving others, fiery wyverns using their size and strength for evil, or Protectors craving too much magical power. Within their governments, they would watch for signs of this and act to cure the problem before it caused harm. Ambassadors between the governments would keep a watchful eye, each upon the other, to aid in this. External powers, such as Zhu's empire, would be brought to the attention of all, and they would work together to stop the spread of such evil.

The representatives for the new treaty were Von and the departmental heads for the Protectors, Princess Isladora and her Betrothed Tobin for the Juna, Queen Ariah and her bond-mate Json for the Draconians, and the Commander and Kaigen on behalf of the Annites. The pact was signed and sealed, and Isladora was confident her father the king would immediately see the benefits and would agree with the philosophy of seeking out and preventing evil from growing.

With the treaty ink dried, the Draconians and humans returned to Sybaris and spent some time exchanging stories and lore, especially in the healing arts. Then, with eager wyvern volunteers to carry the humans down to Horn and to defend them if necessary, Isladora and Tobin descended to where they'd left Fashi, with promises to visit, again with wyvern help as emissaries came and went, as soon as they could.

In Issedones, Von had been true to his word. Not once did he kiss Kaigen more than one chaste peck on the cheek, and it was driving her crazy! She was frustrated beyond bearing and growing angry, thinking of a little earthquake to shake him up a bit.

As the sun began to set on the eve of the Draconians' departure, Von approached her with a pack on his back. He held out his hand and drew her in for one of those oh! so! frustrating! little! kisses! This one was a little different, somehow, however and her brows furrowed as he ran his hand along her cheek and traced his thumb gently across her lips. "Come along, my scowling Kaigen," he said, leading her to a transport pad.

"Hold still," he said, and she stuck her tongue out at him as if to say she remembered, was he an idiot? The transport, as it had before, seemed to have no effect on her whatsoever, though she was still frustrated that she couldn't seem to feel the magic it used. She would find it useful to learn that trick!

That was the moment that their surroundings penetrated her grumpy ruminations. She smelled saltwater! She couldn't see the sea, but she could hear the crash of waves, and her eyes got wide indeed.

"Come along, my girl," he said again, leading her down a well-hidden stone path that ended in a massive stone outcropping, a triangle of solid stone that pointed due south out to sea. She recognized it, of course, as the place that Von had described to lovingly to her, his favorite place in the world. Standing on the shores of the Rubian Sea, he gave her an altogether different sort of kiss.

Tobin and Isladora had reached the time to depart Draconia, and the duo of wyverns—blue Firenzi and purple-and-black Drom—were ready to act as their mounts for the journey to Horn. Json would accompany them that far, along with Ariah, in case of trouble, but Petrus had already, it appeared, managed to smooth things over with the townsfolk of Horn with promises of reparations from the queen.

Isladora rolled her eyes at this, but money was often a motive for humans. Sometimes too much of one, but she supposed they did deserve something for Sunny's attack on the fortress.

"Json, I wish Firenzi and Drom could fly us all the way home, but we cannot leave Fashi in Horn Town," Isladora said, and Tobin—who'd learned a lot of the wyvern tongue, at least to listen, while they were there—nodded his agreement.

Json shook his head. "One of us could probably carry him in our claws, but that would terrify him, and he'd undoubtedly struggle to the point we'd either hurt him or worse, drop him," he said with a shrug. "Horses and wyverns only get along when the horse is in a wyvern's belly, as the saying goes." He didn't mean anything by it; it was a fact of nature.

Tobin said, "No, we will just have to find a way around the mountains, since the Silver Roads' entrance collapsed on us. However long that takes." He was as protective as ever of his furry friend.

Mezzi had been listening and said, "We could sedate him heavily and then rig up a sling that a wyvern could carry. I have used the sedation medicines for wyverns and for my dog Unsu so they should work on a pony, I think. He would never know he was being carried by a wyvern."

Darkale said, "That's brilliant, Mezzi."

She smiled shyly at him, saying, "It'll take a bigger wyvern than any of you to carry him. It would probably take Sunny to carry him." She looked even more shyly at the she-wyvern.

Sunny arched her golden head and said, "I will carry him only if you will fly with me, Mezzi. I don't want to be in the sole company of males on the way back." She glared so fiercely at Firenzi and Drom that they backed up several steps, then laughed at their reaction.

Mezzi jumped up and ran, hugging Sunny around her neck, "Really? Oh, Sunny!" She was happy beyond words that Sunny would allow her to ride her. Now though, she wondered how she'd react to the idea of becoming bonded? *A problem for another day*, she decided.

The next day, Isladora and Tobin were honored by the ruling wyverns, and all the ruling Sybaris as they gathered to escort Tobin, Fashi, and Isladora home in order to meet and formalize their agreement with King Elijashen and the Juna nation. "I, I had no idea, Your Majesty," Isladora stammered, and the queen wrapped her arms around her.

"Toyah is my mother, but you are at least an aunt, Isladora," she said, referring to the fact that Isladora had helped Json with her rebirth.

The larger group waited a few miles outside of Horn Town so they wouldn't cause pandemonium while Tobin retrieved Fashi from the stable. The scout fed medicine-laced apple slices to the little pony on the way back, and by the time they reached the wyverns, Fashi was beginning to doze on his feet. They carefully guided him into the sling and Sunny gently lifted it up with her mouth until it was well supported, then Json held the harness in place while Sunny took the air with Mezzi looking down from her back.

"I really never imagined anything like this," Tobin said as they climbed onto their mounts. "Not in my wildest dreams." If Fashi was aware that a twelve-ton flying predator was holding him suspended over the forest floor, he gave no sign.

Flying across unknown territory, the wyverns were arranged in a V-shaped combat pattern, the Commander in front flanked by Silverback and Bedaiko, then by Firenzi and Drom in turn, then Abraxis on the right corner. Sunny and Mezzi, carrying Fashi, flew behind the Commander in the middle, and Json and his Queen made up the left corner of the formation.

When the Juna spotted the wyverns, there was at first a lot of commotion and crying out until the warriors began to recognize Json, and then others spotted Isladora and Tobin riding two others. The wyverns landed in a field outside of the walls, and Sunny was extra careful to set down the little pony and hold the harness gently while they carefully lowered it and released a heavily drugged Fashi to lay on his side in the grass.

King Elijashen and his wife Anyumay, escorted by the king's soldiers, came running to see if it was true that their daughter was found unharmed. "Isladora?" King Elijashen demanded. He was impressed, seeing her riding unharmed on a winged giant, but he was also unhappy in the extreme that she'd chosen to disappear.

"Father, Tobin has found me and brought me home," she said, dropping to the ground beside Firenzi to bow deeply to her father. "I know I have a lot of explaining to do, but we have guests." She spread her arms to encompass the Draconians.

The King looked on, bemused, as his daughter began conversing in the wyvern language. The strikingly beautiful golden Sybaris replied to her in the same tongue, and Isladora turned back to her parents. "Our new friends would like to remain until they can bear witness to my marriage to Tobin," she said, gazing in her father's eyes steadily as she made this announcement. "Queen Ariah here would also like you to read through a treaty draft so that, hopefully, you can sign it into force between our nation and hers. I have signed it as Princess of the Juna, but of course the final decision is yours."

"Oh, it is my decision, is it?" the king replied grumpily to his head-strong daughter, but he couldn't prevent his pride from showing through. She'd clearly been through a lot—again—and he wanted to hear her story, and that of the wyverns and Sybaris as well. The King of the Juna turned and bowed gracefully to Ariah. "Welcome Draconians!"

Only Queen Ariah, Darkale, and Json could understand him but they all nodded their heads.

To his daughter, King Elijashen opened his arms and held her in a crushing embrace. He said, "Welcome home, daughter; our hearts are full again now that you are here." He looked up at Tobin. "Now that you and your *betrothed* are here."

Tobin swallowed, and suddenly the warriors with the king saluted him, fists to heart, in Juna fashion. Tobin and Isladora were to be married, and no one in Juna could gainsay it. The wyverns grasped the importance of the salute and threw their heads up to the sky, lighting the field with their flames in their own salute and clear approval of the couple.

Isladora gave her parents a joyful look and then turned to embrace To-bin openly for the first time before her people. She smiled at him with a knowing smile, and he gave the look right back with interest. It had been an eternity, to wait for the king's approval, and now, all their dreams would come true.

The End.